TEXTBOOK OF MEDICAL PARASITOLOGY

Textbook of Medical Parasitology

SECOND EDITION

R PANJARATHINAM
Ph.D. (Bact); Ph.D. (Med. Microbiology)
Fellow of the Zoological Society (Kolkata)
Department of Microbiology
B.J. Medical College
Ahmedabad, Gujarat, India

Orient Longman

Dedicated
to

Divine Mother
Shri Aurobindo Ashram
Pondicherry

Orient Longman Private Limited

Registered Office
3-6-752 Himayatnagar, Hyderabad 500 029 (A.P.) India
email: cogeneral@orientlongman.com

Other offices
Bangalore/Bhopal/Bhubaneshwar/Chennai/Ernakulam/Guwahati/
Hyderabad/Jaipur/Kolkata/Lucknow/Mumbai/New Delhi/Patna

First edition/published 1990
Second edition 2007

ISBN 13: 978-81-250-3159-8
ISBN 10: 81-250-3159-6

Illustrations by
Sigma Publishing Services
Chennai 600 033

Typeset by
Sigma Publishing Services
Chennai 600 033

Printed at
Novena Offset Printing Co.,
Chennai 600 005.

Published by
Orient Longman Private Limited
160 Anna Salai
Chennai 600 002
Email: chegeneral@orientlongman.com

Preface

The primary purpose of this book is to serve as a textbook for undergraduate medical students. With the ever-increasing pressure of a crowded medical curriculum, the study of protozoan, helminthic and arthropod parasites has become more difficult to cope with in a very short time. While preparing this book, this aspect was taken into consideration. I hope that this book will be useful not only to medical students but also to physicians, nurses and laboratory technicians as well.

A lot of importance has been given to the most common parasites prevalent in India. To enable the students to understand the subject more easily, simplified diagrams of lifecycles of parasites have been included. A chapter on pseudoparasites has been added to remove the confusion between parasites and pseudoparasites, especially while examining stool samples. Besides, the chapters on stool and blood examinations, serological tests, treatment, signs and symptoms of parasitic diseases, parasites of various organs, common parasites prevalent in India and a glossary of technical terms will be useful to students as they provide quick reference. The book has been generously illustrated to further aid the student in his learning of the subject.

A spectrum of parasitic opportunists found in association with human immunodeficiency virus (HIV) infection, chapters on immuno parasitology, recent parasitic serology, culture media, free living amebae, microsporidia, cryptosporidium, larva migrans, tumour associated parasites and 300 zoonotic parasites have been added with up to date information in this second edition.

Accuracy and proportion of diagrams are compensated by colour microphotographs with magnification, although all diagrams were drawn enlarged to identify easily certain unique anatomical characteristics of the parasites. Colour microphotographs were taken under a fluorescence microscope fitted with a camera.

R PANJARATHINAM

Acknowledgement

I am grateful to Dr. RC Shah, MBBS, MSc (Med), Deputy Director of Medical Education Research, Gujarat State, Ahmedabad, and Dr. VV Kollali, MD (Path. Bact), DCP, Professor and Head, Microbiology Department, B.J. Medical College, Ahmedabad, for their kind permission and encouragement in writing this textbook.

I am grateful to Dr. Shrinivas, MD, DCP, FAMS., Professor and Head, Department of Microbiology, All India Institute of Medical Sciences, New Delhi; Dr. Sambasiva Rao, MD, MNAMS, Professor and Head, Department of Microbiology, Jawaharlal Institute of Postgraduate Medical Education and Research, Pondicherry; Dr. S Subramanian, MBBS, MD, D Bact (Lond.), FAMS, FTASc, FIMSA, FMMC, Emeritus Professor of Post Graduate Institute of Basic Medical Sciences, Taramani, Chennai, and Principal, Rajah Muthiah Medical College, Annamalai University, Annamalainagar, for having spared their valuable time to examine the manuscript.

Mr. DN Zaveri, MSc (Med) is also acknowledged for his assistance during photography.

I am indeed indebted to all Professors and Heads of Department of Microbiology of various Medical Colleges of India for having kindly reviewed the first edition and for their valuable suggestions which are incorporated in this second edition. Besides, I am very much encouraged by the constructive advice of the Pathological Society of Great Britain and Ireland, London, which has also been incorporated into this edition.

My sincere thanks are due to my wife and children for their support and encouragement, and to Orient Longman, for having elegantly published this book.

R PANJARATHINAM

CONTENTS

Colour Plates

GENERAL INTRODUCTION

Medical parasitology is a branch of medical science which deals with parasites and their relationship with the host. It consists of

1) Protozoology (the study of protozoa)
2) Helminthology (the study of helminths) and
3) Entomology (the study of insects or vectors).

A ***parasite*** is an organism which adapts itself to live in or on another organism on which it is dependent for its nutrition or metabolism. Literally, 'parasite' means 'eating from another's table'.

Most of the parasites which affect mankind are of animal nature, i.e., they belong to any one of the three main divisions of the animal kingdom – protozoa, helminths and arthropods.

Parasites can be classified, on the basis of their relationship with their hosts, as follows:

- An ***ectoparasite*** is one which lives on the surface of the body, e.g., the human louse, *Pediculus humanus*.
- An ***endoparasite*** is normally found inside the human body, e.g., the roundworm, *Ascaris lumbricoides,* which lives in the human intestine.
- A ***commensal*** is a parasite which lives in or on a host for its own benefit but does not produce disease, e.g., *Entameba coli.*
- ***Pathogens*** are parasites which are pathogenic to humans, living at the expense of the tissues, fluids and metabolites of their hosts, e.g., *Entameba histolytica.*
- ***Symbionts*** are two organisms which live in close association, so that each derives benefit from the presence of the other.

Infection occurs when a parasite establishes itself within a host, and ***infestation***, when a parasite lives superficially on the host.

A ***host*** is any animal that harbours a parasite. A host may be

- Definite
- Intermediate or
- A reservoir.

A ***definite*** host is one that harbours the vegetative, the adult or the sexual stage of the parasite. Humans are definite hosts for *Taenia saginata.* An ***intermediate*** host is an animal which harbours the cystic, larval, immature or asexual stage of the parasites. Cattle are the intermediate hosts for

T. saginata. The infected person or animal may act as a ***reservoir*** (source of parasitic infection) for transmission by insect bite during the parasitic lifecycle in the host. A reservoir host is an animal, which takes the place of the human in the lifecycle of a parasite. The antelope is the reservoir host of African Trypanosomiasis.

There are several states of parasitism which are described below:

- ***Facultative parasites*** are those parasites which have free living and parasitic forms, e.g., *Strongyloides stercoralis.*
- ***Obligatory parasites*** are those which are incapable of free living and completing their lifecycle in the absence of their hosts, e.g., *Toxoplasma gondii.*
- An ***erratic*** or ***ectopic parasite*** is found in organs or tissues of the body which it does not normally invade, e.g., *Ascaris lumbricoides* are occasionally found in the bile duct or liver which they do not normally parasitize.

Mechanisms of disease production by animal parasites Parasites may damage host tissues either by mechanical injury, or by the detrimental effect of toxic substances. These two effects may, sometimes, take place together as in *Plasmodium falciparum.* When this malarial parasite grows in the human red blood cells, it can destroy mechanically the architecture of the red blood cells. At the same time, it liberates toxic substances which cause the rigors and clinical symptoms of malaria. Similarly, *Entameba histolytica* damages the human intestine by mechanical injury and by the production of a histolytic enzyme, ultimately leading to amebic dysentery.

Mechanical injury may be

1) By means of pressure as the parasite grows larger (hydatid cyst) or
2) By obstruction of ducts in the following ways:
   a) Obstruction of the blood vessels (strongyloides) causing infarction
   b) Obstruction of the lymph vessels (filaria) causing elephantiasis and
   c) Obstruction of the intestines *(Ascaris lumbricoides)* causing perforation and necrosis.

By competing with the host for food, e.g., the fish tapeworm, *Diphyllobothrium latum,* deprives its host of vitamin B_{12}, thus causing megaloblastic anemia. Similarly, hookworm *(Ancylostoma duodenale)* infestation leads to iron deficiency.

Table 1 Classification of parasites

	Termination	*Example*
Phylum		Platyhelminths
Class	(-idea)	Cestodes
Order		Cyclophyllidea
Superfamily	(-oidea)	Taenioidea
Family		Taeniidae
Genus	(-idae)	Taenia
Species		Taenia saginata

Bacteria may contaminate the wound or ulcer which is initially produced by a parasite, e.g., the guinea worm, *Dracunculus medinensis,* can indirectly cause tetanus.

Host reactions to the parasites Host reactions may be tissue reactions or immunological responses. When parasites invade certain tissues of the human body, there is excessive proliferation of the tissue, e.g., fibrosis (or cirrhosis) in the liver due to ova deposited by *Schistosoma mansoni* in the liver; hepatic fibrosis and hyperplasia of the biliary epithelium in liver fluke infection (*Clonorchis sinensis* and *Fasciola hepatica*).

Scheme of study Parasites of medical importance have been described in this book under the following headings:

1. History of the discovery of the parasite
2. Geographical distribution
3. Habitat inside the human body
4. Morphology
5. Lifecycle
6. Modes of infection
7. Pathogenicity and clinical features
8. Laboratory diagnosis
9. Treatment and prophylaxis

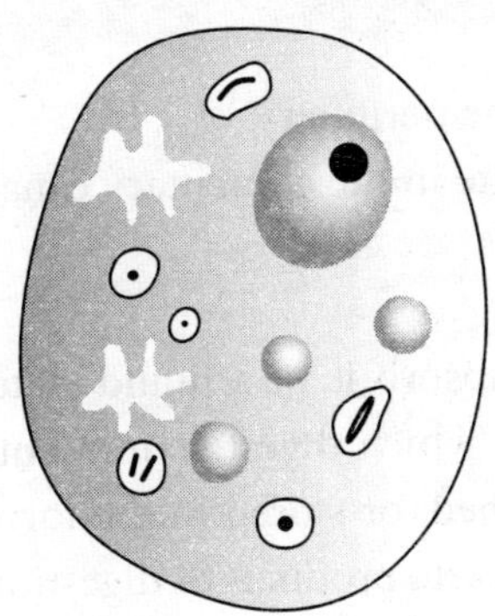

Section I

PROTOZOOLOGY

1 PROTOZOA

Protozoa are single-celled or unicellular animals which are microscopic in size (*Proto* primitive; *zoa* animal).

Morphology In general, there is a protoplasmic body or ***cytoplasm*** in which one or more nuclei are embedded. The cytoplasm is usually divided into an outer ectoplasm and an inner endoplasm.

The ectoplasm performs the functions of locomotion, respiration, excretion and protection, whereas the function of the endoplasm is nutritive and reproductive.

The ***nucleus*** controls various functions and regulates reproduction. It consists of a nuclear membrane which encloses a network of fine delicate filaments. Usually, there is a mass in the centre of the nucleus, the ***karyosome,*** which may be minute. The nuclear membrane and fine filaments contain chromatin granules. The nucleus is useful to differentiate the genera and species.

Classification On the basis of the organ of locomotion, pathogenic protozoa can be classified into the following groups:

1. ***Rhizopoda*** which move with the help of pseudopodia (*pseudo* false; *podia* feet). These pseudopodia are also used by amebae to engulf food (Entameba)
2. ***Mastigophora*** which have elongated, threadlike filaments, flagella (Trypanosoma)
3. ***Sporozoa*** which exhibit no movement, e.g., the malarial parasite
4. ***Ciliata*** which move about by means of shorter processes called *cilia,* e.g., *Balantidium coli.*

Lifecycle Protozoa have three stages in their lifecycle.

1. ***Trophozoite***: This is the motile stage which exhibits gliding movement and is capable of enclosing itself in a resistant wall to form a cyst (encystment)

2. ***Pre-cystic stage:*** It has a blunt pseudopodium projecting from the periphery
3. ***Cystic stage:*** It is a resistant stage. On reaching the anatomical site in the alimentary canal, the cyst gives rise to one or more trophozoites (excystation).

Metabolism The protozoa may engulf food in a solid form or absorb it in a liquid state. Food material is digested in the endoplasm in 'food vacuoles' into which digestive ferments and enzymes are secreted. Following digestion, food may be absorbed, or stored in the form of glycogen, volutin, chromatoid bodies and other substances. The waste products of digestion pass out into the medium in which the animal lives.

Nutrients metabolized by protozoa: *In vitro* cultivation studies of protozoa show that the malarial parasites and African trypanosomes metabolize large quantities of carbohydrates, e.g., glucose. The end product of metabolism in African trypanosomes is pyruvic acid; and lactase is known to accumulate in the case of malarial parasites. Blood inhabiting protozoa require the following constituents of plasma for their growth and multiplication: amino acids, vitamins, inorganic salts and metabolic cofactors. The intestinal protozoa, however, differ from others in that they can only thrive on bacterial flora.

Reproduction Reproduction of protozoa may be by asexual multiplication or sexual reproduction.

1. ***Asexual multiplication:*** This may take place
   a) By binary fission, that is, simple division into two, e.g., *E. histolytica* in the human large intestine or
   b) By multiple fission or schizogony in which more than two individuals are produced, e.g., *Plasmodia* in the liver and red blood cells of the mammalian host.
2. ***Sexual multiplication*** may be achieved
   a) By conjugation in which a temporary union of two individuals takes place with the interchange of nuclear material, e.g., Ciliata or
   b) By syngamy or sporogony, that is, the process by which a male parasite unites with a female to produce a fertilized ovum or zygote which undergoes division into numerous, thin, rod-like structures known as sporozoites.

Members of the genus *Trypanosoma* of the class Mastigophora also reproduce asexually. In the African trypanosomes *(T. gambiense* and *T. rhodesiense)*, asexual reproduction takes place in the blood by repeated longitudinal fission. In the American trypanosome *(T. cruzi)*, it occurs in the tissue cells where the protozoa roll themselves up into round shapes, dividing repeatedly to produce intracellular aggregations or 'nests' of young rounded parasites. These elongate afterwards to the trypanosome form and re-enter the bloodstream.

SUMMARY

- Protozoa are microscopic, primitive unicellular animals with
  - (a) An outer cytoplasm (ectoplasm) responsible for movement, respiration, excretion, protection;
  - (b) Inner cytoplasm (endoplasm) with a nucleus which controls nutrition, reproduction.
  - (c) Karyosome (minute mass) in the centre of the nucleus can be useful to distinguish genera and species.
- They are grouped as:
  1. Rhizopoda which move with pseudopodia (false feet) to engulf food (Entameba)
  2. Mastigophora which move with long hair-like filaments, flagella (Trypanosoma)
  3. Sporozoa, these do not move (Plasmodium)
  4. Ciliata, these move with their cilia (short processes) – *Balantidium coli.*
- Their lifecycle stages:
  - (a) Trophozoite (motile stage) transforms into cyst (encystment)
  - (b) Precystic stage with blunt pseudopodia.
  - (c) Cystic stage (resistant form) gives rise to trophozoite (excystation)
- Solid or liquid food can be engulfed by protozoa, digested by enzymes in food vacuoles. After digestion, it is stored as glycogen, volutin, chromatoid. Waste products are passed out.
- Glucose is metabolized into pyruvic acid (end product) by trypanosome and to lactase by Plasmodia.
- Blood protozoa require aminoacids, vitamins and salts, whereas intestinal protozoa live on bacterial flora.
- They reproduce:
  1. Asexually (binary fission of Entameba; multiple fission or schizogony of Plasmodium)
  2. Sexually (temporary union, conjugation, of two protozoans to interchange their nuclear material – Ciliata); male and female unite to form a zygote (sporogony or syngamy) which produces sporozoites (infective form).

  African trypanosome reproduces asexually by repeated longitudinal fission; whereas American trypanosome occurs in round shapes in tissue and elongates into trypanosome and re-enters the blood circulation.

QUESTIONS

Q *What are protozoa?*

- Protozoa are microscopic single-celled primitive animals.

Q *Why are protozoa called primitive animals?*

▶ Protozoa are called primitive animals because they are microscopic and single-celled with animal physiological activities.

Q *What is the function of the nucleus?*

▶ Nucleus controls nutrition and reproduction.

Q *What is the function of the ectoplasm?*

▶ Ectoplasm controls movement, respiration and excretion. It also provides protection.

Q *What is a karyosome? State its use.*

▶ Karyosome is a minute mass in the center of the nucleus. It is useful in distinguishing between genera and species.

Q *What are rhizopoda?*

▶ They are motile protozoa which move with pseudopodia.

Q *What are pseudopodia? What are its functions?*

▶ Pseudopodia are false feet which help protozoal movement to engulf food material.

Q *What are mastigophora?*

▶ They are protozoa which move with flagella.

Q *What is a flagellum?*

▶ It is a hair-like, long filament, arising from the ectoplasm, which helps in movement.

Q *What are sporozoa?*

▶ They are non-motile protozoa.

Q *How are ciliata motile?*

▶ They are motile, because of their cilia.

Q *What are cilia?*

▶ Cilia are short processes; they arise from the ectoplasm and are responsible for the movement of protozoa.

Q *What is a trophozoite? Mention its role.*

▶ Trophozoite is a protozoal developmental stage. It is motile and can engulf food material and invade the tissue.

Q *What is the cystic stage of protozoa?*

▶ Cyst is a resistant form of protozoa which gives rise to trophozoites (infective forms).

Q *Mention the end product of glucose metabolism by African trypanosome and the malarial parasite.*

▶ The end product of glucose metabolized by African trypanosome is pyruvic acid; whereas in the case of malarial parasite it is lactase.

Q *Which protozoa require aminoacid, vitamins and inorganic salts in the blood for their growth and multiplication?*

▶ Blood protozoa.

Q *Which protozoa thrive on bacterial flora?*

▶ Intestinal protozoa.

Q *Enumerate the different types of multiplication.*

▶ 1. Asexual multiplication by protozoa. (a) Binary fission of Entameba; (b) Multiple fission of Plasmodium; (c) Repeated longitudinal fission of African trypanosome. (d) Rounding and elongation of American trypanosome.
2. Sexual multiplication (a) Conjugation of ciliata; (b) Sporogony of Plasmodium in mosquito.

2 RHIZOPODA

The genus *Entameba* contains six species or associated species which have been recovered from the human alimentary tract. These are *Entameba histolytica, E. coli, E. gingivalis, Iodameba bütschlii, Dientameba fragilis* and *E. nana.* Of these gut amebae, only *E. histolytica* is pathogenic to mankind. The medical importance of other amebae lies in the fact that they may be confused with *E. histolytica.* In *Entameba,* the nuclear membrane is lined by chromatin granules and the compact karyosome is either centrally *(E. histolytica)* or eccentrally *(E. coli)* placed.

In *Endolimax,* the karyosome is a large irregular mass situated peripherally; it may be connected with another small mass *(E. nana).*

In *Iodameba,* the karyosome is a large circular mass surrounded by refractile globules *(I. bütschlii).*

In *Dientameba,* the karyosome consists of six chromatin granules. There are two nuclei *(D. fragilis).*

ENTAMEBA HISTOLYTICA

E. histolytica, which causes diarrhea, dysentery, hepatitis and liver abscess in humans, was first discovered by Lambl (1859). Losch (1875) proved its pathogenic nature. It is found worldwide, but more commonly in the tropics and subtropics. Trophozoites of *E. histolytica* live in the mucosa and submucosa of the human large intestine.

Morphology The organism takes the following forms:

1. ***Trophozoite***: It exhibits a slow gliding movement and contains cytoplasm and nucleus. The cytoplasm consists of an outer, clear, translucent ectoplasm and an inner granular endoplasm which has the nucleus, and vacuoles which may contain food material,

leucocytes, erythrocytes and bacteria. The pseudopodia, the organs of locomotion, are composed of hyaline ectoplasm. In addition to locomotion, they serve as feeding organs by flowing around solid food particles, bacteria and erythrocytes, which are then easily engulfed by amebae.

The nucleus is spherical in shape and is bounded by a thin limiting membrane on which small granules of chromatin are arranged in a regular circle of dots. In the centre of the nucleus, there is a slightly larger granule called the karyosome. This morphological appearance of the nucleus is characteristic of all species of Entameba and therefore it is important from the diagnostic point of view (Fig. 2.1 and 2.2a).

The trophozoite causes acute amebic dysentery and tissue amebiasis.

2. ***The pre-cystic forms:*** Special pre-cystic forms are developed first, and they have a blunt pseudopodium (Fig. 2.2b).
3. ***The cysts*** are round or oval in outline, refractile and pearly white in colour. Each measures 6–15 μm in diameter. There is a definite cyst wall and the cysts may contain one, two or four nuclei (Fig. 2.2 c, d and e).

   The newly formed cyst consists of:

   a) A ***nucleus*** which is stained with iodine
   b) A ***glycogen*** mass visible on staining and
   c) ***Chromidial bars*** which are rod-like structures with rounded ends. Their function is not fully understood yet.

As the cyst grows older, it may ultimately give rise to four nucleated cysts. The glycogen mass and chromidial bars are used up and disappear gradually. In iodine-stained preparations of feces, the cysts stain a light brown to yellow colour, and the nuclei and glycogen masses are clearly visible.

Lifecycle *E. histolytica* passes its lifecycle in one host only, i.e., human.

When the fully developed cysts containing four nuclei are swallowed by humans, they pass down the intestine without being affected by the gastric juices, though they can be digested by trypsin in the intestine. A process of ***excystation*** takes place in the lower part of the large intestine, where the pH is neutral or slightly alkaline. During this process, the cytoplasmic body retracts and loosens itself from the cyst wall. The tetra-nucleate ameba escapes and produces

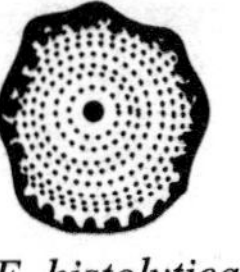
E. histolytica

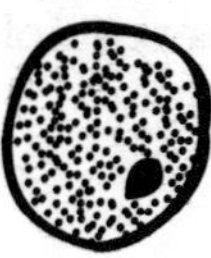
E. coli

Dientameba

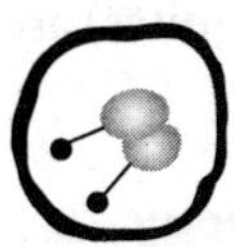
Endolimax

Iodameba

Fig. 2.1 Nuclear character of various genera under amebida.

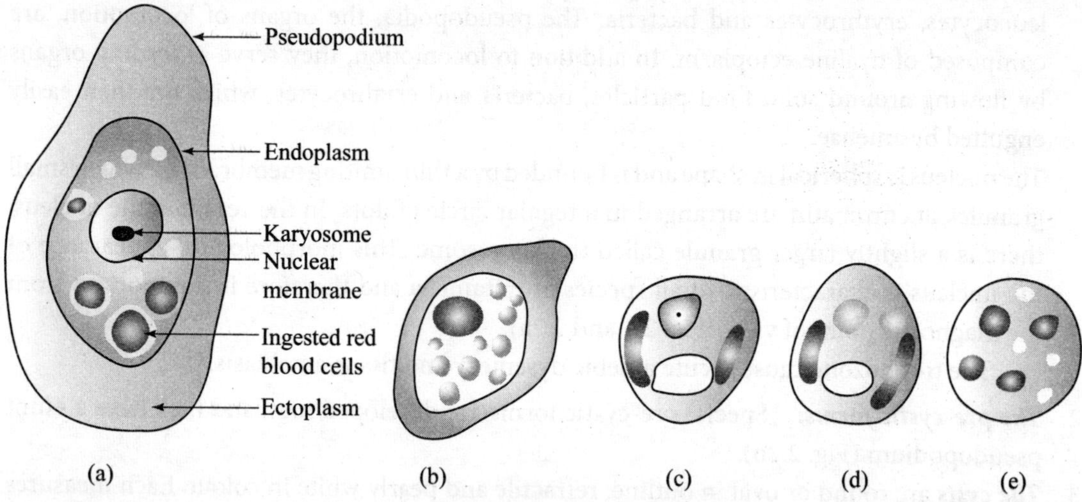

Fig. 2.2 a) Trophozoite of *E. histolytica;* b) pre-cystic stage; c) uninucleate cyst; d) binucleate cyst; e) multinucleate cyst (enlarged).

eight uninucleated amebae by binary fission. These trophozoites grow and multiply rapidly, the nucleus dividing before cytoplasmic division takes place.

The amebae invade the mucous membrane of the large intestine, multiply there and cause ulceration. The factors which determine their invasiveness are still obscure, but the important ones among them are proteolytic ferment (cytolysin), symbiosis with the gut bacterial flora and the size and genetic make up of the ameba. Trophozoites may, in some cases, enter the portal of the bloodstream and be carried to other organs, i.e., liver, lungs, brain and skin, and cause extra-intestinal amebiasis

After a period of growth and multiplication in the submucosa of the intestine, the trophozoites are discharged in the lumen of the gut, and are transformed into small ***pre-cystic*** forms from which adult cysts develop. This process is known as ***encystment*** which takes place within a few hours. To cause the infection, the cysts must be ingested within a few hours of being passed in the stool. (As the trophozoites are easily destroyed by acidity and the gastric juices, they fail to infect humans, whereas the cysts do.) The motile trophozoite is the only form which parasitizes mankind. In the case of cysts, infection occurs in humans, only when they are swallowed and when those once formed in the lumen do not excyst in the same host. Vegetative amebae (trophozoites) are normally found in loose stools and cysts in formed stools (Figs. 2.3 and 2.4).

Pathogenicity and pathology

1. ***Intestinal pathology***: In the primary infection in the large intestine, the lesions are found more commonly at the points of stasis, i.e., the cecum, hepatic flexure, splenic flexure and recto-sigmoid junction. In light infections, they may be confined to these points alone and

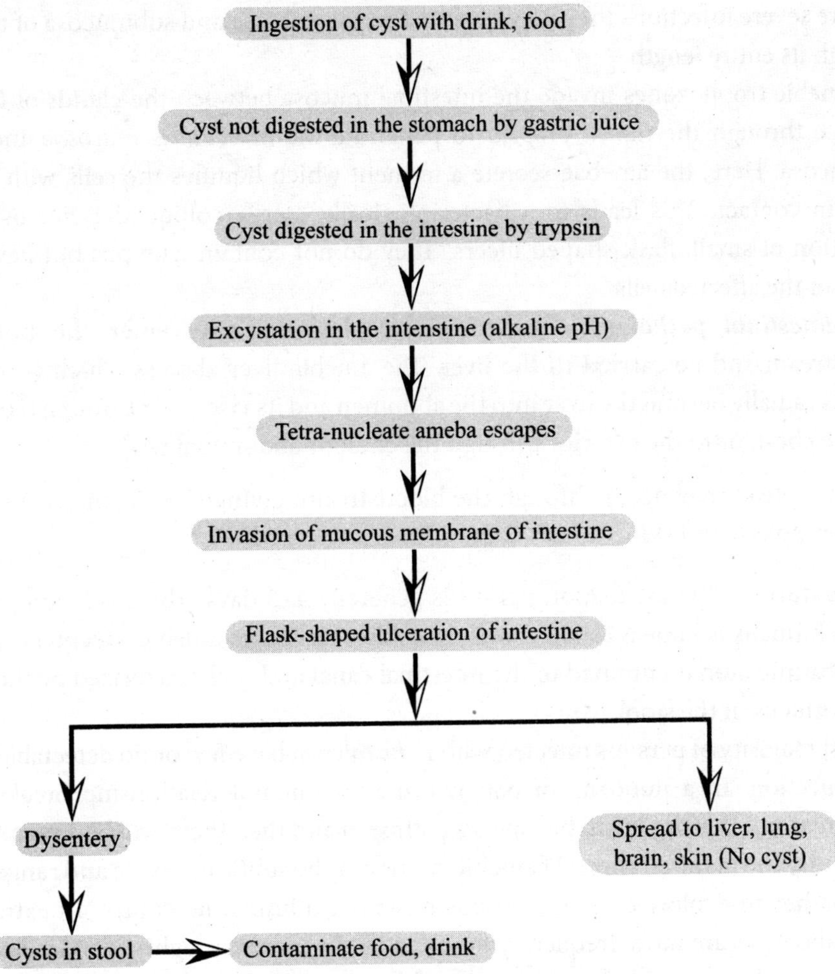

Fig. 2.3 Lifecycle of *E. histolytica*.

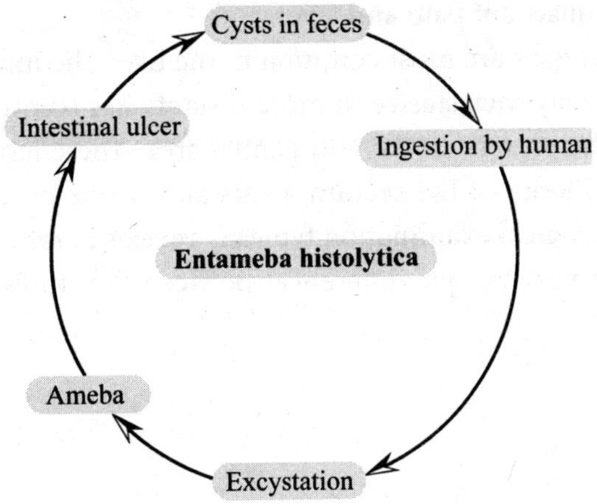

Fig. 2.4 Lifecycle of *E. histolytica*.

in more severe infections they may be found in the mucosa and submucosa of the large gut through its entire length.

The amebic trophozoites invade the intestinal mucosa between the glands of Lieberkuhn, advance through the *tunica propria* to penetrate the *muscularis mucosae* and reach the submucosa. Here, the amebae secrete a ferment which liquifies the cells with which they come in contact. This leads to a bacteriologically 'sterile colliquative necrosis' with the formation of small, flask-shaped ulcers. They do not contain true pus but have the lysed debris of the affected cells

2. ***Extra-intestinal pathology***: Sometimes, trophozoites may enter the portal of the bloodstream and be carried to the liver. The amebic liver abscess which is formed here extends radially beyond the liver into the abdomen and its viscera or through the diaphragm into the chest, or to the exterior through the chest or abdominal wall.

Embolic spread may occur through the bloodstream, giving rise to amebic abscess in the lungs, brain, spleen and skin.

Clinical features The incubation period is generally 4–5 days. The condition produced by amebae in humans is known as *amebiasis. E. histolytica* causes amebic dysentery, a condition in which the infection is confined to the intestinal canal and is characterized by the passage of blood and mucus in the stool.

The vast majority of persons infected with *E. histolytica* have few or no detectable symptoms of their infection. In a minority of patients, the commensal relationship breaks down for unknown reasons, this organism becomes a pathogen and then there will be a manifestation of amebic colitis. The manifestations of amebic colitis may be subtle or severe and range from mild watery diarrhea to explosive bloody dysentery with a fulminating course. In extra-intestinal infection, abscesses are more frequently found in the liver, where right-sided lesions are much more common than left-sided ones (presumably owing to the vascular supply to the liver). Important clues to the presence of an amebic liver abscess include elevation of the right hemi-diaphragm, right-upper quadrant pain and fever.

Although amebic abscesses are most common in the liver, the infection may extend to the lung or peritonuim and may metastasize to more distant sites (central nervous system). Less frequently, lesions may be present in the ano-genital area. These lesions have been confused with squamous cell carcinoma of the rectum, penis and cervix on the basis of macroscopic appearance, though histological examination typically reveals *E. histolytica* trophozoites.

The macroscopic and microscopic differences between the stools of amebic and bacillary dysentery are:

Table 1 Amebic and Bacillary dysentry-differences

	Amebic dysentery	*Bacillary dysentery*
Macroscopic differences		
Frequency	6–8 motions per day	Over 8 motions per day
Quantity	Relatively copious	Small
Odour	Offensive	Odourless
Colour	Dark red	Bright red
Nature	Blood and mucus, mixed with feces	Blood and mucus only, no feces
Reaction	Acidic	Alkaline
Consistency	Not adherent to the container	Adherent to the container
Microscopic differences		
RBC	In clumps; yellow green in colour	Discrete or in rouleaux; Bright red in colour
Pus cells	Scanty	Numerous
Macrophages	Very few	Large and numerous
Eosinophils	Present	Scarce
Pyknotic bodies	Very common	Nil
Ghost cells	Nil	Numerous
Parasite	Trophozoite of *E. histolytica.*	Nil
Bacteria	Many motile bacteria	Many non-motile bacteria
C.L. crystals *	Present	Nil

* Charcot–Leyden crystals. In saline preparations, they appear as diamond-shaped crystals, clear and refractile. Their presence is indicative of the necessity for a careful examination of the stool for *E. histolytica*.

Diagnosis In ***intestinal amebiasis,*** a definite diagnosis can be made by

1. Stool examination, in which the cysts (in formed stools), and the trophozoites (in diarrheal stools) are identified. Cysts of *E. histolytica* can be demonstrated by acridine orange (AO) staining technique with fluorescence microscopy.
2. Sigmoidoscopy, in which scrapings from any lesions in the rectum or recto-sigmoid are examined for trophozoites. *E. histolytica* can be grown in Balamuth's monophasic medium, modified Boeck and Drobohlov's diphasic medium, Schaffer, Ryden and Freye's transparent medium, Philip's medium.

In ***extra-intestinal amebiasis,*** the following procedures are followed:

1. Clinical diagnosis: Most cases of extra-intestinal amebiasis are diagnosed by the clinical features and later confirmed by the presence of cysts of *E. histolytica* in the stool or trophozoites in the tissues.
   In amebic liver abscess, a clinical diagnosis is usually based on the presence of an enlarged liver, pain in the right hypochondrium, epigastrium or lower chest, an abdominal mass, fever and sweating.
2. Stool examination is important to confirm the clinical diagnosis.
3. X-ray examination: X-ray, ultrasonography of the abdomen should be done for all patients.
4. Immuno-diagnostic tests: The hemagglutination, complement fixation and gel diffusion tests are very useful. The antigen used is an amebic extract. The most recent and equally satisfactory tests are the fluorescent antibody, precipitin and immuno-electrophoresis tests.

Western Blot may become one of the very recent, more accurate methods for the successful immuno-diagnosis and epidemiology of acute intestinal amebiasis.

ELISA test is performed currently for the detection of an antibody to *E. histolytica* by using purified antigen instead of crude soluble antigen.

A new fluorescence (FIAX) technique, in which fluorescence is measured in a fluorometer, is a new test adapted to routine diagnosis. Invasive amebiasis is detected by another very recent technique, cellulose acetate precipitin (CAP) test. Besides, recently, both Dot immuno-binding assay (DIB) and sandwich ELISA are used in the diagnosis of invasive amebiasis. Both are equally specific and sensitive. DIB is easier to perform, is cheaper and recommended for the detection of the antibody in patients with invasive amebiasis in India.

Treatment ***Severe amebic dysentery*** may be treated as follows: dehydroemetine dihydrochloride 60 mg intramuscularly daily for 1–3 days is followed by metronidazole 400 mg, three times daily, on days 4–8.

Less acute dysenteric amebiasis can be treated with metronidazole 800 mg, three times daily, for five days.

Amicline is a complete current amebicide containing chloroquine phosphate and diiodohydroxy quinoline for the eradication of extra-intestinal and intestinal amebiasis. Tinidazole two times daily for three days is effective for intestinal amebiasis. Dependal (metronidazole, furazolidine) and recently, Amicline plus (oxytetracycline, chloroquine phosphate and diiodohydroxy quinoline), are very effective for both amebic and bacillary dysentery.

Prophylaxis

Personal prophylaxis consists of

1. Use of boiled drinking water
2. Protection of food and drink from flies, cockroaches and rats
3. Avoiding eating unwashed raw vegetables and fruits and
4. Personal cleanliness while taking food.

Community prophylaxis comprises

1. Effective sanitary disposal of feces
2. Protection of water supplies from fecal pollution
3. Avoidance of the use of human excreta as fertilizer and
4. Detection and isolation of carriers.

ENTAMEBA COLI

E. coli are found worldwide and live in the human large intestine.

Morphology They have all the stages of *E. histolytica* in their lifecycle (Fig. 2.4).

Lifecycle The lifecycle of *E.coli* is similar to that of *E. histolytica*, but during excystation, the original eight nuclei of *E. coli* may be reduced to four.

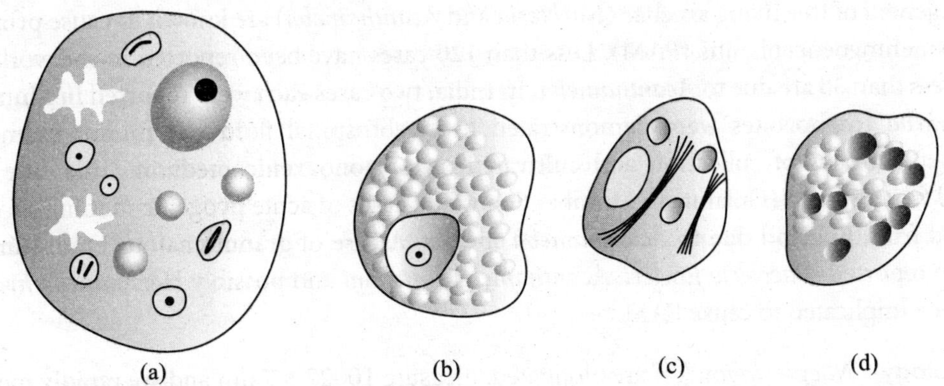

Fig. 2.5 a) Trophozoite of *E. coli*; b) pre-cystic stage; c) cyst of *E. coli* with chromatoid; glycogen vacuoles, nuclei; d) cyst with eight nuclei with eccentric karyosomes.

Pathogenicity *E. coli* is a commensal.

Diagnosis *E. coli* is commonly found in dysenteric stool.

FREE LIVING OR COPROZOIC AMEBAE

Free living amebae, which are coprozoic, are recovered from feces. They may have been ingested through contaminated water and survived transit through the gastrointestinal tract; hence they are often contaminants of the passed stool specimens of water used for the preparation of fecal films.

Table 2 Trophozoite and Cyst of *E. histolytica* and *E. coli*

TROPHOZOITE		
Fresh preparation		
Size	20–30 μm	20–40 μm
Motility	Very active	Sluggish
Cytoplasm	Clearly defined into ectoplasm	Not defined; ectoplasm scarcely seen
Cytoplasmic inclusions	Red blood cells; leucocytes and tissue debris, but no bacteria. Not visible in unstained preparation	Bacteria and other materials, but never red blood cells. Visible in unstained preparation
Nucleus		
Stained with iodine		
Nuclear character	Central karyosome; fine chromatin granules line the delicate nuclear membrane	Eccentric karyosome; chromatin granules line the thick nuclear membrane
CYST		
Fresh preparation		
Chromatoid bodies	Rounded bars	Filamentous, thread-like, with square or pointed ends
Stained with iodine		
Size	6–15 μm	15–20 μm
Nucleus	1–4; central karyosome	1–8; eccentric karyosome
Glycogen mass stage	Visible in uninucleate stage	Large and visible in the binucleate stage

The genera of free living amebae (*Naegleria* and *Acanthameba*) are known to cause primary amebic meningoencephalitis (PAM). Less than 120 cases have been reported in the world, of which less than 30 are due to *Acanthameba*. In India, two cases each were reported in Mumbai. *Acanthmeba* trophozoites were demonstrated in cerebrospinal fluid wet mount examined within 20 minutes of collection and cultivated on a monoaxenic medium. This case was referred from Baroda (Gujarat) to Mumbai. Four fatal cases of acute pyogenic meningitis were reported from England due to *Acanthameba* species. A case of granulomatous brain tumour was also reported. *Naegleria fowleri, Acanthameba castellani* and possibly *Hartmanella hyaline* have been implicated to cause PAM.

Morphology *Naegleria fowleri* are elongated, measure 10–22 × 7 μm and are rapidly motile. Their vacuoles are seen in the cytoplasm (the nucleus with its large nucleolus is not usually visible in an unstained preparation); they do not contain ingested red blood cells. *Naegleria* will remain motile for several hours at room temperature and up to 24 hours at 35–37°C. They can be stained with Giemsa stain, but not by Gram stain; in distilled water they develop flagella after 2–4 hours and can be identified by their utilization of *Escherichia coli* and by their ability to become ameflagellates in water, their cysts can be distinguished from those of *Acanthameba castellani* which are angular in shape with a double wall.

Pathogenicity and clinical features Most cases have developed in children who were swimming in warm soil-contaminated pools, sometimes indoors, but usually outdoors. The amebae, primarily *N. fowleri*, apparently enter via the nose and cribriform plate of the ethnoid, passing directly into the brain tissue where they rapidly form nests of amebae that cause extensive hemorrhage and cause damage, chiefly in the cerebrum and cerebellum. In most cases, death ensues in less than a week. Entry of *Acanthameba* into the central nervous system from skin ulcers or traumatic penetration such as keratitis, from puncture of the corneal surface or ulceration from contaminated saline used with contact lenses, has also been reported. The more subacute form of PAM associated with immuno-compromised hosts is caused by *Acanthameba,* but not by *Naegleria.*

Laboratory diagnosis Diagnosis is by microscopic examination of the cerebrospinal fluid which contains the trophozoites and red blood cells, but no bacteria. Free-living amebae can be readily cultured on non-nutrient agar plate, seeded with *Escherichia coli*. These soil amebae are distinguished by a large, distinct nucleus, by the presence of contractile vacuoles and mitochondria (absent in Entameba) and by cysts that have a single nucleus and lack of glycogen or chromatoid bodies. *Acanthameba* may encyst in invaded tissues, whereas *Naegleria* does not.

Treatment Treatment with amphotericin B has been successful. Sulphonamide and α̃hydroxy stibamide isethionate have been recommended for acanthamebiasis.

Prophylaxis Avoidance of swimming in warm, soil-contaminated pools. Contaminated saline should not be used with contact lenses.

SUMMARY

Entameba histolytica

- Among the six species of Entameba, *E. histolytica* is pathogenic to humans. It causes diarrhea, dysentery, hepatitis, amebic abscess in the lungs, brain, spleen and skin.
- Infection in humans starts within a few hours after swallowing fresh mature four-nucleated cysts; these cysts, unaffected by gastric juices, are digested by trypsin in the large intestine, where the excystation process is initiated at neutral pH; by binary fission, eight uninucleated amebae are liberated to perpetuate their lifecycle. These amebae (trophozoites) invade the mucosa of the large intestine, multiply and cause ulceration (flask-shaped ulcers). Some trophozoites may escape into the blood circulation system, settle in the liver, lungs, brain and skin and cause extra-intestinal amebiasis.
- After multiplication in the mucosa, they re-enter the lumen of the gut and transform into cysts (encystation) which are passed out in the stool.
- Pathological changes:
  1. Intestinal flask-shaped ulcer
  2. Extra-intestinal amebic abscess in lung, brain, spleen, skin.
- Amebic dysentery is characterized by the presence of blood and mucus in the stool. The stool is dark red, offensive and copious. In amebic liver abscess, the clinical symptoms are the presence of enlarged liver, pain in the right hypochondrium, epigastrium or lower chest, abdominal mass, fever, sweating.
- Cyst is formed in the stool; trophozoites in diarrheal stool can confirm the diagnosis of intestinal amebiasis, in addition to ultrasonography, X-ray of abdomen and immuno-diagnostic tests.
- Amebiasis can be treated by appropriate drug; it can be controlled by personal, community prophylaxis.
- *E. coli* is nonpathogenic to humans and can be identified by the presence of eight nuclei with an eccentric karyosome.

QUESTIONS

Q *How many species of Entameba are found in the human alimentary tract? Enumerate them.*

- There are six species: *E. histolytica, E. coli, E. gingivalis, Iodameba bütschlii, Dientameba fragilis and E. nana.*

Q *Why are the other non-pathogenic species of medical importance?*

- All non-pathogenic species are confused with *E. histolytica*, hence they are medically important for differentiation and identification.

Q *Enumerate the diseases caused by E. histolytica.*

- It causes diarrhea, dysentery, hepatitis, amebic abscess in the lung, brain, spleen, skin.

Q *Who first discovered E. histolytica?*
▶ Lambl first discovered *E. histolytica* in 1859.

Q *Though E. histolytica is distributed worldwide, where is it very common?*
▶ It is very common in the tropics and subtropics.

Q *Where does E. histolytica live?*
▶ It lives in the mucosa and submucosa of the large intestine.

Q *What is the importance of the karyosome in Entameba?*
▶ The karyosome is important from the diagnostic point of view. Different species can be differentiated by the position of the karyosome in the nuclei. In *E. histolytica*, it is in the center, in *E. coli*, it is eccentric.

Q *What is excystation?*
▶ It is a process in which the cyst wall retracts, tetra-nucleated amebae are liberated and by binary fission, eight uninucleated amebae (trophozoites) are produced.

Q *How do trophozoites invade the mucosa of the intestine?*
▶ They invade the mucosa by production of their cytolysin and by symbiosis with gut bacterial flora.

Q *From which structure of E. histolytica does the first division start for their multiplication?*
▶ The first division starts from the nucleus of *E. histolytica*.

Q *How can you differentiate E. histolytica from E. coli?*
▶ The differentiation can be made by the position of the karyosome in the nucleus.

Q *Where are the lesions confined in primary, light and severe infections of the intestine?*
▶ In primary infection, they are more commonly found at the points of stasis (cecum, hepatic flexure, splenic flexure, recto-sigmoid junction).

In light infection, the lesions are restricted to these points only. In severe infection, more severe lesions are found in the muscosa and submucosa of the large intestine.

Q *How are bacteriologically sterile colliquative necrosis and ulcer in the large intestine formed?*
▶ When the amebae come in contact with the intestinal mucosa, they secrete a ferment which liquefies cells, ultimately forming sterile colliquative necrosis and a flask-shaped ulcer which contains lysed cells and no bacteria.

3 ZOOMASTIGOPHOREA

Class zoomastigophorea (sub-phyllum Sarcomastigophora, sub-class Mastigophora) includes the flagellate protozoa. The flagellates are one-celled animals that possess one to several long, delicate, thread-like extensions of the cytoplasm, termed ***flagella*** (singular, ***flagellum***), which are responsible for motility. According to their habitat, these flagellates are classified as follows:

GIARDIA INTESTINALIS

Common name: *Giardia lamblia*

This flagellate was first discovered by Leeuwenhoek (1681) in his own stools. Lambl (1859) gave it the name *G. intestinalis.* A new binomial, *Giardia lamblia,* was created in honour of

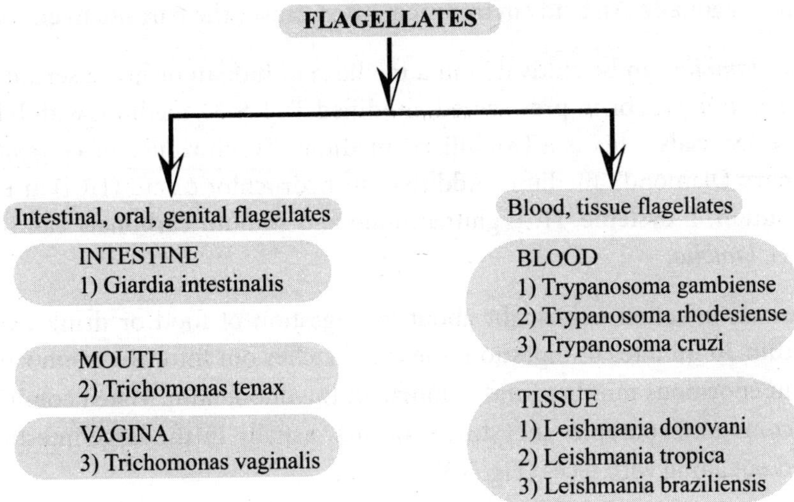

Fig. 3.1 Flagellates.

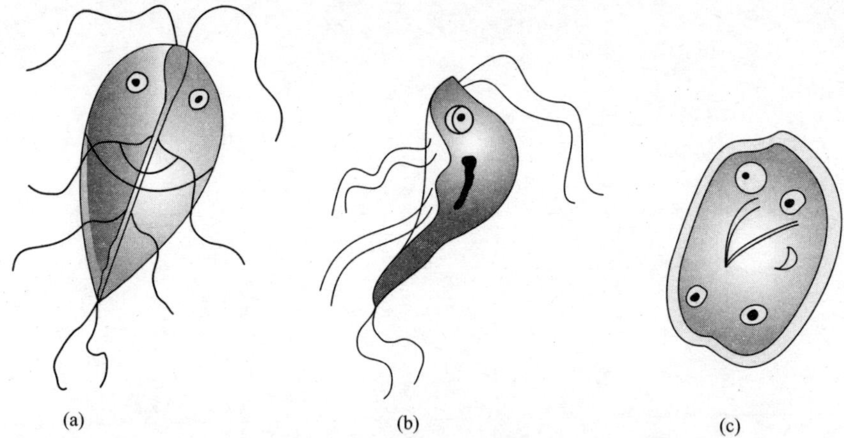

Fig. 3.2 Trophozoite of *G. lamblia,* a) ventral view; b) profile view; c) mature cyst.

Giard and Lambl, the discoverers. It is a universal parasite with a reported 200 million cases and 500,000 new cases occurring every year. It lives in the duodenum and the upper part of the human jejunum.

Morphology *G. lamblia* has both trophozoite and cyst stages. The ***living trophozoite*** (Fig. 3.2a and b) is rounded anteriorly and pointed posteriorly. Dorsally, it is convex and ventrally, it is provided with a concave notch (sucking disc). The trophozoite is 9.5 µm in length and 5.0 µm in breadth. A pair of nuclei, one on each side of the middle and near the anterior end of the body, is ovoidal and contains a central karyosome. Four pairs of flagella arise from the ventral side of the body. There are two axostyles. The ***cysts*** (Fig. 3.2c) are ovoidal and measure 8.0 µm in length and 7.0 µm in breadth. They have a finely granular cytoplasm, clearly separated from the cyst wall. Recently formed cysts have two nuclei and mature cysts have four nuclei. The axostyles lie diagonally. An acid environment often causes the parasite to encyst.

Cultivation *G. lamblia* can be cultivated in a medium of human or horse serum containing a seeding of *Saccharomyces* or in prewarmed, modified TYI-S-33 medium with bile salts and antibiotics in sealed vials. This is a lyophilized medium. Trophozoites of *G. lamblia* can be grown in ordinary Diamond's medium. Additives to hydrochloric acid (HCl) at PH_2 such as Hank's salts solution, L-cysteine, HCl, gluthathione and sodium carbonate can improve the excystation of *G. lamblia*.

Lifecycle Human infection is brought about by ingestion of food or drink contaminated with cysts. Within 30 minutes of ingestion, the cyst hatches out into two trophozoites, which then multiply in enormous numbers and colonize in the duodenum. When conditions in the duodenum become unfavourable, encystment occurs, usually in the large intestine, and the cysts are passed out along with feces (Fig. 3.3).

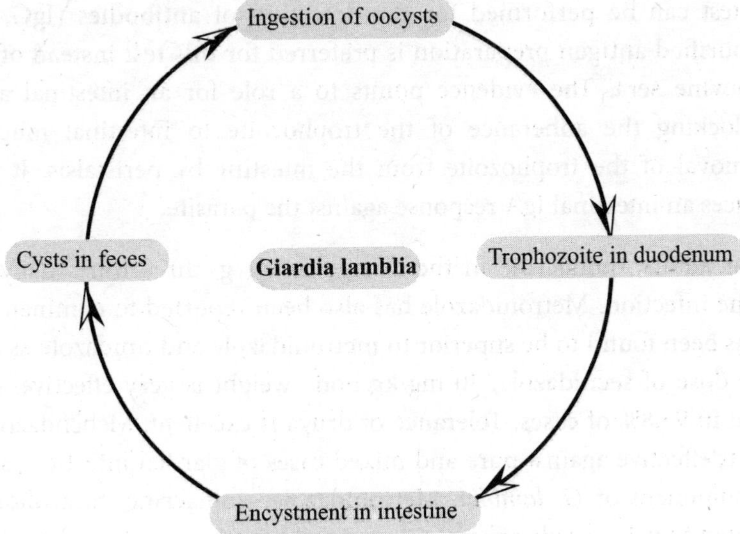

Fig. 3.3 Lifecycle of *G. lamblia*.

Pathogenicity and clinical features With the help of the sucking disc, the trophozoite attaches itself on the convex surface of the epithelial cells of the intestine and disturbs the intestinal function, leading to malabsorption of fat. Consequently, there is mild steatorrhea (passage of stools with excess fat), loose motions, chronic enteritis and cholecystopathy.

The majority of infections with *G. lamblia* are asymptomatic. In those patients who are ill, the disease ranges from mild diarrhea to severe debilitating malabsorption and weight loss. Reversible lactose deficiency and malabsorption of fat and vitamin B_{12} have been documented. There are recent concepts regarding the role of cyclic adenosine monophosphate (cAMP) and calmodulin etc in the pathogenesis of giardiasis. The majority of symptoms result from malabsorption and include abdominal distension, cramps, nausea, flatulence and frequent loose, bulky, foul and pungent stools. Upper gastrointestinal symptoms such as nausea and epigastric pain may distinguish giardiasis from infectious disorders of the colon.

Diagnosis Diagnosis is by

1. Microscopic demonstration of trophozoites in diarrheic stools and cysts in formed stools
2. Demonstration of trophozoites in the duodenal aspirate
3. Fluoroscopy which may demonstrate the hypermotility of the jejunum and
4. X-ray, ultrasonography which may reveal mucosal defects.

G. lamblia can be cultivated in Diamond's medium or a modified TYI-S-33 medium with bile salts and antibiotics. ELISA is highly sensitive and specific, either visually or by optical density determination, when compared with microscopy for the detection of the Giardia fecal antigen. ELISA is an extremely effective tool for the epidemiological investigation of giardiasis.

An ELISA test can be performed for the detection of antibodies (IgG, IgM, IgA) to *G. lamblia.* A purified antigen preparation is preferred for this test instead of crude soluble antigen, i.e., bovine sera. The evidence points to a role for an intestinal antitrophozoite antibody in blocking the adherance of the trophozoite to intestinal mucosa, with the consequent removal of the trophozoite from the intestine by peristalsis. It is shown that *G. lamblia* induces an intestinal IgA response against the parasite.

Treatment For adults, quinacrine in the dosage of 0.1 g, three times daily for five days, can eradicate the infection. Metronidazole has also been reported to eliminate the infection. Albendazole has been found to be superior to metronidazole and tinidazole as an antigiardial agent. A single dose of secnidazole, 30 mg/kg body weight is very effective. Parasitological cure is obtained in 95.8% of cases. Tolerance of drugs is excellent. Mebendazole 600 mg/day up to five days is effective against pure and mixed cases of giardial infection, as it targets the microtubule component of *G. lamblia.* Metronidazole, quinacrine, furazolidine have been prescribed, though they have side effects and may result in therapeutic failure. Prevention can be achieved only by personal hygiene.

GENUS TRICHOMONAS

These flagellates exist only in the trophozoite stage, they are provided with a cytostome (a cleft-like depression) at the side, 3–5 free flagella, an additional flagellum on the margin of an undulating membrane and an axostyle which usually protrudes through the posterior end of the body.

Genus Trichomonas has been classified according to habitat into three groups:

1) *Trichomonas vaginalis* (vagina and urinary tract) (Fig. 3.4)
2) *Trichomonas hominis* (ileo-caecal region) (Fig. 3.5) and
3) *Trichomonas tenax* (oral cavity) (Fig. 3.6).

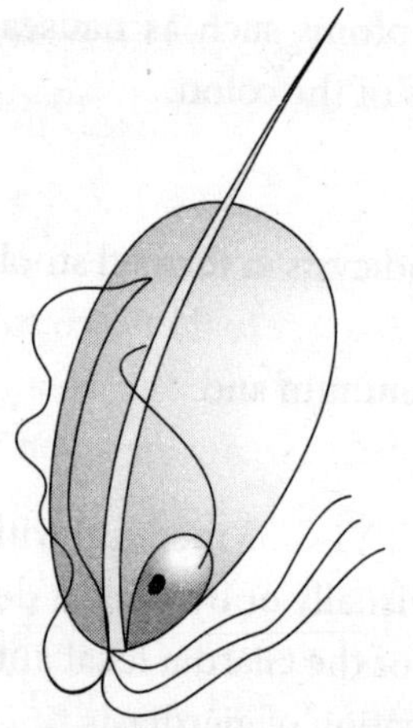

Fig. 3.4 *Trichomonas vaginalis.*

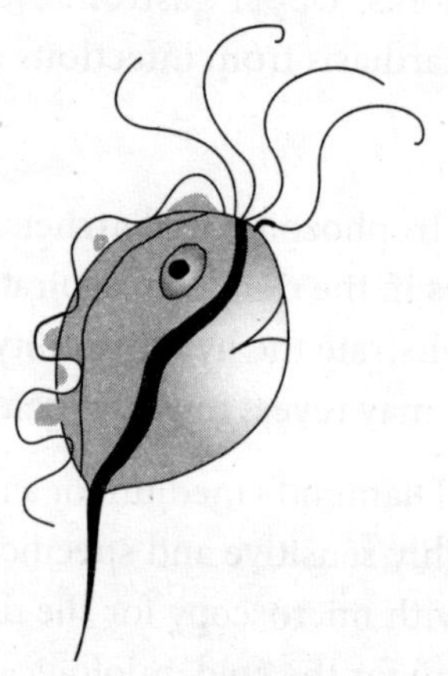

Fig. 3.5 *Trichomonas hominis.*

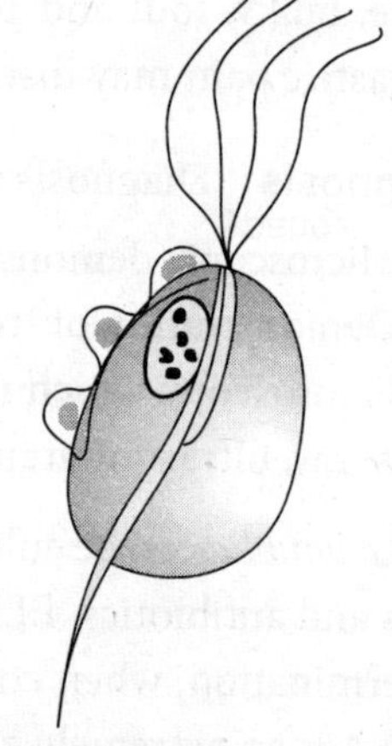

Fig. 3.6 *Trichomonas tenax.*

Trichomonas vaginalis

Donne (1836) first observed this species in female and male genital organs. This flagellate is commonly found in the human vagina and prostate gland.

Morphology *T. vaginalis* exists only in the trophozoite stage (Fig. 3.4). It is considerably larger (13 μm), its undulating membrane is shorter and its cytostome is much less conspicuous than the other trichomonas flagellates.

Biology and lifecycle In the female, this parasite feeds on the mucosal surface of the vagina, ingesting bacteria and leucocytes. It grows in the more acid condition of the vagina with an acidic pH than in a healthy one. The infected female is the reservoir of *T. vaginalis* and the infection is acquired by the male from her during intercourse.

Pathogenicity and clinical features T. *vaginalis* causes degeneration and desquamation of the vaginal epithelium, followed by leucocytic inflammation of the tissue layer. Very large numbers of trichomonads and leucocytes begin to be present in the vaginal discharge which is greenish or yellow. The vaginal secretions are extremely irritating, and cause itching and excoriation.

T. vaginalis inhabits the urethra, urinary bladder, vagina and prostate. Nearly half of the infections are asymptomatic. Recognized symptoms are yellow creamy vaginal discharge associated with itching and burning. Dysuria may be prominent. Infection of the male is generally asymptomatic; occasionally it is associated with mild urethral burning of brief duration.

Diagnosis In the female, *T. vaginalis* may be found in the centrifuged urine and vaginal secretions or scrapings. Care should be taken to distinguish it from *T. hominis* which is present in the feces. Indirect hemagglutination test is considered to be highly specific.

Immunoflorescence detects antibodies in urogentital trichomoniasis. Under acridine orange fluorescent microscopy, flagellated *T. vaginalis* appears red brown. *T. vaginalis* can be grown on Trussel and Johnson's medium, Lash's casein hydrolysate serum medium, Feinberg medium, modified liquid medium (Fuji).

Treatment and prevention Metronidazole is the most effective drug. The infection in the symptomless male must be diagnosed and treated to avoid spread through sexual intercourse.

Treatment of both partners is advised, for this is a sexually transmitted disease. Treatment with a single 2 g dose of metronidazole is also effective as 250 mg three times daily for seven days. It is frequently associated with nausea as a side-effect, a metallic taste and alcoholic intolerance. Each vaginal tablet contains clotrimazole USP (100 mg), a six-day course of one tablet is to be inserted in the vagina at bedtime for six consecutive days. A single course of four tablets, each tablet containing Tinidazole 500 mg is to be taken at bedtime on the first day of treatment, with the vaginal tablets.

A single course of four tablets (Tinidazole 500 mg) is to be taken by the male sexual partner to break the vicious cycle of repeated relapses of Trichomonas vaginitis. These are current chemotherapeutic agents. *T. vaginalis* is susceptible to mebendazole *in vitro*; whereas *T. hominis* is susceptible to it clinically.

GENUS TRYPANOSOMA

The genus Trypanosoma was established as a flagellate protozoon recovered from the blood. It has a typical trypanosomal structure (Fig. 3.7) i.e., an elongated, spindle-shaped body, more or less tapering at both ends, a centrally situated nucleus, a kinetoplast posterior to the nucleus, an undulating membrane arising from the kinetoplast and proceeding forward along the margin of the cell membrane, and a single free flagellum at the anterior end. Volutin granules are not observed during the acute stage of the infection, but appear in chronic and relapsed cases.

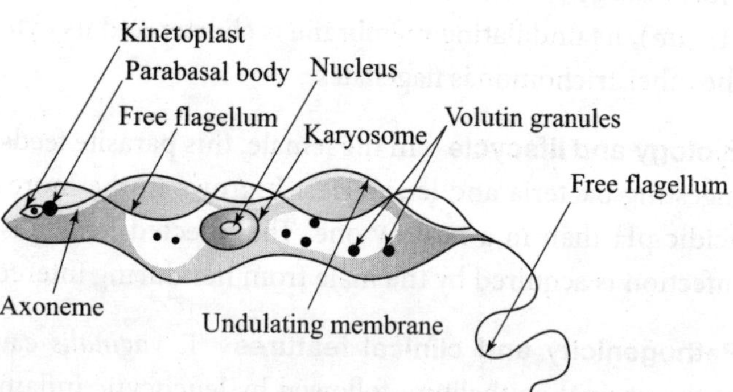

Fig. 3.7 Trypanosome - typical morphology.

Human pathogenic trypanosomes are classified as follows:

1) *Trypanosoma brucei-rhodesiense-gambiense* group (the human strain is *T. rhodesiense* (Fig. 3.8). *T. gambiense* (Fig. 3.9) causes African trypanosomiasis
2) *T. cruzi* (Fig. 3.10) causes South American trypanosomiasis (Chagas' disease).

Trypanosoma gambiense

Forde (1901) first observed *T. gambiense* in the blood and Dutton (1902) proposed the name *Trypanosoma gambiense*. It is found commonly in Uganda, Kenya, Tanzania, Zambia and Rhodesia.

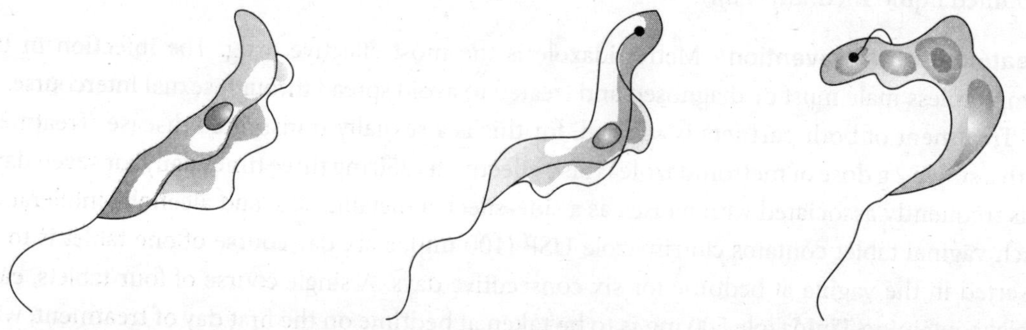

Fig. 3.8 *T. rhodesiense*. **Fig. 3.9** *T. gambiense*. **Fig. 3.10** *T. cruzi*.

Morphology *T. gambiense* occurs in three forms: long, short and intermediate. It measures 14.0 μm in length and 1.5 μm in breadth.

In the early stage, *T. gambiense* occurs in the blood and lymph nodes, and after cerebral symptoms develop, it is found in the cerebrospinal fluid.

Lifecycle In humans, the definite hosts, *T. gambiense* lives in the blood and multiplies by longitudinal binary division (Figs 3.11 and 3.16).

In the invertebrate intermediate host (*Glossina palpalis,* Glossina fly or tse-tse fly), after ingestion, the trypanosomes (Fig. 3.12) reach the intestine and reproduce in the lumen, never intracellularly; they transform into crithidial forms (Fig. 3.13) (long, slender forms) and migrate back to gain access to the salivary glands, where they multiply and fill the cavity of the gland. These metacyclic trypanosomes (infective forms) are introduced into humans by the bite of the fly. The entire lifecycle in the fly takes about 20 days. This type of development in the fly is known as 'development at the anterior station' (Figs 3.14–16).

Pathogenicity and clinical features Once introduced into the skin, the metacyclic trypanosomes produce at the site of the 'bite' an initial trypanosomal chancre, which is elevated, indurated and painful to touch. With the invasion of the lymph nodes, there is general enlargement of the lymph nodes. The spleen and liver are enlarged and congested.

With the invasion of the nervous system, the chronic or 'sleeping sickness' stage of infection is initiated. The headache is severe, and there is progressive mental dullness and apathy. There is disinclination to work, the patient becomes morose or excitable and has a weary gait. The sleepiness becomes so pronounced that the patient falls asleep while eating, standing or sitting. The patient sleeps continuously and cannot be aroused even to eat. Convulsions and death follow ultimately.

The signs and symptoms of sleeping sickness differ according to the infecting organisms. Rhodesian sleeping sickness, due to *T. rhodesiense,* causes a rapid progressive disease, often resulting in cardiac failure and acute neurological

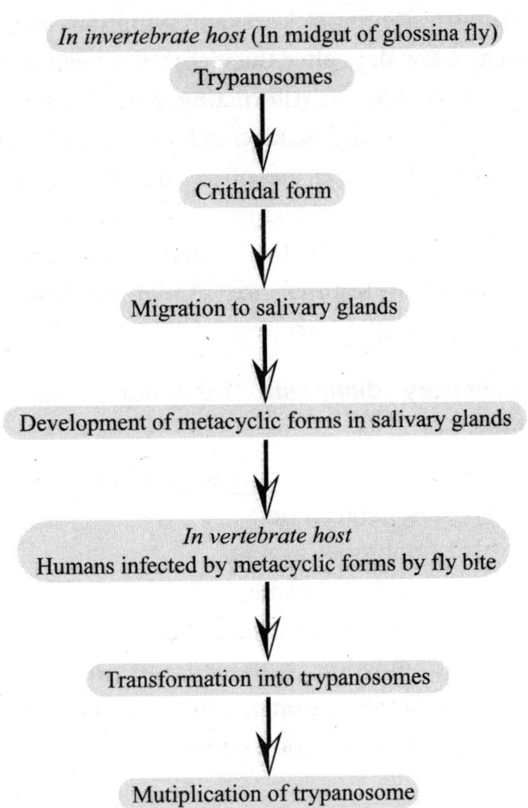

Fig. 3.11 Lifecycle of Trypanosoma gambiense.

manifestations. Gambian sleeping sickness, caused by *T. gambiense*, is typically a more chronic illness with primarily neurological features. Sometimes, Gambian sleeping sickness can progress rapidly and occasionally, Rhodesian sleeping sickness may follow a more chronic course. Fever, headache, dizziness and weakness occur in a majority of Gambian sleeping sickness patients. Lymphadenopathy with prominent supra clavicular and posterior cervical enlargement is seen in 80% of Gambian sleeping sickness patients. These enlarged lymph nodules are usually discrete, rubbery and painful. Moderate splenomegaly may occur; urticaria and erthematous rashes have also been observed. Clinical signs of heart disease are unusual. Rhodesian sleeping sickness is more acute than Gambian sleeping sickness and symptoms usually occur a few days after the victim has been bitten by the tse-tse fly. Alternating periods of high fever, malaise and headache, followed by several days of well being are often misinterpreted as acute malarial infection. Lymphadenopathy is not prominent in this variety of the disease. Neurological features are similar to those of Gambian sleeping sickness

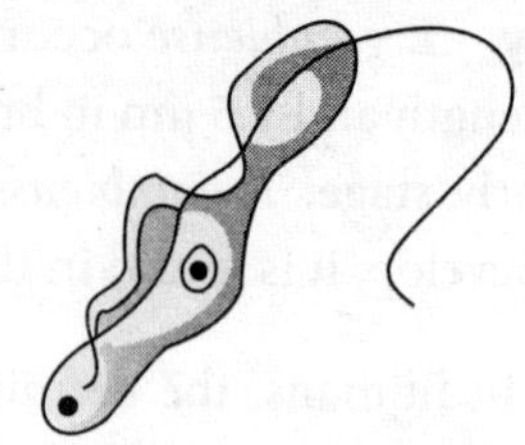

Fig. 3.12 Trypanosome after ingestion.

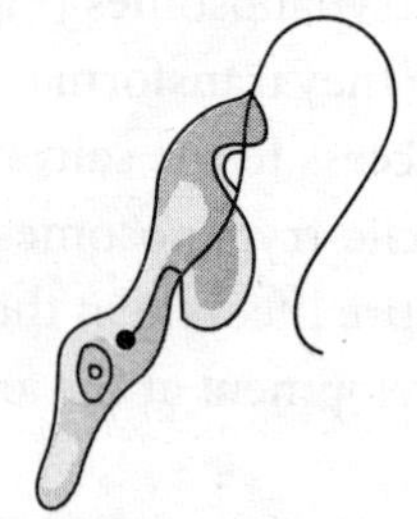

Fig. 3.13 Crithidial form.

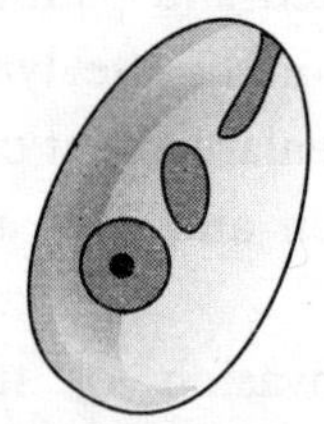

Fig. 3.14 Leishmania.

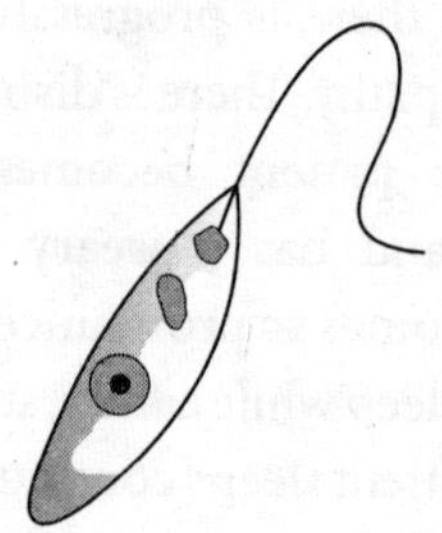

Fig. 3.15 Leptomonas.

Laboratory diagnosis Laboratory diagnosis consists of

1. Demonstration of trypanosomes in
   a) Peripheral blood
   b) Lymph node aspirate
   c) Bone marrow smear and
   d) Cerebrospinal fluid, by microscopic examination of stained and unstained films. Trypanosomes can also be easily seen by acridine orange (AO) staining technique adapted for rapid diagnosis of malarial parasites in blood smears.

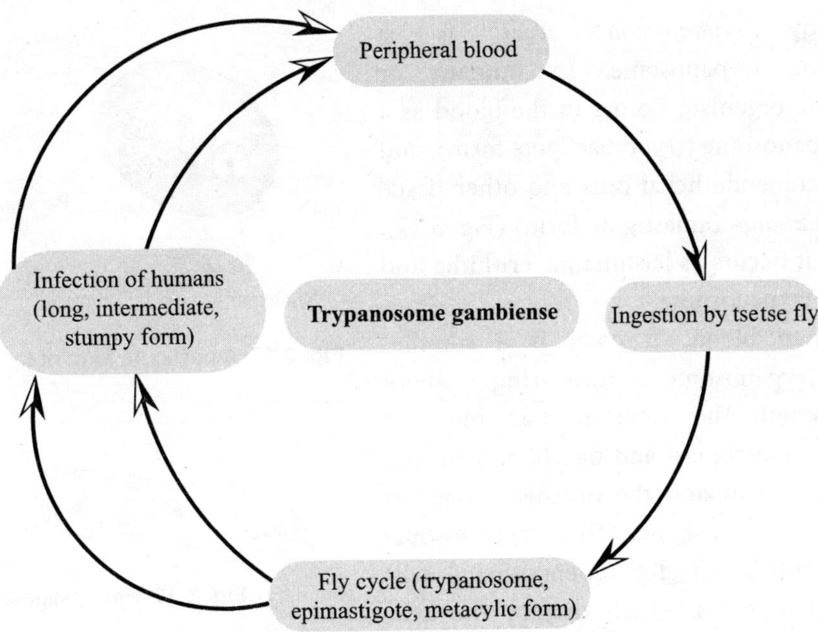

Fig. 3.16 Lifecycle of *T. gambiense.*

2. Cultivation in suitable media (Weinman's medium and Tobie, Von Brand and Mehlman's medium)
3. Animal inoculation
4. Serological tests: agar gel precipitation; indirect fluorescent antibody test and complement fixation test. Besides ELISA, capillary passive hemagglutination (HA) also has been developed. Antigens are not commercially available. A card agglutination test (CAT) has also been introduced. It is simple, specific and sensitive. It is yet to be fully evaluated.

Treatment Tryparsamide, suramin and pentamidine have been effectively used for treatment. Recent additions include melarsen, an antimony compound and berenil. They will not cure the disease once CNS invasion has developed.

Prophylaxis This includes destruction of vectors, isolation of human population from infected areas and chemoprophylaxis by pentamidine.

Trypanosoma cruzi

Chagas (1909) discovered *Trypanosoma cruzi,* first in the intestine of a triatomid bug, and later in the blood of a sick child. It is widely prevalent in Brazil, Chile, Argentina, Peru and Colombia. It has been estimated that 35 million persons in Latin America are likely to get this infection (WHO, 1960). Chagas' disease strikes 12 million victims annually. Only one million of these cases are diagnosed. It kills 60,000 people a year (WHO, 1990).

Morphology *Trypanosoma cruzi* is a pleomorphic trypanosome. In humans or animals, the organism occurs in the blood as a typical trypanosome (trypomastigote form), and in the reticuloendothelial cells and other tissue cells as *leishmania* (amastigote form) (Fig. 3.17). In insects, it occurs as leishmania, crithidia and metacyclic trypanosome.

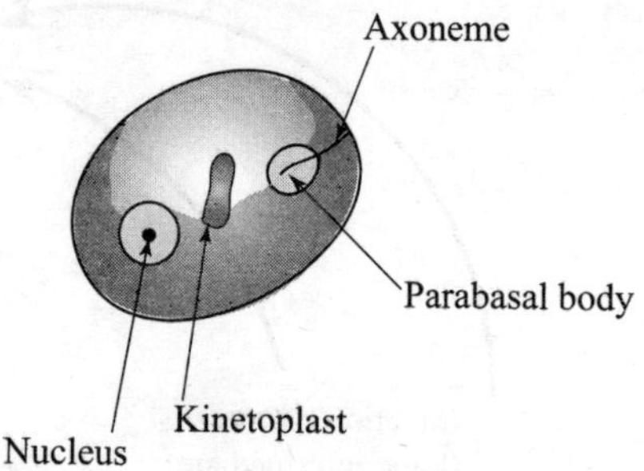

Fig. 3.17 Amastigote form of trypanosome.

In human blood, *T. cruzi* is a spindle-shaped trypanosome, measuring about 20 μm in length. The cytoplasm stains blue and the nucleus, kinetoplast and flagellum stain red with Giemsa stain and the organism assumes a characteristic C-shape. This trypanosome multiplies only in the reticuloendothelial cells as leishmania forms, which destroy the cells after repeated division. The leishmania forms are round or ovoidal in shape, measuring 1.5–4 μm in diameter and they are almost indistinguishable from *Leishmania donovani.*

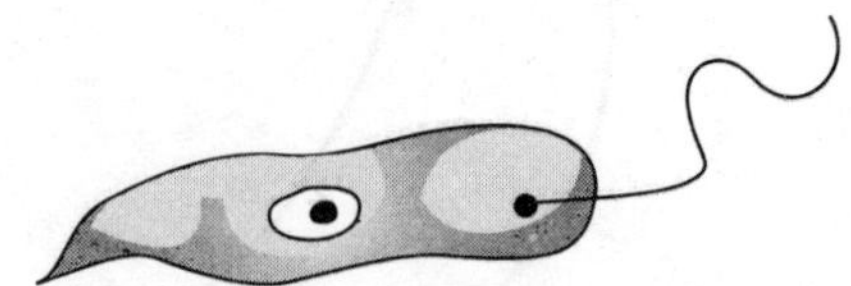

Fig. 3.18 Promastigote.

T. cruzi is easily cultivated on Novy, MacNeal and Nicolle's (NNN) medium, Weinmann's medium and Tobie, VonBrand and Mehlman's medium.

Lifecycle *T. cruzi* passes its lifecycle in two hosts: human and in the reduvid bug, *Triatoma infestans* or the assassin bug. It is also called kissing bug – when the infected bug bites the lips of a sleeping child to transmit Chagas' disease, it creates the impression that it is kissing the child.

Development in reduviid bug: The trypomastigote forms are ingested by the bug while biting an infected individual. In the midgut (stomach) of the bug, they are transformed into amastigote forms which multiply by binary fission, and later transform into epimastigote forms (Fig. 3.19). These migrate to the hindgut, multiply by longitudinal fission and transform into metacyclic trypanosomes which are excreted in the feces of the bug. This type of development in 8–10 days is known as 'development at the posterior station'.

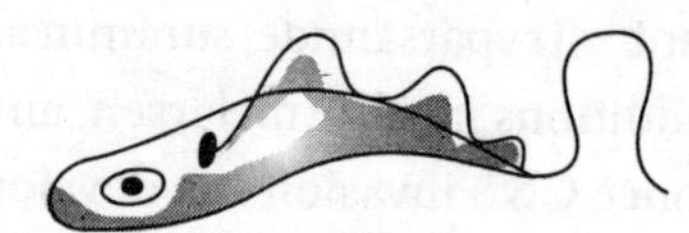

Fig. 3.19 Epimastigote.

Development in humans: These metacyclic trypanosomes, infective to humans, when rubbed into the puncture wound made by the bug or into any abrasion of the skin or on the exposed mucous membrane of the eye, nostrils or lips, invade the adipose cells of the subcutaneous tissues and the nearby muscle cells immediately below the site of inoculation. Then they transform into amastigote forms, multiply by binary fission, pass through the promastigote and epimastigote forms which are again transformed into trypomastigote forms and liberated into the blood (Fig. 3.20).

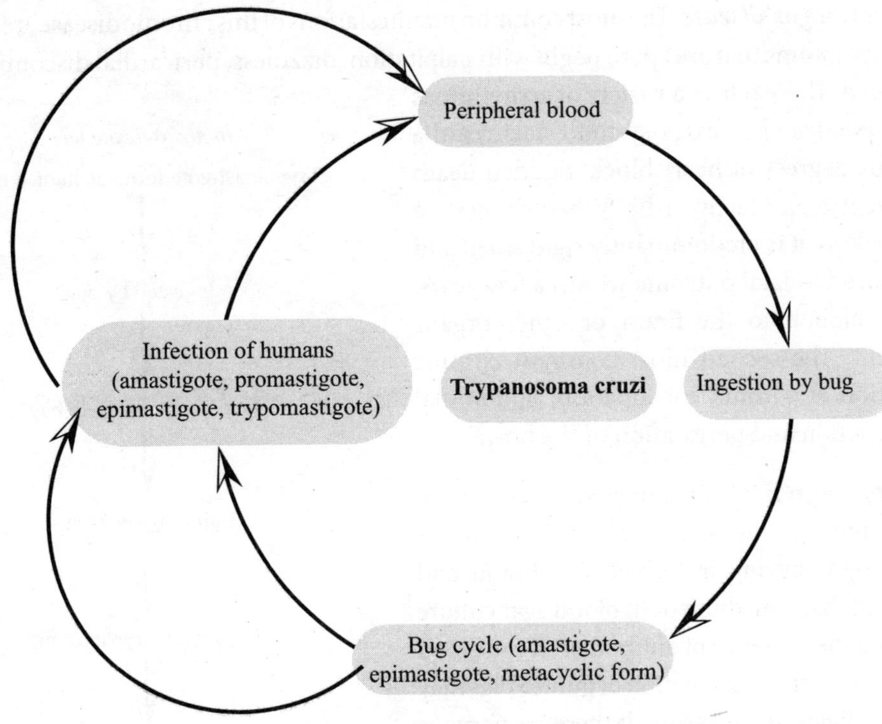

Fig. 3.20 Lifecycle of *T. cruzi*.

Pathogenicity and clinical features In the skin, there is a characteristic primary lesion (chagoma), which blocks the lymphatic capillaries and produces edema of the area. Chagas' disease occurs in the acute and chronic forms.

The acute form, which is usually found in children, lasts for 20 to 30 days and is characterized by high fever. The face is swollen, there is marked edema of the eyelids (Romana's sign) and keratitis.

The chronic form follows the acute form in children who survive and is common in adults. The symptoms of the chronic form are probably related to damage sustained during the acute phase. The chronic infection is characterized by disturbances of cardiac rhythm. When motor centres are destroyed, there is paraplegia, diplegia and spastic paralysis. Cardiomyopathy may be a complication.

Acute Chagas' disease can occur commonly in children at any stage with an incubation period of a week. Other signs of this acute disease include generalized lymphadenopathy, hepatosplenomegaly, myocarditis accompanied by tachycardia and nonspecific electrocardiographic changes. Meningoencephalitis is another serious complication in infants, fatal outcome is rare in the acute form and when it does occur, it is due to myocarditis and congestive failure or to meningoencephalitis. Sometimes signs and symptoms may subside within a week to several months even without treatment.

Chronic Chagas' disease. The most common manifestations of this chronic disease are cardiac signs and symptoms that are apt to begin with palpitation, dizziness, pericardial discomfort and even syncope. These reflect a variety of arrhythmias including ventricular extra-systolic tachycardia and various degrees of heart block. Sudden death is due to ventricular tachycardia. When congestive failure develops, it is predominantly right sided and is likely to lead to fatal outcome within a few years. Peripheral emboli to the brain or other organs are frequent. The second most common chronic manifestation is chronic constipation, abdominal pain, obstruction and perforation of the bowel.

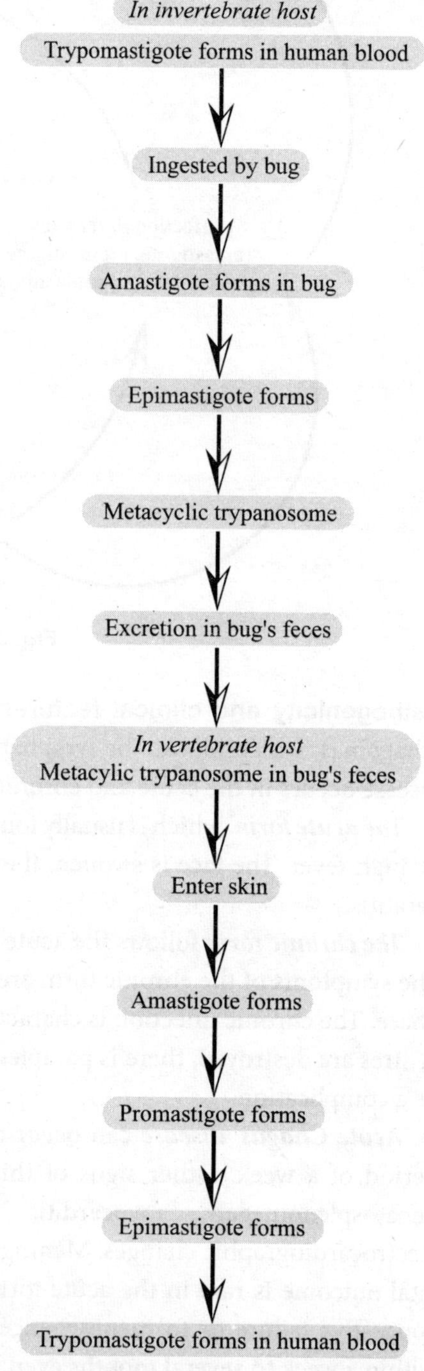

Fig. 3.21 Lifecycle of *T. cruzi.*

Laboratory diagnosis Diagnosis of this infection rests on demonstration of *T. cruzi* in the blood or tissues, or by culturing in Tobie, Von Brand and Mehlman's diphasic medium or in blood agar culture medium and the presence of antibodies. If the blood is negative for *T. cruzi,* inoculation of guinea pigs may be done as a diagnostic measure. If there are nervous symptoms, inoculation of the cerebrospinal fluid into susceptible animals is effective in demonstrating trypanosomes. Xenodiagnosis has been employed frequently, allowing trypanosome-free, laboratory bred triatomids to 'bite' the individual suspected of having the disease. If the infection is present in the blood meal, the trypanosomes multiply in the intestine of the bug and an examination of the intestinal contents in 10–30 days will reveal metacyclic trypanosomes.

The complement fixation test using antigen obtained from cultures of *T. cruzi* is both specific and practical. Serological testing is generally not needed for diagnosis of acute disease. Parasitic specific IgM antibody detected by immunofluorescence or direct agglutination does not become positive until 20 to 40 days after the onset of symptoms. The diagnosis of chronic Chagas' disease requires demonstration of antibody to *T. cruzi* in the presence of characteristic cardiac abnormalities. Indirect hemagglutination (HIA) test is recommended. Very recently, WHO used a G-agglutination test to diagnose Chagas' disease in blood donors in Brazil. Indirect Flouorescence Antibody test (IFAT) is also used. ELISA is the best choice.

It is necessary to differentiate *kala azar* from Chagas' disease by culture, immunologic tests or xenodiagnosis.

Treatment Only one case of *T. cruzi* infection in a laboratory attendant was reported as being successfully treated with nitrofurazone. Very recently, oral allopurinol in a dose of 600 to 900 mg/day/for 60 days has been found as effective as the nitrofurans or benznidazole for Chagas' disease without side effects. Early in 1990, it was found that a few mg of Azardirachtine, a substance in neem seeds is effective in blocking the development of *T. cruzi*. Thus, its lifecycle is broken. This is still under experiment.

Prophylaxis Prophylaxis consists of

1) Destruction of bugs by effective insecticides, BHC (gammexane)
2) Avoiding bug bites by using mosquito nets and
3) Vaccination.

   An attempt has been made very recently by American scientists to develop a vaccine against Chagas' disease.

GENUS LEISHMANIA

This genus was established to include *Leishmania donovani*.

The Leishmania species have a nucleus, a kinetoplast, an axoneme and, in the leptomonas stage, a single flagellum arising from the latter, but no undulating membrane.

There are three species of Leishmania:

1) *L. donovani* which causes *kala azar*
2) *L. tropica* which causes oriental sore or the cutaneous leishmaniasis of the Old World and
3) *L. braziliensis* which causes mucocutaneus leishmaniasis or Espundia or American leishmaniasis or the cutaneous leishmaniasis of the New World.

Leishmania donovani

In 1900, Leishman discovered *Leishmania donovani* in the spleen smears of a dead soldier at Dum Dum, India. The condition is therefore known as Dum Dum fever or *kala azar*. Later, in 1903, Donovan reported it from Chennai. *Kala azar* affects 15 million people worldwide and the last epidemic in India resulted in 20,000 deaths. It still continues in Bihar state sporadically.

L. donovani is found commonly in America, Africa, Asia (China, eastern India in Assam and Bengal, and also in Bihar, Orissa, Tamilnadu and in eastern Uttar Pradesh) and Europe. The amastigote forms (leishmania) are always present in the human reticuloendothelial cells.

Morphology L. *donovani* occurs in two stages – the aflagellar leishmania (amastigote) stage in humans and reservoir mammals, and the leptomonas (promastigote) in the sand fly and in cultures. Leishmania is an ovoidal body, measuring about 2–3 m in length and living intracellularly in the monocytes or polymorphonuclear leucocytes of humans. In preparations stained with Giemsa's stain, the cytoplasm stains pale blue and the nucleus stains red; there is a deep red, rod-like body, known as the parabasal body. The kinetoplast is at a right angles to the nucleus. The axoneme is a delicate filament extending from the kinetoplast to the anterior tip.

Leptomonas forms are long, slender and spindle shaped, have a single flagellum and possess marked motility. They measure 15 μm in length and 1.5 μm in breadth. The flagellum measures 15 μm in length and projects from the anterior end. The nucleus is centrally situated, and the kinetoplast lies transversely near the anterior end. These forms can be grown on NNN medium.

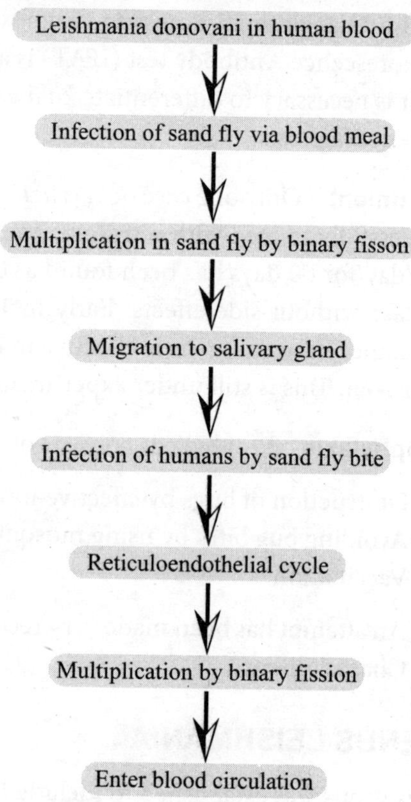

Fig. 3.22 Lifecycle of *L. donovani.*

Lifecycle After entry into the human body, the organism is engulfed by the reticuloendothelial cells, in which it multiplies by binary fission as a leishmania until the host cell is destroyed. It parasitizes the new macrophage cells, and the free leishmania and the parasitized macrophage cells enter the circulation.

A blood sucking insect, the sand fly, *Phlebotomus argentipes* (Indian vector), draws in these circulating leishmania and macrophage cells during a blood meal. In the intestine of the sand fly, the leishmaniae become leptomonas forms and divide by longitudinal fission into two individuals. Enormous numbers of leptomonas are found in the midgut, and later in the pharynx and buccal cavity of the sand fly. This type of development is known as 'anterior station development'. The transmission is thus effected through the bite of the infected insect and the cycle is repeated (Figs 3.22 and 3.23). Rapid multiplication in the insect and in cultures gives rise to the so-called 'rosette forms' in which several organisms are arranged with their innermost flagella entangled.

Pathogencity and clinical features When an infected sand fly bites a human prey, the leptomonas stage is inoculated into the victim's skin, and the macrophages nearby engulf the organisms which metamorphose into the leishmania stage within the cytoplasm of the host cells. Sometimes, parasitized macrophages are set free into the bloodstream and are carried from the skin to the viscera where they lodge and develop rapidly. In the spleen or liver, the leishmanias are taken up by fixed macrophages, such as Kupffer's cells in the liver, and they

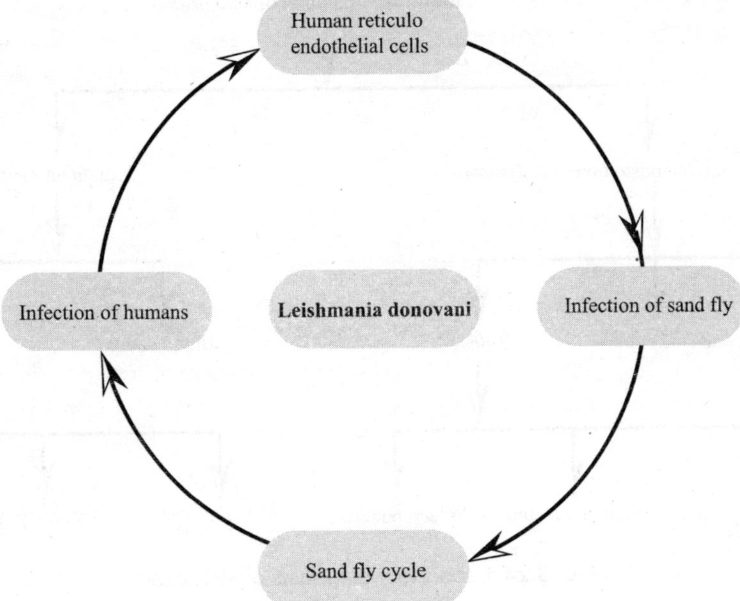

Fig. 3.23 Lifecycle of *L. donovani.*

multiply in these cells and destroy them. These are called '*kala azar* bodies'. When the red bone marrow is involved, there is diminished production of erythrocytes with ensuing anemia.

The incubation period is usually limited to 2–4 months. The first symptoms are malaise, headache and irregular fever, with progressive enlargement of the spleen and occasional acute abdominal pain. There is edema of the skin, emaciation of the chest, dysentery or diarrhea, bleeding of the mucous membranes of the gums and nostrils and cachexia, accompanied by a progressive and marked enlargement of the spleen and a lesser enlargement of the liver.

The skin over the entire body is dry, rough and harsh and is often pigmented (darkened). The hair tends to be brittle and falls out. Death frequently occurs from complications (amebic and bacillary dysentery, pulmonary tuberculosis, pneumonia, etc.).

Though the incubation period is usually long (2–4 months), it may be as short as 10–14 days. Under conditions of immuno-suppression, latent infection of several years may be activated. The onset is usually insidious. Fever accompanied by sweating, weakness and weight loss, gradually becomes noticeable. The symptoms, perhaps including nonproductive cough and abdominal discomfort produced by an enlarging liver and spleen, may continue for months. In some patients, the course is rapid with high temperature and chills simulating typhoid fever or acute brucellosis. The most pronounced physical findings are fever, splenomegaly and cachexia which are especially evident in the thorax and shoulder girdle. Fever pattern often exhibits characteristic elevation twice daily to 38 to 40°C for some time. Generalized adenopathy is common in some patients. In light-skinned persons, hyper pigmentation of the skin may be noted; the term *kala azar* is Hindi for black sickness. Spleen enlargement is extreme

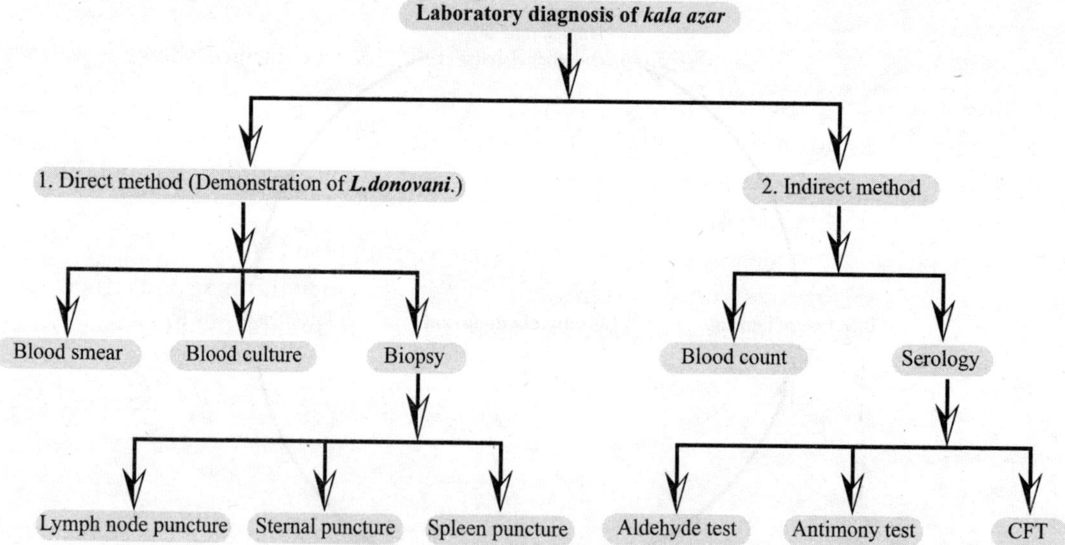

Fig. 3.24 Laboratory diagnosis of *kala azar*.

in this disease. The organ is firm and tender. Some typical cases may involve only modest hepatosplenomegaly. As the disease progresses, weight loss, anemia and other signs become clinically more apparent. Subcutaneous edema, ascites and other evidence of hypoalbuminemia may develop. Another cause of death is massive gastrointestinal bleeding.

Pathogenic lesions:

Spleen

1. Macroscopic appearance:
   a. The organ is enormously enlarged
   b. The capsule of the enlarged spleen is often thickened due to peri-splenitis
   c. The organ is soft in consistency and cuts easily without any resistance
   d. The cut surface shows marked congestion, and has a dull red or chocolate colour
   e. The substance of the splenic tissue is friable and can easily be broken down by the pressure of the thumb, signifying the absence of fibrosis.
2. Microscopic appearance:
   a. The vascular spaces are widely dilated and engorged with blood
   b. The reticular cells of Billroth cords are markedly increased and are packed with the amastigote forms of *L. donovani;* the sinus lining cells (littoral cells) do not contain any parasite
   c. There is no evidence of fibrosis in the parenchyma
   d. The trabeculae are thin and atrophic
   e. The Malpighian corpuscles disappear almost completely due to the pressure of the hyper-plastic pulp tissue
   f. There is often an increase of plasma cells.

Liver

1. Macroscopically, the liver is enlarged and congested. The cut surface shows a nutmeg appearance
2. Microscopically, the organ shows the following:
   a. The Kupffer's cells are greatly increased in size and number and their cystoplasms are packed with amastigote forms of *L. donovani*
   b. The sinusoidal capillaries are dilated and engorged with blood
   c. The liver cells are free from parasitization. They may undergo thinning and atrophy due to the pressure of dilated sinusoidal capillaries. A certain amount of fatty changes may be present
   d. The fibrous tissues in the liver are not increased, but there is a slight increase in the reticulum fibrils.

If the liver is greatly damaged, jaundice appears as a manifestation of *kala azar*. A profound anemia with a hemoglobin level of 5–10 g/100 ml may occur in *kala azar*. In the past, the cause of this anemia was thought to be bone marrow hyperplasia. Careful studies have shown that marrow hyperplasia is not the main cause of anemia. It is thought that hemolysis, as a possible mechanism, plays an important part in the production of anemia in *kala azar*.

Bone marrow The reticuloendothelial cells undergo extensive hyperplasia due to the stimulus of *L. donovani*. This causes profound disturbance of the hemopoietic activities in the bone marrow, particularly of the leucoblastic elements, resulting in leucopenia (neutropenia). The leucopenia increases as the disease advances.

Microscopically, the bone marrow shows considerable replacement of the hemopoietic tissues by the proliferated and parasitized macrophages, and the plasma cells are increased. The amastigote forms of *L. donovani* can be demonstrated in the smear prepared from the bone marrow obtained by sternal or iliac crest puncture. This is useful in the diagnosis of *kala azar*.

Lymph nodes The changes are not constant. Parasites have been observed in the lymph nodes of patients in China and the Mediterranean areas, but not in India where, so far, only two cases of lymphadenopathy in *kala azar* with numerous parasites have been recorded.

Intestine These intestinal ulcers are not characteristic features of *kala azar*; they may be due to secondary infection, and not due to *L. donovani*.

1. ***Direct method***: One of the most conclusive methods for the diagnosis of *kala azar* is by the demonstration of *L. donovani*.

   The direct method consists of:

   a. Blood smear: Microscopic examination of a stained film has been found to be successful in demonstrating the presence of the amastigote forms of *L. donovani* in peripheral blood. The chance of finding *L. donovani* is greatly increased by adopting the following procedures:

      i) By making a thick film as recommended for malarial parasites

ii) By producing a straight leucocytic edge by abruptly lifting off the spreading slide. The straight line will contain a large number of white blood cells and

iii) By centrifuging citrated blood. The sediment can be pipetted off with a capillary pipette, smeared, dried and examined.

b. Blood culture: About 1–2 ml of blood is taken aseptically from the vein and diluted with 10 ml of citrated saline solution (0.85% normal saline containing 2% sodium citrate). The cells are either allowed to settle in a cool incubator (22°C) overnight or centrifuged. The cellular sediment is then inoculated into the water of condensation of NNN medium and incubated at 22°C for 1–4 weeks. Each week, a drop of condensation fluid is examined for the promastigote forms of *L. donovani.* It is time consuming (about one month), but a positive result is obtained in many cases.

L. donovani (Indian strain) can be propagated in a chemically defined media suitable for cultivation and cloning of promastigotes: defined medium (S-α-MEM) based on a minimum essential medium supplemented with glutamine, glucose, folic acid, biotin, hematin, HEPES and adenine; another defined medium (S-RPM1) is based on S-RPM1-1640, suitably supplemented. Better growth was seen in S-α-Mem and improved by the addition of heat inactivated fetal bovine serum. Nutrient broth containing fetal calf serum, antibiotics is cheap, an easily prepared medium satisfactory for Leishmania growth.

Leihmania can also be cultured in Schneider's enriched medium or in Tobie, Von Brand and Mehlman's diphasic medium. Amastigote *L. donovani* can be cultivated in a murine tumour cell, dog sarcoma cell, vero cell.

c. Biopsy:

i) Spleen puncture is one of the best methods, if the spleen is considerably enlarged. Amastigote forms are found in stained film and promastigote forms of *L. donovani* in culture. The only risk of spleen puncture is that there may be continuous bleeding from the puncture wound in the soft and enlarged spleen, which will result in death

ii) Bone marrow puncture: Sternal or iliac crest puncture is one of the important methods of diagnosis of *kala azar*. It can be adopted in the early stages, when the spleen is not enlarged. Compared to spleen puncture, it is more painful but safer. When the parasites are scanty, it may give negative results. The amastigote forms of *L. donovani* can be demonstrated in stained films and the promastigote forms in NNN medium.

2. ***The indirect method*** comprises the following:

a. Blood count: Examination of the leucocyte count reveals leucopenia. The average total count is 3000/mm³ of blood and there is progressive diminution during the course of the disease, the count falling to 1000/mm³ of blood or even below.

b. Serological tests are based mostly on an increase in serum gammaglobulin and a decrease in serum albumin, and they are not very reliable.

   i) Aldehyde (formol gel) test of Napier: One or two ml of serum from the *kala azar* patient should be taken in a test tube and one or two drops of 40% formalin should be added to it. Jellification of milkwhite opacity like that of the white of a hard boiled egg will take place. If the reaction takes place within 20 minutes, the test is said to be strongly positive, and the test becomes positive mostly after three months' duration. The test is also positive in infection with *Schistosoma japonicum* and *Trypanosoma brucei,* in multiple myeloma and cirrhosis of the liver. The test is negative in infection with *Leishmania tropica*

   ii) Antimony test of Chopra: Neat or 1:10 diluted serum from the *kala azar* patient is taken in a test tube and a 4% urea stibamine solution in distilled water is added to it. In positive cases, there will be formation of a profuse flocculent precipitation

   iii) Complement fixation test: This test is based on the demonstration of immune bodies in the blood sera of *kala azar* patients. In this type of test, the human tubercle bacilli of Witebsky, Klingenstein and Kuhn called the WKK antigen is used *(Leishmania* and *Mycobacterium tuberculosis* share a common antigen). This test is also positive in the lepromatous type of leprosy and pulmonary tuberculosis. Hence, it is considered nonspecific. Complement fixation test, using the human tubercle bacilli of Kedrowsky as antigen, has been employed successfully in the diagnosis of *kala azar* in India.

3. ***Other serological tests*:**
   a) The immunofluorescent test is very valuable in the diagnosis of *kala azar*. Promastigote forms of *L. donovani* are used as antigen and the serum diluted to 1:100
   b) The indirect hemagglutination (HIA) test is also used
   c) The specific complement fixation test may be performed by using the promastigotes of *L. donovani* and the spleen or liver from an infected hamster as antigen.

4. ***Leishmanin (Montenegro) test*** for immunity is employed to diagnose *kala azar*. About 0.1 to 0.2 ml of antigen (containing 6–10 millions of killed promastigotes of *L. donovani* or *L. tropica* per ml) is injected intradermally and the result is read after 72 hours. Delayed reaction develops in cured individuals. The test is negative in early cases but becomes positive six to eight weeks after the completion of treatment. The test is positive in African *kala azar,* but not in Indian and Mediterranean *kala azar*. There appears to be no cross immunity between strains of *L. donovani* and *L. tropica.*

5. ***Adler's test:*** The development of the promastigote forms of leishmania in Locke's serum agar can be inhibited by a specific immune serum. Thus, the three species, *L. donovani, L. tropica* and *L. braziliensis,* can be differentiated serologically to some extent.
   Several techniques have been developed to detect and measure specific leishmanial antibodies in patient sera. They are indirect fluorescent antibody test (IFAT), counter immuno-electrophoresis (CIEP) and enzyme-linked immunosorbent assay (ELISA). IFAT is a sensitive technique to detect the antibody in 93% of patients of visceral leishmaniasis. The test results are positive in the early stage. CIEP also becomes positive in 80% of patients in the early stage and in almost all patients with late infection. ELISA is specific and sensitive, but further evaluation has indicated that it is the most practical test. As compared to ELISA and IFAT, the direct agglutination test (DAT) was found to be most sensitive, specific and easy to perform at the field level and economic enough to be cost effective. The rate of positivite results with DAT (96.3%) was comparable and slightly better than that of splenic smear examination (94%), the 'gold standard' test for the diagnosis of *kala azar.* DAT appears to be the future diagnostic tool of *kala azar.*

Laboratory diagnosis of acute kala azar:

1. Demonstration of parasites
   a) In the peripheral blood by thick film and by blood culture and
   b) In a sternum or iliac crest puncture, sufficiently enlarged at this stage to be punctured
2. Blood count which shows leucopenia
3. Serological test: Complement fixation test with WKK antigen is positive within three weeks of infection, whereas the aldehyde test becomes negative at the early stage and positive later on.

Treatment

Supportive treatment: This includes good nursing care, a diet rich in vitamins and iron, liver therapy and at times, transfusion.

Specific treatment: Sodium or potassium antimony tartarate in 2% freshly prepared solution administered intravenously was the common drug used in the early years. Pneumonia may complicate the treatment with antimony tartarate. Certain pentavalent preparations of antimony have proved to be highly effective in the treatment of this infection. Of these, ethylstibamine is the most satisfactory; it is less toxic and produces a cure in the shortest time. The adult initial dose is 0.1 g; a second dose of 0.2 g and a third dose, has to be continued daily until the symptoms disappear. For Indian cases, 12 intramuscular administrations are required.

Sodium stibogluconate or sodium antimony gluconate gives excellent results and is least toxic. Though sodium antimony gluconate, 20 mg/kg twice daily for 20 days, is an effective drug for the treatment of visceral leishmaniasis in India, very recently, oral ketoconazole in a dose of 600 mg daily in three divided doses for four weeks was found to cure the patient clinically and parasitologically, within four weeks.

Earlier, in India (Bihar), pentamadine was found to be effective against *kala azar*, but it is costlier than sodium stibogluconate. It has side effects like the onset of diabetes in many cases. Besides, it was found that curative treatment is costlier than preventive treatment. Aminosidine is also used for the treatment of visceral leishmaniasis. Liposomised amphothericin B has increased efficacy against *L. donovani* infection. It may be largely due to enhanced drug tolerance rather than altered drug distribution at the site of infection. Amphotericin B administered intravenously is very effective to multidrug (sodium stibogluconate, allopurinol plus ketoconazole and pentamidine isothionate) resistant *L. donovani* in low dosage (dose of 1 mg stepped up daily) and safer in the treatment of antimony unresponsive to *kala azar*.

Prophylaxis

1. All human cases should be treated adequately with antimony
2. Infected dogs should be destroyed, especially in China and the Mediterranean countries
3. Decaying vegetation from the ground which may harbour or breed sand flies should be removed
4. Adult sand flies should be caught and destroyed every morning and evening
5. Mosquito nets should be used regularly
6. Houses should be well lit and ventilated
7. Sleeping quarters should be above the ground floor because sand flies do not usually fly many feet above the ground
8. Sand flies should be destroyed by insecticides, e.g., DDT.

Dermal Leishmanoid

It is a non-ulcerative cutaneous lesion. Usually, it develops in 10% of *kala azar* patients after completion of sodium or potassium antimony tartarate treatment for the original disease (*kala azar*), when the visceral infection disappears and the skin infection persists. Its occurrence indicates the need for intensive treatment with a pentavalent antimony preparation. It also develops in spontaneously cured *kala azar*.

It is distributed in endemic areas of *kala azar* (Assam, Tamilnadu and West Bengal). It has also been reported in Africa and China, but not in Mediterranean countries.

Clinical features These are of three types:

1. ***Depigmented macules:*** These are early lesions which appear most commonly on the trunk, extremities and less commonly on the face. The loss of pigmentation is not complete.
2. ***Erythematous patches:*** These are also early lesions which are distributed on the nose, cheek and chin, often having a butterfly distribution, therefore referred to as 'butterfly erythema'. They are highly photo-sensitive, and become prominent towards the middle of the day.
3. ***Yellowish pink nodules:*** In this type, earlier lesions are replaced by these nodules which are mostly found on the face, skin, rarely on the mucous membrane of the tongue and eyes,

and may appear on any part of the body. These nodules are soft, painless, granulomatous growths of various sizes, and do not ulcerate as in oriental sore.

Laboratory diagnosis Diagnosis can be made by microscopic demonstration of amastigote forms of *L. donovani* in a smear of the nodular lesion after Leishman or Giemsa staining; but these cannot be found in the depigmented nodules.

Treatment The condition can be treated by the administration of pentavalent antimony compounds at double the dose used for visceral leishmaniasis. The second dose, if required, should not be repeated within two months of the first course. Post *kala aza* dermal leishmaniasis (PKDL) is never fatal, it can remain alive and act as a potential source of sand fly infection in an untreated patient for at least 35 years. Recently, it has been shown that all cases of PKDL can be completely cured if antimonials are given in the correct dosage and for a longer period, till the lesions disappear.

Leishmania tropica

Cunningham (1885) first observed the parasite in the tissue of a 'Delhi boil' in Kolkata. A Russian military surgeon, Borovsky (1898), described it accurately, and Luhne (1906) gave it the name *Leishmania tropica.*

Cutaneous leishmaniasis is distributed in Africa, America, Asia, Europe, Sri Lanka and West Pakistan, western and northwestern India. In India, the oriental sore is limited to the dry parts of western India, whereas *kala azar* is confined to the moist eastern parts.

In human beings, *L. tropica* is a parasite of the skin, found in the endothelial cells of the capillaries of the affected areas. This species is not found in peripheral blood. Oriental sore, found in dogs in Mumbai, is caused by leishmania identical to *L. tropica.* It has been concluded that it is a parasite of both humans and dogs.

Morphology The morphology of *L. tropica* is identical to that of *L. donovani.* This flagellate is found in the leishmania form in humans and in the leptomonas form in cultures and in sand flies *(Phlebotomas papatasii* – a western Indian vector).

L. tropica can be cultivated in an NNN medium. Infectivity for humans can be retained in cultures for a very long period of time. Laboratory animals can be infected with *L. tropica.*

Lifecycle The lifecycle of *L. tropica* is similar to that of *L. donovani* in human beings and sand flies, except that in humans, the leishmania forms live only in the reticuloendothelial cells and the lymphoid tissue of the skin and do not invade the viscera, as does *L. donovani.* The method of reproduction in both the leishmania and leptomonas stages is by binary longitudinal division.

Pathogenesis The leptomonas stage of *L. tropica* is introduced into the skin of the victim by the infected sand fly while sucking a blood meal. The parasites are engulfed by local white blood cells. In macrophages, the parasites roll up to the leishmania form and multiply, and the macrophages rupture. Escaped parasites are taken up by other macrophages in the immediate vicinity.

Pathology At first, the tissue cells in the corneal layer of the skin contain a large number of parasites; later this breaks down to produce a cratiform lesion with a depressed ulcerated centre covered with granulating tissue and an indurated periphery. The growth of *L. tropica* in the cutaneous tissue causes hypertrophy of the stratum corneum. Necrosis and ulceration occur and secondary infections with bacteria are common.

Clinical features The incubation period of oriental sore varies from a few days to several months. The symptoms are also variable. The sores usually occur on the exposed parts of the body and may be single or multiple.

The lesion appears first as a reddish papule which later transforms into a shallow ulcer. The ulcer gradually enlarges and has sharp, cut, raised edges surrounded by an indurated area. These ulcers coalesce to produce large ulcers. Secondary bacterial infection of the sore is common. Then, general symptoms (fever, chills and inflammation) are observed. Verrucose, lupoid forms of oriental sore have been described in India.

Laboratory diagnosis The diagnosis of infection with *L. tropica* may be done by microscopic examination of Leishman or Giemsa-stained smear prepared from the punctured indurated edge of the sore. These flagellates are not found in the blood. Smears made by scraping the floor of the ulcer are often negative, because *L. tropica* cannot exist along with the bacteria in the ulcer. If smears are negative, biopsy of the lymphoid under the ulcer provides specific proof of infection. In all cases, cultures should be made in the NNN medium.

Montenegro reaction (Skin test): This can be invoked by intradermal inoculation of the dead or washed leptomonads of *L. tropica.* A positive leishmanin skin test and serum antibody can be demonstrated in patients by the time a cutaneous lesion has ulcerated. These tests remain positive in mucocutaneous disease. Serological tests can reflect a previous rather than a current leishmanial infection.

A recent technique, that may permit direct and rapid diagnosis as well as species differentiation of leishmania, is blotting with radio-labeled DNA probes.

Treatment Pentavalent antimony preparation is the drug of choice. Dehydroemetine orally in doses of 100 mg daily for 10–21 days gives satisfactory results. Patients with different forms of cutaneous leishmaniasis are given a single exposure to CO_2 laser rays. The lesions are totally cured without side effects.

In India, ketoconazole is successful in visceral leishmaniasis treatment and also for cutaneous leishmanisis which does not respond to sodium antimony gluconate. It is used in a dose of 200 mg twice daily for 15 days, increasing to 400 mg twice daily for another 15 days.

Amphoterion B is indicated in cases in which antimonials have failed to control the disease. Side effects are common and severe. Other drugs are rimfapin and metronidazole, but they are inferior to antimony. Mebendazole is effective clinically.

Prophylaxis

1. If possible, the ulcers should be protected from insects with a gauze bandage
2. Transmission to others must be prevented by covering the ulcer
3. The patient should be warned regarding auto-inoculation
4. Spray of DDT is the most effective method of control of sand flies
5. Fly repellents can be applied over the skin
6. Mosquito nets are very effective
7. All natural reservoirs (dogs, rodents, etc.) of *L. tropica* should be destroyed.

Leishmania braziliensis

Lindenberg (1909) found leishmanias in ulcers in patients in Brazil. Later, Carinii (1911) found leishmanias in the naso-pharyngeal mucous membrane and in ulcerative lesions in patients in the same country and named it *Leishmania braziliensis.* Morphologically, this parasite is identical with *L. donovani* and *L. tropica,* and these three parasites have distinct agglutination and complement fixation reactions.

L. braziliensis is found commonly in America and Argentina. Human Immunodeficiency Virus (HIV) associated leishmaniasis has been reported from South America, the Mediterranean basin, Iberian peninsular and in other states where leishmaniasis is endemic. Recrudescent and new infections have occurred with *L. donovani, L. tropica, L. infantum* and *L. braziliensis* have also been identified. Visceral leishmaniasis with cutaneous dissemination is common and in Brazil, disseminated cutaneous leishmaniasis has been reported in those with AIDS.

Morphology The morphology of *L. braziliensis* in both the leishmania and leptomonas forms is identical with that of *L. tropica* and *L. donovani.*

L. braziliensis can be cultivated in the NNN medium and in the chorio-allantoic membrane of the chick embryo. The rhesus monkey is at times susceptible to infection, but Syrian hamsters have been refractory.

Lifecycle The lifecycle of *L. braziliensis* and its method of reproduction are identical with those of *L. donovani* and *L. tropica.* The insect hosts of this species of parasite are sand flies (Phlebotomas). The adaptation of leishmania species to their local vectors is associated with the genetic factor in leishmania.

Transmission The disease is typically endemic. Direct contact may cause infection, as the condition is inoculable and auto-inoculable.

Pathogenesis and pathology Following inoculation of the leptomonas stage of *L. braziliensis* by an infected sand fly, a small papule appears; this soon transforms into a red, itchy vesicle. Within one to four weeks, the lesion begins to show ulceration, often with a round or oval contour but at times with ragged, irregular, indurated edges.

Histologically, the elevated circumference shows epithelial hyperplasia and intense dermal inflammation with edema. Beneath the epithelial proliferation, there is a zone of leishmaniae. This primary lesion tends to be self-healing in six to fifteen months, unless secondary invasion develops. The primary lesion is mostly found on the ear lobe. The secondary lesions in the mucous membrane may be ulcerative or indurative.

Clinical features The period of incubation varies from a few days to several weeks. The primary lesion appears as a papule which develops into a painless ulcer and may disappear after a few months, or it may transform into an open weeping sore which is very painful. The characteristic secondary lesions of the mucous membranes may appear before the initial sore is healed. The first signs usually noted are thickening of the mucosa in the nasal septum, followed by the development of nodules which necrose and form ulcers involving the mucous membrane of the mouth, and hard and soft palates. Constitutional symptoms are fever, anemia, pain in the affected region and malaise.

Laboratory diagnosis Diagnosis is established by

1. Demonstration of amastigote forms of *L. braziliensis* in material obtained by puncture of the edge of the initial ulcer stained with Giemsa stain
2. Culture on the NNN medium for promastigote forms and
3. The Montenegro intradermal reaction which is the method of choice for diagnosis of mucocutaneous leishmaniasis.

Treatment The treatment of the initial sore is the same as that of oriental sore, while that of the stage involving the mucous membrane consists of intravenous injection of one of the antimony preparations.

Prophylaxis Prophylaxis consists of avoiding forests where the sand flies breed; protection from sand flies by application of fly repellents; and avoiding direct contact with infected cases.

SUMMARY

- Mastigophora (flagellates) are single-celled animals with several long, delicate, thread-like filaments (organ of locomotion). They are intestinal, oral, genital, blood, tissue flagellates

Giardia lamblia

- Giardia lamblia (intestinal flagellate). Its name is given in honour of Giard and Lambl (1859). It lives in the duodenum and jejunum of human beings. Its lifecycle has trophozoite and cystic stages. Trophozoite has two nuclei and a ventral sucking disc and can be cultivated in an artificial medium.
- Human beings get the infection within 30 minutes after ingestion of mature cysts in food or drink. These cysts give rise to two trophozoites which multiply enormously and colonize in the duodenum. In the large intestine, under unfavourable conditions, they encyst and the cysts are passed out in the stool.
- The intestinal function is disturbed because they attach to the mucosa with their sucking disc causing loose motions with excess fat (steatorrhea), chronic enteritis and cholecystopathy.
- Diagnosis can be confirmed by the presence of trophozoites or cysts in the stool; or trophozoites in duodenal aspirate; by the hyper motility of the jejunum by fluoroscopy; mucosal defects by x-ray.
- Quinacrine, metronidozole can be useful to eliminate the infection; only personal hygiene can control the infection.

Genus trichomonas

- These flagellates have only the trophozoite stage in their lifecycle. According to their habitat they are grouped into:
  1. *Trichomonas vaginalis* (vagina, urinary tract)
  2. *Trichomonas hominis* (ileocaecal region)
  3. *Trichomonas tenax* (oral cavity).

Trichomonas vaginalis

- It was first observed by Donne (1936) in the male and female genital tract and in the human prostate gland. It is the largest among protozoa (13 μm) with an undulating membrane. It feeds on the vaginal mucosal surface, ingests bacteria and leucocytes in the more acidic condition of the vagina. Males get infected during sexual intercourse with infected females.
- Degeneration and desquamation of vaginal mucosa with leucocytic infiltration are pathological changes. Greenish or yellowish discharge may contain many *trichomonas vaginalis* and leucocytes. It is extremely irritating; causes itching and excoriation.
- Its infection can be diagnosed by the presence of *Trichomonas vaginalis* in the centrifuged urine and vaginal secretion and by a specific indirect hemagglutination test.
- Metronidazole is the most effective drug. The disease can be controlled by avoiding sexual intercourse with infected individuals.

Genus trypanosoma

- It is a spindle-shaped blood flagellate, it has a free flagellum at the anterior end and an undulating membrane arising from the kinetoplast which is at the posterior end and has volutin granules.
- Human pathogenic trypanosomes are classified into two.
  1. Trypanosoma brucei–rhodensiense–gambiense group causes African trypanosomiasis (sleeping sickness)
  2. *T. cruzi* causes South American trypanosomiasis (Chagas' disease).
- **Trypanosoma gambiense** *T. gambiense* occurs in three forms: long, short and intermediate. In the early stage, it occurs in blood and lymph nodes, in the cerebrospinal fluid (CSF) after cerebral infection.
- In their lifecycle, ingested trypanosomes in the midgut of the fly, transform into crithidial forms which migrate to the salivary gland of the fly, where they develop into metacyclic forms which are infective to humans, especially by the bite of the glossina fly. This type of development in the fly is known as 'development at anterior station.' In the blood, these metacyclic forms transform into trypanosomes which multiply by longitudinal binary fission. An elevated, indurated, painful initial 'trypanosomal chancre' develops in the skin after glossina fly-bite. After invasion in the lymph nodes, the spleen and liver are enlarged and congested.
- The chronic or 'sleeping sickness' stage of the infection is initiated after the invasion of the nervous system. The headache is severe, with mental dullness, apathy, disinclination to work, profound sleep – the patient falls asleep while eating, standing, will not be aroused even to eat, ultimately there is convulsion and death.
- Laboratory diagnosis can confirm the infection by demonstration of trypanosomes in blood, lymph node, bone marrow, CSF, by microscopical examination of stained films; by cultivation in media; animal inoculation and by serology.
- The infection can be treated by suitable drugs (tryparsamide, suramin, pentamidine) and be controlled by destruction of vectors, isolation of patients.
- **Trypanosoma cruzi** *T. cruzi* is a pleomorphic trypanosome occurring in human blood as a typical trypanosome (trypanomastigote form), in other tissues as leishmania (amastigote form), whereas in insects, it occurs as leishmania, crithidial and metacyclic trypanosomes, infective to humans. *T. cruzi* can be cultivated in Novy, Mac Neal and Nicolle (NNN.) medium.
- Lifecycle requires two hosts (humans and the reduviid bug). The bug (*Triatoma infestans*), ingests trypanosomes, while biting an infected human, and are transformed into mastigote forms which multiply by binary fission, and later transform into epimastigote forms which migrate to the hindgut, multiply by longitudinal fission and transform into metacylic forms which are excreted in the feces of the bug. This is the 'development at the posterior station' in the bug.
- These metacyclic forms (infective to humans) when rubbed into the wound made by the bug, invade the adipose cells of subcutaneous tissue of humans, transform into amastigote, promastigote, epimastigote which at last transform into trypomastigote forms which are liberated into the human blood.

- In Chagas' disease, the primary lesion appears in the skin which is known as 'Chagoma' which produces edema by blocking lymphatic capillaries. Chagas' disease occurs in two forms:
  1. The acute form is common in children with fever lasting for 30 days, swollen face with edema of the eyelids (Romana's sign), keratitis.
  2. The chronic form is common in adults and is characterized by the disturbance of cardiac rhythm. There is paraplegia, diplegia and spastic paralysis. When motor centers are affected, there may be cardiomyopathy complication.
- In the laboratory, the infection can be diagnosed by the demonstration of *T. cruzi* and antibodies in the blood. If the blood is negative, guinea pigs can be inoculated for the presence of *T. cruzi* in guinea pig blood. Xenodiagnosis can be done by allowing trypanosome-free laboratory bred triatomids to bite individuals suspected for the disease. Metacyclic trypanosomes can be detected in the intestinal content of the bug.
- Destruction of bugs, avoiding bug bite and vaccination can control the infection.

Genus leishmania

- It includes three species:
  (a) *Leishmania donovani* which causes *kala azar*
  (b) *L. tropica* which causes oriental sore
  (c) *L. braziliensis* which causes mucocutaneous leishmaniasis.
- **Leishmania donovani** Leishman discovered *L. donovani* from the spleen smear of a dead soldier at Dum Dum (Kolkata), India; later, Donovan reported it from Chennai.
- Though it is common in other countries; in India, it is more common in eastern India, in Assam, Bengal, Bihar, Orissa; it is often reported in Tamilnadu and eastern Uttar Pradesh.
- Leishmania (amastigote form) lives in the reticuloendothelial cells of human beings.
- Morphologically, Leishmania has two stages:
  1. Amastigote (Leishmania) in humans; 2. promastigote (leptomonas) in sand fly and cultures
  2. Amastigote is an oviodal body living in mononuclear or polymorphonuclear human leucocytes. It has a parabasal (rod-like) body and a delicate filament extending to the anterior tip
  3. Leptomonas is long, slender and spindle-shaped with a single flagellum and can be grown on an NNN medium.
- In their lifecycle, metacyclic trypanosomes are engulfed by macrophages when they enter the human body after it is infected by sand fly bite. After multiplication by binary fission in the macrophages, they enter into blood circulation, after these host macrophages are destroyed and are drawn up by the sand fly during its blood meal.

- In the intestine of the sand fly, they transform into leptomonas forms, which by their longitudinal fission, divide into numerous leptomonas and migrate into the pharynx of the fly. This is known as 'development in anterior station.' Then they are transmitted by the bite of the infected sand fly to humans. This cycle is repeated. Metacyclic trypanosomes, engulfed by macrophages, metamorphose into leishmania within the host cells. These parasitized macrophages are carried away from the skin to the viscera by the bloodstream. In the spleen or liver, leishmania are taken up by fixed macrophages such as Kupffer's cells in the liver.They multiply in these cells and destroy them. These are called '*kala azar* bodies' Erythrocyte production is diminished with the ensuing anemia when the bone marrow is involved.
- After an incubation period of 2–4 months, the symptoms (malaise, headache, fever, enlargement of spleen, acute abdominal pain, pigmented, 'darkened,' rough, dry skin) are observed. Death may be due to complications (tuberculosis, dysentery, pneumonia).
- Diagnosis of *kala azar* can be done in the laboratory by
  (a) Direct method (demonstration of *L. donovani* in blood or biopsy)
  (b) Indirect method (blood count or serology).
- Supportive and specific treatment should be undertaken. The infection can be controlled by
  1. Destruction of sand fly by insecticides
  2. Bedrooms should be above the ground floor
  3. House should be well lit and ventilated
  4. Mosquito net should be used
  5. All human cases should be treated with effective drugs.
- **Dermal leishmanoid** It is a non-ulcerative extraneous lesion. It develops in 10% cases of *kala azar* after completion of antimony treatment. Skin infection may persist when visceral infection disappears. This lesion may also develop in spontaneously cured *kala azar*. It is very common in endemic areas of *kala azar* (Assam, West Bengal, Chennai – Tamil Nadu).
- Clinically, the lesions are of three types:
  1. Depigmented macules appearing on the face, trunk and extremities
  2. Erythematous patches on the nose, cheek with butterfly distribution
  3. Yellowish pink nodules on the skin, face, eyes; rarely in the tongue which does not ulcerate as in oriental sore.
- *L. donovani* can be demonstrated in the smear of the modular lesion.
- This condition can be treated with a double dose of antimony.
- **Leishmania tropica** It was first observed in the tissue of a Delhi boil in Kolkata. It causes cutaneous leishmaniasis or Delhi boil or oriental sore in humans and is distributed in Sri Lanka, Pakistan, Western and west northern India. Oriental sore is limited to the dry parts of India, whereas *kala azar* is found in the moist eastern parts of India. This parasite resides in the capillary endothelial cells of the blood vessels.

- Leishmania, identical to *L. tropica,* causes oriental sore in dogs in Mumbai and is a parasite of both dog and humans and can be grown in NNN medium.
- Its lifecycle in humans and sand flies is similar to that of *L. donovani,* except that it does not invade the viscera, but is confined only to the reticuloendothelial cells of the skin. It occurs in both.
- The skin containing numerous parasites breaks down to produce a cratiform lesion with an ulcer at the center and an indurated periphery. Secondary bacterial infection is common. Fever, chills and inflammation are the clinical symptoms.
- In the laboratory, it can be diagnosed by demonstration of *L. tropica* in a smear prepared from the punctured edge of the ulcer. As *L. tropica* cannot live with bacteria, the scraping from the floor of the ulcer will be negative. They can be cultivated in NNN medium. Skin test (Montenegro reaction) can also be used in the diagnosis.
- It can be treated with antimony and can be controlled by following the same prophylactic methods as for *L. tropica and L. donovani.*
- **Leishmania braziliensis** It causes mucocutaneous leishmaniasis in humans in America and in Argentina. Mophologically, it is identical to *L. tropica* and *L. donovani.* These three leishmania have distinct agglutination and complement fixation reactions, though they are similar in all other characteristics.

QUESTIONS

Genus trypanosoma

Q *What is Trypanosoma?*
- It is a flagellate blood protozoon.

Q *How many flagella do they have?*
- They have a single free flagellum.

Q *At what stage of the infection do volutin granutes appear in Trypanosoma?*
- The volutin granules appear in the chronic stage of infection and in cases of relapse.

Q *Enumerate the human pathogenic trypanosomes.*
- Human pathogenic trypanosomes are classified into:
  1. Trypanosoma brucei–rhodesiense–gambiense group causing African Trypanosomiasis
  2. *T. cruzi* causing South American trypanosomiasis.

Trypanosoma gambiense

Q *At which stage is T. gambiense found in the cerebrospinal fluid?*
- It is found after the onset of cerebral symptoms.

Q *Name the definite host and the intermediate host involved in the lifecycle of T. gambiense?*
- Humans are definite hosts; the glossina fly or the tsetse fly is the invertebrate intermediate host.

Q *Which are the forms of T. gambiense that cause infection to humans?*
▶ Metacyclic forms are infective to humans.

Q *Where does T. gambiense live in humans and how does it multiply?*
▶ It lives in human blood and it multiplies by longitudinal binary fission in the blood.

Q *Describe the multiplication of T. gambiense in the intermediate host?*
▶ After ingestion of *T. gambiense* trypanosomes by fly bite, these flagellates reach the intestine of the fly, multiply in the lumen, not intracellularly, and transform into crithidial forms which migrate to the salivary gland of the fly for further development into the metacyclic form, which is infective to humans. This type of development in the fly is known as development at the anterior station, as in the case of the sand fly (intermediate host of *L. donovani*).

Q *What is trypanosomal chancre?*
▶ At the site of glossina fly bite, an initial (indurated, elevated painful to touch) trypanosomal chancre develops.

Q *When does the sleeping sickness stage of the infection develop?*
▶ This stage develops when the nervous system is affected.

Q *Describe the symptoms of sleeping sickness?*
▶ Severe headache, mental dullness, apathy and disinclination to work. Sleepiness becomes so pronounced that the patient cannot be aroused even to eat. Convulsions and ultimate death follow the symptoms.

Q *How can the disease be diagnosed in the laboratory?*
▶ The infection can be diagnosed by microscopic examination of stained blood, lymph nodes, bone marrow and cerebrospinal fluid; by cultivation in NNN medium, animal inoculation and by serological tests.

Q *How is this disease treated and controlled?*
▶ The disease is treated by effective drugs and can be controlled by destruction of the vector (glossina fly) and isolation of infected individuals.

Trypanosoma cruzi

Q *How can T. cruzi be differentiated from T. gambiense morphologically in stained smear under a microscope?*
▶ *T. cruzi* has a characteristic C-shape, whereas *T. gambiense* is elongated and spindle shaped.

Q *Name the intermediate host of T. cruzi.*
▶ The intermediate host of *T. cruzi* is the reduviid bug (*Triatoma infestans*) in which the amasitgote, epimastigote and the metacyclic trypanosome forms are found.

Q *In which host of the lifecycle of T. cruzi are the amastigote, promastigote and epimastigote forms found?*
▶ All these three forms are found in the vertebrate definite host (human beings).

Q *What is Chagoma?*

▶ It is a characteristic primary lesion in the skin of patients with Chagas' disease, caused by *T. cruzi.*

Q *What is Romana's sign?*

▶ Romana's sign is usually found in the acute form of Chagas' disease in children and is characterized by high fever, swollen face, marked edema of the eyelids and keratitis.

Q *When do paraplegia, diplegia and spastic paralysis occur in the chronic form of Chagas' disease?*

▶ They occur when the motor centers are destroyed.

Q *What is xenodiagnosis?*

▶ It is employed by allowing trypanosome-free laboratory bred triatoma (bug) to bite suspected individuals for Chagas' disease. If the trypanosomes are recovered from the intestinal content of the bug, then it is positive for Chagas' disease.

Genus leishmania

Q *What is Leishmania?*

▶ It is a tissue flagellate.

Q *How many species of Leishmania cause disease in human beings?*

▶ 1. *Leishmania donovani* causes kala azar

2. *L. tropica* causes oriental sore

3. *L. braziliensis* causes mucocutaneous leishmaniasis.

Leishmania donovani

Q *Where was L. donovani first discovered in India?*

▶ *L. donovani* was first discovered in the spleen smears of a dead soldier at Dum Dum, Kolkata, later it was reported from Tamilnadu; it is limited to the moist eastern parts of India.

Q *How was L. donovani named?*

▶ It was named in honour of Leishman and Donovan (discoverers).

Q *In how many stages does L. donovani occur in its lifecycle?*

▶ *L. donovani* occurs in two stages:

1. Aflagellar Leishmania (amastigote) stage in humans and reservoir
2. Leplomonas (promastigote) in the sand fly.

Q *Where does Leishmania live in humans?*

▶ It lives intracellularly in human polymorphs and is an ovoidal body.

Q *Where are leptomonas found in its lifecycle?*

▶ They are found in the intestine of the sand fly and later migrate to the salivary gland and the buccal cavity.

Q *Why should leptomonas migrate to the salivary gland?*

▶ They migrate to the salivary gland for further development before infecting humans.

Q *Why is this type of development called 'anterior station development?'*

▶ Because it develops in the salivary gland of the sand fly.

Q *What is a rosette form?*

▶ Rosette form occurs when several leptomonas are arranged with their innermost flagella entangled. This form is seen in insects or in culture.

Q *Why are leptomonas carried away from the victim's skin after their inoculation into the skin by the bite of an infected fly?*

▶ Leptomonas are set free into the bloodstream. After parasitized macrophages are ruptured, they are carried from the skin to the spleen and liver through the blood for their multiplication in fixed macrophages which will be destroyed to produce 'kala azar bodies;' later anemia develops, when the bone marrow is affected.

Q *Describe in brief the clinical features of kala azar.*

▶ Symptoms are fever, malaise, headache, abdominal pain, edema of the skin, emaciated chest, dysentery, skin is dry, rough and 'darkened' Death is due to complications (tuberculosis, dysentery).

Q *How will you diagnose kala azar in the laboratory?*

▶ *Kala azar* can be diagnosed directly and indirectly. In the direct method, by demonstration of *L. donovani* in blood smear, culture, biopsy, in the indirect methods by blood count, serology.

Q *How can kala azar be treated and controlled?*

▶ Treatment can be specific and supportive. Control is by destroying the sand fly, using mosquito nets; the sleeping quarter should be above the ground floor.

Leishmania tropica

Q *Who first observed L. tropica and where?*

▶ Cunningham (1885) first observed *L. tropica* in the tissue of Delhi boil in Kolkota.

Q *Where is it confined to in India?*

▶ It is confined to the dry parts of India (western and north-western India), causing oriental sore or cutaneous leishmaniasis.

Q *How does L. tropica differ from L. donovani?*

▶ Though *L. tropica* is identical to *L. donovani*, it differs mainly by its limiting multiplication only in the reticuloendothelial cells of the skin, not invading into the viscera.

Q *What is a cratiform lesion in oriental sore and how is it produced?*

▶ Cratiform lesion is a depressed ulcerated center covered with granulating tissue and an indurated periphery. It is produced when the skin cells containing a large number of *L. tropica* break down to produce this lesion.

Q *Describe its clinical features.*

▶ Symptoms are fever, chills and inflammation. A reddish papule develops first and later transforms into a shallow ulcer.

Q *How can oriental sore be diagnosed in the laboratory?*

▶ *L. tropica* can be demonstrated microscopically in the stained smear prepared from the punctured indurated edge of the sore, not in the blood smear.

Q *Why does scraping of the floor of the ulcer result in a negative reading?*

▶ Because *L. tropica* cannot exist along with the bacteria in the ulcer.

Q *When the smear from the floor of the ulcer is negative, where are L. tropica demonstrated?*

▶ It can be demonstrated in the biopsy material of the lymphoid under ulcer.

Dermal leishmanoid

Q *Define dermal leishmaniasis and how it develops?*

▶ It is a non-ulcerative cutaneous lesion which develops in 10% of *kala azar* patients after completion of antimony treatment.

Q *Where is it distributed in India?*

▶ It is common in endemic areas of *kala azar* (Assam, Tamilnadu, West Bengal).

Q *Enumerate the clinical types of dermal leishmanoid.*

▶ There are three types:

1. Depigmented macules
2. Erythematous patches
3. Yellowish pink nodules.

Q *How can it be diagnosed and treated?*

▶ It can be diagnosed by demonstration of leishmania in the nodules and treated with pentavalent antimony.

Leishmania braziliensis

Q *How is the name L. braziliensis derived?*

▶ It is so named, because Lindenberg (1909) first found leishmania in a patient's ulcers in Brazil.

Q *What disease is caused by L. braziliensis in humans?*

▶ It causes mucocutaneous leishmaniasis in humans.

Q *How can all these three species (L. donovani, L. tropica and L. braziliensis) be distinguished, as they are morphologically identical?*

▶ They can be differentiated by agglutination and complement fixation reactions.

Q *Among these three species of leishmania, which one can be cultivated in a chorio-allantoic membrane (CAM) of the embryo of a chick?*

▶ *L. braziliensis* can be grown in the CAM of chick embryo, though all species can be grown in NNN medium.

Q *Among all these species of leishmania, which species can also be transmitted by direct contact?*

▶ Only *L. braziliensis* can be transmitted by direct contact, though it is transmitted by the sand fly as in other cases.

Q *Name a common skin test for all these three species.*

▶ Montenegro intradermal test is common to all.

Q *Where is the primary lesion commonly found in mucocutaneous lieshmaniasis and how does it heal?*

▶ The primary lesion is mostly found on the ear lobe and it tends to be self-healing in six months.

4 SPOROZOA

Sporozoa do not possess special organs of locomotion such as flagella or cilia, they show only a slight ameboid change of form. They are parasitic protozoa that live in the body fluids and tissues of vertebrates or invertebrates. They produce spores and have a lifecycle characterized by an alternation of generation, one sexual and one asexual, occurring completely in the same host or requiring an alternation of hosts (Plasmodium). In the asexual cycle of development, multiplication is by segmentation, or ***schizogony***, while in the sexual cycle of development, multiplication occurs after fertilization of female cells by the male, which is referred to as ***sporogony.***

Species of sporozoa which parasitize humans may be classified as follows:

Sub-phyllum:	Sporozoa
Class	Telosporea
Sub-class:	Coccidia
Order	Eimeriidea
Family:	Eimeriidae
Genus	Isospora
Species	*Isospora hominis*
Sub-class:	Haemosporina
Family	Plasmodiidae
Genus	Plasmodium
Species	*P. vivax, P. falciparum, P. malariae, P. ovale.*
Class	Toxoplasmea
Order	Toxoplasmida
Genus	Toxoplasma, Sarcocystis
Species	*Toxoplasma gondii, Sarcocystis lendemanni*
Class	Haplosporea
Genus	Pneumocystis
Species	*Pneumocystis carinii*

FAMILY EIMERIIDAE

Genus Isospora

(*Isospora belli* and *Isospora hominis*)

History: *Isospora hominis (belli)* is believed to have been seen by Kjellberg in 1860 in the villi of the human small intestine.

Geographical distribution: Species of human *Isospora* are relatively uncommon. Isolated cases have been reported from Belgium, Egypt, Iraq, Iran, Italy, Africa, Japan, China and Indochina. Mukherjee (1947) reported 14 cases among British troops in the Arakan, Bengal (India).

Habitat: *Isospora belli* and *I. hominis* are parasites of the small intestine of human beings.

Morphology: Oocysts and sporocysts of these species have been studied. Oocysts (Fig. 4.1) are elongated, ovoidal in shape and measure 20 μm in length and 10 μm in breadth. The oocyst wall consists of two layers and is smooth, thin and colourless. The inner layer is membranous and the outer layer is hard. A small micropyle is present at the narrow end of the oocyst. Sporozoites are formed within each sporocyst. They are long, crescent-shaped bodies, with a single nucleus. They remain clumped together with the sporocystic residue.

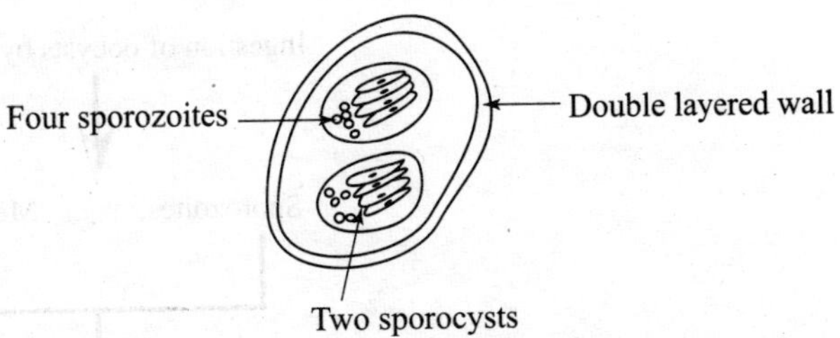

Fig. 4.1 Oocyst of *Isospora hominis*.

Lifecycle: After ingestion by humans, the mature oocysts liberate sporocysts in the small intestine and these sporocysts penetrate the cells of the villi, undergo schizogony (trophozoite, schizont, merozoite) and eventually sporogony with the development of the oocysts. These are later found in the feces and, when swallowed, repeat their lifecycle.

Pathogenicity: The lesions produced by *Isospora* in humans are unknown, since human coccidiosis has never been observed at autopsy. Merozoites invade the mucosal cells of the intestine with traumatic and erosive damage, which is sufficient to produce the mucous diarrhea characteristic of the disease in calves.

Clinical features: The symptoms consist of anorexia, nausea, abdominal pain and diarrhea. The infection in humans is usually self-limited. In immuno-compromised (AIDS) patients *I. belli* causes severe complications (diarrhea).

Laboratory diagnosis: Diagnosis depends on the demonstration of the oocysts of *Isospora belli* or *I. hominis* in the feces by the examination of unstained or iodine stained preparations. There is no permanent staining method for this parasite.

Treatment: No specific treatment is known for human coccidiosis. Rest with bland diet appears to aid the process of recovery. A large dose of bismuth salicylate is effective.

Prophylaxis: This consists of

1. Avoidance of ingestion of food or drink contaminated with feces containing oocysts or sporocysts
2) Adopting the methods recommended for amebiasis and giardiasis, which are effective.

Genus Eimeria

This genus contains coccidia that are characterized by the production of oocysts containing four sporocysts, each of which has two sporozoites. It is an animal parasite common in India. Fish and animals are natural hosts. Species of Eimeria have been demonstrated in human stools and are in transit through the digestive tract, as a result of ingestion of fish or through animal contact.

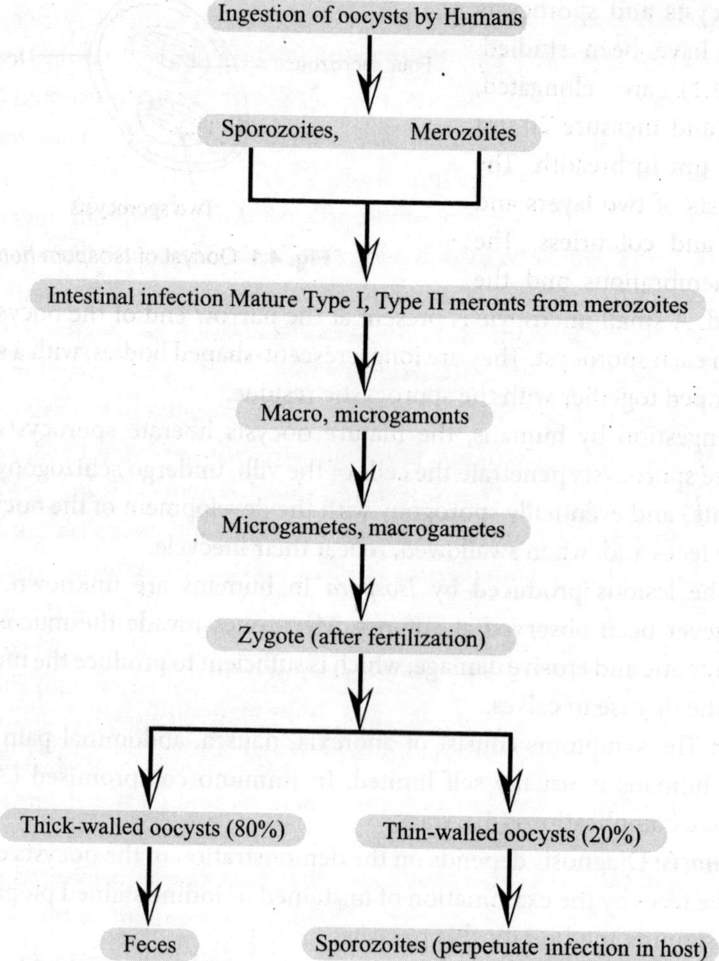

Fig. 4.2 Lifecycle of *C. parvum*.

Cryptosporidium parvum

C. parvum infects the intestine of immuno-compromised (e.g. those with AIDS) and immuno-competent individuals and causes severe intractable diarrhea. These organisms are *coccidian*, related to Isospora. They have long been known as parasites of fowl, rodents and cattle and have probably been an unrecognized cause of self limited mild gastroenteritis and diarrhea in humans. It is distributed in India – North India (5%), South India (13%), and also in Bangladesh (6.5%), Kuwait (16%) and Liberia (7.9%). However, in India it has been reported from Vellore, Kolkata, Bangalore and Chandigarh.

Morphology: Cryptosporidium species are minute (2–5 μm), intracellular spheres found in great numbers just under the mucosal epithelium of the stomach or intestine. The mature trophozoites (schizonts) divide into 8 arc-shaped merozoites which are released from the parent cell to begin a new lifecycle. Oocysts measuring 4–5 μm and containing four sporozoites may be seen, but not the sporocysts. Oocysts passed in the feces are presumed to be infective agents. Oocysts appear faintly blue with reddish or purple corpuscles, if stained by modified Ziehl–Neelsen staining.

Lifecycle of C. parvum which causes human cryptosporidiosis Human infection occurs by ingestion of thick-walled oocysts. Host cells are infected by sporozoites and merozoites which emerge from oocysts and meronts respectively (mature type I and II meronts contain eight and four merozoites respectively). Sexual phases of the lifecycle consist of fertilization of macrogamonts by microgametes, released from microgamonts, with zygote formation. Most (80%) zygotes mature into thick-walled oocysts which are excreted in the feces; the rest of the zygotes mature into thin-walled oocysts which remain in the host and release sporozoites to perpetuate the infection.

Pathogenicity and clinical features Cryptosporidium inhabits the brush border just within the outer limiting membrane of mucosal epithelial cells of the gastrointestinal tract, especially the surface of villi of the lower small intestine. Patients infected with cryptosporidiosis have watery diarrhea, cramps, upper abdominal pain (exacerbated by food ingestion), weight loss and flatulence, nausea, vomiting, anorexia, myalgia, malaise, dehydration, fever is not common. The predominant clinical features of cryptosporidiosis is diarrhea which is mild and self limited (1–2 weeks) in normal persons, but may be very severe and prolonged in immuno-compromised (AIDS) patients or very young or old individuals. Reversible lactase deficiency and fat malabsorption have been documented in severe chronic cryptosporidiosis.

Recent work supports the view that *C. parvum* infection can be prevented or interrupted by an antibody that binds to cryptosporidium lifecycle stages present in the intestinal lumen (sporozoites and merozoites).

Diagnosis depends upon the detection of oocysts in fresh stool samples. Direct wet mounts, concentration by floatation techniques and modified Ziehl–Neelsen staining can be used for the detection of cryptosporidium with reddish or purple corpuscles. A serological test has been described and it is in an experimental stage.

Treatment is unnecessary for patients with normal immunity. For those receiving immuno-suppressant drugs, cessation of immuno-suppressants may be indicated; for those with AIDS or congenital immuno-deficiency, only supportive therapy is available. Spiramycin may be temporarily effective. A successful use of Diclazuril (benzene acetonitrate compound) in crysptosporidium sp. infection in a 20 year old male (an intravenous drug user) with AIDS and chronic persistent hepatitis B was reported. This success in a single case should be viewed cautiously. Paromomycin has recently been reported to be effective in the treatment of cryptoporidiosis in patients with AIDS. It is commercially available and approved for treatment. Though Paromomycin significantly inhibits *in vitro C. parvum* infection, further clinical trials of this drug are warranted for treatment of chronic cryptosporidiosis in immunocompromised patients.

Epidemiology and prophylaxis: Though initially recognized in animals, cryptosporidial infection is increasingly recognized as an important cause of diarrhea in both immunocompromised and immuno-competent individuals. Previously, it was thought that the source of cryptosporidial infection was animals, but now transmission from human to human is possible. Cryptosporidiosis is acquired from infected animals or human feces or feces-contaminated food or water. Mild cases are common in farm workers. For those at high risk (young or old persons), avoidance of feces and careful attention to sanitation are required.

Microsporida

Microsporida are an unnatural group of unicellular parasites (Protozoa) with unusual biologic characteristics, especially with respect to their subcellular organization and spore structure. They lack mitochondria and have ribosomes that resemble those of bacteria in subunit size and nucleotide sequences. It has been suggested that microsporidia arose as an early branch from the stock leading from the prokaryotes of the higher cells and have been accorded status as a separate phylum – Microsporidia.

Microsporidian lifecycles are composed of proliferative (merogonic) and spore producing (sporogony) phases. In the latter phase, a sporont divides into sporoblasts that mature into thick-walled Gram positive spores.

The spores have an extrusion apparatus consisting of a coiled polar filament and anchoring disk and contain the infective agent known as sporoplasm. The obligate intracellular habitat is reached in a new host when the coiled polar filament is extruded, usually in the gut of the host, to form a hollow tube through which the sporoplasm passes to be inoculated in the host cell. Microsporidia have great reproductive potential, multiplying within cells and spreading from cell to cell. Although they have long been known as parasites of widespread occurrence in populations of invertebrates and fish, the potential of Microsporidia for infecting warm-blooded vertebrates is only now being recognized. Infection with *Encephalitozoon cuniculi*, a species that has a wide host range in mammals (rodents, rabbits, carnivores and primates) has been diagnosed once in Japan, and even in Sweden, in children with neurological illness.

Microsporidia are ubiquitous obligate intracellular protozoan parasites found commonly in laboratory animals. They are unicellular Gram positive organisms with mature spores 0.5 – 2 × 1–4 um in diameter. Significant microsporidiosis in humans is increasing in association with the increase in patients with Acquired Immuno Deficiency Syndrome (AIDS). There are four genera of microsporidia known to infect human beings:

1. *Enterocytozoon bieneusi*, the most common microsporidian observed in AIDS patients, infects the intestinal mucosa and causes diarrhea. Its estimated prevalence may be as high as 10% in AIDS patients.

2. *Pleistophora* species was reported in an immuno-compromised Human Immunodeficiency Virus (HIV) negative patient with myositis. Its spores are arranged in large groups enclosed by a membrane (Pansporoblastic membrane).
3. *Encephalitozoon cuniculi*, most common in laboratory animals, was reported in several immuno-compromised patients and also in AIDS patients with peritonitis; hepatitis. Previously, *E. cuniculi* was the only available mammalian microsporidian for use in serological test. Antibodies to *E. cuniculi* were found in patients. *E. cuniculi* was characterized by its development within a parasitophorous vacuole in macrophages, vascular endothelial and perithelial cells, kidney tubule cells and by its unpaired nuclei and disporous sporogony (i.e., sporont gives rise to two spores). Very recently, Didier *et al.* isolated and characterized a new human microsporidian, *E. hellum* (new species) from three AIDS patients.
4. *Nosema corneum* (new species), parasite causing ocular infection or nosematosis of the cornea, was first reported in HIV positive patients. *N. connori* was characterized by virtue of the paired (diplokaryotic) arrangement of its nuclei in the spores. It caused a generalized infection in a severely immuno-compromised infant who died in the U.S.A.

Besides, infection with an *E. cuniculi*-like organism was reported in several AIDS patients with conjunctivitis and very recently, a new microsporidian, *E. hellum* (new species) was isolated and characterized from three AIDS patients with keratoconjunctivitis as follows:

***In vitro* growth of microsporidia** *E. cuniculi, N. corneum* and *N. algerae* were grown in Madin–Darby canine kidney (MDCK) cells using RPMI 1640 culture medium supplemented with 5% heat inactivated fetal bovine serum and antibiotics.

Corneal tissue and conjunctival scrapings from HIV seropositive patients with microsporidal keratoconjunctivitis were mixed and added to monolayer MDCK cells. The culture was incubated at 37°C with 5% CO_2 except for *N. algerae* culture which was incubated at room temperature.

Electron microscopy of microsporidia. The larger proliferative stages (meronts) were attached to a parasitophorous vacuole membrane. The spores displayed relatively thick electron lucent endospores and irregular electron dense exospore structures.

Serology The new ocular isolated *E. hellum* displayed immunological reactivity and morphological similarities to *E. cuniculi*. The serological diagnosis of microsporidiosis in AIDS patients are possible, because in all cases, positive antibody binding to *E. hellum* could be demonstrated. The availability of new human isolate provides antigen for testing sera and increases the likelihood of detecting positive sera.

FAMILY PLASMODIIAE

Malarial Parasites of Humans

The World Health Organization (WHO) in 1963 recommended that the term 'malarial parasites' be restricted to the family plasmodiiae (Fig. 4.3). The plasmodia infecting human beings are *Plasmodium vivax, P. ovale, P. malariae* and *P. falciparum*.

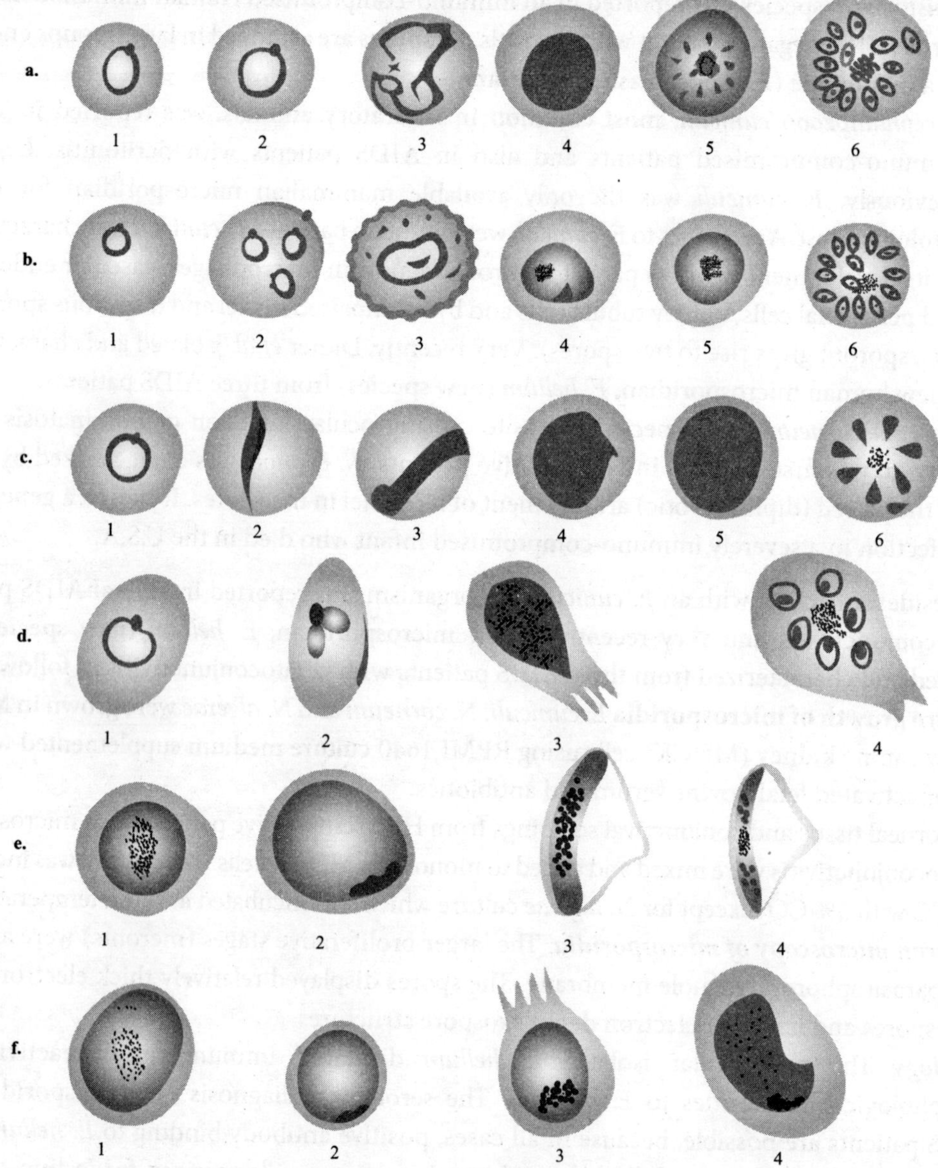

Fig. 4.3 Malarial parasites of humans.

a. *P. vivax* (1–3, trophozoites; 4–5, schizonts; 6 merozoites).

b. *P. falciparum* (1–3, trophozoites; 4–5, schizonts, 6, merozoites)

c. *P. malariae* (1–3, trophozoites; 4–5, schizonts; 6, merozoites).

d. *P. ovale* (1–2, trophozoites, 3, schizonts, 4, merozoites).

e. *P. vivax* (1, microgametocyte, 2, macrogametocyte); *P. falciparum* (3, microgametocyte; 4, macrogametocyte).

f. *P. malariae* (1, microgametocyte; 2, marcogametocyte); P. ovale (3, microgametocyte; 4, macrogametocyte).

Plasmodium vivax causes vivax or tertian malaria, *P. ovale* causes ovale malaria, *P. malariae* causes malariae or quartan malaria, and *P. falciparum* malignant tertian or falciparum malaria.

Laveran (1880) first observed *P. vivax*. The staining method for malarial parasites was discovered by Romanowsky (1891). Bigmani et al. (1898) worked out the mosquito cycle of human plasmodia, and Ross in Kolkata demonstrated the same with the avian Plasmodium. MacFie and Ingram first described *P. ovale*, in 1917 and Short et al. (1949) demonstrated the pre-erythrocytic schizogony of *P. falciparum*.

Geographical distribution Malarial parasites are worldwide in distribution. The endemic area of these parasites is the tropical zone. Vivax infections are more common in temperate than in tropical regions. Ovale malaria occurs mostly in tropical Africa and is endemic in Ethiopia. *P. malariae* is common in Africa, Burma, Sri Lanka and India. It is widely prevalent in certain areas of Malaysia and Indonesia. *P. falciparum* is common in the tropics and subtropics.

A recent study (WHO, 1991) shows that malaria kills 2 million people a year worldwide, and afflicts 100 million more. Multi-drug resistant *P. falciparum* is widespread and is a health hazard. Chloroquine-resistant *P. falciparum* extends from Pakistan and India to other countries. There are two recent reports of *P. vivax* resistance to chloroquine in Australia. The first case of chloroquine-resistant *P. falciparum* was reported in Assam (India).

Habitat The malarial parasites undergo a development stage in the parenchyma cells of the liver, reside in the red blood cells of humans and are carried through the bloodstream to various organs.

Lifecycle The malarial parasites pass their lifecycle in two different hosts:

1. ***Intrinsic phase (human)***: A human acts as the intermediate host for malarial parasites. Here, plasmodia reside inside the hepatic cells and red blood corpuscles and reproduce by the asexual method (schizogony). Only in malaria and hydatid disease, humans are the intermediate host.
2. ***Extrinsic phase***: **(*Female Anopheles mosquito*)**. The mosquito represents the definite host of malarial parasites, because of the sexual method of reproduction of the malarial parasites. For the initiation of the mosquito cycle, sexual forms (male and female gametocytes) are first developed in the human host. Then they are transferred to the definite host (female Anopheles mosquito), where they develop further and transform into sporozoites which are minute, thread-like, curved organisms tapering at both ends, measuring 9–12 μm in length with a central elongated nucleus without any pigment. Sporozoites are infective to humans. Only the female mosquito can transmit the sporozoites to the intermediate host (human); because of their well-developed serrated maxillae and mandibles, they have stout proboscis which can pierce the human skin like a needle. Host specificity is possibly determined by the presence or absence of certain amino acids in the mosquito.

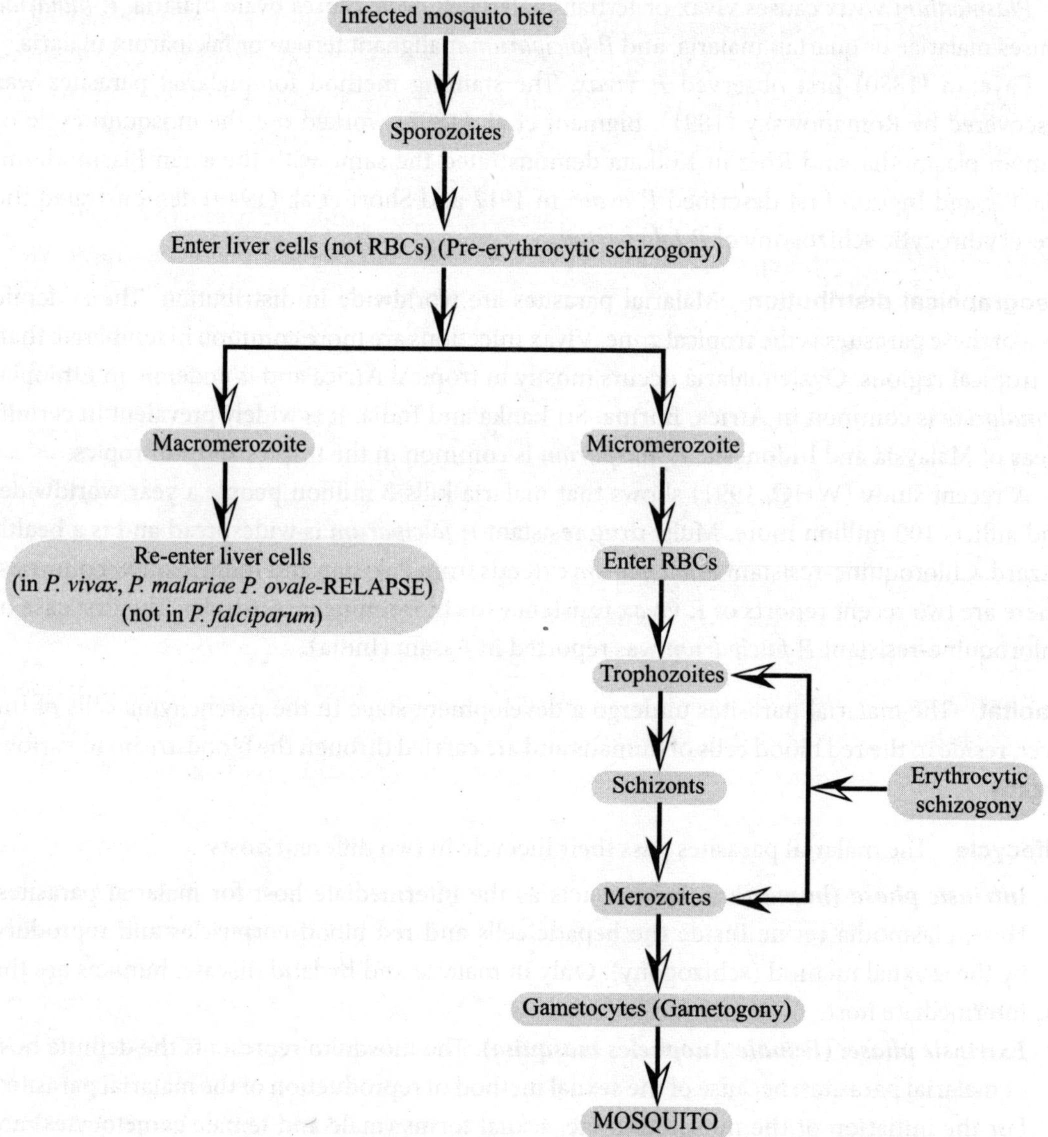

Fig.4.4 Human cycle of Plasmodium.

Human cycle The human cycle (asexual cycle of malarial parasites) starts with the introduction of sporozoites into humans by the bite of an infected Anopheles mosquito. It consists of four stages:

1) Pre-erythrocytic schizogony
2) Erythrocytic schizogony
3) Gametogony and
4) Exo-erythrocytic schizogony.

1. ***Pre-erythrocytic schizogony***: The sporozoites do not enter directly into the red blood corpuscles to start their erythrocytic stage, but undergo the development phase inside human tissues (liver). This stage is referred to as ***pre-erythrocytic schizogony*** or primary exo-erythrocytic schizogony and consists of only one generation of pre-erythrocytic schizonts, the cycle lasting approximately eight days in *P. vivax*, six days in *P. falciparum* and nine days in *P. ovale*. Pre-erythrocytic schizogony occurs inside the parenchyma cells of the liver. The liberated merozoites are called cryptozoites. The smaller ones (micromerozoites) enter the bloodstream and they bind with sialoglycoproteins or glycoproteins of red blood cell membrane; when these antigens are altered, no binding takes place. The interaction of malarial parasites with the red blood cells consists of a sequence of events starting with the initial recognition of specific erythrocyte molecules by parasite surface receptors, followed by a series of structural and metabolic adjustments of both the red blood corpuscles and the parasites, finally leading to a truly interactive relationship between the red blood cells and parasites. The large ones (macromerozoites) re-enter the liver cells. During pre-erythrocytic schizogony, the parasites are not found in the peripheral blood, and inoculation of such blood does not produce any infection, i.e., the blood is sterile. When the parasites develop inside the liver, there is no clinical manifestation and pathological damage.
2. ***Erythrocytic schizogony***: During this phase, the parasite passes through the stages of ***trophozoite, schizont*** and ***merozoite*** inside the red blood corpuscles. These asexual forms can be demonstrated in the thick smear of peripheral blood, 3–4 days after completion of pre-erythrocytic schizogony, i.e., in *P. vivax* after about 12 days, and in *P. falciparum* infection nine days after exposure to mosquito bite. Each erythrocytic schizogony lasts 48–72 hours. In *P. vivax, P. ovale, P. falciparum*, it is 48 hours, but in *P. malariae* it is 72 hours. The parasitic multiplication during the erythrocytic phase is responsible for bringing about a 'clinical attack of malaria' (overt malaria). The schizogony cycle may be continued for a considerable time, but sometimes the infection may die out or the parasites may have the urge for sexual multiplication as they are exhausted with asexual multiplication and the spontaneous destruction of parasites.
3. ***Gametogony***: After the erythrocytic schizogony stage, some of the merozoites do not develop directly into trophozoites and schizonts, but they transform into sexual forms which are capable of sexual reproduction outside the human host. These forms are known as gametocytes. These gametocytes are produced to propagate and to continue the lifecycle in the mosquito. They develop in the red blood cells of the capillaries of the internal organs (spleen and bone marrow). Only the mature gametocytes are found in the peripheral blood. The complete maturation takes about 96 hours (four days), i.e., twice the time taken by an erythrocytic schizont to mature completely. The individuals who harbour these gametocytes are called 'carriers'.

4. ***Exo-erythrocytic schizogony***: After the micromerozoites infect the red blood corpuscles, the pre-erythrocytic phase disappears completely in *P. falciparum*, whereas in the case of *P. vivax, P. ovale, P. malariae*, it persists in the form of a local liver cycle. This tissue phase (liver cycle) is described as 'exo-erythrocytic schizogony'. This is responsible for relapse of vivax, ovale and malariae malaria, but there is no relapse in *P. falciparum*, i.e., there is no exo-erythrocytic schizogony of *P. falciparum*. The merozoites (both micro- and macromerozoites) liberated from this exo-erythrocytic schizogony are called ***phanerozoites*** (Figs 4.4 and 4.6).

Recrudescence of falciparum malaria Recrudescence, becoming active again after a dormant period, of clinical falciparum malaria due to the parasites persisting in the circulation at a subclinical level following a previous attack is referred to as 'recrudescence'; this is different from malaria relapse. There is no relapse stage in *P. falciparum*. Recrudescence may occur due to inadequate drug therapy, drug resistance or when a person's natural acquired immunity is reduced e.g., during pregnancy. It may occur within a few weeks or months of a previous attack. Most of the recrudescence dies out within a year of the original attack. Partially resistant parasites recrudescence up to two months in the non-immune, after the treatment.

Mosquito cycle In the sexual cycle of the malarial parasite, when a female Anopheles mosquito bites an infected human host, it sucks blood during its blood meal from the infected person. It ingests both the sexual and asexual forms of the malarial parasites, but only the mature sexual forms which are capable of development survive and the remaining asexual forms die immediately. It has been suggested that a mosquito can transmit the infection of humans, if the blood of a human carrier contains at least twelve gametocytes per mm^3 of blood; the number of female gametocytes should be more than that of male ones to initiate infection.

In the proventriculus (stomach or midgut) of the mosquito, one male microgametocyte gives rise to four to eight thread-like filamentous structures known as ***microgametes***. This process of development is called ex-flagellation, whereas one female macrogametocyte develops into one macrogamete without forming any flagellation. Its nucleus shifts to the surface where a projection is formed. These gametes are ready for fertilization. By the process of chemotaxis, the male microgametes are attracted towards the female macrogametes. One of the male gametes attaches itself to the periphery of the female parasite at the site of this projection and penetrates through this projection into the body of the female gamete. Then there is fusion of their pronuclei, thereby the macrogamete is fertilized, which is called the ***zygote***. This zygote formation takes 20 minutes to two hours after the mosquito's blood meal.

After about 20 minutes, the zygote puts out a pseudopodium into which its protoplasm flows to form a fusiform body, the ***ookinete*** (a motile zygote).

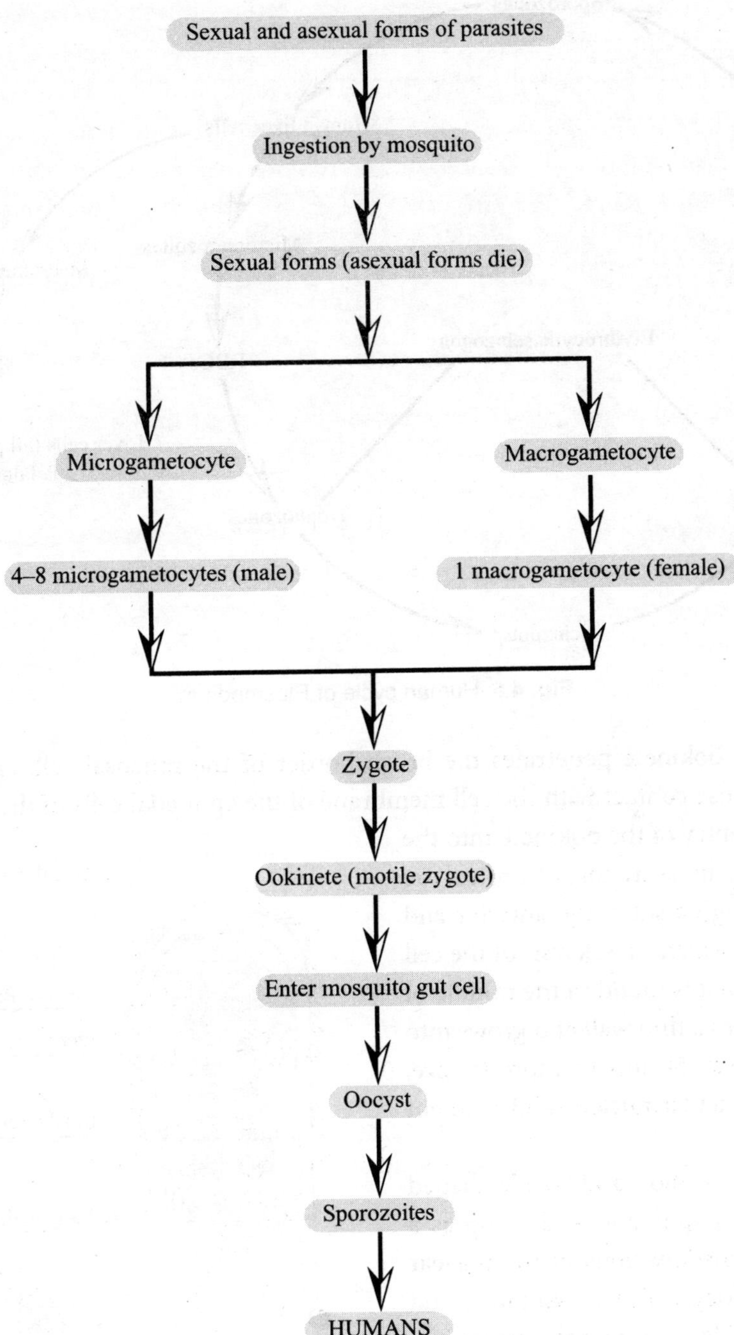

Fig. 4.5 Mosquito cycle of Plasmodium.

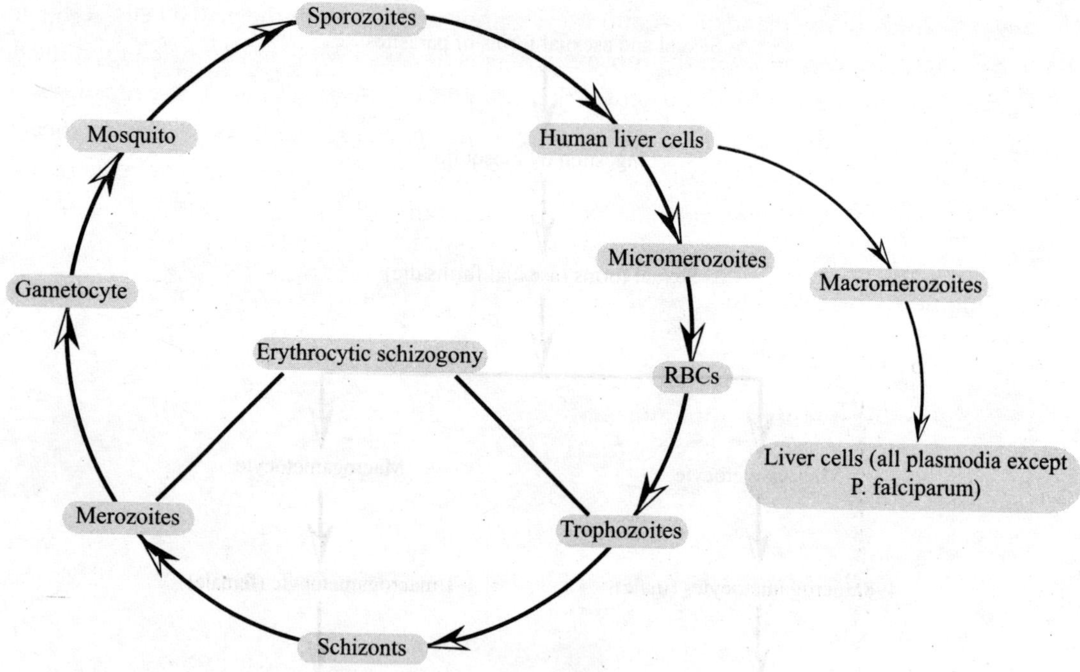

Fig. 4.6 Human cycle of Plasmodium.

This mature ookinete penetrates the brush border of the mucosal cell, and its anterior end comes in close contact with the cell membrane of the epithelial cells of the midgut of the mosquito. The entry of the ookinete into the cell is made by the secretion of proteolytic substance, through a slit at the anterior end of the ookinete, which causes lysis of the cell membrane. Then it is found in the middle of the cell; it secretes a thin wall and grows into a spherical oocyst, 50 µm or more in size, with a single vesicular nucleus and pigment granules.

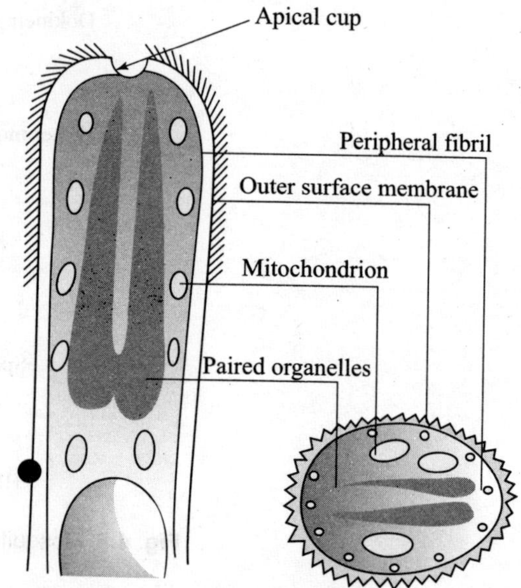

Fig. 4.7 Longitudinal and transverse sections of sporozoite.

As many as a thousand sickle-shaped bodies, known as sporozoites, develop as a result of successive divisions of the nuclear material of the oocyst. The oocyst bursts and the sporozoites (Fig. 4.7) enter the mosquito's body cavity (hemocele) from which they disperse throughout the mosquito's body, except to the ovaries. Those that come in contact with the salivary glands bore into these glands and, through the acinal cells, lodge in the acinal ducts. Therefore, when the mosquito injects its saliva while obtaining a blood meal, it also injects sporozoites which thus enter the human host. A single bite of the mosquito is sufficient to transmit the infection. Only the female ***Anopheles*** mosquitoes take blood meals. Different species of malarial parasites can develop in the same mosquito and may give rise to 'mixed infection', i.e., *P. falciparum* and *P. vivax* (Figs 4.5 and 4.8).

Ookinete: Under the electron microscope:

1) The ookinete is enclosed in a two-layered envelope. The inner one is smooth, whereas the outer one is corrugated
2) The inner layer appears denser at the anterior end
3) There are peripheral fibrils under the envelope
4) There is a granular nucleus with nucleolus
5) There is no micropyle and
6) Cytoplasmic inclusions (mitochondria, lysosome and black pigment granules) are in the vacuoles of the cytoplasm (Fig. 4.9).

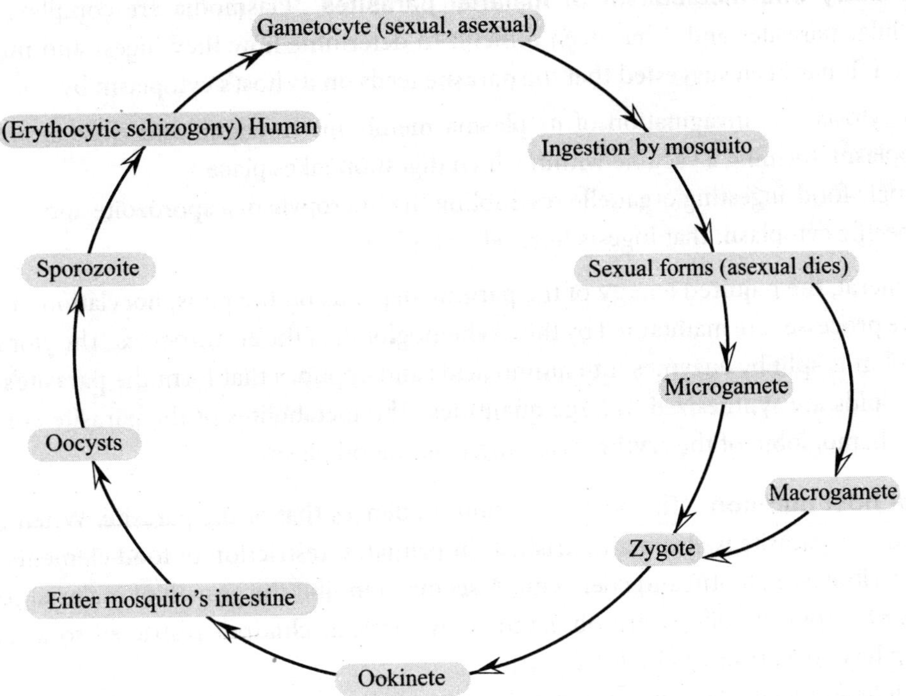

Fig. 4.8 Mosquito cycle of Plasmodium.

Sporozoites:

1) They are infective forms of malarial parasites
2) They have a complex structure held together by a relatively thick membrane
3) Their shape varies from narrow, slightly curved (vivax), thick (malariae), to sickle shaped (falciparum)
4) They measure about 10–14 μm in length
5) They have peripheral fibrils which may have locomotory functions
6) They possess mitochondria, but no pigment
7) They have a deep depression in the surface membrane which is called the micropyle. The micropyle may represent the point of exit of the emergent sporoplasm, i.e., the infective material from the sporozoite.

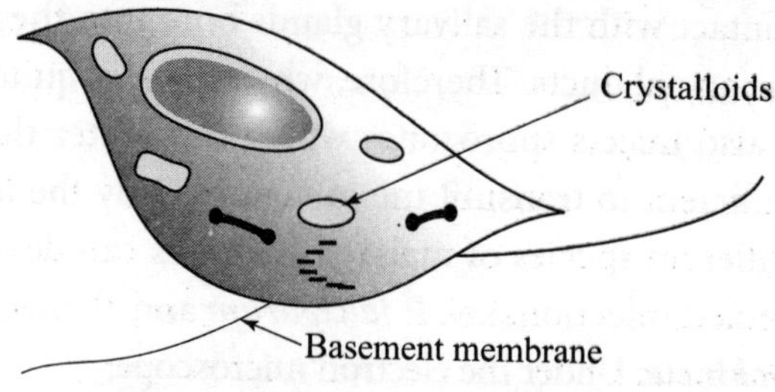

Fig. 4.9 Ookinete of Plasmodium.

Biochemistry and metabolism of malarial parasites Plasmodia are complex, obligate intracellular parasites and it has been difficult to determine how they ingest and metabolize their food. It has been suggested that the parasite feeds on its host's cytoplasm by

1) Pinocytosis, i.e., invagination of its plasma membrane to engulf and close around some cytoplasm, forming a vacuole within which digestion takes place
2) A single food-ingesting organelle resembling the micropyle of a sporozoite and
3) A specific cytoplasm that ingests host cell cytoplasm.

In general, the required energy of the parasite depends on the phosphorylation of glucose; oxidative processes are maintained by the oxyhemoglobin of the erythrocytes. The globin of the hemoglobin is split by enzymes into amino acids and peptides that form the parasite's protein and the lipids are synthesized in large quantities. The metabolites of the parasite are derived from the hemoglobin of the erythrocytes and from blood plasma.

Effect of host nutrition The host's nutrition influences that of the parasite. When the host is starved, the parasite is also malnourished. In primates, restriction of food elements such as thiamine, riboflavin, biotin and coenzyme A seems to inhibit the growth of malarial parasites, but in birds, opposite effects are observed. West African children restricted to a milk diet remained heavily parasitized by *P. falciparum*.

G-6PD deficient trait: A genetic deficiency known as the Glucose-6 phosphate dehydrogenase deficient (G-6PD) trait seems to confer some protection against *P. falciparum* infection. African Americans and East Africans inherit this trait. The low activity of this enzyme results in an abnormal concentration of reduced glutathione in the red blood corpuscles and also in the limitation of the hexose monophosphate shunt metabolic pathway. In their metabolism, plasmodia use the hexose monophosphate shunt pathway. Hence, this genetic glucose-6 phosphate trait appears to confer some protection against *P. falciparum*.

***Sickle cell anemia trait*:** This is also responsible for resistance to malaria. The sickle cell trait, common in Africa, Asia and Europe, results in an abnormal hemoglobin, the molecules of which, when deoxygenated, tend to collect in rigid, rod-like masses which distort the red cells into a sickle shape. *P. falciparum* schizonts appear to have difficulty in utilizing this abnormal hemoglobin so that their growth and schizogony are stunted.

Thalassemia hemoglobin and hemoglobin E provide some protection against *P. vivax* and human fetal hemoglobin against all plasmodia. Oocysts develop better when the host mosquito has blood rather than a glucose diet. The host specificity is determined by the presence or absence of certain amino acids in the mosquito.

Plasmodium vivax

The specific name 'vivax' is derived from Latin *vivere* (to live) and indicates 'movement'. *P. vivax* is almost worldwide in distribution and is more common in temperate than in tropical regions.

***Gametes*:** The microgametocyte of *P. vivax* usually ex-flagellates six microgametes, each 20–25 μm in length. The macrogametocyte becomes a macrogamete. A microgamete penetrates into the small projection of the macrogamete and the ookinete is formed. The process takes from ten minutes to one hour in the mosquito's gut.

***Ookinete*:** Vivax ookinetes are 15–22 μm in length and 3 μm in width. They are motile and penetrate the epithelial cell of the mosquito's midgut, 24–48 hours after the blood meal is ingested.

***Oocysts*:** Their maturing period is 7–8 days. Pigment granules are present.

***Sporozoites*:** Vivax sporozoites are narrow and slightly curved, measuring about 14 μm in length.

***Exo-erythrocytic (EE) stages*:** Primary vivax exo-erythrocytic schizogony is completed in 7½–8 days. After seven days, the schizont is ovoid, 40 μm in length and with blue staining cytoplasm. At maturity, the schizont gives rise to 10,000 merozoites, which are spherical (1.2 μm), and are released to enter the host's circulation.

Secondary exo-erythrocytic schizonts have been observed fourteen days to nine months after infection.

***Erythrocytic stages*:** The sporozoites leave the bloodstream within an hour after injection and a pre-patent period of about eight days ensues with the bloodstream free of plasmodia. On the eighth day, exo-erythrocytic merozoites invade the younger red blood cells. *P. vivax* shows a greater tendency to invade younger red blood corpuscles. The asexual cycle of *P. vivax* usually takes 48 hours (Figs 4.10, 4.11, 4.12).

***Gametocytes*:** Vivax gametocytes usually appear on the fifth day.

6

Morphology

Unstained preparation: The *P. vivax* trophozoite appears within the red blood corpuscles as a small hyaline ring which becomes ameboid with the characteristic movement, which justifies its name 'vivax'. In a few hours, it begins to show delicate granules of pigment. At the end of 36 hours, it fills most of the infected cells dividing the organisms into 12–24 daughter cells or ***merozoites.***

Stained preparation: In blood smears stained by Giemsa's stain, the Plasmodium cytoplasm stains blue and the nuclear chromatin stains violet, while the cytoplasm of the infected erythrocytes stains yellow or salmon pink.

The earliest erythrocytic ***trophozoite*** is a delicate blue-stained ring of cytoplasm with a red chromatin dot. The erythrocyte is stained salmon pink.

As the Plasmodium enlarges, the ring form becomes irregular and larger and contains dots or threads of red stained chromatin and granules of dark pigment. Orangish-pink or pink spots known as 'Schuffners' dots' may appear in the cytoplasm of red blood corpuscles.

P. vivax segments, round blue bodies, each having a bright red or violet chromatin dot situated at or near the periphery of the red blood cells, are produced. These bodies are the merozoites, typically 16 in number. They are liberated in the blood plasma, enter the red blood cells and appear as oval, blue-stained bodies with a red dot of chromatin near the centre.(Figs 4.10–4.12)

The ***microgametocyte*** cytoplasm stains pale blue, while that of the ***macrogametocyte*** stains deep blue. The macrogametocyte of *P. vivax* has a smaller nucleus than the microgametocyte, and the chromatin is arranged in a complex mass near the periphery. The cytoplasm stains bright blue and the chromatin deep red. The pigment in fine granules is arranged in small masses.

The gametocytes of *P. vivax* appear in the peripheral blood from the first day of fever (16 days after inoculation of sporozoites), i.e., 4–5 days after the initial appearance of the asexual parasites in thick smears. If these gametocytes are not taken up by the insect host, they do not live for more than a week in the human host.

The differences between the microgametocyte and macrogametocyte of *P. vivax* are as follows:

	Microgametocyte	*Macrogametocyte*
Size	9–10 μm	10–12 μm
Cytoplasm	Stains light blue.	Stains deep blue.
Nucleus	diffuse, large; lies laterally.	small, compact; lies peripherally.

PLASMODIUM FALCIPARUM

The specific name 'falciparum' (Latin, *falx,* a sickle) is derived from the sickle shaped gametocyte. *P. falciparum* is most prevalent in the tropics and sub-tropics and is also common in tropical and sub-tropical Asia.

Gametes: The microgametocytes of *P. falciparum* produce 4–6 microgametes by ex-flagellation which begins in the host insect's gut, at 33°C about ten minutes after ingestion. The microgametes

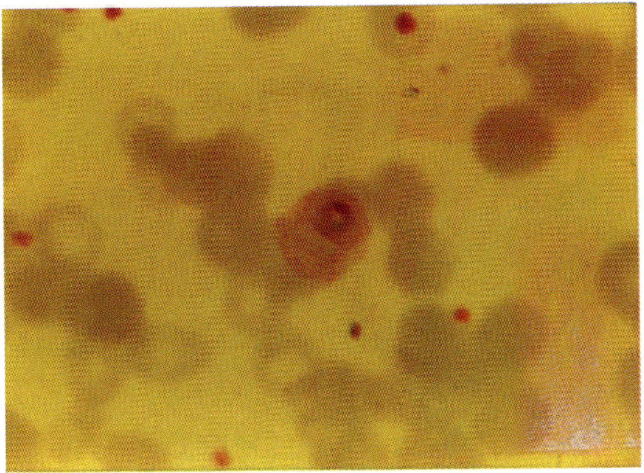

Fig. 4.10 *P. vivax* trophozoite ring form.

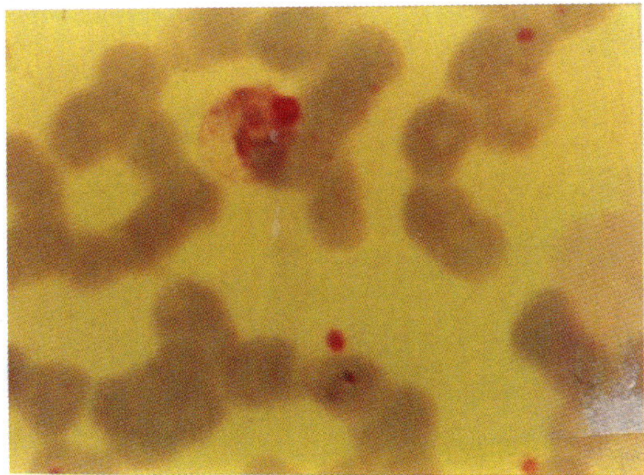

Fig. 4.11 *P. vivax* mature schizont.

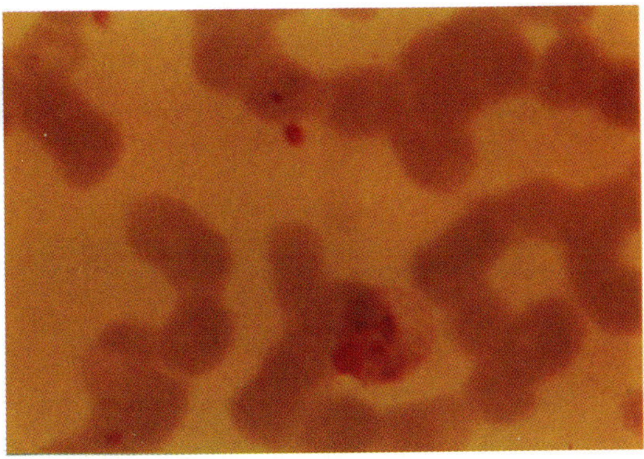

Fig. 4.12 *P. vivax* trophozoite.

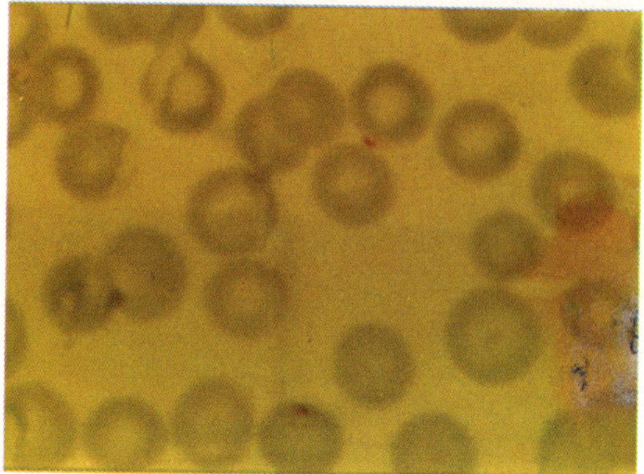

Fig. 4.13 *P. falciparum trophozoite* accolé.

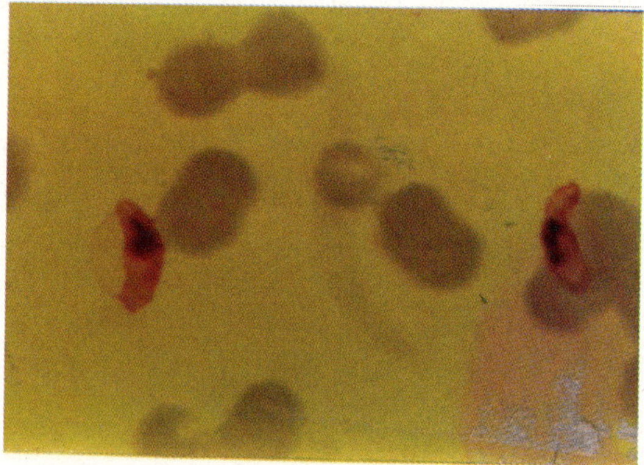

Fig. 4.14 *P. falciparum* gametocytes–male and female.

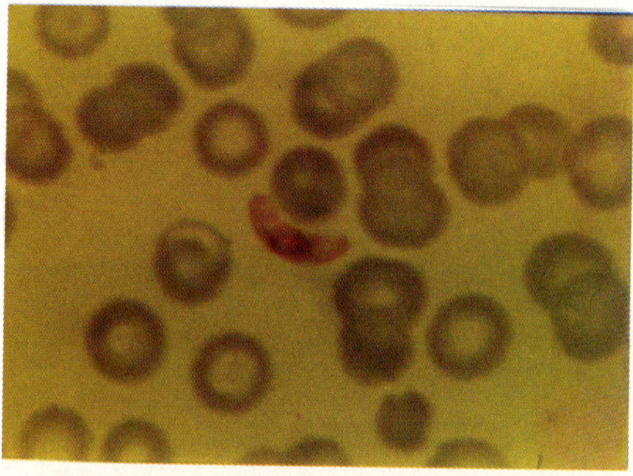

Fig. 4.15 *P. falciparum* female gametocyte.

are slender and measure about 16–25 μm in length. The macrogametes become spherical. Their nuclei approach the edge of the parasite, forming a protuberance into which a microgamete will penetrate.

Ookinetes: Falciparum ookinetes form 12–18 hours after the insect takes its blood meal. These are more slender than those of *P. vivax*. They measure about 25 μm in breadth and 13 μm in length.

Oocysts: Falciparum oocysts are generally smaller than those of the other malarial parasites of humans.

Sporozoites: Falciparum sporozoites are sickle-shaped, with equally pointed ends measuring about twelve μm in length. They invade the salivary glands of the host mosquito in nine days or more after the insect's blood meal and remain infective for up to 40–45 days.

Exo-erythrocytic stages: In *Plasmodium falciparum*, exo-erythrocytic schizogony appears to be limited to a single generation. There is no secondary exo-erythrocytic schizogony and it is completely absent. Hence, there is no relapse. The exo-erythrocytic schizonts grow rapidly, measure some 60 μm in diameter and may liberate some 30,000 exo-erythrocytic merozoites.

Erythrocytic stages: The exo-erythrocytic merozoites invade both young and old red cells. The schizogony cycle is completed in 36–48 hours. Multiple infection of red blood cells is very common in this species.

1. **Trophozoites:** The early ring form measures 1.5 μm in diameter. It consists of a fine and uniform cytoplasmic ring with the nucleus often projecting beyond the edge or lying outside the ring. The parasite often attaches itself to the margin or edge of the host's cell. The nucleus and a small part of the cytoplasm remain almost outside. This form is known as ***'applique'*** or ***'accole'***. (Fig. 4.13)

   The nucleus is often divided into two parts which may remain close together or be situated at opposite poles.

   The pigment granules formed by *Plasmodium falciparum* are dark brown or black in colour and collect to form a single mass at an early stage.

   The infected red blood cells remain unaltered, but the cells containing the large-sized rings occasionally show a crenated appearance at the periphery. The colour of the cell is reddish violet. Maurer's dots, staining brick red with Leishman's stain, are seen.
2. **Schizont:** As the growth continues, the nucleus divides into 8–32 masses and the cytoplasm forms many segments. The mature schizont measures 4.5–5 μm in diameter.
3. **Merozoites:** Its average number is 18–24 and measures 0.5–0.7 μm in diameter.
4. **Gametogony:** At first, the falciparum gametocytes are round or ovoid, but become spindle, cigar or diamond-shaped later. They appear in the peripheral circulation after 8–11 days of parasite potency and by then they have assumed their typical crescent or sickle shape. The microgametocyte is more banana-shaped than crescent and is thicker and blunter than the female macrogametocyte, which stains a darker blue and has a more compact nucleus.

Gametocytes of *P. falciparum* persist in the blood for weeks after asexual forms have been successfully eliminated. They do not cause the disease and their presence does not indicate treatment failure (Figs 4.13, 4.14 and 4.15).

The differences between a microgametocyte and a macrogametocyte of *P. falciparum* are listed below:

	Microgametocyte	*Macrogametocyte*
Shape	Broader, shorter; ends blunt	Longer, narrow; ends pointed
Size	8–10 µm by 2–3 µm	10–12 µm by 2–3 µm
Cytoplasm	Stains light blue	Stains deep blue
Nucleus	Scattered in fine granules over a wide area	Condensed into a small compact mass at the centre
Pigments	Scattered throughout the cytoplasm.	Aggregate like a wreath around the nucleus.

Plasmodium malariae

This species was first studied by Laveran in 1880; the specific name malariae was given and is still retained. The quartan parasite is common in tropical Africa, Burma, Sri Lanka and parts of India. It is prominent in certain parts of Malaysia and Indonesia.

***Gametes*:** Malariae gametes are smaller than those of vivax and falciparum. Typically, the microgametocytes form eight microgametes. The microgamete measures about 16 µm in length.

***Ookinetes*:** They seem to be denser than those of other species.

***Oocysts*:** *P. malariae* do not develop easily in mosquitoes and are scanty in malarial infections.

***Sporozoites*:** Malariae sporozoites are thicker and coarser than those of other species that infect humans. They measure 13–14 µm in length.

***Exo-erythrocytic stages*:** Primary *P. malariae* exo-erythrocytic (EE) schizogony is probably completed in 13–16 days. In secondary EE schizogony, relapses are common. Such relapses may occur as long as 40 years after infection.

***Erythrocytic stages*:** *P. malariae* are scanty in the red blood corpusu1es and show a special tendency to invade mature and older erythrocytes. The cycle of schizogony is completed in 72 hours (three days) and occurs mostly in the peripheral circulation.

***Trophozoites*:** The characteristic feature of the trophozoite of *P. malariae* is that the parasite stretches right across the red blood cells and assumes a band-like appearance. When the parasite is 6–8 hours old, coarse pigment granules, dark brown or black in colour, appear in the cytoplasm.

***Schizont*:** It is circular and measures about seven µm in diameter. When segmentation is complete, the schizonts arrange themselves in a 'daisy head' form.

***Merozoite*:** It measures 2–2.5 µm in diameter.

***Gametocyte*:** Malariae gametocytes are slow to appear. They appear between the tenth and fourteenth days. Peak gametocyte density occurs about six days after that of the asexual parasites. They measure 7–7.5 µm in diameter and are large. The morphological differences between the female and male gametocytes are the same as those of *P. vivax*. The host cell is not enlarged.

Plasmodium ovale

P. ovale, the least common of the species infecting humans, occurs mostly in tropical Africa. It is endemic in Ethiopia.

***Gametes*:** The ovale gametes produce up to eight microgametes somewhat smaller in size than those of *P. vivax*.

***Ookinetes*:** The ovale ookinetes appear 18–20 hours after the mosquito ingests the gametocytes. These ookinetes are smaller than those of *P. vivax*.

***Oocysts*:** The ovale sporozoites are plump, elongated, pointed at one end and measure 11–12 µm in length.

***Exo-erythrocytic stages*:** The ovale exo-erythrocytic schizogony is completed in nine days after the sporozoites enter the liver parenchymal cells. The schizont is unusually large and distinctive, confirming the validity of *P. vivax* as a distinct species. Its special characteristic is its relatively enormous nuclei.

***Erythrocytic stages*:** Erythrocytic schizogony in this species requires 49–50 days, a little longer than in *P. vivax*. There may be prolonged latency up to four or more years.

***Trophozoite*:** The ring form measures 2–2.5 µm in diameter and resembles that of *P. malariae,* more closely, but the band form is not seen. The pigment granules are coarse and dark brown in colour. Even at the early ring stage of the parasite, the infected red blood cells show granules like Schuffner's dots and take on a violet tinge; these are known as James' dots. The infected red blood cell is slightly enlarged, often oval.

***Schizont*:** It is round or oval in shape and measures 6.2 µm in diameter. The unclear material is divided into 6–12 masses (usually eight).

***Merozoite*:** It measures 2–2.5 µm in diameter. The nucleus is crescentic.

***Gametocyte*:** The ovale gametocytes appear on the fifth day of parasite patency. In about three weeks, they become sufficiently numerous to infect the mosquitoes.

Morphology In quick-dried, very thinly stained blood films, the ovale-infected red cell is moderately enlarged and presents a characteristic feature – an oval shape with fimbriation of one or both ends. This feature is not seen in unstained blood.

Stippling with Schuffner's dots appears earlier and is more prominent than in *P. vivax*. Ovale stipplings (James' dots) are fewer but more prominent and more violet than in vivax-infected cells.

The ovale parasites are fairly compact, generally smaller than the corresponding stages of *P. vivax*. The mature *ovale* schizonts display fewer and larger merozoites, averaging about eight, each with a prominent nucleus. The stained ovale gametocytes closely resemble those of *P. vivax*. The pigment seems darker than that of *P. vivax*. The diagnostic features of *P. ovale* are:

1) A large nucleus with clear-cut borders
2) The absence of much ameboidicity
3) The low average number of merozoites in the primary attack
4) Darker colour and
5) Smaller size.

Laboratory study of malarial parasites

***Staining method*:** Leishman and Giemsa stains can be used to study the detailed structure of malarial parasites.

Leishman stain can be prepared by dissolving the dry powder in acetone-free, pure methyl alcohol and used in 0.15%. Giemsa stain is obtained in a readymade solution. Hence, the fixation of the film with alcohol is only necessary when Giemsa stain is used. Quantitative Buffy Coat (QBC) method for malaria provides markedly increased levels of accuracy and sensitivity. It does not require more than a minute. In thick smear films, more than 100 fields may take ten minutes.

Very recent Polymerase Chain Reaction (PCR) detects specimens containing *P. falciparum* DNA, when parasite densities are below the microscopic threshold. Elevation of Plasma Lactase Dehydrogenase (LDH) can be demonstrated in severe cases of malaria with anemia.

Cultivation Recently, *P. falciparum* was cultivated *in vitro* in umbilical cord human erythrocytes in China. Continuous *in vitro* cultivation of *P. falciparum* was done by using the candle jar method and the type AB Rh + plasma. Antigen from this *P. falciparum* can be used for the malaria fluorescent antibody test. Sorbitol synchronization of *P. falciparum* culture has proved a reliable and simple method and has achieved worldwide use.

Epidemiology Malaria is ***endemic*** where there is a constant and measurable incidence of cases and natural transmission over a succession of years. It is ***epidemic*** when the incidence of cases in an area rises rapidly and notably above the usual level or when the disease suddenly occurs in an area previously considered non-malarious. When an epidemic spreads far beyond the usual limits, it becomes ***pandemic***.

Cases of malaria contracted locally are called ***autochthonous;*** when acquired outside the area and brought in, they are called ***imported.*** Cases proved to be locally derived from imported malaria are called ***introduced,*** in contrast to autochthonous. Malaria cases are ***indigenous*** if the disease is natural to an area. Malaria is ***sporadic*** when autochthonous cases are few and scattered.

Malaria is ***holo-endemic*** when the spleen rate (frequency of splenomegaly) in children (two to nine years) is constantly over 75% and adult populations have high tolerance; it is ***hyperendemic*** where the children's spleen rate is constantly over 50% and the rate is also high in adults; ***meso-endemic*** when the children's spleen rate is 11–50%; and ***hypo-endemic*** when the spleen rate is 10% or less.

Animal inoculation: Human species of malarial parasites are now transferable to several species of primates.

Reservoir of infection: Lower animals do not harbour the human species of malarial parasites. Children in an endemic area act as the only reservoir of infection. In some parts of Africa, chimpanzees may act as a reservoir for *P. malariae*.

Method of transmission The infection is transmitted by the inoculative method. During the act of biting, the mosquito's proboscis pierces the skin, and the salivary secretion is injected into the puncture wound. The salivary secretion carries a large number of sporozoites which are directly introduced into the bloodstream and cannot be found in the blood after half an hour.

The female Anopheles mosquito is the transmitting agent. The skin is the portal of entry and the site of localization is first in the liver cells and then in the erythrocytes.

Pathogenicity Infection with Plasmodium causes intermittent fevers which are together known as 'malaria'. (The word malaria is derived from two Italian words, *mala* and *aria*, meaning 'bad air'). Each of the four species causes a characteristic fever and the diseases are named as follows:

1. *Plasmodium vivax:* Vivax malaria (benign tertian malaria)
2. *Plasmodium malariae:* Quartan malaria (malariae malaria)
3. *Plasmodium falciparum:* Falciparum malaria (malignant tertian malaria). It also causes pernicious malaria and black water fever
4. *Plasmodium ovale:* Ovale malaria.

The sporozoites leave the bloodstream soon, without having caused apparent harm, and they lodge in the parenchyma cells where exo-erythrocytic schizogony takes place. The destruction of liver cells occurs, but without noticeable host reaction. The exo-erythrocytic merozoites (micromerozoites) invade the red cells and pathogenic effects then become significant.

A major factor in the pathogenesis of malaria is the disturbance in oxygen usage caused by the infection. This may occur in two ways:

1. Oxygen supplies may be reduced below the minimum physiological needs leading to a state of anoxic anemia, and
2. The host may not utilize adequate oxygen because of pathological changes in the metabolizing cells, which results in a state of cytotoxic anoxia.

Table 1 Malarial Parasites of Humans

Differential characters of erythrocytic phases (after staining)

	P. vivax (48 hours)	*P. falciparum* (48 hours) or under	*P. malariae* (72 hours)	*P. ovale* (48 hours)
Schizogony forms in peripheral blood	Trophozoites, schizonts and gametocytes	Rings, crescents only.	Trophozoites, schizonts, gametocytes.	Trophozoites, schizonts, gametocytes.
Trophozoites; Ring form	Size, 2.5/μm. cytoplasm opposite nucleus is thicker.	Size l.25/μm–1.5/μm cytoplasm fine, regular accolé form.	Same as *P. vivax*.	Same as *P. malariae*.
Growing form	Irregular with a vacuole. Actively ameboid.	Assumes compact form. Pigments collect into a single mass early.	Band-like. Slightly ameboid. Vacuole disappears early.	No ribbon shape. Slightly ameboid.
Schizont (mature)	Size, 9–10 /μm. Regular, completely fills enlarged red blood cells.	Size, 4.5–5/μm. Fills two-thirds of a red blood cell which is not enlarged.	Size, 6.5–7 /μm. Regular, almost fills a normal sized red blood cell.	Size, 6.2/μm. Fills three-quarters of a red blood cell which is slightly enlarged.
Merozoites	12–24. Arranged in an irregular grape-like cluster.	18–24 or more. Arranged in a grape-like cluster.	6–12. Arranged around a central mass of pigment like a 'daisy' or a 'rosette'.	6–12. Irregularly arranged.
Malarial pigments	Yellowish brown fine granules.	Dark brown or blackish, one or two solid blocks.	Dark brown; coarse granules.	Dark yellowish brown; coarser than *P. vivax*.
Infected RBC.	Enlarged, pale, Schuffner's dots present.	Unaltered, crenation reddish violet colour, Maurex's dots.	Not enlarged, not pale and no dots.	Enlarged, oval. James' dots.
Gametocyte	Spherical, much larger than a red blood cell. Schuffner's dots.	Crescentic. Larger than red blood cell. Host cell hardly recognizable.	Round, oval. Size of red blood cell.	Oval. Size of red blood cell. Host cell slightly enlarged with James' dots.

Female: Cytoplasm blue; nucleus small and compact.
Male: Cytoplasm pale blue; nucleus large and diffuse.

A state of shock may occur in acute severe malaria, e.g., in the so-called 'algid malaria'. Low blood pressure and low cardiac output and vasoconstriction may result in local anoxic anemia with cellular damage in the liver or kidney.

Incubation period In *Plasmodium ovale, P. vivax* and *P. falciparum,* it is 10–14 days, and in *P. malariae* it is 18 days to six weeks.

Clinical features The clinical features of malaria are 1. Febrile paroxysm, 2. Anemia and 3. Splenomegaly.

Each febrile paroxysm has three stages:

1. The cold stage (lasting 20 minutes to an hour)
2. The hot stage (lasting 1–4 hours) and
3. The sweating stage (lasting 2–3 hours). The total duration of the febrile cycle is 6–10 hours.

Types of fever

1. In quotidian fever, the fever recurs at intervals of 24 hours, observed in vivax and malariae malaria
2. In tertian fever, it recurs every third day
3. In quartan fever, the fever recurs every fourth day.

Fever, occurring at regular intervals, depends upon the time of segmentation of infecting Plasmodium. *P. falciparum* segments more irregularly and produces a paroxysm every 36–48 hours. Some cause daily fever.

Paroxysm of malaria occurs at the time of rupture of schizonts and is caused by pyrogens and other toxins released from ruptured schizonts, although none has been identified to date.

Periodicity It is produced by synchronized infection in which all the schizonts rupture simultaneously. Partial immunity reduces parasitemia and symptoms may disappear. This immunity depends upon persistent latent infection known as infection or premunition. The B lymphocytes produce IgG and IgM antibodies against merozoites which are coated with these antibodies. Coated merozoites do not enter RBCs and are removed by phagocytic cells. T lymphocytes stimulate the pagocytosis.

Anemia After the paroxysm, anemia of the microcytic hypochromic type, with iron deficiency, develops due to the break down of the red blood cells during the segmentation of parasites.

Splenomegaly One of the important signs in malaria is enlargement of the spleen. Initially, the enlargement is slight and by the second week, it is much enlarged and palpable.

Symptoms The onset is usually sudden in vivax. Ovale and malariae malaria start with shivering, succeeded by fever reaching 104° or 105°F (40° or 40.6°C), accompanied by symptoms of acute febrile infection such as headache, muscular pains, malaise and increased pulse and respiration. Pernicious symptoms such as coma, convulsions and cardiac failure frequently occur in falciparum malaria.

No signs or symptoms are pathognomonic of malaria. Fever need not be accompanied by the characteristic malarial paroxysm. The paroxysm begins with a chilly feeling, bed-shaking chills and a rise in temperature. The skin appears pale with cynosis of the lips and nail beds. The patient experiences headache, nausea and may vomit. Within one to two hours, the temperature rises towards 40–40.6°C. The patient feels fatigued, weak and often sleeps. This is a typical clinical feature of benign malaria. Fever may persist and may be prolonged in malignant falciparum malaria. Fever is not usually periodic in malignant falciparum malaria. Periodicity of fever occurs only in synchronized infection, when the majority of infected erythrocytes containing mature schizonts rupture at the same time. This occurs at intervals determined by the length of the asexual erythrocytic cycle. The cycle in *P. vivax, P. ovale* malaria takes 48 hours and thus the fever occurs every other day. *P. malariae* matures in 72 hours and causes fever every third day.

The pulse rate is elevated but commensurate with the fever, the nonproductive cough may occur during fever. Hypotension is common in falciparum malaria and weakness may persist for weeks. Splenomegaly occurs frequently and hepatomegaly less frequently. Tenderness on palpation of liver and spleen may be due to sudden stretching of their capsules; splenic rupture is a fatal complication. The absence of splenomegaly does not exclude the diagnosis of malaria.

Most falciparum infections are eliminated in one year; a few persist for up to three years, *P. malariae* may persist as an asymptomatic infection for the life of the patient.

Relapses differ from recrudescence in that the infection that induces the relapse persists as a latent form in hepatic parenchymal cells. Relapses occur only in *P. vivax, P. ovale* and *P. malariae*.

Table 2 Clinical differences between the four strains of Plasmodium

P. falciparum	*P. vivax*	*P. ovale*	*P. malariae*
High parasitemia, severe anemia, renal failure, cerebral malaria, pulmonary edema, death.	splenic rupture, anemia, rare severe neurological complications.		RBC infection persists for years, nephritis

Pernicious malaria: During the course of *P. falciparum* infection which is inadequately treated, a series of phenomenon occur, known as pernicious malaria and it may cause death within one to three days. The pathogenesis of pernicious malaria is due to certain biological features of *P. falciparum* which cause agglutination of red blood cells, which may lead to the blockage of capillary vessels of internal organs. The features are:

1. Erythrocytic schizogony of *P. falciparum* occurring inside the capillary vessels of internal organs
2. Segmenting forms of parasites unable to alter their shape during their passage inside the capillary vessels may act as emboli
3. The growing trophozoites and sexual forms adhere to each other, as well as to the vessel wall, resulting in agglutination and blockage of the vessel.

The peripheral blood smear shows heavy parasitemia, schizonts and ring forms being predominant. The series of symptoms is classified as comatose, algid, bilious, cardialgic, choleraic, delirious, dysenteric, eclamptic, hemorrhagic, hemiplegic and pneumonic. The patient may be cold, pulseless and unconscious (algid type), comatose or restless, at times even violent (cerebral type), bleeding from the skin or mucous membrane (hemorrhagic type), or vomiting and with acute dysentery (gastro-intestinal type). Malaria may simulate many other diseases because of its protean manifestations.

Black water fever Black water fever appears to be a manifestation of repeated infections with falciparum malaria, inadequately treated with quinine.

Congenital malaria It is considered an intra-uterine transmission of malaria and is more common in non-immune infected mothers than in highly immune mothers whose placentae are more frequently heavily loaded with P. falciparum schizonts. It has been reported in each of the four species of Plasmodium. Blood examination of mothers, of the umbilical cord during delivery and of babies within five hours after delivery reveals that the malaria is usually connatal, i.e., acquired during parturition.

Pathology of Malaria

Malarial parasites reside in the red blood cells of the human host. The schizogony lifecycle is completed within the host cell, resulting in the destruction of red blood cells. During their growth, they produce pigment (hematin) from the hemoglobin and also multiply asexually to form daughter individuals (merozoites). On completion of schizogony, merozoites, pigment granules, unused portions of the cytoplasm of the infected red blood cells and 'malarial toxins' are liberated in the bloodstream.

Malarial pigment (hematin): The World Health Organisation (1963) does not recommend the term 'hemozoin' for the malarial pigment. The pigment granules, liberated in the plasma at the time of rupture of segmenting parasites, are filtered out from the circulating blood by the activity of the reticuloendothelial cells and they may be found in any quantity inside these cells. Therefore, the organs rich in reticuloendothelial cells become densely pigmented, i.e., slate grey to black, the characteristic pigmentation of organs. Although, the malarial pigment contains iron, it does not give a Prussian blue reaction when stained with potassium ferrocyanide, but stains black. Other pigments which are also found because of blood destruction are not specific products of malarial parasites. They are

1. Hemosederin (containing iron) and
2. Hematoidin (which is converted into the bile pigment, cholebilirubin).

During the erythrocytic phase, malarial parasites require para-amino-benzoic acid (PABA) for their metabolism. The deficiency of PABA inhibits their growth.

Pathological changes in organs

Spleen

***Macroscopic appearance*:**

1. The spleen is enlarged
2. The colour is slate grey or black

3. The capsule is thin and stretched in acute falciparum malaria
4. The ***consistency*** is soft in acute cases and firm in chronic cases
5. The cut surface has a homogenous black area.

Microscopic examination:

1. Hematin and hemosiderin are found scattered throughout
2. The sinusoids are congested
3. The macrophages are increased in number
4. The parasites appear as black dots in the red blood corpuscles, when sections of the spleen are stained with hematoxylin and eosin
5. The parasites and the pigment are not seen in the malpighian corpuscles (white pulp)
6. In chronic cases, ***reticulin fibrils*** are increased.

Liver

Macroscopic appearance:

1. The liver is enlarged
2. The ***colour*** is slate grey or black.

Microscopic appearance:

1. Parasitized red blood cells fill up the central veins of the lobules and sinusoidal capillaries.
2. Kupffer's cells are increased in number
3. The malarial pigment (hematin) and the parasitized erythrocytes fill up the cytoplasm of Kupffer's cells
4. There is no increase in fibrous tissue
5. Fatty degeneration, atrophy and necrosis are observed in the parenchyma cells of the liver.

Bone marrow

Macroscopic appearance: In acute cases, there is very little change in the marrow of the long bone. In chronic cases, the upper and lower thirds of the long bone are reddish brown in colour or slate grey or black.

Microscopic examination:

1. Parasitized red blood cells are present
2. The reticuloendothelial cells are filled with malarial parasites.

Kidney The kidneys are congested and may reveal acute or sub-acute glomerular nephritis with hemorrhagic areas.

The urine is usually normal in *P. vivax* or *P. malariae* patients; but in *P. falciparum*, it may sometimes show albumin and hyaline and granular casts.

Testes A case of epididymo-orchitis due to falciparum malaria has been reported in Punjab (India).

Brain

1. The brain is congested
2. The cortex may be greyish or slightly brownish.

Lungs They may be pigmented and the capillaries may carry free pigments, pigmented leucocytes, phagocytes and infected erythrocytes.

Stomach and Intestines The stomach and intestines sometimes show marked congestion of mucous membrane with slight pigmentation, while ulceration may be due to blockage of capillaries by the pigment, infected erythrocytes and macrophages.

Heart The heart may show fatty degeneration. In falciparum malaria, coronary occlusion or thrombosis may occur due to the adhesion of infected red blood cells and parasites to the capillary walls.

Laboratory diagnosis The only certain method of diagnosis of malaria is the demonstration of the causative organism, Plasmodium, in the blood. It is better to have both thin and thick films on the same slide or on two different slides. The thick film is preferable for the quick detection of Plasmodium. If the Plasmodia are few, the thin film is examined for identifying the species of Plasmodium. (For laboratory methods, refer to Chapter 12 on 'Blood examination for parasites'.)

In rapid diagnosis of microscope and interference filter in thick and thin blood smears stained with acridine orange (AO), the parasites are quickly detected and easily differentiated from leucocytes as they fluoresce green and red.

The detection of Plasmodium becomes difficult if blood films are taken

1. After an anti-malarial drug
2. During an apyrexial interval *of P. falciparum* infection and
3. During the first 2–3 days of primary infection.

Serodiagnostic methods for malaria, such as complement fixation, slide flocculation, latex agglutination, indirect hemagglutination (HIA) and fluorescent antibody tests, are still at an experimental stage and their use is handicapped by a shortage of antigenic material (WHO, 1968).

Sedimentation, centrifugation and the use of fluorochrome stains and of new wide angle microscope objectives are all under study. The fluorescent antibody test is especially useful in the measurement of development, persistence and specificity of antibodies in human malaria.

In recent years, a variety of serological tests has been developed for malaria, but is not usually used for the diagnosis of clinical infection. They are particularly useful for epidemiological survey and detection of infected blood donors. Those most commonly used are the indirect immuno-fluorescent (IIF) and the indirect hemagglutination (IHA) test. IIF titres equal to or greater than 1:64 are suggestive of recent infection with Plasmodium. These serological tests show a false positive rate of 1% or less or have a sensitivity of over 95%.

In India, the IIF test is used for the diagnosis of malaria by using *P. falciparum* antigen. The diagnostic titre is 1:80. Besides, 80% seropositivity was observed by mean ELISA optical density values to both *P. falciparum* and *P. vivax*. Development of natural immunity in *P. falciparum* malaria can be detected by Western Immunoblot. DNA probe provides a useful epidemiological tool for vivax malaria control programs.

In recent years, ELISA is used to assist in the diagnosis of malaria. ABC, ELISA 'new' test correlated with IIF was better then the conventional ELISA. Plasmodial antigens can be detected by monoclonal antibody.

The recent new genetic engineering method of Padmanabhan (1989) can detect falciparum malaria very specifically, by using radioactive chemicals. This method is very accurate and can detect as few as 50 parasites in the blood sample. Though the currently used slide method is cheap, it is also time consuming and subject to personal errors. Similarly, another method has been developed to detect vivax malaria in India. Magnetic Resonance Imaging (MRI) is most recently used to diagnose cerebral malaria due to *P. falciparum*.

Treatment

Curative treatment: Chloroquine, amodiaquine (the drug of choice) and quinine (for drug resistant *P. falciparum)* are potent schizonticidal drugs acting on the early erythrocytic phases of the parasites.

Anti malarial drug (turmaric), which is one of the ingredients obtained from turmeric (*haldi* in Hindi) is found to be effective against human malaria. It is a very cheap drug (Padmanabhan, 2005—television news discussion on 10.8.2005).

Multidrug resistant *P. falciparum* can respond to mefloquine. This drug is very costly and is not easily available in India. However, there is a very recent report of four cases of prophylaxis failure with mefloquine in Africa. Rarely, mefloquine causes disorientation, hallucination and lapses of consciousness two to three weeks after drug administration. Cinchonism (nausea, vomiting and vertigo) commonly results from treatment with quinine and is not an indication to alter or discontinue therapy. In France, a patient, who had inadvertently received 5.25 g of mefloquine over six days, instead of a single dose of 1.5 g, developed cardiac, hepatic and neurological symptoms. All symptoms disappeared rapidly when mefloquine was discontinued. During mefloquine therapy, 35% of patients vomited at least once within 30 minutes of receiving the drug and there was some probable reinfection in children less than five years old.

Chloroquine-resistant *P. vivax* can be treated with amodiaquine. A combination of sulfadoxine and pyrimethamine (Fansidar) or chlorproguanil and dapsone are superior to chloroquine for clearing parasitemia in falciparum malaria and the longest protection was with the first mentioned combination of drugs.

Recent WHO (1992) recommendations for chloroquine-resistant *P. falciparum* malaria:

1. Mefloquine 15 mg/kg body weight up to 1000 mg in two doses, 12 hours apart. Mefloquine should not be administrated until 12 hours have elapsed after completion of parenteral quinine administration. It should not be given to pregnant women in the first trimester of pregnancy.
2. Halofantrine 8 mg base/kg body weight, every six hours for three days is highly effective. It is not advocated for pregnant women.
3. Quinine tablet 10 mg/kg body weight every eight hours to complete seven days of treatment.
4. Sulfadoxine/pyrimethamine single dose following a shorter course of quinine.
5. Mefloquine – sulfadoxine – pyrimethamine in the prophylaxis of *P. falciparum* provides support for the use of the drug for the treatment of resistant malaria in indigenous African population and is safe for 24 weeks in endemic areas and is comparable to standard antimalarials.

The optimum treatment dose of mefloquine is 25 mg/kg body weight in the Thai-Burmese border for multidrug resistant falciparum malaria.

Pyronaridine is highly active *in vitro* against chloroquine-resistant strains of *P. falciparum* and may be a promising candidate for the treatment of resistant malaria. In China, it is clinically effective against *P. falciparum*.

The multiple resistant blood smear over three weeks and abnormal lumbar puncture are sufficient data to exclude the diagnosis of cerebral malaria with mefloquine-resistant falciparum malaria.

Relapse in malaria can be prevented by the use of 8-aminoquinoline which acts on the exo-erythrocytic phases of the parasites in the liver. It also acts on the gametocytes, but has little action on the erythrocytic stages of the parasites.

Prophylactic treatment: Unless resistant strains of *P. falciparum* are involved, chloroquine and amodiaquine in weekly doses will prevent an acute attack of malaria. These drugs act on the pre-erythrocytic phase of the parasites in the liver and also inactivate the gametocytes which cannot develop further in the mosquito.

Prophylaxis consists of 1. Personal prophylaxis, and 2. Community prophylaxis.

Personal prophylaxis consists of protection against mosquitoes by using mosquito nets and the systematic use of anti-malarial drugs.

Community prophylaxis comprises prevention of the carrier state with anti-malarial drugs; and anti-mosquito measures, which include destruction of adult mosquitoes by spraying insecticides, DDT or gammexane and the use of larvicides (DDT dissolved in oil).

Biological Control Adult dragon flies feed mainly on adult mosquitoes, whereas, their larvae feed only on mosquito larvae. It is termed 'larvicidal fish' and introduced into wells and open tanks.

Efforts to control malaria have been less effective because the mosquito that carries Plasmodium is less susceptible to insecticides and Plasmodia have become more drug-resistant. In 1991, WHO reported that bed nets impregnated with a biodegradable insecticide, permethrin, can deter mosquitoes from entering homes, it kills a large number of mosquitoes that come in contact with it, has no adverse effect on people and can reduce by two thirds the mortality among children.

Vaccination Very recently, it has been realized that the best approach for human vaccination against malaria is via monoclonal antibody to the protective antigen of Plasmodium. Once isolated, this antigen may be synthesized (assuming it is a protein) and mass produced. The world's first vaccine (synthetic peptides) against malaria, developed by a Colombian scientist Dr. Manuel Patarroya in 1987, prevents the invasion of red blood cells by raising antibodies against the micromerozoites. The vaccine is given in three doses, the second dose after one month and the last after 150 days. It would cost Rs. 7 (Indian currency) to vaccinate a single person. This vaccine protects against malaria caused by *P. vivax* and *P. falciparum*. The only major adverse reaction was inflammation at the site of injection which disappeared after a few days. Over 30,000 people in Latin America have been vaccinated against malaria. The vaccine is cheap, safe and effective in 60–83% of cases, with a maximum efficacy in children under five. In late 1992, this technology of vaccine preparation has been provided to India, free of cost.

Babesia

It is a sporozoan parasite mainly affecting cattle. Few human cases have been reported and almost all of them were splenectomised persons (Garnham et al., 1969). Later, the infection that had been reported in a non-splenectomised individual by Western blot (1970) created interest in Babesiosis.

Organisms resembling atypical *P. falciparum* were found in the blood smear of infected individuals. Babesia (Fig. 4.16) does not contain pigment; it is somewhat pear-shaped and divides within infected blood cells. Babesia antibodies can be demonstrated by complement fixation and tube latex agglutination tests.

Chloroquine has been of some value in the treatment of human Babesia infection (babesiosis).

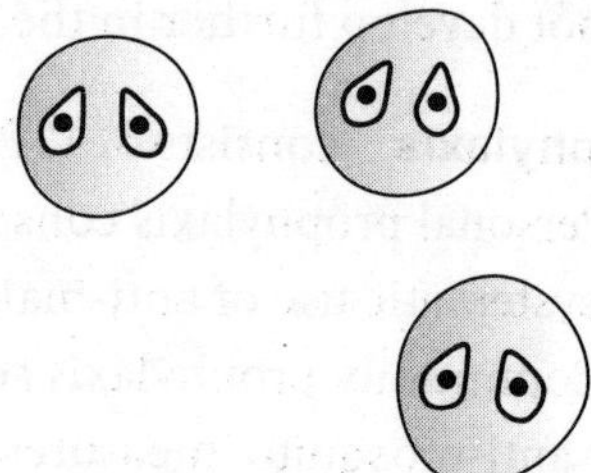

Fig. 4.16 Babesia.

Toxoplasma gondii

This parasite was discovered by Nicolle and Manceaux in 1908 in a small rodent, gondii, of North Africa. It is found distributed all over the world. Human infection has been reported from Africa, Europe, the Middle East, Sri Lanka, North, Central and South America, Australia, Hawaii and the United Kingdom.

Morphology It is an obligatory, intracelluar, ***coccidial*** parasite. It may occur in two forms:

1. *Extracellular form:* It is a slender, crescent-shaped organism, one end being rounded and the other pointed. It is somewhat sickle-shaped and measures 2–7 μm by 2–3 μm in size.
2. ***Intracellular form***: Under the electron microscope, the following structures are found in the cytoplasm:
   a. Mitochondria
   b. Conoid (a spindle-like object at the pointed end)
   c. Toxonemes (a bundle of long bodies) (Fig. 4.18).

Staining reaction: When stained with Giemsa stain, the cytoplasm appears blue, the nucleus reddish purple and the para-nuclear body, red.

Reproduction: It multiplies by binary fission.

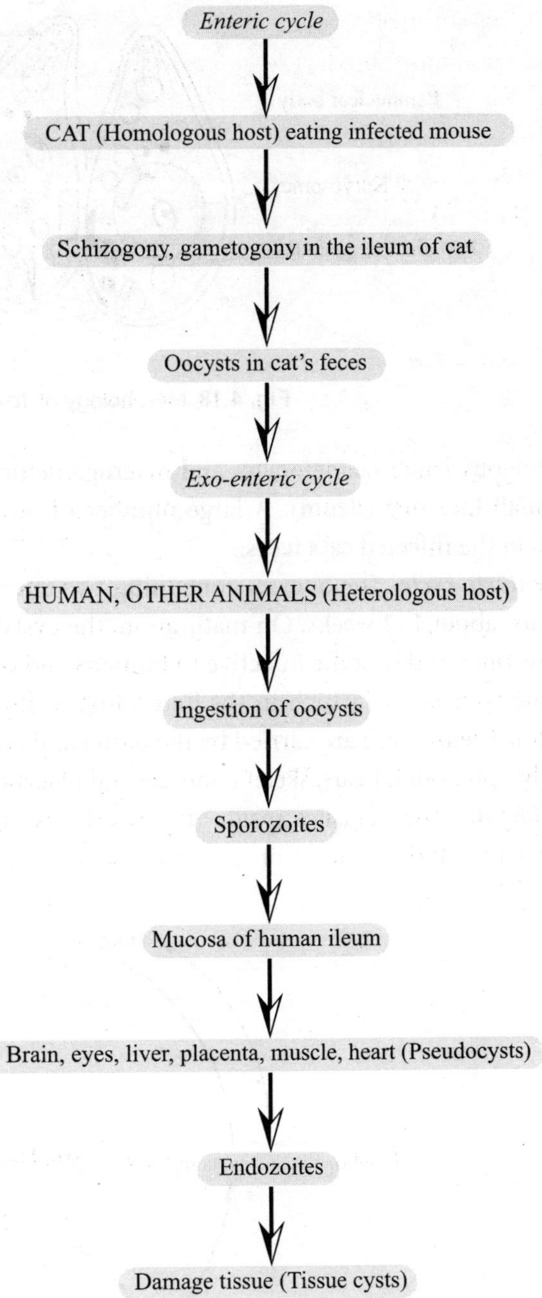

Fig. 4.17 Lifecycle of *T.gondii*.

Lifecycle The lifecycle of *T. gondii* may be
1. Enteric, and 2. Exo-enteric.

Enteric cycle: In cats (homologous host) eating a mouse brain which contains cysts (tissue cysts) of *Toxoplasma gondii,* cycles of schizogony (trophozoite, schizont, merozoite) and

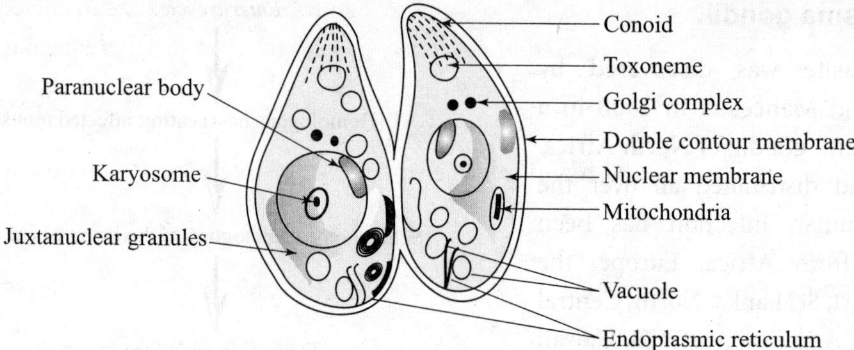

Fig. 4.18 Morphology of *Toxoplasma gondii.*

gametogony (microgametocytes and macrogametocytes) develop inside the epithelial cells of the small intestine (ileum). A large number of oocysts resembling those of *Isospora* can be found in the infected cat's feces.

Exo-enteric cycle*:** The oocysts containing two sporocysts (*Isospora*) are excreted in the cat's feces for about 1–2 weeks. On maturation, the cysts develop into four sporozoites resembling trophozoites and become infective to humans and other animals. The oocysts, after ingestion, liberate sporozoites which in the heterologous host (human) penetrate the mucosa of the intestine (ileum) and are carried by the blood and lymph stream to distant organs (brain, eyes, liver, lymph nodes, heart, skeletal muscle and placenta of the pregnant uterus) where they form ***pseudocysts. The parasites inside the pseudocyst are known as ***endozoites***. The parasitized cells rupture and the endozoites escape and continue their intracellular multiplication. Hence,

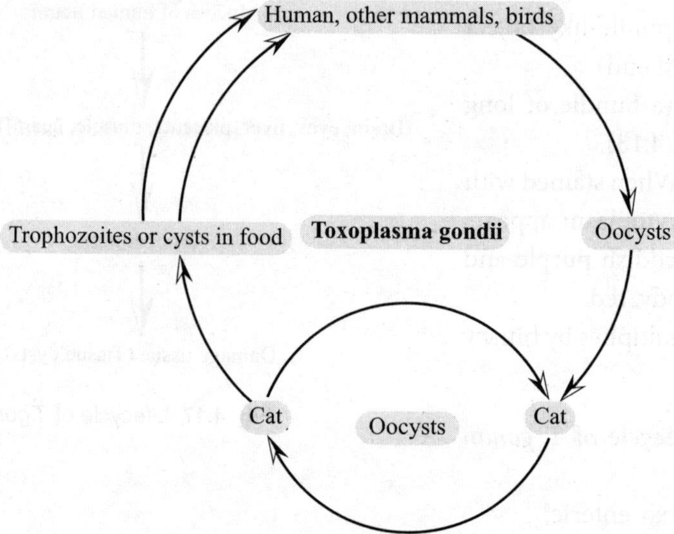

Fig. 4.19 Lifecycle of *T. gondii.*

this causes damage to the tissues. Some of the sporozoites tend to localize in the central nervous system and musculature, and later they transform into ***tissue cysts*** where the parasites also multiply. Both pseudo-cysts and tissue cysts are infective to humans and animals (Fig. 4.19). The organism has a predilection for the following:

1. Tissues rich in ***reticuloendothelial cells***, causing their enlargement, e.g., lymphadenopathy
2. ***The central nervous system***, where it produces encephalitis, chorioretinitis (pigmented, ringed scar) and depletion of cerebral tissue
3. ***The heart***, especially in the acquired form, where it produces cardiomegaly, myocarditis and endocardial fibrosis
4. ***The uterus***, where it produces abortion.

Clinical features Toxoplasmosis may be congenital or acquired.

1. ***Congenital toxoplasmosis*:** This results from congenital infection in infants and young children. It usually appears as a form of encephalitis, accompanied by chorioretinitis, hydrocephalus or microcephaly, mental retardation and convulsions.

   The infection passes from the mother through the placenta, late in pregnancy, when any neutralization of antibody cannot take place. The child is usually born jaundiced with purpuric or maculopapular rash, and enlarged liver and spleen. In cases in which the infection occurs late during gestation or involves very few organisms, the infants will probably have no immediate clinical manifestation, but will have positive humoral and cellular immune response to *T. gondii*. Cysts of *T. gondii* will persist in the brain, retina, myocardium and/or skeletal muscle for the infant's lifetime.

   In infants who are infected early during gestation or with large inocula, the clinical sequelae can be severe. Spontaneous abortion, stillbirth and prematurity may result. The infant may be born with microphthalmia, microcephaly, severe cerebral calcification, bilateral retinochoroiditis, rash, lymph adenopathy, pneumonitis, fever or hepatosplenomegaly which may be severe.
2. ***Acquired toxoplasmosis*:** Toxoplasmosis is very rare in adults, often fatal. It is followed by prolonged remittent fever with erythematous rash.

   ***Acquired toxoplasmosis in the immuno-competent individual*:** The majority of individuals who are infected with *T. gondii* after birth have no apparent clinical symptoms. In the small number of individuals with symptomatic illness, lympadenopathy (90%), fever (40%), are the common manifestations. The nodes are characteristically rubbery and non-tender. Splenomegaly occurs in 30% of patients. The fever is usually low grade but on occasion can be high, rapidly fluctuating and prolonged. Fatigue can be a prominent feature. For most patients with clinically apparent disease, toxoplasmosis is self limiting. Death due to toxoplasmosis in immuno-competent patients is extremely rare. Toxoplasmosis causes 20–35% retinochoroiditis in children and adults. Patients complain of blurred vision, pain or epiphora. Panuveitis and papillitis with optic atrophy can occur.

Toxoplasmosis in immuno-deficient patients: The disease occurs with particular frequency in patients with AIDS and occasionally in Hodgkin's disease patients. The clinical manifestations are variable. Fever, hepatosplenomegaly, pneumonitis, maculopapular rash, myositis, myocarditis, meningoencephalitis may be seen. The most common manifestations, particularly in patients with AIDS, are central nervous system involvement with fever, headache and confusion, progressing to coma, local neurological signs and seizures.

Laboratory diagnosis The following tests are used to diagnose toxoplasmosis:

1. ***Complement fixation test of Warren and Sabin.***
   Tests for IgM antibody (IgM fluorescent antibody or double sandwich ELISA technique) are particularly useful for establishing recent Toxoplasma infection, because titres appear early (as early as five days after infection) and disappear within several months. IgM antibodies are elevated in acute disease.
   CFT using soluble Toxoplasma antigen becomes positive three to six weeks after infection, rises for two to eight months and falls to a very low level after one to two years. Recent PCR can detect *T. gondii* DNA in the CSF of AIDS patients with cerebral toxoplasmosis. HIA and IFA are sensitive, specific and simple to perform. The direct agglutination test with 2 mercaptoethanol (2AD-2ME) and the IFA test are used in the diagnosis of toxoplasmosis. The former is a little superior to the latter. A modified agglutination test can also be used.
2. ***Skin test of Frenzel*** is done by injection of 0.1 ml of 1:500 dilution of antigen intradermally. The test is positive when, after 24–48 hours, an area larger than 0.5 cm persists.
3. ***The dye test of Sabin and Feldman*** is perhaps the most popular diagnostic technique. It consists of
   a) Mixing equal parts of peritoneal exudate from infected mice and of the patient's serum
   b) Incubating for an hour at 37°C
   c) Adding one drop of saturated solution of methylene blue to a drop of this mixture, and
   d) Examining this under a high power microscope.

   In the absence of antibody, 99–100% of Toxoplasma takes up the stain, whereas in its presence less than 50% is stained. *In vitro* culture and cloning of *T. gondii* can be made in a newly established line derived from TG 180.
4. ***Radiological diagnosis*** (Ventriculogram): X-ray of the skull to show cerebral calcification is done. Computed Tomography (CT) scan can be used to diagnose *Toxoplasma gondii* encephalitis.

Treatment Treatment is unsatisfactory at present. Sulphonamides and pyrimethamine are currently used.

Prevention Careful disposal of the feces of cats and other domestic animals is the only effective method to prevent toxoplasmosis.

Sarcocystis lindemanni

It was first observed in humans by Lindemann in 1868 and was named by Rivolta, after its discoverer Lindemann, in 1876 as *Sarcocystis lindemanni*. This organism is found worldwide. It has been reported in India (Mumbai) from a 40-year old labourer.

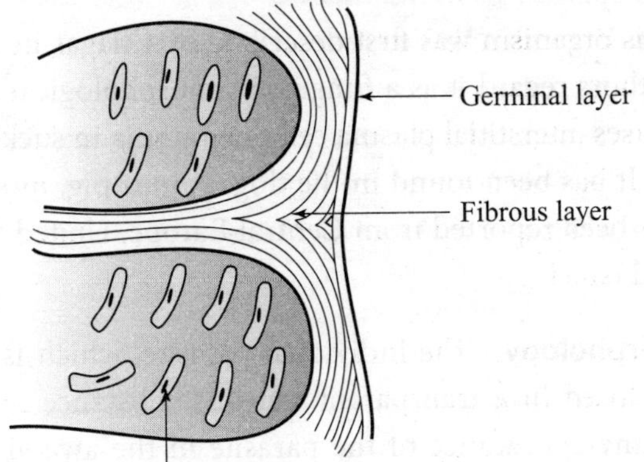

Fig. 4.20 Section of Miescher's tube in muscle. *Sarcocystis lindemanni*.

Morphology *S. lindemanni* (Fig. 4.20) consists of a cylindrical, elongated or fusiform body, hyaline in appearance, with pointed ends, lying lengthwise in the affected muscle fibres. It is enclosed in a membrane and contains myriads of round and crescent-shaped spores, known as 'Miescher's tubes'. They vary in length from being microscopic to up to five cm. Macroscopically, they appear as minute white streaks in the muscle fibres. Each parasite consists of a cylindrical whitish tube with pointed ends. In its compartment, it contains 'Rainey's corpuscles' or 'spores', known to be trophozoites. These are banana-shaped, similar to Toxoplasma. It has not yet been cultivated.

Lifecycle There is no sexual stage and no intermediate host is required. Humans ingest infected meat or drink containing the trophozoites, which on reaching the intestine, pass through the wall, enter the blood vessels and are carried to striated muscles. Each trophozoite divides by binary fission producing round bodies, 4–8 μm in diameter, enclosed in a cyst wall which enlarges and matures.

Pathogenicity and clinical features The secretion of the toxic byproduct, ***sarcocystin***, affects the central nervous system, heart, adrenals and intestinal wall. The organism is found in the myocardium and muscles of the larynx, tongue and limbs. Infections in sheep and other animals may be fatal. A toxin enables the ***sarcocystis*** to penetrate the intestinal wall. Miescher's tubes in the muscle fibres do not produce serious injury or irritation.

Diagnosis and treatment Demonstration of Miescher's tubes in the affected muscles is an effective method of diagnosis. *S. lindemanni* is rarely observed in humans. The Sabin–Feldman dye test gives positive reactions with both *Sarcocystis* and *Toxoplasma,* but the latter may be distinguished by the complement fixation test.

There is no specific treatment. Prognosis is, however, excellent in human infection.

Food contaminated with infected animal excreta and uncooked infected meat should be avoided.

Pneumocystis carinii

This organism was first described by Chagas in 1909 and by Carinii in 1910. Although some authors regard it as a fungus, its morphological appearance resembles that of a protozoon. It causes interstitial plasma cell pneumonia in suckling infants.

It has been found in the dog, guinea pig, mouse, rat, rabbit, sheep, goat and humans, and has been reported from Central Europe, United States, Canada, Australia, Chile, South Africa and Israel.

Morphology The individual parasite, which is a single cell about 1.5–2 μm in diameter, is enclosed in a transparent mucous substance in the interior of a sphere. The characteristic foamy appearance of the parasite in the alveoli of the lung is due to the heaping up of the mucous spheres.

Lifecycle The sporozoites, after escaping from the sporocysts ingested by mouse or guinea pig, pass through the gut wall and enter the endothelial cells. After repeated schizogony, the merozoites finally spread as far as the kidney and lungs, where sporogony occurs. Sporogony ends with the formation of moderately thick-walled cysts (Fig. 4.21) containing eight characteristically large, oval shaped, spore-like structures, 1–2 μm in diameter. These eight daughter cells of the sporocysts are arranged in a rosette formation in the sphere body. The parasites divide repeatedly in the spheres by binary fission.

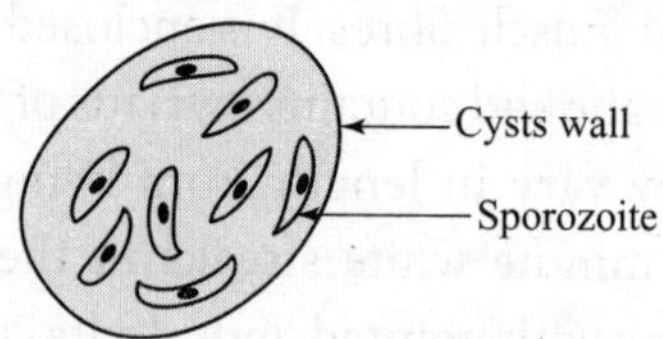

Fig. 4.21 *Pneumocystis carinii* (A small round cyst containing eight uninucleated bodies - sporozoites).

Clinical features *Pneumocystis carinii* interstitial pneumonia is mainly a disease of premature and debilitated children. The incubation period is 20–30 days and the duration of the attack is 1–4 weeks. The course of the disease is acute and is occasionally fatal. Death is due to asphyxia caused by the blockage of the alveoli and bronchioles by proliferating masses of parasites. The major symptoms of pneumocystis are dyspnea, tachypnea, chest tightness, cough, fever and cynosis. The clinical syndrome can progress rapidly over several days or can appear insidiously over weeks or months. The rapidly progressive form is characteristic of patients with malignant neoplasm, especially during corticosteroid withdrawal. The insidious form is typically seen in children with congenital immuno-deficiencies and in adults with AIDS. Patients may have signs of respiratory distress (tachypnea, dyspnea and cynosis), associated fever, but some patients, particularly those with AIDS, may have a paucity of signs. Auscultation of lungs shows no abnormalities, although scattered rales of bronchi may be heard.

Diagnosis and treatment

1. Detection of this parasite in sections of lung tissue stained by Gram Weight *P. carinii* stain. Because most patients infected with *P. carinii* lack adequate antibodies, serological methods of diagnosing the disease (which can cause pneumonia) particularly in AIDS patients, are limited. Gram weight stain is one option as it demonstrates the presence of *P. carinii* in smears or imprints of bronchovascular lavage specimens or bronchial brushing and transbronchiol or open lung biopsy specimens. Smears and imprints are fixed and air dried before staining and the results (the organisms appear blue or deep purple against a pink background) are obtained within 30 minutes. It is a very recent staining technique.
2. Radiological appearance of pneumocystis pneumonia, and
3. Complement fixation test using lung tissue as antigen.

The most effective treatment appears to be pentamidine isothionate. The combination of clindamycin–primaquine in acute therapy of *P. carinii* pneumonia (PCP) in human immunodeficiency virus (HIV)-infected patients is an effective and alternate therapy to the standard regimen. There is no specific preventive measure as the mode of infection is not well understood yet.

SUMMARY

- Sporozoa are protozoa showing no locomotion. They produce spores and have a lifecycle characterized by alternation of generation, one sexual and one asexual, occurring completely in one host (Eimeria, Isospora) or an alternation of hosts (Plasmodium).

Genus isospora

- *Isospora belli* and *Isopora hominis* produce oocysts and sporocysts. Oocysts are elongated or ovoidal, have two layers – the inner layer is thin and the outer layer is hard. At one end, they have a small micropyle and have two sporocysts with four sporozoites, which are long, crescent-shaped with a single nucleus. It causes self limited disease in humans.

Genus eimeria

- This genus produces oocysts containing four sporocysts. Each sporocyst contains two sporozoites (schizogony). It is an animal parasite causing coccidiosis (common disease) in calf. Human infection is accidental after ingestion of water contaminated with oocysts of Eimeria.

Genus plasmodium

- This genus consists of the following species:
  1. *Plasmodium vivax* causing vivax or tertian malaria
  2. *P. ovale* causing ovale malaria
  3. *P. falciparum* causes malignant tertian or falciparum malaria.
- Laveran (1880) first observed *P. vivax*. Romannowsky (1891) developed a staining method for malarial parasites. Bigmani *et al.* (1898) described the mosquito lifecycle of human Plasmodium.
- The endemic area of these Plasmodia is the tropical zone. *P. falciparum* is common in the tropics and subtropics. Plasmodia develop in liver cells, reside in red blood cells and they are carried to various organs through the blood stream.
- Two hosts are required for their lifecycle:
  1. Humans (intermediate host)
  2. Mosquito (definite host)
- In humans, Plasmodia reside in hepatic cells and red blood cells and multiply asexually (schizogony). Humans are also an intermediate host for hydatid disease (caused by the tapeworm). In the female Anophelos mosquito (definite host), Plasmodia multiply sexually; male and female gametocytes are ingested by the mosquito from the blood of the infected human and forms a zyote in the mosquito intestine after fertilization and later become ookinete (motile zygote). On reaching the salivary gland of the mosquito, they liberate sporozoites, infective to humans.
- Sporozoites injected by the infected mosquito bite into the human victim and enter directly into the liver cells (not RBCs) – pre-erythrocytic schizogny. Macromerozoites re-enter liver cells (in *P. vivax, P. malariae, P. ovale* there is RELAPSE). There is no relapse in *P. falciparum*. Micromerozoites enter RBCs, develop into trophozoites, schizonts, merozoites (erythrocytic schizogny), then at last into gametocytes (gametogony), which are ingested by mosquito.
- The individuals who harbour these gametocytes are called 'carriers'.
- ***Phanerozoites*** are merozoites liberated from the liver cycle.
- ***Sporozoites*** are infective forms cf malarial parasites. Their shapes vary from narrow, curved (vivax), thick (malaria), sickle-shaped (falciparum). They have an apical cup, mitochondria, paired organelles. The ookinete is enveloped by two layers: the inner one is smooth; the outer one is corrugated and has cytoplasmic inclusions (mitochondria, black pigment granules).
- Malarial parasite feeds on its host cytoplasm by pinocytosis. It gets energy by phosphorylation of glucose; oxidative process is maintained by the oxyhemoglobin of erythrocytes. The globin of hemoglobin is split by enzymes into amino acids and peptides to form the parasite's protein. Its metabolites are derived from the hemoglobin and blood plasma.

- The malarial parasite is malnourished, when the host is starved. Restriction of thiamine, riboflavin and biotin may inhibit the growth of the parasite. *P. falciparum* heavily infects West African children restricted to a milk diet.
- ***Glucose-6 phosphate dehydrogenase deficient*** (G6 PD) trait may confer some protection against *P. falciparum* infection.
- Sickle cell anemia trait may also cause resistance to *P. falciparum* infection, as this parasite cannot utilize the abnormal hemoglobin (rod-shaped masses) which distorts red blood cells into a sickle-like shape.
- ***Thalasemia hemoglobin and hemoglobin E*** can provide protection against *P.vivax* and human fetal hemoglobin against all Plasmodia.

P. vivax Vivax is derived from the Latin 'vivere' which means to live. *P. vivax* has worldwide distribution and is common in India.

- ***Gametes*** Its microgamete penetrates into the small projection of the macrogamete and forms ookinetes. This process takes 10 minutes to one hour in the mosquito's gut.
- Schizogony forms of *P. vivax* are found in peripheral blood, 48 hours after staining.
- Trophzoites ring form 2–5 µm, cytoplasm opposite to nucleus is thicker.
- Growing form is irregular with a vacuole, actively ameboid.
- Schizont (mature), 9–10 µm, regular, completely fills enlarged RBCs.
- Merozoites, 12–24, arranged in an irregular grape-like cluster.
- Pigment is yellowish brown with fine granules, infected RBCs are enlarged, pale, Schuffner's dots are present.
- Gametocyte is spherical, much larger than an RBC. Cytoplasm of the female gametocyte is blue; the nucleus is small and compact. Cytoplasm of the male is pale blue; its nucleus is large and diffuse.

Plasmodium falciparum The name falaciparum (Latin, *falx* for sickle) is derived from the sickle-shaped gametocyte of *P. falciparum*. Its distribution is worldwide. It is very common in India.

- ***Gametes*** Macrogamete is spherical, with its nucleus approaching the edge of the parasite, forming a protuberance into which a microgamete will penetrate.
- Sporozoites are sickle-shaped.
- Schizogony forms of *P. falciparum* in the peripheral blood after 48 hours (after staining)
- Trophozoite (ring form) 1.25 µm–1.5 µm, cytoplasm fine, regular ***accolé form*** nucleus. Growing form assumes compact form, pigments collect into a single mass early.
- Schizont (mature) 4.5 µm–5 µm, fills two thirds of RBCs which are not enlarged. Merozoites 18–24 or more, arranged in a grape-like cluster.
- Pigments are dark brown or blackish, (one or two solid blocks). Infected RBCs are unaltered, crenated, reddish violet colour, Maurer's dots. Gametocytes are

spherical, much larger than RBCs. Host cells are hardly recognizable. Cytoplasm of female gametocyte is blue, nucleus is small and compact.

- Cytoplasm of male gametocyte is pale blue, nucleus large and diffuse.

Plasmodium malariae Schizogony forms of *P. malariae* of the peripheral blood. Trophozoites are the same as *P. vivax*. Growing forms are band like, slightly ameboid, their vacuoles disappear early.

- Schizont (mature) measures 5–7 μm, regular, almost fills a normal sized RBC.
- Merozoites are 6–12, arranged around a central mass of pigment, like a daisy or rosette. Pigments are dark brown, coarse granules. Infected RBCs are not enlarged, not pale and have no dots.
- Gametocyte is round, oval, size of RBC. The cytoplasm of the male is pale blue; its nucleus is large and diffuse; whereas that of female is blue and its nucleus is large and diffuse.

Plasmodium ovale Its name is derived from its shape which is oval. Its schizogony forms:

- Trophozoite (ring form) is the same as *P. malariae*. Growing form has no ribbon shape, slightly ameboid.
- Schizont (mature) is 6.2 μm, fills three quarters of RBC which is slightly enlarged.
- Merozoite 6–12, is irregularly arranged. Pigment is dark yellowish brown, coarser than *P. vivax*. Infected RBCs are enlarged, oval with James's dots; gametocyte is oval, size of RBC. Host cell is slightly enlarged with James's dots. Male gametocyte cytoplasm is stained pale blue by Leishman stains, its nucleus is large and diffuse; whereas that of the female is stained blue; its nucleus is small and compact.

Pathogenicity of plasmodium Intermittent fevers caused by plasmodium infection are called 'malaria' (Lat. *mala* and *aria* means 'bad air')

- Each species causes characteristic fever
  1. Quotidian fever (daily fever) is caused by vivax and malariae malaria
  2. Tertain fever (every third day) occurs in *P. falciparum* malaria
  3. Quartan fever (recurring every fourth day) is caused by malariae malaria.
- Sporozoites injected into the blood by mosquito bite, leave the bloodstream and enter the liver cells without any host reaction. Micromerozoites liberated from the liver cells after schizogony enter into red cells and pathogenic effects become noticeable.
- The infection may cause disturbance of oxygen usage which may occur in two ways:

oxygen supply may be reduced below the physiological level resulting in a state of anoxic anemia. Because of pathological changes in the metabolizing cells, the host may not utilize adequate oxygen supply, which is responsible for a state of cytotoxic anoxia.

- Acute severe malaria (algid malaria) may cause a state of shock, in which there will be local anoxic anemia with liver or kidney damage. The incubation period is 10–14 days in *P. vivax, P. ovale* and *P. falciparum,* whereas in *P. malariae*, it is 18 days to 6 weeks (longest period)
- Fever is the main clinical feature and has three stages – cold, hot and sweating stage. Total duration of fever is 6–10 hours.
- During schizogony of *Plasmodium* in red cells, these RBCs break down and cause microcytic hypochromic type anemia, with iron deficiency which occurs after paroxysm.
- Splenomegaly is the main sign, showing steady enlargement of the spleen; after two weeks, it is much enlarged and palpable.
- Shivering with high fever (104°F), headache and muscular pain are main symptoms. Pernicious symptoms (coma, convulsion, cardiac failure) are frequently observed in falciparum malaria. Because of its protean manifestations, malaria may simulate other diseases.
- Black Water fever develops in falciparum malaria due to repeated falciparum infection which is inadequately treated with quinine.
- Congenital malaria is due to intra-uterine transmission of malaria and is common in non-immune infected mothers, whose placentae are heavily loaded with *P. falciparum*. Co-natal malaria is acquired during parturition.
- Laboratory diagnosis can be done by:
- Direct detection of plasmodium in stained blood smear.
- It is an easy accurate method; when parasites are scanty, thick smears are preferred, while a thin smear can be used to identify Plasmodium species.

  Various serological methods Treatment may be curative or prophylactic
- Curative: Padmanaban (2005) obtained one of the ingredients of turmeric (haldi –Hindi word) found to be effective against human malaria. It is a very cheap anti-malarial drug still under trial
- Prophylactic: Anti-malarial vaccine prepared by DNA recombinant technique is proved successful in animal experimentation and is under human trial (Padmanaban, 2005)

Babesia

- It is a protozoan parasite affecting mostly cattle; however, a few human cases have been reported. This protozoa is similar to *P. falciparum* and found in blood smear. Babesia is pear shaped, divides within red cells and has no pigment. Complement fixation and latex agglutination tests can detect Babesia antibodies. Chloroquine has some value in human babesiosis.

Toxoplasma gondii

- Its name is derived from gondii (*gondii* means a small rodent). It has a worldwide distribution. It is an obligatory, intracellular, coccidial parasite occurring in two forms:
  1. Extracellular form is sickle, crescent shaped
  2. Intracellular form has mitochodria, conoid.
- Its lifecycle may a) enteric and b) exo-enteric.
  (a) Enteric cycle occurs in the epithelial cells of the ileum of the cat (i.e. schizogony, gametogony). Oocysts similar to those of Isospora may be detected in the infected cat's feces.
  (b) Exo-enteric cycle: Isospora (oocysts containing two sporozoites) are excreted in the cat's feces. Sporozoites liberated from the oocysts are infective to humans and animals, penetrate the mucous membrane of the ileum and are carried by the blood to various organs (brain, eyes, lymph node, liver, heart, placenta of pregnant uterus where they produce pseudocysts. The parasites inside these pseudocysts are known as endozoites, which escape to continue their multiplication in the cells and cause damage to the tissues and transform into ***tissue cysts*** which are infective to humans and animals.
- *T. gondii* has a predilection for reticuloendothelial cells causing lymphadenopathy; for central nervous system causing encephalitis, chorionetinitis, for the heart (cardiomegaly, myocarditis), for the uterus (abortion)
- Clinically, toxoplasmosis may be congenital or acquired.
  1. ***Congenital toxoplamosis*** is common in children characterized by encephalitis, chorio-retinitis, hydrocephalus, mental retardation and convulsion, enlarged liver and spleen. This infection passes from the infected mother in late pregnancy through the placenta to the fetus.
  2. ***Acquired toxoplasmosis*** is often fatal and very rare in adults (prolonged remittent fever with erythematous rash).
- ***Laboratory diagnosis***: Complement fixation test, dye test of Sabin and Feldman are useful, in addition to radiological diagnosis.
- Treatment is not satisfactory and prevention can be done by the proper disposal of cat's feces.

Sarcocystis lindermanni

- Linderman first discovered *Sarcocystis lindermanni* (which was so named in honour of its discoverer). This parasite is worldwide in distribution. In India, (Mumbai) only one case (40 year old labourer) has been reported.
- It is a cylindrical, elongated body lying in the affected muscle, contains crescent shaped spores known as 'Miescher's tubes'. Each tube contains 'Rainey's corpuscle' or spores known as trophozoites (banana-shaped)

- Humans get the infection by ingestion of infected meat or drinks containing the trophozoites, which pass through the intestinal wall and blood to the striated muscles, where they produce round bodies enclosed in a cyst.
- Sarcocystin (toxic byproduct) affects the CNS, heart, adrenals and the intestinal wall. The infection in animals is fatal. Miesher's tubes do not produce serious injury. The best method of diagnosis is the demonstration of Miescher's tubes in the affected muscles. Serology can also be useful. Treatment is not specific and the infection can be controlled by avoiding the ingestion of food contaminated with the trophozoites.

Pneumocystis

- **Pneumocystis carinii** It causes interstitial plasma cell pneumonia in sucking infants. It is a single cell parasite, with a foamy appearance found in the alveoli of the lungs, enclosed in the spores.
- The sporozoites after escaping from the spores enter into the gut wall. After repeated schizogony, the merozoites spread to the kidney, lungs where sporogony occurs. Oocyst contains eight sporozoites, clinically the disease is acute. Death may be due to asphyxia.
- Detection of this parasite is the best method of laboratory diagnosis; in addition, radiology and serology can be used. Pentamidine isothionate is very effective and there is no specific preventive measure.

QUESTIONS

1. *What is a sporozoa?*
   - Sporozoa is a non-motile protozoan which produces spores.
2. *Why do sporozoa require an alternation of generation?*
   - They require it because they multiply both sexually and asexually in their lifecycle.
3. *Mention a species of sporozoa which requires an alternation of hosts for its lifecycle.*
   - Plasmodium requires an alternation of host (human – intermediate host; mosquito – definite host).
4. *For what purpose does Plasmodium require the mosquito?*
   - Plasmodium requires the mosquito for sexual multiplication.
5. *What is sporogony?*
   - Sporogony is sexual multiplication which occurs after fertilization of female gametes by male gametes in the gut of the mosquito where oocysts are formed.
6. *What is schizogony?*
   - Schizogony is an asexual cycle of development; multiplication is by segmentation in RBCs in humans (intermediate host).

7. *How would you differentiate between Isospora and Eimeria?*

▸ Eimeria is identified by its oocyst containing four sporocysts, each one has two sporozoites.

Isospora is identified by its oocyst containing two sporocysts with four sporozoites (in each sporocyst which undergoes schizogony (trophozoite, schizont, merozoites) and eventually, sporogony with the development of oocysts.

8. *Describe in brief the clinical features of Isospora and Eimeria.*

▸ Isospora causes anorexia, nausea, abdominal pain and diarrhea. Human infection is self limited. Eimeria causes coccidiosis (common) in calf and is found in the human stool during its transit after accidental ingestion.

Plasmodia

1. *Who recommended that the term malarial parasites should be restricted to the family Plasmodiae?*

▸ The World Health Organization (WHO) recommended this.

2. How many species of Plasmodium cause malaria?

▸ There are four species which cause malaria: *Plasmodium vivax; Plasmodium falciparum, P. ovale* and *P. malariae.*

3. Who first discovered the following (1) *P. vivax*; (2) Staining method for Plasmodium, (3) Mosquito cycle of human plasmodia; avian plasmodia?

▸ 1. *P. vivax* by Laveran (1880)

2. Staining method by Romanowsky (1891)

3. Mosquito cycle of human Plasmodia by Bigmani et al (1898)

4. Mosquito cycle of avian Plasmodia by Ross in Kolkata (India).

4. *Where do Plasmodia undergo development and reside?*

▸ Plasmodia undergo a development stage in the parenchyma cells of the liver, reside in the RBCs of humans and are carried via the bloodstream to various organs.

5. *Name two diseases in which humans act as intermediate hosts?*

▸ (i) Malaria; (ii) Hydatid disease.

6. *Why does the mosquito represent the definite host of malarial parasites?*

▸ It does so because of the sexual method of reproduction of malarial parasites.

7. *What forms of Plasmodia are required to initiate the mosquito cycle?*

▸ To initiate the mosquito cycle, sexual forms (male and female gametocytes) are first developed in the human host and they are transferred to the definite host (female Anopheles mosquito), where they develop further and transform into sporozoites infective to humans.

8. *Why can only the female Anopheles mosquito transmit malaria?*

▸ The female Anopheles mosquito has a stout proboscis which can pierce the human skin like a needle.

9. *Why is the proboscis of the female mosquito stout?*
▶ It is stout because of the presence of well-developed serrated maxillae and mandibles in the proboscis.
10. *Why is it that the male Anopheles mosquito cannot bite human beings?*
▶ This is because the proboscis of the male is not stout, it is flexible; hence it cannot pierce through the skin.
11. *How is host specificity observed in Plasmodium?*
▶ Host specificity is determined by the presence or absence of certain amino acids in the mosquito required by Plasmodium for its sexual development.
12. *How many stages of the human cycle are involved in Plasmodium? Cite them.*
▶ There are four stages. They are
   1) Pre-erythrocytic schizogony
   2) Erythrocytic schizogony
   3) Gametogony
   4) Exo-erythrocytic schizogony.
13. *Why do the sporozoites (infective forms) not enter directly into the RBCs to initiate the infection?*
▶ This is because they have to undergo the developmental stage in the parenchyma cells of the liver (human tissues). This is known as pre-erythrocytic schizogony. After this schizogony, the merozoites are liberated.
14. *What are cryptozoites?*
▶ Merozoites liberated from the liver are called cryptozoites or phanerozoites (both micromerozoite and macromerozoite).
15. *What is the main function of cryptozoites or merozoites?*
▶ Merozoites give rise to micromerozoites and macromerozoites.
16. *What is the role of micromerozoites and macromerozoites?*
▶ Micromerozoites enter RBCs to initiate the infection, whereas macromerozoites re-enter the liver cells for exo-erythyrocytic schizogony which is responsible for relapse of vivax, ovale and malariae malaria.
17. *What is a relapse? Why is there no relapse in P. falciparum?*
▶ *P. vivax, P. ovale* and *P. malariae* undergo pre-erythrocytic schizogony in the form of a focal liver cycle (tissue phase) which is necessary for relapse of malaria.
   In the case of *P. falciparum*, there is no relapse because it has no exo-erythrocytic schizogony or liver cycle.
18. *When is blood sterile in malaria?*
▶ Blood is sterile when the parasites (Plasmodia) are not found in the peripheral blood during pre-erythrocytic schizogony.
19. *When is there no clinical manifestation and pathological damage in malaria?*
▶ When Plasmodia develop inside the liver there is no clinical manifestation and pathological damage.

20. *Why is the liver cycle in malaria necessary?*
▶ Liver cycle is necessary for the development of micromerozoites which can only enter into RBCs to initiate the infection. If there is no liver cycle, there are no micromerozoites.
21. *How many stages of plasmodium are seen in the RBCs during erythrocytic schizogony?*
▶ Three stages – tropozoites, schizonts and merozoites – are seen in erythrocytic schizogony.
22. *When does a clinical attack of malaria (overt malaria) occur?*
▶ Clinical attack of malaria occurs during parasitic multiplication in the erythrocytic phase.
23. *When do Plasmodia have the urge for sexual multiplication?*
▶ They have the urge for sexual multiplication when they are exhausted with asexual multiplication and when there is spontaneous destruction of the parasites (Plasmodia).
24. *After erythrocytic schizogony, why do some of the merozoites not develop directly into trophozoites?*
▶ This is because some of the merozoites transform into sexual forms which are capable of sexual reproduction outside the human host. These forms are known as gametocytes. These gametocytes are required to propagate and continue their lifecycle in the mosquito. This stage is called gametogony.
25. *Who is a carrier?*
▶ An individual who harbours these gametocytes is called a 'carrier'.
26. *Why does pre-erythrocytic schizogony disappear completely in P. falciparum?*
▶ It disappears because the pre-erythrocytic schizogony of *P. falciparum* does not persist in the form of a focal liver cycle and there is no exo-erythrocytic schizogony, hence no relapse.
27. *What is exflagellation in the mosquito cycle?*
▶ Exflagellation is a process of development in which one male micro-gametocyte gives rise to four to eight thread-like filamentous structures known as microgametes which move towards the female by the process of chemotaxis.
28. *Where will the male gamete get attached to the female?*
▶ The male gamete will get attached to the site of projection which is at the periphery of the female.
29. *What is a zygote?*
▶ A zygote is formed when the male gamete penetrates into the projection of the female and fertilizes it, thus forming a zygote.
30. *What is an ookinete?*
▶ It is a motile zygote with pseudopodium; it enters into the mucosa of the mosquito intestine, it forms oocysts which burn to give rise to sporozoites.
31. *What is a sporozoite?*
▶ A sporozoite is a sickle-shaped body liberated from the oocyst and is spread throughout the body of the mosquito, except in the ovaries. It is infective to humans and is injected into humans by mosquito bite.

32. *When is Plasmodium malnourished?*
▶ When the host is starved.

33. *When is the growth of malarial parasites inhibited?*
▶ The growth of Plasmodia is inhibited when the food element (thiamine, riboflavin and biotin) is restricted.

34. *In which country are the children heavily parasitized by P. falciparum?*
▶ In Africa, when they are restricted to a milk diet.

35. *What are the traits responsible for resistance to malaria?*
▶ They are G-6PD deficient traits, sickle cell anemia traits.

36. *How will you differentiate between the male and female gametocytes of P. falciparum?*
▶ The male microgametocyte is more banana-shaped than crescentic; it is thicker and blunter than the female macrogametocytes which stain darker blue with a small and compact nucleus.

37. *What is the average number of merozoites of P. falciparum and their size inside RBCs?*
▶ The average number of merozoites is 18–24 inside RBCs. It measures 0.5–0.7 μm in diameter (less than the size of the bacteria (cocci)).

38. *How is the word 'malaria' derived?*
▶ It is derived from the Italian words, *mala* and *aria*, meaning 'bad air'.

39. *Can you notice a host reaction when the destruction of liver cells occurs?*
▶ Host reaction is not noticeable when the liver cells are destroyed during the liver cycle of Plasmodium.

40. *When is a pathogenic effect significant?*
▶ The pathogenic effect is significant when the exo-erythrocytic merozoites (micromerozoites) invade RBCs and multiply.

41. *What is a major factor in the pathogenesis of malaria?*
▶ A major factor is the disturbance in oxygen usage caused by the infection; (i) Oxygen supplies may be reduced; (ii) Adequate oxygen supply may not be utilized by the host due to pathological changes in the metabolizing cells.

42. *What is algid malaria?*
▶ Algid malaria is acute severe malaria with low blood pressure, low cardiac output and vasoconstriction leading to liver or kidney damage with a state of shock.

43. *How many types of fever are common in malaria?*
▶ There are three types 1) quotidian, 2) tertian, 3) quartan fever.

44. *What type of anemia develops in malaria?*
▶ Anemia of the microcytic hypochromic type with iron deficiency develops in malaria.

45. *In malaria, which organ is much enlarged and palpable after the second week of infection?*
▶ The spleen is much enlarged and palpable after the second week (splenomegaly).

46. *Describe in brief the symptoms of malaria, succeeded by fever (104°F), headache, muscular pain, malaise, increased pulse and respiration.*

▶ In *P. falciparum* malaria, pernicious symptoms (coma, convulsion, cardiac failure) are observed.

47. *What is Black Water fever?*

▶ It is a manifestation of repeated infections with falciparum malaria, inadequately treated with quinine.

48. *What is congenital malaria?*

▶ It is an intra-uterine transmission of malaria and is common in non-immune mothers whose placentas are heavily parasitized with *P. falciparum* schizonts.

49. *What is connatal malaria?*

▶ Connatal malaria is malaria acquired by babies during parturition.

50. *What is a certain method of laboratory diagnosis of malaria?*

▶ A certain method is the demonstration of Plasmodium in the blood smear under microscope.

51. *When is a thick blood smear required?*

▶ It is required for quick detection of Plasmodium.

52. *When is a thin blood smear required?*

▶ It is required for the identification of the species.

53. *When does the detection of Plasmodium become difficult?*

▶ It becomes difficult if the blood films are taken

1) After anti-malarial drug use 2) During an apyrexial period of *P. falciparum* 3) During the first three days of primary infection.

54. *Enumerate serodiagnostic methods for malaria.*

▶ Serological methods (serology) are complement fixation, slide flocculation, latex agglutination, indirect hemaglutination and fluorescent antibody tests.

55. *Cite other methods which are under study?*

▶ They are sedimentation, centrifugation, flurochrome staining, new side angle microscope objectives, new genetic engineering methods.

56. *Describe in brief, the new genetic engineering method of Padmanabhan for the detection of P. falciparum.*

▶ Padmanabhan (1989); Indian scientist, Bangalore, can detect falciparum malaria very specifically by using radioactive chemicals in his genetic engineering method. This method is very accurate and can detect as few as 50 parasites in the blood sample.

57. *How can malaria be treated?*

▶ Malaria can be treated by

i. ***Curative treatment*** Chloroquine, amodiaquine (drug of choice), Mefloquine and quinine (for drug resistant *P. falciparum*). Primaquine can be used to prevent relapse in malaria.

ii. ***Prophylactic treatment*** Chloroquine, amodiaquine in weekly doses will prevent an acute attack of malaria.

58. *How can primaquine prevent relapse in malaria?*

▶ Primaquine can prevent relapse in malaria by acting on the exo-erythrocytic phases of the parasites inside the liver. It also acts on the gametocyte but has little action on the erythrocytic stages of the parasites.

59. *What are the recent (2005) findings on malaria treatment by Padmanabhan at Bangalore (India)?*

▶ a) Curative treatment of malaria by turmeric (Hindi–*haldi*) is under experimentation with great hope

b) Prophylactic treatment. Anti malarial vaccine prepared by the use of DNA recombinant technique is very effective in annual experimentation and is under human trial.

60. *How can prophylaxis of malaria be carried out?*

A. It can be done by personal prophylaxis and community prophylaxis.

a) Personal prophylaxis by protection against mosquito by using mosquito nets and by systemic anti-malarial drugs

b) Community prophylaxis by the destruction of mosquito by spraying insecticides; DDT or by the use of larvicides (DDT dissolved in oil), by treating carriers with anti-malarial drugs.

61. *Is there any hope for a malarial vaccine in the near future?*

▶ There is a great hope for successful malarial vaccination in the near future.

Babesia

1. *What is Babesia?*

▶ It is a protozoa affecting mostly cattle, very rarely human beings; it resembles *P. falciparum* and is found in RBCs. Chloroquine has some value in the treatment of human babesiosis.

Toxoplasma gondii

1. *What is T. gondii?*

▶ It is a protozoon affecting the small rodent, gondii. It is an elongated, intracellular, coccidial parasite.

2. *How many hosts does it require?*

▶ It requires two hosts: cat and human.

3. *How do human beings get the infection?*

▶ Human beings get the infection by ingestion of food contaminated with oocysts found in cat's feces. Trophozoites liberated from oocysts infect, penetrating into the human ileum and carried by the bloodstream to various organs (brain, liver, placenta of woman) which are damaged. It causes abortion in pregnant woman.

4. *How many types of clinical toxoplasmosis are seen?*

   a) Congenital and b) Acquired toxoplasmosis.

Sarcocystis lindemanni

1. *Where was the parasite reported in India?*

► It was reported in Mumbai (India) in a 40-year-old labourer.

2. *How do humans get infected?*

► Humans get the infection by ingestion of infected meat or drink containing the trophozoites which pass the mucosa of the intestine, enter the bloodstream and are carried to the striated muscles where they form round bodies enclosed in a cyst which enlarges. Thus, the toxic product sarcocystin affects the CNS, heart and the intestine.

3. *How can it be diagnosed and treated?*

► It can be diagnosed by demonstration of Miescher's tubes in the affected muscles and there is no specific treatment.

Pneumocystis carinii

1. *Describe in brief P. carinii?*

► It resembles a protozoon. It causes interstitial plasma cell pneumonia in suckling infants and is common in AIDs patients as a secondary invader. It is enclosed in a sphere which is foamy in appearance in the alveoli of the lung. This foamy mass causes asphyxia leading to death. It is diagnosed by detection of *P. carinii* in lung tissue; by radiological examination of the lung and by complement fixation test. Pentamidine isothionate is an effective drug for *P. carinii*.

5 CLASS CILIATEA

Members of this group of protozoa are classified in the sub-phylum ciliophora. Ciliata has

1) Its body covered with cilia (short hair-like extensions of its ectoplasmic membrane)
2) Two distinct nuclei (large macronucleus and small micronucleus) and
3) Its body shape defined by a cell membrane. The pathogenic species is *Balantidium coli.*

BALANTIDIUM COLI

Balantidium coli was first observed by Malmsten (1857) in the dysenteric stools of two patients. Panjarathinam (Pondicherry, 1972) reported it for the first time in pig's stool. *B.coli* has a cosmopolitan distribution and is found in humans and in pigs.

Balantidium coli is the largest protozoon parasitizing the large intestine of humans, monkey and pig, where the trophozoites feed on the cells of the intestinal wall or on bacteria and mucus. The pig is the common reservoir of infection and does not suffer from the infection.

Morphology *Balantidium coli* has two stages (see Figs 5.1 and 5.2.)

1. ***The trophozoite*** stage is found in dysenteric stools
2. ***The cystic*** stage is found in chronic cases and carriers.

Trophozoite: It is oval in shape and its body is covered with cilia. The cilia which line the mouth parts appear to be longer and are called 'adoral cilia'. The anterior end is somewhat pointed and, on one side of the longitudinal axis, there is a deep, slightly curved, inverted conical depression called the ***cytostome.*** The posterior end is broadly rounded. At the posterior end, there is a small opening in the membrane called the ***cytopyge.*** The trophozoites vary in length from 50 to 200 μm and in breadth from 40 to 70 μm. The most distinctive objects within the cytoplasm are

1. Two nuclei:
    a) The large trophic nucleus (macronucleus) has the shape of a narrow bean or is kidney shaped and is densely packed with chromatin granules which stain as a single mass

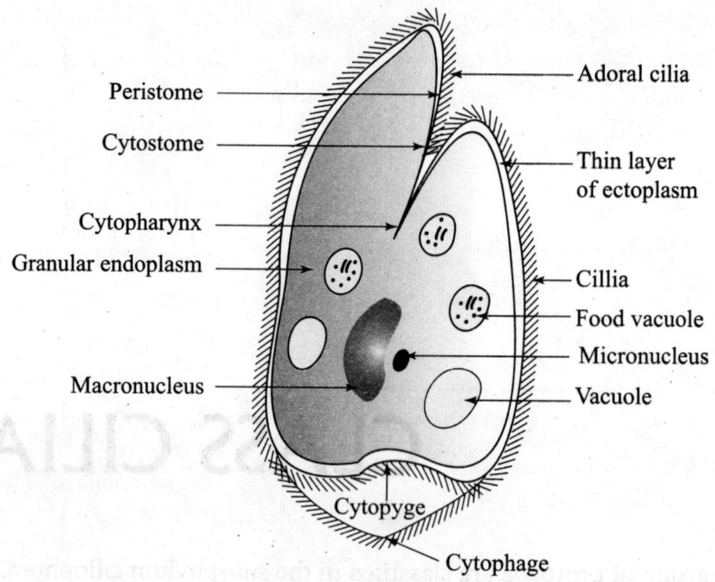

Fig. 5.1 Trophozoite of *B. coli*.

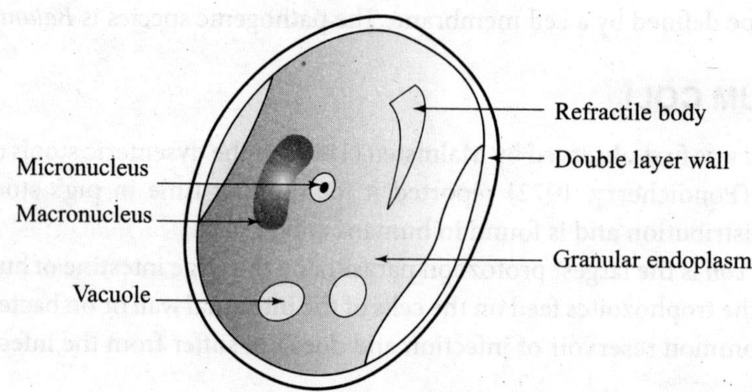

Fig. 5.2 Cyst of *B. coli*.

b) The smaller nucleus (micronucleus) lies in the centre of the inner curvature of the macronucleus. It is a round mass which takes a very deep stain and is believed to function as a kinetic organelle

2. Two contractile vacuoles, one near the middle of the body and the other at the posterior end and
3. Numerous food vacuoles containing debris of red blood corpuscles and white blood corpuscles.

Cyst: It is smaller than the trophozoite form, and measures 50–60 μm in diameter. The cytoplasm is granular and contains the macronucleus, the micronucleus and a refractile body. The cyst is surrounded by a thick transparent double-layered wall.

Balantidium coli is cultivated in various nutrient media, with or without associated bacteria.

Lifecycle *Balantidium coli* passes its lifecycle only in one host (either in a human host or in a pig).

When the cyst (infective form) is ingested (mode of entry) accidentally by farmers or workers in meat factories, the cyst liberates trophozoites in the large intestine and only one individual is formed from each cyst. The liberated, free trophozoites enter the submucous coat of the large intestine where they grow and multiply by binary transverse fission. After binary fission, two daughter trophozoites are formed and consequently, numerous trophozoites are produced. The micronucleus divides first, which is followed by the division of the macronucleus and finally the body splits into two by a transverse partition. The daughter trophozoite formed from the anterior half retains the cytostome of the original trophozoite and reconstructs the posterior end of the body. The individual formed from the posterior end, develops its own cytostome and other structures. When the trophozoites find conditions unsuitable for their existence, they encyst. These cysts are passed out with the feces. In this way, the lifecycle is perpetuated in only one host and no intermediate host is involved (Fig. 5.3, 5.4).

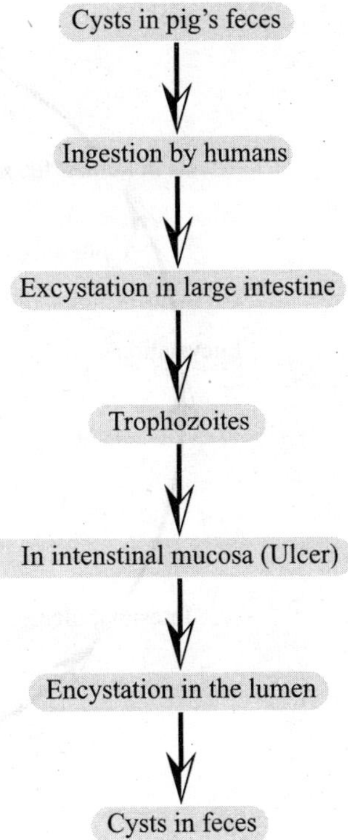

Fig. 5.3 Lifecycle of *B.coli.*

Pathogenicity Once established in humans, *Balantidium coli* never fail to invade the tissue. Free trophozoites come in contact with the mucous surface of the intestine, burrow into the cells and set up colonies. *B. coli* produce an enzyme, hyaluronidase, which helps the organism's ability to invade the tissue. The characteristic early lesion is the opening into the mucosa of the intestine. The opening is of larger diameter. The 'neck' of the ulcer is short and the base is broadly rounded and covered with pus and necrotic material.

Balantidium coli feeds mainly on starchy food found in abundance in the pig's intestine and does not invade the mucous surface of the intestine of the pig; hence, they are harmless to the pig. *Balantidium coli* rarely invade extra-intestinal sites.

Clinical features In a majority of cases, dysentery is characteristic, accompanied by abdominal colic, tenesmus, nausea and vomiting. Loss of appetite, headache, insomnia, muscular weakness

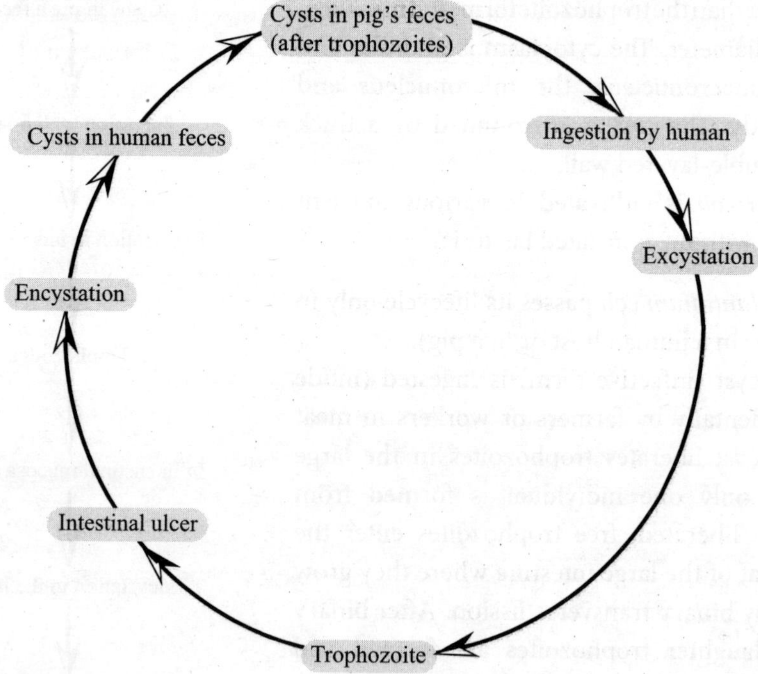

Fig. 5.4 Lifecycle of *B. coli*.

and loss of weight have all been observed in the infection with this parasite. The great majority of human infections are non-invasive, asymptomatic, self limited and infrequently, a cause of disease. *B. coli* can penetrate the colonic mucosa with formation of deep ulcers, illness consists of dysentery, usually bloody, often with resulting dehydration and prostration at the site of the ulcers, infection may extend to the mesenteric lymph nodes and less commonly, the appendix and terminal ileum. Isolated reports of infection of vagina, liver, lung and pleura have been documented, but extra-intestinal migration of the organism is rare.

Poor nutrition and debilitating illness seem to predispose to symptomatic balantidiasis. When crowding and poor hygienic conditions exist, there is person to person spread.

Laboratory diagnosis Diagnosis depends upon the demonstration of *Balantidium coli* in the feces of the patient. Motile trophozoites are present when the stools are dysenteric in character and cysts are found in semi-formed and formed stools. The methods employed to demonstrate the parasite in the feces are similar to those used for intestinal amebae. *B. coli* can be cultivated in Rees medium, Balamuth's medium with rice flour.

Treatment Carbarsone has been employed in treating human cases of balantidiasis, but recurrence of infection is possible. Diiodohydroxyquin is more effective in eliminating the parasite. Tetracycline appears to be more dependable.

Therapy is reserved for patients with symptomatic infection and consists of tetracycline, 500 mg four times daily for 10 days or metronidazole, 250 mg, two times daily for seven days, is also effective.

Prophylaxis Methods of prevention are similar to those employed for *Entameba histolytica.* These are

1) Avoidance of contact with the infected animal and
2) Prevention of contamination of food and drink with the feces of infected pigs.

SUMMARY

Class Ciliatea

- Ciliatea are motile protozoa which move with the help of cilia (short hair-like extensions of its cytoplasmic membrane). They are covered with cilia; have two distinct nuclei (large macronucleus and small micronucleus), their shape is maintained by a cell membrane.
- **Balantidium coli** Malmstein (1857) first observed this protozoan in two human patients; Panjarathinam (1972) first reported it from pig in Pondicherry (India), though this protozoan (*B. coli*) has worldwide distribution. It is the largest protozoan of the large intestine of humans, pigs. Its trophozoites feed on the intestinal mucosal cells, bacteria and mucus. Pig is the reservoir of *B.coli* and does not suffer from infection.
- It has two stages: Trophozoites and cysts.
  1. Trophozoite is found in acute dysentery patient's stool
  2. Cyst is detected in chronic cases and carriers.
- The cyst (infective) ingested by humans liberates only one trophozoite which gives rise to two trophozoites. These free trophozoites burrow into the intestinal mucosa with the help of hyaluronidase enzyme and form an ulcer with a 'short neck' and a broad base containing pus and necrotic material. These trophozoites are harmless to pigs as they feed on the abundant starchy food in the pig's intestine. Clinically, dysentery is accompanied by abdominal pain, tenesmus, nausea and vomiting. Besides, loss of appetite, headache, insomnia and loss of weight is observed. Diagnosis can be done by the microscopic demonstration of trophozoites and cysts in the stool. Tetracycline, carbarsome can be used for human treatment. Diiodohydroxyquin can eliminate the parasite.
- **Prophylaxis** It can be prevented by the methods used for *E. histolytica*.

QUESTIONS

Q *What are ciliata?*

- Ciliata are protozoa which move with cilia.

Q *What are cilia?*

▶ Cilia are short hair-like extensions of the cytoplasmic membrane.

Q *How many nuclei do they have?*

▶ They have two nuclei (large macronucleus and small micronucleus)

Q *Which species of ciliata is pathogenic to humans?*

▶ *Balatidium coli* are pathogenic to humans.

Balantidium coli

Q *Who first observed B. coli in humans?*

▶ Malmstein first observed *B.coli* in humans in 1857.

Q *Who first reported B. coli in pig in Pondicherry (India)?*

▶ Panajarathinam (1972) first reported *B. coli* in pig in Pondicherry (India).

Q *Which is the largest protozoan infecting the large intestine of humans, pigs?*

▶ *B. coli* is the largest protozoan of the intestine of humans, pigs.

Q *On what cells do trophozoites of B. coli feed?*

▶ They feed on intestinal cells, bacteria, mucus.

Q *Why does the pig not suffer from this infection though it is a reservoir of B.coli?*

▶ Because *B.coli* feeds on intestinal starchy food, as a result it does not enter the intestine.

Q *How many stages does B. coli have?*

▶ It has two stages: Trophozoite and cyst stage.

Q *Describe trophozoites of B. coli*

▶ The Trophozoite is oval, covered with cilia. It has two nuclei, cyctostome, cytopage.

Q *Where is the smaller nucleus (micronucleus) of B. coli situated?*

▶ It is situated in the centre of inner curvature of the large nucleus (macronucleus) of *B. coli.*

Q *What is the function of the micronucleus?*

▶ It is believed to function as a kinetic organelle and divides first.

Q *What is a cytostome?*

▶ Cytostome is a deep, slightly curved, inverted conical depression situated on one side of the longitudinal axis of the pointed anterior end of *B. coli.*

Q *What are adoral cilia?*

▶ Adoral cilia are longer cilia which line the mouth part of *B. coli*

Q *What is a cytopyge?*

▶ Cytopyge is a small opening in the membrane at the posterior end of *B. coli.*

Q *What are the positions of the contractile vacuoles in B. coli?*

▶ One contractile vacuole is near the middle of the body and the other at the posterior end.

Q *What does a food vacuole contain?*

▶ Food vacuoles contain debris of RBCs and WBCs.

Q *In which media can B. coli be grown?*

▸ It can be grown in various nutrient media with or without associated bacteria.

Q *Cite a protozoan which has only one host in its lifecycle?*

▸ *B.coli* has only one host (human or pig) in its cycle.

First Report of Protozoa

E. histolytica – Lamb (1858)

G. lamblia – Leeuwenhoek (1681)

T. vaginalis – Donne (1836)

Trypanasoma gambiense – Forde (1901)

T. cruzi – Chagas (1900)

L. donovani – Leishman (1900)

L. tropica – Cunningham (1885)

L. braziliensis – Lindenberg (1909)

I. hominis (belli) – Kjellberg (1860)

P. vivax – Larveran (1880)

P. ovale – Ingram (1917)

P. falciparum – Short et al. (1949)

Babesia – Garnham (1969)

T. gondii – Nicolle and Manceaux (1908)

Sarcocystis lindemanni – Lindemann (1868)

B. coli – Malmsten (1857)

Section II

HELMINTHOLOGY

HELMINTHOLOGY

The word 'helminth', from Greek, means 'worm'. All species of helminths belong to the sub-kingdom Metazoa, and all are provided with tissues and organs derived from three embryonic body layers: the ectoderm, endoderm and mesoderm. Helminths of medical importance are classified into two main divisions:

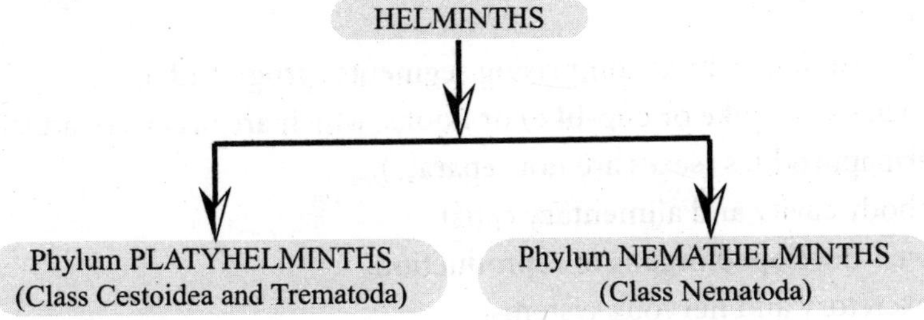

Characteristics of Phylum Platyhelminths:

1. Flattened, leaf-like or tape-like and segmented
2. Mostly hermaphrodite
3. Alimentary canal incomplete or entirely lacking
4. Body cavity absent

Characteristics of Phylum Nemathelminths:

1. Elongated, cylindrical, unsegmented bodies
2. Sexes separate
3. Alimentary canal complete
4. Body cavity present

6 CESTODES

1. They are long, dorso-ventrally flattened, segmented and tape-like, so they are known as 'tapeworms'.
2. They vary in size from a few millimetres to several metres.
3. They are found in the intestine of humans and animals.
4. The adult worm has three regions:
   a) A head (scolex)
   b) A neck and
   c) A body or trunk (strobila) comprising segments (proglottids).
5. They bear suckers (slit-like or cup-like) or hooks, which are organs of attachment.
6. They are hermaphrodites (sexes are not separate).
7. There is no body cavity and alimentary canal.
8. They have well-developed organs of reproduction.
9. They have excretory and nervous systems.

Differences between pseudophyllidean cestodes and cyclophyllidean cestodes:

The pseudophyllidean cestode has

1. Two slit-like grooves (bothria)
2. No branching uterus
3. A uterine pore
4. A common genital pore lying ventrally in the middle line and
5. Operculated eggs hatching out ciliated larvae.

The cyclophyllidean cestode has

1. Four cup-like suckers
2. A uterus with lateral branches
3. No uterine pore

4. A laterally situated common genital pore and
5. Non-operculated eggs which do not hatch out ciliated larvae.

PSEUDOPHYLLIDEAN TAPEWORMS OF HUMANS

Superfamily: Bothriocephaloidea
Genus: DIPHYLLOBOTHRIUM
Species: *Diphyllobothrium latum*
Pseudophyllidean cestodes have the following features:

1. A long chain of segments
2. A head bearing two slit-like grooves called ***bothria***
3. ***Ventrally*** situated genital pores, not marginal (three genital orifices in each segment, one male orifice and two female orifices)
4. Scattered vitelline glands in the parenchyma
5. Uterus opening to the exterior through which eggs come out
6. Operculated eggs which can develop only in water and give rise to a single ciliated embryo (first stage larva - ***coracidium***)
7. Two more larval development stages – the second stage larva is called ***procercoid*** and the third stage larva ***plerocercoid*** in fish flesh.

Diphyllobothrium latum (fish tapeworm)

Linnaeus (1758) called *Diphyllobothrium latum* by another name *Taenia lata*. Later, in 1910, Luhe described it as *D. latum*, which is a common parasite of humans, and is found commonly in northern Italy, Switzerland, Germany, North America, Japan and Eastern Canada. It has not yet been reported from India. *D. latum* inhabits the small intestine of humans, dogs and cats.

Morphology When freshly expelled from the human intestine, *D. latum* is ivory or yellowish grey in colour. It measures from 3–10 (young mature specimen from humans) metres or more in length. The head (scolex) is small, spatulated or spoon shaped and elongated. It has a pair of slit-like grooves (bothria or deep sulci), one on the ventral surface and the other on the dorsal surface. The measurement of each bothrium is about 1 mm across and 2.5 mm long. It bears no rostellum (a beak-like projection on the head) and no hooklets (Fig. 6.1).

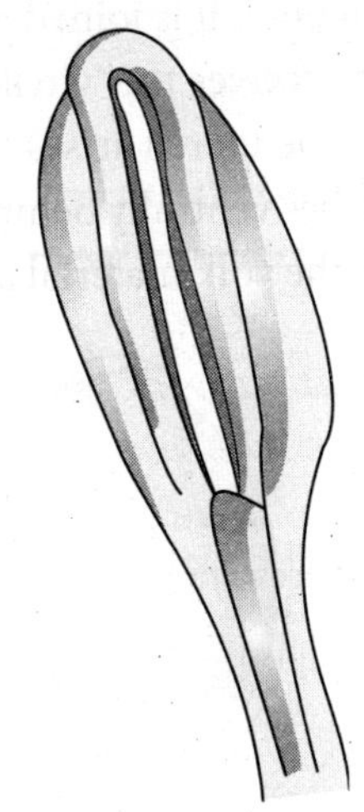

Fig. 6.1 Head of *D. latum*.

Immediately behind the scolex, there is an unsegmented 'neck' region, several times the length of the head.

About four-fifths of the entire worm consists of as many as 3000 or more maturing and mature segments (proglottids). The typical mature proglottid (Fig. 6.2) is somewhat broad

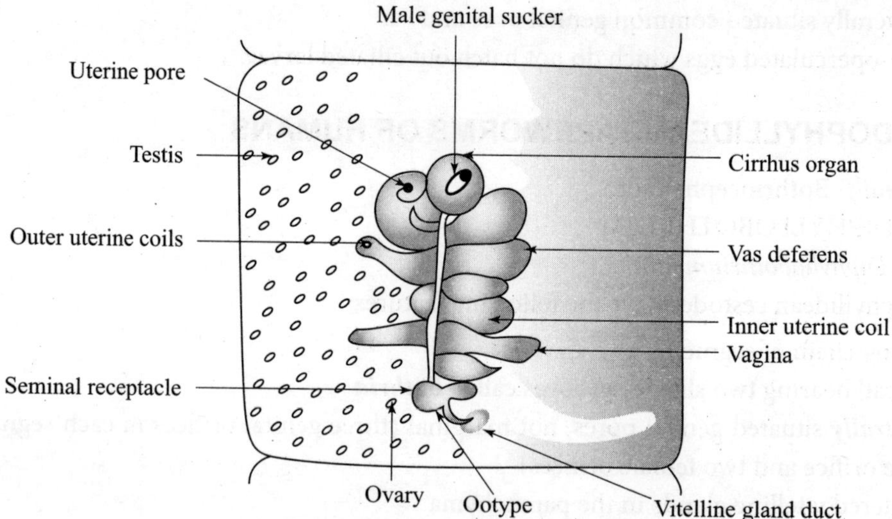

Fig. 6.2 Mature proglottid of *D. latum*.

more than long and practically filled with male and female genitalia. The measurement of each segment varies from 2–4 mm in length and 10–20 mm in breadth. Eggs are discharged through the uterine pore of mature proglottids.

The mature proglottid has the following structures: the testes are minute follicles situated in both the lateral fields in the dorsal plane of the body. The vas efferentia is just in front of the ootype to form the deferens, which proceeds as a convoluted tubule to the upper border of the common genital atrium. Near its outer terminus, there is a seminal vesicle and a muscular cirrhus organ. In the posterior third of this proglottid, the symmetrically bilobed ovary is present in the ventral position. Between its two lobes is the ootype surrounded by Mehli's glands. A vagina proceeds directly from the ootype and opens externally just below the male genital pore. It is joined at its inner end by the oviduct and by the common vitelline gland duct which receives the 'vitelline' material from the minute multiple follicles situated in the lateral fields. The uterus arises from the ootype and proceeds in convolutions up to the uterine pore, which lies ventrally behind the vaginal pore. Spermatozoa fertilize the naked ova in the ootype, where the yolk material and shell are then added and the egg is passed into the uterus. Eggs are

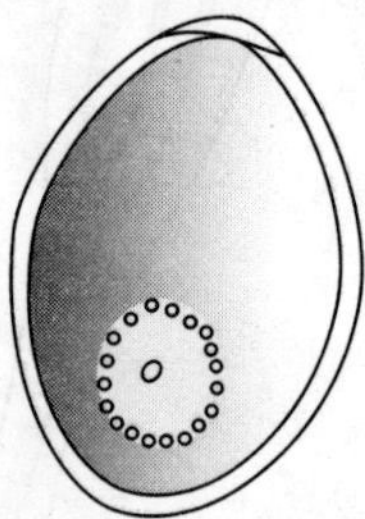

Fig. 6.3 Egg of *D. latum*.

Fig. 6.4 Free swimming coracidium of *D. latum*.

evacuated periodically through the uterine pore. In this way, a single worm may discharge as many as one million eggs per day.

Egg of D. latum (Fig. 6.3): The egg of *D. latum* is 1) broadly ovoidal 2) operculated 3) thick shelled 4) light golden yellow in colour 5) measures 58–76 µm by 40–51 µm (average 66 by 44 µm) 6) contains immature embryo when oviposited and discharged in the feces and 7) upon maturing, the hexacanth embryo (oncosphere) escapes through the opercular opening of the shell, casts off its embryonal envelope and a ciliated embryo *(Coracidium)* swims about in the water (Fig. 6.4).

Lifecycle *D. latum* passes its lifecycle in one ***definite host*** (human, dog or cat) and two ***intermediate hosts;*** first in the Cyclops (Figs 6.5 and 6.6) and then in fish.

When the egg of *D. latum,* which is passed out along with the feces of the infected host (human) comes in contact with water, the ciliated embryo (coracidium) escapes through the opercular opening of the shell of the egg and swims in the water. Within about 12 hours, it must be ingested by an appropriate copepod (Cyclops) in order to continue its development. The most common Cyclops is *Diaptomus vulgaris.* In the midgut of the Cyclops, the embryo casts off its ciliated coat, and by using its three pairs of hooklets, and probably an anterior pair of penetration glands also, the embryo penetrates into the hemal cavity, where in the course of two or three weeks it becomes transformed into ***procercoid*** larva measuring 550 µm in length and still having three pairs of hooklets (Fig. 6.7a).

If the infected Cyclops is now ingested by a freshwater fish (salmon), the procercoid larva works its way with the help of three pairs of hooklets through the tissues of the fish and comes to lie between the muscle fibres, where it grows into a ***plerocercoid*** or ***sparganum*** larva (measuring six mm in length). The plerocercoid larva (Fig. 6.7b) is infective to humans; it has an invaginated anterior end representing the inverted head of the future adult worm and is unsegmented. On consuming the raw or insufficiently cooked infected fish, humans (the definite hosts) become infected. In the course of five or six weeks, eggs appear in the feces after the plerocercoid has developed into an adult worm in the human intestine (Figs 6.8 and 6.9).

Pathogenicity *D. latum* grows and discharges its metabolic wastes into the human intestinal lumen. Its pathogenic effect depends 1) Partially on the mass of worm 2) Type and amount of byproducts absorbed into the host's tissue and, 3) The host's susceptibility to these foreign substances.

D. latum is most frequently attached to the wall of the ileum and causes impairment between the intrinsic and extrinsic factors of Castle, thus bringing about the pernicious type of anemia. It contains a large amount of vitamin B_{12} and this may deprive the host of essential nutritional components, which also causes pernicious anemia. Leucocytosis with eosinophilia is the only significant blood finding.

Clinical features The presence of adult worms in the intestinal tract causes no symptoms in most infected persons. Sometimes, non-specific abdominal symptoms have been ascribed to this infection. Clinical vitamin B_{12} deficiency develops if the worms attach themselves to the proximal portion of the jejunum.

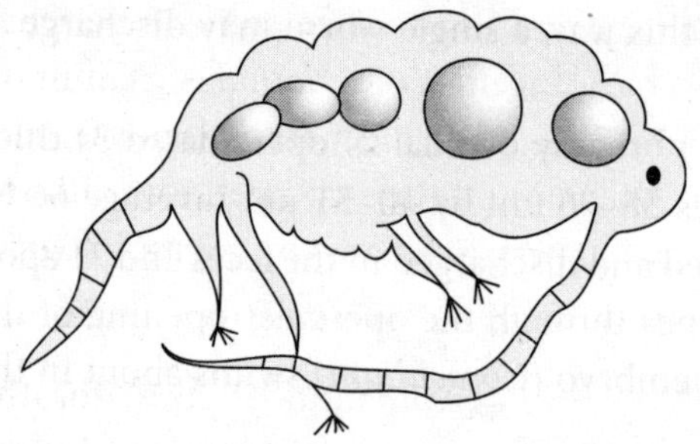

Fig. 6.5 *Diaptomus vulgaris* with developing procercoids of *D. latum* in the hemocele cavity.

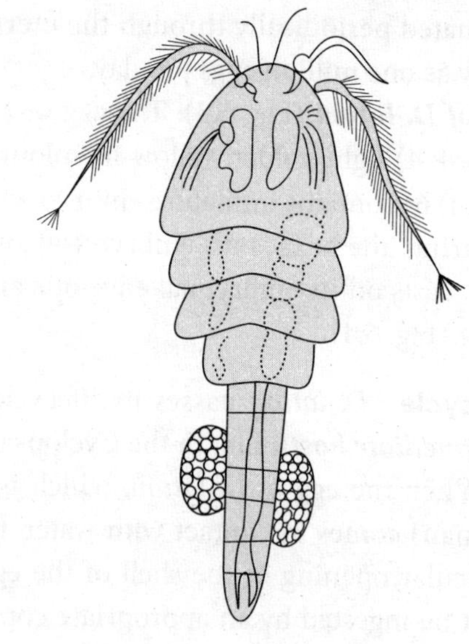

Fig. 6.6 Cyclops – dorsal view.

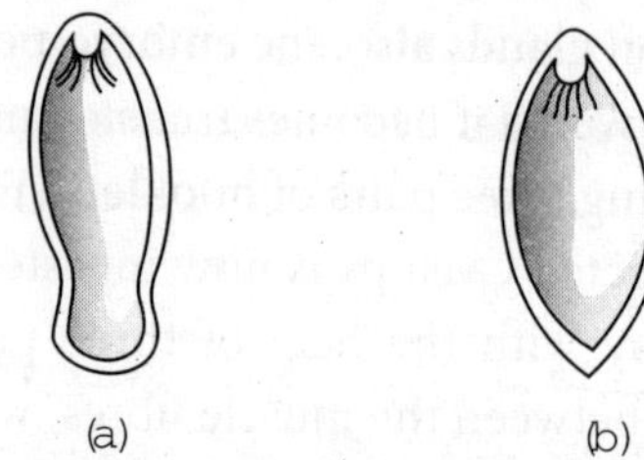

Fig. 6.7 a) Procercoid larva, b) Plerocercoid larva.

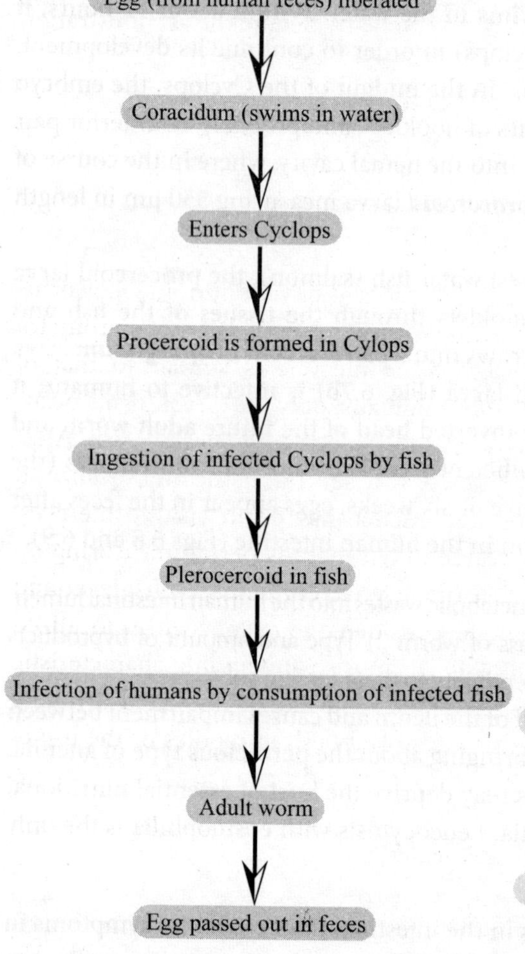

Fig. 6.9 Lifecycle of *Diphyllobothrium latum*.

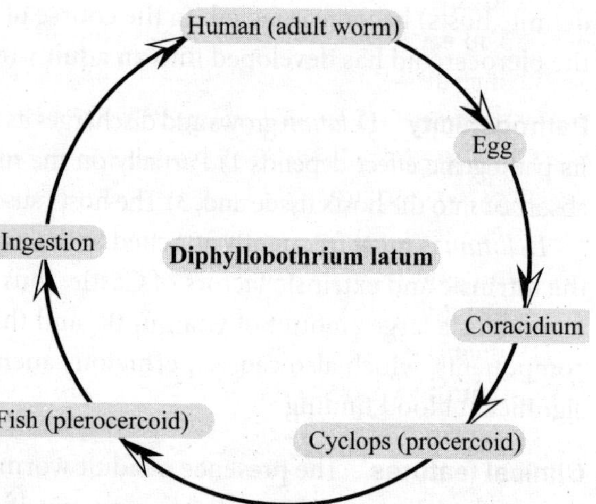

Fig. 6.8 Lifecycle of *D. latum*.

Most of the patients infected with *D. latum* are asymptomatic, but some experience intestinal symptoms from mucosal irritation. The most harmful effect of *D. latum* is vitamin B_{12} malabsorption, and rarely, a megablastic pernicious anemia. The exact mechanism is not certain, but it is related to the absorption of vitamin B_{12} by the worms and their competition with the human host for the available supply of vitamin B_{12} which has been evaluated by microbiological assay and radioactive tracer technique. This is reported primarily in Scandinavia.

Laboratory diagnosis This is based on the microscopic examination of feces for the operculated eggs. Proglottids, if passed out along with the feces, may be identified by the presence and position of the genital pore and the character of the rosette-shaped uterus and there is no satisfactory serological method of diagnosis.

Treatment The drug of choice is Quinacrine hydrochloride. Niclosamide and paromomycin have also been found to be effective.

Pernicious anemia associated with *D. latum* infection can be treated by the administration of folic acid, 20–30 mg daily for seven to ten days.

Prophylaxis

1) Thorough cooking of suspected freshwater fish is important
2) Pollution of water can be prevented by efficient disposal of sewage
3) In endemic areas of infection, dogs and cats should not be given fish.

Sparganosis is an uncommon infection of humans with larval diphyllobothroid tapeworms closely related to *D. latum*. It is caused by the sparganum or plerocercoid larva of spirometra which measures up to several centimeters in length. The lifecycle is similar to that of *D. latum*. Adult forms are found in dogs and cats and in humans, only the larval forms occur in the Far East. Humans get the infection by ingestion of the infected raw flesh of fish. After penetrating the intestinal wall, the larvae usually migrate through the tissue and localize in the subcutaneous or muscular tissue. Localization and edema may occur around the eyes. A slowly growing pruritic nodule develops over a three to ten months period measuring up to three centimeters. Local induration, periodic urticaria, edema, erythema, chills, fever and marked eosinophilia may occur. The parasite should be considered in anyone with a localized subcutaneous swelling and a possible exposure history. Diagnosis is by finding characteristic larvae in the removed nodules. Infection can be prevented by avoiding untreated drinking water in endemic areas and avoiding the ingestion of uncooked flesh of reptiles or the use of this flesh in the Far East.

CYCLOPHYLLIDEAN TAPEWORMS OF HUMANS

Cyclophyllidean cestodes have the following features:

1. A chain of segments
2. A head which is quadrate in outline with four cup-like structures at each of the four angles. In the centre of the quadrate head, there is an apical rostellum with hooklets

3. Vitteline glands concentrated into a single mass behind the ovary and situated near the posterior margin of each segment
4. A common genital pore situated laterally or marginally in each segment, alternating irregularly between the right and left margins
5. No uterine pore, the eggs therefore escaping only when the gravid segment detaches, ruptures or disintegrates in the feces
6. Non-operculated egg with non-ciliated embryo
7. Larval development in the intermediate host.

Taenia saginata

Superfamily: Taenioidea
Genus: Taenia

Taenia saginata, the common 'unarmed tapeworm' parasitizing humans, was observed even in ancient times, but was not differentiated from *Taenia solium* until 1782. *T. saginata* has a cosmopolitan distribution and in most countries, its incidence is considerably greater than that of *T. solium*. In India, it seems to be prevalent particularly in the Muslim community, due to their beef eating habit. It is practically unknown in Ethiopia and is common in the United States. *T. saginata* is endemic throughout Germany, Austria, Britain, Switzerland, Yugoslavia and Italy.

The adult worms live with their heads embedded in the mucosa of the small intestine.

Morphology The adult worm is white and semitransparent. Under favourable conditions, they may attain a length of 25 metres or more, but usually they measure 5–10 metres.

The head ***(scolex)*** is quadrate in cross-section and is provided with four pigmented hemispherical or circular suckers of 0.7–0.8 mm diameter, situated at the four angles of the head and serving as the organs of attachment. The apical region of the head is somewhat concave, pigmented and is not provided with the rostellum (a beak-like projection) (Fig. 6.10). The neck is narrow (about 0.5 mm in width) and somewhat long.

Segments (proglottids): The neck is followed by a series of immature, mature and gravid proglottids which range from 1000 to 2000. The mature segments are more broad (12 mm) than long and the gravid segments are narrower and longer (5–7 mm broad, 20 mm long). In the gravid segment, the uterus is filled with eggs and the other reproductive organs are atrophied. The central longitudinal stem of the uterus has 15–30 lateral branches (Fig. 6.11). The adult worm may live up to about 10 years.

Eggs of T. saginata: They are liberated after the rupture of the gravid segment, because of the absence of the uterine pore.

The characteristics of the egg (Fig. 6.12) are as follows:

1. The eggs are spherical and brown in colour
2. They measure 31–43 μm in diameter
3. Sometimes, they have a thin, outer, transparent shell

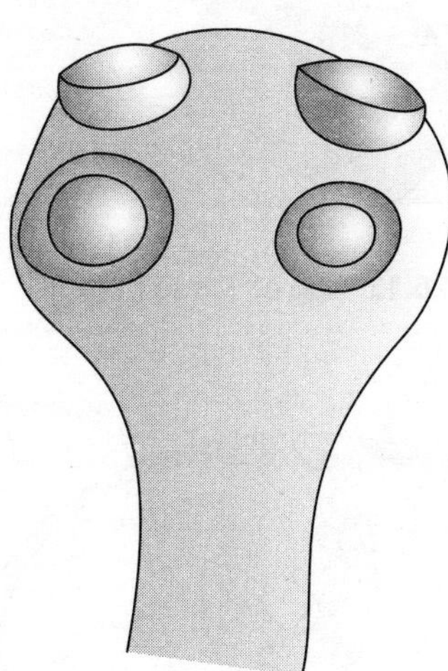

Fig. 6.10 The unarmed scolex (head) of *T. saginata*.

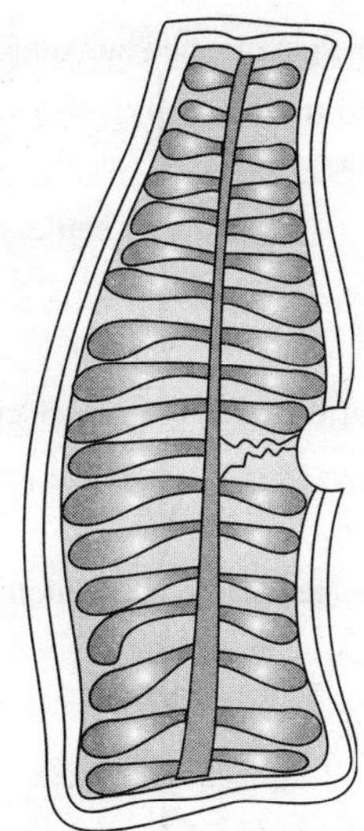

Fig. 6.11 A gravid segment of *T. saginata* showing 15—30 lateral branches from the central longitudinal stem of the uterus.

4. The inner embryophore is brown, thick walled and radially striated
5. The eggs contain an oncosphere (14–20 μm in diameter) with three pairs of hooklets
6. They do not float in a saturated solution of common salt
7. They remain viable for eight weeks and are infective only to cattle.

Lifecycle The worm passes its lifecycle in two hosts: 1) The definite host (human) and 2) The intermediate host, cattle (cow, buffalo).

The eggs of the gravid segments are passed out along with the feces of the infected individual. While grazing on the polluted ground, the mature eggs are ingested by cattle. These eggs reach the duodenum of the cattle and the hatching of the oncospheres takes place after rupture of the radially striated wall (embryophore) of the egg, caused by the gastric juice. The embryos penetrate the intestinal wall with the help of their hooklets and, possibly aided by lytic secretions, reach the mesenteric venules or lymphatics. They are then carried through the circulation and reach the following organs: the liver, the right side of the heart, the lungs, the left side of the heart and the systemic circulation, in that order. The naked oncospheres are filtered out in the striped muscles, particularly the pterygoid muscle, those of the tenderloin region and the myocardium, where in 60–75 days, they metamorphose into the bladder worm *(Cysticercus bovis,)* which is characterized by the presence of invaginated unarmed scolex (Fig. 6.14). The mature cysticercii are ovoidal in shape, milky white, opalescent and measure 7.5–10 mm in length by 4–6 mm in breadth.

During their metamorphosis, oncospheres lose their hooklets after settling in their site of predilection—striped muscle or myocardium—and their cells in the centre are liquified. Each oncosphere forms an oval vesicle containing the larva at its bottom (the scolex of the future

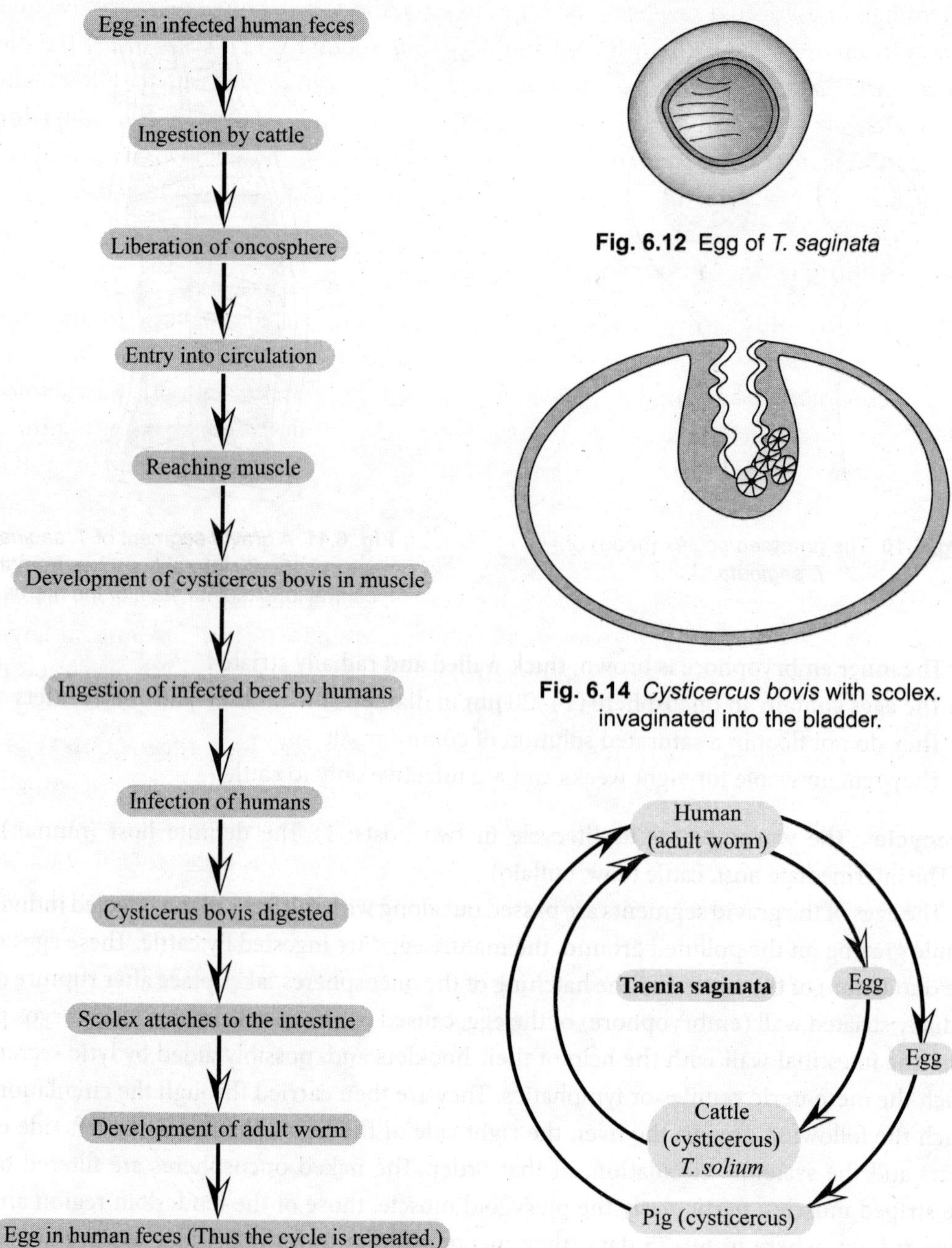

Fig. 6.12 Egg of *T. saginata*

Fig. 6.14 *Cysticercus bovis* with scolex. invaginated into the bladder.

Fig. 6.13 Lifecycle of *T. saginata*.

Fig. 6.15 Lifecycle of *T. saginata* and *T. solium*

adult worm) and takes about 60–70 days to metamorphose into the cysticercus, which can live for about eight months in the muscle of cattle. Beef containing the cysticercus is called 'measly beef' and can become infective to humans.

On ingesting infected raw beef, the human being, the sole definite host, becomes infected with cysticercus larvae with an incubation period of about 10–12 weeks. Inside the human stomach, the larva is digested out of the beef. The scolex comes in contact with the bile, evaginates, attaches itself to the intestinal wall with the help of suckers and develops into an adult worm by gradual strobilisation (formation of scolex, neck and segments). The adult worm starts liberating eggs which are passed out in the feces. Thus, the lifecycle is repeated (Figs 6.13 and 6.15).

Taenia solium (pork tapeworm)

Knowledge that this 'armed' tapeworm' parasitized humans dates back to the time of Hippocrates. *T. solium* was not specifically differentiated from *T. saginata* until 1782. *T. solium* has a cosmopolitan distribution. It is rare in Muslims as they do not eat pork. Larval infection with *T. solium* in the human host is relatively common in populations harbouring the adult worm. Cysticercosis is common in Africa, China and India. The adult *T. solium* lives attached to the wall of the human small intestine.

Morphology *T. solium* attains a length of 2–7 metres. The scolex (head) is roughly quadrate or globular with a diameter of about one mm. It possesses four unpigmented, large, deeply cupped suckers (0.5 mm diameter) and a rounded rostellum armed with a double row of large and small hooklets, numbering 22–32 and measuring 160–180 µm and 110–140 µm, respectively, in length. The hooklets are dagger shaped (Fig. 6.16).

***Proglottids* (Segments):** Immature proglottids are broader than long. Mature ones (Fig. 6.17) are nearly square and gravid ones are longer than broad. The total number of mature proglottids is less than 1000. The genital pore is marginal, thick lipped and situated near the middle of the lateral margin of each segment, alternating irregularly between the right and left margins. The vaginal opening is not guarded by a muscular sphincter. The gravid uterus consists of a median longitudinal stem with 5–10 lateral branches on each side. The gravid segments are expelled in chains of 5–6 at a time and not singly. The adult worm lives for about 25 years.

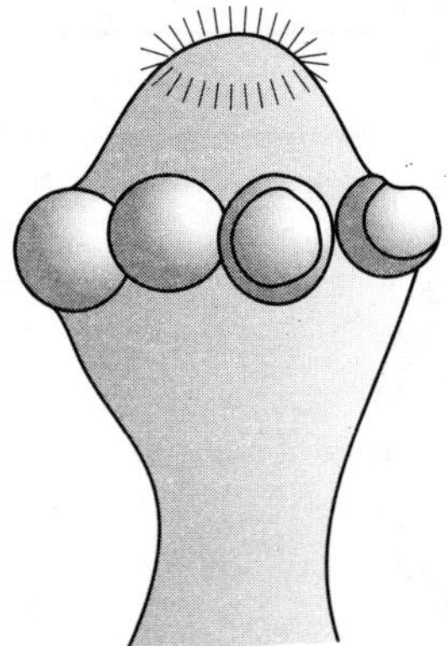

Fig. 6.16 Scolex of *T. solium*.

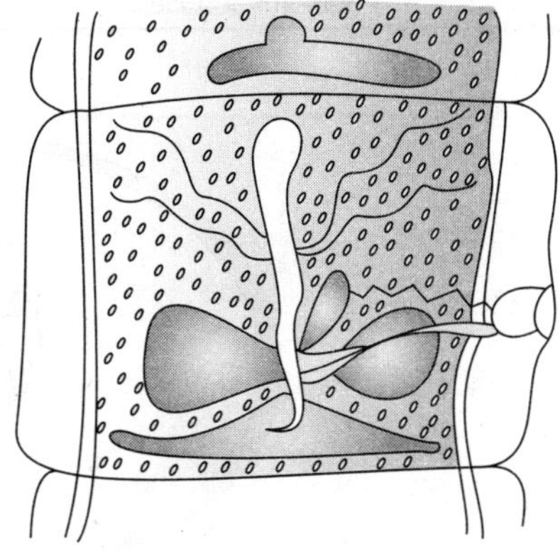

Fig. 6.17 Mature proglottid of *T. solium*.

Egg of T. solium: The eggs escape from the uterus through a ventral longitudinal slit, either before or after the ripe proglottids become free. They are infective to both pigs and humans. The characteristics of the egg of *T. solium* are similar to those of *T. saginata.*

The mature proglottid of *T. solium* differs from that of *T. saginata* in only a few essential details.

Lifecycle of T. solium: The lifecycle of *T. solium* is similar to that of *T. saginata*. The intermediate host is the pig. The pork 'measle' or 'measly pork' or 'bladder worm' *(Cysticercus cellulosae)* is an opalescent ovoidal body. It measures about 810 mm in length and 5 mm in width. It can live for about eight months in the flesh of the pig and sometimes also in humans (Fig. 6.18).

Pathogenicity and clinical features Because of its large size, the mature *T. saginata* is frequently responsible for considerable disturbance in the normal functioning of the digestive tract. *T. solium* on the other hand may cause a lot of irritation, but produces intestinal obstruction less frequently. Ordinarily, the adult worm produces no serious damage, but it can cause vague abdominal discomfort, hunger pains, chronic indigestion and persistant diarrhea or diarrhea alternating with constipation. The nutritional needs of tapeworms are met by obtaining digested material from the host's body. Sometimes, individual proglottids may initiate acute

Table 1 Differences between the adult worms of *T. saginata* and *T. solium*

	T. saginata	*T. solium*
Length :	5–10 metres	2–7 metres
Head :	Large quadrate; without rostellum and hooks; pigmented suckers	Small, globular, with rostellum and hooks; suckers not pigmented
Proglottid :		
Number :	1000–2000,	Under 1000
Expulsion	Expelled singly	Expelled in chains of 5–6
Uterus :	15–30 thin lateral branches on each side	5–10 thick lateral branches
Vagina :	Vaginal sphincter present	Vaginal sphincter absent each side
Ovaries :	Two in number without accessory lobe	Two in number with an accessory lobe
Testes :	300–400 follicles	150–200 follicles.

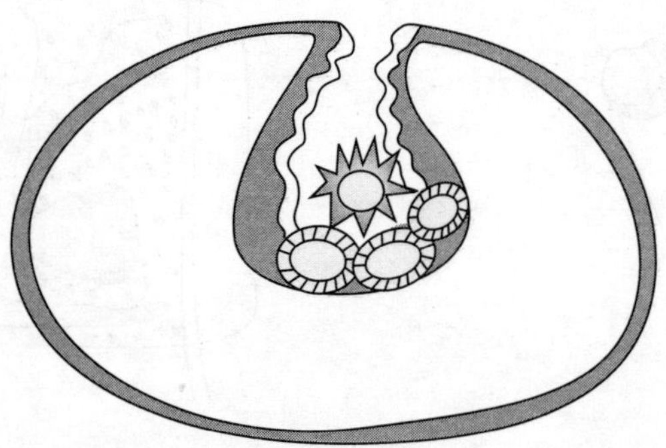

Fig. 6.18 *Cysticercus cellulosae* of *T.solium*.

appendicitis. More often, the absorbed by-products of the worm create systemic intoxication in the patient. In rare cases, the scolex may perforate the intestinal wall and initiate peritonitis. In weak patients, the presence of Taenia in the intestine may cause anorexia, loss of weight and nervous disorders of toxic origin. The larvae *(Cysticercus bovis)* of *T. saginata* are not found in humans, but those *(Cysticercus cellulosae)* of *T. solium* are occasionally found in humans.

Cysticercus cellulosae produces cysticercosis cellulosae in humans. The larval stage of this worm has been found in every organ and tissue of the body. The symptoms vary according to the number of bladder worms *(Cysticercus cellulosae)* and the tissues which they have invaded. They are frequently found in the subcutaneous tissues and finally the brain, where they develop in superficial cyst capsules or visible nodules. Following the lodging of the larva in the brain, there is hardly any disturbance during its lifetime, but as soon as the larva dies, tissue reactions begin to take place around it. As a result, a variety of brain symptoms may develop. Epileptiform seizures may occur commonly and may produce a rapidly fatal outcome. A patient harbouring an adult worm may auto-infect himself due to the gravid segments being thrown back into the stomach by the reversal peristaltic movement of the intestine or due to unhygienic habits. Sometimes, humans may become infected, as in the pig, by eating raw vegetables contaminated with eggs or by drinking polluted water.

T. saginata. Usually one worm can cause the infection, but multiple infections can occur rarely. In most cases, the adult worms are in the upper jejunum and cause no damage or symptom. Irritation, however, may cause flatulence, cramps or diarrhea. Eosinophilia occurs in almost half of those infected and usually in less than 10%. Infection is recognized by the spontaneous passage of gravid proglottids out of the anus or in the feces.

T. solium (Human cysticercosis) Intestinal infection is usually with one adult worm and this seldom causes anything more than local irritation and mild eosinophilia. ***Cysticerci*** may develop in any tissue or organ of the body. The cysticercus matures in the human host in a few months and forms a translucent cyst which gradually becomes surrounded by a fibrous capsule. Eventually, the larvae die and calcify. No serious effects develop from cysticera in the most frequent locations, the subcutaneous tissues and skeletal muscles, although palpable or visible subcutaneous nodules can be recognized in approximately half of those with established infections. These are most frequently felt in the pectoral and abdominal superficial tissues than in the limbs and simulate neurofibromatosis.

The invasive stage often causes no symptoms, but fever, eosinophilia, muscle ache and fatigue have been described. In the brain, cysticerci may be present in the cortex, meninges, ventricles or in the substance of the cerebrum. Cysts in the ventricles may cause hydrocephalus. When parasites die in the brain, they provoke a severe inflammatory reaction that can lead to increased pressure symptoms. Calcification occurs after the parasite has been dead for some years. CSF changes occur more often in the presence of cysts in contact with the subarachanoid space rather than with parenchymatous cysts. Patients with larvae in the brain may present with epilepsy, intracranial hypertension, motor or sensory or personality changes many years after initial infection. Cysticercus is the most common larval tapeworm to invade the eye where it reaches through the retinal artery. It may lodge anywhere in the orbit, conjunctiva or anterior chambers. Reactions to live larvae are usually minimal, but dead parasites produce iridocyclitis, clouding of the vitreous and severe retinal inflammation or detachment. Patients may present with intra-orbital pain, light flashes and the presence of blurred vision. Cysts may rarely localize in all layers of the heart tissue and may produce myocarditis or congestive heart failure.

Human cysticercosis is suggested by a history of infection with adult worm, the presence of multiple subcutaneous nodules, typical symptoms and earlier residence in endemic areas and moderate eosinophilia. Definite diagnosis is done by removal of subcutaneous nodules or brain cysts. Ocular cysticercosis is confirmed by the characteristic movement and scolex of worm. After calcification of larvae, roentgenologic eletrocardiogram (ECG), computed tomography (CT) and magnetic resonance imaging (MRI) can confirm the space occupying lesions. With CT, MRI, the cerebral cysticercosis must be differentiated from hydatid cyst or coenurus cyst, brain tumour.

An indirect hemaggluatination (HIA) test is presently the best available serological method and is positive in a significant number of human cysticercosis cases. However, a negative result cannot be ruled out for human cysticercosis. ELISA or CFT on CSF may be positive, particularly when inflammatory changes are present in CSF. A dot-ELISA using fresh fluid of cysticercus cellulosae from swine, as antigen, was studied to detect *C. cellulosae* antibody in sera and CSF of patients with neurocysticercosis (96.1% positive). There was cross reaction with sera of *Paragonimus westermanii, Clonorchis sinensis* infected subjects.

Praziquantel is very effective against human cysticercosis.

Diagnosis The presence of characteristic Taenia eggs in the stool does not permit differential diagnosis between *T. solium* and *T. saginata.* Recovery of gravid proglottids and count of the main lateral branches of the uterus (5–10 on each side for *T. solium* as distinguished from 15 to 30 for *T. saginata)* constitute the only specific pre-treatment diagnosis. When the proglottids are pressed between two slides and examined with a hand lens, the number of main lateral branches of the uterus can be determined.

Treatment Quinacrine is the drug of choice for tapeworms. Essentially, 100% eradication may be obtained by oral administration of this drug. Niclosamide, mebendazole, albendazole and bithionol have also been found effective.

Praziquantel (a very recent anthelminitic agent) in a single dose of 10 mg/kg body weight is very effective against *T. saginata*, it is well tolerated and has no side effect.

Prophylaxis It consists of 1) Personal hygiene 2) General sanitary measures 3) Avoidance of ingestion of raw pork or beef and vegetables irrigated by sewage water 4) Rigid quality inspection of pork and beef in all slaughter houses and 5) Avoidance of fecal contamination either from self or from others infected with the adult worms.

Infection with adult worm can be prevented by heating the pork from 49 to 53°C for a half hour or freezing at –5°C for three days which kills the larvae. Pickling and smoking are usually not sufficient to destroy the cysticerci. Proper hygienic measures and disposal of human excrement can prevent human cysticercosis.

Echinococcus granulosus (dog tapeworm)

Family Taeniidae
Genus Echinococcus

In ancient times, Hippocrates and Galen were clinically familiar with hydatid cysts.

The most extensive enzootic regions are the sheep and cattle raising countries including South Australia, New Zealand, Africa and America. In India (Punjab), dogs (28.8%) and cattle (90%) harbour hydatid cysts.

Human infection occurs in Europe and quite frequently, in Siberia, China, Japan and the United States as well. Hydatid disease is cosmopolitan in its distribution.

The adult worm of *E. granulosus* lives attached to the villi of the small intestine of the dog; the larval form develops only in humans, the intermediate host.

Morphology The adult worm (Fig. 6.19) is a minute tapeworm. It has a scolex, neck and strobila comprising three segments. It measures 3–6 mm in length. It has a pyriform scolex (300 μm in diameter), provided with four suckers and a protrusible rostellum armed with two circular rows of hooklets (usually 30–36). The neck is short and thick.

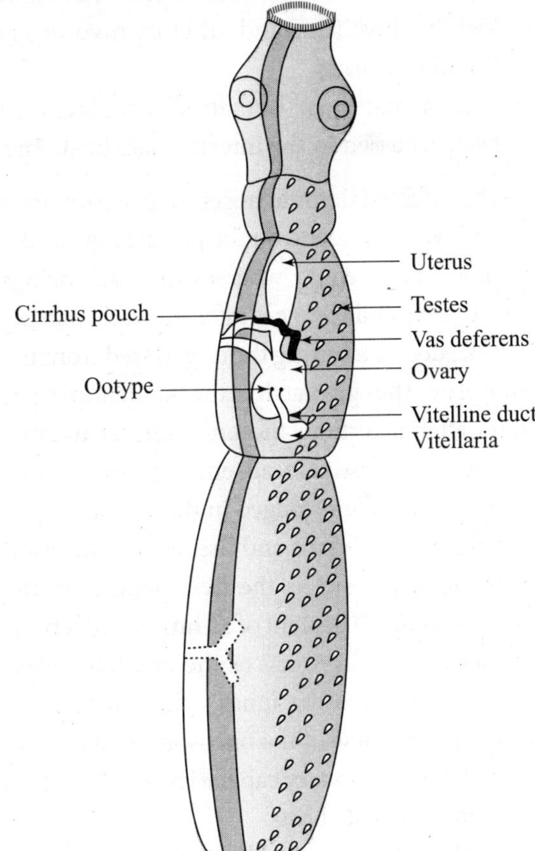

Fig. 6.19 *Eichonococcus granulosus* (adult worm).

1. The strobila consists of three segments, usually one immature proglottid, one mature proglottid and one gravid proglottid. The gravid proglottid is the broadest and longest, measuring 2–3 mm in length by 0.6 mm in breadth. In the gravid unit, the uterus resembles a loosely twisted coil.
2. Egg: It cannot be distinguished from that of Taenia. It is ovoid in shape and measures 32–36 μm in length by 25–32 μm in breadth. It contains a hexacanth embryo. It is infective to humans, cattle, sheep and other herbivorous animals (Fig. 6.20a and b)
3. Larval form: It is found within the hydatid cyst developing inside the intermediate host. It represents the scolex of the future worm and is invaginated (Fig. 6.21) into its own body to protect its rostellar hooklets. When ingested by the definite host (dog), the scolex with its four suckers and rostellar hooklets evaginates and develops into an adult worm.

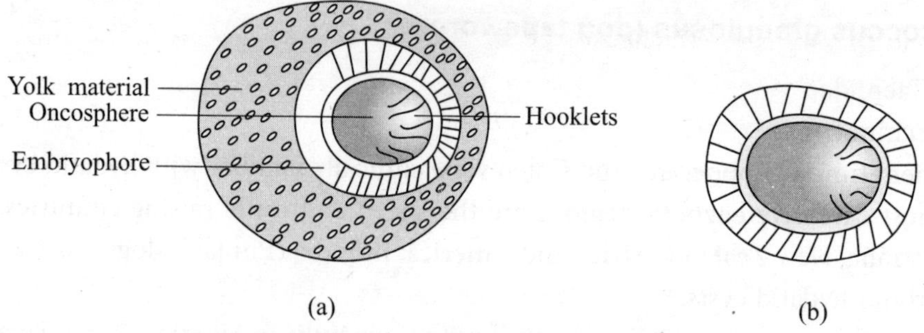

Fig. 6.20 (a) Egg with shell (b) Egg without shell.

Lifecycle The worm passes its cycle in two hosts.

1. Definite host (dog and other carnivorous animals): Dog is the sole optimum definite host for adult worms
2. Intermediate host (human, sheep, goat and cattle): The larval stage, giving rise to the hydatid cyst, is passed in the intermediate host. The optimum intermediate host is the sheep.

The infected definite hosts (dog, carnivorous animals) pass the stool with the eggs onto the ground. While grazing on the polluted ground, the herbivorous animals (sheep, goats and cattle) swallow these eggs, whereas human beings (particularly children) get infected while playing with the dog or allowing the dog to feed from the same plate. The eggs hatch in the duodenum eight hours after ingestion; the oncospheres migrate through the intestinal wall, enter the mesenteric venules and become lodged in the capillary filter beds in various organs and tissues. The first and most important site is the liver; where on the average, about 70 percent of all human infections are located. The liver acts as the first filter. Next in importance are the lungs, which act as the second filter. A few of the oncospheres may pass through the pulmonary capillaries, enter the general bloodstream and lodge in the various organs of the intermediate hosts.

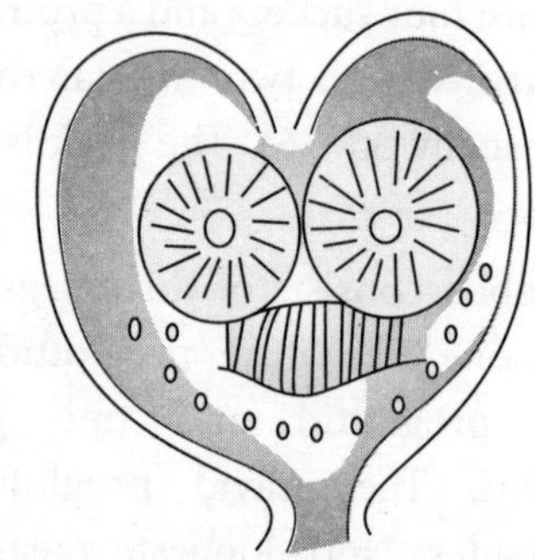

Fig. 6.21 Scolex invaginated into the cyst membrane.

The leucocytes probably attack and kill many oncospheres at the site of predilection. Some usually survive and, by the fourth day, reach a diameter of 40 μm. They then begin to develop into a cystic cavity (hydatid cyst). By the end of three weeks, the young cyst attains a diameter of 250 μm and transforms into a hollow bladder (Gk: *hydatis,* meaning 'drop of water'). By the end of the fifth month, the hydatid cyst (Fig. 6.23) reaches a diameter of one cm and its intrinsic wall by now has become differentiated into 1) The outer, friable, laminated, milky opaque, non-nucleated layer and 2) The inner nucleated germinal layer. From the inner layer, brood capsules develop and may remain attached or be set free into the fluid of the cystic cavity. The free brood capsules and free scolices are called 'hydatid sand'. Some cysts never produce brood capsules; in other cysts, brood capsules never produce scolices, hence these cysts are called ***acephalocysts.***

From the inner wall of the brood capsules, the scolices develop and invaginate into their own bodies to protect the rostellar hooklets from injury. A hydatid cyst developing from the oncosphere may contain thousands of scolices.

When the organs or tissues containing fertile hydatid cysts are ingested by the dog, the cysts grow into adult worms in about 6–7 weeks in the intestine. The eggs are passed out in the dog's feces. Thus, the lifecycle is repeated (Figs 6.22 and 6.24).

Since the dog has no access to the hydatid cyst developed in the human viscera, the lifecycle of *E. granulosus* comes to an end.

Pathogenicity and clinical features The adult worm of *E. granulosus* in the intestine of the dog does not cause much physiological disturbance. The damage produced by the hydatid cyst of *E. granulosus* in the human body is both mechanical and toxic. The young cysts which develop from the

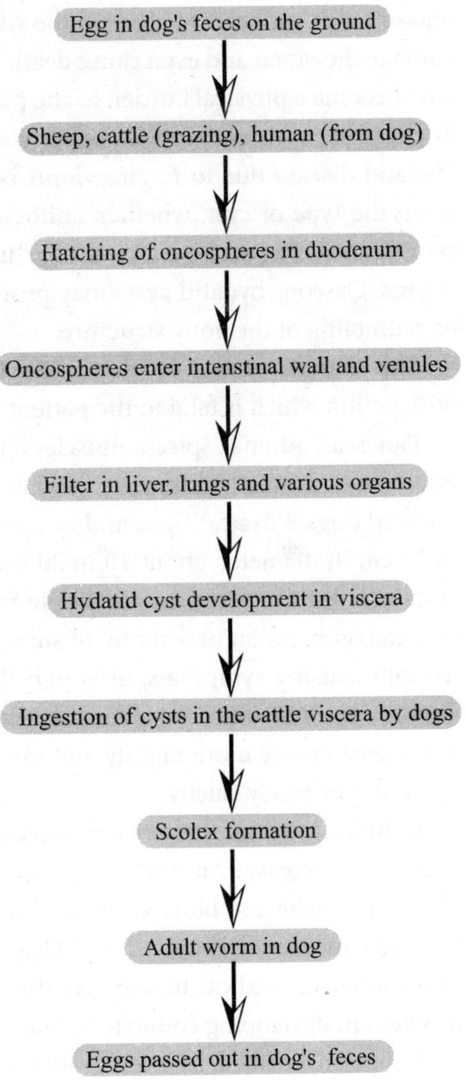

Fig. 6.22 Lifecycle of *E. granulosus.*

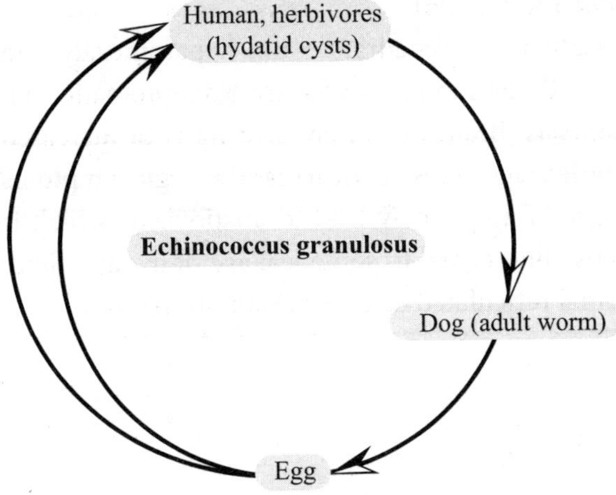

Fig. 6.24 Lifecycle of *E. granulosus.*

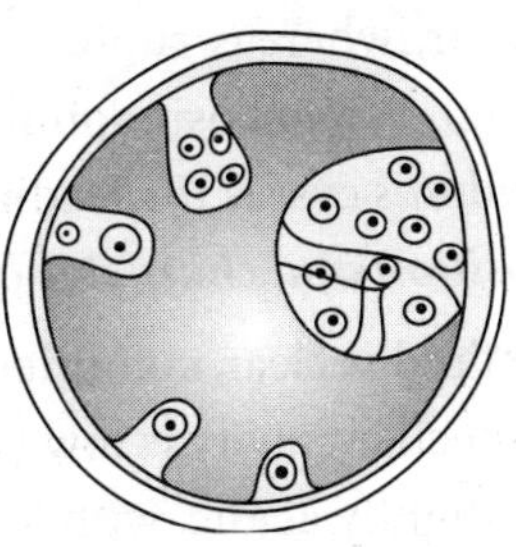

Fig. 6.23 Hydatid cyst.

oncospheres (embryos) lodged in the vital centres may interfere with the function of the organ, damage the organ and even cause death. The benign unilocular cyst may grow to a tremendous size, become a physical burden to the patient and burst, precipitating an anaphylactic reaction. The osseous cysts may erode the bony structure, resulting in permanent injury to the patient. Hydatid disease due to *E. granulosus* is always serious. The gravity of the infection depends upon the type of cyst, whether unilocular or osseous. Unilocular hydatid cyst may produce symptoms 5–20 years later, only after it has reached a sufficient size to press on the adjacent organs. Osseous hydatid cysts may produce rapid erosion of the bone with multiple fractures or crumbling of the bony structure.

The young cyst may develop in the brain, orbital capillary or on the heart valve, cause an obstruction which is fatal to the patient.

Pancreas, adrenal, spleen, muscles and head of femur are also affected. Mostly *E. granulosus* infection occurs in children, by hand to mouth transmission of eggs picked up from the fur of infected dogs. Physical signs and symptoms do not usually occur until the cysts are at least 10 to 20 cm in diameter, about 10 to 20 years after initial infection. Rupture or leakage of viable cysts may lead to secondary multiple implantations of the peritoneum or organs. Cysts may lead to compression or atrophy of surrounding tissue. Cysts may become inactive and calcify without causing symptoms, although there may still be some viability in the calcified cyst. There is less resistance to spherical growth in the lung than in the liver, and lung cysts may attain greater size more rapidly and rarely calcify. Brain cysts are usually present at a younger age and they rarely calcify.

In India, Mumbai doctors removed 400 hydatid cysts of *E. granulosus* surgically on 26 June 2006 with success, from the brain of a Faizabad-based Muslim barbar, 21 years old, who had severe headache and blurred vision. There were 400 large and small cysts in within the skull, the cysts measured about 12.3 × 11.6 × 8.5 cm in size. It is a startling number, previously unrecorded in medical history say doctors. It may be slowly recognized as an public health problem in developing countries (*Times of India* 5 July, 2006)

Symptoms related to liver cysts include right upper quadrant pain, hepatomegaly and jaundice. Approximately half of the patients with pulmonary cysts are asymptomatic, but cysts may cause chest pain, cough and hemoptysis. Brain cysts may give signs of increased intracranial pressure and convulsions. With slow leakage of cyst, urticaria and allergic symptoms may occur, whereas rupture or needle puncture of a cyst may lead to anaphylaxis which is often fatal. When eosinophilia is present, it is usually related to some leakage of hydatid fluid. *E. granulosus* cyst is the leading cause of a normal reticulated calcified lesion in the liver.

Composition and character of hydatid fluid:

1. The fluid is clear, colourless or pale yellow
2. Its specific gravity is low (1.005–1.010)
3. It is slightly acidic, with a pH of 6.7

4. It contains sodium chloride, sodium sulphate, sodium phosphate, sodium and calcium salts of succinic acid
5. It is antigenic, hence used in immunological tests
6. It is highly toxic and gives rise to anaphylactic reaction
7. The hydatid sand consists of liberated brood capsules, free scolices and loose hooklets, which settle in the hydatid fluid as granular deposits.

Laboratory diagnosis

1. Intradermal test or Casoni's test is used as the clinical diagnostic procedure. The antigen employed consists of sterile hydatid fluid obtained by puncture of the unilocular hydatid cyst of sheep or human cases. The antigen is filtered, incubated to test its sterility and placed in sealed ampoules on ice. For the test, 0.2 ml of the antigen is introduced intradermally on the upper arm after sterilization of the area with alcohol. For the control, the same amount of sterile physiologic salt solution is injected into the skin of the opposite arm. The control fades almost immediately, while the tested site of positive cases develops a typical wheal (five cm in diameter) within half an hour. This test indicates that the patient has or has had a hydatid cyst.
2. Serological tests:
   a. Precipitin test: 0.4 ml of the patient's fresh serum is added to an equal amount of the antigen in small agglutination tubes and allowed to stand for 36 hours at room temperature. In a serum with high precipitin content, the precipitate forms in two to three hours. The flocculation has been designated as '+++'; fine precipitate with granules in suspension, '++' and microscopic granularity '+'. The precipitin test closely parallels the complement fixation test reaction.
   b. Complement fixation test: Sterile hydatid fluid is used as antigen. The test is sensitive, specific; it is not anti-complementary and does not give false positive reactions.
   c. Hemagglutination test: Fresh or formalinized sheep red cells, sensitized with tannic acid and coated with echinococcus antigen, is used as antigen. It is more sensitive than the complement fixation test.
   d. Bentonite flocculation test: Bentonite particles coated with sterile hydatid cyst is used as antigen in the test.
   e. Latex slide agglutination test: It is a simple and inexpensive diagnostic screening method for hydatid disease. It employs polystyrene latex particles coated with hydatid cyst fluid obtained from human cases. The test is equal or superior to the complement fixation, hemagglutination or bentonite flocculation tests
   f. Fluorescent antibody test: It is a very sensitive method for the diagnosis of hydatid disease.
3. Other diagnostic aids are:
   a. The X-ray: The technique is frequently helpful in hydatid cysts of the lungs or other thoracic involvement.

b. Exploratory cyst puncture: This is an accurate method, but is dangerous due to anaphylactic shock resulting from escape of hydatid fluid.
c. Eosinophilia: Generalized eosinophilia is present in 20–25 per cent of infected cases.
d. Radioactive scanning, CT, MRI or sonography is useful in localizing non-calcified cysts. Pulmonary cysts present as regular, well-defined, round shadows which cannot be differentiated from a tumour. Immunological techniques are quite valuable and should always be employed pre-operatively to alert the surgeon to the likely presence of a hydatid cyst. When Casoni's skin test shows an immediate negative reaction, there is good, but not absolute evidence of the absence of hydatid disease and a false positive reaction may occur. The immuno-electrophoresis is the only absolutely specific test for hydatid disease, but it is presently not readily available. Dot-blot ELISA is a confirmative test of hydatid disease. This 30-minute test is based on the detection of antibodies to antigen B of hydatid cyst fluid. The use of capture ELISA can be advocated to detect specific immune complexes in serum, this could be valuable in monitoring a certain endemic area of active hydatid disease.

Treatment All non-surgical procedures are usually unsuccessful. Hence, there is no specific drug. Surgical technique is helpful only in patients with unilocular cysts in operable sites. Most recently, clinical trails with albendazole at a daily dose of 15 mg per kg body weight for 14 days was satisfactory with immediate effect on *E. granulosus*.

Prophylaxis This consists of 1) avoidance of handling infected dogs 2) avoidance of ingestion of raw vegetables polluted with eggs 3) personal hygiene (cleaning hands before eating) 4) preventing dogs from eating the carcasses of sheep, cattle and dogs in infected areas 5) destroying eggs with arecoline hydrobromide 6) discarding all infected viscera in slaughter houses by dumping them into pits, inacessible to dogs, and 7) educational propaganda in schools.

Echinococcus vogeli

This species causes Polycystic Hydatid Disease (PHD). It is distributed throughout America and its intermediate host is the wild rodent.

Surgical treatment of polycystic hydatid disease is frequently unfeasible, because the multiple cysts involve extensive portion of the liver and other organs and are disseminated throughout the peritoneum.

Albendazole 10 mg/kg body weight orally is effective in the treatment of patients with polycystic hydatid disease.

Hymenolepis nana (dwarf tapeworm)

Family: Hymenolepididae
Genus: Hymenolepis

This species was discovered by Bilharz in 1851 in the small intestine of a boy. The name Hymenolepis is derived from Greek, ***hymen***, membrane and ***lepsis***, shell. It is cosmopolitan in its distribution. It is particularly common in India, Europe, the USSR and the United States of America.

Hymenolepis nana remains attached to the wall of the small intestine of humans and rodents (rats, mice).

Morphology

1. Adult worm: The entire worm is small, measuring up to 25–40 mm in length by one mm in diameter. It lives for about two weeks (Fig. 6.25).
2. The scolex is minute (0.32 mm in diameter), rhomboidal or globular and has four hemispherical suckers (80 μm in cross-section) and a short retractile rostellum armed with 20–30 hooklets in one single row, capable of invagination into the apex of the organ. The rostellar hooklets are shaped like tuning forks (Fig. 6.26). The neck is long.
3. Proglottids (segments): There are about 200 segments. Immature proglottids at the beginning are very short and narrow, whereas the distal proglottids become increasingly wider and broader. At the distal end, the general contour of the strobila is rounded. The maximum size of the proglottid is 0.15–0.3 mm in length and 0.8–1 mm in breadth. The genital pores are marginal and situated on the same side. The uterus is a transverse sac and there are three testes (Fig. 6.27).

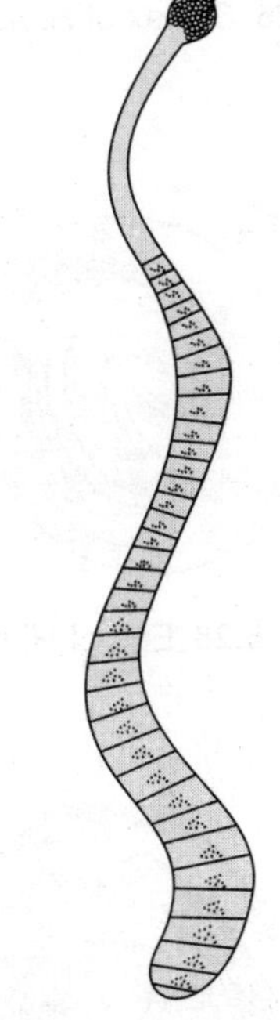

Fig. 6.25 *Hymenolepis nana* (complete worm).

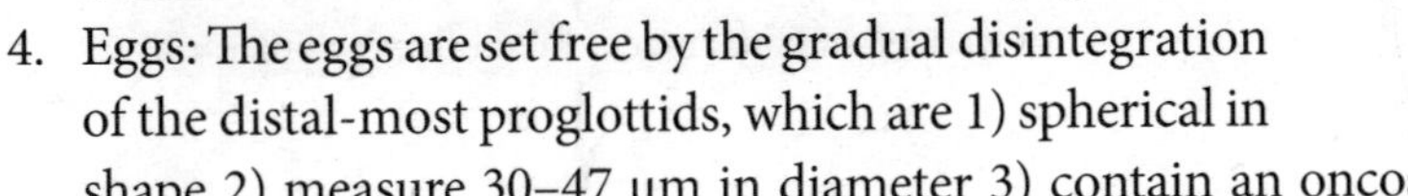

4. Eggs: The eggs are set free by the gradual disintegration of the distal-most proglottids, which are 1) spherical in shape 2) measure 30–47 μm in diameter 3) contain an oncosphere which is enclosed in an inner envelope (embryosphore) with two polar thickenings, from each of which arise 4–8 polar filaments. Within the oncosphere are three pairs of tuning-fork shaped hooklets. The space between the inner and outer envelopes is filled with yolk granules and polar filaments and 4) float in a saturated solution of common salt (Fig. 6.28).

Lifecycle The lifecycle (Figs 6.29 and 6.31) of *H. nana* takes place only in one host; no intermediate host is involved.

Fully embryonated eggs, recently passed in the feces are ingested by humans. They hatch in the stomach or small intestine, and the free oncospheres penetrate into the villi of the anterior part of the small intestine and metamorphose into young cercocysts or *cysticercoids* (Fig. 6.30).

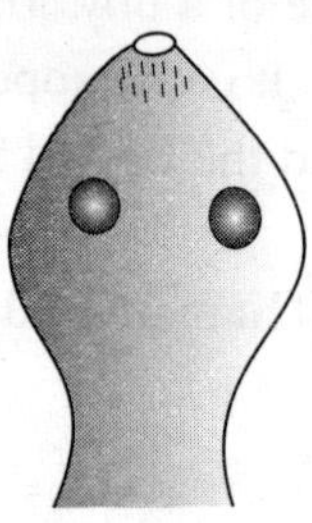

Fig. 6.26 Scolex of *H. nana*.

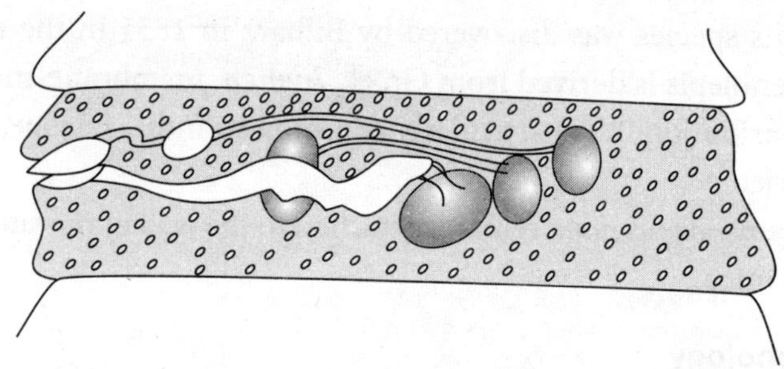

Fig. 6.27 Mature proglottid of *H. nana*.

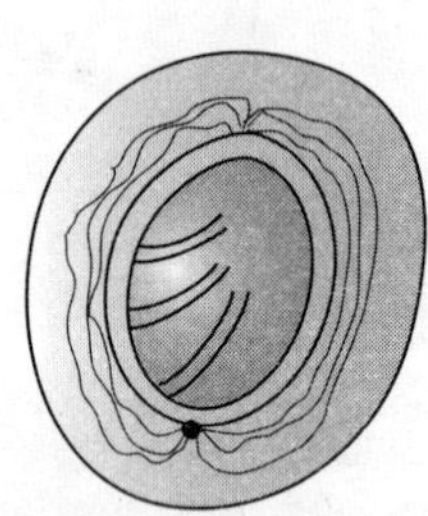

Fig. 6.28 Egg of *H. nana*.

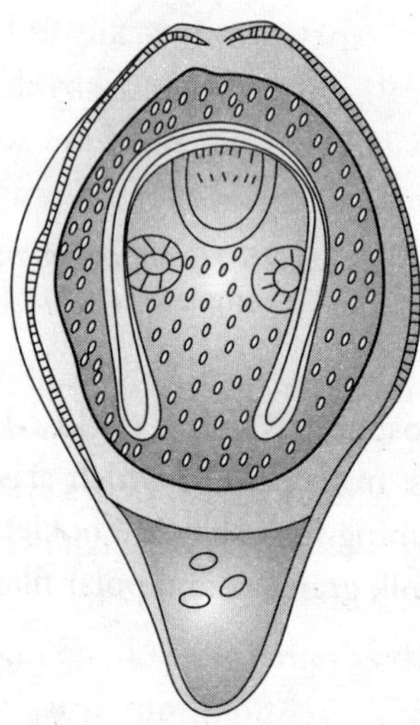

Fig. 6.30 Cysticercoid *Hymenolepis nana*.

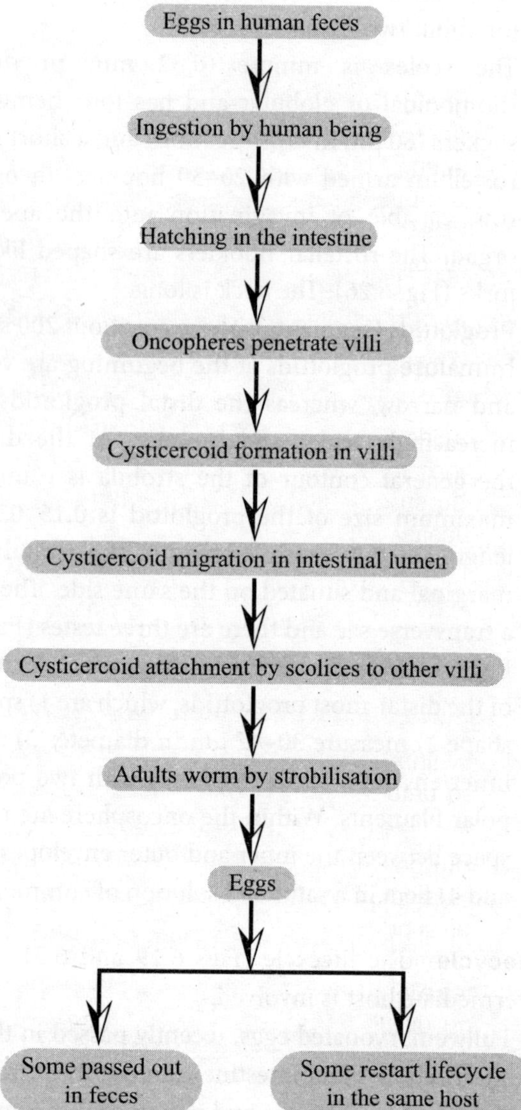

Fig. 6.29 Lifecycle of *Hymenolepis nana*.

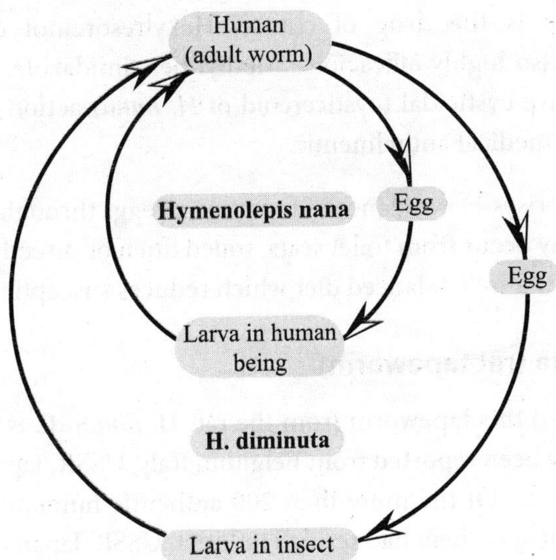

Fig. 6.31 Lifecycle of *H. nana* and *H. diminuta*.

These larvae then migrate into the lumen of the small intestine, become attached by their scolices to other villi farther down in the small intestine, and in the course of two weeks or more, develop into mature worms. Strobilisation (the process of producing or growing new segments) is rapid, and in about 30 days after ingestion, the adult worms start to lay eggs. Some of them are passed out in the feces and those eggs remaining in the intestine restart the lifecycle in the same host, i.e., human. *H. nana* is the only 'human' tapeworm typically utilizing no intermediate host and is one of the exceptions to the general rule that helminths do not multiply inside the body of the definite host. Humans are probably the only common source for human infection. This is the ***direct*** lifecycle; besides this, there is an ***indirect*** (common in Argentina) lifecycle, in which the rat flea *(Xenopsylla cheopis)* and beetle act as intermediate hosts and transmit the infection from mice to human beings.

Pathogenicity and clinical features A large number of *H. nana* attached to the wall of the small intestine produce considerable irritation of the intestinal mucosa. There is generalized toxemia due to the absorption of the metabolic wastes of the parasites by the patient's systems. The general symptoms are headache, dizziness, anorexia, pruritus of nose and anus, periodic diarrhea and abdominal pain.

Infection with 1000 worms can occur in humans. In most cases of light infection, no injury is caused to the mucosa and there are no symptoms, but the mucosal irritation from heavy worm loads may lead to anorexia, abdominal pain and diarrhea. Mild eosinophilia is often present.

Laboratory diagnosis Characteristic eggs in the patient's stool should be demonstrated microscopically and identified by their typical polar filaments.

The ELISA for *H. nana* may be useful for defining the epidemiology of *H. nana* infection, especially in areas free from cysticercosis and hydatidosis.

Treatment Niclosamide is the drug of choice. Hexylresorcinol crystoid is frequently effective. Quinacrine is also highly efficacious. Methyl benzimidazole, a new broadspectrum anthelmintic, with effective cysticidal (cysticereoid of *H. nana*) action experimentally in rats makes it a candidate as a medical anthelmentic.

Prophylaxis This comprises 1) avoidance of ingestion of eggs through contaminated food or drink (contamination may occur from toilet seats, soiled linen or directly from anus to mouth) 2) personal hygiene and 3) a well balanced diet which reduces susceptibility to infection.

Hymenolepis diminuta (rat tapeworm)

Rudolphi (1819) recovered this tapeworm from the rat. *H. diminuta* is a common parasite of the rat. Human cases have been reported from Belgium, Italy, USSR, Japan, China, Philippines, India, Africa and Venezuela. Of the more than 200 authentic human cases from the United States, it was found that most of them had resided in India, USSR, Japan or Italy. This tapeworm lives in the intestine of the rat.

Morphology The adult worm measures 20–60 cm in length, its width at the distal end is 4 mm. The scolex is round, has four-cupped suckers and a retractile unarmed pyriform rostellum. The terminal proglottid measured 0.75 mm in length and 2.5 mm in width, has three ovoidal testes and the genital organ. The gravid proglottids become detached from the strobila, disintegrate and discharge their eggs which are passed in the feces. The adult worm lives in the rat for more than 13 years.

The eggs are subspherical and have a slightly yellowish transparent outer membrane, and an inner membrane around the oncosphere which has two polar thickenings, but no polar filament. Between the two membranes, there is a colourless gelatinous matrix. The six lanceolate hooklets of the oncosphere are arranged in a fan-shaped pattern.

Lifecycle The lifecycle of *H. diminuta* requires two hosts: a human, the definite host and *xenopsylla cheopis*, the intermediate host.

In the intestine of the intermediate host, the egg hatches and the oncosphere penetrates into the hemal cavity, where it metamorphoses into a cysticercoid larva. Accidental ingestion of the parasitized intermediate hosts cause infection of the definite host. The cysticercoids liberated from the rat flea develop into adult worms. Cachexia is a common symptom.

Diagnosis Diagnosis is based on the recovery of the characteristic egg. The evacuated worm can be easily identified as well.

Treatment Quinacrine is effective, but Niclosamide is preferred.

Prophylaxis The only effective method of prophylaxis is the avoidance of accidental swallowing of the ectoparasites.

Dipylidium caninum (double-pored dog tapeworm)

Family: Dilepididae
Genus: Dipylidium

Dipylidium caninum (from Greek *dis,* two; *pylis,* gate; *dipylidium* means 'having two entrances') was first observed by Linnaeus (1758). It is a common tapeworm of the dog (Panjarathinam, 1991) and cat throughout the world, including the Indian palm cat, and from time to time, human beings (mostly children).

Morphology The adult worm measures 100–700 mm in length. The scolex is small and rhomboidal, and has four deeply cupped oral suckers and a median apical, club-shaped rostellum, capable of protrusion to a length of 185 μm or invagination into the scolex. The rostellum is armed with circles of spines. The anterior spines are the largest and the posterior ones are the smallest. Mature and gravid proglottids are pumpkin-seed shaped. Each is provided with two sets of reproductive organs with a genital atrium on each lateral margin. The gravid proglottid is filled with uterine blocks. Each block contains 8–15 eggs enclosed in an embryonic membrane.

The eggs are spherical, thin-shelled and hyaline. They measure 25–40 μm in diameter and have delicate hooklets, 12–15 μm in length. They consist of an outermost yolk shell, an innermost embryonic membrane and an intermediate albuminous layer. Sometimes, groups of eggs within the mother embryonic membrane are passed in the feces.

Lifecycle Eggs deposited on the ground are ingested by the dog flea *(Ctenocephalides canis)* in the larval stage. The dog flea is similar to the rat flea in appearance. The eggs hatch in the intestine of the flea and migrate into their hemal cavity where they develop into procercoid and, later, cysticercoid larvae. Infected fleas, when ingested by the mammalian host, produce infection.

Pathogenicity and clinical features Pathogenicity in humans is due to the metabolic wastes of the worm being absorbed into the system. Clinical manifestations are intestinal disturbances, indigestion, loss of appetite and toxic nervous symptoms. The proglottids of *D. caninum* are motile and may migrate from the anus and can be mistaken for pin worms by case history.

Diagnosis Diagnosis is by demonstration of characteristic eggs in the mother capsules.

Treatment Quinacrine, mebendazole and niclosamide are effective.

Prophylaxis consists of avoiding handling dogs which are infested with fleas; and dusting of dogs with Gammaxene or DDT.

Treatment for tapeworms Drug of choice for *D. latum, Taenia sp., H. nana* and *D. caninum* is niclosamide (adult single 2 gram dose chewable tablet), side effects are rare. Another effective drug is paromomycin. Mebendazole is also effective against *Taenia sp.*

Praziquantel (current anthelmintic agent) in a single dose of 300 mg twice daily for three days is effective against human cysticercosis of the brain and subcutaneous and muscular tissue (50 mg per kilogram body weight per day, in three divided doses for 14 days). Calcified cysticerci do not respond to this treatment, and it is not recommended for ocular cysticerci. *T. saginata*: in a single oral dose of 10 mg/kg body weight is well tolerated and has no side effects. Mebendazole is effective against human cysticercosis due to *E. granulosus* and *T. solium*, but it is teratogenic and embryotoxic, therefore it is contraindicated in pregnancy and childhood. It is less effective than albendazole (10 mg/kg body weight daily in four courses of 30 days with 15 day intervals between courses). The treatment of patients with systematic echinococosis by albendazole may no longer require surgery.

SUMMARY

- All species of Helminths (Greek, helminth means 'worm') belong to the sub-kingdom Metazoaoa, which are provided with tissues, organs derived from the embryonic endoderm, ectoderm and mesoderm. Helminths of medical importance are as follows. They may be Phylum
  I. Platyhelminths (class Cestoidea and Trematoda)
  II. Nemathehelminths (class Nematoda)

Phylum Platyhelminths

- They are leaf or tape-like, segmented, hermaphrodite and have no alimentary canal and no body cavity.

Phylum Nemathelminths

- They are elongated, cylindrical, unsegmented, and they have separate sexes, body cavity, and alimentary canal.

Cestodes

- They are long, dorso-ventrally flattened, segmented and tape-like. So, they are also called 'tapeworms'; they measure from a few millimeters to several metres in length and are found in the intestine of humans and animals. They have regions a) A head (scolex); b) Body (strobila) c) Segments (proglottids) suckers (slit-like or cup-like), have no separate sexes; no body cavity and alimentary canal, they have reproductive, excretory and nervous systems.
- They are pseudo-phyllidean and cyclo-phyllidean cestodes.
  Pseudophyllidean Cestodes

Diphyllobothrium latum

- It is a parasite of humans, has worldwide distribution, but has not yet been reported from India. It lives in the intestine of humans, dog, cat.

- It is yellowish, measures 3–10 metres. Its head is small, spoon-shaped and long. It has two bothria (slit-like grooves) on both ventral, dorsal surfaces; has no rostellum (a beak-like projection on the head) and no hooklets. Its neck is longer than the head; it has 3000 proglottids. Each proglottid is broader and is filled with male and female genitalia. Operculated eggs are discharged through the uterine pore of the mature proglottid.
- One definite host (human, dog, cat) and two intermediate hosts (first in the Cyclops, second in fish) are required *by D. latum* to complete its lifecycle. When the egg of *D. latum* comes in contact with water, coracidium (first stage larva, ciliated embryo) escape through the opercular opening of the egg, swim in the water and are ingested by Cyclops. In the midgut of the Cyclops, the ciliated embryo casts off its ciliated coat, transforms into a procercoid larva (second stage larva). If the fresh water fish ingests the infected Cyclops, the procercoid larva grows into plerocercoid or sparganum (third stage larva) in the muscle fibres of fish. On ingestion of infected raw or insufficiently cooked fish, human beings (definite host) become infected, because pleroceroid is infective to humans, it develops into an adult worm, in the human intestine, where it lays eggs. It takes five or six weeks for the development from pleroceroid to egg appearance in the feces.
- When *D. latum* gets attached to the ileum, it brings about the pernicious type of anemia. It contains large amounts of vitamin B_{12} and deprives the host of essential nutritional components, which also causes pernicious anemia.
- Clinically, nonspecific symptoms and vitamin B_{12} deficiency develops.
- Demonstration of operculated egg of *D. latum* is accurate. Laboratory diagnosis: Treatment with broadspectrum anthelmintic drugs is effective. Pernicious anemia responds well to folic acid therapy.
- *D. latum* infection can be prevented by thorough cooking of infected fish; proper disposal of sewage to avoid pollution of water; not feeding dogs with infected fish.

Taenia saginata (Beef tapeworm)

- *T. saginata* is called the common unarmed tapeworm. It has been known to infect humans since ancient times. It has a cosmopolitan distribution. In India, it is prevalent in the Muslim community, as they eat beef.
- It lives with its head embedded in human intestinal mucosa. It is white and semi-transparent, measuring 5–10 metres. It may live up to 10 years.
- Its head is quadrate with suckers situated at four angles of the head and it is not provided with a rostellum. Its neck is narrow, followed by 2000 proglottids. The mature gravid segments are narrower and longer, with the uterus filled with eggs and atrophied reproductive organs. The central longitudinal stem has 15–30 lateral branches. Because of the absence of uterine pores, the eggs are liberated after the rupture of the gravid segment.
- Its eggs are spherical (31–43 µm in diameter.) The egg has a thin outer transparent shell and the inner brown, thick-walled, radially striated embryophore; it contains

an oncosphore (14–20 μm in diameter), with three pairs of hooklets. The oncosphere is infective to humans.

- When cattle (intermediate host) graze the ground polluted with eggs in human feces, they ingest the eggs which hatch out after rupture of the embryophore caused by gastric juices. The oncosphore liberated from the embryophore penetrates the intestinal wall of cattle, reaches the mesenteric venules or lymphatics and is carried to various organs (liver, right side of the heart, lungs, left side of heart, systemic circulation in that order). This naked oncosphore is filtered in the striped muscle, where it transforms into *cysticercus bovis*.
- On ingestion of beef containing cysticercus (called 'measly beef'), human beings (definite hosts) get infected. The larva (cysticercus) develops into adult worm, liberating eggs to repeat its lifecycle.

Taenia solium (Pork tapeworm)

- This 'armed tapeworm' is known since Hippocrates' time, has worldwide distribution, it is not common among Muslims, as they do not eat pork. Its larval infection is common in populations infected with *T. solium*, causing cysticercosis in the brain. It is very similar to *T. saginata*. Its length is 2–7 metres. Its head is small, globular, with rostellum and hooklets. Its proglottid number is under 1000 and expelled in chains of 5–6. Its uterus has 5–10 thick lateral branches on each side. The gravid proglottid is longer than broad.
- Its vaginal sphincter is absent. Its ovaries are two in number with an accessory lobe. Its testes have 150–200 follicles. It lives attached to the human intestinal wall for about 25 years.
- Its lifecycle is similar to that of *T. saginata.* The definite host is human; the intermediate host is the pig. The pork 'measle' or 'measly pork' or 'bladder worm' (cysticercus cellulosae) is an opalescent ovoid body, measuring 10 mm in length and 5 mm in width. It can live for eight months in the flesh of pig and sometimes in humans.
- Clinically, the adult worm produces no serious damage, but it can cause vague abdominal pain, hunger, diarrhea. Less frequently, it causes intestinal obstruction as in *T. saginata*.
- The larva (cysticercus bovis) of *T. saginata* is not found in humans, but the larva (cysticercus celluosae) of *T. solium* is found in humans.
- *Cysticercus cellulosae* produces cysticercosis cellulosae in humans. It is found in every organ and tissue of the body. Finally, in the brain, it develops into visible nodules without any disturbance during its lifetime. As soon as the larva dies, a variety of symptoms develop: epileptiform seizures and fatal outcome. Sometimes human beings may get infected, as in the pig, by ingestion of food or drink contaminated with eggs. Treatment is by specific recent anthelmintic drugs. Prophylaxis is by 1) personal hygiene 2) community sanitation 3) avoiding the ingestion of pork or beef 4) rigid inspection in slaughter houses.

Echinococcus granulosus (dog tapeworm)

- This cestode is also called dog tapeworm. It has been known since ancient times for causing hydatid disease in humans. It is widely distributed. In Punjab (India), dogs (28.8%) and cattle (90%) harbour hydatid cysts.
- The adult worm lives attached to the small intestinal villi of dog. Its larval form develops only in humans (the intermediate host).
- It is a minute (dwarf) worm. It comprises three regions (scolex, neck, strobila), measures 3–6 cm in length, has a pyriform scolex with four suckers and a protrusible rostellum armed with two circular rows of hooklets. Its neck is short. The strobila consists of one immature, one mature and one gravid proglottid. The gravid proglottid is the broadest and longest. Its uterus resembles a loosely twisted coil. Its egg is similar to other Taenia eggs and is infective to humans, cattle and sheep. It contains a hexacath embryo (oncosphere). Its larval form is within the hydatid cyst, developing in the intermediate host. It represents the scolex of the future worm and is invaginated. When ingested by the definite host (dog), the scolex with its four suckers and rostellar hooklets evaginates and develops into an adult worm.
- For perpetuation of the lifecycle, sheep, cattle ingest it while grazing on the ground contaminated with the eggs in dog's feces; humans while playing with dogs ingest the eggs which later hatch out as oncospheres in the duodenum. Oncospheres enter into the intestinal wall and venules, are first filtered in the liver, next in the lungs and then in various organs, hydatid cysts develop in the viscera. These hydatid cysts in cattle, sheep viscera are ingested by the dog; the scolex is evaginated and develops into adult worm, which lays eggs. These eggs are passed out in the dog's feces to repeat the lifecycle.
- The adult worm of *E. granulosus* may not cause much disturbance in the intestine of dog. The damage caused by its hydatid cyst is both toxic and mechanical. The cysts in the vital organs may interfere with the function of the organ, damage the organ and even cause death. The osseous cyst may erode the bony structure. If the cyst increases to a tremendous size it may cause a physical burden to the patient and burst, precipitating an anaphylactic reaction. Cyst in the brain, heart valve may cause death.
- Hydatid fluid is clear, colourless and slightly acidic with low specific gravity, is antigenic and is highly toxic causing anaphylaxis.
- Hydatid sand contains brood capsules, scolices and hooklets and settles in the fluid as granular deposits.
- Diagnosis can be done by Intradermal test or the Casoni's test (routine test), serological and other diagnostic tests (roentgenogram, exploratory cyst puncture).
- Treatment: Although all non-surgical procedures are unsuccessful, Ivermectin injection was found effective on adult *E.granulosus* in dog (Panjarathinam, 2005; is under publication).
- Prophylaxis can be by 1) avoiding infected dogs 2) ingestion of polluted vegetables, drink 3) Personal hygiene 4) Preventing dogs from eating infected carcasses 5) Strict inspection in slaughter houses.

Hymenolepis nana

- Its common name is dwarf tapeworm. The name hymenolepis is derived from Greek, ***hymen***, membrane, and ***lepsis,*** which means shell. Though it is cosmopolitan in its distribution, it is common in India. It remains attached to the villi of the human small intestine and rodents (rats, mice), lives for about two weeks. It is small (25–30 mm in length). Its scolex is minute, globular with four hemispherical suckers with a short retractile rostellum, armed with 20 hooklets in one single row, which can invaginate into the apex. These hooklets are shaped like tuning forks. Its neck is long. Proglottids are about 200 in number. The genital pores are marginal on the same side. Its uterus is transverse and there are three testes.
- Eggs liberated after disintegration of the distal proglottid are spherical and contain an oncosphere enclosed in an inner envelope (embryophore) with two polar thickenings, from which four or more polar filaments arise. The oncosphere contains three pairs of tuning fork-shaped hooklets. The space between the outer and inner envelopes is filled with yolk granules and polar filaments. Its lifecycle requires only one host, no intermediate host is required. It is an exception to the general rule that the helminth does not multiply inside the definite host.
- Humans ingest eggs in human feces. These eggs are hatched out in the intestine; the free oncospheres penetrate villi, transform into cercocysts or cysticercoids, migrate farther down in other villi and transform into adult worms which lay eggs, some eggs are passed out in feces, some restart their lifecycle in the same host. *H. nana* irritates the intestinal mucosa. The absorption of parasitic metabolic wastes by the patient's system may cause generalized toxemia, headache, anorexia, pruritus of nose and anus, diarrhea and abdominal pain.
- Demonstration of eggs with typical polar filaments in the stool is an accurate diagnosis.
- Prophylaxis is similar to that of other cestodes.

Hymenolepis diminuta (rat tapeworm)

- It is mainly the tapeworm of rat. Some human cases have been reported in India. It lives in the intestine of rat for about 13 years and is morphologically similar to *H. nana*. Its eggs are similar to those of *H. nana*, except that they have no polar filaments. Their six lanceolate hooklets are arranged in a fan shape on the oncosphere.
- It requires two hosts: human (definite host), and Xenopsylla cheopis – rat flea (intermediate host). In the intestine of the rat flea, the eggs are hatched out and the free oncospheres penetrate into the hemal cavity and develop into cysticercoid. Accidental ingestion of infected rat flea causes the infection in humans. The cysticercoids liberated from rat flea develop into adult worms. Cachexia is a common symptom. Demonstration of typical eggs and adult worm in the stool is a definite diagnosis. It can be treated by effective drugs. Accidental swallowing of ectoparasites should be avoided.

Dipylidium caninum

- Its common name is double pored dog tapeworm. It is the common tapeworm of dog (Panjarathinam, 1989), it is small. Its scolex is small with four cup-shaped oral suckers. The gravid proglottid is pumpkin-seed shaped, is filled with uterine blocks. Each block contains 8–15 eggs. Eggs are spherical, thin-shelled and hyaline and have delicate hooklets.
- Dog flea (*Ctenocephlaides canis*) ingests eggs deposited on the ground. Dog flea is similar to rat flea. These eggs are hatched in the intestine of the dog, migrate into the hemal cavity and develop into cysticercoid larvae. When these infected fleas are ingested by the definite host, they produce the infection. Clinical manifestations (intestinal disturbance, indigestion, loss of appetite, toxic nervous symptoms) are noticed when the metabolic wastes of the worm are absorbed into the human system. Diagnosis is by the demonstration of characteristic eggs in the mother's capsules.

Treatment by effective drugs

- The disease can be prevented by the destruction of dog flea by insecticides and by avoiding dogs.

QUESTIONS

Q *What is a helminth?*
- Helminth means worm.

Q *What are metazoa?*
- It is a parasite of the subkingdom to which all species of helminths belong.

Q *Classify helminths?*
- Helminths are Platyhelminths (cestodes, trematoda), Nemathelminths (Nematoda).

Q *Define Cestodes?*
- Cestodes are long, dorso-ventrally flattened, segmented and tape-like; they are also known as 'tapeworm'.

Q *What is the meaning of the following: scolex, strobila, proglottid, sucker, hook, hermaphrodite?*
- Scolex – head; strobila – body or trunk; proglottid – segment; sucker – slit-like, cup-like depression or groove; hook – organ of attachment, hermaphrodite – sexes are not separate, bothria - groove.

Q *How many types of cestodes are known?*
- There are two types of Cestodes. 1. Pseudophyllidean 2. Cyclophyllidean cestodes.

Q *What is coracidium, procercoid, plerocercoid?*
- Coracidium – first stage larva of *diphyllobothrum talum* or ciliated embryo liberated from operculated egg in the water. Procercoid is second stage larva in Cyclops. Plerocercoid – third stage larva in fish flesh, this third stage larva is also called sparganum, which is infective to humans.

Diphyllobothrium latum

Q *What is the common name of D. latum?*

▶ The common name *D. latum* is broad fish tapeworm.

Q *Why is it called Diphyllobothrium?*

▶ It is called Diphyllobothrium because it has a bothrium on both surfaces.

Q *What is the shape of its scolex?*

▶ It is spoon-shaped.

Q *How are its eggs discharged?*

▶ Its eggs are discharged through the uterine pore.

Q *How many eggs can a single worm discharge?*

▶ It may discharge about one million eggs per day.

Q *How can you diagnose in the laboratory?*

▶ By direct demonstration of operculated egg.

Q *How is a pathogenic effect produced?*

▶ The pathogenic effect is due to the absorption of parasite waste products.

Q *How is pernicious anemia caused?*

▶ Pernicious anemia is due to deprivation of the host of essential nutritional compounds. Thus *D. latum* contains a large amount of Vitamin B_{12}.

Q *What are the clinical symptoms?*

▶ Clinical vitamin B_{12} deficiency develops if the adult worms are attached to the jejunum, adult worms in the intestine may cause no symptom.

Q *How will you treat pernicious anemia associated with D. latum.?*

▶ It can be treated by folic acid administration.

Taenia saginata

Q *What is the common name of T. saginata?*

▶ It is called beef tapeworm or unarmed tapeworm.

Q *Why it is called beef tapeworm or unarmed tapeworm.*

▶ Since its larva is lodged in the beef and since its scolex is not provided with a rostellum.

Q *Why is T. saginata very common among Muslims in India?*

▶ It is common because Indian muslims consume beef.

Q *For how many years can the adult worm live?*

▶ It may live for 10 years.

Q *How many gravid proglottids does it give rise to and how is it expelled?*

▶ It may range to 2000 and is expelled singly at a time.

Q *Since it has no rostellum how does it get attached to the intestine?*

▶ It gets attached to the intestine with the suckers.

Q *Why are its eggs liberated after rupture of gravid segment?*
▶ They are liberated because of the absence of a uterine pore.

Q *For how many weeks do their eggs remain viable?*
▶ They remain viable for eight weeks.

Q *Why is hatching of their eggs necessary?*
▶ Hatching is necessary to liberate oncospheres.

Q *What is the function of oncosphere?*
▶ It is infective to cattle and is carried through the circulation to various organs and transforms into *Cysticercus bovis* in the beef.

Q *For how many months can this cysticercus live?*
▶ Cysticercus can live for eight months in the muscle of cattle.

Q *What is 'measly beef'?*
▶ Beef containing the cysticercus is called 'measly beef' and it can become infective to humans.

Taenia solium

Q *What is the common name of T. solium?*
▶ Its common name is 'pork tapeworm' or 'armed tapeworm'.

Q *Why it is called 'pork tapeworm' or 'armed tapeworm'.*
▶ 1. Since its larva is found in pork it is called pork tapeworm

2. Since its scolex is armed with a double row of large and small hooklets.

Q *What is the shape of the hooklet?*
▶ The hooklet is dagger shaped.

Q *Why is T. solium rare in the Muslim community?*
▶ It is rare among Muslims as they do not eat pork.

Q *How many proglottids are produced and expelled at a time?*
▶ It produces 100 and it is expelled in chains of 5–6 at a time.

Q *How many lateral branches are present on each side of a median longitudinal stem of the gravid uterus of 1) T. solium and 2) T. saginata?*
▶ 1) There are 5–10 thick lateral branches in *T. solium.* 2) There are 15–30 thin lateral branches.

Q *What is a measle?*
▶ It is a bladder worm found in muscle. If it is found in beef, it is called 'measly beef' (*Cysticercus bovis*); if it is found in pork it is called 'measly pork' or bladder worm (*Cysticercus cellulosae*)

Q *Is intestinal obstruction by T. solium frequent?*
▶ Intestinal obstruction is less frequent, but it may cause a lot of irritation, when compared to *T. saginata* which causes a considerable disturbance because of its large size.

Q *What are the symptoms of T. solium?*
▸ *T. solium* produces no serious damage, but it causes vague abdominal discomfort, hunger, pain, diarrhea, sometimes appendicitis.

Q *Which Cysticercus is found in humans?*
▸ *Cysticercus cellulosae* is found in humans, but *Cysticercus bovis* of *T. saginata* is not found in humans.

Q *When do brain symptoms develop in cysticercosis, caused by Cysticercus cellulosae in humans?*
▸ As soon as the larva (*Cysticercus cellulosae*) dies, tissue reaction begins around the dead larva and symptoms develop.

Q *What are the brain symptoms?*
▸ Symptoms like epileptiform seizures are common and may produce fatal outcome.

Q *How does auto-infection take place in humans?*
▸ Auto-infection may occur in humans harbouring an adult worm and is due to the gravid segments being thrown back into the stomach by the reversal peristaltic movement of the intestine.

Echinococcus granulosus

Q *What is the common name of E. granulosus?*
▸ Its common name is dog tapeworm.

Q *Where was it reported in animals in India?*
▸ It was reported in Punjab.

Q *What is the name of the disease caused by E. granulosus?*
▸ It is a hydatid disease.

Q *Name a minute tapeworm.*
▸ *E. granulosus* is minute like a grain.

Q *What type of rostellum does this tapeworm have?*
▸ It has a protrusible rostellum.

Q *Name a tapeworm with a strobila consisting of only three segments?*
▸ It is *E. granulosus.*

Q *Why is E. granulosus the smallest tapeworm?*
▸ It is smallest because of its minimum number of three segments.

Q *What is the function of larval form of E. granulosus found within the hydatid cyst?*
▸ It represents the scolex of the future worm and is invaginated into its own body to protect its rostallar hooklets.

Q *What is hydatid cyst?*
▸ It is a cystic cavity formed by the developing oncosphere in the viscera, it may transform into a bladder worm ('hydatis' meaning a 'drop of water'.)

Q *What is hydatid sand?*

▶ Free brood capsules and free scolices set free in the fluid of cystic cavity are called hydatid sand.

Q *What is acephlocyst?*

▶ The cyst which produces brood capsules alone never produces scolices.

Q *What are the pathological effects produced by hydatid cyst?*

▶ The young cyst lodged in the vital centers may interfere with the function of the organs and even cause death. The cyst may grow a tremendous size, may become a physiological burden and burst, causing an anaphylactic reaction. Osseous cyst may erode the bone with multiple fracture. Thus, hydatid cyst may cause both mechanical and toxic damage, it may damage even the brain and heart valve.

Q *When and where were 400 hydatid cysts removed surgically from the brain of a 21-year-old patient?*

▶ The cysts were removed from the patient on 26/6/2006 at Mumbai (India)

Hymenolepis nana

Q *What is the common name for H. nana?*

▶ It is also called dwarf tapeworm.

Q *Is it common in India?*

▶ It is common in India.

Q *How are its eggs set free?*

▶ Its eggs are set free due to disintegration of the proglottid.

Q *What are the characteristics of its egg?*

▶ It is spherical, its oncosphere is enclosed by an embryophore with two polar thickenings; from each arise 4–8 polar filaments. Within the oncosphere there are three pairs of tuning fork-shaped hooklets.

Q *Name the tapeworm which liberates eggs containing oncospheres with tuning fork-shaped hooklets.*

▶ Only *H. nana* can liberate such an egg with tuning fork-shaped hooklets.

Q *The oncosphere of which metamorphoses into young cercocysts or cysticercoids?*

▶ Oncospheres of *H. nana* transform into cysticercoids after penetrating into the villi of the small intestine.

Q *Cite a tapeworm which does not utilize an intermediate host?*

▶ *H. nana* has no intermediate host.

Hymenolepis diminuta (rat tapeworm)

Q *Cite another species of Hymenolepis having an intermediate host.*

▶ *H. diminuta* has an intermediate host (Xenospsylla cheopis).

Q *What is its common symptom?*
▶ Cachexia is a common symption.

Dipylidium caninum

Q *What is the common name of D. caninum tapeworm?*
▶ It is called double-pored dog tapeworm.

Q *Who reported this tapeworm in dog in India.*
▶ Panjarathinam reported this tapeworm in dog in India.

Q *How are the eggs of this tapeworm passed out in feces?*
▶ Groups of eggs within the mother embryonic membrane are passed out in feces.

Q *How is a pathogenic effect produced?*
▶ It is produced by the absorption of the metabolic wastes of the worm.

Q *What are its clinical manifestations?*
▶ Intestinal disturbance, indigestion, loss of appetite, toxic nervous symptoms.

First Report of Cestoda

D. latum – Linnaeus (1758)

T. saginata – (1782)

E. granulosus – Hippocrates and Galen in ancient times.

H. nana – Bilharz (1851)

D. caninum – Linnaeus (1758)

H. diminuta – Rudolphi (1819)

Tapeworm (natural size)

Scolex of *Taenia saginata*

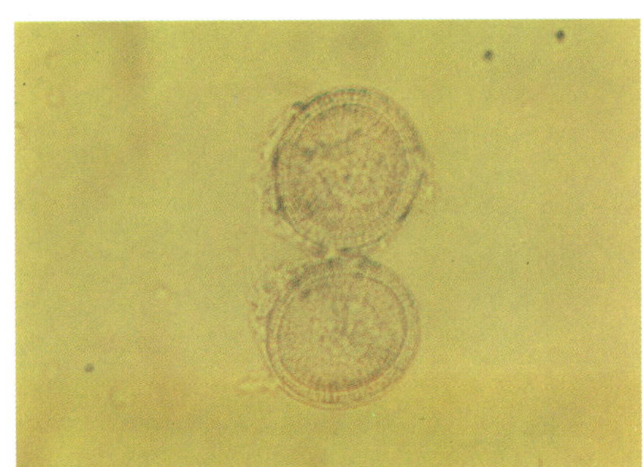

Egg of Taenia

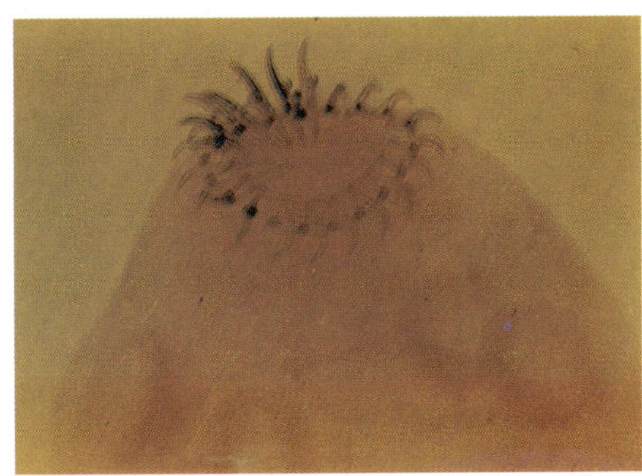

Scolex of *T. solium*

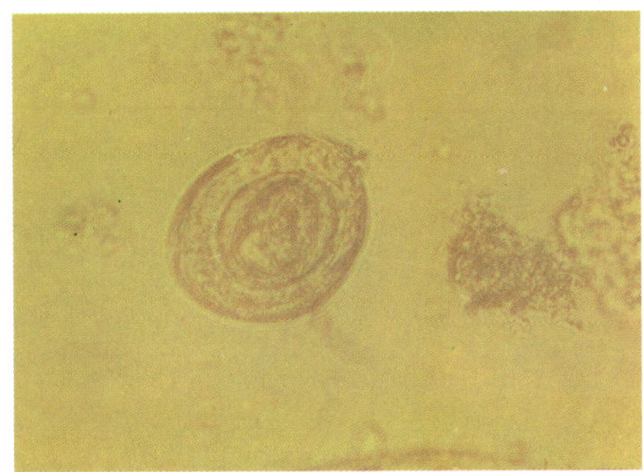

Egg of *H. nana*

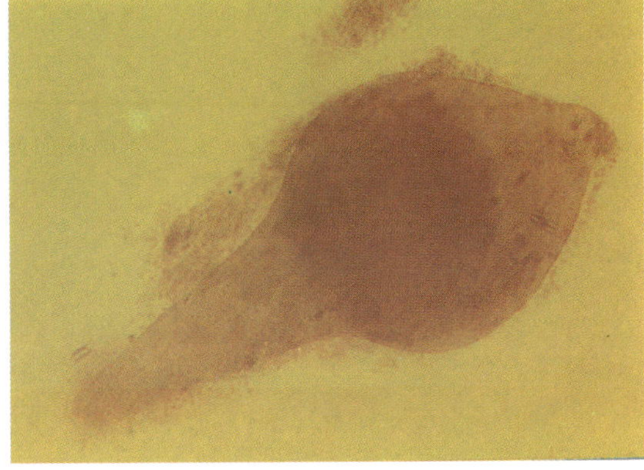

Cystercercoid of *H. nana*

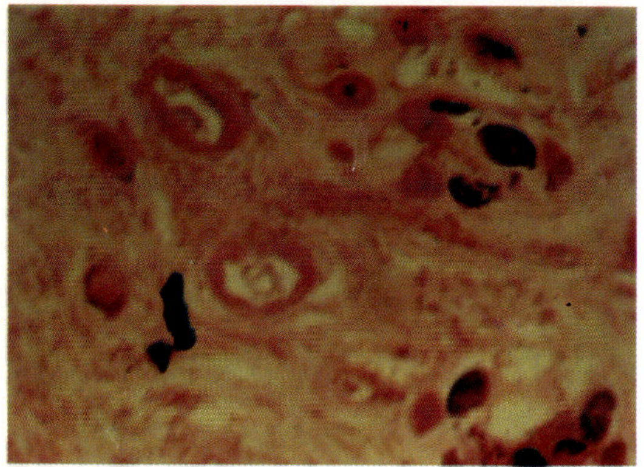

Mature egg of *S. haematobium*

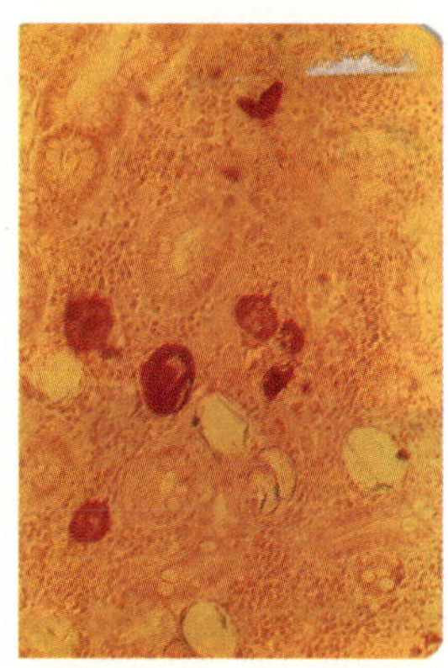

Mature egg of *S. japonium*

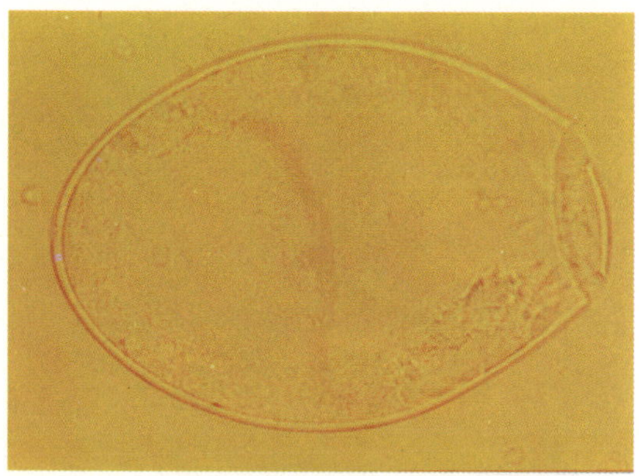

Mature egg of *F. hepatica*

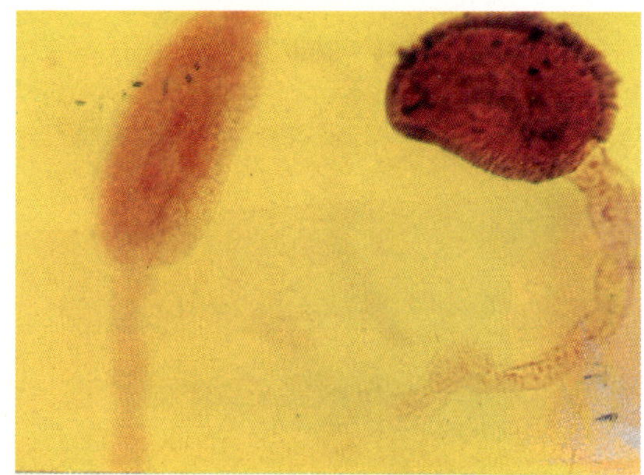

Cercaria of *F. hepatica*

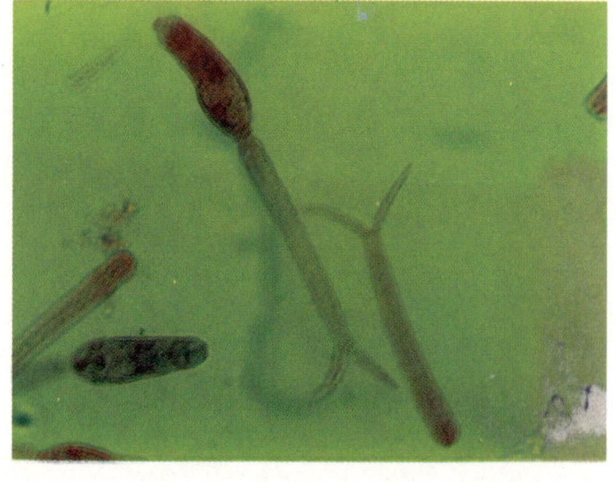

Cercaria of schistosoma with bifid tail

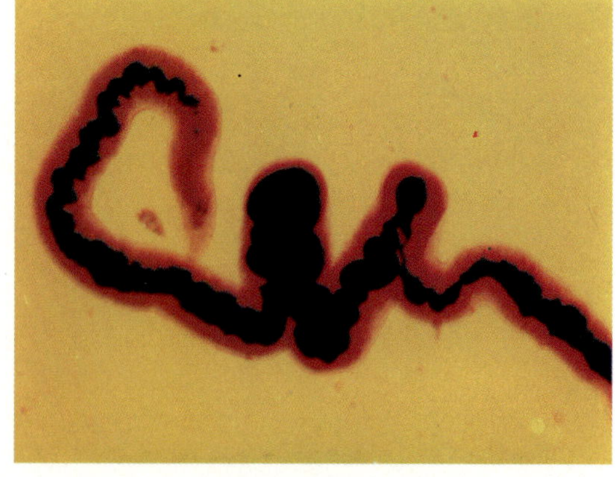

Female schistosoma

7 CLASS TREMATODA

The name Trematoda is derived from the Greek ***trematos***, which means 'pierced with holes.' Trematoda is a flatworm with suckers.

Trematodes are unsegmented, dorsoventrally flattened or leaf-shaped; hence they are called 'flukes'. Their size is variable (from one mm to several centimetres in length). The largest human trematode is *Fasciolopsis buski*. Trematodes have two suckers (ventral and oral), which are cup-like structures acting as organs of attachment.

Trematodes are generally hermaphrodites (sexes are not separate), except in Schistosoma.

They have no body cavity, an incomplete alimentary canal, a complete and highly developed reproductive, as well as excretory and nervous system. They are oviparous (lay eggs) and their eggs are operculated (except those of Schistosoma) and do not float in a saturated solution of common salt.

Trematodes have complex lifecycles, involving one or more intermediate hosts.

Trematodes have been classified according to their habitats:

1. Blood trematode:
   a) *Schistosoma haematobium* in the vesical venous plexus
   b) *S. mansoni* in the rectal venous plexus and
   c) *S. japonicum* in the portal venous system
2 Hepatic trematode *(Fasciola hepatica, Clonorchis sinensis)*
3. Intestinal trematode *(Fasciolopsis buski)* and
4. Lung trematode *(Paragonimus westermani).*

SCHISTOSOMA HAEMATOBIUM

Family: Schistosomatidae

Genus: Schistosoma

Schistosoma haematobium, the vesicle blood fluke causing schistosomiasis hematobia, vesicle schistosomiasis, urinary bilharziasis and schistosomal hematuria, was first recovered by

Bilharz (1851), from the mesenteric veins of a native of Cairo, Egypt, and was demonstrated by him to be the cause of hematuria. It is found widely distributed in Africa, Egypt and Tanzania. In 1952, an autochthonous (cases contracted locally) focus was identified by Gadgil and Shah in Ratnagiri district, about 140 miles from Mumbai, India. The eggs of *Schistosoma nasalis* (animal trematode) were found in the nasal washing of the nasal granuloma of cattle for the first time, in Pondicherry, in 1972, by the author.

Morphology The adult worms of *Schistosoma haematobium* live in the vesicle and pelvic plexuses of the venous circulation. The ***male*** adult worm is a shorter, stouter organism, measuring 10–15 mm in length and 0.8–1 mm in breadth. It is covered with minute integumentary tuberculation and has two muscular suckers, of which the ventral sucker is larger. Behind the ventral sucker, the body of the male is folded all the way to the caudal extremity to form the ***gynecophoric canal***, in which the female is held during copulation and oviposition. There is a bulbous cluster of glands around the esophagus. The paired caeca fuse to form a single trunk, which ends blindly near the caudal extremity. The testes are behind the ventral sucker. The ***female*** is long and slender, measuring about 20 × 0.25 mm. The suckers are small and are not muscular. Tuberculation is confined to the extremities of the worm. The digestive tract is similar to that of the male (Fig. 7.1).

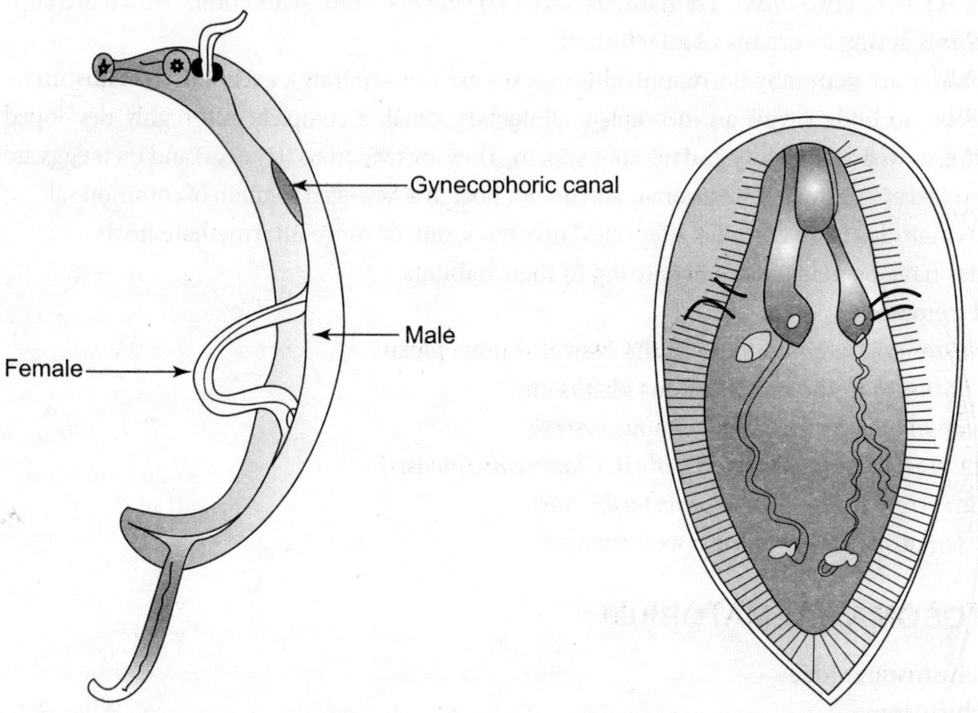

Fig. 7.1 Female *S. haematobium* in the gynecophoric canal of the male.

Fig. 7.2 Mature egg of *S. haematobium* with fully embryonated miracidium.

Egg: The egg measures 112–170 μm long and 40–70 μm wide, and possesses a distinct terminal spine. The egg shell is transparent and light yellowish brown (Fig. 7.2). Every time an infected person urinates, he releases 40,000 eggs.

Lifecycle *Schistosoma haematobium* passes its lifecycle in two hosts:

1. ***Definite host*** – human, and
2. ***Intermediate host*** – freshwater snail, particularly, *Ferrissia tenuis* in India.

The eggs are discharged in the urine of the infected person, usually towards the end of micturition. When these eggs are discharged in the water, the ciliated larvae (***miracidium***, the first larval stage) hatch out. These ciliated larvae swim in search of a suitable intermediate host (snail). On contact with the appropriate species, they infect the snails by penetrating their soft tissues and ultimately reach the liver and other organs, where they lose their cilia. In the course of eight weeks, they develop into the first and second generation of ***sporocysts*** (second larval stage) and finally, a generation of fork-tailed cercariae (Fig. 7.3), which break out of the snail and are viable for a period of 10–25 days.

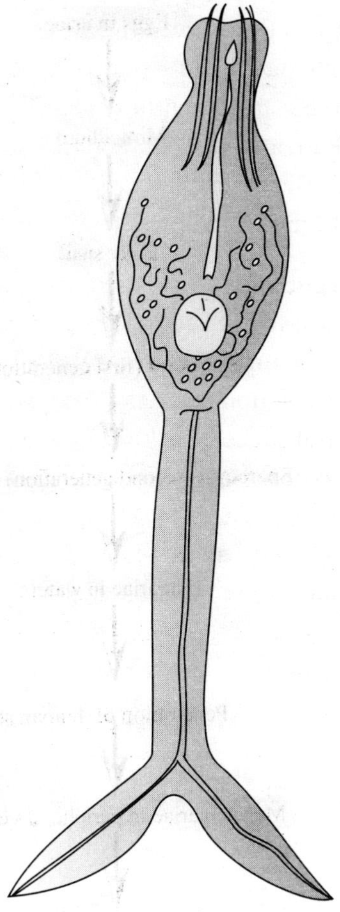
Fig. 7.3 Cercaria (enlarged).

When human beings bathe or wade in cercariae-infested water, the cercariae come in contact with the human skin. As the water on the skin evaporates, they enter the skin, casting off their tails (cercariae without tails are called metacercariae or ***schistosomules***). They achieve this with the help of the digestive action of the secretions of the penetration gland in less than 30 minutes. The metacercariae (infective to humans) enter the peripheral venules, are transported to the right part of the heart, pass into the pulmonary capillaries and are carried through the left part of the heart into the systemic circulation. The majority of them are shunted into the abdominal aorta, gain access to the mesenteric artery, pass through the mesenteric capillaries and enter the portal circulation.

In the intrahepatic portal vessels, the larvae begin to feed and grow, become sexually differentiated in about 20 days after skin penetration, and migrate against the bloodstream. They pass through the inferior mesenteric veins, rectal venous plexuses and pelvic veins and at last, enter the vesical plexus of veins, within three months after the initial exposure of the skin.

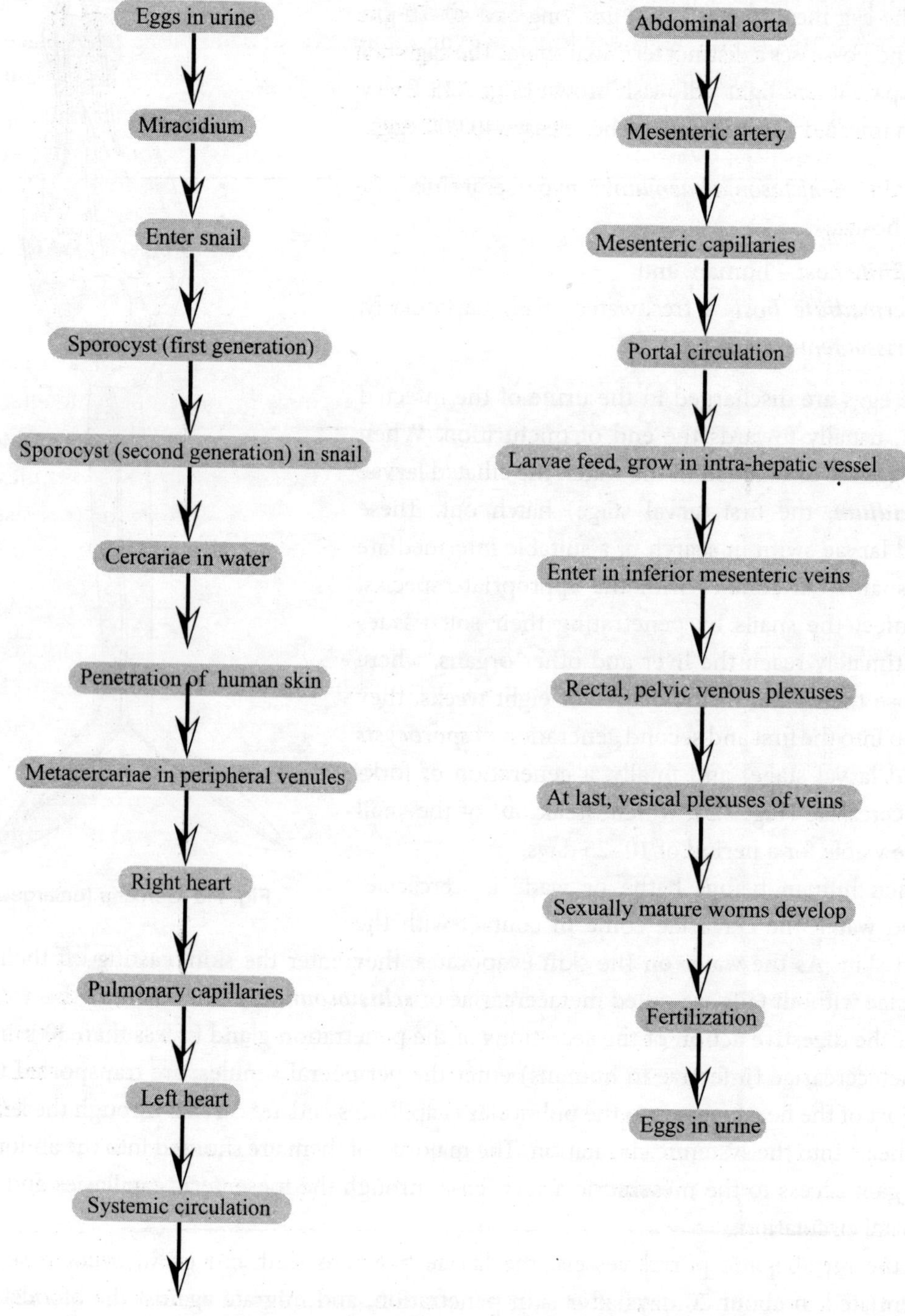

Fig. 7.4 Lifecycle of *Schistosoma haematobium.*

Upon arrival in the vesical venules (site of predilection), the worms become sexually mature. The male worm holds the female within the gynecophoric canal and mating takes place. The female begins to lay eggs in quick succession in the smallest venules by extending its anterior end. The venules are thus filled with eggs, which are held in position by their terminal spines. Because of the contraction of vessels, the eggs work their way through the vessels and the mucosa of the urinary bladder, enter the cavity and are excreted in urine (Figs 7.4 and 7.5).

Pathogenesis During the period of development, the metabolites of *Schistosoma haematobium* are discharged and provoke an allergic reaction in the patient. In vesical schistosomiasis, the damage occurs in the wall of the urinary bladder due to the escaping of the eggs. Infiltration of eggs into the tissues may lead to fibrosis with resultant miliary pseudo-tubercle formation. This eventually causes fibrosis of the entire organ. Pathogenic effects of *Schistosoma haematobium* consist of 1. generalized and localized reaction to metabolites of growing and mature worms 2. trauma with hemorrhage as eggs escape from the venules and 3. pseudo-abscess and pseudo-tubercle formation around the eggs lodged in the perivascular tissues.

Clinical features The incubation period is about 10–12 weeks. The earliest manifestations are irritation and minute hemorrhages at the site of entry on the skin. There is a gradual onset of toxic symptoms, consisting of anorexia, headache, malaise, generalized pain in the back and the limbs and fever, followed by rigors and night sweating. There is pronounced urticaria, at first on the limbs, later more generalized in distribution. The abdomen may be enlarged and tender, the liver and spleen may be hypertrophic and there may be difficulty in breathing. After several months, there is painless passage of small volumes of blood at the end of micturition – ***hematuria.*** There is a burning sensation and increased frequency of micturition.

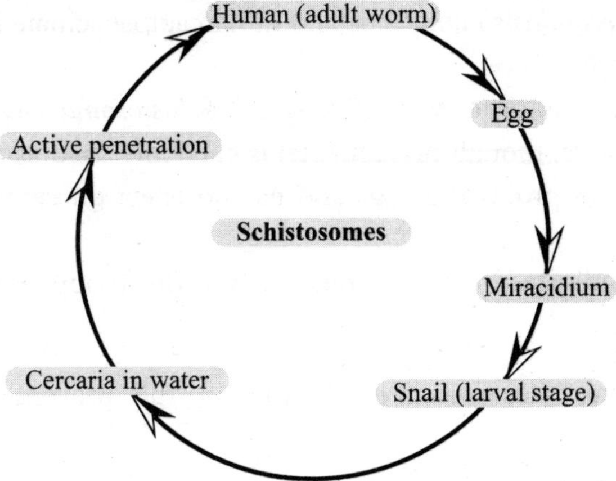

Fig 7.5 Lifecycle of *Schistosomes.*

Most of the pathologic changes in infected individuals are seen in the bladder wall and the lower end of the ureters. In the urinary bladder, the formation of egg granulomas leads to hyperemia, tubercle, ulcers and polyps. Other urinary tract lesions (urinary calculi and bladder cancer) are associated with *S. hametobium* infection. Swimmer's itch and acute schistosomiais are rarely described in *S. hametobium* infection. In endemic areas, 50 to 60% of infected subjects complain of dysuria, hematuria or frequency of urination. Hematuria is characteristically terminal, but with extensive ulceration, the whole stream of urine may be bloody with the passage of clots. In late cases, symptoms related to secondary infection of urinary tract, severe obstructive uropathy or neoplasia may occur. Cystoscopic examinations show some degree of pathology (being hyperemic near the urethral opening). Radiologically, bladder calcification is a characteristic feature of urinary schistosomiasis. Once *S. haematobium* is established, assessment of urinary tract pathology by ultrasonography is recommended.

Laboratory diagnosis

Specific diagnosis can be made by

1. Microscopic demonstration of terminal spined eggs in the centrifuged deposit of urine and
2. Examining under the microscope, a piece of biopsied vesical mucosa, obtained through a cystoscope, by compressing it between two slides and locating the eggs.

Serological tests: Fairley's complement fixation test, in which antigens from cercariae and adult worms are used, gives group-specific reaction and is sensitive in detecting acute infection.

The intradermal, precipitin, hemagglutination and bentonite flocculation tests are all group-specific for schistosomal infection. The precipitin test is more sensitive in chronic than in acute infection. Recent ELISA tests can also be used for the diagnosis of schistosomiasis.

Treatment Specific chemotherapeutic agents are potassium antimony tartarate or sodium antimony tartarate. Among trivalent antimony compounds, stibophen is better tolerated, but is less efficacious for *Schistosomiasis hematobia* and dimercaptosuccinate has high cure rates. Miracil D has a 55% cure rate.

Niridazole and TAC pomoate are fairly effective against *Schistosoma haematobium*. Recently, Mebendazole is found effective, though praziquantel is currently used as a chemotherapeutic agent against *S. haematobium* producing eggs and has no effect on cercarial penetration in swimmer's itch.

Successful treatment is indicated by the demonstration of the disappearance of eggs in urine and the absence of hematuria.

Prophylaxis The following measures are effective in the prevention of *Schistosoma haematobium* infection:

1. Eradication of snails by molluscicides
2. Sanitary improvement of the environment

3. Prevention of pollution of water by infected persons
4. Avoiding swimming or wading in polluted water and
5. Proper disposal of human excreta.

Schistosomal cercarial dermatitis There are three types of cercarial dermatitis (swimmer's itch, cercarial itch):

1. ***Schistosome dermatitis Type I:*** It is caused by *Trichobilharzia ocellata,* a non-human schistosome which develops in the snail, *Lymnaea.* It is prevalent in the USA (Oregon, Washington, California), Canada, Germany, Switzerland, France, Burma and India.
   As the water evaporates from the skin, a prickling sensation is experienced, followed by urticarial wheals. After half an hour, the initial dermatitis subsides, leaving only a few macules. Several hours later, intense itching of the area develops with edema and the papules transform into pustules.
2. ***Schistosome dermatitis Type II*** is caused by the cercariae of the avian species of blood flukes, particularly *Trichobilharzia.*
3. ***Schistosome dermatitis Type III*** results from penetration into the human skin by cercariae of the mammalian species of the blood fluke, *Schistosoma spindalis.* It has been reported in paddy field workers in Malaysia and Thailand. Trimeprazine is given orally for treatment.

SCHISTOSOMA MANSONI

Schistosoma mansoni or Manson's blood fluke produces schistosomiasis mansoni or Manson's intestinal schistosomiasis, often called bilharziasis. Bilharz first observed lateral spined eggs in female schistosoma recovered from a patient in Cairo, Egypt. *Schistosoma mansoni* is common in the Nile delta, Sudan, the East African coast and in the United States (New York).

Adult worms of *Schistosoma mansoni* are mostly found in the mesenteric veins of the sigmoid-rectal area and live for 26 years. *S. mansoni* can be kept in the laboratory for research purposes.

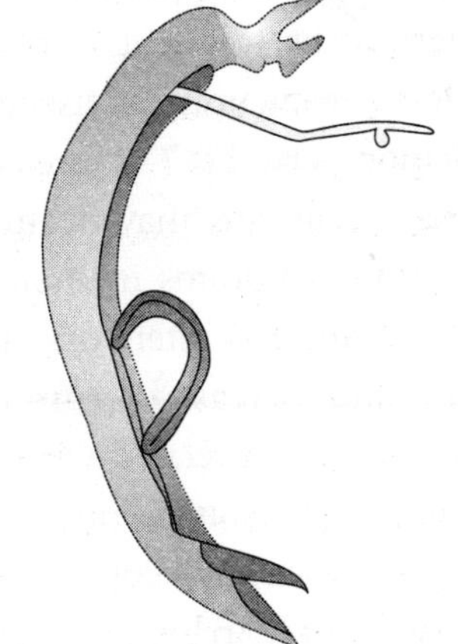

Fig 7.6 Male and female *S.mansoni.*

Morphology Adult worms (Fig. 7.6) resemble those of S. *haematobium,* but both the male (6.4–12 mm long) and the female (7.2–17 mm long) S. *mansoni* are smaller. The integumentary tuberculations of the male *S. mansoni* are also more conspicuous and have 6–9 testes. In the female, the ovary is situated at the anterior half of the body. The uterus is short and contains only a few lateral spined eggs.

The eggs have a yellowish-brown transparent shell, a characteristic lateral spine and measure 114–175 μm in length and 45–68 μm in diameter (Fig. 7.7).

The miracidium is larger than that of *S. japonicum* and *S. haematobium* and has larger anterior penetration glands and its lifecycle in the snail is similar to that of *S. japonicum* and *S. haematobium.*

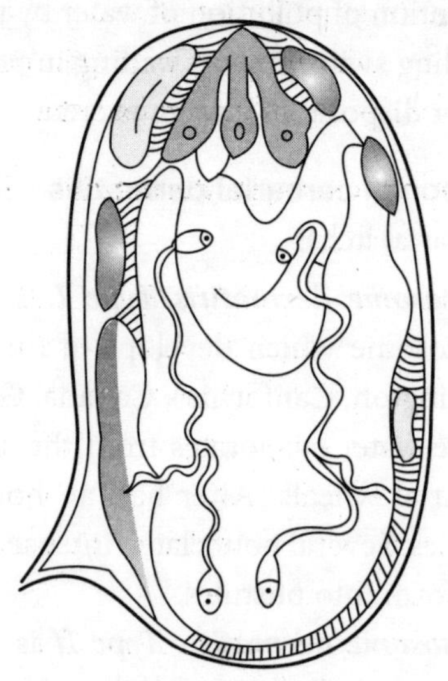

Fig. 7.7 Mature egg of *S. mansoni.*

Lifecycle It parallels that of *S. haematobium.* The definite host is a human; the intermediate host is the fresh water snail, *Biomphalaria glabrata,* in America.

Pathogenicity The lesions produced by *S. mansoni* are similar to those of *S. haematobium* and *S. japonicum* infection, except that the production of granuloma around the eggs in the tissues is delayed, because of the smaller number of eggs produced by *S. mansoni.* The colon and rectum are mostly involved. In the liver, there are pathological changes like hepatic cirrhosis. A living immature male *S. mansoni* has been recovered from the anterior chamber of the right eye of a patient.

Clinical features Initially, there is papular rash with pruritus over the skin of the feet. The liver is enlarged and tender, and there is accompanying fever. In classical schistosomiasis, dysentery is characterized by frequent stools with lateral spined eggs and abdominal pain. Dysentery becomes less conspicuous, as tissue reaction takes place around the eggs in the intestinal wall. The incubation period is 7–8 weeks.

Cercarial dermatitis may occur, following skin penetration by the larvae of *S. mansoni.* The presenting symptoms in their order of occurrence are fever, anorexia, abdominal pain and headache, and less often, diarrhea, nausea and vomiting may occur. Hepatosplenomegaly, eosinophilia and increased serum immunoglobulin are the main clinical signs. Most of these manifestations are correlated with the intensity of infection. Nervous system involvement in schistosomiasis mansoni is rare. The underlying pathologic lesions are usually granuloma-forming eggs in the spinal cord. Other frequent nonspecific symptoms and signs are weakness, inability to work or diarrhea. Enlargement of liver usually occurs in the left lobe. Simultaneously, gross enlargement of the spleen may occur, the organ is characteristically rubbery and hard. An association between schistosomal hepatosplenomegaly and hepatitis B antigen and antibody presence has been described.

Laboratory diagnosis

1. Diagnosis is readily accomplished by the recovery of the characteristic lateral spined eggs in the stool, which can be seen under the microscope. There were no significant differences between the two-egg counting techniques (Teesdale glass sandwich and the Kato Katz technique), for the diagnosis of *S. mansoni.*
2. Microscopical examination of the rectal tissue obtained by rectal biopsy is done as in *Schistosoma haematobium.*
3. Serological tests include complement fixation and slide flocculation tests which are satisfactory and far superior to the intradermal test. In India, ELISA with *S. mansoni* and *S. haematobium* antigens is used for the diagnosis of schistosomiasis, even for infections of low intensity. Counter immunoelectrophoresis (CIEP) test can be used for rapid and specific diagnosis of acute fascioliasis and schistosomiasis. This test is able to identify a mixed infection of *Fasciola hepatica* and *S. mansoni* which did not become positive for schistosomiasis by stool examination, until the fourth week after infection.
4. Blood examination in the early stage reveals leucocytosis with marked eosinophilia. Moderate leucopenia and macrocytosis may develop later.

Treatment The only effective old drug is potassium antimony tartarate or sodium antimony tartarate. Niridazole is most effective. Recently, mebendazole has been found to affect *S. mansoni,* though Praziquantel is the current anthelmintic that is prescribed.

Prophylaxis

Prophylaxis is similar to that of *S. haematobium.* Sodium pentochlorophenate has been used with considerable success to control snails.

Patients should be treated with tartaremetic.

Construction of public baths, laundry tanks and sanitary drainage canals can control the infection. Disinfection of night soil with ammonium nitrate before it is used as fertilizer in the field may kill the eggs.

SCHISTOSOMA JAPONICUM

Schistosoma japonicum, the Oriental blood fluke, produces schistosomiasis japonica or Oriental schistosomiasis. This disease was first mentioned by Fuji, a Japanese physician, in 1847; Fuginami (1904) first found the female worm in the portal vein and Katsurada (1904) described the adult worm from infected dogs and cats. This infection is confined to areas such as Japan, China and the Philippines.

Adult worms of *Schistosoma japonicum* mostly inhabit the radicles of the superior mesenteric veins, draining the ileo-cecal region.

Morphology The adult worm of *S. japonicum* resembles *S. haematobium* and *S. mansoni,* but lacks integumentary tuberculations. The male worm measures 12–20 mm in length and

0.5–0.55 mm in diameter. There are seven testes. The female averages 26 mm in length and 0.3 mm in diameter. The ovary lies behind the mid-plane of the body. The uterus is a long straight tube which can contain 50 eggs at a time (Fig. 7.9).

Egg: The egg measures 70–100 μm by 50–65 μm. It is hyaline, oval or biconvex and has an abbreviated spine on the upper right border of the shell (Fig. 7.10).

Lifecycle It is similar to that of S. *mansoni* and S. *haematobium* and takes place in two hosts:

1. ***Definite host:*** human, cat, dog, pig or cattle, and
2. ***Intermediate host***: freshwater snail of the genus *Oncomelania.*

Eggs which are excreted in the feces require only the dilution of the feces in the water to hatch, allowing the miracidium to escape from the egg and to swim in the water. This miracidium is smaller in size, but similar to that of *S. haematobium* and *S. mansoni.* It enters the soft tissues of the snail *(Oncomelania quadrasi* in the Phillipines) and produces the first and second generation of sporocysts, and then the fork-tailed cercariae.

On contact with human or animal skin, the cercariae cast off their tails, penetrate the skin and enter the venous circulation. They are carried

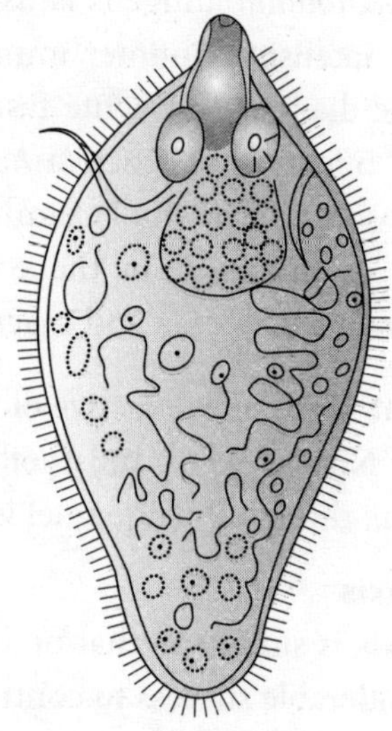

Fig. 7.8 Miracidium.

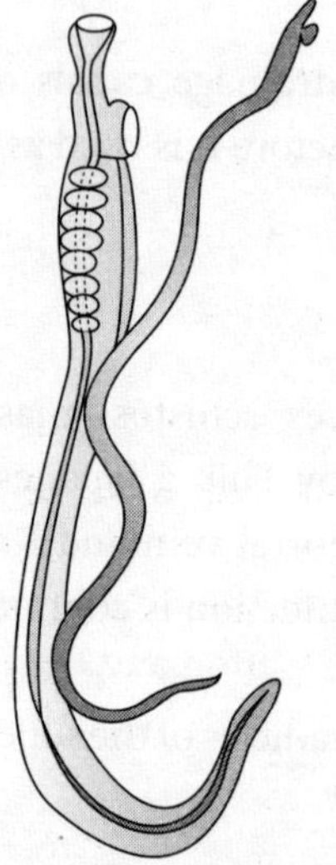

Fig. 7.9 Male and female of S. *japonicum*.

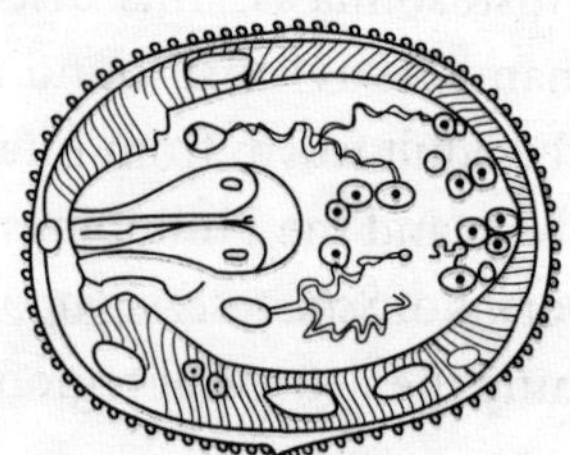

Fig. 7.10 Mature egg of S. *japonicum*.

through the right part of the heart to the lungs, and through the pulmonary capillaries, they are carried through the left part of the heart into the systemic circulation. On reaching the intrahepatic portal circulation, they feed, grow and migrate into the superior mesenteric venules. There, the adult worms mate and the females lay eggs which are passed out with the feces.

Pathogenicity *S. japonicum* produces lesions which are similar to those produced by *S. mansoni* and *S. haematobium*. The intestinal tract and liver are mostly involved. The pseudo-tubercles around the eggs produce fibrosis and papillomatous growths. The intestinal and hepatic schistosomiasis of the Orient is also called 'Katayama disease'.

Clinical features The manifestations include dysentery, hepatic cirrhosis, splenomegaly, appendicitis, intestinal obstruction, pneumonitis, cerebral syndrome and intoxication. Urticarial rashes, accompanied by fever, may develop into characteristic wheals of varying sizes in the skin.

Cercarial dermatitis is not a prominent feature of *S. japonicum* infection. Katayama fever, or acute schistosomiasis, was named after a district in Japan, endemic for *S. japonicum* infection. Symptoms usually begin 5–7 weeks after infection and are similar to those associated with schistosomiasis mansoni. The clinical features subside in a few days, but the infection may last for several months and have been so reported. The chronic manifestations of schistosomiasis japonicum are related to ova deposited in the intestine and liver. Adult worms produce ten times more eggs than those of *S. mansoni*. Schistosomiasis japonicum granulomas vary tremendously in size and tend to show signs of necrosis. Acute schistosomiasis japonicum has disappeared in Japan, but patients with the chronic stage of the disease are still alive in the previously endemic areas of Japan and develop hepatocellular carcinoma, associated with hepatitis C virus infection.

The major pathologic lesions in *S. japonicum* are seen in infected, rather than in uninfected individuals. The most frequent manifestation of cerebral schistosomiasis japonica is focal Jacksonian epilepsy. *S. mekong* is the most recent schistosoma species that has been described to infect and cause disease in humans and it is endemic in some parts of South East Asia. Their eggs are similar to those of *S. japonicum*. Symptoms are also similar to those of *S. japonicum*; they include abdominal pain, diarrhea and hepatosplenomegaly. Diagnosis is established by fecal examination for parasitic ova.

Laboratory diagnosis Specific diagnosis rests on the recovery of characteristic eggs from the stools. The eggs can be demonstrated in proctoscopic aspiration and biopsy.

Complement fixation and slide flocculation tests along with the clinical history will support the diagnosis.

Treatment Potassium antimony tartarate or sodium antimony tartarate is the most effective drug. Fuadin and anthiomaline have proved to be as effective.

Praziquantel (current anthelmintic) treatment can be repeated weekly for up to three weeks in the treatment of intestinal schistosomiasis. It has marked antiparasitic activity with low toxicity, and side effects are usually mild, rare and self-limiting; side effects include abdominal pain, headache, dizziness and skin rashes. Metrifonate and oxamniquine are two additional antischistosomial chemotherapeutic agents and have therapeutic efficiency similar to praziquantel.

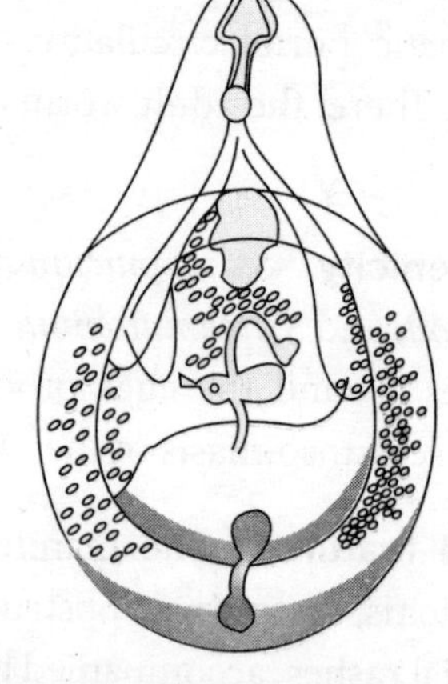

Fig. 7.11 Adult worm of G. *hominis.*

Prophylaxis This consists of the following measures:

1. Proper disposal of night soil
2. Treatment of night soil with ammonium nitrate to kill eggs before it is used as fertilizer
3. Destruction of snails by molluscicides
4. Avoiding bathing and wading through polluted water
5. In the Philippines, cats, pigs, dogs, water buffaloes and wild rats are commonly infected. These reservoir hosts constitute an important handicap to the control of *Schistosomiasis japonicum.*

GASTRODISCOIDES HOMINIS

Family: Gastrodiscidae
Genus: Gastrodiscoides

Gastrodiscoides hominis was first discovered and described by Lewis and McConnell in 1876 from the cecum of an Indian patient. It is a human parasite found commonly in Assam. Human infections have been reported from India (Bengal, Bihar and Orissa), Vietnam, Philippines, Kazakhstan and among Indian immigrants in Guyana. The pig is the common reservoir host. Rhesus monkeys in India have also been found infected.

The adult worms live in the large intestine of the definite host.

Morphology The living worm (Fig. 7.11) is bright pink in colour and pyriform in outline. It has a conical anterior portion and a discoidal posterior portion. It measures 8–14 mm in length and 5.0 mm in breadth. There are two parts 1) The anterior conical portion (with a length of two mm) and 2) The posterior hemispherical portion with a genital cone which characterizes the genus. It has two large, lobate testes, and the spheroidal ovary lies in the centre of the disc, the uterus coils dorsal to the testes. The eggs of *G. hominis* are ovoid, operculated and measure 150 by 60 μm.

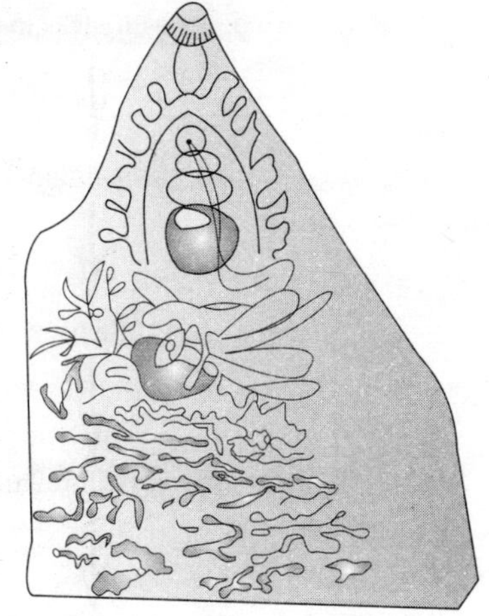

Lifecycle It is unknown; but in India, the planorbid snail, *Helicorbus coenosus*, has been found to act as the intermediate host.

Pathogenicity and clinical features *Gastrodiscoides hominis* attached to the cecum and ascending colon, produces a mucous diarrhea in humans.

Diagnosis This is by demonstration of the typical eggs in the feces.

Treatment Carbon tetrachloride or tetrachlorethylene is an efficient anthelmintic.

FASCIOLA HEPATICA

Family: Fasciolidae
Genus: Fasciola

Fasciola hepatica, the sheep liver fluke, producing sheep liver rot or fascioliasis hepatica was the first trematode to be described by de Brie in 1379; besides, it was also the first for which the complete lifecycle was demonstrated.

This fluke is prevalent among animals in all the sheep and cattle raising countries, the United States and India. Human infections have been reported from Argentina, Venezuela, Chile, China, Soviet Russia, England, France and Italy. It has a cosmopolitan distribution and is common in France and Algeria.

The adult worms live in the biliary passages.

Fig. 7.12 *Fasciola hepatica* (adult).

Morphology *Fasciola hepatica* (Fig. 7.12) is a fleshy fluke measuring 30 mm in length, 13 mm in breadth, but it is relatively flat and leafy along the margins. It is brown in colour. At the anterior end, there is a conical projection which bears the oral sucker. The posterior end is rounded. The oral sucker which is smaller, measures about one mm in diameter and the ventral sucker, 1.6 mm. The digestive tract has branched ceca, which extend to the posterior end of the worm. The testes, which lie one behind the other, are dentritic. The vittellaria are highly branched. The dentritic ovary is situated on the right side of the anterior testes. The uterus is short and surrounded by Mehli's glands. The adult worm lives in sheep for five years and for 9–13 years in humans.

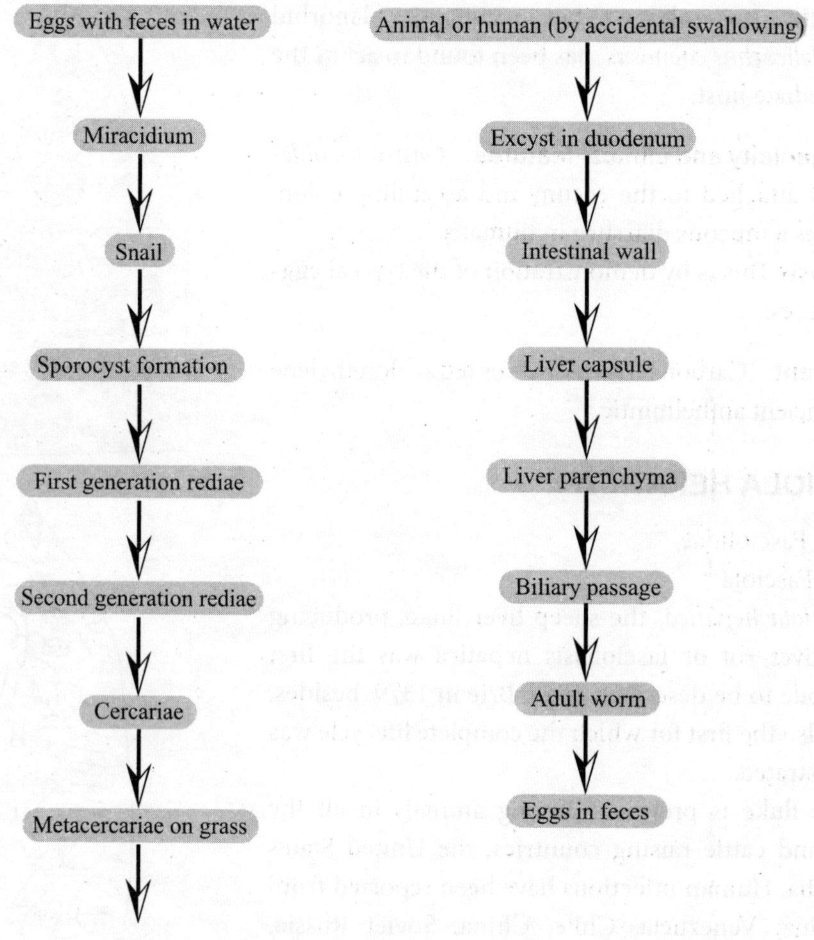

Fig. 7.13 Lifecycle of Fasciola hepatica.

The eggs are large, ovoid, operculated, light yellowish brown in colour and measure 150 μm by 90 μm. They contain a large unsegmented ovum and do not float in an unsaturated solution of common salt (Fig. 7.14).

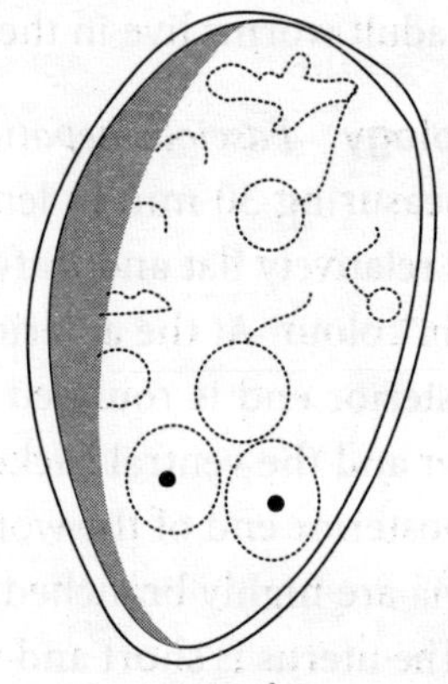

Fig. 7.14 Mature egg of *F. hepatica*.

Lifecycle The lifecycle of *F. hepatica* requires two hosts:

1. ***Definite host*:** sheep, goat, cattle or human and
2. ***Intermediate host*:** snails of the genus, *Lymnaea.*

The eggs are evacuated in the feces of the definite host and mature in water. The miracidium escapes from the egg into the water, swims in search of a suitable intermediate host, the snail, and enters the snail's tissues. It loses its cilia, and within three weeks after penetration, the sporocysts start producing the first generation rediae (redia, are the third larval stage of all trematodes in the snail, except in Schistosoma, where there is no stage of redia formation). In another week, the second generation rediae and finally, the cercariae (Fig. 7.15) develop. They swarm out of the snail and swim about in the water. After casting off their tails, they encyst (Fig. 7.16) on the blades of grass, and other aquatic vegetation. These metacercariae (infective forms) are swallowed along with grass by herbivorous animals (definite hosts), and occasionally human beings contract the infection through consumption of raw vegetables. The metacercariae excyst in the duodenum and migrate through the intestinal wall into the peritoneal cavity. From there, through the liver capsule, they traverse the liver parenchyma to the biliary passages, where they settle down and grow to maturity (It takes one month for them to migrate.) Adult worms liberate eggs in the feces through the bile in three to four months after the infection. The cycle is thus repeated (Figs 7.13 and 7.17).

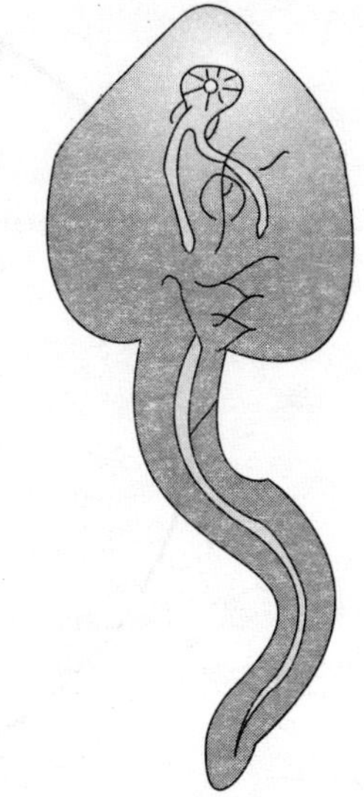

Fig. 7.15 Cercaria of *F. hepatica*.

Pathogenicity Traumatic and necrotic lesions are produced only during the migration of the larva through the liver parenchyma. Adult worms in the bile ducts provoke inflammatory and edematous changes of the biliary epithelium with fibrosis of the ducts. Moreover, the gall bladder undergoes pathological changes in the same way as the bile ducts.

Clinical features The clinical manifestations are hepatic and obstructive jaundice with coughing and vomiting, generalized abdominal rigidity, abdominal pain on pressure; urticaria, early leucocytosis and eosinophilia, irregular fever, persistent diarrhea, later, marked anemia and rarely, hemoglobinuria. Cholelithiasis is a frequent complication.

Acute fascioliasis. Invasion and maturation occur during the first three months after ingestion of the metacerecariae. The immature flukes produce no signs or symptoms or there may be abdominal pain, hepatomegaly, fever, vomiting and jaundice. Leucocytosis and marked eosinophilia are present, but *F. hepatica* eggs are not found in the stool at this stage.

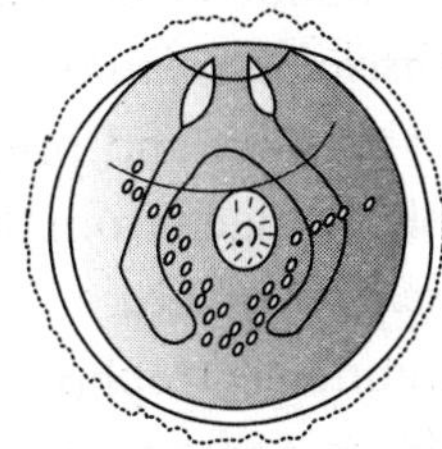

Fig. 7.16 Encysted metacercaria of *F. hepatica*.

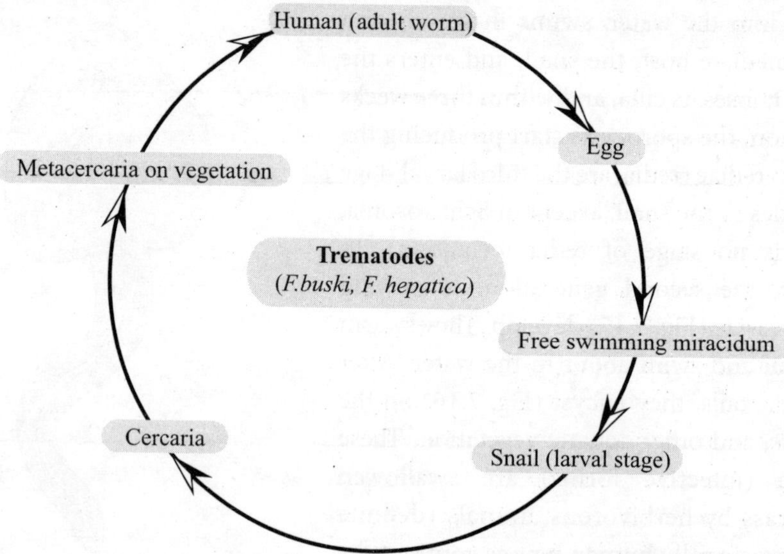

Fig. 7.17 Lifecycle of Trematodes (through ingestion of aquatic vegetation).

Established infection. The mature flukes now produce metabolites that irritate the biliary passage resulting in hyperplasia. Obstruction and dilatation of the biliary passage and cholecystitis may occur. There may be abdominal pain, hepatomegaly, recurrent urticaria, jaundice, irregular fever, diarrhea and loss of weight. Anemia from blood loss can be severe. The obstruction and irritation may produce thickening of the biliary tree, atrophy of the hepatic cells and biliary cirrhosis. Cholelithiasis is common. A relationship of fascioliasis and biliary cancer is not proved.

Extra biliary fascioliasis. Ingestion of raw sheep or goat liver containing young flukes causes the condition called 'halzoun' (suffocation).The pharyngeal fascioliasis is due to lodgement of flukes in the upper respiratory and digestive tracts. Inflammation and edema may lead to dysphagia, dyspnia and even asphyxiation. Cutaneous fascioliasis usually, in the upper abdomen, presents as migratory modules that are pruritic, painful and inflamed and vary in size from 2 to 3 cm. Rarely, they are found in the lungs, peritoneum, muscle, eye and brain.

Laboratory diagnosis Specific diagnosis is based on the recovery of the eggs in the patient's stool or from the duodenal or biliary tract drainage. The eggs are practically indistinguishable from those of *Fasciolopsis buski.*

Complement fixation and precipitation tests are helpful, but they cannot be adapted for routine diagnosis. Antigen from the adult worm of *Fasciola hepatica* gives specific intradermal reaction for *Fasciola hepatica.*

Counter immunoelectrophoresis (CIEP) tests can be used for rapid and specific diagnosis of acute fascioliasis and schistosomiasis. This test is able to identify a mixed infection of *F. hepatica* and *S. mansoni,* which did not become positive for schistosomiasis by stool examination until the fourth week of infection. In chronic infection, the stool contains characteristic large operculated eggs (150 × 90 μm) of *F. hepatica.*

Treatment Emetine hydrochloride has been used with success. Bithionol is possibly curative. Recently, hexachloroparaxylene has given favourable results in Russia.

Chloroquinine was also used in the past with some success. Praziquantel is now the drug of choice for *F. hepatica* infection. The dosage is 75 mg/kg of body weight, divided into three doses per day for two days. Ectopic flukes are removed surgically.

Prophylaxis

This consists of

1. Eradication of adult worms in reservoir hosts by adequate chemotherapy
2. Killing of snails by the use of 1:50,000 solution of copper sulphate and
3. Education of the local population about the danger in eating raw vegetables.

FASCIOLOPSIS BUSKI

Family: Fasciolidae
Genus: Fasciolopsis

Fasciolopsis buski, the giant intestinal fluke, which produces fasciolopsiasis, was discovered in 1843 by Busk for the first time in the duodenum of a sailor who died in London. This is a common parasite of humans and the pig, found in central and south China, Taiwan, Vietnam, Thailand, India (Assam, Bengal) and other parts of the Orient.

The adult worm of *F. buski* remains attached to the duodenum and jejunal wall of humans and pig.

Morphology The adult worm (Figs 7.18 and 7.19) is the largest fleshy trematode of the intestine, usually elongate and ovoidal, 20–75 mm in length, 8–20 mm in breadth and 0.5–3 mm in thickness. There is no cephalic cone. The oral sucker measures about 0.5 mm in diameter and the nearby acetabulum, 2–3 mm. The intestine includes two unbranched caeca. The highly dentritic testes lie one behind the other. The branched ovary lies to the right of the midline. The uterus is between the ootypes. The adult worm lives for about six months.

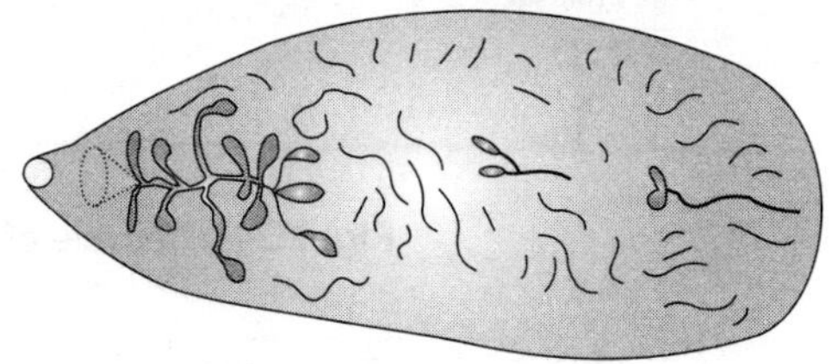

Fig. 7.18 *Fasciolopsis buski* (adult).

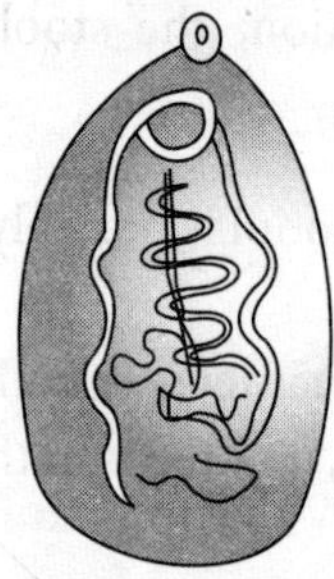

Fig. 7.19 *F. buski* (adult).

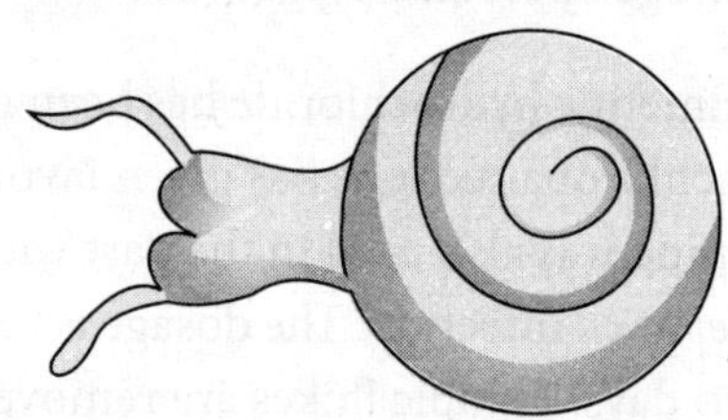

Fig. 7. 20 Segmentina snail.

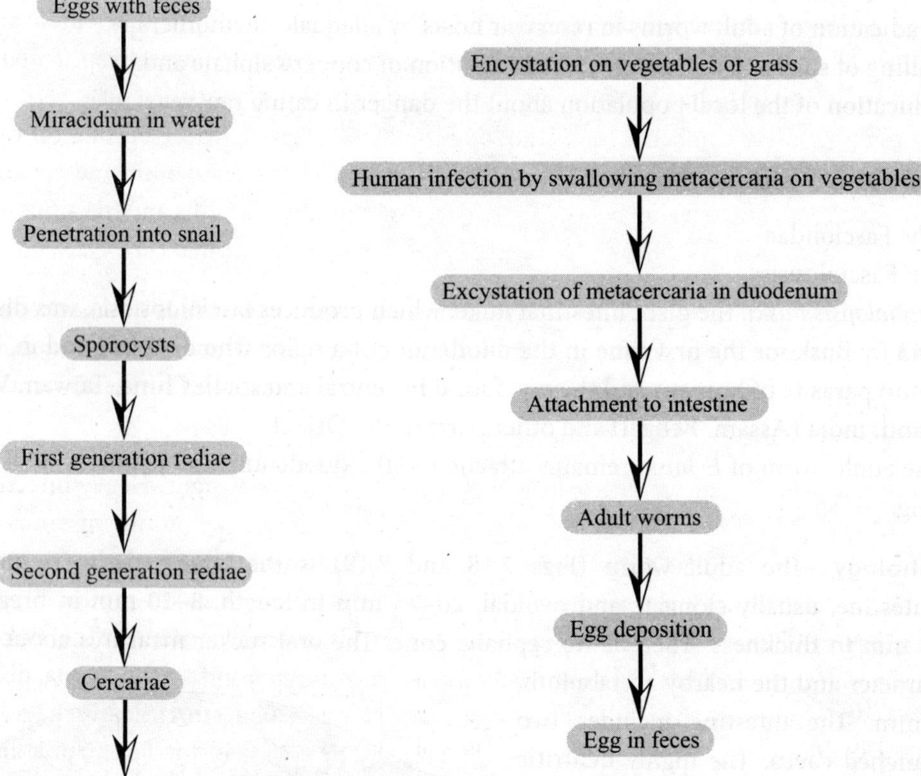

Fig. 7.21 Lifecycle of Fasciolopsis buski.

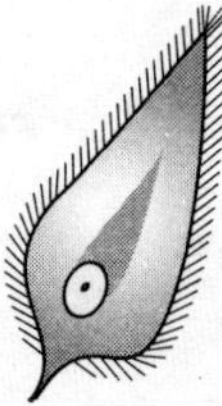

Fig. 7.22 Miracidium of *F. buski*.

The eggs of *F. buski* are large (like a hen's egg) and are identical with those of *F. hepatica.* They measure 130–140 μm by 80–85 μm and are embryonated when laid.

Lifecycle The lifecycle of *F. buski* requires two hosts:

1. ***Definite host*** – human or pig; and
2. ***Intermediate host*** – snail of the genus, *Segmentina* (Fig. 7.20).

The lifecycle of *F. buski* is similar to that of *Fasciola hepatica.* When immature eggs are discharged in the feces, they mature in water and hatch out, and the emerging miracidium (Fig. 7.22) swims about in the water. On contact with an appropriate snail, *Segmentina trochoideus,* it penetrates the soft tissues and within a few weeks the sporocysts, first and second generation rediae and cercariae are consecutively produced. These cercariae are similar to those of *Fasciola hepatica.* They encyst on the seed pods of the water caltrop, *Trapa bicornis,* found commonly in India (Bengal).

Human beings are infected by swallowing the metacercariae, while peeling off the skin of infected plants with their teeth. The metacercariae excyst in the duodenum and get attached to the intestinal wall and develop into adult worms in about three months and the adult worms lay eggs which are passed out with the feces. The lifecycle is thus repeated (Fig. 7.21).

Pathogenicity The physiological damage caused by the adult worms is traumatic, obstructive and toxic. At the site of attachment, there is inflammation and deep ulceration of the mucosa. Many worms obstruct the passage of food. The intoxication is caused by the absorption of the worm's metabolites into the system.

Clinical features Toxic diarrhea and hunger pains are the first signs. Heavy infections have symptoms similar to gastric ulcer. Generalized toxic and allergic symptoms appear as edema of the face, abdominal wall and lower limbs. There is absolute eosinophilia.

Many light infections are asymptomatic, but a heavy load of flukes produces symptoms, especially in children. The worm load may be up to several thousands. The flukes attach themselves to the duodenal and jejunal mucosa and produce symptoms of trauma, obstruction and toxin production. There may be abdominal pain, gastrointestinal hemorrhage, diarrhea and intestinal obstruction. In severe cases, there may be edema of the face, trunk and legs as well as ascites.

Laboratory diagnosis Specific diagnosis depends upon the recovery of the eggs and their microscopic identification. The eggs of *F. buski* and *Fasciola hepatica* are considerably similar. Recovery of characteristic adult *F. buski* is a definite diagnosis. Eosinophilia is common and may exceed 50% of white blood cells. Serological tests, such as the indirect fluorescent antibody test, are available in some laboratories in America. The specificity of the serological test can be improved and definite diagnosis cannot be based on serological tests alone. This is also true for the skin test.

Treatment Hexylresorcinol crystoids is the drug of choice. Tetrachlorethylene is also effective. Praziquantel is the current drug of choice. The recommended dose is 75 mg/kg of body weight divided in three doses per day for two days.

Prophylaxis Destruction of snails by 1:50,000 copper sulphate solution, sterilization of night soil, before it is used as fertilizer, and cooking raw vegetables properly or immersing them in boiling water for a few seconds before eating are all effective measures in prophylaxis.

CLONORCHIS SINENSIS

Family: Opisthorchiidae

Genus: Clonorchis

Clonorchis sinensis, the Chinese liver fluke, producing clonorchiasis, was first identified by McConnell (1875) in the bile passage of a Chinese carpenter who died in India (Kolkata).

Japan, Korea, China, Taiwan and Vietnam are endemic areas of this infection. The heavy infections are, however, confined to Okayama and Niigata.

The adult worms live in the bile passage or pancreatic duct of humans, dogs, cats or pigs and have a very long lifespan of up to 50 years.

Morphology The adult worm of *Clonorchis sinensis* is flat, transparent, flabby and spatulate. It measures 10–25 mm in length and 3–5 mm in breadth. The oral sucker is slightly larger than the ventral sucker. The testes are large, deeply lobulated or branched, and are situated one behind the other. The ovary is small and slightly lobed. The uterus arises from the ootype and proceeds in compact coils to the genital atrium (Fig. 7.23).

The eggs are ovoid and have a moderately thick, light yellowish-brown shell. They are provided with a convex operculum and possess a terminal hook-like spine (resembling an electric bulb). Each egg measures 29 µm by 16 µm. The eggs are fully embryonated (miracidium) and are infective to snails and hatch out only in the snail. They do not float in a saturated solution of common salt (Fig. 7.24).

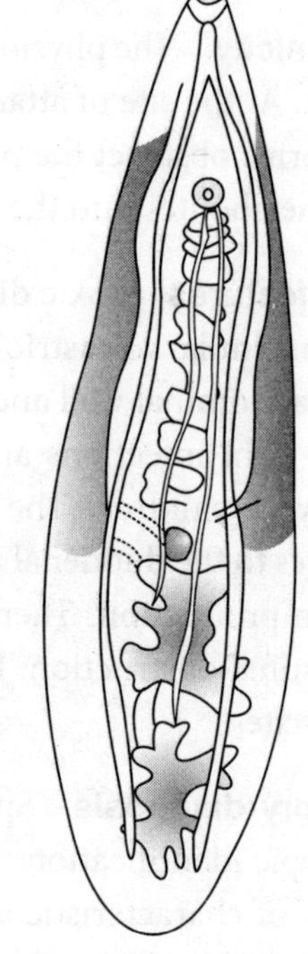

Fig. 7.23 Adult worm of *Clonorchis sinensis*.

Lifecycle The lifecycle of *C. sinensis* requires three hosts, one definite host and two intermediate hosts.

1. ***Definite host:*** human, dog, cat or pig
2. ***First intermediate host***: snail *(Bulimus)*
3. ***Second intermediate host***: fish belonging to the family Cyprinidae or crayfish *(Caridina, Palaemonetes sinensis).*

Fully embryonated eggs (Fig. 7.24) containing miracidium are passed with the feces of the definite host into the water. These eggs are ingested by the suitable species of snails *(Bulimus, Alocinma)* and the miracidium hatches out from the egg. Within the snail, the first generation sporocyst and the second generation rediae develop. These rediae produce cercariae (Fig. 7.26). After escaping from the snail, these cercariae swim in the water. On contact with freshwater fish (cyprinidae or cray fish), the cercariae become attached to the fish, discard their tails, penetrate under the scales and encyst in the skin or in the flesh. On ingestion of the infected flesh by humans, the encysted cercariae (metacercariae) excyst in the duodenum, and enter the common bile duct through the ampulla of Vater, where they mature in a month. The eggs are discharged with the feces. The entire lifecycle requires about three months. Thus, the lifecycle is repeated (Figs 7.25 and 7.27).

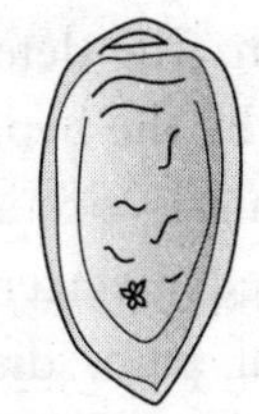

Fig. 7.24 Egg of *C. sinensis.*

Pathogenicity The larvae of C. *sinensis* may initiate the proliferation and inflammation of the biliary epithelium, and ultimately fibrosis of the bile duct may ensue. Twenty-one thousand worms were recovered from one case in Indochina.

Clinical features There are three stages in the manifestation of symptoms:

1. The mild, essentially symptomless stage
2. The progressive stage, with irregular appetite fullness in the abdomen, diarrhea and hepatomegaly and
3. The severe stage, with portal cirrhosis syndrome.

Catarrhal cholangitis occurs due to the occlusion of the bile passages by sticky masses of eggs and by tissue proliferation. Symptoms of systemic toxemia are palpitation of the heart, tachycardia, vertigo, tremor, cramps and mental

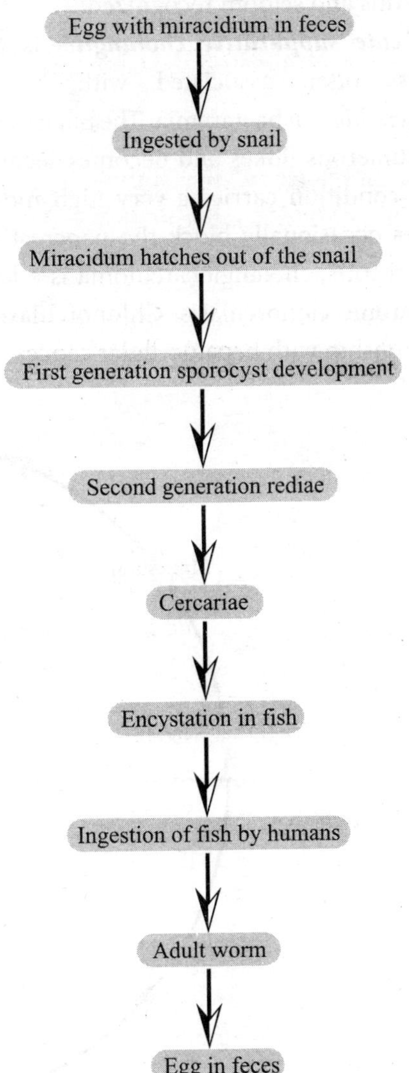

Fig. 7.25 Lifecycle of *Clonorchis sinensis.*

depression. The detoxifying properties of the liver are impaired by the byproducts of the adult worms. Acute chlonorchiasis occurs 1–3 weeks after the ingestion of encysted metacercaria. There may be fever, chills, abdominal pain, diarrhea, tender hepatomegaly and mild jaundice. The white blood cells count is raised with massive eosinophilia, and serum alkaline phosphate, SGOT, SGPT and bilirubin levels are elevated. The clinical presentation is often confused with acute viral hepatitis and seldom recognized.

Acute suppurative cholangitis is a severe febrile illness often associated with hypoglycemia and *Escherichia coli* bactaremia. The biliary system is blocked by numerous flukes and becomes secondarily infected. This condition carries a very high mortality rate. The flukes occasionally block the pancreatic ducts causing pancreatitis, cholangiocarcinoma is a late complication of chronic clonorchiasis. Chlonorchiasis has no causal relationship with hepatocellular cancer.

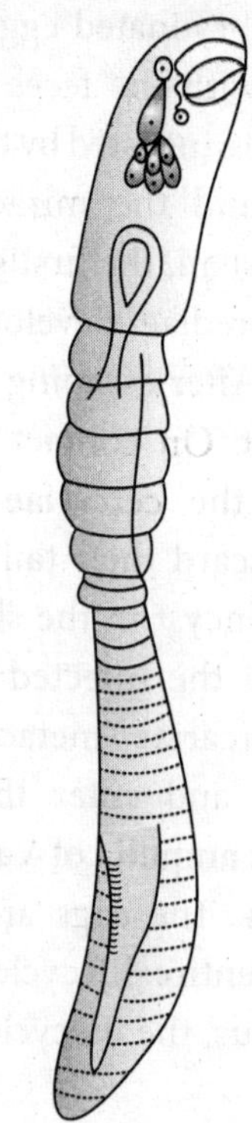

Fig. 7.26 Cercaria of *C. sinensis*.

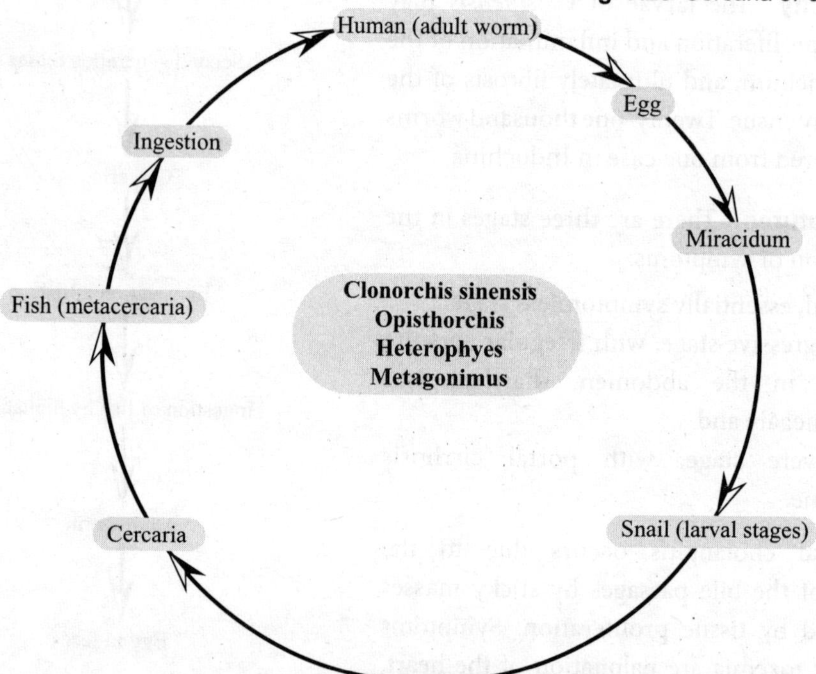

Fig. 7.27 Lifecycle of Trematodes (through ingestion of raw fish).

Laboratory diagnosis Diagnosis is not made mainly on the basis of the recovery of characteristic eggs in the feces or in the duodenal aspiration, which are similar to those of Opisthorchis, Heterophyes and Metagonimus. The adult fluke should be demonstrated for definite diagnosis. Radioisotope scan and ultrasound of the liver are normal.

Acute chlonorchiasis must be distinguished from hepatic amebiasis and visceral larva migrans. In the former, eosinophilia is absent and serology for amebiasis is positive. In the latter, the serology for toxocariasis is positive. However, serologic and skin tests for chlonorchiasis are not sufficiently specific and sensitive for clinical use.

Treatment Sodium antimony tartarate, chloroquine diphosphate, dithiazanine iodine, hexachloro-paraxylol and bithionol are found to be effective to some extent. Praziquantel is the recent drug of choice. The dose is 75 mg/kg body weight divided in three doses on the same days and is well tolerated. Albendzole is equally good.

Prophylaxis The following prophylactic measures are useful:

1. Cooking all freshwater fish thoroughly will protect the human population
2. Addition of ammonium sulphate to night soil can act as a sterilizing agent
3. Pollution of water with feces should be prevented.

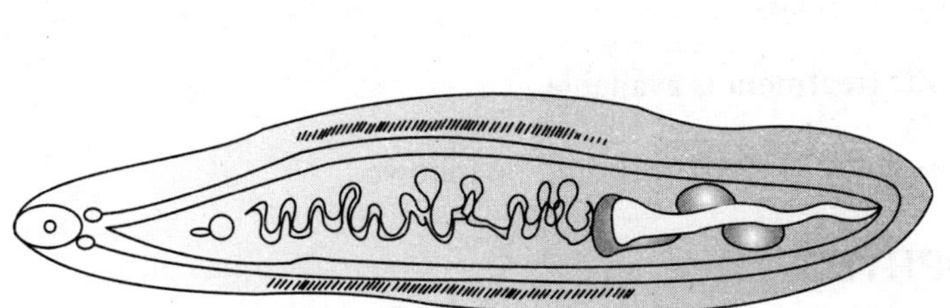

Fig. 7.28 Adult worm *Opisthorchis felineus*.

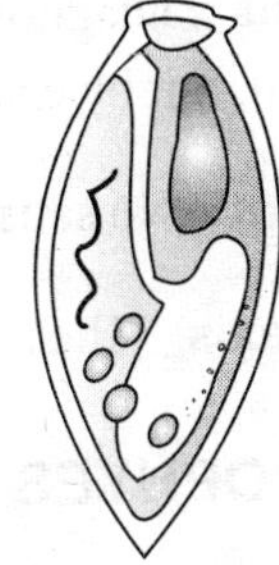

Fig. 7.29 Egg of *O. felineus*.

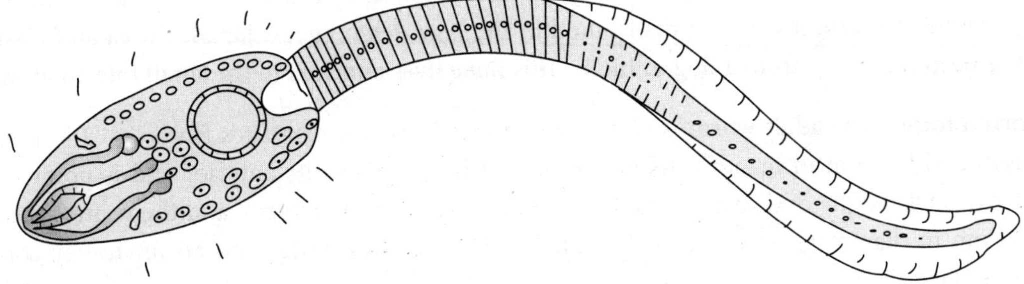

Fig. 7.30 Cercaria of *O. felineus*.

OPISTHORCHIS FELINEUS

Family: Opisthorchiidae
Genus: Clonorchis

Opisthorchis felineus, the cat liver fluke, producing opisthorchiasis, was first reported as a human infection in Siberia in 1892. It is common in Europe, Vietnam, France, Germany and Poland, and has also been recovered from patients in Japan and India (Kolkata).

Adult worms live in the biliary and pancreatic passages of the definite host.

Morphology *Opisthorchis felineus* is morphologically similar to *C. sinensis,* except that the testes are not branched, but are lobed (Fig. 7.28). The eggs are similar to those of *C. sinensis.* At the posterior end of the shell, there is a minute tubercular thickening (Fig. 7.29).

Lifecycle The lifecycle of *O. felineus* is the same as that of *C. sinensis.* The cercariae (Fig. 7.30) attack fish.

Pathogenicity and clinical features
These are similar to those of *C. sinensis.* Cholangiocarcinoma can also result from chronic opisthorchiasis.

Diagnosis Diagnosis is not based on the recovery of the typical egg in the stool and duodenal aspiration, but by examination of adult fluke.

Treatment No satisfactory specific treatment is available.

Prophylaxis The same measures as for *C. sinensis* should be followed.

HETEROPHYES HETEROPHYES

Family: Heterophyidae
Genus: Heterophyes

This minute fluke causing heterophyiasis was first found by Bilharz, in 1851, at the autopsy of a native of Cairo. It is found distributed in the Nile delta, Egypt, Japan, Korea and China. It has been recovered from a dog in India. This fluke lives attached to the small intestinal wall.

Morphology The adult worm is elongate and pyriform and measures from 1 to 1.7 mm in length and 0.3 mm in breadth. Its posterior end is broad and its anterior end is pointed. It has two suckers: the oral sucker which is minute (90 μm in diameter), and the ventral sucker (230 μm in diameter) which is thick walled. It has two oval testes and an intricately coiled uterus (Fig. 7.32).

The eggs are minute, operculated and ovoid. They are light brown in colour and measure 30 μm by 17 μm. They contain well developed miracidium (Fig. 7.31).

Lifecycle The lifecycle of *H. heterophyes* requires a definite host (human, dog, cat, fox) and an intermediate host (marine or brackish water snail, *Pironella conica,* in Egypt). The eggs hatch only after ingestion by the freshwater snail *(Pironella conica),* which is common in Egypt. A sporocyst and one or two rediae generations are developed, from which the cercariae emerge. They encyst in the mullet *(Aphanius fasciatus* found in Egypt) and, on ingestion of this uncooked fish, the definite host (human) becomes infected. Ultimately, adult worms deposit eggs which are passed out with the feces. Thus, the lifecycle is repeated.

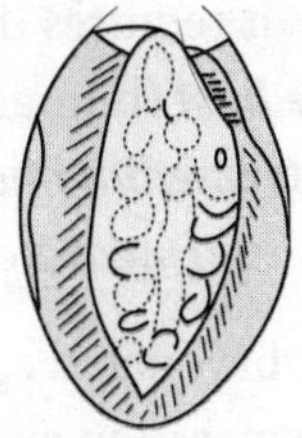

Fig. 7.31 Egg of *H. heterophyes.*

Pathogenicity and clinical features There is mild inflammation at the sites of attachment to the intestinal mucosa. The clinical manifestations are colicky pains, mucous diarrhea with excess mucous production. Sometimes, eggs may enter the intestinal wall and the mesenteric lymphatics and may filter into the cardiac valves and myocardium where they produce tissue reactions, ultimately causing cardiac failure. If they are carried to the brain, they cause fatal cerebral hemorrhage.

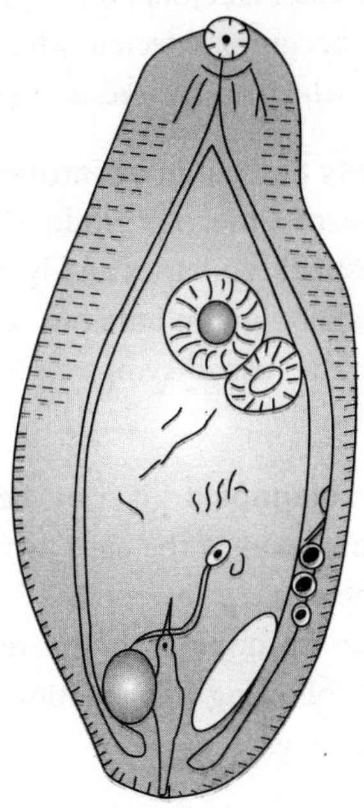

Fig. 7.32 Adult worm of *Heterophyes heterophyes.*

Laboratory diagnosis It can be done by the demonstration of typical eggs in the feces. These eggs are similar to those of *C. sinensis.*

Treatment Tetrachloroethylene is effective. Praziquantel is a recent drug of choice.

Prophylaxis Avoidance of eating raw freshwater fish and destroying snails by using molluscicides are effective methods of prophylaxis.

METAGONIMUS YOKOGAWAI

This worm which produces metagonimiasis was first described by Katsurada in 1912. It is common in East Asia, Spain and Siberia.

Adult worms remain attached to the intestinal mucosa.

Morphology This fluke (Fig. 7.34) resembles *Heterophyes heterophyes* in its size and shape. The eggs of *Metagonimus yokogawai* cannot be distinguished from those of *H. heterophyes.*

Lifecycle It requires three hosts:

1. ***Definite host*** (human, fish-eating mammals, pelican),
2. ***First intermediate host*** (snail: *Melania libertina),* and
3. ***Second intermediate host*** (freshwater fish: *Salmo perryi).*

Fully embryonated eggs are ingested by the snail. Inside the snail, they develop into the first sporocyst generation and then into two generations of rediae. From there, the cercariae escape from the snail, swim in the water and become encysted under the scales, in the skin or in the flesh of freshwater fish *(Salmo perryi).*

Humans becomes infected when they eats the uncooked freshwater fish. Adult worms liberate eggs which are passed in the feces.

Pathogenicity and clinical features Inflammation develops around the sites of attachment, followed by excess mucous production, sloughing and necrosis. Sometimes, the eggs infiltrate into the intestinal capillaries and lymphatics, and are carried to the myocardium, brain, spinal cord, etc. where granulomatous changes take place. The usual symptom is mild diarrhea.

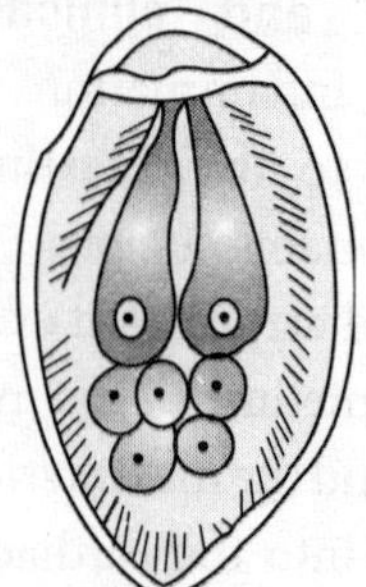

Fig. 7.33 Egg of *M. yokogawai.*

Laboratory diagnosis It can be done by the identification of the eggs, which are similar to those of *H. heterophyes.* Specific diagnosis can be done with the recovery of flukes following evacuation with anthelmintic drugs.

Treatment Tetrachloroethylene is effective. Praziquantel is a current chemotherapeutic agent which is very effective against *M. yokogawai*

Prophylaxis Eating the raw flesh of infected freshwater fish should be avoided.

Alaria americana is an intestinal trematode of dog, fox and wolf. Two cases of human infection by the mesocercaria of this fluke have been reported in Ontario. Mesocercaria is a stage of development between cercaria and metacercaria. The cercariae emerging from the snail penetrate the tadpole. As the tadpole grows into

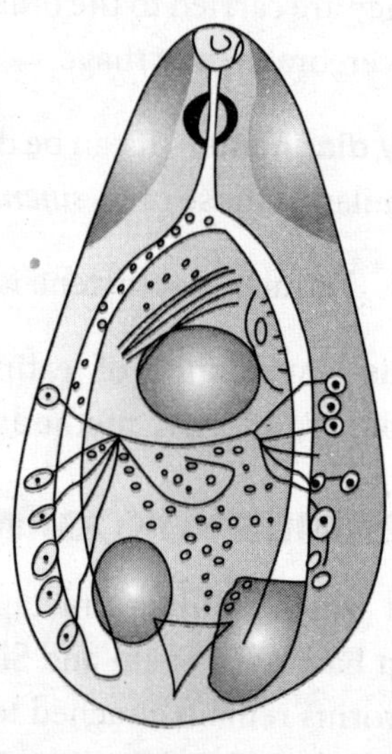

Fig. 7.34 *Metagonimus yokogawai* (adult worm).

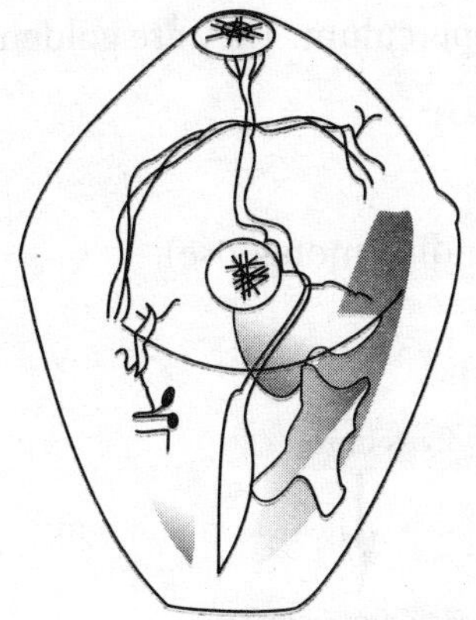

Fig. 7.35 Adult worm of *P. westermani.*

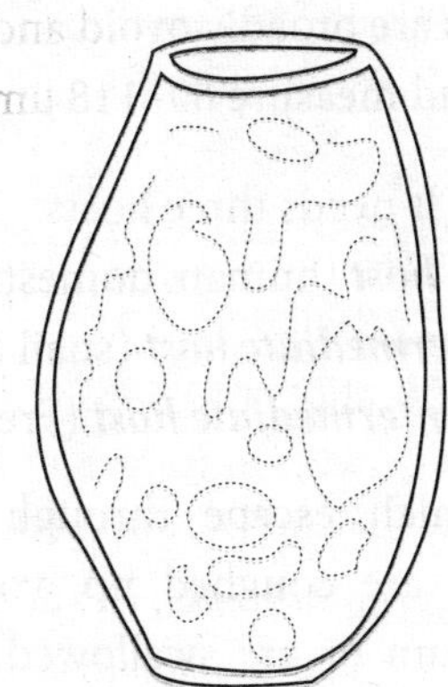

Fig. 7.36 Egg of *P. westermani.*

a frog, the mesocercariae tend to concentrate in the hind leg. When the frog is eaten by a carnivore, the mesocercariae develop into metacercariae and adult flukes, in the lungs and the gut respectively. When a human, not a normal host, eats the frog, the mesocercariae migrate all over the body. In the first reported case, the mesocercaria was removed from the retina of the eye. The second case was a fatal systemic infection manifested by severe respiratory stress, coma, a coagulation abnormality and vasculitis. At autopsy, the mesocercariae were found in all organs.

Treatment There is no known treatment although Praziquantel may be useful.

PARAGONIMUS WESTERMANI

Family: Troglotrematidae
Genus: Paragonimus

Paragonimus westermani, the oriental lung fluke, or the lung distome, which produces paragonimiasis, pulmonary distomiasis or endemic hemoptysis, was first found by Kerbert in the lungs of two Bengal tigers which had died in the Amsterdam Zoological Gardens. In Sri Lanka, wild carnivores are often infected with the Paragonimus species. In 1879, Ringer found a pulmonary fluke in a human patient.

The heavily infested areas are East Asia, Japan, Korea and Taiwan. Isolated foci exist in China, Vietnam, Malaysia and India (Bengal, Malabar, Chennai, Assam).

The adult worm of *Paragonimus westermani* lives in the lungs for six to seven years.

Morphology It is a reddish brown, plump, ovoid fluke with a rounded anterior end and a somewhat tapering posterior end. It measures 7.5–12 mm in length, 4–6 mm in breadth and 3.5–5 mm in thickness. The oral sucker and ventral suckers are sub-equal (0.75–8 mm in diameter). The testes are deeply lobed, and the ovary is also a large, lobed organ consisting of a tightly coiled rosette (Fig. 7.35).

The eggs are broadly ovoid and have a distinct flattened operculum. They are golden brown in colour and measure 80–118 μm by 48–60 μm (Fig. 7.36).

Lifecycle It needs three hosts:

1. ***Definite host*** (human, domestic animals, tiger, leopard, Indian mongoose),
2. ***First intermediate host*** (snail *Melania libertina),* and
3. ***Second intermediate host*** (Freshwater fish: crayfish, crab).

Eggs which escape through the bronchioles are coughed up, voided in the sputum or are swallowed and passed out in the feces, They complete their embryonation in water, where they hatch out and the miracidia escape as free swimming organisms in search of their suitable intermediate snail host *(Melania libertina).* Within the snail, a sporocyst and two generations of rediae (Fig. 7.38) are produced, followed by the development of cercariae (Fig. 7.39). The cercariae erupt from the snail, swim in the water and invade the viscera or muscles of crayfish *(Cambaroides similis)* or crabs *(Eriocheir japonicus),* where the metacercariae encyst.

The definite host (human) becomes infected after the ingestion of parasitized crab or crayfish viscera (which is soaked in rice wine or salted in China). The metacercariae excyst in the duodenum and migrate through the intestinal wall and reach the abdominal cavity. They once again travel through the diaphragm to the pleural cavity and lungs. Finally, they settle in the vicinity of the bronchioles where they grow into adult worms in tissue capsules formed by the host. Their development in the definite host requires several weeks.

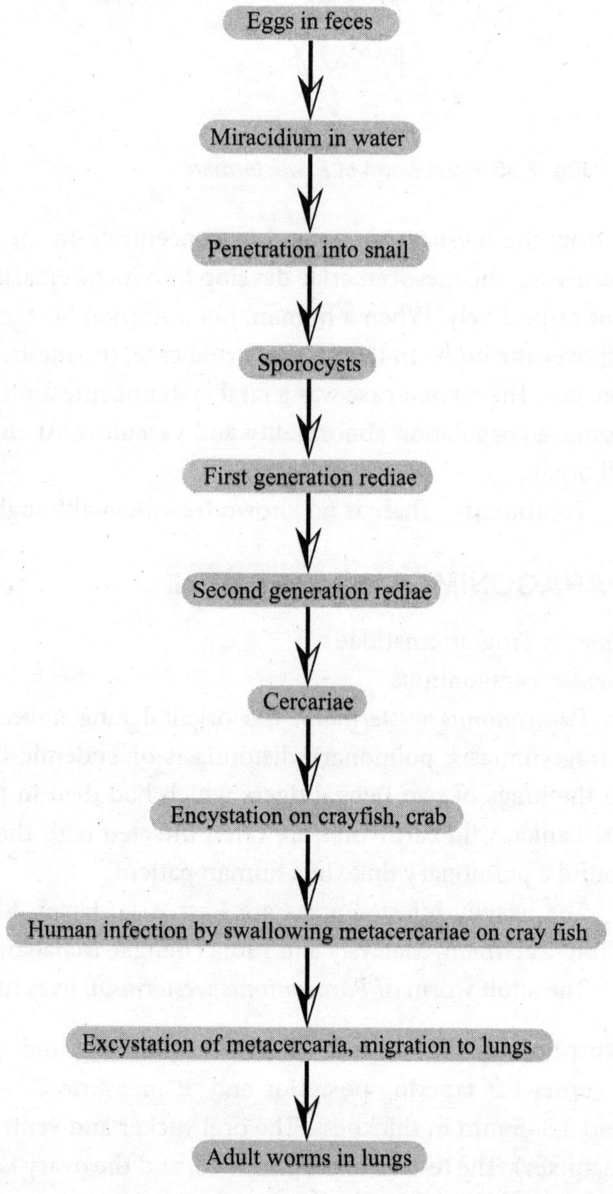

Fig. 7.37 Lifecycle of *Paragonimus westermani.*

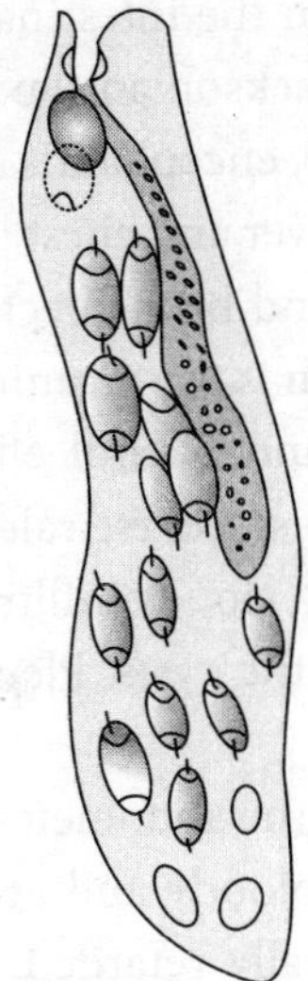

Fig. 7.38 Redia of *P. westermani.*

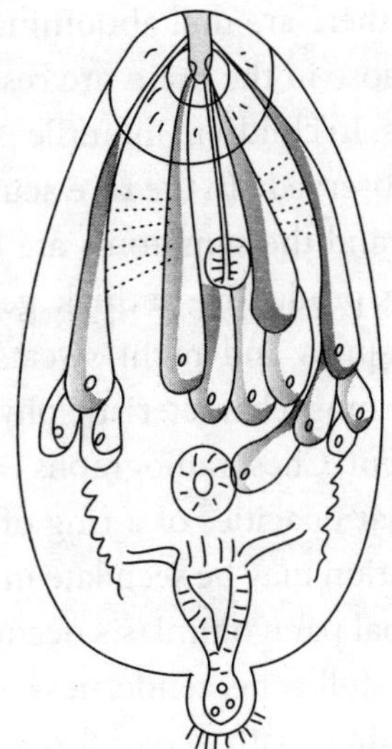

Fig, 7.39 Cercaria of *P. westermani.*

Eggs deposited by the adult worms in the bronchioles are coughed up, voided in the sputum, swallowed and passed in the feces. Thus, the lifecycle is repeated (Figs 7.37 and 7.40).

Pathogenicity The worms in the tissues may provoke granulomatous reactions. In the abdominal cavity, an abscess may develop around the worm, and the eggs may become the centres for pseudo-tubercles. In the lung, there is a thick, cystic encapsulation of the parasite. Besides, these cysts may be found in the liver, intestinal wall, mesenteric lymph nodes, muscles, testes, brain, peritoneum or pleura.

Clinical features Chest pain and night sweats are common symptoms. Following paroxysmal coughing, there is occasional profuse hemoptysis after physical exertion. The manifestations are severe. Bronchopneumonia or bronchiectasis with pleural effusion is the physical sign.

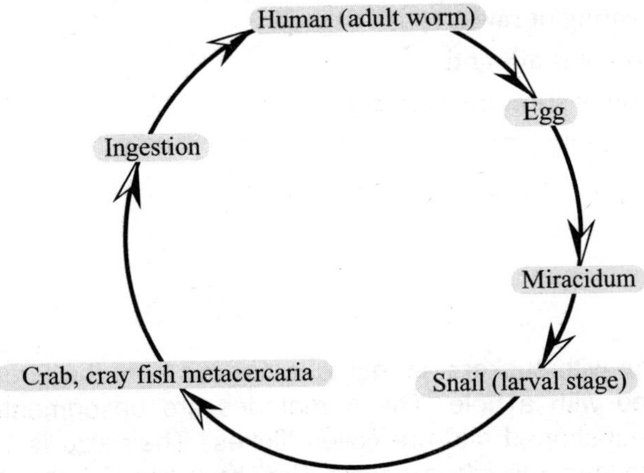

Fig. 7.40 Lifecycle of *P. westermani.*

Usually, there are dull abdominal pains. The worms lodged in the intestinal wall provoke diarrhea. Those in the brain are responsible for epilepsy of the Jacksonian type as in cerebral cysticercosis. In children, infantile paralysis, cerebral hemorrhage, encephalitis and meningitis have been observed. In the rare acute case, there may be chills, fever and chest pain. The onset is insidious and the symptoms are those of chronic bronchitis and bronchiectasis. Cough in the morning, productive of thick, gelatinous, blood-tinged sputum is the prominent symptom. External dyspnea and night sweats are common. Chest pain and pleural effusion may be present. The most characteristic physical finding is persistent, moist, coarse rales over the area of involvement. Chest radiographs early in the disease show patchy, cloudy infiltration, but later dense nodular opacities of a ring of shadows indicate the site of the cysts. Pleural thickening and calcification may be seen late in the disease.

Abdominal paragonimiasis occurs when the flukes localize in the abdomen. Symptoms are nonspecific, dull ache, tenderness and diarrhea, which may be bloody and accompanied by mucus. Children with cerebral paragonimiasis are usually mentally retarded. Subcutaneous localization of the fluke results in abscess formation.

Laboratory diagnosis The finding of the characteristic eggs in the sputum or feces is specific diagnosis. The complement fixation test is positive only during the life of the parasite. Recent Dot Immuno Binding (DIB) assay can also be adopted. Intradermal tests may remain positive for many years, hence they are not reliable. Chest X-ray may reveal abnormal shadows, ultrasonography is more useful.

Treatment Emetine hydrochloride, bithionol and hexachloroparaxylol are found effective. Praziquantel, because of its safety, ease of use and high degree of efficacy, has replaced bithionol and niclofolan. The recommended dosage of praziquantel is 75 mg/kg of body weight divided into three doses daily for two days.

Prophylaxis This consists of

1. Avoiding eating of raw crayfish or crab
2. Destruction of snails and
3. Disinfection of sputum and feces.

SUMMARY

Trematoda

- It is a flatworm with suckers. Its name is derived from the Greek *trematos,* which means pierced with a hole. The trematodes are unsegmented, dorso-ventrally flattened or leaf-shaped and are called 'flukes'. Their size is variable; the largest human trematode is *Fasciolopsis buski*. They have two cup-shaped (ventral and oral) suckers, which are organs of attachment. They are hermaphrodites, except schistosoma. They lay operculated eggs, except schistosoma. Their lifecycle requires one or more intermediate hosts.

- According to their habitats, they are classified as
  1. Blood trematode
  2. Hepatic trematode
  3. Intestinal trematode
  4. Lung trematode

Schistosoma haematobium

- It is commonly called a vesical blood fluke causing schistosomiasis hematobia. In India, Gadgil and Shah identified an autochthonous focus in the Ratnagiri district of Maharashtra. Panjarathinam (1972) reported *Schistosoma nasalis* in the nasal washing of the nasal granuloma of cattle for the first time in Pondicherry (India).
- *Schistosoma haematobium* lives in the vesical plexuses of venous circulation. The adult ***male*** is shorter and stouter and is covered with tuberculation; it has two ventral and oral suckers and has at the caudal end, a gynecophoric canal in which the female is held during copulation and ovipositon. The ***female*** is long and slender. Its suckers are small and its tuberculations are confined. Its definite host is human; its intermediate host is the fresh water snail (*Ferrisia tenuis* in India), which is involved in its lifecycle. Its eggs have a distinct terminal spine. When its eggs in the urine are discharged into the water, the ciliated larva (miracidium, the first stage larva) hatches out. This miracidium swims in water, comes in contact with the snail, penetrates into the snail, reaches the liver and other organs where it loses its cilia, transforms into the first and second generation of sporocysts (the second larval stage), finally, a generation of fork-tailed cercariae breaks out of the snail, swims in water, penetrates into the human skin and casts off its tail. This tail-less cercaria is called metacercariae or schistosomule. It is infective to humans; it enters the peripheral veinules, the right part of the heart, pulmonary capillaries and the left part of the heart, systemic circulation, abdominal aorta and mesenteric arteries. This larva feeds, grows in the intra-hepatic vessel, becomes sexually differentiated, migrates against the bloodstream, enters the inferior mesenteric veins, rectal pelvic venous plexuses, and lastly, the vesical plexuses of veins, it becomes sexually mature. The male worm holds the female within the gynecophoric canal. After fertilization, the eggs are passed out in the urine to restart its lifecycle. Its pathogenic effects are due to:
  1. Generalized and localized reaction to metabolites of growing and mature worm
  2. Trauma with hemorrhage as their eggs escape from the venules
  3. Pseudo-abscess and pseudo-tubercle formation around lodged eggs in the tissues. Clinically, there is irritation, minute hemorrhage at the site of entry on the skin, followed by toxic symptoms (anorexia, headache, malaise, pain, rigor, night sweating, urticaria), liver and spleen are hypertrophied, hematuria at the end of micturation.

- In the laboratory, the diagnosis is by microscopic demonstration of terminal spined eggs in urine deposits, by serological tests. Treatment is by the use of specific drug (antimony compound). Prophylaxis is by eradication of snails; sanitary improvement; prevention of pollution of water by infected persons; by avoiding wading in polluted water and proper disposal of human excreta.

Schistosomal cercarial dermatitis

- There are three types:
  1. ***Schistosome dermatitis type I*** is caused by *Trichobilharzia ocellata*. Their intermediate host is the *Lymnea* snail. It is also reported in India. Clinically, there is a prickling sensation, followed by urticaria, in the initial stages. After several hours, intense itching of the area develops, with edema, and the papules transform into pustules.
  2. ***Schistosome dermatitis type II*** is caused by cercaria, an avian species of trichobilharzis cercariae.
  3. ***Schistosome dermatitis type III*** is caused by the penetration into the human skin by cercaria of the mammalian species of blood fluke (*Schistosoma spindalis*). Oral trimeprazine is effective.

Schistosoma mansoni

- It is commonly called Manson's blood fluke. It causes Manson's intestinal schistosomiasis (bilharziasis). It is found in the mesenteric veins of the sigmoid rectal area and lives for 26 years.
- It resembles *S. haematobium,* but is smaller; its egg has a characteristic lateral spine. Its miracidium is larger than that of *S. japonicum* and *S. haematobium*. Its lifecycle in snails is similar to that of *S. japonicum* and *S. haematobium*. The definite host is human; the intermediate host is the fresh water snail, *Biomphalaria glabrata*. The lesions produced by *S. mansoni* are smaller than those of *S. haematobium* and *S. japonicum*. The colon and rectum are mostly involved. Initially, there is papular rash, with pruritus over the skin of the feet, fever, dysentery, abdominal pain. Diagnosis can be by the demonstration of characteristic lateral spined eggs in the stool, by various serological tests and by blood examination. Antimony compounds are effective and prophylaxis is similar to that of *S. haematobium*.

Schistosoma japonicum

- Its common name is the oriental blood fluke. It lives in the radicles of the superior mesenteric veins, draining the ileo-cecal region and causes oriental schistosomiasis. It is similar morphologically to the other two schistosoma, but it lacks tuberculation. Its egg has an abbreviated spine on the upper right border of the shell. Its lifecycle is also similar to that of the other two schistosoma; but its intermediate host is the fresh water snail of the genus *Oncomelania*. Its miriacidium is smaller in size. Its pathogenic lesions are also similar to those of the other two schistosoma. Intestine and liver are mostly affected. The intestinal and hepatic schistosomiasis in oriental schistosomiasis is also called Katayama disease.

- Its clinical features are dysentery, hepatic cirrhosis, splenomegaly, appendicitis, intestinal constriction, pneumonitis, cerebral syndrome, intoxication, urticaria, fever. Diagnosis, treatment and prophylaxis are the same as in other schistosoma.

Gastrodiscoides hominis

- Human infections have been reported from India (Assam, Bengal, Bihar, Orissa) and other countries. Rhesus monkeys have also been found to be infected in India.
- Pig is the common reservoir host. It lives in the large intestine of the definite host (human). It is pyriform, has a conical anterior portion and a discoid posterior portion. Its eggs are ovoidal, operculated. This worm causes mucous diarrhea. Typical egg can be demonstrated in feces. Treatment is by the use of an effective drug.

Fasciola hepatica

- It is commonly known as sheep liver fluke causing fascioliasis hepatica. It was the first trematode to be described along with its complete lifecycle. It lives in the biliary passage for 13 years in humans. It has a cosmopolitan distribution, including in India. It is a fleshy fluke, with oral and ventral suckers. The oral sucker is the conical projection. Its eggs are large, ovoidal and operculated. They contain a large unsegmented ovum.
- Definite host (sheep, goat, cattle or human) and intermediate host (snail–lymnea) are involved in its lifecycle.
- ***Lifecycle*** Eggs, passed in feces, mature in water. The miracidium escapes from the egg, swims, enters into the snail, forms a sporocyst after losing its cilia. This sporocyst produces first and second generation rediae and finally, cercariae (redia is formed only in all trematodes in snail, but not in schistosoma). These cercariae, liberated from the snail, swim in water and encyst into metacercaria (infective form) on the grass. Cattle get infected by grazing, humans by accidental swallowing of metacercariae which excyst in the duodenum, enter into the intestine, peritoneal cavity, liver capsule, liver parenchyma and at last settle in the biliary passage and mature into adult worms liberating eggs in feces. During migration its larvae produce traumatic, necrotic changes: inflammation, edema on biliary epithelium, fibrosis of biliary ducts. Clinically, there could be obstructive jaundice, coughing, vomiting, abdominal pain, urticaria, fever, diarrhea, anemia. Cholelithiasis is a complication.
- Diagnosis is by the recovery of eggs from stool or biliary drainage. Its egg is similar to that of *Fasciolopsis buski*. It can be treated by suitable drugs (Albendazole is a recent effective drug). Prophylaxis is by eradication of the worm, by killing of snails by chemicals; education of the public.

Fasciolopsis buski

- It is called the giant intestinal fluke causing fasciolopsiasis in humans and pigs. It is fleshly, elongate and ovoidal and has no cephalic cone. It lives for six months attached to the duodenum. It has a worldwide distribution, including in India (Assam, Bengal). Its lifecycle is similar to that of *F. hepatica,* except its intermediate host, *Segmentina triochoideus*. Its cercariae encyst on the seed pod of the water caltrop *Trapa bicornis*, commonly found in India (Bengal). Humans get infected by swallowing the metacercariae, on the seed pod, which get attached to the duodenum and transform into adult worms laying eggs similar to those of *F. hepatica*. All other characteristics are similar to those of *F. hepatica*

Clonorchis sinensis

- It is commonly known as Chinese liver fluke producing clonorchiasis. It was first identified by McConnell (1875), in the bile passage of a Chinese carpenter who died in Kolkata (India). It lives in the biliary passage of humans, pigs, cats. It is distributed worldwide. It is flat, transparent and spatulate. Its eggs are ovoidal, resemble an electric bulb with a terminal hook like spine, have an operculum. They are fully embroyonated (miracidum) and are infective to humans. Three intermediate hosts are required: one definite host (human, cat, dog); a first intermediate host, snail (*Bulimus*) and a second intermediate host crayfish (*Caridina*)
- ***Lifecycle*** When fully embryonated eggs are ingested by the snail (*Bulimus, Alocinma*), the miraciduim hatches out from the egg. Within the snail the rediae are developed, produce cercariae which become attached to the fish, lose their tail and enter into the flesh. Humans get infected by the ingestion of infected fish. The metacercariae excyst in the duodenum and enter into the common duct through the ampulla of vater, mature into adult worms whose eggs are discharged with the feces. Proliferation, inflammation, fibrosis of bile duct may ensue. Clinically, there are three stages: mild, progressive and severe. Cholangitis may occur. It can be diagnosed by the recovery of its characteristic egg from the stool. It can be treated by effective drugs. The infection can be prevented by properly cooking infected fresh water fish; sterilizing night soil; avoiding pollution of water with feces.

Opisthorchis felineus

- Its common name is the cat liver fluke. It is prevalent in several countries. It was first reported from India (Bengal). It is morphologically similar to *C. sinensis*, except its testes are lobed. Its egg is also similar to *C. sinensis*, but there is a minute tubercular thickening. In all other aspects, it is similar to *C. sinensis,* but there is no specific treatment.

Heterophyes heterophyes

- It is a minute fluke causing heterophyiasis. It is distributed in many countries including India, where a worm was recovered from a dog. It is elongated and pyriform. Its eggs are minute, operculated and ovoidal. The well-developed egg has a miracidium. Definite host (human, dog, fox) and intermediate hosts, marine water snail and fresh water fish, are required for its lifecycle. Snail ingests the eggs which are hatched out. A sporocyst, one or two rediae are developed, from which the cerecariae emerge and encyst in the mullet fish. On ingestion of this infected fish, humans get infected. Adult worm deposits eggs. There is mild inflammation at the site of intestinal attachment by the worm, colic pain and mucous diarrhea. Some eggs may enter into the circulation, filter into the cardiac valves and myocardium causing tissue reaction and cardiac failure; if carried to the brain, they cause fatal cerebral hemorrhage. Recovery of typical egg from feces is correct laboratory diagnosis. It can be treated by effective drugs. Prevention is by eating cooked fresh water fish and destroying the snail.

Metagonimus yokogawai

- It causes metagonimiasis. It is attached to the intestine. It resembles *H. heterophyes*. Its egg cannot be distinguished from that of *H. hetrophyes*. Three hosts
  1. Definite host (human, pelican);
  2. First intermediate host (snail);
  3. Second intermediate host (fresh water fish).
- Snails ingest fully embryonated eggs. These eggs develop first into sporocyst, and then into two generations of rediae. At last, the cercariae escape from the snail, swim in water, encyst in the fish skin or flesh of fresh water fish. Humans get infected by consuming infected fish. Adult worms lay eggs, later found in feces. Pathogenicity and clinical features are similar to those of *H. hetrophyes*. Diagnosis, treatment and prophylaxis are the same as in the case of *H. heterophyes*.

Paragonimus westermani

- Its common name is oriental lung fluke. It causes paragonimiasis. Many countries are heavily infested with this fluke including India (Assam, Bengal, Tamilnadu). It is reddish brown, plump and ovoidal and has a flattened operculum. Three hosts are involved in its lifecycle:
  1. Definite host (human, tiger, leopard, Indian monkeys);
  2. First intermediate host (snail);
  3. Second intermediate host (fresh water fish, crayfish, crab)
- Miracidium hatched out from eggs swims in the water and enters the snail. Within the snail, a sporocyst, two generations of rediae and cercariae are produced, liberated and swim in the water, enter into the muscle of the crayfish and encyst. After ingestion of infected crayfish, humans get infected. The metaceriae excyst in the duodenum, migrate through the abdominal cavity, the diaphragm, pleural cavity and to the lungs and finally settle in the bronchioles and mature into an adult worm which deposits eggs. The eggs are coughed up or voided in the feces to repeat its lifecycle. Granulomatous reactions may take place around the worm, abscess in the abdominal cavity, with pseudo-tubercles around the eggs. The cysts may be found in the liver, intestine, muscle, brain, pleura.

QUESTIONS

Q *Define Trematode.*
▶ Trematode is a flatworm with suckers.

Q *Why are they called flukes?*
▶ They are so called because they are unsegmented, dorso-ventrally flattened or leaf-shaped.

Q *Which is the largest human trematode?*
▶ *Fasciolopsis buski* is the largest human trematode.

Q *Why are all trematodes hermaphrodites?*
▶ This is because they do not have separate sexes.

Q *Why are Schistosoma (blood fluke) not hermaphrodites?*
▶ This is because they have separate sexes.

Q *Which trematode does not produce operculated eggs?*
▶ Schistosoma does not produce operculated eggs.

Schistosoma haematobium

Q *What is the common name of S. haematobium?*
▶ The common name is vesical blood fluke.

Q *Where was S. haematobium reported in India?*
▶ *S. haematobium* was reported from the Ratnagiri district of Maharashtra State (India).

Q *What is a gynecophoric canal?*
▶ Behind the ventral sucker, the body of the male Schistosoma is folded all the way to the caudal extremity to form the gynecophoric canal in which the female is held during copulation.

Q *What is a miracidium?*
▶ Miracidium is the ciliated larva of Schistosoma and its first larval stage.

Q *What is the function of miracidium?*
▶ Its function is to infect the snail (intermediate host).

Q *What is a sporocyst?*
▶ It is the second larval stage of Schistosoma.

Q *What is a schistosomule?*
▶ It is cercaria without a tail.

Q *Where do Schistosoma feed, grow and become sexually differentiated?*
▶ In the intrahepatic portal vessels.

Q *Where is the site of predilection of S. haematobuim?*
▶ The site of predilection of *S. haematobium* is the vesical venule.

Q *What is the use of the terminal spine of the egg of S. haematobium?*

▶ It helps the eggs to work their way through the vessels and the mucosa of the urinary bladder.

Q *How is an allergic reaction provoked in the patient?*

▶ It is due to the discharge of metabolites of *S. schistosoma.*

Q *How are fibrosis and miliary pseudo-tubercles formed in schistosomiasis haematobium infection?*

▶ They are formed due to the infiltration of eggs into the tissues.

Q *What is the main clinical feature of schistosomiasis hematobium?*

▶ There is painless passage of small volumes of blood at the end of micturition – hematuria, a burning sensation and increased frequency of micturition.

Q *What is the synonym of cercarial dermatitis?*

▶ It is also called swimmer's itch or cercarial itch.

Q *How many types of cercarial dermatitis are reported?*

▶ There are three types: they are schistosome types I, II and III.

Q *Which type of cercarial dermatitis is reported in India?*

▶ Type I is reported in India.

Schistosoma mansoni

Q *What is the common name of S. mansoni?*

▶ It is also called Manson's blood fluke.

Q *What is bilharziasis?*

▶ Manson's intestinal schistosomiasis is also called bilharziasis.

Q *What is the site of predilection of S. mansoni?*

▶ It is found in the mesenteric veins of the sigmoid rectal area.

Q *What is the lifespan of S. mansoni?*

▶ It lives for 26 years.

Q *Which schistosoma can be kept in the laboratory for research purposes?*

▶ *S. mansoni* is used for research purposes.

Q *Why is the production of the granuloma around the eggs delayed in the case of S. mansoni?*

▶ The production of granuloma is delayed because of the smaller number of eggs produced by *S. mansoni.*

Q *Which schistosoma was recovered from the anterior chamber of the eye of a patient?*

▶ *S. mansoni*

Schistosoma japonicum

Q *What is the common name of S. japonicum?*

▶ Its common name is oriental blood fluke.

Q *What is the site of predilection of S. japonicum?*
▶ It inhabits the radicles of the superior mesenteric veins draining the ileo-cecal region.

Q *How does the adult worm of S. japonicum differ morphologically from other schistosoma?*
▶ The adult worm of *S. japonicum* lacks integumentary tuberculations.

Q *What is Katayama disease?*
▶ It is intestinal and hepatic schistosomiasis of the Orient.

Gastrodiscoides hominis

Q *In which states of India is G. hominis prevalent?*
▶ It is prevalent in Bengal, Bihar and Orissa.

Q *In which country is the Rhesus money infected with G. hominis?*
▶ In India, the Rhesus money is infected with *G. hominis.*

Q *In which country is the lifecycle of G. hominis known?*
▶ Its lifecycle is known in India.

Q *Which disease is produced by G. hominis?*
▶ *G. hominis* produces mucous diarrhea.

Fasciola hepatica

Q *What is the common name of F. hepatica?*
▶ It is known as sheep liver fluke.

Q *For how many years does it live in humans?*
▶ It lives for 9–13 years in humans.

Q *In which trematode is redia formation observed?*
▶ Redia formation is observed in *Fasciola hepatica.*

Q *What is redia?*
▶ Redia is the third larval stage of all trematodes in the snail, except in schistosoma.

Q *What is cercaria?*
▶ It is the final larval stage after redia.

Q *What is metacercaria?*
▶ Metacercaria is encysted cercaria and is infective to cattle or humans.

Q *How do metacercaria of F. hepatica migrate from the intestine to its site of predilection (biliary passage)?*
▶ It migrates from the intestine, peritoneal cavity, liver capsule and parenchyma to the biliary passage.

Q *Why do the metacercaria of F. hepatica settle down in the biliary passage?*
▶ It settles to grow to maturity.

Q *How much time does it take to reach the site of predilection (biliary passage)?*
▶ It takes one month to reach the biliary passage.

Q *What are the lesions produced during migration of the larva of F. hepatica?*

▸ Traumatic and necrotic lesions are produced in the liver parenchyma.

Q *What are the pathological changes produced by the adult worm of F. hepatica in the bile duct and gall bladder?*

▸ Inflammatory and edematous changes of the biliary epithelium with fibrosis of the bile ducts and gall bladder are produced.

Q *What are the clinical features of F. hepatica?*

▸ Hepatic, obstructive jaundice, coughing, vomiting, abdominal pain, diarrhea, fever, anemia, hemoglobinuria.

Q *What is a frequent complication of F. hepatica infection?*

▸ Cholelithiasis is a frequent complication.

Fasciolopsis buski

Q *What is the common name of F. buski?*

▸ It is also known as giant intestinal fluke.

Q *In which states of India is F. buski prevalent?*

▸ It is prevalent in Assam, Bengal, Orissa (India).

Q *Which is the largest intestinal trematode?*

▸ *F. buski* is the largest intestinal fluke.

Q *What is the lifespan of F. buski?*

▸ Its lifespan is six months.

Q *On which plant, do the cercariae of F. buski encyst?*

▸ They encyst on the seed pods of the water caltrop (plant).

Q *Where is this water caltrop (water plant) common in India?*

▸ It is common in Bengal (India).

Q *Why do adult worms of F. buski obstruct the passage of food?*

▸ Many adult worms may obstruct the food passage because of their giant size.

Q *Why is there edema of the face, abdominal wall and lower limbs in F. buski infection?*

▸ There is edema because of the generalized toxic and allergic reactions provoked by adult worm of *F. buski*.

Clonorchis sinensis

Q *What is the common name of C. sinensis?*

▸ Its common name is Chinese liver fluke.

Q *What is the appearance of the egg of C. sinensis?*

▸ Its egg looks like an electric bulb.

Q *In which country were 21,000 worms recovered from one patient?*

▸ In Indo-China.

Q *How many stages are there in clinical manifestations in C. sinensis infection?*

▶ There are three stages. They are

1. Mild symptomless stage
2. Progressive stage
3. The severe stage.

Q *In which stage does portal cirrhosis syndrome occur in C. sinensis infection?*

▶ In the severe stage.

Q *How does catarrhal cholangitis occur in C. sinensis infection?*

▶ Catarrhal cholangitis occurs due to occlusion of the bile passage by sticky masses of eggs and by tissue proliferation.

Q *Why do the following symptoms – palpitation of heart, tachycardia, vertigo, tremor, cramps and mental depression, occur in C. sinensis infection?*

▶ These symptoms are due to the byproducts of adult worms of *C. sinensis*.

Opisthorchis felineus

Q *How is O. felineus called commonly?*

▶ It is commonly called cat liver fluke.

Q *From which places in India has the adult worm of O. felineus been recovered?*

▶ In Kolkata.

Q *Cite two passages in which O. felineus lives?*

▶ It lives in the biliary and pancreatic passages of humans.

Heterophyes heterophyes

Q *Why are clinical manifestations (like colicky pain, mucous diarrhea with excess mucous production) produced?*

▶ These clinical manifestations are due to mild inflammation at the sites of attachment of adult worms to the intestine.

Q *How is cardiac failure caused by H. heterophyes?*

▶ Sometimes its eggs may enter the mesenteric lymphatics, filter into the cardiac valve and myocardium where they produce tissue reactions, ultimately causing cardiac failure.

Q *What will happen if these eggs are carried to the brain?*

▶ They cause fatal cerebral hemorrhage.

Metagonimus yokogawai

Q *What changes will take place if the eggs of M. yokogawai are carried to the myocardium, brain, spinal chord etc.*

▶ Granulomatous changes will take place.

Paragonimus westermani

Q *What is the common name of P. westermani?*

▶ Its common name is Oriental lung fluke.

Q *Cite the places in India where P. westermani is reported?*

▶ It is reported in Assam, Bengal, Malabar, Tamil Nadu.

Q *For how many years does P. westermani remain alive in the lungs?*

▶ It lives for six to seven years.

Q *How does the metacercaria of P. westermani migrate from the intestine to the bronchioles (site of predilection)?*

▶ It travels through the abdominal cavity, diaphragm, pleural cavity, lungs and bronchioles.

Q *What will happen if the adult worm of P. westermani is present in the lungs?*

▶ If it is present in the lungs, there will be a thick, cystic encapsulation of the parasite. Similar changes may also be observed in other organs.

Q *What will happen if the adult worm of P. westermani reaches the brain of an adult or a child?*

▶ It causes epilepsy of the Jacksonian type as in cerebral cysticercosis in adults; in children, infantile paralysis, cerebral hemorrhage, encephalitis and meningitis are observed.

First Report Of Trematodes

Q – Who reported for the first time the following trematodes: *S. haematobium, S. mansoni; S. japonicum; S.nasalis, Gastrodiscoids hominis; F. hepatica; F. buski; C. sinensis; O. felineus; H. heterophyes; M. yokogawai; P. westermani.*

▶
S. hematobium – Bilharz (1851)
S. mansoni – Bilharz (1851)
S. japonicum – Fuginami (1904)
S. nasalis – (animal trematode) Panjarathinam (1972)
G. hominis – Lewis and McConnell (1876)
F. hepatica – de Brie (1379)
F. buski – Busk (1843)
C. sinensis – McConnell (1875)
O. felineus – unknown in 1892
H. heterophyes – Bilharz (1851)
M. yokogawai – Katsurada (1912)
P. westermani – Ringer (1879)

8 CLASS NEMATODA

GENERAL CHARACTERISTICS

Structure

Nematodes are elongated, cylindrical in shape and tapering at both ends. They are typically non-segmented worms. Their sizes are variable, ranging from the smallest *(Trichinella spiralis* and *Strongyloides stercoralis)* measuring less than 5 mm to the largest *(Dracunculus medinensis)* measuring up to one metre. They have a rough protective covering or cuticula.

The nematodes have a rudimentary nervous system, complete genitalia and a digestive tract with both oral and anal openings. The oral cavity, if present, may have teeth or cutting plates or it may be continuous with the esophagus. The muscular esophagus of certain nematodes is of uniform calibre (filariform esophagus) throughout. If the esophagus is expanded posteriorly into a bulb which contains a valve mechanism, it is referred to as rhabditiform esophagus. Frequently, the free-living stages of a worm have the rhabditiform type of esophagus; while the parasitic forms of the same worm have the filariform structure.

The rudimentary excretory and nervous systems, the genitalia and the digestive tract float in the body cavity.

Reproductive Systems

The sexes are separate, so nematodes are referred to as 'diecious helminths'. The males are generally much smaller than the females, and the reproductive organs are tubular and lie coiled within the body cavity. In the male, there is a single tubule which, at its smaller end, consists of testicular cells. It expands into a vas deferens and a seminal vesicle, and terminates into an ejaculatory duct opening into the cloaca. In some males, accessory copulatory organs (spicule and gubernaculum) are also present. In some other male forms, the posterior end of the male expands into a thin-walled copulatory bursa supported by thickened rays.

The female worm has two cylindrical ovaries, which expand into uteri. The uteri may each open to the exterior through a single vulva or there may be a common vagina between the vulva and the uteri. The vulva is frequently located near the middle of the body, but its position varies in different species.

In contrast to the trematodes and cestodes, which are parasitic, the female nematodes may be;

1) ***Viviparous***, giving birth to larvae (e.g., *Dracunculus medinensis, Wuchereria bancrofti, Brugia malayi* and *Trichinella spiralis*)
2) ***Oviparous,*** laying eggs (*Ascaris lumbricoides, Trichuris trichiura* which lay eggs with unsegmented ovum, *Ancylostoma duodenale, Necator americanus* which lay eggs with segmented ovum, *Enterobius vermicularis* which lay eggs containing larvae) or
3) ***Ovo-viviparous***, laying eggs containing larvae which hatch out immediately (*Strongyloides stercoralis*).

TRICHINELLA SPIRALIS

Superfamily: Trichuroidea
Genus: Trichinella

Trichinella spiralis, the 'trichina' worm, producing trichinosis or trichinelliasis was first discovered in the encysted larval stage in muscles, during autopsies conducted by Peacock in London (1828). *T. spiralis* has a cosmopolitan distribution. In Great Britain, Holland, Germany and Spain, the incidence is relatively low, whereas in Poland, Ukraine, West USSR, Hungary and Bulgaria, it is high. It is not prevalent as a human infection in Africa and India.

Adult worms of *T. spiralis* remain buried in the duodenal or jejunal mucosa and their larvae encyst in the striated muscles of humans, pigs or rats, harbouring the adult worms.

Morphology The adult worm is one of the 'smallest' nematodes infecting humans. The male (Fig. 8.1) measures 1.4–1.6 mm in length and 40–60 μm in diameter. The anterior end is more delicate than the posterior one. The caudal extremity, the cloaca, which is evertible during coitus, is guarded by two conspicuous conical papillae. The female (Fig. 8.2) is more than double in length compared to the male and is one and a half times wider. It is viviparous and discharges embryos (larvae) as long as it is alive.

The larvae measure 100 μm in length and 6 μm in diameter (Fig. 8.3).

Lifecycle The lifecycle passes in only one host (human, pig or rat).

When a human consumes raw meat, infected (mode of infection) with the cysts of *T. spiralis,* the cysts (Fig. 8.5) are digested out of the meat, in the stomach. After excystation in the duodenum, the larvae invade the duodenal and jejunal mucosa and develop into minute, thread-like adult

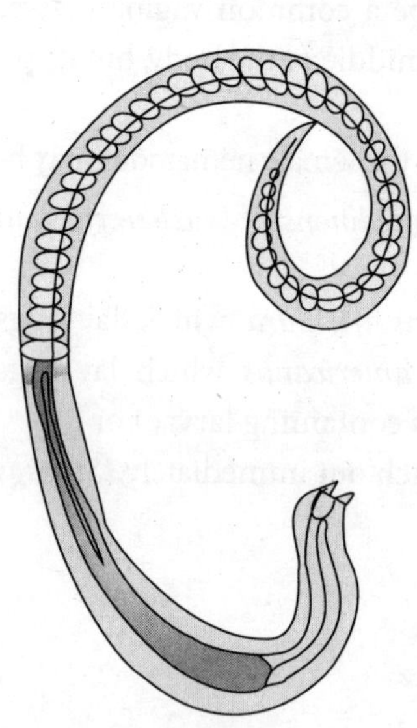

Fig. 8.1 Adult male of *T. spiralis*.

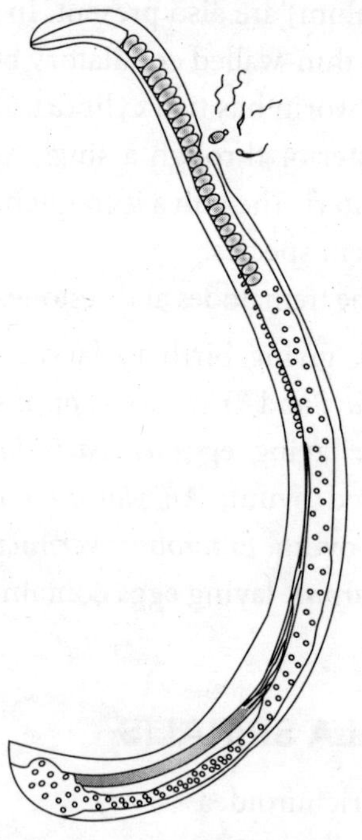

Fig. 8.2 Adult female of *T. spiralis*.

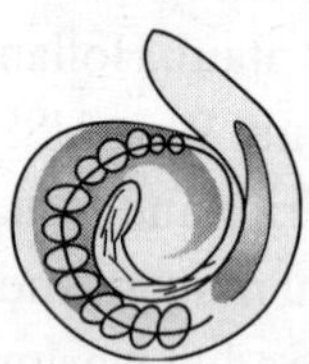

Fig. 8.3 The larva of *T. spiralis*.

males and females within two days. At first, the adult worms may be lodged in the glandular crypts. The females burrow into the villi, the deeper layers of the intestinal wall and the mesenteric lymph nodes. The males die after fertilizing the females. The fertilized females discharge at least 1500 progenies during 16 weeks or more, as long as the mother worms are alive. Some may escape into the intestinal lumen and the majority reach the intestinal mesenteric lymphatics. They are carried through the right part of the heart and lungs, to the arterial circulation and are lodged temporarily in various tissues, including the myocardium, brain, cerebrospinal fluid and body cavities from which they may re-enter the bloodstream and are finally distributed in the striated muscle, where they encyst. The encysted larvae may remain alive for many years. The long axis of the cyst parallels that of the muscle fibres. The cyst wall results from the host tissue reactions and is not secreted by the larvae. The diaphragm, muscles of the larynx, tongue, abdomen, intercostal spaces, biceps, gastrocnemius and deltoid are mostly infected (Fig. 8.5). There are three principal maintenance cycles: 1) Pig to pig 2) Rat to rat and 3) Sylvatic, perpetuated by carnivorous wild hosts (Fig. 8.6).

Pathogenicity and clinical features They are divided into three successive stages: 1) Invasion (incubation) 2) Migration of the larvae and 3) Encystation and tissue repair.

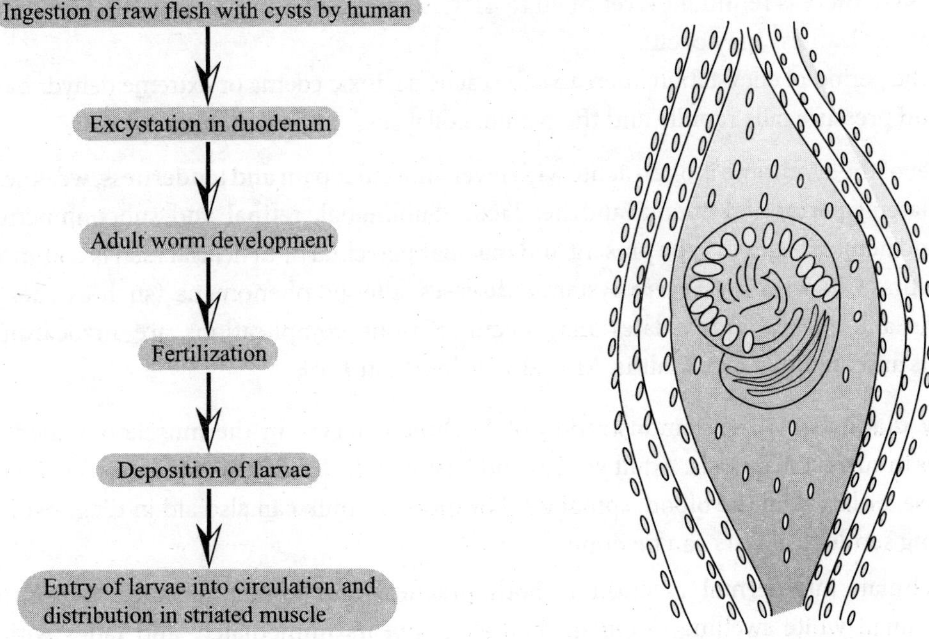

Fig. 8.4 Lifecycle of *Trichinella spiralis*.

Fig. 8.5 Young cyst of *T. spiralis in muscle* fibres.

1. During the invasion of the larvae into the duodenal mucosa, the symptoms of nausea, vomiting, toxic diarrhea or dysentery, colic and profuse sweating are similar to those of acute food poisoning.
2. During the migration of the larvae, there are muscular pains, indicating the inflammatory processes in the muscles and edema around the eyes, nose and hands. The lymph nodes

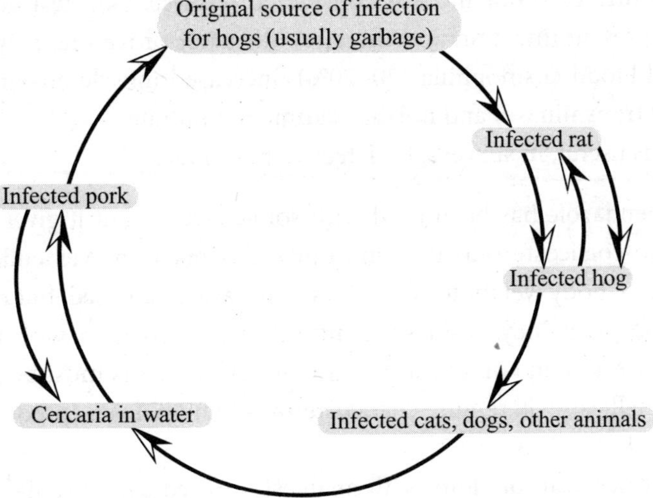

Fig. 8.6 Lifecycle of *T. spiralis* (common method of exposure).

are enlarged, there is remittent fever of 40 to 41°C, and encephalitis, meningitis and ocular disturbance; deafness may occur.

3. During the period of encystation, there may be cachexia, toxic edema or extreme dehydration. The blood pressure falls rapidly and the patient collapses.

The onset of the syndrome is often acute with fever, muscular pain and tenderness, weakness, malaise, bilateral periorbital edema and headache. Sublingual, retinal and subconjunctival petechiae and hemorrhages may be present and macular petechial or urticarial rash is common. Within the first two weeks of severe systemic diseases, allergic phenomena (such as edema, pneumonitis and pleural transudate) may occur. Serious complications are myocarditis, pneumonitis and meningoencephalitis. Mortality is less than 1.5%.

Laboratory diagnosis The demonstration of Trichinella larvae in the muscle obtained by biopsy helps in correct diagnosis. Adult worms and larvae in the feces during the diarrheic stage of the disease, or larvae in the blood, spinal fluid or mother's milk can also aid in diagnosis. The following serological tests can be done:

1) The Bechman intradermal reaction is both practical and highly specific. In positive cases, a small white swelling, 5 cm in diameter, appears immediately and fades within 15–20 minutes. It is advisable to conduct a precipitin test to confirm the intradermal test.
2) The precipitin test is more accurate and reliable than the other serological tests.
3) Bentonite flocculation and skin tests give good correlation with the disease.
4) The fluorescent antibody technique using larval antigen has been found to be specific.

Antibodies are not detected until three weeks after the onset of infection. Counter immunoelectrophoresis (CIEP), ELISA, passive hemagglutination (HA) and indirect immunofluorescence (IF) are rapid screening tests. The bentonite flocculation test is the most widely used and a titre of 1:5 or more is considered positive. Skin test does not distinguish between past and present infection and therefore does not prove the active disease. There is marked peripheral blood eosinophilia (20–70%), increased muscle enzyme in serum (CPK, LDH, aldolase and transminase) and normal sedimentation rate.

Xenodiagnosis is useful, in surveys, to detect viable larvae.

Treatment Thiabendazole has been used with some success, but it gives rise to side effects like allergy. Adreno-corticosteroids may minimize this reaction. Mebendazole and pyrantel pamoate (10 mg/kg of body weight for four days) have also been used, but none of these drugs is advocated during pregnancy. Mild systemic infection is treated with rest and analgesic, recovery may take weeks and complications are rare. All patients must be carefully observed. Acute severe trichinelliasis will require corticosteroids in high doses (prednisone, 60 mg daily) for two or more weeks.

Supportive treatment can be done with analgesics to reduce muscular pain, Glauber salt (Na_2 So_4) to dislodge the adult worm from the intestine and sterile isotonic saline solution infusion for dehydrated patients.

Prophylaxis It consists of

1) The destruction of all carcasses and viscera of pigs dying on farms;
2) The elimination of raw garbage feeding;
3) Extermination of rats and mice; and
4) Thorough cooking of all pork to be consumed by humans.

TRICHURIS TRICHIURA

Genus: Trichuris

Trichuris trichiura, the human whipworm producing trichuriasis, was first described by Linnaeus in 1771. Well-preserved eggs of this worm were observed in the feces, in the preserved body of a girl whose death had occurred 450 years ago. This whipworm has a cosmopolitan distribution but is more common in the warm, moist regions of the world. It is prevalent in Asia, USSR, Europe, Africa and America.

T. trichiura remains attached to the wall of the human cecum.

Morphology The adult worm is brown in colour. Three-fifths of the anterior end is very thin and hair-like. The posterior two-fifths are fleshy, thick and stout. The worm, therefore, resembles a whip with a handle. On the ventral portion of the anterior part, there is a broad, longitudinal ***bacillary*** band, which is an area of cuticular pores. The anterior portion contains a minute, delicate esophagus. The posterior portion contains the intestine and sex organs.

The male worm (Fig. 8.7) measures 30–45 mm in length and its caudal extremity is coiled ventrally through 360° degrees. The genitalia consist of a long testis, vas deferens and an ejaculatory tubule which empties into the cloaca. A single spicule protrudes through a retractile penial sheath which has a bulbous termination covered with small spines (Fig. 8.8).

The adult female (Fig. 8.9) measures 35–40 mm in length and is bluntly rounded at the posterior end. The genitalia consist of a single ovary, oviduct and uterus which constrict behind the vulva and end in the external pore situated at the anterior extremity of the fleshy portion of the worm. The female of *T. trichiura* is oviparous.

The egg (Fig. 8.10) of *T. trichiura* is barrel shaped with mucoid plugs at both ends. It measures 50–54 μm by 22–23 μm. It has a triple shell in addition to a vitelline membrane, and the outermost shell is bile stained. The egg contains an unsegmented ovum and floats in a saturated solution of common salt. The egg laying capacity of this worm is about 5000–7000 per day.

The egg containing the unsegmented ovum is evacuated in the humans feces. It develops into a fully embryonated egg in moist soil. This egg containing the rhabditiform larva is infective to humans who become infected by swallowing the fully embryonated egg. The egg shell is digested in the human small intestine and the larva emerges through one of the mucoid plugs of the egg. The liberated larva gets attached, for nourishment, to the small intestine. It then passes down into

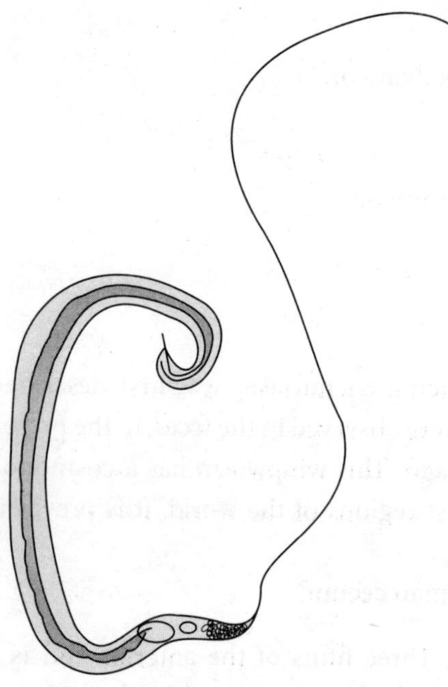

Fig. 8.7 Adult male of *T. trichiura*.

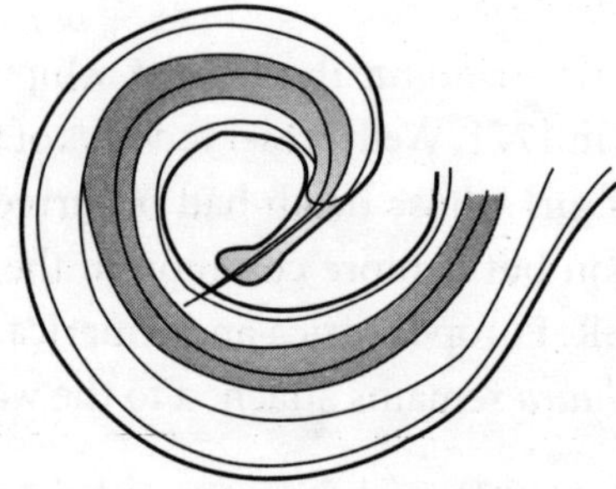

Fig. 8.8 Posterior end of adult male of *T. trichiura* showing copulatory sheath and spicule.

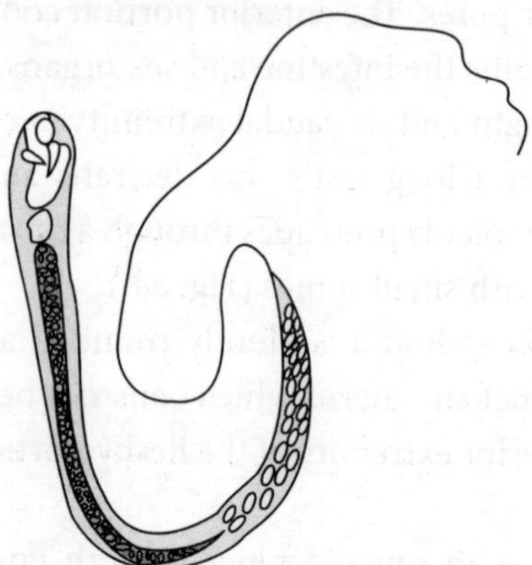

Fig. 8.9 Adult female of *T. trichiura*.

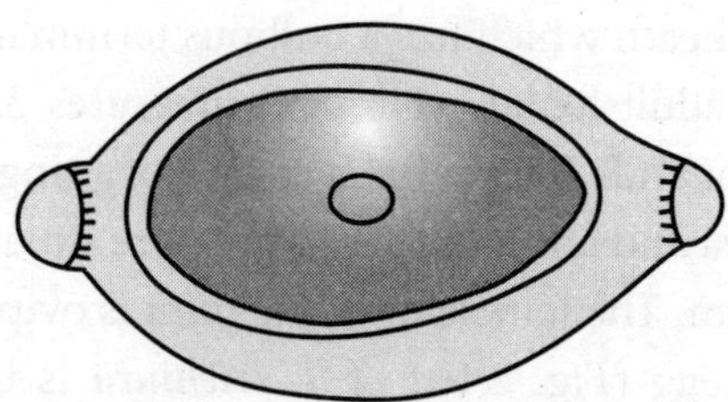

Fig. 8.10 Egg of *T. trichiura*.

the cecum, the site of predilection, where it grows into an adult worm in about three months. The gravid female starts laying eggs which are passed out in the human feces. Thus, the lifecycle is repeated (Figs 8.11 and 8.12).

Lifecycle No intermediate host is required in the lifecycle of *T. trichiura*.

Pathogenicity and clinical features The exact mechanism of pathogenicity of *T. trichiura* is not completely understood yet. The processes of infection may be traumatic or allergic. Many worms together may block the lumen of the appendix, cause irritation and inflammation of the cecum and produce colitis and secondary anemia which may be due to prolonged dysentery. One worm may suck up to 0.005 ml of blood per day. The presence of only a few worms provokes hardly any allergy or blood loss. The common symptoms are abdominal pain, vomiting, constipation, abdominal distension and systemic intoxication. The skin is dry and the patient is emaciated. The clinical picture is similar to that of hookworm disease, acute appendicitis or amebic dysentery.

Light infections are often asymptomatic. Heavy infections are accompanied by abdominal pain and diarrhea, which may be severe and prolonged. Though the infection is limited to the large intestine, malabsorption does not occur; rectal prolapse is a complication of heavy infection.

Laboratory diagnosis The characteristic egg of *T. trichiura* can be demonstrated in the patient's stool.

Treatment Dithiazanine iodide, thiabendazole and mebendazole are effective. Mebendazole, 100 mg twice daily for three days can be used for light and heavy infections, with precautions for children under two years. It is contraindicated to pregnant women. Methyl benzimidazole, a new broadspectrum anthelmintic, has produced a high cure rate when used in minute amounts.

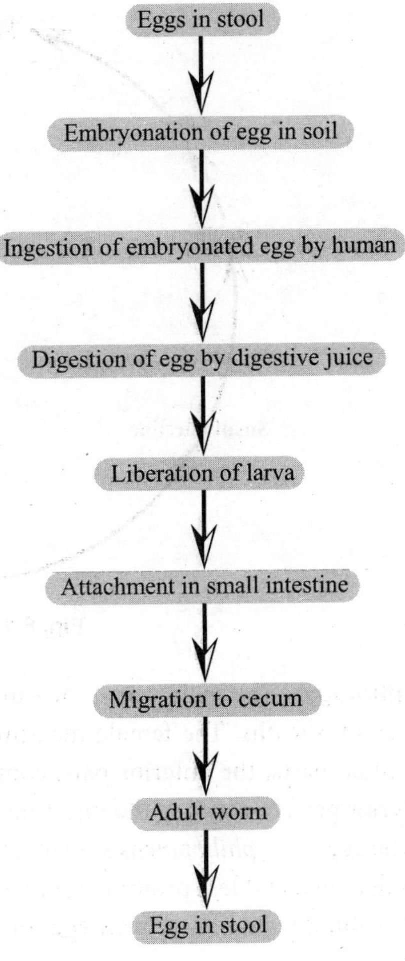

Fig. 8.11 Lifecycle of *T. trichiura*

Prophylaxis Proper disposal of feces, thorough cleaning of hands before meals, children not being allowed to defecate on the ground, avoiding putting dirty fingers into the mouth and consumption of properly cooked vegetables are effective measures of prophylaxis.

CAPILLARIA PHILIPPINENSIS

Superfamily: Trichinelloidea

Genus: Capillaria

Capillaria philippinensis producing intestinal capillariasis, was first reported in 1963 from a male patient in the Philippines. This parasite is found commonly in the Philippines. The worm *Capillaria philippinensis* remains burrowed in the mucosa of the jejunum, with both ends free.

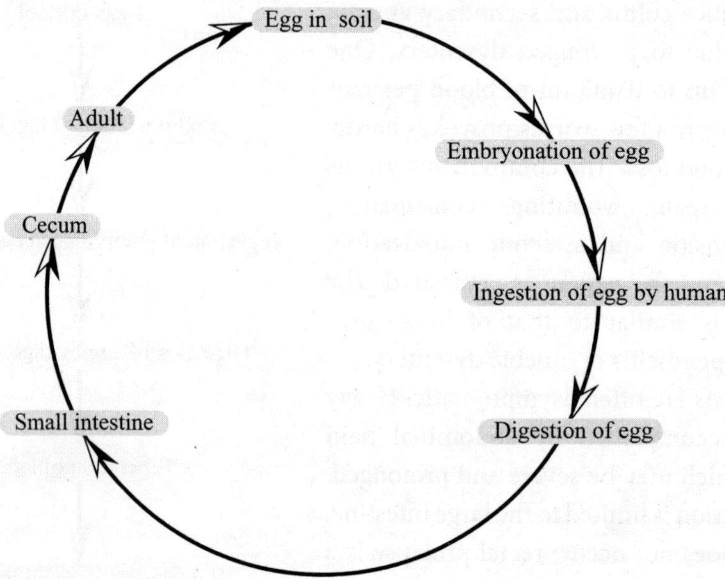

Fig. 8.12 Lifecycle of *T. trichiura*.

Morphology The male worm measures 2.3–3.17 mm in length. It has caudal alae and long non-spiny sheaths. The female measures 2.5–4.3 mm in length. The body of the female has two equal parts, the anterior part, containing the esophagus and esophageal glands, and the posterior part, containing the intestine and the reproductive organ with a prominent vulva.

The egg of *C. philippinensis* is similar to that of *T. trichiura*, but it is smaller and more oval with flattened and less prominent bipolar plugs.

The differences between the eggs of *C. philippinensis* and *T. trichiura* are as follows:

	C. philippinensis	*T. trichiura*
Size	45 × 21 μm	52 × 26 μm
Shape	Peanut-shaped	Elliptical
Plugs	Bipolar, flattened	Bipolar, protuberant
Shell	Pitted	Smooth

Lifecycle It has not yet been established, but all stages of development can occur only in humans. This infection is caused possibly by eating raw fish.

Pathogenicity and clinical features The mode of infection is by the fecal–oral route. The epithelial cells of the jejunum, in most cases, show degenerative changes and the lamina propria is inflamed. The chief symptoms are diarrhea, emaciation, weakness and abdominal pain. Death may be due to cachexia.

Laboratory diagnosis Adult worms and eggs can be detected in the feces. The intradermal test which is highly sensitive and specific can also be used.

Treatment Thiabendazole and dithiazanine are effective.

Prophylaxis In endemic areas where the infection seems to be acquired by eating raw fish, people should be advised to cook the fish thoroughly.

STRONGYLOIDES STERCORALIS

Superfamily: Rhabdiasoidea

Genus: Strongyloides

Strongyloides stercoralis, the threadworm, producing strongyloidiasis or strongyloidosis, was first discovered by Normand (1876) in the feces of French soldiers. This threadworm is found distributed in Asia, America and the Pacific Islands.

The parasitic females remain buried in the mucous membrane of the small intestine (duodenum and jejunum) of humans.

Morphology The parasitic ***female*** (Fig. 8.13) measures 2.5 mm in length and 40–50 μm in diameter. The cylindrical muscular esophagus occupies the anterior third of the body (Fig. 8.14), whereas the intestine fills up the posterior two third. The anus opens mid-ventrally, a short distance in front of the pointed caudal tip, and a short vulva is situated at the junction of the middle and posterior thirds of the body. The genitalia are paired and extend from the vulva; one set of genitalia is situated anteriorily; and another posteriorly. Adult worms are ovo-viviparous.

The parasitic males are similar to the free living males (Fig. 8.15). They are shorter and broader than the parasitic females; they cannot penetrate the mucous membrane of the intestine, so they remain in the lumen of the human intestine.

The developing eggs (Fig. 8.16) fill the uterus and occupy a major portion of the body. They are transparent, thin-shelled and oval. They measure about 50 μm in length

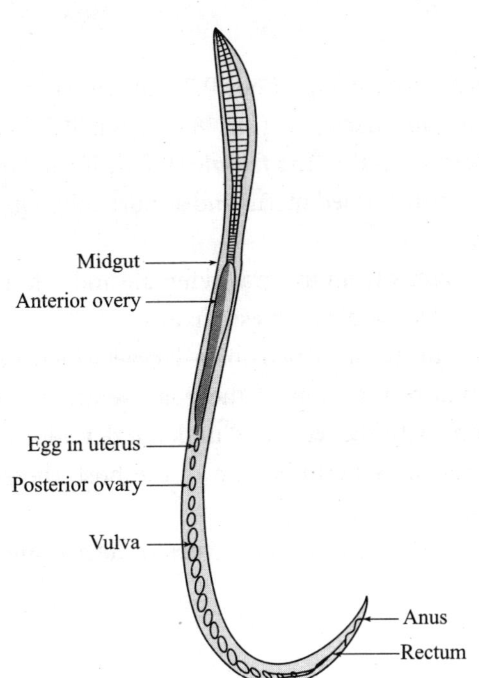

Fig. 8.13 Parasitic female of *S. stercoralis.*

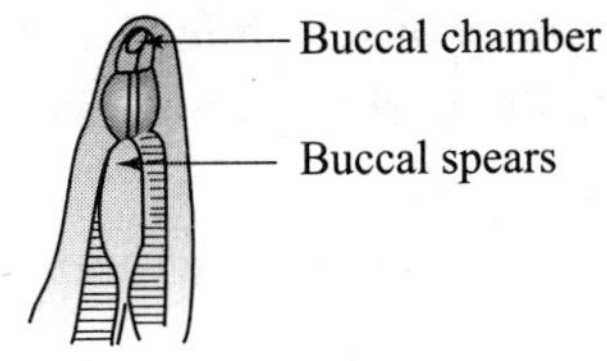

Fig. 8.14 Anterior end of parasitic female of *S. stercoralis.*

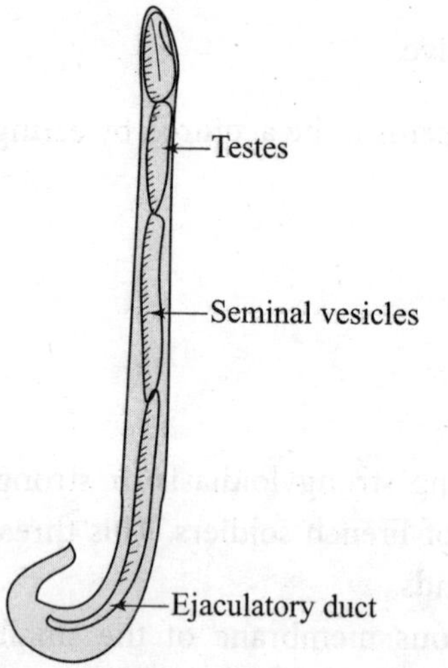

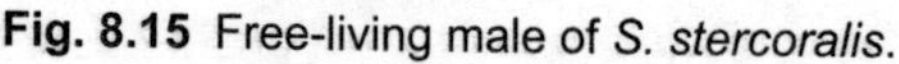

Fig. 8.15 Free-living male of *S. stercoralis.*

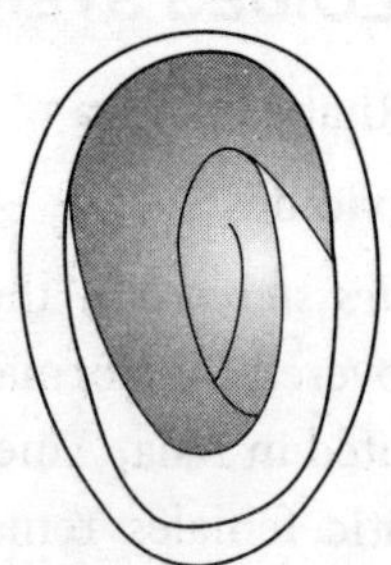

Fig. 8.16 Egg of *S. stercoralis.*

and 30 µm in breadth. As soon as the eggs are laid, the rhabditiform larvae are hatched out and come out of the mucous membrane of the human intestine into the lumen, from where they are passed in the feces. Therefore, the larvae are found in the feces, but not in the eggs.

There are two types of larvae:

1) The rhabditiform larvae and
2) The filariform larvae.

The male rhabditiform larva is broadly fusiform, measuring about 0.7 mm in length by 40–50 µm in diameter. It has two spicules and a gubernaculum (Fig. 8.17), but it has no caudal alae and the tail portion is pointed and curved ventrally. The ***female*** rhabditiform larva is stout, measures about 1 mm by 50–75 µm and has a two-horned uterus and a short vulva which opens near the middle of the ventral side of the body.

The rhabditiform larva (Fig. 8.19) is developed directly from the gravid female and is found in the lumen of the intestine. It has a short mouth and a double bulb esophagus.

In the lumen of the bowel, the larvae metamorphose into filariform larvae which may penetrate into the intestinal mucosa, causing internal re-infection. If these larvae are carried further down the bowel, they may be passed out along with the feces and undergo development in the soil. Sometimes, they may penetrate the perianal or perineal skin of the host, thereby becoming a source of auto-infection (hyper-infection).

If the free living rhabditiform larvae are voided with the feces, two types of development take place in the soil:

1) Direct (host → soil → host) and
2) Indirect cycles.

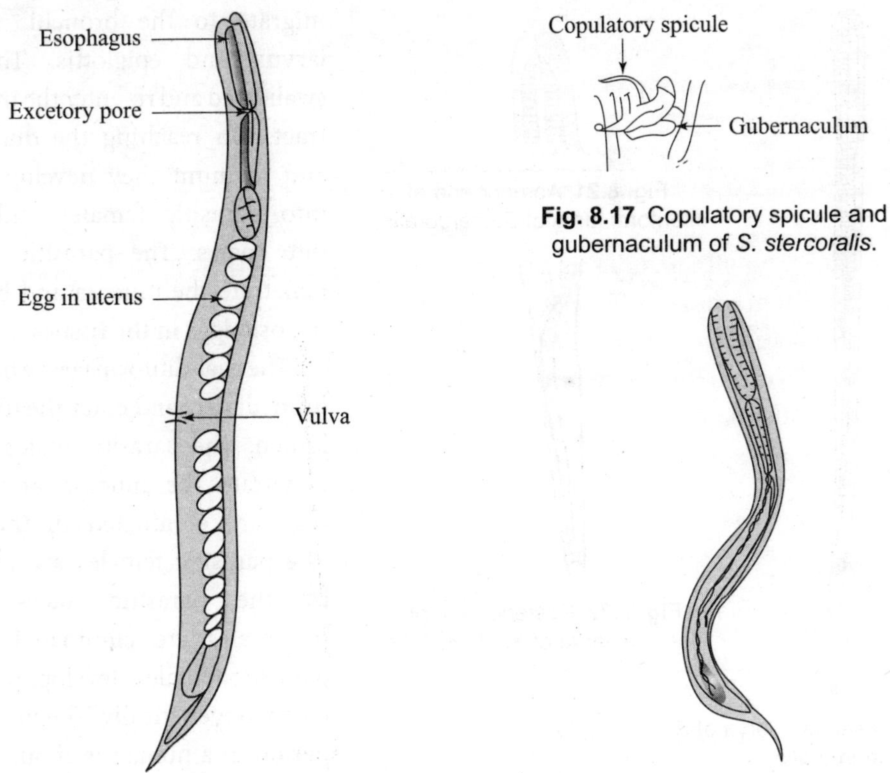

Fig. 8.17 Copulatory spicule and gubernaculum of *S. stercoralis*.

Fig. 8.18 Free-living female of *S. stercoralis*.

Fig. 8.19 Rhabditiform larva of *S. stercoralis*.

In the direct cycle, the rhabditiform larvae in the soil directly metamorphose, in three to four days, into filariform larvae. One rhabditiform larva gives rise to only one filariform larva, and there is no sexual phase.

In the indirect cycle, the male and female free-living rhabditiform larvae copulate and produce a batch of rhabditiform larvae which are indistinguishable from those produced by the parasitic females. In three to four days they transform into filariform larvae, i.e., each pair gives rise to 30 filariform larvae.

The filariform larvae (infective stage – Figs 8.20–8.22) are longer and more slender than the rhabditiform larvae. They have short mouths and a cylindrical esophagus. They enter the human body through the skin. Filariform larvae may develop directly from the rhabditiform larvae in the soil or from fertilized female rhabditiform larvae.

Lifecycle Humans are the optimum hosts and no intermediate host is required.

When a person walks barefoot on soil contaminated with feces containing filariform larvae of *S. stercoralis,* these filariform larvae penetrate directly through the skin (portal of entry) of the bare foot, and enter the venous circulation. They are carried through the right part of the heart to the lungs and break out of the pulmonary capillaries into the alveoli. They then

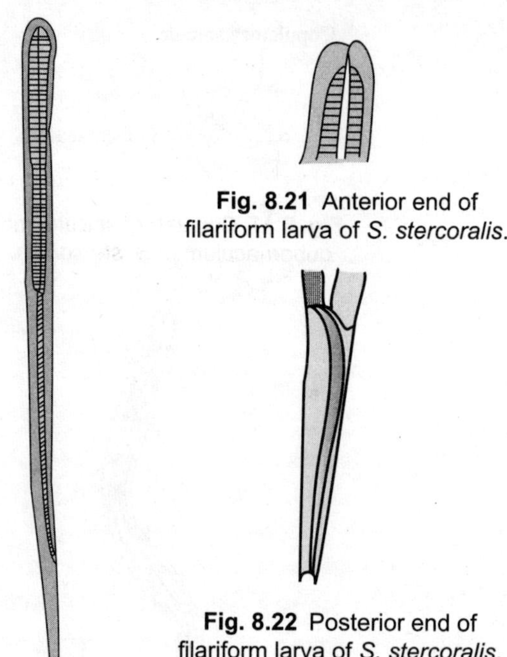

Fig. 8.21 Anterior end of filariform larva of *S. stercoralis*.

Fig. 8.22 Posterior end of filariform larva of *S. stercoralis*.

Fig. 8.20 Filariform larva of *S. stercoralis*.

migrate to the bronchi, trachea, larynx and epiglottis. They are swallowed and re-enter the intestinal tract. On reaching the duodenum and jejunum they develop mostly into parasitic females and rarely into males. The parasitic females penetrate the mucosa and begin to deposit eggs in the tissues.

The rhabditiform larvae hatch out immediately and enter the intestinal lumen. The parasitic males cannot penetrate the mucosa and hence they are eliminated in the feces. The parasitic females are fertilized by the parasitic males before the males are eliminated or the parasitic females develop, probably, parthenogenetically. The incubation period in a human is about 28 days (Figs 8.23 and 8.24).

Pathogenicity and clinical features

1. Skin lesion: While invading the skin, the filariform larvae produce a petechial hemorrhage at the site of entry, followed by intense pruritus, congestion, edema with a macular erythematous spot (0.5–1 mm in diameter) and urticarial rash.
2. Pulmonary lesion: As the larvae break out of the pulmonary capillaries into the alveoli, hemorrhage and cellular infiltration into the air sacs and bronchioles may develop. While passing through the lungs, young worms may produce broncho-pneumonia with consolidation of the lobules. The symptoms are frequent coughing, pleural effusion and pyothorax.
3. Intestinal lesion: In heavy infestation, the mucosa of the intestine may be honey-combed by the adult worms and larvae, and sloughing of excessive patches may occur. Three types of enteritis occur:
   a) Catarrhal enteritis
   b) Edematous enteritis and
   c) Ulcerative enteritis.

There is accompanying diarrhea with mucus and blood, which can be very painful.

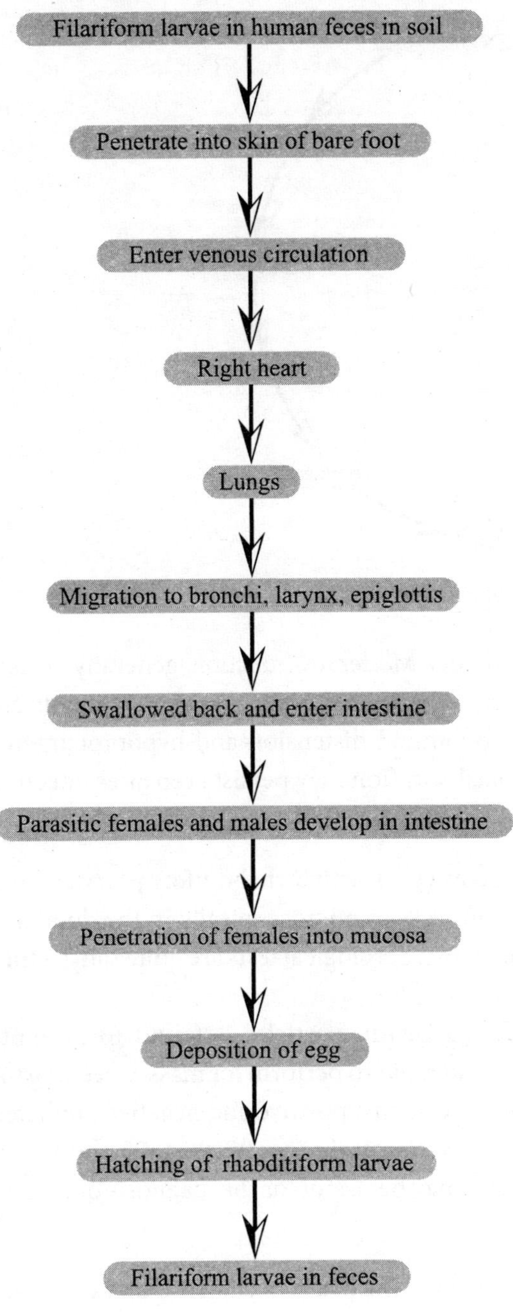

Fig. 8.23 Lifecycle of *S. stercoralis*.

Alternatively, strongyloides larvae may develop to the infective stage in the intestine and penetrate the intestinal wall to reach circulation and enter the cycle of infection. This process of ***internal auto-infection*** is unique to this species among trematodes. Infective larvae may also penetrate the perianal skin after being passed with the stool to enter the host by ***external auto-infection***. This process may enable an infection to persist for 30 to 40 years in the absence of re-exposure of the host.

In immunosuppressed or malnourished patients, internal auto-infection may assume proportions with ectopic migration of the larvae, resulting in the ***hyperinfection syndrome***.

In the hyperinfection syndrome and in other severe cases of strongyloidiasis, intestinal changes are more pronounced. Parasites are found in all layers of the intestinal wall which is thickened by edema and fibrosis. Pulmonary involvement in the hyperinfection syndrome is characterized by extensive larval migration and hemorrhagic pneumonia. As the larvae migrate through the lungs, they sometimes cause a pneumonitic process similar to Loeffler's syndrome in ascariasis. Larvae may be found throughout the body, especially in the kidney, brain and heart. In the small intestine, microscopic abnormalities are stunted, with swollen or fused villi, eosinophilic infiltration of lamina propria and mononuclear infiltration of the mucosa.

As the larvae penetrate the skin, particularly in the case of external auto-infection, they may cause a migratory pruritic eruption known as ***larva currens***. Larval migration through the lung may cause pneumonia with cough, dyspnea and hemoptysis, but this is common. Infection may be accompanied by recurrent urticaria.

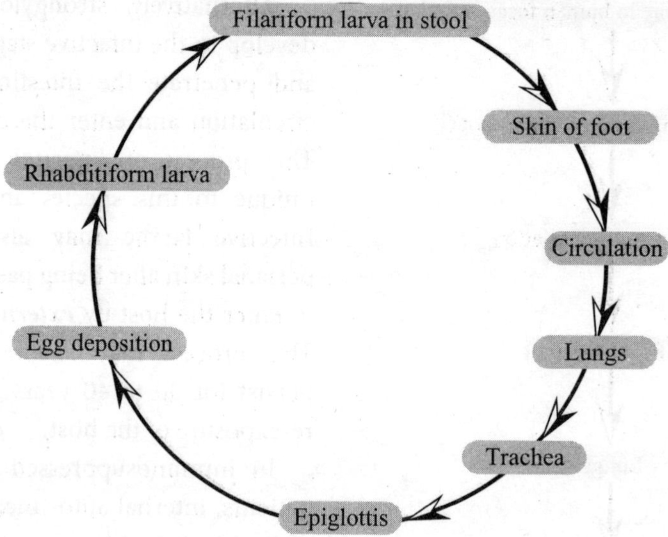

Fig. 8.24 Lifecycle of *S. stercoralis*.

Mild intestinal infections are often asymptomatic. Moderate infection generally results in epigastric pain and intermittent diarrhea, whereas heavy infections may cause significant malabsorption with bulky foul-smelling stools, abdominal distension and hypoproteinemia with edema. In patients who are malnourished, malabsorption may persist even after infection is adequately treated.

Laboratory diagnosis This depends on the recovery of active rhabditiform larvae from the stool and sputum. The larvae of *S. stercoralis* can be seen microscopically in the duodenal washing and in the material obtained from jejunal biopsy. Serological tests are quite satisfactory in the diagnosis of this disease.

Indirect agglutination test with newly developed gelatin particles is found to be quite comparable with HIA and ELISA. The test is simple and rapid to perform for mass-screening for human strongyloides. Very recently, the sensitivity, specificity, positive and negative predicted values of ELISA test using F_2, protein fraction from *S. stercoralis* was 95, 96.4, 95 and 96.4% respectively. Another recent immuno-blot technique may be useful for the diagnosis of human strongyloidiasis.

Treatment Thiabendazole and albendazole are currently the drugs of choice. Other drugs are pyrvinium pamoate, mebendazole, diethylcarbamazine. None of these drugs are recommended for pregnant women.

Prophylaxis consists of the following measures: 1) The human body must be protected from infective soil and from contaminated feces 2) Constipation should be avoided by the use of cathartics 3) Possible auto-infection should be avoided by careful cleaning of the anal sphincter 4) Diagnosed cases should be treated specifically.

SUPERFAMILY STRONGYLOIDEA

General characters The superfamily strongyloidea possesses a well-developed mouth cavity (buccal capsule), which may contain teeth or cutting plates. The male has a bursa (copulatory bursa) which surrounds the cloaca. The egg has a transparent shell and contains a segmented ovum, and the larva develops in moist soil.

This superfamily contains two families:

1) Family Ancylostomatidae (having teeth or cutting plates in the mouth cavity) and
2) Family Strongyloidae (lacking teeth or cutting plates in the mouth cavity).

Family Ancylostomatidae has two subfamilies:

1) Sub-family Ancylostomatinae (tooth like processes):
   a) Two pairs of teeth *Ancylostoma duodenale*
   b) One pair of teeth *A. braziliense*
   c) Three pairs of teeth *A. caninum* and
2) Sub-family Uncinariinae (cutting plates) – *Necator americanus.*

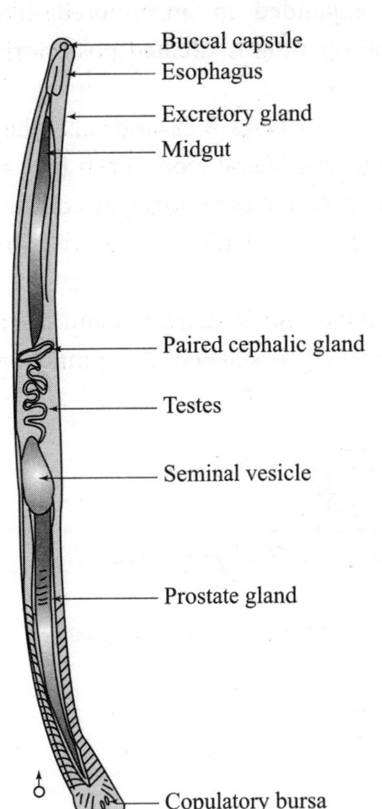

Fig. 8.25 *Ancylostoma duodenale* (male).

Ancylostoma duodenale

Ancylostoma duodenale, the 'Old World' hook-worm, producing ancylostomiasis was first written about in Egypt (1600 BC) and the first accurate description was given by Dubini in 1843 from autopsy material. *Ancylostoma duodenale* is mainly a parasite of Southern Europe, Africa, northern India (Punjab and Uttar Pradesh), Sri Lanka, Japan, China and Chile. Ancylostomiasis in dogs has been reported by the author (1972) from Pondicherry, India.

The adult worm lives mainly in the jejunum.

Morphology The adult worm (Figs 8.25 and 8.26) is a small, stout, greyish-white, cylindrical worm. Due to the ingested blood in its intestine, the living worm is pinkish or creamy grey in colour. The anterior end is bent dorsally like a hook, hence the name 'hookworm'. The oral aperture is also directed towards the dorsal surface. The large buccal capsule (Fig. 8.27) is provided with six teeth, of which the four on the ventral surface are hook-like and the two on the dorsal surface are knob-like.

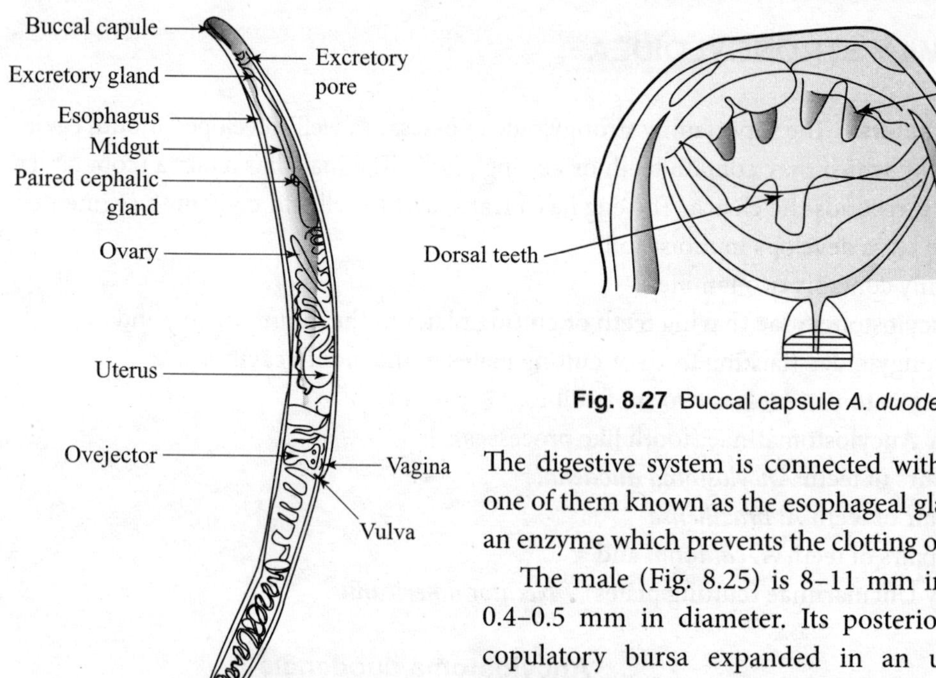

Fig. 8.26 *A. duodenale* (female).

Fig. 8.27 Buccal capsule *A. duodenale*.

The digestive system is connected with five glands, one of them known as the esophageal gland secreting an enzyme which prevents the clotting of blood.

The male (Fig. 8.25) is 8–11 mm in length and 0.4–0.5 mm in diameter. Its posterior end has a copulatory bursa expanded in an umbrella-like fashion. The genital opening is situated posteriorly with the cloaca.

The copulatory bursa (Figs 8.25 and 8.28) has three lobes: one dorsal and two lateral lobes. Each lobe is supported by chitinous rays, the dorsal lobe being supported by three rays (a single ray and two externo-dorsal rays) and the two lateral lobes by ten rays (three pairs of lateral rays and two pairs of ventral rays). Totally, there are thirteen rays.

The female (Fig. 8.26) measures 10–13 mm in length and 0.6 mm in diameter, and has a tapering posterior end and no expanded bursa. Its genital opening is situated at the junction of the posterior end and the middle third of the body. Insemination occurs when the male applies its copulatory bursa around the vulva, inserts the pair of copulatory spicules and secretes cementum to provide an uninterrupted discharge of spermatozoa. Because of the position of the genital opening, the worm assumes a Y-shaped

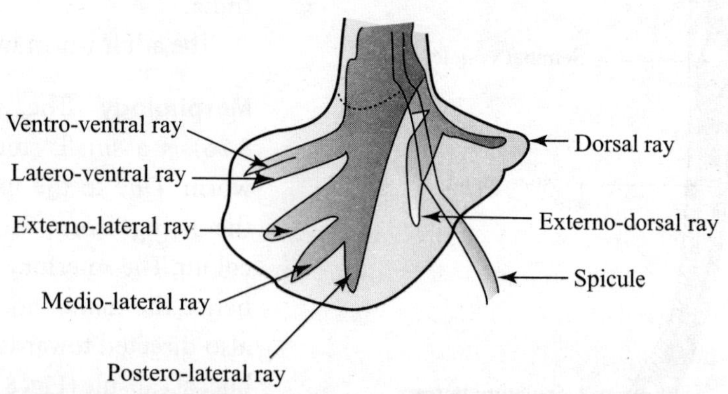

Fig. 8.28 *A. duodenale* (The dorsal ray is single but partially divided at the tip and each division is tripartite. Total number of rays – 13).

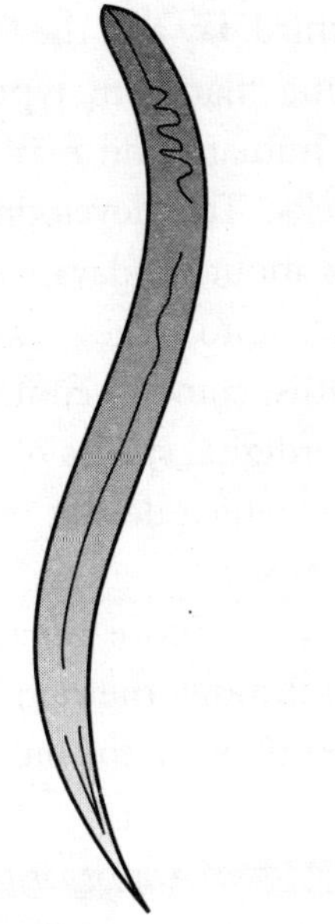

Fig. 8.29 Rhabditiform larva.

figure during copulation. The adult worm lives in the human intestine for about three to four years.

The rhabditiform larva (Fig. 8.29) measures 0.25–0.3 mm in length and 17 μm in diameter. It has a long narrow buccal chamber, a flask-shaped muscular esophagus occupying the anterior third of the digestive tract, a midgut, a short rectum and a very small genital opening. These characteristics may be useful to distinguish this from the strongyloides larvae and other free-living nematodes.

The filariform larva (Fig. 8.30) which is a long, delicate organism with a short esophagus, without the notch in the caudal extremity, is infective to humans.

The egg (Fig. 8.31) measures 65 μm in length and 40 μm in breadth. It is oval or elliptical in shape with bluntly rounded ends, colourless (not bile-stained) and is surrounded by a transparent hyaline shell membrane. It contains a segmented ovum with four blastomeres, and there is space between the egg shell and the segmented ovum. The ovum of the freshly laid egg is unsegmented. When the fertilized egg passes through the bowel, the segmentation of the ovum proceeds to four blastomeres. The egg is not infective to humans, and floats in a saturated solution of common salt.

Lifecycle The human is the optimum host for *A. duodenale*.

Stage 1 consists of the passage of eggs from the infected host. The fertilized eggs with four blastomeres are discharged in the feces of the human host.

Stage 2 is the development of the egg in the soil. In the soil of a moist, shady and warm place, the eggs usually hatch in 24–48 hours and the emerging larvae (rhabditiform larvae) begin to feed on bacteria and organic debris (mode of feeding same as in first stage hookworm larva).

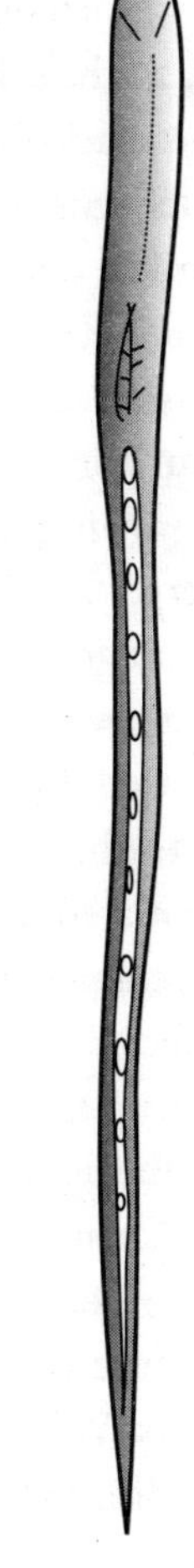

Fig. 8.30 Filariform larva *stercoralis*.

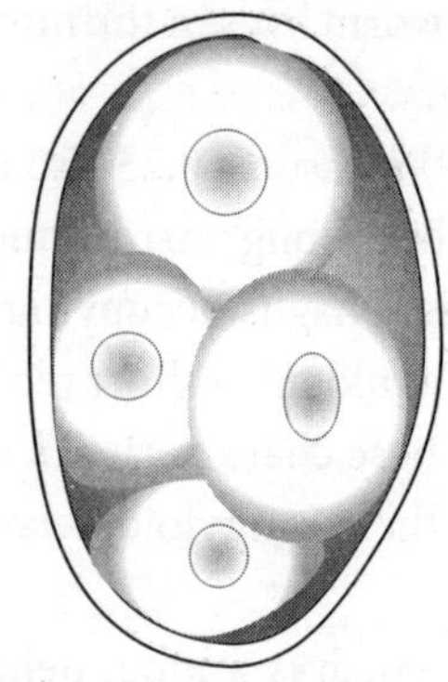

Fig. 8.31 Egg of *A. duodenale* showing four blastomeres (enlarged).

Then they moult twice, on the third day and the fifth day, and transform into the non-feeding filariform type (third larval stage), which is infective to humans and may remain viable in the soil for several weeks. The development of filariform larvae from the egg takes about ten days.

Stage 3 constitutes the entrance into a new host. The filariform larvae cast off their sheaths, come in contact with the exposed human skin of the interdigital spaces of the feet and penetrate the skin. Those larvae which do not reach the venules usually die and are phagocytosed.

Stage 4 is the migration of the larvae. Those larvae which invade the bloodstream are carried through the right part of the heart to the lungs, where they break out of the pulmonary capillaries into the alveoli. Then they migrate to the bronchi, trachea, larynx and epiglottis and are swallowed back. During their migration through the esophagus, a third moulting takes place and a terminal buccal capsule is formed. This stage takes about ten days.

Stage 5 consists of the development of the larva into an adult worm and the laying of eggs. The growing larvae settle in the jejunum, undergo a fourth moulting and develop into adolescent worms. During this stage, the provisional toothless buccal capsule is replaced by the definite buccal capsule with teeth. The worms become sexually differentiated and grow into adults. The fertilized females lay eggs which are passed in the feces. A period of about five weeks elapses from the time of the patient's exposure until the females lay eggs. When the mature filariform larvae of *A. duodenale* are swallowed, very rarely, they may develop into mature worms without passage through the lungs. Within a year, 70% of the worms may be eliminated in the absence of re-infection, although few may persist for up to nine years (Figs 8.32 and 8.33).

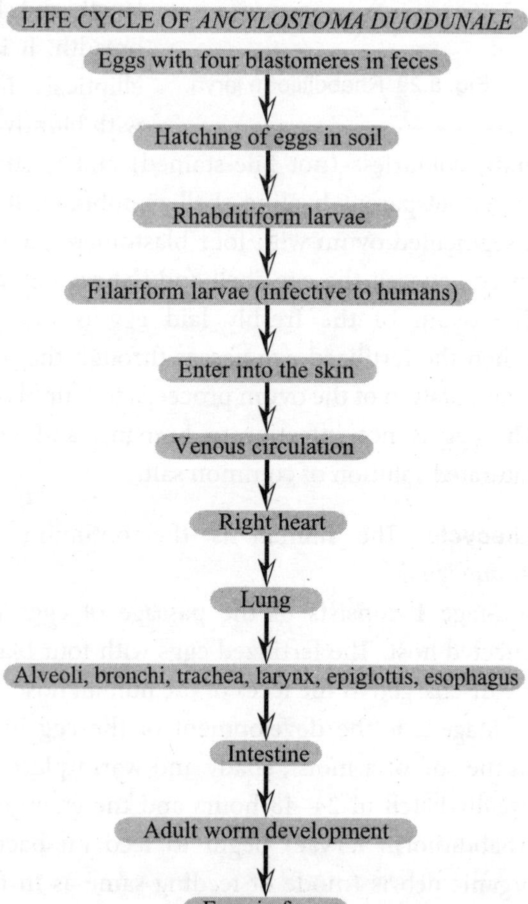

Fig. 8.32 Lifecycle of *A.duodenale*.

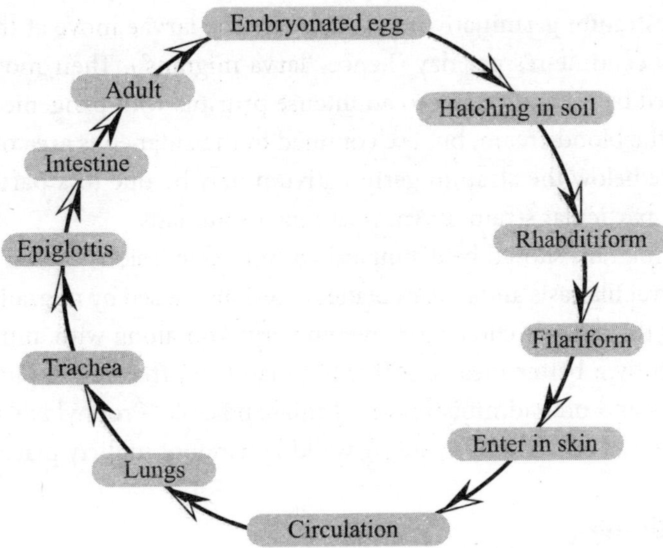

Fig. 8.33 Lifecycle of *A. duodenale.*

Pathogenicity The filariform larvae of *A. duodenale* penetrate the thin skin of the interdigital spaces of the human host. The common sites of entry are

1) The thin skin between the toes
2) The dorsum of the feet and
3) The inner sides of the soles.

Pathogenic effects may be caused by ancylostome larvae or adult worms. These are

1) Cutaneous lesions (ancylostome dermatitis and creeping eruption) and
2) Visceral pulmonary lesions (minute hemorrhages, bronchitis and bronchopneumonia).

Cutaneous lesions: At the site where the filariform (the third stage) larvae of *Necator americanus* and *A. duodenale* penetrate the skin, they produce 'ground itch', characterized by itching and burning, edema and erythema which develops into a papular eruption, then a vesicle.

Cutaneous larva migrans

(Creeping eruption): Cutaneous larva migrans is a skin lesion produced by the entry of the filariform larvae of canine or feline and sometimes human Ancylostoma *(A. braziliense, A. duodenale, A. caninum* or *Necator americanus* into the skin of an unprotected foot). Such lesions due to *N. americanus* have been observed in Indian garden labourers.

The infective stage larvae of *A. braziliense* are unable to enter below the stratum germinativum of the human skin. Thus, they produce a reddish, itchy papule at the site of invasion which is followed in 2–3 days by a serpiginous tunnel in the stratum germinativum with the corium as the floor and the stratum germinativum as the roof. The larvae move at the rate of several millimeters to a few centimetres per day (hence, 'larva migrans'). Their movements and the tissue reaction caused by them give rise to an intense pruritus with pyogenic infection. These larvae do not enter the bloodstream, but are confined to the cutaneous area of the body. Their inability to penetrate below the stratum germinativum may be due to a partial physiological inadaptability of the particular strain of Ancylostoma for humans.

Cutaneous larva migrans should be distinguished from skin lesions caused by strongyloides larvae, cutaneous larval filariasis and linear cutaneous lesions caused by migrating fly maggots.

Thiabendazole is the drug of choice for creeping eruption along with anti-histamines, but albendazole is currently a better means of therapy than local freezing, topical application of certain anthelmintics and oral administration of thiabendazole. Prophylaxis is by eradicating this infection in dogs and cats and by avoiding walking barefoot in dirty places.

Visceral larva migrans

In natural hosts under unsuitable conditions or in natural hosts, when nematode larvae gain entrance into extra-intestinal viscera, they produce visceral larva migrans which is surrounded by phagocytic cells resulting in granulomatous lesions.

When the unnatural hosts (human and mouse) ingest infective stage eggs of *Toxocara canis* (dog ascarid) and *T. cati* (cat ascarid), these eggs hatch out in the small intestine and these free larvae invade the intestinal wall, lymphatics and are carried into the capillaries of the extra-intestinal viscera (liver, less common, lungs, brain, eye, musculature), the larvae are attacked by host cell reaction of a granulomatous nature and their further migrations are intercepted. In humans, the larvae do not grow or moult but remain alive for weeks or months within the host cell granuloma. Visceral larva migrans can also be demonstrated in *S. stercoralis* intestinal auto-infection.

Hypereosinophilia, hepatomegaly, pulmonary diseases, cardiac dysfunction, nephrosis, cough, cerebral lesions with central nervous system involvement are the clinical features. There is no specific drug, but thiabendazole and albendazole may be helpful.

Pulmonary lesions: Minute hemorrhages are produced when the hookworm larvae break out of the pulmonary capillaries. During their migration in the lungs, if the larvae cause considerable damage, blood may accumulate in the alveolar spaces and cause difficulty in respiration. Pneumonitis is not common. The symptoms are cough, dyspnea, high eosinophilia and frequently, nausea and vomiting. Bronchitis and bronchopneumonia may occur.

The adult worm produces severe progressive anemia of the microcytic hypochromic type. The anemia may be due to chronic blood loss or nutritional defects.

1. Chronic blood loss may occur because the parasites may obtain blood for food, and chronic hemorrhages from the circumscribed lesions in the submucosa. Recently established human ancylostomes remove as much as 0.67 ml of blood per day. The major portion of the blood

may pass through the gut of the worm, but some portion may come out from the sides of the attached head of the worm. Each worm, which has been in the intestine for months or years, draws 0.2–0.5 ml of blood per day. Blood loss depends upon the number of parasites and their length of stay in the intestine. A large number of parasites over a long period may cause anemia. It has been estimated that the loss of hemoglobin for every 12 worms may be 1%. It has been suggested that the blood-sucking hookworms are in need of oxygen supplied by the red blood cells in the low oxygen environment of the intestine.

2. Nutritional defects: Iron deficiency and other hemopoietic substances in the diet are the contributory factors. It has been found that a balanced diet, to which iron and liver have been added, compensates for blood loss due to hookworm disease, even without deworming. Patients suffering from severe hookworm infection are usually poorly nourished and, hence, have poor resistance to infection.

The type of anemia depends upon the nature of the nutritional defect. In hypochromic microcytic anemia, there is iron deficiency. In the macrocytic type, there is deficiency of folic acid and vitamin B_{12}, and in the dimorphic type, there is deficiency of both iron and vitamin B_{12} or folic acid.

Blood loss is higher in *A. duodenale* infection, because it is a larger worm, which is armed with teeth and is highly migratory, therefore leaving more bleeding points.

Clinical features Based on the severity of symptoms, cases may be classed as mild, moderate and severe types. In the mild type (with blood compensation), the anemia is negligible. This type is clinically unimportant.

In the moderate type (with appreciable blood decompensation), the symptoms are heart-burn, flatulence, fullness in the abdomen and epigastric pain. These are relieved by eating clay, mud or earth (which is known as *pica* or *geophagy).* There may be low grade, intermittent fever, lassitude, dyspnea and palpitation of the heart.

In the severe type, the classical picture of hookworm disease is present. There is constipation or diarrhea and the food is not properly digested. The skin is dry, harsh and pale yellow. Even in a hot climate, the patient is cold. The patient eats clay which relieves the pain in the intestinal tract. The hair is dry and lifeless. There is edema of the face and around the eyes. 'Pot belly' is a typical physical sign in children. In the late cases, the pulse is weak; there is mental dullness, apathy and melancholia. Finally, there is physical exhaustion, cardiac failure and anasarca.

A local inflammatory response occurs at the site of skin penetration of the filariform larvae and as the larvae migrate through the lungs, an eosinophilic and mononuclear infiltration takes place, along with local hemorrhage. A heavy passage of larvae through the lungs may cause a pneumonitic process similar to Loeffler's syndrome in ascariasis. In the intestine, the adults attach themselves to the mucosa and actively suck the blood. *A. duodenale* ingests more blood (0.15 ml per worm per day) than *A. necator* (0.03 ml per worm per day). The wall of the intestine becomes edematous and a mononuclear and eosinophilic infiltration surrounds each parasite. In light infection, clinical manifestations are asymptomatic, whereas in heavy infection, they are frequent.

A pruritic, vesicular or papular eruption, known as ground itch, may develop at the site of larval invasion. This is pronounced after multiple exposures to the parasite. The passage of larvae through the lungs is sometimes associated with wheezing, dyspnea and cough productive of blood-streaked sputum.

Abdominal pain and diarrhea may be caused by adult worms in the intestine, particularly as the parasites attach themselves to the mucosa. The most important clinical manifestations are those of anemia and hypoalbuminemia, resulting from chronic blood loss. Weakness, fatigue, lassitude and growth retardation are characteristic findings in patients with hookworm disease. Signs and symptoms of high output, congestive heart failure may be present and peripheral edema may occur as a result of heart failure and hypoalbuminemia.

Laboratory diagnosis It comprises two methods:

1) The direct method and
2) The indirect method.

1. ***Direct method:***
   a) Examination of stool: The adult worm can be detected in the stool, macroscopically. The characteristic hookworm egg can be demonstrated by microscopic examination of the stool, using the concentration method. Various egg counting methods may be employed to estimate the intensity of hookworm infection. Stoll technique is not recommended for routine laboratory diagnosis.
   b) Duodenal intubation: The egg of the adult worm of Ancylostoma can be demonstrated in the material obtained by duodenal intubation.
2. ***Indirect method:***
   a) Blood examination: The nature of anemia and presence of eosinophilia can be ascertained by an examination of the blood.
   b) General examination of stool: Charcot-Leyden crystals are found in the stool. The test for occult blood in the stool is positive in hookworm infection.

Morphological examination of the adult worm or the mature infective filariform larvae can only differentiate *A. duodenale* from *Necator americanus.* The examination of their eggs cannot show the differentiation, as their eggs are similar.

Treatment This consists of supportive treatment followed by specific treatment.

1. Supportive treatment: Anemia due to hookworm disease should be treated for several days to improve the general condition of the patient before starting the specific treatment. Rich balanced diet and iron preparations such as ferrous sulphate, ferrous gluconate, ferrous carbonate should be administrated to build up the patient's condition.
2. Specific treatment: If the hemoglobin level of the blood has reached above 50%, the specific treatment should be commenced. The more recently developed anthelmintic drugs, tetrachloroethylene, mebendazole, albendazole, pyrantel pamoate, methyl benzimidazole (minute amount) and hexylresorcinol crystoids, are being employed with great success.

Prophylaxis Personal protection by wearing gloves and boots, disinfection of feces or soil and prevention of soil pollution, and treatment of carriers, affected persons and the entire community, are effective methods of prophylaxis.

Necator americanus

Necator americanus, the New World hookworm or American hookworm, producing necatoriasis, was first described by Stiles in 1902 as a new species. It is a human hookworm common in the United States, Africa, Asia, Sri Lanka, Burma, Malaysia, the Philippines, Indonesia and southern India. Its lifecycle, general morphology, pathogenicity, diagnosis and treatment are the same (Figs 8.34 and 8.35).

It can be cultivated successfully in undefined media based on chick embryo extract (CEE), serum, tissue extract.

Ancylostoma braziliense

This hookworm was reported in 1910 from cats and dogs in Brazil. Adult *A. braziliense* had been wrongly reported from humans in Indonesia, Sri Lanka, Thailand, Africa, Brazil and India.

This parasite is similar to *A. ceylanicum* but is smaller. The ***male*** measures 7.75 mm in length and 0.35 mm in diameter. Its buccal capsule is diagnostic and it has a pair of small, inconspicuous median teeth and a pair of large outer teeth. The bursa of the male is also small but distinct. The ***female*** measures 9.0 mm in length and 0.37 mm in diameter. Its eggs are similar to those of other Ancylostoma.

The filariform larva of *A. braziliense* causes creeping eruption in humans. As they cannot penetrate below the stratum germinativum of the human skin, they produce a serpiginous tunnel. *A. ceylanicum* does not produce cutaneous larva migrans in humans.

A. ceylanicum

There are instances where the adult worms of *A. ceylanicum* have been found in the human intestine, but they are common in the intestine of cats in Sri Lanka and their filariform larvae do not produce creeping eruption. It is considered to be a variant of *A. braziliense.*

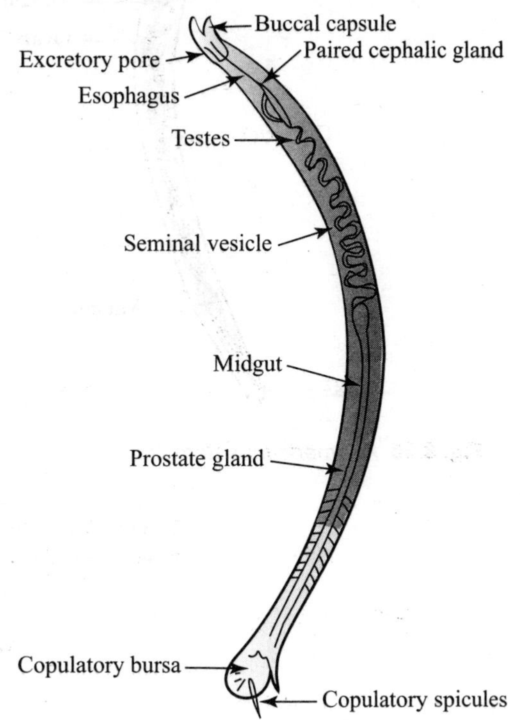

Fig. 8.34 *Necator americanus* (male).

Differentiating features of *A. duodenale* and *N.americanus*

	A. duodenale	*N. americanus*
Size	Adult worm, larger and thicker	Adult worm, smaller and more slender
Anterior end	Bends in the same direction to the body curvature	Bends in the opposite direction as the body curvature
Buccal capsule	Six teeth: four hook-like on the ventral surface and two knob-like on the dorsal surface	Four chitinous plates: two on the ventral surface and two on the dorsal surface
Copulatory bursa	Dorsal ray is single. Total number of rays–13	Dorsal ray is split from the base. Total number of rays–14
Posterior end of female	A spine is present	A spine is absent
Vulval opening	Behind the middle of the body	In front of the middle of the body
Pathogenicity	More pathogenic	Less pathogenic

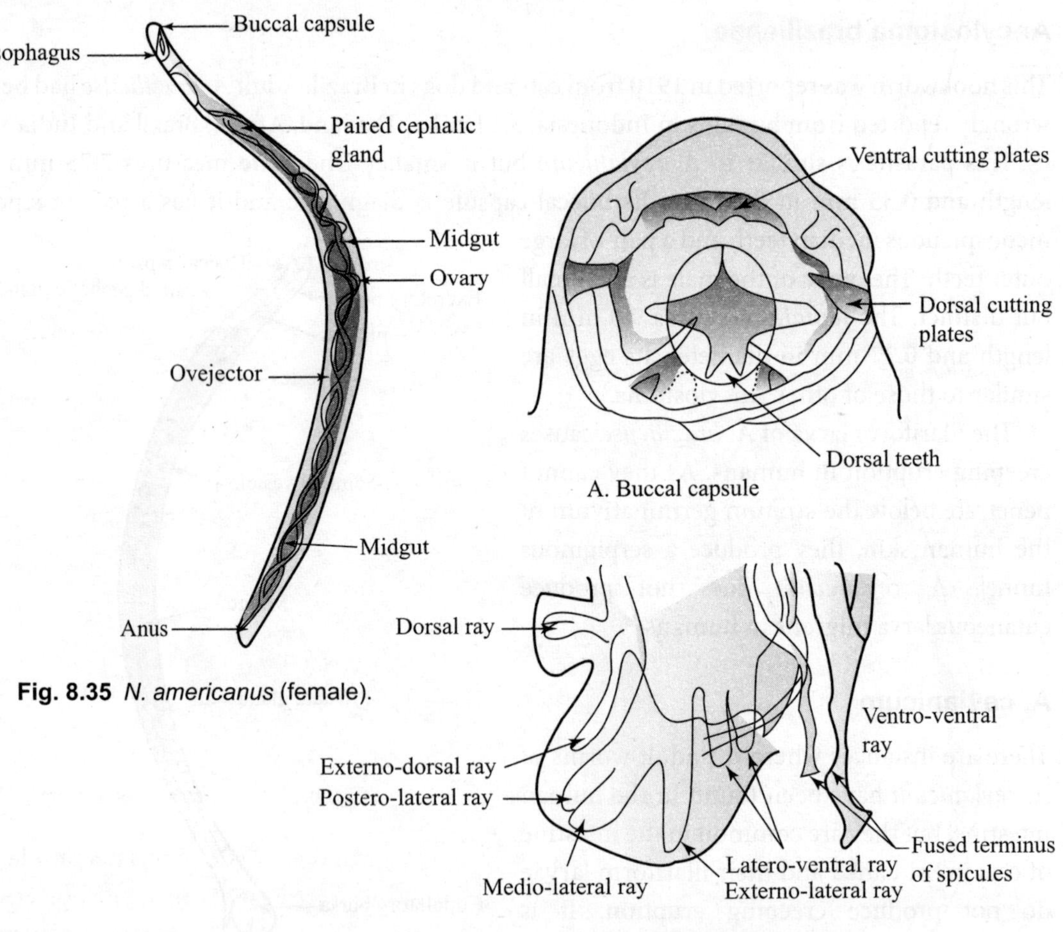

Fig. 8.35 *N. americanus* (female).

Fig. 8.36 *Necator americanus*.

A. malayanum

This is found in bears in India and Malaysia, and is the largest hookworm. This species was reported once from humans.

A. caninum

This is a common intestinal parasite of dogs in Pondicherry, India (Panjarathinam, 1972) and has been reported once as a human parasite in the Philippines.

SUPERFAMILY: OXYUROIDEA

Enterobius vermicularis

Genus: Enterobius

Enterobius vermicularis, the human pinworm or seatworm, producing enterobiasis or human oxyuriasis, has been known since ancient times. The worm has a cosmopolitan distribution. It is more common in temperate climates. In India, the author (1978) reported the finding of a gravid female in the peri-anal skin of a little girl, confirmed later in the laboratory, microscopically. The uterus of the worm was found to be filled with typical eggs.

E. vermicularis remains attached to the mucosa of the cecum, appendix, colon and ileum by its head.

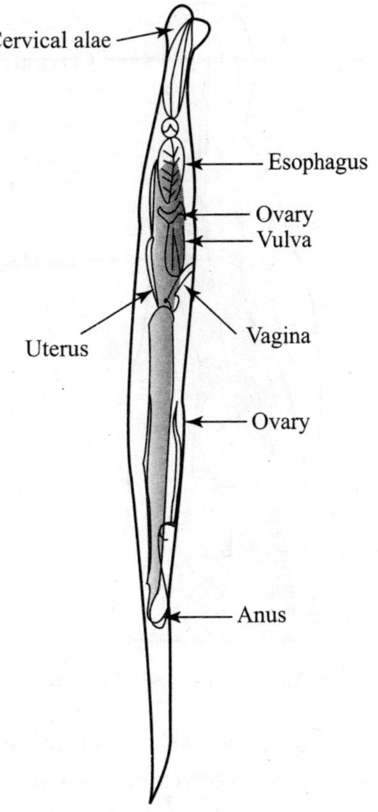

Fig. 8.37a *E. verrnicularis* female.

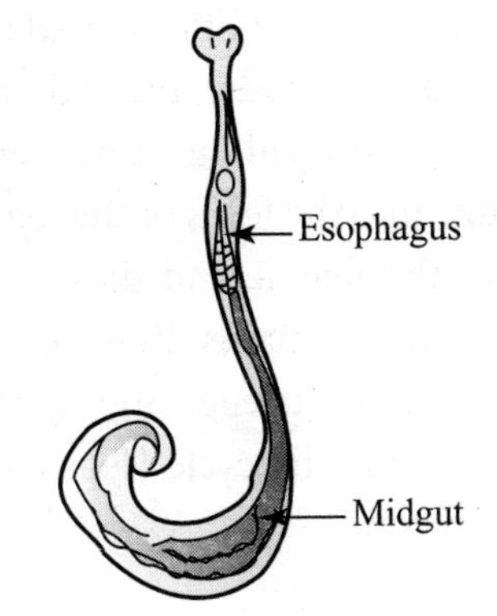

Fig. 8.37b *E. vermicularis* male.

Morphology The adult worm (Fig. 8.37a, b) is small, white and similar to a small piece of thread. It is more or less spindle shaped. The oral end has no buccal capsule, but is provided with three lips. The anterior extremity has cervical alae (bladder-like or wing-like expansions of the cuticula). The posterior end of the esophagus is dilated into a small globular bulb (a double-bulb esophagus–Fig. 8.38). It is an important characteristic of this nematode.

The male measures 2–5 mm in length by 0.1–0.2 mm in its greatest diameter, its posterior end is strongly curved ventrally. It has a single small copulatory spicule (70 µm in length), but it lacks a gubernaculum. The cloaca is near the copulatory spicule. Its reduced bursa is called

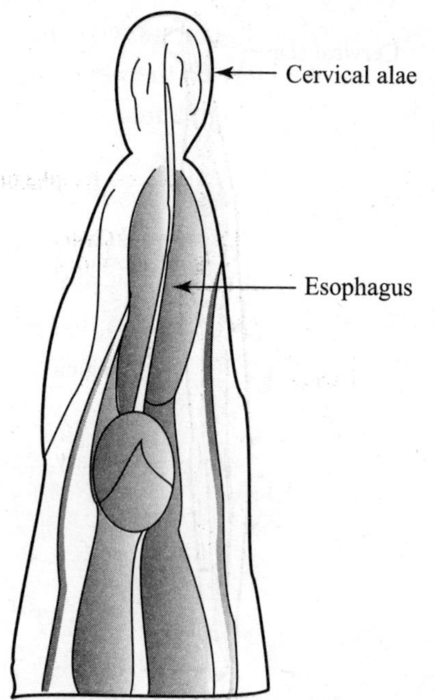

Fig. 8.38 Anterior end of *E. vermicularis.*

'caudal alae' supported by a pair of caudal papillae (Figs 8.39 and 8.40). The male usually dies after fertilizing the female, and so is rarely seen.

The female measures 8–13 mm in length and 0.3–0.5 mm in diameter. Its tail end is sharply pointed and constitutes about a third of the entire length. The vulva opens mid-ventrally, just in front of the middle third of the body. The vagina is relatively long and extends posteriorly from the vulva, and joins the paired genital organs, i.e., the uteri, oviducts and ovarian tubules. The gravid female loosens her attachment to the intestinal wall, migrates freely in the lumen and crawls out of the anus on to the peri-anal and perineal skin. This migration occurs 15–43 days after ingestion of the infective eggs. The gravid female dies within 2–3 weeks after oviposition.

The eggs (Fig. 8.41) are colourless, i.e., not bile stained, and measure 50–60 μm by 20–30 μm. They are plano-convex in shape (the ventral side is flattened and the dorsal side is convex). The shell is composed of a thick hyaline, albuminous outer layer. The eggs contain a motile embryo (coiled, tadpole-like larva) and float in a saturated solution of common salt.

When the fully embryonated (infective stage) eggs are ingested (mode of entry) by a human, they reach the duodenum and are dissolved by the digestive juices. The larvae hatch out and pass down the small intestine. Without migration through the lungs, they moult twice *en route* and lodge into the folds of the jejunum and ileum. They then became sexually mature; the male fertilizes the female and dies. The gravid female then migrates down the cecum, colon and appendix and remains there till the eggs develop. Finally, it crawls out of the anus during the night and deposits eggs on the peri-anal skin. A single female may deposit as many as 11,105 eggs. The entire lifecycle (Figs 8.42 and 8.43) is then repeated by anus to mouth transmission (auto-infection).

Lifecycle For the lifecycle of *E. vermicularis,* no intermediate host is required.

Mode of infection Enterobiasis (oxyuriasis) is more common in children than in adults. The methods of transmission are of four kinds:

1) The anus-to-mouth transmission by finger contamination (auto-infection which is very common) and through soiled night clothes
2) Sleeping in the same bedroom with the carriers

3) Air-borne eggs, which are dislodged from the linen, being inhaled or swallowed and
4) Retro-infection: The infective larvae are hatched out from the eggs on the peri-anal skin, then they migrate through the anus back to the colon and develop into adult worms.

Pathogenicity and clinical features Minute ulcerations with hemorrhages may develop in the mucosa of the cecum and appendix due to the attachment of mature *E. vermicularis*. Pathogenic bacteria may enter the ulcers and produce submucosal abscess, and appendicitis may be produced. Absorbed metabolites may cause a characteristic helminthic toxemia. Gravid females, migrating out of the anus, may oviposit on the peri-anal and perineal skin of the anus and cause severe pruritus with severe scratching which is characteristic of this infection. Sometimes, it may enter the female genital tract causing salphingitis and at last encyst in the peritoneal cavities. There may also be urethritis, nocturnal enuresis (frequency of micturition) and masturbation. Loss of appetite, loss of weight, nervousness, insomnia, nightmares, convulsions, nail biting and nose picking and grinding of teeth at night may be observed in children.

Laboratory diagnosis It can be performed by

1) The identification of the recovered adult worm and
2) The demonstration of the characteristic egg.

1. Recovery of adult worm:
    a) The worm may be found by the children themselves or by the parents at night on the peri-anal skin
    b) After enema, the adult worm can be eliminated with the stool
    c) The worms thus collected should be preserved in alcohol or in 10% formaldehyde for examination.
2. Demonstration of characteristic egg: The characteristic egg of *E. vermicularis* can be demonstrated in the stool by the direct method or by the concentration method. Eggs can be demonstrated generally in the scrapings from the peri-anal skin by using a cellophane anal swab, referred to as the National Institute of Health (NIH) swab. At least seven consecutive swabs should be taken before declaring the specimen negative.

The **NIH** swab consists of a glass rod (8–10 cm long and 4.0 mm wide), one end of which is covered with a piece of transparent cellophane one inch square and is held in position by a rubber band. The end of this rod is used for swabbing the anal region, and to obtain material from fingernails and garments. The other end passes through the rubber cork with which the test tube is closed.

After swabbing, the cellophane with the stool is placed in the test tube and sent to the laboratory for examination. A drop of saline is placed on a glass slide and the cellophane end is held over it. The rubber band is pushed up with the help of forceps until the cellophane is free. The cellophane is spread over the saline with the help of the rod in such a way that the cellophane adheres to the slide and the eggs are between the cellophane and glass slide. A drop

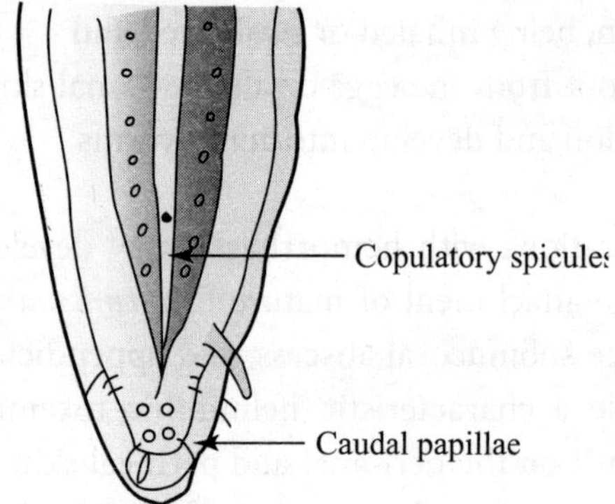

Fig. 8.39 Posterior end of male of *E. vermicularis* (ventral view).

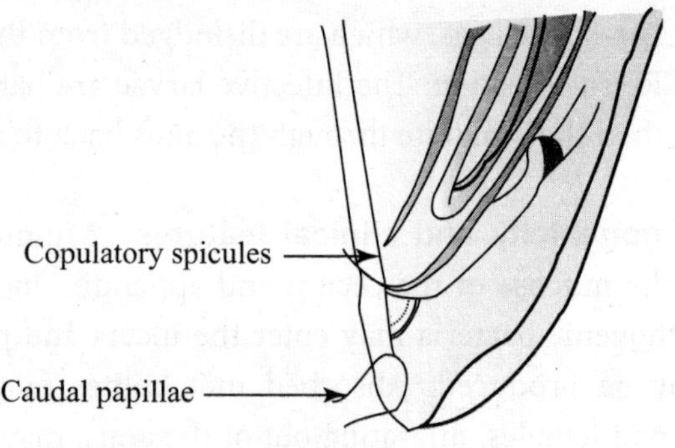

Fig. 8.40 Lateral view of posterior end of male *E. vermicularis* (lateral view).

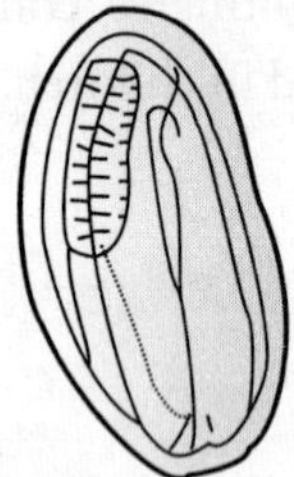

Fig. 8.41 Egg of *E. vermicularis*.

of saline is applied again over the cellophane and a cover slipped over it. The eggs can then be demonstrated microscopically.

Treatment Piperazine adipate, thiabendazole and mebendazole are effective anthelmintics.

Prophylaxis This consists of the following measures:

1) Personal hygiene should be strictly observed
2) The clothes and garments of patients should be sterilized by boiling
3) Fingernails should be cut short and thoroughly cleaned several times each day
4) Toilet seats should be regularly scrubbed and sterilized

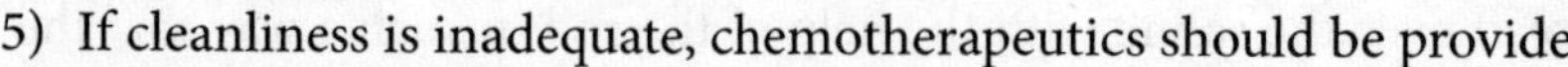

5) If cleanliness is inadequate, chemotherapeutics should be provided.

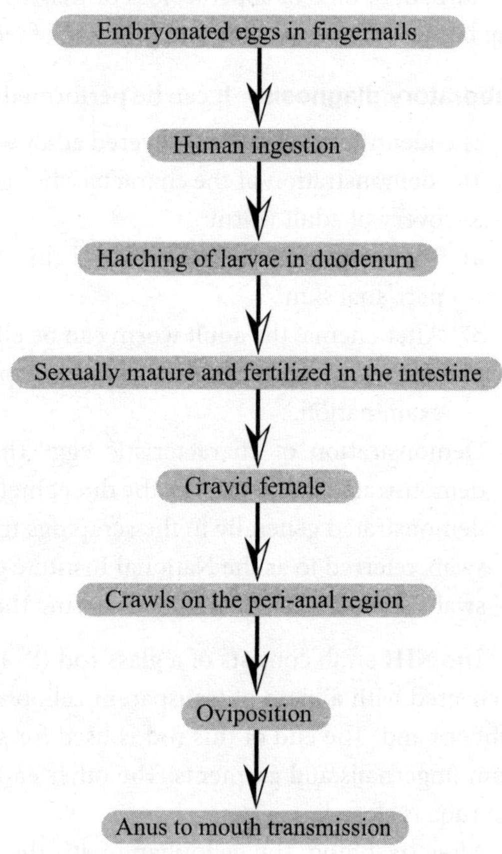

Fig. 8.42 Lifecycle of *E. vermicularis*.

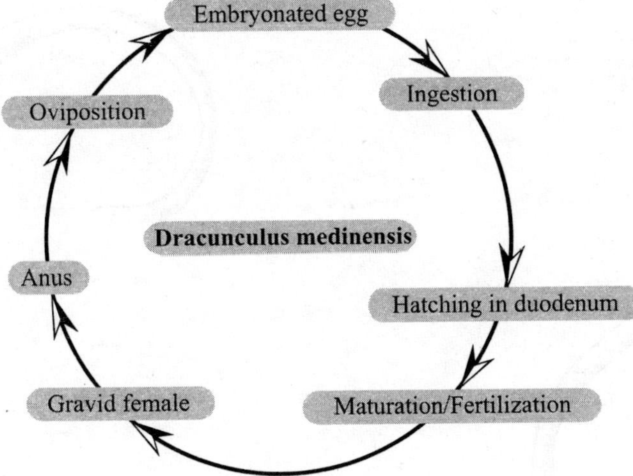

Fig. 8.43 Lifecycle of *E. vermicularis*.

SUPERFAMILY ASCARIDOIDEA

The worms of this superfamily are large and stout. The mouth has three small lips without the buccal capsule. Males do not have bursa copulatrix and caudal alae.

Ascaris lumbricoides

Genus: Ascaris

Ascaris lumbricoides, the giant intestinal roundworm, causing ascariasis, was known as a parasite even in ancient times. It is the most common of all helminths. There is high prevalence of this worm among children of the rural communities of China. It is also prevalent in India among children living in unhygienic rural environments, and has also been found in calves (by the author in Pondicherry, 1972). Bovine and porcine ascariasis is not a zoonotic disease.

Morphology The adult worm is the largest of the common human intestinal nematodes (Figs 8.44, 8.45). It is light brown or pink in colour, when freshly voided in the feces. It is elongated, cylindroidal, tapering more bluntly at the anterior end (Figs 8.46 and 8.47) than the posterior end (Figs 8.48 to 8.50). Its anterior end has three, small, finely dentriculate (toothed) lips, one dorsal and two ventral. Each lip has minute papillae on its lateral margins. A small triangular buccal cavity is located centrally among the lips (Fig. 8.51).

The male measures 15–31 cm in length and 2–4 mm in diameter. The posterior end of the male is curved ventrally. Its genitalia consist of a long single tubule (testes), vas deferens and an ejaculatory duct opening into the cloaca which is subterminal. A pair of equal or unequal, simple, cylindrical copulatory spicules, measuring 23.5 mm in length, with pointed ends, is located in the genital tubule, and there is no gubernaculum. The papillae are situated symmetrically in the peri-cloacal region of the male. The anus opens with the ejaculatory duct into the cloaca.

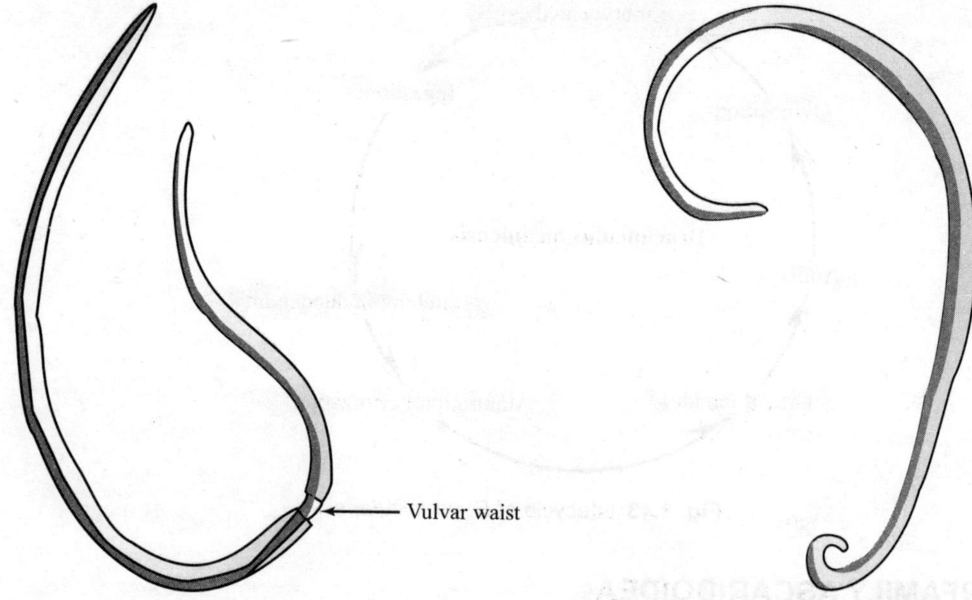

Fig. 8.44 Female adult worm of *Ascaris lumbricoides.*

Fig. 8.45 Male adult worm of *A. lumbricoides.*

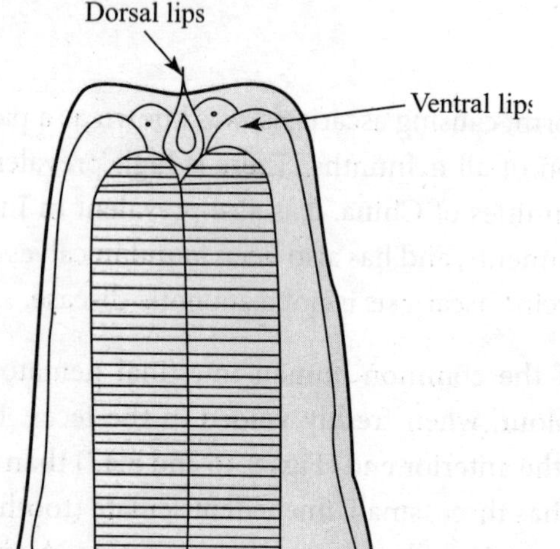

Fig. 8.46 Ventral anterior extremity of mature worm.

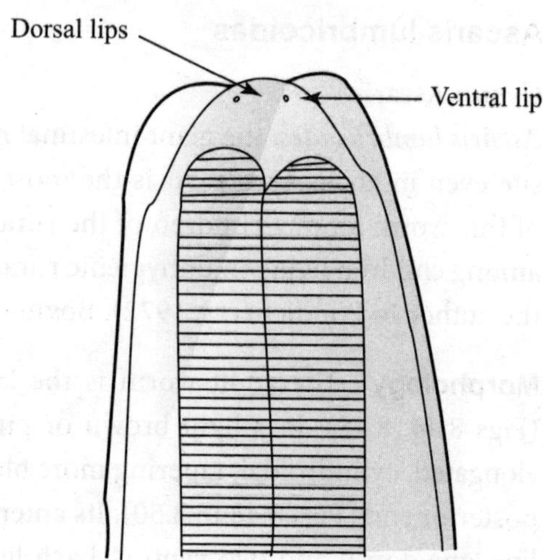

Fig. 8.47 Dorsal anterior extremity.

The female measures 20–35 cm in length by 3–6 mm in diameter. The vulva of the female is located mid-ventrally near the junction of the anterior and middle thirds of the body. It is narrower and is called the vulvar waist. A single vagina is connected with two genital tubules, each tube consisting of the uterus, seminal receptacle, oviduct and ovary. Each female deposits about 200,000 eggs per day. The reproductive and digestive organs float inside the body which

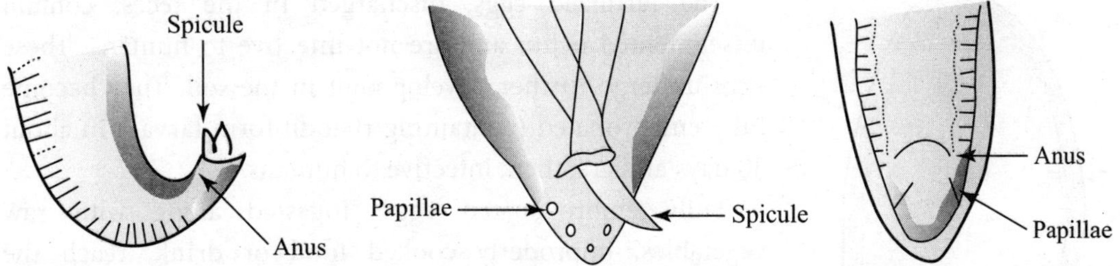

Fig. 8.48 Posterior end of male (lateral view).

Fig. 8.49 Posterior end of male (ventral view).

Fig. 8.50 Posterior end of female (ventral view).

also contains an irritant fluid. The action of this fluid is due to the ascaron or ascarase present in it. Ascarase is proteose in nature and is responsible for the allergy in the infected persons. The lifespan of the adult worm is less than two years.

The fertilized egg (Fig. 8.52) measures 45–75 μm in length and 35–50 μm in diameter. It is ovoidal, bile stained and its shell is transparent, thick and has three layers, a nonpermeable innermost membrane, not found in the unfertilized egg, the thick middle layer, and an outermost, coarsely mammillated, albuminoid layer, usually stained golden brown. The innermost membrane protects the embryo from toxic substances which injure the embryo. The ovum is unsegmented, and there is a clear crescentic area at each pole, The egg floats in a saturated solution of common salt.

The unfertilized egg (Fig. 8.53) measures 88–94 μm by 44 μm. It is narrower and longer and is bile stained. It has a thinner shell with an irregular albuminoid coating, and contains a small, atrophied ovum with various sized refractile granules. This egg is the heaviest of all helminthic eggs, and therefore does not float in salt solution.

The presence of unfertilized eggs in the feces shows that the host is harbouring the female worm. Ascaris eggs may remain infective for many months.

Lifecycle No intermediate host is required. Humans are the only optimum definite hosts for *A. lumbricoides.*

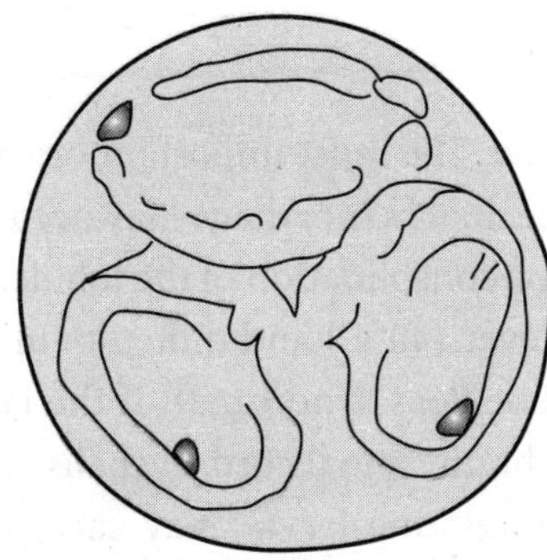

Fig. 8.51 Head-on view of worm, showing lips and papillae.

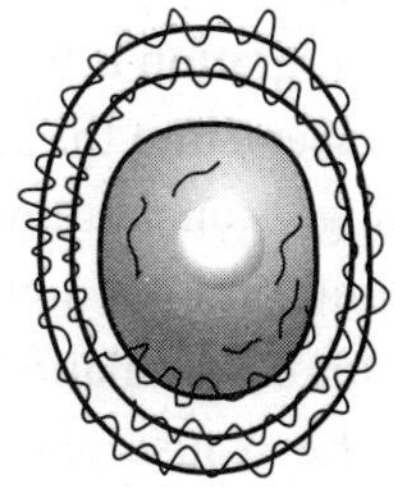

Fig. 8.52 Fertilized egg.

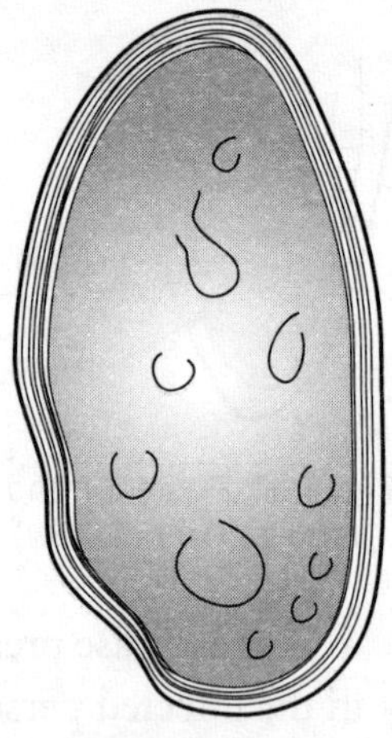

Fig. 8.53 Unfertilized egg.

The fertilized eggs, discharged in the feces, contain unsegmented ovum and are not infective to humans. These eggs undergo further development in the soil. They become fully embryonated (containing rhabditiform larvae) in about 30 days and are, then, infective to humans.

Fully embroyonated eggs, ingested along with raw vegetables, improperly cooked food or drink, reach the duodenum. Their shells are digested by the digestive juice and the enclosed embryo (measuring 0.2–0.3 mm in length by 13–15 μm in diameter) is activated and emerges out of the shells through a rent. These rhabditiform larvae penetrate the wall of the small intestine. Instead of becoming adult worms, they reach the portal hepatic venules, are carried through the right part of the heart to the lungs and usually break through the pulmonary capillaries into the alveoli. These larvae crawl up the bronchioles, bronchi, trachea and epiglottis, and are swallowed. (The migration period through the lungs takes about 15 days.)

On arrival in the small intestine, the larvae mature sexually and develop into adult worms. The ***female*** worms are fertilized. The gravid females discharge the eggs in the stool within about 60 days from the time of infection. Thus, the lifecycle is repeated (Figs 8.54A and B).

Mode of infection Consumption of raw vegetables, food and water contaminated with the fertilized eggs of *A. lumbricoides* in human excreta or contaminated by dirty fingers is a common mode of infection.

Sometimes, the dried eggs in the dust may be inhaled. These eggs, instead of being swallowed, may hatch on the moist mucous surface of the upper air passage. The larvae enter through the pulmonary capillaries into the systemic circulation and are filtered out in various organs and tissues (spleen, brain, spinal, thyroid), where they cause acute tissue reaction. If these larvae settle in the kidneys, they may be excreted in the urine. They occasionally pass through the placental filter and reach the fetus.

Pathogenicity and clinical features

1. Pathological effects produced by the migrating larvae: The most important organ involved during migration is the lungs. Some trauma and petechial hemorrhage may occur when the larvae escape into the alveoli. As a result, there will be consolidation of the lobule, spasms of coughing, bronchial rales, urticaria, eosinophilia, fever (40°C) and difficulty in breathing. This condition is known as *Ascaris pneumonitis* (Loeffler's syndrome). If the larvae enter the systemic circulation, they are filtered out in the brain, spinal cord, eyeballs and kidneys where they cause physiological disturbance. The migrating larvae may carry along with them the micro-organisms from the intestine to other organs. The adult worm may migrate to extra-intestinal sites in response to drug administration.

2. Pathogenic effects produced by the adult worm: These worms obtain their food by sucking the liquid nutriment present in the intestinal fluid, thus depriving the host of its nutrition. This is known as spoliative action. They may also cause vitamin A deficiency (night blindness). Lowered serum vitamins A and C and protein values have been reported in infected children. The worms are protected from enzymatic digestion because of the anti-enzymes liberated by them in the intestine. Digestion may be disturbed by the worms themselves causing fever, which may cause the worms to be passed out spontaneously through the anus or vomited through the nares. They may enter the Eustachian tube and cause otitis media (ectopic Ascariasis). Generalized toxemia or specific nervous system symptoms like insomnia, twitching, restlessness and even manifestations simulating meningitis and paraplegia, including urticaria, may occur in persons sensitive to absorbed foreign proteins. Cerebral symptoms may occur in children.

Some of the mechanical effects are intussusceptions in the intestines, penetration of the worms through the ulcers of the intestine, and intestinal obstruction which may be induced by the bolus formed by a large number of worms.

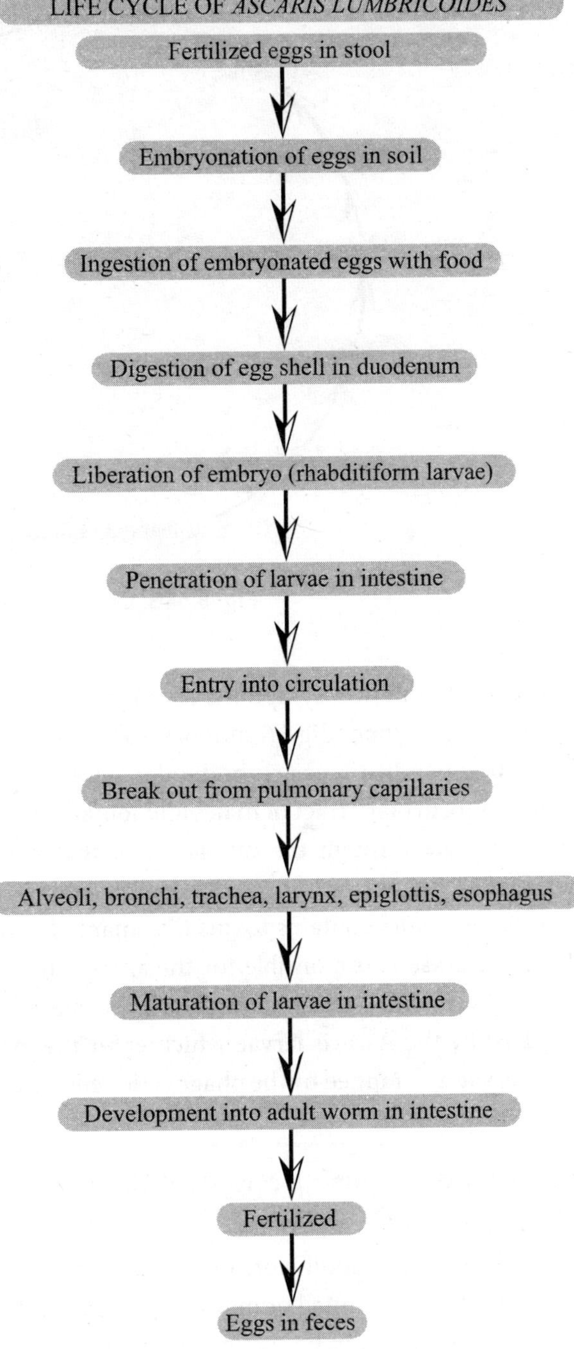

Fig. 8.54A Lifecycle of *Ascaris Lumbricoides*.

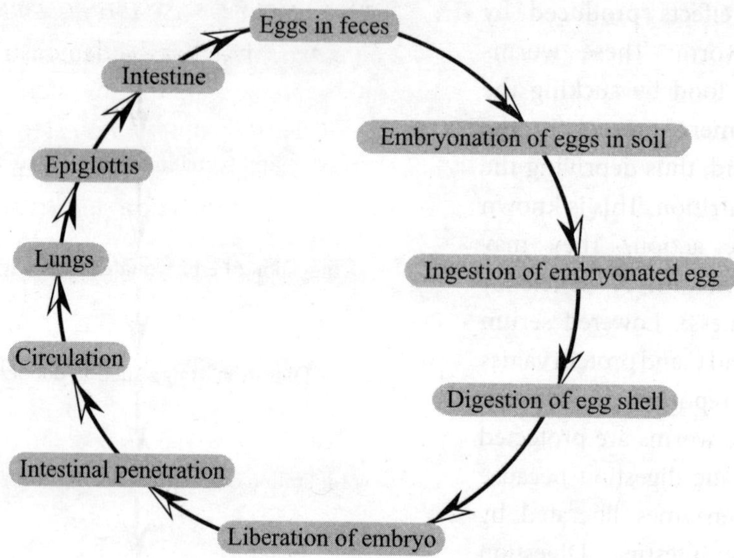

Fig. 8.54B Lifecycle of *A. lumbricoides*.

The most common symptoms are vague abdominal discomfort, acute colicky pain in the epigastric region, poor digestion, diarrhea and fever. The wandering worms may cause symptoms like acute appendicitis, gastric or duodenal trauma, esophageal perforation, severe involvement of the genito-urinary tract of males and females and invasion of the heart. Moreover, the larvae which migrate through the capillaries of the brain and eyeball may produce symptoms of meningitis, epilepsy, retinitis and palpebral edema.

A. lumbricoides contains toxins like anaphylaxins, neurotoxins, hemolysins and endocrino toxins. Ascarase is responsible for the allergic manifestations in laboratory workers handling the worms. In small children, ascariasis is frequently complicated by ***visceral larva migrans*** produced by the Ascaris larvae which enter the extra-intestinal viscera of an unnatural host. These larvae are trapped by the phagocytic cells and initiate granulomatous reactions simulating neoplastic growths.

Laboratory diagnosis It consists of direct and indirect methods.

1. ***Direct method***
   a) Detection of adult worm in stool or vomit: The adult worm may be passed out in the stool or be vomited or may escape through the nares. Expulsion of the adult worm from the intestine can be carried out by the administration of a specific anthelmintic.
   b) X-ray diagnosis: Barium emulsion, when administered, can be ingested by the worm within 4–6 hours. The adult worm of *Ascaris lumbricoides* can thus be detected radiologically, because barium emulsion casts an opaque shadow.

c) Demonstration of eggs:
   i) In the stool: Characteristic eggs of *A. lumbricoides* can be demonstrated by direct microscopic examination of the saline preparation of the stool. Eggs can be concentrated by the floatation method (refer to chapter 13 on stool examination). Unfertilized eggs do not float in salt solution, so only fertile eggs can be detected.
   ii) In the bile: Bile can be collected by duodenal intubation and examined for eggs under the microscope.

2. ***Indirect method***
   a) Blood examination: There may be pronounced eosinophilia in the circulating blood.
   b) Allergic test (skin reaction): The 'scratch test' is performed by using powdered Ascaris antigen. It may be found positive but the results are variable.

Treatment Piperazine (citrate, hydrate, adipate or phosphate), hexyl resorcinol, thiabendazole and mebendazole are very effective. Santonin is not effective and the oil of chenopodium is very toxic. In India (Kashmir), hepatobiliary and pancreatic ascariasis has been treated recently with mebendazole along with a palliative treatment. More recently, albendazole is also very effective and is the drug of choice. Mebendazole is useful in mixed infection (Ascaris and Tricthuris infection); the dosage is 100 mg twice a day for three days. Pyrantel pamoate is also effective in a single dose of 11 mg per kg. There is no specific treatment for Ascaris pneumonitis.

Prophylaxis Proper disposal of human excreta, treatment of infected individuals, educating children about sanitation and hygiene, and avoidance of consumption of raw vegetables, food or drink contaminated with the feces of infected persons.

Toxocara canis

Larvae of *T. canis* do not complete their lifecycle in humans, but migrate through the body including various organs and produce a symptom known as 'visceral larva migrans'. When the eye is involved, other organs are usually spared; this is known as ocular larva migrans.

Lifecycle Humans are infected by ingestion of soil contaminated with feces of infected dogs. Swallowed eggs hatch in the small intestine and the larvae penetrate the intestinal wall to enter the circulation. When they reach the smallest blood vessels, they bore into the surrounding tissue. Larvae are found in the liver, lungs, heart, brain and eyes.

Pathogenicity and clinical features Migrating larvae leave tracks of hemorrhages, necrosis and inflammatory cells. Eosinophilic granulomas of abscess remain at the site of destruction of larvae; other larvae are walled off and may resume their migration years later.

Common symptoms of visceral larva migrans are fever, coughing, wheezing, malaise and weight loss. Physical findings are wheezes, rales and hepatomegaly. Occasionally, the central nervous system is involved, resulting in sneezing or behaviour disturbance. White blood cells are increased with 50 to 90% eosinophilia. Serum immunoglobulin IgG, Ig M and Ig E are usually elevated as isohemagglutinins.

In ocular larva migrans, the presentation may be of visual loss, strabismus or less often, eye pain. Funduscopic findings may range from a retinal granuloma to severe exudative ophthalmitis with retinal detachment.

Diagnosis Visceral larva migrans should be considered in any child with persistent eosinophilia after the child's contact with a dog. Diagnosis may be confirmed by ELISA.

Treatment In severe cases, thiabendazole in a dose of 25 mg/kg body weight twice a day may be given.

Anisakis marina

This nematode is a parasite of sea mammals and fish. It has been reported from Holland and Japan. Humans acquire the infection (anisakiasis) by consuming raw fish or inadequately pickled fish.

The larva liberated from the digested fish enters the mucosa of the stomach and intestine producing an eosinophilic granulomatous growth, simulating malignancy. The lifecycle of this nematode is still not fully understood. Colicky abdominal pain and symptoms of intestinal obstruction are the main clinical features.

Laboratory diagnosis Demonstration of the larvae in the surgically removed tissue aids in the diagnosis. Indirect hemagglutination test is positive.

SUPERFAMILY FILARIOIDEA

Filariform worms have a simple mouth. The mouth is circular or dorso-ventrally elongated and surrounded by papillae. They have a rudimentary buccal cavity without lips. Males may or may not have caudal alae. Those causing human infections are *Wuchereria bancrofti, Brugia malayi, Onchocerca volvulus, Dipetalonema perstans, D. streptocercum, Mansonella ozzardi* and *Loa loa.*

Wuchereria bancrofti

Ancient Hindu (Susruta, 600 BC) and Persian physicians recognized the dramatic symptoms of filariasis. The microfilariae were first demonstrated by Demarquay in 1863 in human hydrocele fluid. Later in 1866, Wucherer found them in chylous urine and in 1872, Lewis in India, observed them in human blood. Adult female worms were found in 1876 by Bancroft, and the specific name *Wuchereria bancrofti* was given in honour of the discoverers, Wucherer and Bancroft.

This parasite is found distributed in Europe (Hungary, Yugoslavia and Turkey), Japan, Korea, Central Africa, South America, India, Southern China, Southern Spain, Nile Delta, Tangier, Australia, Philippines, Malaysia and Thailand.

In India, it is distributed mainly along the sea coast and the banks of big rivers (except the Indus). It has been reported from Rajasthan, Punjab, Uttar Pradesh, Delhi and Gujarat. Stoll (1947) estimated the combined figures of those affected by Bancroft's filaria and Malayan filaria to be 25 million in the endemic areas of India. Ramachandran (1990) reported that 45 million, out of 200 million filariasis cases in the world, were in India. Most recently, an incidence of 31% has been found in those attending the special filariasis clinic in Kerala.

Morphology The adult worm (Figs 8.55, 8.56) is a long, minute, thread-like and creamy white nematode. The head is slightly swollen and carries two rings of inconspicuous papillae.

The male measures 20–40 mm in length and 0.1 mm in diameter. Its tail end is curved (Fig. 8.57) ventrally and contains two spicules of unequal length and a gubernaculum (Fig. 8.58). Caudal alae are lacking. The male worm is rarely recovered.

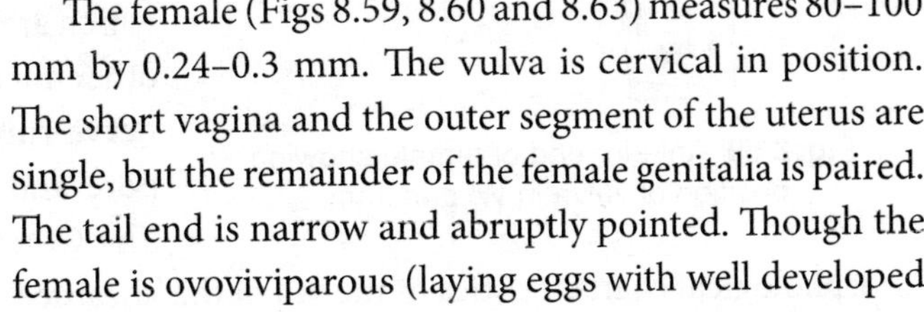

The female (Figs 8.59, 8.60 and 8.63) measures 80–100 mm by 0.24–0.3 mm. The vulva is cervical in position. The short vagina and the outer segment of the uterus are single, but the remainder of the female genitalia is paired. The tail end is narrow and abruptly pointed. Though the female is ovoviviparous (laying eggs with well developed

Fig. 8.55 Male adult worm of *W. bancrofti.*

Fig. 8.56 Female adult worm of *W. bancrofti.*

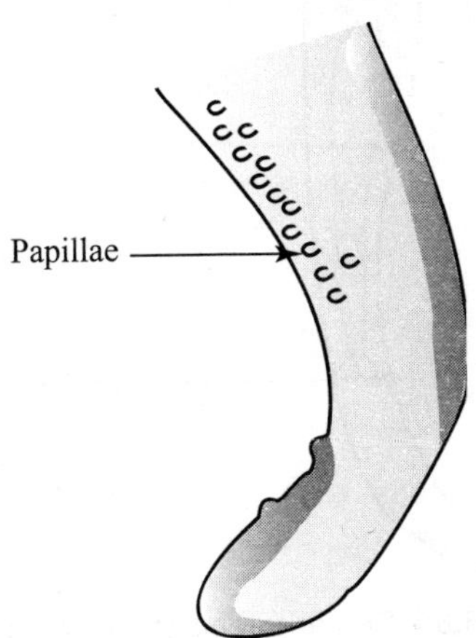

Fig. 8.57 Posterior end of male (lateral view).

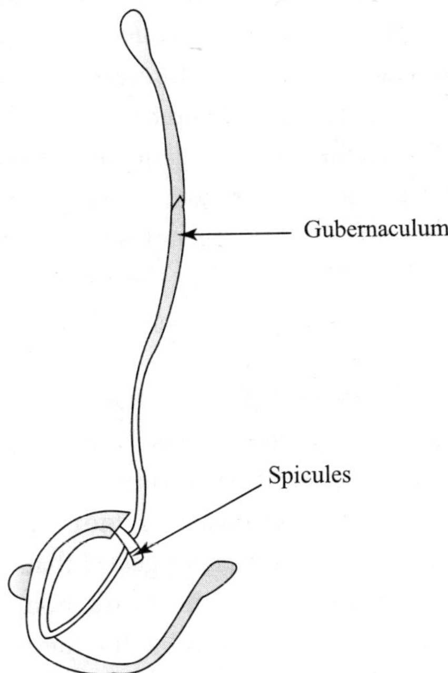

Fig. 8.58 Male worm of *W. bancrofti.*

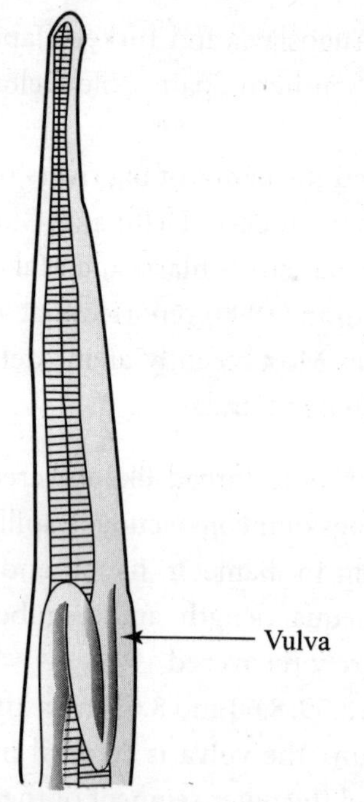

Fig. 8.59 Anterior end of female showing position of vulva in *W. bancrofti.*

embryo), it liberates active embryos (38 by 25 μm in size). The shell of the embryo becomes elongated to accommodate the active embryo. It is known as the 'sheath' of the embryo (i.e., microfilariae). At this stage, the microfilariae escape from the female worm into the lymph and blood vessels.

The microfilariae (Fig. 8.61) measure 244 μm in length and 75 μm in diameter. The anterior end is round and has a stylet, and the posterior end is pointed. The internal structure can be studied only after staining. There is a central column of nuclei extending from the head to the tail. In the column of the nuclei, there are important anatomical landmarks which are used to differentiate this species from other microfilariae. The landmarks consist of the nerve ring, excretory pore, excretory cell, anal pore and genital cells – the so-called G-cells. The G-cells are in front of the anal pore. The morphological characteristics of the tail of the 'sheathed' microfilariae of *Wuchereria bancrofti, Brugia malayi* and *Loa loa,* the 'unsheathed' microfilariae of *Dipetalonema perstans, Mansonella ozzardi, Onchocerca volvulus* are illustrated in Figs 8.62 and 8.63.

For further development, the microfilariae require an appropriate intermediate host (mosquito). If they are not sucked up by the mosquito, they may die. The microfilariae are able to pass the placental filter and have been found in the newborn.

Microfilarial periodicity: There is a nocturnal surge of the microfilariae of *W. bancrofti* in the peripheral circulation between 10 p.m. and 2 a.m. Its mechanism is not yet clearly understood. It has been suggested that:

1) The relaxation of the host's body during sleep may be responsible for the migration of microfilariae to the periphery at night

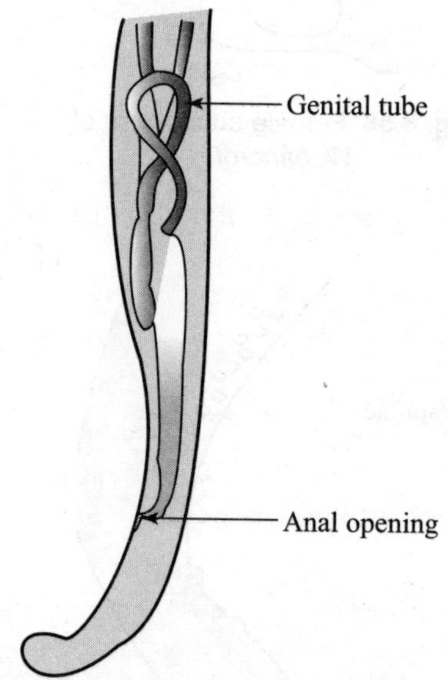

Fig. 8.60 Posterior end of female in *W. bancrofti.*

2) There is response to O_2 and CO_2 supply
3) The microfilariae adapt themselves to the feeding habits of the mosquito, *Culex pipiens quinquefasciatus,* a night feeder. The non-periodicity type utilizes the daytime feeder, *Aedes* and
4) During the daytime, they retire inside the capillaries of the lungs, kidneys, heart and carotid.

In the Pacific Islands, *Mf. bancrofti* does not exhibit any periodicity.

Lifecycle It requires two hosts:

1) The only known definite host – human and
2) The intermediate host, mosquito – *Culex, Aedes, Anopheles.*

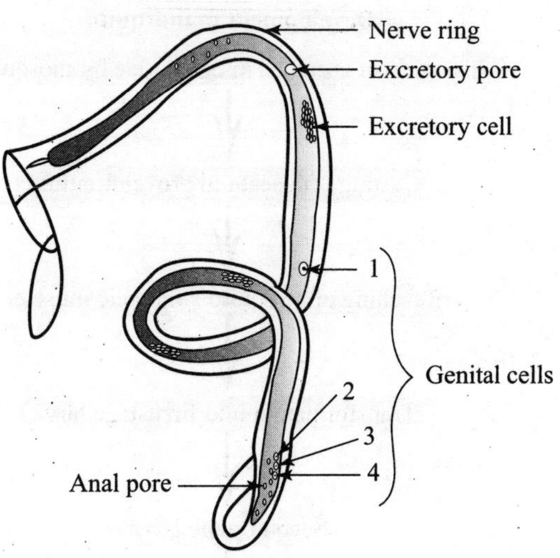

Fig. 8.61 Sheathed microfilaria of *W. bancrofti.*

Development in mosquito When a mosquito bites an infected human, sheathed microfilariae are ingested during its blood meal. These microfilariae arrive at the anterior end of the proventriculus (stomach) of the mosquito, the microfilariae cast off their sheaths within 2–6 hours and penetrate the wall of the proventriculus and ultimately reach the thoracic muscles in 4–17 hours. During the next two days, the slender, snake-like organisms (Fig. 8.65a) transform into a

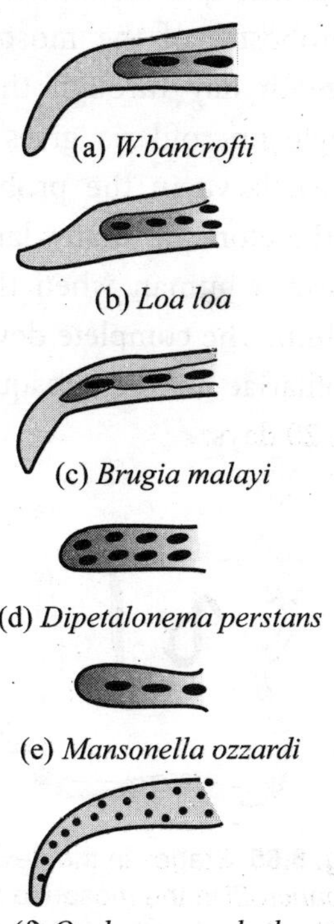

Fig. 8.62 Posterior extremity of human microfilaria.

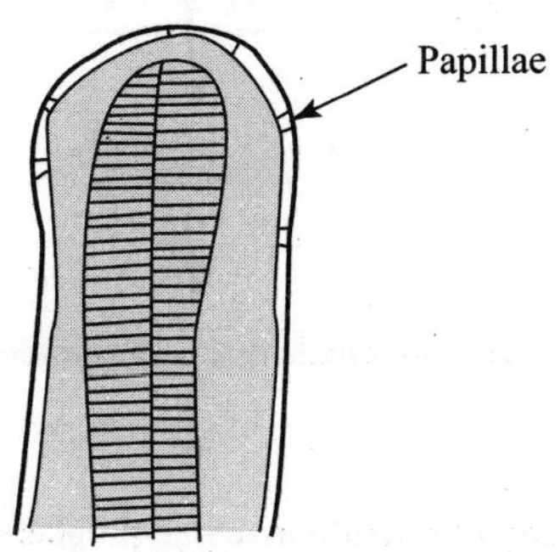

Fig. 8.63 Head of adult worm of *W. bancrofti.*

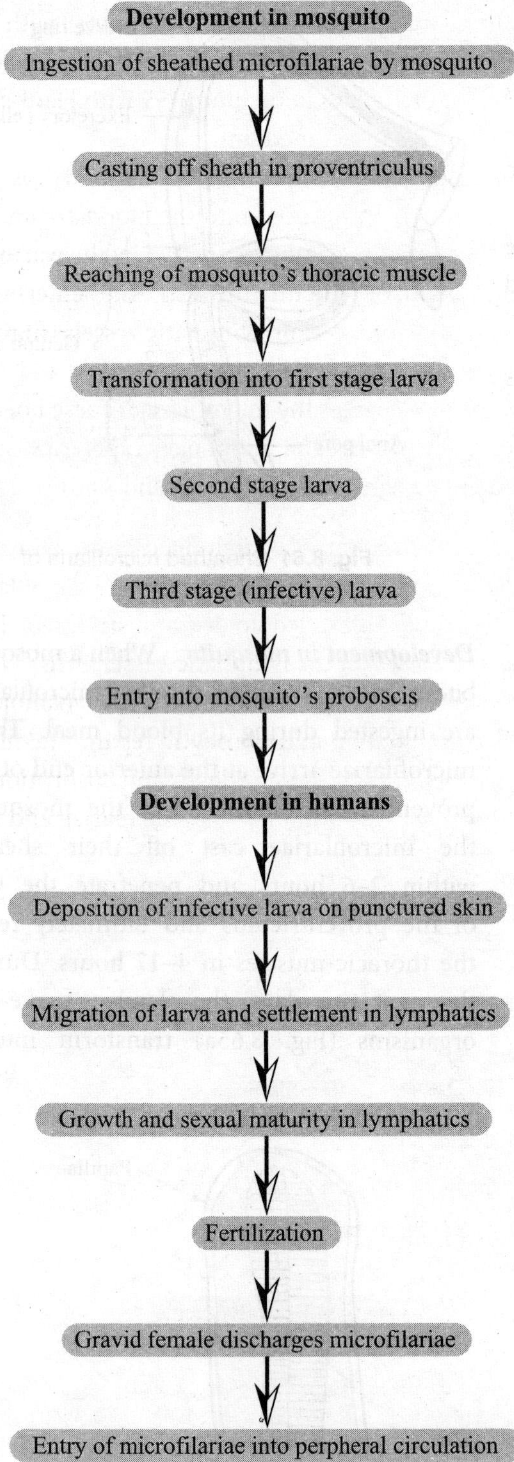

Fig. 8.64 Lifecycle of *Wucheraria bancrofti*.

thick, short, sausage-shaped organism (measuring 124–250 µm in length and 10–17 µm in diameter). This is the first stage larva (Fig. 8.65 b). On the fifth and sixth days, its tail is atrophied to a mere stump and the intestinal tract becomes well differentiated. This is the second stage larva (Fig. 8.65 c). It measures 225–330 µm in length and 15–30 µm in diameter.

In the beginning of the second week, there is a complete metamorphosis. The digestive system, body cavity and genital organs become well developed. The worm elongates into a filiform mature larva (the third stage larva). It measures, 1.4–2 mm in length and 18–23 µm in diameter (Fig. 8.65 d). This third stage larva is infective to humans and enters the proboscis of the mosquito on the fourteenth day through the hemocele. A single microfilaria gives rise to one infective larva in the proboscis. There may therefore be many larvae waiting to infect a human when the mosquito bites him. The complete development of microfilariae in the mosquito requires about 20 days.

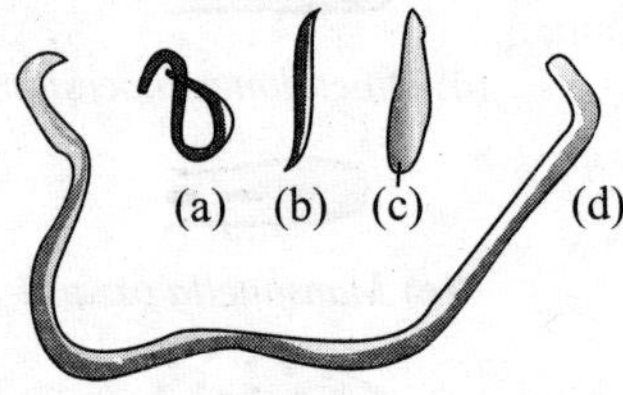

Fig. 8.65 Stages in the development of *W. bancrofti* in the mosquito a) Microfilaria without its sheath; b) First stage larva; c) Second stage larva; d) Third stage or mature infective larva.

The microfilariae can be kept in an artificial medium (Franke's NI medium) with 10% human serum under 5% CO_2 atmosphere for 20 days.

W. bancrofti can be cultured with 95% viability for 10 days in medium 199 with Hank's salts supplemented with organic acids and sugars of Grace's insect medium.

Development in humans When a healthy human being is inoculated by the infected mosquito, the third stage larvae (infective forms) are not directly introduced into the bloodstream as in malaria, but are deposited on the skin around the puncture wound. Attracted by the warmth of the skin, the third stage larvae migrate into the wound, or puncture the skin. After entering the skin, they reach the lymphatic channels and settle down in certain lymphatic vessels (inguinal, scrotal, abdominal lymphatics) where they grow, mature sexually, become adult and mate. The male fertilizes the female and the gravid female discharges the microfilariae. These liberated microfilariae enter the thoracic duct, then the venous system and pulmonary capillaries, and at last reach the peripheral circulation. Thus, the lifecycle is repeated (Figs 8.64 and 8.66).

Pathogenicity and clinical features If the living microfilariae are lodged in the lymphatic vessels and lymph nodes, the reticuloendothelial cells infiltrate to attack these microfilariae. The endothelial layer of the lymphatic vessels becomes thickened, folded and stratified. There is fibrin deposition on the endothelial surface and edema of the lymphatic vessel wall.

When the living worms are trapped in the lymph nodes, they are surrounded by eosinophils. Cellular granulation is followed by proliferative granulation and fibrocytic repair. The filarial granulation tissue is pathognomonic of this disease. Finally, there is death and absorption (or calcification) of the parasite. The initial tissue responses are stimulated by the filariae and their metabolic products.

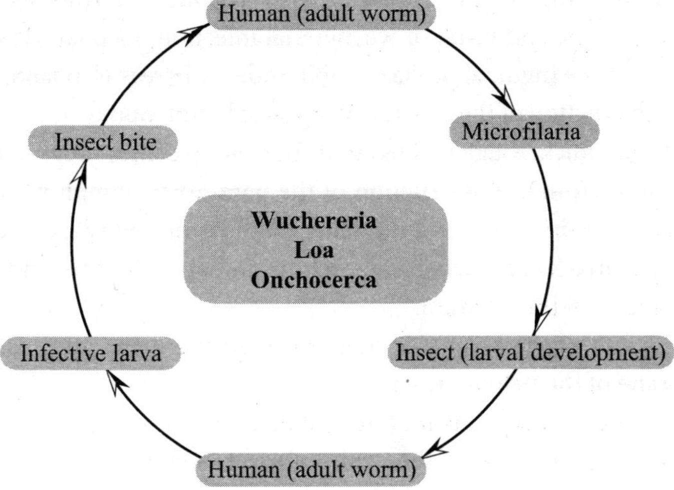

Fig. 8.66 Lifecycle of human filarial worms.

The adult worms produce obstruction in the lymphatic vessels, followed by lymph stasis and edema. As the worms die, lymphangitis ensues. The end result is usually lymph varix or elephantiasis.

1. Lymphangitis: In this condition, the lymphatics of the testicle and the epididymis (epididymo-orchitis) of the spermatic cord (funiculitis) and the lymphatics of the upper and lower extremities are involved. The globus major of the epididymis is the site for the adult *W. bancrofti*. The lymphatic trunks are red, congested, palpable and painful. When the abdominal lymphatics are involved, acute abdominal symptoms may result. The wuchererial lymphangitis may occur periodically once every month and sometimes it is related to the lunar cycle, but the relationship is not well established.
   The causes of lymphangitis are:
   1) Metabolites liberated by the growing larvae and toxic fluid by fertilized females
   2) Absorption of the toxic products of dead worms
   3) Mechanical irritation due to the movement of the worms in the lymphatic vessels and
   4) Secondary bacterial invasion which may cause lymphangitis.

   The causes of lymphatic obstruction are
   1) Fibrosis of the afferent lymph nodes draining a particular area
   2) Obstructive endolymphangitis and
   3) Mechanical blocking of the lumen by the dead worm.
2. Lymphadenitis: It is the inflammation of the regional lymph nodes (lymphadenitis) which precedes an attack of lymphangitis. It is mostly found in the groin or in the axilla. It is soft and lobulated and is not painful and tender. The skin over the swelling is not adhered.
3. Elephantiasis is due to the obstruction of the lymphatic tracts caused by dead worms or due to recurrent attacks of lymphangitis. The affected part becomes enormously enlarged and looks like a tumour. This is the end result of wuchererial infection. Elephantiasis of the legs is due to the obstruction of the inguinal or iliac lymph nodes, whereas elephantiasis of the scrotum results from the obstruction of the superficial inguinal lymph nodes. The surface of the skin of the scrotum becomes thick, rough and fissured. The hair becomes rough and sparse.
4. Hydrocele: It results from the obstruction of the para-aortic lymph nodes which interfere with lymph drainage from the tunica vaginalis, epididymis and spermatic cord. It may also be due to repeated attacks of wuchererial orchitis and epididymitis, and may exist with or without elephantiasis of the scrotum.
5. Chyluria: This is due to the escape of chyle through the urine after passing through the mucous membrane of the urinary tract.
   In chyluria, the urine is milky in colour. It contains
   a) Fat particles which dissolve in ether, chloroform or xylol
   b) Albumin which precipitates on boiling and
   c) Fibrinogen which forms coagulation on standing.

Microfilariae can be demonstrated microscopically in the sediment of chyluria. Chyluria is rare in India.

The three most common clinical presentations of lymphatic filariasis are asymptomatic. A fourth presentation, the tropical eosinophilia syndrome is considered. Filarial fevers are acute febrile episodes characterized by high temperature (often with shaking chills), lymphatic inflammation (i.e., lymphadentis, lymphangitis) and transient local edema. They occur as often as 6–10 times per year in affected persons. The lymphangitis characteristically develops in a retrograde fashion, extending peripherally from the drainage node where the adult parasites reside. Regional nodes are enlarged and painful and the entire lymphatic tract often becomes indurated and inflamed. Concomitant local thrombophlebitis is common. Involvement of genital lymphatics is almost exclusively a feature of *W. bancrofti* infection. Funiculitis, epididymitis, scrotal pain and tenderness are acute bancrofti episodes. Patients with filarial fevers may be microfilaremic. As the lymphatic damage progresses, pitting edema develops. Pressure in the renal lymphatic causes rupture of the renal pelvis or tubules leading to chyluria which is intermittent.

Laboratory diagnosis It consists of two methods:

1) The direct method and
2) The indirect method.

1. The direct method depends upon the demonstration of sheathed microfilariae (with tail-tip free from nuclei) in the peripheral blood, chylous urine, exudate of lymph varix and hydrocele fluid. Microfilariae can be demonstrated in thin or thick smear as in malaria (refer to chapter 12, on blood examination). Microfilariae are also easily seen by acridine orange (AO) staining technique as in rapid diagnosis of malaria by fluorescence microscopy with light microscope and interference filter, the parasites fluoresce green and red.
   Microfilariae are not found in the following conditions:
   a. In cases of elephantiasis, due to lymphatic obstruction
   b. After an attack of lymphangitis, due to the death of the adult worm
   c. In early allergy and
   d. In occult filariasis.

   The direct method also depends on the detection of adult worms in the lymph node biopsy, and the calcified worm in X-ray.
2. The indirect method (immunological test) comprises allergic tests, immunologic tests and xenodiagnosis.

In the allergic tests, blood examination will reveal eosinophilia (5–15%). In the intradermal test (an immediate hypersensitivity reaction), *Dirofilariae immitis* (dog heartworm) antigen in a dilution of 1: 8000 provides 100% positive intradermal reaction in suspected cases of *W. bancrofti*. A wheal of 2 cm or more appears within 30 minutes in positive cases.

A new diagnostic skin test for filarial infection has been put forward by Malladi Drugs and Pharmaceuticals. The antigen is specific to filaria alone and does not react with other helminthic parasites. The antigen is very sensitive and the test is quick, cheap and operational in field survey. The results are available within 15 minutes of intradermal injection and it does not matter at what time of the day or night it is carried out. It appears that this test will probably play a significant role in monitoring the filaria vector control programme.

Among the immunological tests, the complement fixation test was found to be positive for human filariasis by employing a 1% alcoholic extract of dried *D. immitis* powdered antigen. The florescent antibody technique is not satisfactory. Serological tests using extracts of *D. immitis* as antigen include IHA and BF, but they allow only a diagnosis of filarial group rather than the species. Dot ELISA in the detection of *W. bancrofti* filarial antibody was compared with standard ELISA in India and found to be more sensitive. It is a very recent technique in India. Western blot is also used.

In xenodiagnosis, microfilariae can be demonstrated in the stomach blood of the specific mosquito vector which had been allowed to bite the infected person. However, it is not a very useful method.

Treatment The drugs act on specific stages:

1) Adult worm – synthetic arsenical Mel Wand antimonial M sb B;
2) Microfilariae – Diethyl-carbamazine (Hetrazan). Centperazine is the drug of choice;
3) Infective larvae and immature adult worms – paramelaminyl phenyl sibonate *(MSb).* Ivermectin (dose $\geq$ 100 mg/kg body weight) is effective for treatment and control of filariasis due to *W. bancrofti* in India. This is a new drug primarily used in veterinary practice.

Prophylaxis consists of treatment of carriers by using Hetrazan, protection against mosquito bite and destruction of mosquitoes. Biological control programmes were implemented in India, using *Bacillus sphaerius* by the Vector Control Research Institute, Pondicherry, India.

69–K Da *B.malayi* antigen corresponding to recombinant protein is highly immunogenic in naturally infected children and adults.

Brugia malayi

Brugia malayi, the Malaysian filarial worm producing Malaysian filariasis, was first observed by Lichtenstein in blood films and was described by Brug (1927) as a new species. Adult females and males were studied and described by Rao and Maplestone (1940). This filaria is a parasite of humans in India (Kerala, Hyderabad, Orissa, Madhya Pradesh, Assam), Sri Lanka, Sumatra, Java, Celebes, Malaysia, China and Japan. The adult worms of *Brugia malayi* remain coiled up in the lymphatic system.

Morphology *B. malayi* resembles *W. bancrofti.* It is a delicate, whitish, thread-like roundworm. The tapering anterior end (Fig. 8.67) is provided with a non-labiate mouth surrounded by two rows of minute papillae (Fig. 8.68), an inner row of six and an outer row of four (Fig. 8.69), just as in *W. bancrofti,* except that the papillae are slightly larger and more prominent in *B. malayi.* Adult females measure 43.5 mm in length and 130 μm in breadth and adult males 13.5 mm and 70 μm. The anterior end of the female has the reproductive organ. The posterior end of the

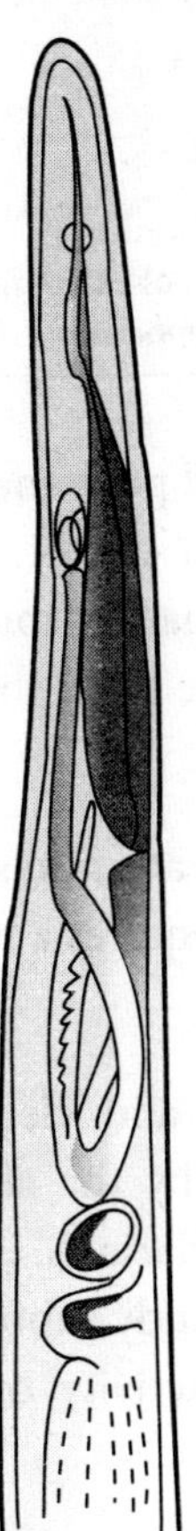

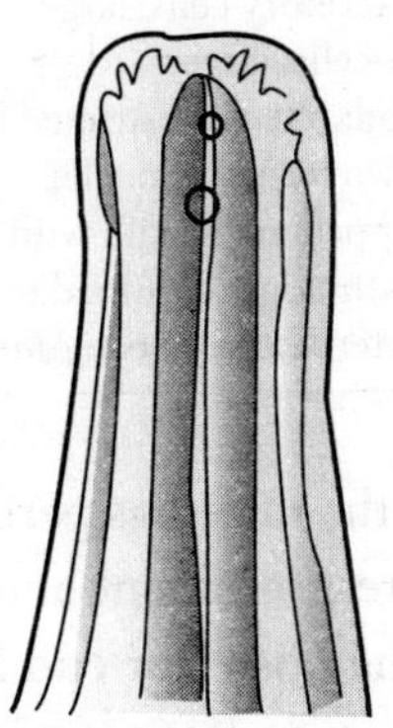

Fig. 8.68 Anterior extremity lateral view of *B. malayi*.

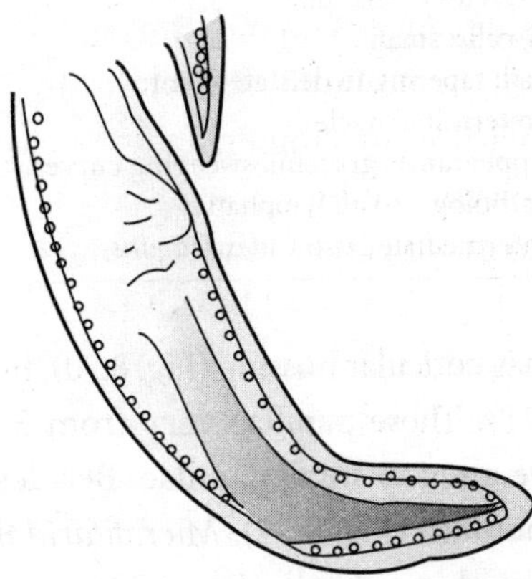

Fig. 8.70 Posterior end of female of *B. malayi* showing cuticular bossing.

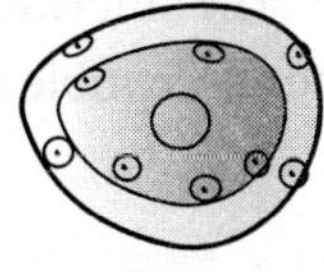

Fig. 8.69 *B. malayi* head-on view of anterior tip showing pattern of peri-oral papillae.

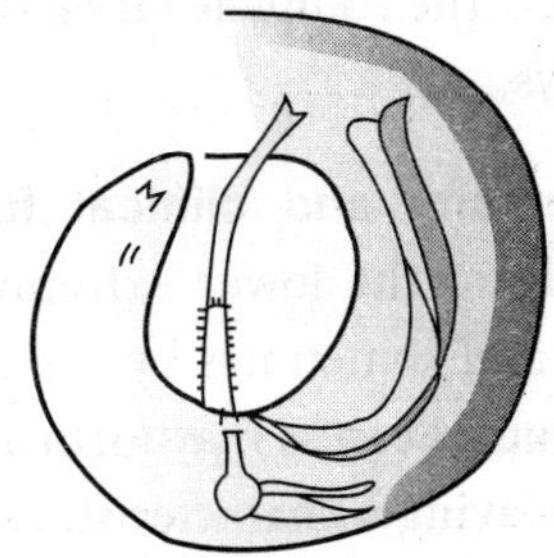

Fig. 8.71 Posterior end of male of *B. malayi* (lateral view).

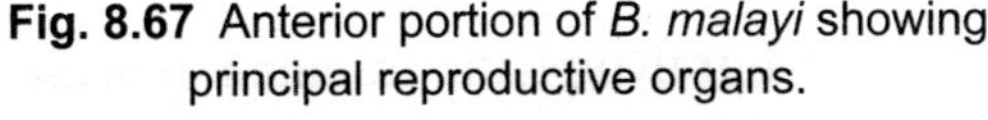

Fig. 8.67 Anterior portion of *B. malayi* showing principal reproductive organs.

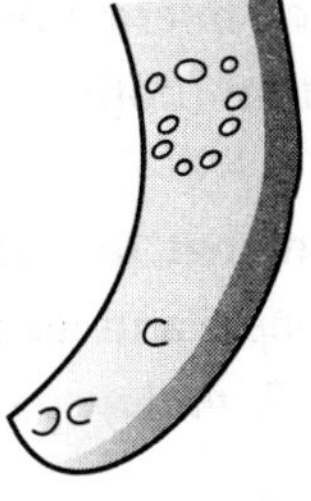

Fig. 8.72 Posterior tip of male of *B. malayi* (lateral view).

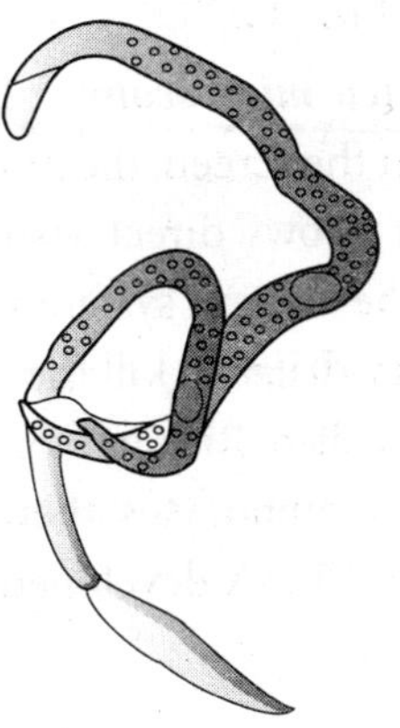

Fig. 8.73 Microfilaria of *B. malayi*.

Mf. bancrofti	Mf. malayi
1. Nocturnal periodicity.	Nocturnal periodicity.
2. Anterior end has one stylet.	Anterior end has two stylets.
3. Cephalic space is long and broad.	Cephalic space is broader.
4. Length: 244 μm	Length: 177 μm
5. Excretory cells: small.	Excretory cells: large.
6. G-cells: small.	G-cells: larger.
7. Tail: tapering to delicate point; no terminal nuclei.	Tail: often constricted between two terminal nuclei.
8. Appearance: graceful, sweeping curves.	Appearance: stiff; with secondary kinks.
9. Pathology: in all lymphatics.	Pathology: confined to lymphatics of extremities.
10. Intermediate host: *Culex fatigans*	Intermediate host: *Mansonia, Anopheles*

female has cuticular bossing (Fig. 8.70), but that of the male has peri-anal and post-anal papillae (Fig. 8.71). These papillae vary from 3–4 and are prominent and unequal. At the tip of the tail there are 4–6 small papillae. Besides these, the posterior end has copulatory spicules and gubernaculum (Fig. 8.72). *Microfilaria malayi* has two discrete nuclei at the tip of the tail and is enveloped in a sheath (Fig. 8.73).

Lifecycle It is the same as that of *W. bancrofti*. The intermediate hosts are *Mansonia* and *Anopheles*. The complete larval development in the susceptible mosquito requires a minimum of six days.

Pathogenicity and clinical features *B. malayi* causes lymphangitis and elephantiasis (primarily of the lower extremities). Malayan filariasis is characterized by the absence of chyluria and sometimes by the presence of scrotal swellings. In Brugian filariasis, especially, a single local abscess may form along the inflamed lymphatic and subsequently rupture to the surface, leaving a characteristic scar which is an indication of the clinical 'activity' of Brugian filarial infection.

Laboratory diagnosis is based on the detection of the characteristic micro-filariae in the peripheral blood.

Recent video-microscopy: Recent video-microscopy of intralymphatic-dwelling *B.malayi* captures on the screen, the hidden intraluminal events in the lifecycle of the lymphatic dwelling worm and allows direct visualization and documentation of interaction between host and parasite. The camera system may also permit direct observation (both *in vitro* and *in vivo*) of the capillary drugs to kill the adult worm and its progeny.

The so-called Rickenberg reaction raises the speculation that the adult worm feeds on circulatory lymphocytes, thereby averting immuno-resposiveness and its own destruction.

In India, ELISA developed using soluble antigen of adult *B. malayi* gave positive response to 95% cases.

Treatment It is the same as that of W. *bancrofti* infection. Both filariasis can be treated by a new drug – Ivermectin. In recent trials, it has shown promise for the treatment of *W. bancrofti*. Single oral dose of Ivermectin of 25–200 mg/kg body weight has been shown to rapidly clear blood microfilariae of *W. bancrofti* within five days and microfilariae may reappear by the third month, whether it may prove useful for periodic *B. malayi* insection, is yet to be determined.

Prophylaxis is also the same as in W. *bancrofti*. In addition, certain water plants should be destroyed, as *Mansonia* grows on these plants. In Kerala, India, where *Mansonia annulifera* is the chief vector of *B. malayi*, the destruction of the water plant *Pistia stratioides* has greatly reduced new infections.

The exeretary–secretory antigens of *B. malayi* are effective in inducing resistance against filarial parasites and thus have potential in immuno-prophylaxes. 69-K-Da *B. malayi* antigen corresponding to recombinant protein is highly immunogenic in naturally infected children and adults.

Onchocerca volvulus

The generic name Onchocerca means 'hooked tail'. This convoluted filaria or 'bending' filaria, producing onchocerciasis, onchocercosis, coastal erysipelas, blinding filariasis and river-blindness was demonstrated by Brumpt in 1919. *Simulium* was reported as the intermediate host by Blacklock in 1926.

This nematoda is prevalent in Africa and America. Adult worms remain tightly coiled in the subcutaneous connective tissue tumours (nodules).

Morphology The adult worms are white, opalescent and transparent with transverse cuticula. They are wire-like, filiform and blunt at both ends. The adult female of *O. volvulus* can live for more than 11 years and produce microfilariae for 9–10 years.

The males measure 42 mm in length by 210 μm in diameter. The posterior end of the male is tightly re-curved ventrally, and has peri-anal and caudal papillae.

The female measures 50 cm by 400 μm. The vulva opens slightly behind the posterior extremity of the esophagus. *In utero,* the embryos are first ovoidal, but later become elongated, are discharged and escape from their 'sheath'. The microfilariae are of two sizes (368 by 9 μm; 287 by 7 μm - Fig. 8.74). Both ends are nuclei-free. The microfilariae are unsheathed and rarely appear in the

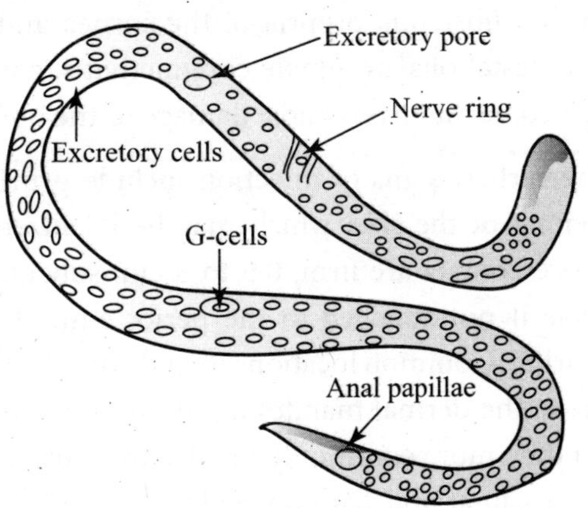

Fig. 8.74 Microfilaria of *O. volvulus*.

peripheral blood, but are mostly found in the lymphatics of the connective tissues and cutaneous layer (stratum germinativum) and corneal conjunctiva.

Lifecycle Humans are the definite hosts and *Simulium* (black fly) acts as the intermediate host. The complete development of the microfilariae of *O. volvulus* in *Simulium* is the same as that of *Mf. bancrofti* in the mosquito (Fig. 8.75).

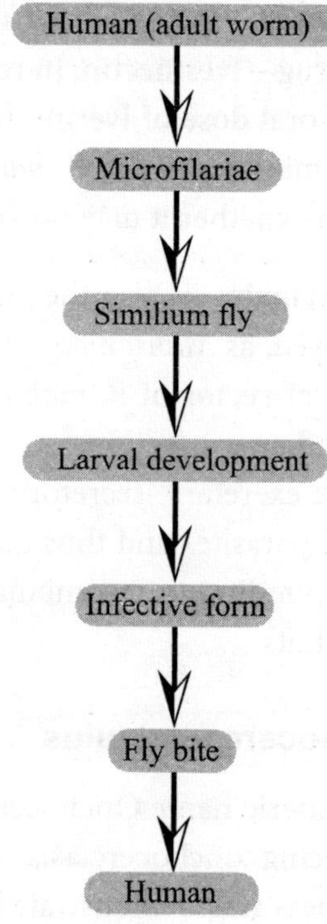

Fig. 8.75 Lifecycle of *O. volvulus*.

Pathogenicity and clinical features Two pathological processes are involved in onchocerciasis.

1. The first process is caused by the adult worm. The mature or adult worms in the skin provoke local cellular reaction (eosinophilia) resulting in the formation of a fibrous nodular encapsulation of the worms. The primary lesion is a non-abscessing fibrous tumour. This nodule is hard on palpation, firm, greyish-white superficially and yellowish around the worms. Pruritic dermatitis is due to the movement of microfilariae in the skin or to the toxic metabolites of the embryos. The unusual elephantiasis of the external genitalia of males and females, resembling that of Bancroft's filariasis, has been reported in Congo.
2. The second pathological effect is produced by the microfilariae which are discharged by the female worms in the fibrous nodules. These embryos escape into the cutaneous and subcutaneous lymphatics and circulate throughout these layers of tissue. These microfilariae circulate into the eyeball and cause corneal opacity. Sometimes they may be found moving in the substantia propria of the cornea and in the anterior chamber of the eye. Clinical manifestations are simple conjunctivitis, corneal opacity, keratitis, iridocyclitis, secondary glaucoma and irreversible damage to the optic nerve leading to blindness.

The earliest signs of infection include pruritus and intermittent papular rash with some thickening of the skin which may be localized to one area of the body and conjunctivitis. Onchocercomata are firm, 0.5 to 3 cm, subcutaneous nodules that are nontender and freely movable if not attached to the periosteum. These frequently occur in clusters that can be disfiguring. Common locations include the skin overlying the scalp and head region. In Central America, the dermal manifestations are most prominent around the head and neck, while in Africa they more commonly involve the trunk, buttocks and lower extremities. Lymph nodes of the inguinal and femoral regions are enlarged. Early ocular manifestations are punctate keratitis and anterior uveitis. Chronic changes include sclerosing keratitis, chorio-retinitis (which leads to progressive construction of visual fields), optic atrophy, glaucoma.

Laboratory diagnosis This consists of demonstration of the microfilariae in the biopsy of a small piece of the epidermis, and the adult worms in the enucleated nodules. Puncture of the suspected tumour may produce severe allergic reaction. Microfilariae can be detected in the ocular lesion by ophthalmoscopic examination. If the embryos are accidentally found in the peripheral blood, eosinophilia (20–75%) is significant.

The complement fixation test gives specific reaction, using alcoholic extracts of the worm. Antigens from the adult *Dirofilaria immitis* give satisfactory intradermal reaction in *O. volvulus* infection.

Skin test (Mazzotti's test): Within 24 hours after the oral administration of 50–100 mg of diethylcarbamazine, a pruritic papular rash appears suggesting the presence of microfilariae in the cutaneous tissue. This reaction is due to *O. volvulus* being killed by the drug.

Pruritus may occur on its own or in association with onchocercosis skin disease. It may interfere with work and prevent sleep. Residents in endemic villages may be seen using wooden sticks to scratch their skin in an attempt to obtain relief.

(*a*) ***Acute papular onchocerciasis***: This consists of small itchy papules which may be widely scattered on the arms. In severe cases, the lesions progress to form vesicles or pustules. Edema of the skin may be present.

(*b*) ***Chronic papular onchocercosis*** which consists of papules which tend to be larger than those in the acute papular eruption. Itching is common. Buttocks and waist areas are common sites followed by shoulders. Atrophy is commonly seen on the buttocks. Itching is not usual at this site.

Depigmentation is most commonly seen on the shins, but may also occur on the calf of the leg, inguinal regions, external genitalia and axillary folds. Nodules are mainly seen on the bony prominences which are easily visible.

Ocular lesions: Microfilariae are seen in all ocular tissues. Clinically, the patient should be asked to rest his head on his knees when sitting and the eye should be examined by using a slit lamp. Dead microfilariae in the cornea are opaque; they lie straightened out and are surrounded by an inflammatory infiltrate.

The more serious and potentially blinding ocular lesions of onchocercosis are sclerosing keratitis, iridocyclitis, choroido-retinitis, choroido-retinal atrophy, optic neuritis and optic atrophy.

A fluorescent antibody technique has been adapted using the *O. volvulus* antigen. Recent immunoblot can be used for the diagnosis of Onchocercosis. Immunological tools using a cocktail recombinant *O. volvulus* antigen are under investigation.

Treatment Enucleation of the nodules is the simplest method and it may also reduce the ocular complications and infection. Diethylcarbamazine kills the circulating microfilariae and Suramin kills the adult worms. They are effective drugs in the treatment of onchocerciasis, but they produce side effects, i.e., severe pruritus, urticaria and ocular changes (including temporary blindness). These side effects can be relieved by anti-histamines. Ivermectin is effective against *O. volvulus* microfilaria at a single dose of 50 mg/kg body weight, it is better tolerated and long lasting. Its activity against adult worms is poor. It is currently used. It is nontoxic, it causes mild Mazzotti reaction; it is a recent anthelmintic drug of ocular onchocercosis.

Prophylaxis The breeding foci of the intermediate host *(Simulium)* should be sprayed with DDT emulsifiable concentrate.

Dipetalonema Perstans

Dipetalonema perstans, the persistent filaria, producing dipetalonemiasis, was first found by Daniels (1898). Later, Manson described microfilariae in blood smear, in Congo. *Dipetalonema perstans* has an extensive distribution in Africa and America. The adult worms live in body cavities (peritoneal and pleural) and rarely in the pericardium.

Morphology The adult male measures 45 mm by 60 µm. The posterior end of the male has caudal papillae and copulatory spicules. The female measures 80 mm by 120 µm. The vulva is situated in the cervical region. The tail end of the female is split and presents a cuticular thickening, forming two triangular appendages.

The microfilariae of *D. perstans* are sub-periodic (i.e., they are found in the peripheral circulation in the daytime and at night). They are small, measuring 200 µm by 4.5 µm and are unsheathed. Their tail end is blunt and the nuclei extend up to the tail tip (Fig. 8.76).

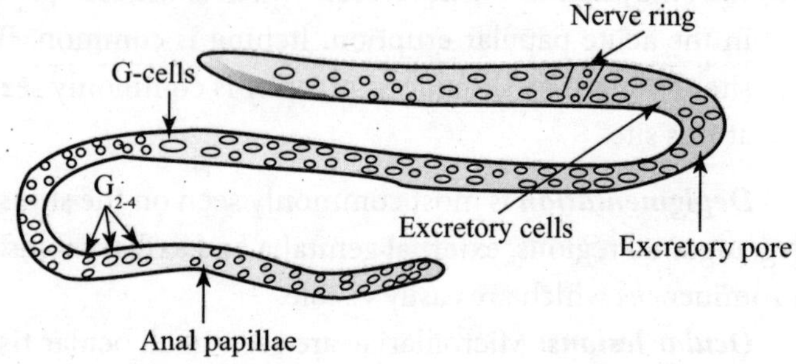

Fig. 8.76 *D. perstans*—microfilaria.

Lifecycle It requires two hosts:

1) Definite host (human) and
2) Intermediate host *(Culicoides austeni).* Like other microfilariae, *Mf. perstans* follows the same larval development in the Culicoides.

Pathogenicity and clinical features No definite pathogenicity is known. However, a few reported cases showed the following symptoms: fatal pericarditis, local irritation with fibrinous exudate in the mesentery, pleura and pericardium where *D. perstans* sew themselves; toxic edema of the eyelid, dyspnea, pericordial pain and eosinophilia with allergic dermatitis.

Laboratory diagnosis This is based on the detection of the microfilariae of *D. perstans* in the peripheral blood by day or night. Hemagglutination or bentonite flocculation test can be employed when the microfilariae cannot be demonstrated in the bloodstream.

Treatment Diethylcarbamazine has no action on the *Mf. perstans* and there is no specific drug.

Prophylaxis The eradication of the intermediate host is not possible as they breed in jungles.

Mansonella ozzardi

Mansonella ozzardi, is also known as the New World filariae or Ozzard's filariae, and produces mansonelliasis ozzardi or Ozzard's filariasis. The microfilaria of this species was recovered by Ozzard from the Carib Indians of Guyana, and was described by Manson as a new species. This worm is found widely-distributed in Argentina, America, Venezuela, Colombia, Panama and the West Indies. It lives embedded in the visceral adipose tissue, mesentery and body cavity.

Morphology The male measures 38 mm in length and 0.2 mm in breadth. The posterior end is strongly curved ventrad and has a slightly bulbous termination. The female measures 80 mm in length and 0.25 mm in diameter. The cuticula is smooth, and the head is unarmed. The posterior end has a pair of fleshy lappets.

The microfilariae are non-periodic, unsheathed (Fig. 8.77) and resemble *Mf. perstans.*

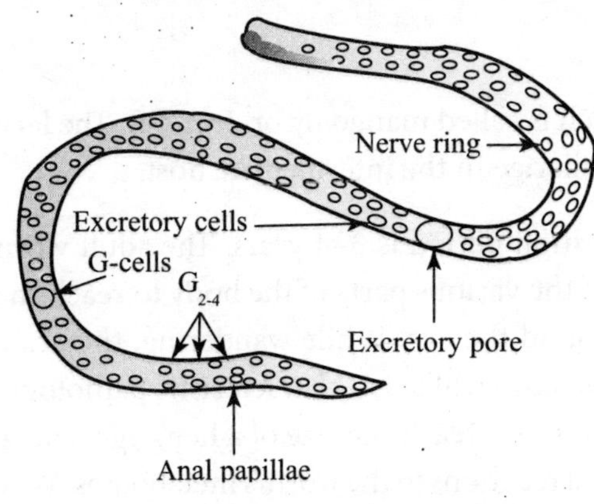

Fig. 8.77 Microfilaria of *M. ozzardi.*

Lifecycle Humans are the definite hosts and *Culicoides furens* is the intermediate host, where the larval development takes place.

Pathogenicity and clinical features There are no clinical manifestations in infected persons. However, there are some reports of associated hydrocele and enlarged lymph nodes with little tissue reaction.

Laboratory diagnosis is based on the recovery and specific identification of the non-periodic unsheathed microfilaria in the peripheral blood.

Treatment Hetrazan has no lethal effect on the microfilaria.

Prophylaxis This has not as yet been studied clearly.

Loa loa

'Loa' is the native West African name of the loa worm or eye worm, producing loaiasis or fugitive swelling. It was identified by Mongin who extracted it from the eye of a native African. This parasite has an extensive distribution in Africa, Sudan and Congo.

The adult worms live in the subcutaneous tissue.

Morphology The adult worms are thread-like and whitish, with a tapering cephalic end. The anterior end is unarmed but is provided with three pairs of small papillae. The male measures 30 mm in length by 0.35 mm in diameter. The caudal end of the male curves ventrally with 'cuticular bosses'. There are about eight pairs of peri-anal papillae with varying sizes and symmetry. The copulatory spicules are unequal and dissimilar in shape. The female measures 50 mm by 0.5 mm. The vulva opens in the cervical region. The lifespan of the adult worm may be 15 years or more.

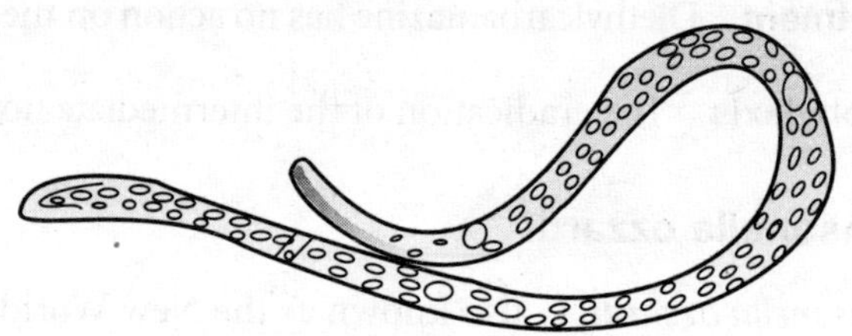

Fig. 8.78 Microfilaria of *L. loa*.

The microfilaria (Fig. 8.78) measures 250 μm by six μm and is sheathed. It has diurnal periodicity; its excretory cells and G-cells are similar to *Mf. malayi;* its tail tapers gradually, and its caudal nuclei are continuous with those of the trunk.

Lifecycle *Loa loa* requires two hosts:

1) The definite host (human) and
2) The intermediate host *(Chrysops dimidiata* which is called mango fly or deer fly). The larval development is the same as that of other microfilariae in the intermediate host.

Pathogenicity and clinical features The incubation period is 3–4 years. The adult worms migrate rapidly through the subcutaneous tissue of the various parts of the body to reach their special site of predilection, for creeping in and around the eye. While wandering, they cause temporary swelling (fugitive swelling or Calabar swelling) which is a characteristic pathological lesion of the infection. The swellings may develop rapidly, reach the size of a hen's egg, and are very painful and last for three days. These are the local reactions to the worm's metabolites. When passing in front of the eyeball or across the bridge of the nose, the adult worms are troublesome, though not very painful. These worms have been removed surgically from the back, groin, axilla, breast, penis, scalp, eyelids, anterior chamber of the eye and bulbar conjunctiva. There is frequent eosinophilia (50–70%). The symptoms are reddened giant urticarial swellings of the skin and mucous membrane, fever and high eosinophilia.

Laboratory diagnosis The microfilariae can be demonstrated in the peripheral blood during the day. The adult worm can be recovered from the swellings. Immunological tests are the same as those adapted for *W. bancrofti* employing *D. immitis* antigen.

Treatment Treatment involves the surgical removal of the adult worm. Suramin and diethylcarbamazine are specific chemotherapeutics. They should be administered with caution as violent allergic reactions may occur in allergic individuals. This allergy may be treated with anti-histamines. Diethylcarbamazine (DEC), 6–10 mg/kg body weight for 2–3 weeks, is extremely effective against microfilaria, but less against the adult worm. Calabar swelling appears to be a hypersensitivity reaction to the adult worm whose presence can be detected in some patients by either as a subcutaneous crawling sensation or the appearance of fine vermiform hives in the skin. Ivermectin rarely causes serious side effects in heavy infection of loa loa, when they co-exist with *O. volvulus.*

Prophylaxis It consists of:

1) Detection and diethylcarbamazine treatment of human cases to destroy circulating microfilariae
2) Anti-larval insecticidal campaigns at breeding places of *Chrysops* and
3) Protection from *Chrysops* bites by application of fly repellent on exposed skin.

Two unfertilized female worms of *Loa inquirenda* were described by Maplestone (1938), one of them from the neck of a European woman in India.

Human Dirofilariasis

Dirofilaria of animals may become adults in humans without producing microfilariae. They are:

1. *Dirofilaria immitis* (dog heartworm), a parasite of dog
2. *D. conjunctivae,* a natural parasite of animals in the USA
3. *D. tenuis,* a parasite of the raccoon in Europe, USSR, Sri Lanka and Asia
4. *D. repens,* a natural parasite of dog in Europe, Asia and America.

Dirofilarial species are filarial parasites, mostly of dogs, cats, that sometimes infect humans, but almost never fully develop to complete their lifecycle in the abnormal host. They have worldwide distribution.

Clinical features Two types:

1) Pulmonary dirofilariasis, caused by the dog heartworm, *D. immitis,* usually presents as an asymptomatic solitary pulmonary nodule, but occasionally chest pain, cough, hemoptysis. Microscopically, there is eosinophilia and granuloma formation around the immature worm.

2) Secondary: Clinical presentation is that of subcutaneous nodule anywhere on the body (or within the eye) that results from infection with *D. repens* or *D. tenuis.*

Diagnosis Immunoblot technique is used to diagnose pulmonary dirofilariasis due to *D. immitis* in humans. It is a very recent technique adapted for diagnosis.

Timor Microfilaria: During an investigation into filariasis on the island of Timor, a new species of microfilaria was found in a blood smear. It is similar to *B. malayi* and has nocturnal periodicity. Clinical features are similar to those of *B. malayi*. Diethylcarbamazine is effective.

SUPERFAMILY DRACUNCULOIDEA

These are long, cord-like worms with a simple pore-like mouth, surrounded by an inner circle of 4–6 papillae and an outer circle of four double papillae. The esophagus and intestine are rudimentary. The females are much larger than the males with the vulva in the middle of the body. The uteri are divergent. These are viviparous. The larvae are typically 'rhabditoid'. The human representative is *Dracunculus medinensis.*

Dracunculus medinensis

Genus: Dracunculus

The medina worm, guinea worm, serpent worm or dragon worm, producing dracunculiasis, dracunculosis or dracontiasis, has been known since the days of antiquity. In the Bible, it is called 'the fiery serpent'. An Arabian physician named this nematode *Vena medina,* because it was common in Medina. *Dracunculus medinensis* is distributed in Africa, Arabia, Burma, Iran, Pakistan, Turkistan, USSR and India (Rajasthan, in Jodhpur, extensive areas in Mumbai, Karnataka, Andhra Pradesh, Punjab, Madhya Pradesh, Maharashtra, Tamilnadu in South India, Panchmahal in Gujarat). Gujarat has the highest incidence with 13 out of 19 districts of the state being affected. Panchmahal district tops the list, followed by Valsad, Sabarkantha and Banaskantha. The disease has been carried to Indonesia from India. It has not yet been reported from Bengal, Assam and Bihar. Recently, an adult worm, one metre long, was removed from the eye of a patient in Orissa.

The adult worms are mostly found lodged in the subcutaneous tissues of the legs, arms and back.

Morphology The adult worm of *Dracunculus medinensis* is elongated and cylindrical. The cuticula is smooth. The posterior end is re-curved to anchor it in position. The anterior end is round, blunt (Fig. 8.79) and surmounted by an oval shield (Fig. 8.80), in the middle of which there is a minute triangular mouth surrounded by an inner circle of six papillae and an outer circle of four papillae. A lateral pair of cervical papillae is situated just behind the nerve ring. A single specimen of male *D. medinensis* has been recovered from a natural human infection in

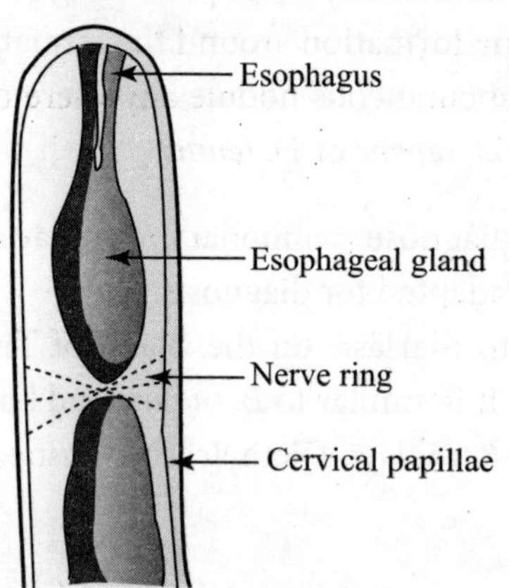

Fig. 8.79 *D. medinensis* anterior end of female (ventral view).

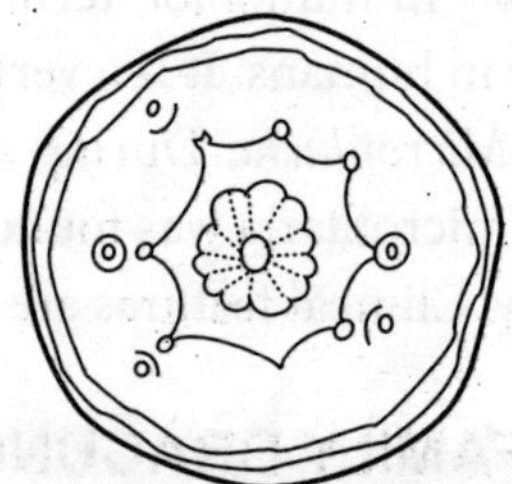

Fig. 8.80 Head end view of *D. medinensis* of worm.

India. It measures 30 mm in length and 0.4 mm in diameter. The posterior end of the male is coiled. There are four pre-anal and six post-anal papillae. The copulatory spicules are subequal, and 490–730 μm long. The gubernaculum is 200 μm long (Fig. 8.81). The female measures 120 cm in length and 1.7 mm in diameter. It is the largest human nematode. It resembles a piece of long twine thread and is milky white. Its ovarian tubules, oviducts and uteri are paired, whereas the vagina is single. There is no vulva in the gravid female. Its posterior end is tapering and bent to form a hook. The female worm is viviparous and discharges embryos. Its body fluid is toxic and causes blisters if it escapes into the tissues. The lifespan of the female is one year and that of the male is about six months.

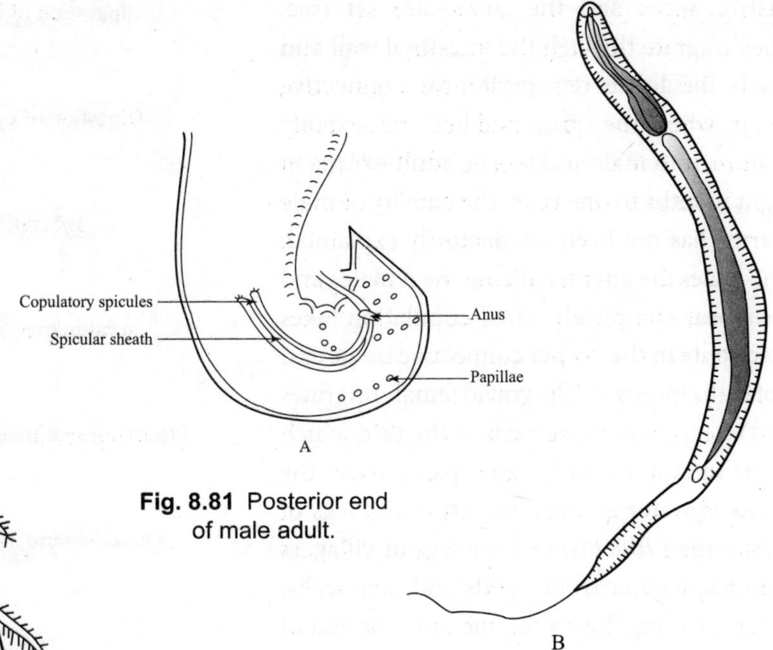

Fig. 8.81 Posterior end of male adult.

Fig. 8.82 Embryo of *D. medinensis*.

Fig. 8.83 Cyclops.

Embryos (Fig. 8.82): The rhabditoid larvae are wiry, coiled organisms with a round head and a long tapering tail. They measure 750 μm long and 25 μm in diameter. When the affected part of the body comes in contact with water, these larvae are discharged and swim in water in search of minute freshwater crustaceans of the genus Cyclops (Fig. 8.83) for their further development. If they are not taken up by the Cyclops, they will die within a short time.

Lifecycle: It requires two hosts:

1) The definite host is human and
2) Cyclops, the intermediate host.

Human infection results from drinking unprotected, unfiltered water containing infected Cyclops (mode of infection). On arriving at the stomach, the Cyclopses are digested by the gastric juices and the larvae are set free. They migrate through the intestinal wall and reach the loose retroperitoneal connective tissue, where they grow and become sexually mature, into male and female adult worms in eight months to one year. The paucity of male worms has not been satisfactorily explained. The males die after fertilizing the females and disappear completely. Their copulation takes place only in the deeper connective tissue and not in the intestine. The gravid female migrates and selects only those parts of the skin which come in contact with water, particularly the backs of water carriers, the arms and legs of washermen *(dhobis)* and the legs of villagers who fetch water from ponds and 'step wells'. After selecting their sites, the anterior end of the gravid female approaches the skin and a papule is formed in the dermis; the worm secretes a toxin, a histamine-like substance which causes a 'blister' within 24 hours. Ultimately, the blister ruptures and forms an ulcer. On contact with fresh water, the worm protrudes from the centre of the ulcer; a loop of the worm's uterus prolapses through its mouth, bursts open and discharges a milky white fluid containing a large number of motile embryos (first stage, rhabditoid larvae). These larvae swim in the water in search of a suitable intermediate host (Cyclops) and are ingested by the Cyclops. On reaching the mid-intestine, they break through the soft intestinal wall, enter the body cavity within 1–6 hours, undergo metamorphosis and increase in size (about one mm in length). It takes about two weeks for the complete development of the embryo. More than 5–6 larvae may kill the Cyclops. Heavy infection may kill them within 15 days. The lifespan of the Cyclops is about three months (Figs 8.84 and 8.85).

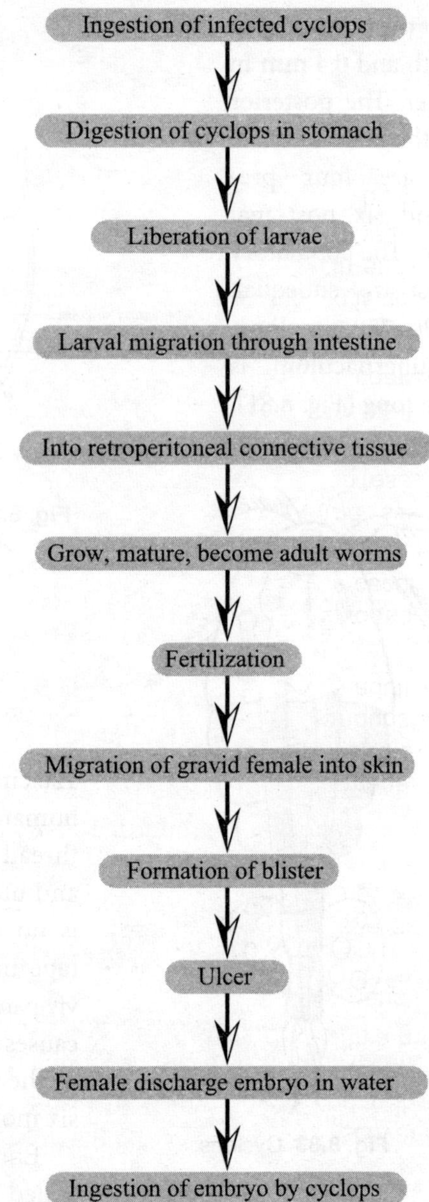

Fig. 8.84 Lifecycle of *Dracunculus medinensis*.

Pathogenicity and clinical features The penetration of the mature larvae into the viscera and deep somatic tissue and their development into mature worms does not produce any

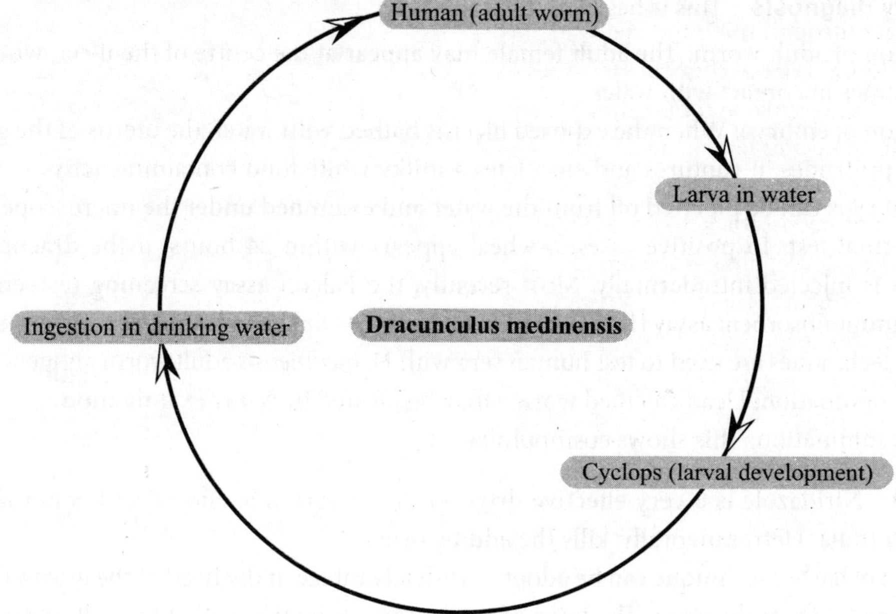

Fig. 8.85 Lifecycle of *D. medinensis*.

pathological lesions. As soon as the gravid female worms begin to migrate to the skin, there is allergic reaction due to a large amount of toxin, which has a histamine-like nature. When the worm reaches the skin, it produces a cutaneous blister which bursts on contact with fresh water. A few hours before the formation of the blister, there may be systemic reaction – erythema, urticaria with intense pruritus, nausea, vomiting, diarrhea and giddiness – due to toxemia, incapacitating the patient and causing much distress. The blister may be on the sole of the feet, ankles, shoulder, hands, arms, trunk, buttocks, scrotum or knee joint (arthritis). Sometimes, the guinea worm emerges out of the breast, tongue or testicles, permanently crippling the patient and even causing death. *D. medinensis* comes out by itself, like a long twine thread, inch by inch daily lasting several days to six months. Extradural abscesses (India), abscess cavity in the pericardium and quadriplegia due to the abscess in the spinal cord have been reported as caused by *D. medinensis.* A guinea worm was removed from the sub-conjunctival space of the eye of a patient in India. *D. medinensis* has been reported as a natural infection in dogs, horse, cattle, wolf, leopard and monkey.

The great social and economic significance of Dracunculiasis which is rarely fatal, derives from the fact that emergence of the worm is very painful and is often associated with swelling, local arthritis and secondary infection. Thus, the victims are often unable to farm and sometimes even walk for weeks or months. Over half the adults in a village may be crippled at the same time and the seasonal infection tends to occur precisely when villagers need to harvest and plant their crops. School attendance is also affected.

Laboratory diagnosis This is based on the following:

1. Detection of adult worm: The adult female may appear at the centre of the ulcer, when the ulcer comes in contact with water.
2. Detection of embryo: When the exposed ulcer is bathed with water, the uterus of the gravid female protrudes, it ruptures and ejaculates a milky white fluid containing active embryo. The embryos can be pipetted off from the water and examined under the microscope.
3. Intradermal test: In positive cases, a wheal appears within 24 hours, if the dracunculus antigen is injected intradermally. Most recently, the Falcon assay screening test–enzyme linked immunosorbent assay (FAST–ELISA) and enzyme linked immuno electrotransfer blot (EITB) techniques are used to test human sera with *D. medinensis* adult worm antigen.
4. X-ray examination: Dead calcified worms may be located by X-ray examination.
5. Blood examination: This shows eosinophilia.

Treatment Niridazole is a very effective drug but has severe side effects, and is not readily available in India. Hetrazan, orally, kills the adult worms.

The Indian barber technique can be adopted with advantage, if the head of the gravid female worm protrudes from the ulcer. The head of the worm can be tied with a fine silk thread to a matchstick and rolled daily inch by inch with gentle traction till the whole parasite is removed. It takes about 15–20 days. Care has to be taken in doing this because if the parasite breaks, it may cause allergic manifestations.

The treatment is difficult, because anthelmintics (thiabendazole or mebendazole) only marginally reduce the duration of emergence and associated pain. Aspirin can help to relieve the pain. Victims can be immunized against tetanus, which is an all too frequent complication. Niridazole (25 mg/kg body weight daily for an adult for 10 days), thiobendazole (50 mg/kg body weight daily for three days) and mebendazole (400 mg for an adult per day for 10–20 days) have no lethal effect on the worm, but they act as anti-inflammatory agents thereby facilitating a less traumatic removal of the worm. Trials with Ivermerctin are proceeding.

Prophylaxis This comprises

1) Preventing infected persons from stepping into water sources
2) Constructing draw wells
3) Providing safe water
4) Boiling water before drinking
5) Filtering water suspected of contamination
6) Spraying insecticides in step wells, ponds, tanks, etc., and
7) Converting step wells into draw wells.

By the end of 1986, India reduced its reported Dracunculiasis by 35% following the method of the International Drinking Water Supply and Sanitation Decade (1981–1990) to provide safe water.

SUPERFAMILY: SPIRUROIDEA

Gnathostoma spinigerum

Genus: Gnathostoma

Gnathostoma spinigerum, producing gnathostomiasis, was first described by Owen from the gastric tumours of a tiger. It has been reported in the domestic cat, wild cat, lion (Zambia) and dog (India). Human cases have been reported from Thailand, Malaysia, China, Japan and India. Except for two cases of possibly spurious parasitism reported by Chandler (1927) from India, almost all human infections have been with the immature worms in the subcutaneous tissue. The adult G. *spinigerum* lives in the tumours in the stomach wall of the cat and dog.

Morphology The adult worm is stout, reddish and transparent with a sub-globose cephalic swelling and is curved ventrally at both ends. The anterior half is covered with leaf-like spines. The posterior half of the cuticula is aspinose. The mouth is guarded by a pair of conspicuous and fleshy lips. The length of the male is about 11–25 mm and it has pseudobursa. The copulatory spicules are chitinoid rods (1.1 mm and 0.4 mm, respectively). The female measures from 25–54 mm in length. The vulva is posto-equatorial and the genital tubes are paired.

The eggs measure 65 by 38 μm, are ovoidal, transparent, superficially pitted, and have a mucoid plug at one pole. They are unembryonated when freshly laid.

Lifecycle The lifecycle of *G. spinigerum* in nature is as follows: The adult *G. spinigerum* lives in tumours in the stomach wall of cats and dogs. Eggs are extruded from the lesions and evacuated in the feces into the water where they embryonate and hatch. These larvae are ingested by the Cyclops in whom they transform into the second stage, with a cephalic bulb provided with pointed spines. When the infected Cyclops is eaten by fish, frog or snakes, the larvae develop into the third stage in the flesh of these animals. When a suitable definite host eats the infected second larval host, the larva develops to maturity in the stomach wall in about six and a half months. Thus, the lifecycle is repeated.

Pathogenicity and clinical features Consumption of inadequately cooked fish containing the encapsulated third stage larva is usually responsible for human *gnathostomiasis.* In humans, gnathostoma is not a fully adapted parasite, but it is the immature worm which produces superficial lesions in the skin, subcutaneous tissue or somatic musculature as it migrates through these tissues. The advanced larval stage causes abscesses including breast abscess. This is referred to as *gnathostomiasis externa* which consists of

1) The development of abscess pockets and
2) The formation of subcutaneous tunnels in which the worms are migrating (i.e., 'larva migrans' causing 'creeping eruption'). Inflammation, toxic and allergic reactions are responsible for these lesions. The erratic migration of the larva into the eye or brain has been encountered.

In cats and dogs, the adult worms are coiled inside the tumours of the digestive tract. This is known as gnathostomiasis interna.

Laboratory diagnosis The removal and identification of the worms aid in specific diagnosis. The intradermal test, by employing 0.05 ml of a 1:50,000 saline solution of an antigen prepared from larval or adult Gnathostoma can be read in 15 minutes. A papule of 10 mm diameter with a peripheral red areola is regarded as positive. The precipitin reaction is also specific.

Treatment Chemotherapy is not effective. The only remedy is the removal of worms.

Gnathostoma hispidum

It is stouter than *G. spinigerum* and has 12 rings of cephalic spines. It is a common parasite in the stomach wall of pigs. It has been found twice as human infection in India.

Angiostrongylus cantonensis

A. cantonensis, the rat lungworm, producing eosinophilic meningo-encephalitis or human angiostrongylosis, was first recovered by Chen (1935) from the lung of a rat. Human infection was first recorded by Nomura and Lin (1945) in suspected cases of meningitis with recovery of worms from the spinal fluid; later, this worm was identified as a human parasite.

This worm is found distributed in China (Canton), Australia, Malaysia, Sumatra and Indonesia. It is found in the lung of the rat.

Morphology *Angiostrongylus cantonensis* is a delicate filiform worm. Its length is 17–25 mm and its diameter is 0.26–0.36 mm. The cuticula is smooth. The cephalic end is simple and has three lips. It has no buccal capsule and the mouth opens into the esophagus. The males measure 15.9 mm in length by 0.26 mm in diameter. The copulatory bursa is curved ventrally. The females measure 21 mm in length by 0.30 mm in diameter. The posterior end is like a blunt horn with a subterminal anal pore and a vulvar opening.

SUMMARY

- The nematodes are elongated, cylindrical, tapering at both ends, non-segmented. Their sizes range from the smallest (*Trichinella spiralis, Strongyloides stercoralis*) to the largest (*Dracunculus medinensis*). They have cuticula (protective covering). They have a nervous system, complete genitalia and digestive tract with both oral and anal openings. The oral cavity has teeth or cutting plates. If the esophagus is uniform, it is called a filarifarm esophagus; if it is expanded into a gill, it is referred to as a rhabditiform esophagus. The free living stages of the worm have rhabiditiform esophagus; the parasite forms have filariform esophagus.

- In contrast to parasitic trematodes and cestodes, the nematodes may be
  1) Viviparous
  2) Oviparous or
  3) Ovo-viviparous.
     1) Viviparous (*Dracunculus medinensis*: giving birth to larva)
     2) Oviviparous (*Ascaris lumbricoides*: laying eggs)
     3) Ovo-viviparous (*Strongyloides stercoralis*: laying eggs containing larva).
- The sexes are separate, so trematodes are 'diecious helminths'. The male worm is smaller than the female, has a tubule of testicular cells, vas deferens, seminal vesicle, an ejaculatory duct opening into the cloaca. In some males, accessory organs (spicule, gubernaculum) are also present. In some other males, the posterior end is expanded into a copulatory bursa supported by rays. Female has two cylindrical ovaries, uteri which may open to the exterior through a single vulva or a common vagina. The vulva is near the middle of the body, but its position varies in different species.

Trichinella spiralis It is commonly known as 'trichina' worm it causes trichinosis. It was first discovered by Peacock (1828). It has worldwide distribution.

- The adult worm of *T. spiralis* remains buried in the duodenal or jejunal muscosa. Its larva encysts in the striated muscle of human, pig, harbouring the adult worm. It is one of the 'smallest' nematodes infecting humans. Its anterior end is delicate. The caudal extremity, the cloaca, is evertible and guarded by two conspicuous conical papillae. The female is two times longer than the male. It is viviparous and discharges embryo (larva).
- Mode of human infection is by ingestion of raw meat infected with cysts of *T. spiralis*.
- In the stomach, these cysts are digested out of the meat; in the duodenum they excyst, these larvae invade the mucosa of the duodenum and the jejunum and develop into minute adult females and males. The females burrow into the villi and the males die after fertilizing the females. These fertilized females discharge 1500 progenies. Some escape into the lumen and the majority enter into the circulation via the mesenteric lymphatics and are carried, lodged in various tissues (myocardium, brain, cerebrospinal fluid and body cavities). From these tissues, they re-enter the blood stream and are distributed in striated muscles where they encyst. The cyst wall formation is due to tissue reaction, but it is not due to larval secretion. Diaphragm, muscles of the lungs, pharynx, tongue and biceps, deltoid are mostly infected.
- Pathogenicity has three stages:
  1) Invasion (incubation)
  2) Migration of larvae
  3) Encystations and tissue repair.
- In the first stage, the clinical symptoms are nausea, vomiting, toxic diarrhea, colic pain and profuse sweating. In the second stage, muscular pain, edema, enlarged lymph nodes, fever, encephalitis, meningitis, ocular disturbance, deafness may occur.

- In the third stage, cachexia, edema, dehydration, low blood pressure, collapse of the patient are observed. In the laboratory, demonstration of the following: larvae in the muscle, adult worm and larvae in the feces; larvae in the blood, spinal fluid, mother's milk can be useful.
- The following serological tests can also be done: intradermal test, precipitin test, flocculation test, fluorescent antibody test, xenodiagnosis can be useful during surveys.
- Curative and supportive treatment can be undertaken. The infection can be prevented by destruction of carcasses, viscera of dead pigs, by consumption of thoroughy cooked pork, destruction of rats, mice.

Trichuris trichiura This 'whipworm' causing trichiuriasis was first discovered by Linnaeus (1771). It has a cosmopolitan distribution. It remains attached to the wall of the human cecum. Its anterior end is thin, hair-like. Its posterior portion is fleshy, thick and stout. It contains intestines, sex organs. It looks like a whip with a handle.

- The caudal extremity of the male worm is coiled ventrally. Its genitalia end in the cloaca. A single spicule protrudes through a refractive penial sheath.
- The posterior end of the adult female is rounded. Its genitalia end in the external pore. Female is oviparous. Its egg is barrel-shaped with mucoid plugs at both the ends. About 5000-7000 eggs are liberated per day.
- Eggs passed in the stool are embryonated in moist soil.
- Embryonated eggs containing rhabditiform larva are infective to humans. After ingestion by a human, these eggs are digested in the small intestine; the larva emerges out of the egg. This larva gets attached to the small intestine for nourishment and migrates to the cecum (site of predilection), where it grows into an adult worm which lays eggs in the stool of humans.
- The process of infection may be traumatic or allergic. Though many worms block the lumen of the intestine, they cause irritation and inflammation of the cecum and produce colitis and secondary anemia and allergic reaction.
- Clinical symptoms are abdominal pain, vomiting, constipation and systemic intoxication. The patient is emaciated with dry skin. Clinically, this infection resembles hookworm disease, acute appendicitis or amebic dysentery.
- Typical egg of *T. trichiura* can be detected in the stool. The infection can be treated by effective drugs and can be prevented by personal hygiene and community prophylaxis.

Capillaria philippinensis This parasite was first reported in 1963 and is common in the Philippines. It remains burrowed in the jejunal mucosa with both ends free. The male has caudal alae. The anterior part of the female has an esophagus with glands, whereas its posterior part has intestines, reproductive organs. Only humans get infected by consuming raw fish, though its lifecycle is not yet established.

- Epithelium of jejunum shows degenerative changes. Clinical symptoms are diarrhea, emaciation, weakness, abdominal pain. Death may be due to cachexia. Adult worm and eggs can be detected in the stool; skin test is sensitive and specific. Treatment is by effective drugs. Prevention is by thoroughly cooking fish.

Strongyloides stercoralis This nematode is also called 'thread worm'. It produces stronglyloidiasis in humans and was first discovered by Normand (1876). Like *T. spiralis*, it remains buried in the mucosa of the duodenum and jejunum. The anterior third of the body of the female contains a cylindrical esophagus, the posterior two thirds are filled with intestine, and the anus opens mid-ventrally. Two sets of genitalia extend from the vulva. It is ovo-viviparous.

- The parasitic male adult worm is shorter than the female; it does not penetrate the intestinal mucosa and remains in the human lumen.
- Its egg is transparent, thin and oval. As soon as the eggs are laid, the rhabditiform larvae hatch and come out of the human intestinal mucosa, then enter the lumen and pass out into the stool.
- There are two types of larvae
  1. Rhabditiform larvae
  2. Filariform larvae.
- The male rhabditiform larvae have two spicules, a gubernaculum and no caudal alae; its posterior end is curved ventrally. The female has two horned uterus and vulva opening in the middle of the ventral side of the body.
- The rhabditiform larva is developed directly from the gravid female and is found in the lumen of the intestine, it transforms into filariform larva, which penetrates into the mucosa of the intestine to cause internal re-infection. Sometimes, they penetrate the peri-anal, perineal skin of the host causing auto-infection (hyper-infection). Some other rhabditiform larva are passed out into the soil and may develop into filariform larva, which may penetrate the skin when a person walks barefooted, enter venous circulation, right part of the heart, lungs, bronchi, trachea, larynx, epiglottis are swallowed back and enter the intestine.
- The free living rhabditiform larvae have two types of cycle:
  1. Direct cycle: in the soil they develop into filariform larvae;
  2. Indirect cycle: the male and female free living rhabditiform larvae copulate and produce batches of rhabditiform larvae, similar to those produced by parasite females.
- Skin lesions (petichial hemorrhage, pruritus, congestion, edema, urticarial rash) are produced by the filariform larvae at the site of entry.
- Pulmonary lesions (hemorrhage and cellular infiltration in air sacs and bronchioles) are produced when the larvae break out of pulmonary capillaries into the alveoli.
- Recovery of adult worms and larvae of *S. stercoralis* from stool and sputum samples is correct direct diagnosis. Treatment is effective.
- The human body should be protected from contaminated soil and feces, avoid by personal hygiene.

Superfamily strongyloidea

- General Characters

- This superfamily has
  1. Buccal capsule (well developed mouth cavity) which may contain teeth or cutting plates
  2. Bursa (copulatory bursa) of male
  3. Egg with unsegmented ovum develops in soil
  4. Two subfamilies:
     a) Sub family Ancylostomadinae (tooth-like processes)
        i) Two pairs of teeth, *Ancylostoma duodenale*
        ii) One pair of teeth, *A. braziliense*
        iii) Three pairs of teeth, *A. caninum*
     b) Superfamily Uncinariinae (cutting-plates) *Necator americanus*

  Ancylostoma duodenale It is commonly named as the old world hookworm causing ancylostomiasis. It was first reported by Dubini (1843). It has worldwide distribution, including in India (Punjab and Uttar Pradesh). Ancylostomiasis in dogs was first reported in Pondicherry (India) in 1972 by Panjarathinam. It lives in the jejunum.

- The adult worm is larger and thicker. Its anterior end bends dorsally like a hook; hence the name 'hookworm', even its oral aperture is bent. Its buccal capsule has six teeth, four hook-like on the ventral surface and two knob-like on the dorsal surface. Its digestive system is connected with the esophageal gland secreting an enzyme which prevents the clotting of blood. The posterior end of the male has a copulatory bursa expanded in an umbrella-like fashion. Its genital opening is connected with the cloaca.
- Dorsal ray of copulating bursa is single. Total number of rays is 13.
- The female has a tapering end and no expanded bursa. Its genital opening is at the middle third of the body. Insemination occurs when the male applies its copulating bursa around the vulva. Its posterior end has a spine. During copulation, the worm assumes a y-shaped figure because of the position of the genital opening. In the human intestine, it lives for four years.
- The rhabditiform larva has a mid-gut, a short rectum, a small genital opening. The filiform larva is long, delicate with short esophagus and is infective to humans. Its egg contains segmented ovum with four blastomeres and is not infective to humans.
- ***Lifecycle***. Eggs with four blastomeres are passed in the feces. In the soil, the eggs hatch out as rhabditiform larvae. These larvae develop into filiform larvae which cast off their sheath and come in contact with the skin of the bare foot. They invade the bloodstream, are carried to right part of the heart, the lungs and then break out from the pulmonary capillaries into the alveoli, bronchi, trachea, larynx, epiglottis, esophagus, and are swallowed back, enter into the intestine, develop into adult worms which lay eggs. The eggs are passed out in the feces.
- Ancylostome adult worm larvae may cause pathogenic effects: cutaneous lesions, ancylostome dermatitis and creeping eruption); pulmonary lesions (minute hemorrhage, bronchitis, bronchopneumonia)

- Filariform larvae of *A. duodenale* and *Nector americanus* penetrate the skin, produce 'ground itch' characterized by itching and burning, edema, erythema, popular eruption, then a vesicle; they also produce cutaneous larva migrans (creeping eruption); anemia, iron deficiency.
- Clinical symptoms are of three types: mild, moderate and severe.
- In the mild type, anemia is negligible; in the moderate type, heart burn, flatulence, epigastric pain, they are relieved by eating clay, mud (which is known as pica or geophagy) mild fever, dyspnea, palpitation of the heart.
- In the severe type, constipation, diarrhea, food is not digested, dry skin; the patient is cold even in hot climate, edema of the face and around the eyes. Pot belly is typical sign in children. Finally, it results in cardiac failure and anasarca.
    1. Direct demonstration of adult worm and its eggs, microscopically
    2. Blood examination can be done to find out indirectly the nature of anemia and the presence of eosinophilia. *A. duodenale* and *N. americanus* can be differentiated by the morphological examination of adult worm and mature filariform larva.
- Supportive treatment should be followed by curative treatment. Prevention is by personal hygiene using gloves, boots and by community prophylaxis.

Necator americanus Its name is the 'New World hookworm or American hookworm'. It causes necatoriasis. It was first described by Stiles (1902). It is prevalent in many countries including southern India. Its lifecycle, morphology, pathogenicity, diagnosis, treatment are the same.

Ancylotoma braziliense It is similar to *A. ceylanium.* Male is smaller than female. Its eggs are similar to those of other ancylostoma. The filariform larvae of *A. braziliense* causes creeping eruption in humans, and also they produce a serpiginous tunnel, as they cannot penetrate below the stratum germinativum of the human skin.

A. ceylanium It does not produce creeping eruption.

A. malayanum It is the largest hookworm found in India and Malaysia in bears and was reported once in humans.

A. caninum It was reported once in a human patient in the Philippines and in dogs in India (Pondicherry) by Panjarathinam (1972).

Enterobius vermicularis Human pinworm or seat worm is a common name. It causes enterobiasis or human oxyuriasis known since ancient times, it has a cosmopolitan distribution. A gravid female was recovered from the peri-anal skin of a child (Panjarathinam, 1978) in Ahmedabad (India). The adult worm remains attached to the mucosa of the cecum, appendix, colon and ileum. It is small, white and spindle-shaped, has no buccal capsule but is provided with three lips. It has a cervical alae, has a characteristic double bulb esophagus. The male has a ventrally curved posterior end. It has a spicule, but it lacks a gubernaculum, it dies after fertilization and hence it is rarely seen.

- The female has a sharply pointed posterior end. Its vulva opens mid-ventrally. Its vagina is long and extends from the vulva. Its cloaca is near the copulatary spicule. It has paired genitalia (uteri, oviducts and ovaries). The gravid female gets detached from the intestinal mucosa, migrates freely in the lumen and crawls out of the anus onto the peri-anal or perineal skin, and dies after oviposition.

- Its eggs are colourless, plano-convex in shape and contain motile embryo. When fully embryonated eggs (infective) are ingested by humans, they reach the duodenum and are digested by the digestive juices. The larvae hatch out and pass down the intestine. Without migrating through the lungs, they moult, lodge in the villi of the jejunum and ileum and become sexually mature and fertilized in the intestine.
- The male dies after fertilization. The gravid female then migrates down the cecum, colon and appendix and remains there till the eggs are developed, then crawls on the peri-anal region for ovipositon. Its eggs are then transmitted from the anus to mouth (auto-infection). Minute intestinal ulcers with hemorrhage caused by adult worm may get infected with pathogenic bacteria, sub-mucosal abscess and appendicitis may be produced. When metabolites of adult worms are absorbed, a generalized helminthic toxemia may ensue. The gravid female may deposit eggs on the peri-anal region and cause severe pruritus with scratching. It may enter the genital tract causing salphingitis, encysts in the peritoneal cavities. It may cause urethritis, nocturnal enuresis.
- Clinical symptoms are insomnia, nervousness, nail biting, nose picking, grinding of teeth at night may be observed in children. Laboratory diagnosis can be done by demonstration of adult worm and its eggs under microscope. Treatment is by specific drugs and prevention can be done by personal hygiene.

Superfamily Ascaridoidea

- The worms of this superfamily are large and stout. They have no buccal capsule, but they have three lips in their mouth. Males have no copulatory bursa.

  Ascaris lumbricoides It is also called giant intestinal roundworm. It causes ascariasis. It is common in children of rural areas in China and India. It has also been recovered from infected calves in Pondicherry (India) by Panjarathinam (1972). The adult worm is the largest nematode of the intestine. It is elongated and cylindrical. Its anterior end has three, small, toothed lips. Each lip has minute papillae; has a small triangular buccal cavity. The male has a ventrally curved posterior end. Its genitalia has testes, vas deferens, ejaculatory duct opening into the cloaca, has copulating spicules, no gubernaculum. The vulva of the female is mid-ventrally situated near the junction of the anterior and middle thirds of the body. Its narrows end is called 'vulvar waist'. Its vagina is connected with two genitalia consisting of uterus, oviduct and ovary. Its body fluid is an irritant due to ascarase which is responsible for allergy. !t deposits about 2, 00,000 eggs per day. Its lifespan is two years. Its fertilized egg is ovoidal, transparent; the ovum is unsegmented. The unfertilized egg contains a small, atrophied ovum with various sized refractive granules. It is heaviest.
- Fertilized eggs in the soil embryonate in the soil. These embryonated (containing rhabditiform larva) eggs are ingested along with food by humans. The egg shell is digested by the digestive juices in the duodenum. The rhabditiform larvae are liberated, penetrate into the intestine. Instead of becoming adult worms, they enter

into the circulation, reach the lungs and break through the pulmonary capillaries into the alveoli. They crawl up the bronchioles, bronchi, trachea and epiglottis and are swallowed. They develop into adult worms in the intestine. The female is fertilized and discharges eggs in the stool. Some trauma and petichial hemorrhage may occur when the larvae escape into the alveoli. As a result, there could be consolidation of the lobules, spasms and coughing, bronchial rales, urticaria, fever and difficulty in breathing. This condition is known as *Ascaris pneumonitis* (Loeffler syndrome). While in circulation, the larvae filter out in the brain, spinal cord, eyelids, kidneys where they cause physiological disturbance. Micro-organisms are carried by these migrating larvae from the intestine to other organs and set up the infection. They deprive the host of its nutrition. They cause vitamin A deficiency (night blindness) Generalized toxemia and mechanical effects are also observed. Common symptoms are vague abdominal discomfort, acute colicky pain in the epigastric region, diarrhea, fever, meningitis, epilepsy. Adult worm and eggs can be detected in the stool. Blood examination and allergic tests can also be undertaken for diagnosis. Effective anthelmitic drugs can be used. Prevention is by personal hygiene; community prophylaxis.

Anisakis marina This nematode is a parasite of sea mammals and fish. Humans acquires the infection (anisakiasis) by consuming raw fish. The fish is digested; the liberated larvae enter the mucosa of the stomach and intestine producing a growth, simulating malignancy. Its lifecycle is not yet known. Colicky pain and obstruction of the intestine are the symptoms. Demonstration of larvae from the incised tissue growth and HA test are useful for diagnosis.

Superfamily Filarioidea

- Filariform larvae have a simple, circular mouth surrounded by papillae, buccal cavity without lips and caudal alae. They are: *Wuchereria bancrofti, Brugia malayi, Onchocerca volvulus, Dipetalonema perstans, D. streptocercum, Mansonella ozzardi and Loa loa.*

  Wuchereria bancrofti Though the symptoms of filariasis have been known since antiquity, microfilariae were demonstrated by Demarquay in 1863. The name *Wucheria bancrofti* was given in honour of the discoverers, Wucherer and Bancrofti.

- This parasite is distributed in many countries including India (Rajasthan, Punjab, Uttar Pradesh, Delhi, Gujarat) along the Indian sea coast and banks of rivers (except the Indus). The adult worm is a long, minute, thread-like nematode. The tail end of the male is curved ventrally with two spicules and a gubernaculum. It has no caudal alae. The male worm is very rare. The vulva of the female is cervical in position. Its female genitalia consists of a short vagina, uterus. Its tail end is pointed. It is ovo-viviparous, it liberates active embryo with the sheath (i.e. microfilariae). These microfilariae enter into lymph and blood circulation. Their anterior end is round with a stylet and the posterior end is tapering. The anatomical 'landmarks' in the central column of their nuclei, extending from head to tail, can differentiate different species. *Wuchereria bancrofti, Brugia malayi* and *Loa loa* are sheathed; whereas *O.volvulus, Dipetalonema perstans, Mansonella ozzardi* are unsheathed.

- Microfilariae of *Wuchereria bancrofti* appear in the peripheral circulation between 10 p.m. and 2 a.m. (nocturnal periodicity) and adapt themselves to the feeding habits of the mosquito, *Culex pipiens*, a night feeder, its length is 244 µm; tail end has no terminal nuclei. They require two hosts in their lifecycle:
  1) The definite host – human, and
  2) The intermediate host – mosquito (*Culex*). When the mosquito bites an infected person, it ingests the sheathed microfilariae. These microfilariae cast off their sheath in the proventriculus (stomach) of the mosquito, penetrate into mosquito's intestinal wall, reach into the mosquito's thoracic muscle, transform into the first, second, third stage (infective) larva. When an infected mosquito bites a human, the infective larvae are deposited on the punctured skin, they migrate into the punctured wound and settle into the lymphatic (inguinal, scrotal, abdominal), grow and sexually mature in the lymphatics, fertilize; gravid females discharge microfilariae which enter into peripheral circulation.
- The filarial granulation tissue is pathognomonic of the disease. As the worm dies, lymphangitis ensues and results in elephantiasis. The following symptoms are common:
  1. Lymphagitis: In this condition, the lymphatics of the testicle, epididymis, are involved; they are red, congested, palpable and painful.
  2. Lymphadenitis: It is the inflammation of the regional lymph nodes which precedes an attack of lymphangitis. It is mostly found in the groin or axilla, it is soft not painful and tender.
  3. Elephantiasis is due to obstruction of the lymphatic tracts caused by recurrent attacks of lymphangitis.
  4. Hydrocele is due to repeated attacks of *Wuchereria orchitis* and epididymitis.
  5. Chyluria is the escape of chyle through the urine. The urine is milky.
- Filariasis can be diagnosed
  1. Directly by the demonstration of microfilariae in the peripheral blood.
  2. Indirectly by various serological tests.
- Effective drug is available for treatment; prophylaxis is by destruction of mosquito and protection from mosquito bite.

Brugia malayi It is prevalent in many countries including India (Assam, Andhra Pradesh, Orissa, Madhya Pradesh, Kerala). It resembles *W. bancrofti*, has a non-labiate mouth. The anterior end of the female has the reproductive organ; its posterior end has cuticular bossing; but that of male has peri-anal papillae, has copulatory spicules and gubernaculum.

- Microfilariae of *B.malayi* have nocturnal periodicity; their anterior end has two stylets, cephalic space is broader; length is 177 µm. Tail is often constructed between two terminal nuclei; their appearance is stiff with secondary kinks. They are confined to lymphatics. Its lifecycle is the same as that of *W. bancrofti.*
- *B. malayi* causes lymphagitis and elephantiasis of the lower extremities. Scrotal swellings are present in *B. malayi*, but chyluria is absent. Microfilariae can be

demonstrated in the peripheral blood. Treatment and prophylaxis are similar to those of *W. bancrofti*.

- In addition, certain water plants should be destroyed as *Mansonia* grows on these plants. These plants grow in Kerala, India.

Onchocerca volvulus Convoluted filaria, bending filaria (common name) causing onchocerciasis. It was reported by Brumpt (1919), remains coiled in nodules (tumours) for 11 years. It is wire-like, filiform and bent at both ends.

- The male of *O. volvulus* is smaller than the female. Its posterior end is re-curved ventrally and it has peri-anal and caudal papillae, it has vulva, uterus. The microfilariae are unsheathed; both ends are nuclei-free.
- The definite host is human and simulium is the intermediate host in its lifecycle. The development of the microfilariae (Mf.) of *O. vulvulus* is the same as that of *Mf. bancrofti* in the mosquito. It produces primary lesion which is a non-abscessing fibrous tumor. Pruritis is due to toxic metabolites of the embryo. The microfilariae circulate in the eyeball and cause corneal opacity. Clinical manifestations are simple conjunctivitis, corneal opacity, keratitis and secondary glaucoma. Microfilariae can be demonstrated in the biopsy of a small piece of the epidermis. They can be detected in ocular lesions. Serological tests can also be useful. Treatment is by effective drugs. Spraying of DDT in the breeding places of simulium.

Dipetalonema perstans *D. perstans* (persistent filaria) causes dipetalonemiasis. It was found by Daniels (1898), distributed in Africa and America, lives in peritoneal and pleural cavities. Male adult worm is smaller than female. Its posterior end has caudal papillae and copulating spicules. The female has vulva situated in the cervical region. Its tail end presents cuticular thickening. Microfilariae of *D. perstans* are subperiodic (i.e. they are found in the circulation in the daytime and at night). Their tail end is blunt and the nuclei extend up to the tail tip. Like *O. volvulus*, it requires two hosts, like other microfilariae, *Mf. perstans'* larval development is the same in the Culicoides (intermediate host). Symptoms are fatal pericarditis, local irritation, toxic edema of the eyelid, dyspnea and pericardial pain. Detection of *Mf. perstans* is by examining the peripheral blood at night or day. Serological tests can be employed. Treatment is by suitable drugs. Prophylaxis is not possible by the eradication of Culicoides, as they breed in the jungle.

Mansonella ozzardi *M. ozzardi* (Ozzard's filariae) produces mansonelliasis. Its microfilariae were recovered for the first time by Ozzard. The male adult worm is smaller than the female. It lives embedded in the visceral adipose tissue; the posterior end is strongly curved ventrad. Female has smooth cuticula. Its head is unarmed. Its posterior end has a pair of fleshy lappets. *Mf. Ozzardi* is unsheathed, non-periodic and resembles *Mf. perstans* during larval development in Culicoides (intermediate host). No clinical manifestations are observed, there are reports of associated hydrocele, enlarged lymph nodes with tissue reaction. Laboratory diagnosis is by the detection of *Mf. ozzardi* in peripheral blood. Hetrazan has no effect on microfilariae. Prophylaxis is not yet established.

- **Loa loa** Loa loa (eye worm) produces loaiasis. It was identified by Mongin from the eye of an African American. It has an extensive distribution. It lives in subcutaneous tissue. Adult worm is thread-like and whitish with tapering cephalic end. Its anterior end is unarmed but it has small papillae. The male is smaller than the female. Its caudal end is curved ventrally, with 'cuticular bosses' has peri-anal papillae and unequal copulating spicules. The vulva of the female is in the cervical region. The adult worm may live for 15 years.

- Its microfilaria is sheathed, has diurnal periodicity. Its tail is tapering. Its caudal nuclei are continuous with those of the trunk. For its lifecycle, it requires a definite host (human) and an intermediate host (*Chrysops dimidiata,* mango fly or deer fly). Its larval development is the same as that of other microfilaraie in the intermediate host.
- After migration through the subcutaneous tissue of the body, the adult worms reach the eye (site of predilection) where they creep in and around the eyes. Temporary swelling (fugitive or Calabar swelling) is caused by wandering worms. They reach the size of a hen's egg, are painful. The worms' metabolites cause the local reaction. The worms are troublesome when they cross the bridge of the nose. Reddened giant urticaria of the skin, fever and high eosinophilia are the common symptoms. The microfilariae can be demonstrated in the peripheral blood in daytime and the adult worm in the swellings. Immunological tests are the same as those adopted for *W. bancrofti.* Treatment is by surgical removal of adult worm and by effective chemotherapy. Prophylaxis is by detection and treatment of human cases; spraying of antilarval insecticides in breeding places of *chrysops*; protection from *chrysops* bites, use of fly repellant.

Loa inquirenda It was recovered from a European woman's neck in India by Maplestone (1938).

Human dirofilariasis *Dirofilaria* of animal (*D. immitis, S. conjunctivae, D. tenuis, D. repens*) microfilariae may become adult without producing microfilariae.

Superfamily Dracunculoidea

- These worms are long, cord-like and have:
  a) Simple pore-like mouth; surrounded by double circles of papillae
  b) Esophagus and intestine are rudimentary
  c) Females are larger than males, with vulva at the middle of body and uteri
  d) They are viviparous, rhabditoid larvae are discharged.
- **Dracunculus medinensis** *D. medinensis* (serpent worm; dragon worm) causes dracunculiasis. It has been known since antiquity. It is widely distributed including in India (Rajasthan, Jodhpur, Mumbai, Karnataka, Andra Pradesh and Gujarat). Gujarat has the highest incidence. Adult worms are mostly lodged in the legs, arms and back. Its anterior end is round and blunt. So, far only one male *D. medinensis* has been recovered in India. Its posterior end is coiled with spicules and gubernaculum. Female is the largest nematode, has paired ovarian tubules, uteri and a single vagina. Gravid female has no vulva. Its posterior end is hook-like, discharges embryos. Its body fluid is toxic and causes blisters when it invades the tissue. Its lifespan is one year, but that of the male is six months.

- Their rhabditoid larvae are coiled, wiry with a tapering tail. In their lifecycle, they require two hosts: human (definite host); Cyclops (intermediate host). If a human being drinks water contaminated with infected Cyclops, in the stomach the Cyclops are digested and their larvae are set free. These larvae migrate through the intestinal wall and reach the retro-peritonial connective tissue, where they grow, sexually mature. Males die after fertilization. The gravid females migrate and select those parts of the body which come in contact with water and form 'blisters', due to the secretion of toxins; the blister ruptures producing ulcer. The females discharge embryo in the water. Allergic reaction occurs when *D. medinensis* migrates under the skin; secretes a toxin which causes blisters and may also produce a systemic reaction (erythema, urticaria with pruritus, nausea, vomiting, diarrhea and giddiness) due to toxemia.
- Detection of adult worm in the ulcer, embryos in water when gravid females ejaculate them into the water. Skin test, X-ray of dead calcified worms and blood examination. Treatment is by effective drugs, removal of the whole parasite by the Indian barber technique.
- Prevention of infected persons from stepping into water sources; drinking of filtered water or boiled water, converting step wells into draw wells.

Gnathostoma spinigerum It causes gnathostomiasis. It was first reported by Owen from the gastric tumour of a tiger; later by Chandler (1927) from India. It lives in the gastric tumours of dog, cat. The male of the adult worm is smaller than the female. The male has pseudo-bursa and copulatory spicules. The female has vulva which is posto-equatorial, paired genital tubes. Its eggs are ovoidal, transparent, pitted and have a mucoid plug at one pole and are embryonated.

- Eggs of *G. spinigerum*, are extruded into the water where they embryonate and hatch. These larvae are ingested by Cyclops, transform into the second stage larva. When the infected Cyclops is eaten by fish, frog, they transform into the third stage in the flesh of these animals. When a suitable host eats the third larval host, the larva develops to maturity in the stomach wall of the host.
- Third stage larva is responsible for human *gnathostomiasis*. Immature worms cause superficial lesions in the skin, subcutaneous tissue. Advanced larval stage causes breast abscess. The formation of tunnels in which the worms are migrating is 'larva migrans', causing creeping eruption (*gnathostomiasis externa*). Toxic and allergic reactions are responsible for these lesions. The erratic migration of the larva in the eye or brain is also encountered.
- In dogs and cats, adult worms are coiled inside the tumour of the digestive tract. This is referred to as *gnathostomiasis interna*. Removal and identification of adult worms is specific diagnosis, skin test is also useful. Treatment is not effective.

Gnathostoma hispidum

- It is stouter than *G. spinigerum*. It is a common parasite of the stomach wall of pigs.

Angiostrongylus cantonensis *A. cantonensis* (rat lungworm) causing eosinophilic meningo-encaphilitis or human angio-strongylosis was first reported by Nemura and Lin (1945). It is distributed in some countries. It is found in the lung of rat. It is a delicate, filiform worm. Its cuticula is smooth. Its cephalic end is simple, has three lips, no buccal capsule, mouth opens into the esophagus. The male is smaller than the female. The copulatory capsule is curved ventrally. The posterior end of the female is like a blunt horn with anal pore and a vulva. Its eggs are elongated, ovoidal. A single female may lay 15,000 per day. Its eggs are hatched out in the lung of the rat and the larvae into trachea. After swallowing, the first stage larvae are expelled in the feces. Then, they infect a molluscum (intermediate host) in which they develop into third stage larva. This infective larva migrates to the brain where it matures, migrates to the pulmonary arteries and begins to lay eggs.

- In human infection, eosinophilic meningo-encephalitis is the main pathological change; symptoms are chronic brain syndrome, low-grade fever, headache, difficulty in urination, later semi-consciousness and death. Detection of mature and immature worms and skin test are useful diagnosis.

QUESTIONS

Q *Define nematode.*

▶ Nematodes are elongated, cylindrical, tapering at both ends. They are unsegmented. Their size is variable, ranging from the smallest to largest and they have protective cuticula.

Q *What is a filariform esophagus of nematode?*

▶ Certain nematodes have esophagus of uniform caliber called filariform esophagus. Parasitic nematodes have a filariform esophagus.

Q *What is rhabditiform esophagus of nematode?*

▶ If the esophagus is expanded posteriorly into a bulb with valve mechanism, it is called a rhabditiform esophagus. Free living types of nematodes have rhabditiform esophagus.

Q *What is a diecious helminth?*

▶ Diecious helminth is a helminth with separate sexes.

Trichinella spiralis

Q *What is the common name of T. spiralis?*

▶ Its common name is 'Trichina' worm.

Q *Where does the adult worm remain buried?*

▶ It remains buried in the mucosa of the duodenum and jejunum.

Q *Where does its larva encyst?*

▶ Its larva encysts in the striated muscles of humans or in pigs harbouring the adult worm.

Q *Which nematode is the smallest?*

▶ *T. spiralis* is the smallest nematode.

Q *For how long is T. spiralis viviparous?*

▶ It is viviparous as long as it is alive.

Q *What is meant by the following terms: viviparous, oviparous, ovoviviparous*

▶ Viviparous are those which give birth to larva.
Oviparous are those that lay eggs.
Ovoviviparous are those that lay eggs containing larvae which hatch immediately.

Q *How many hosts are required for the lifecycle of T. spiralis?*

▶ *T. spiralis* requires only one host for its lifecycle (human or pig or rat).

Q *What happens to males of T. spiralis after fertilization of females?*

▶ Males die after fertilization.

Q *How many progenies are discharged by the females of T. spiralis?*

▶ They discharge 1500 progenies during sixteen weeks.

Q *Where are the progenies of T. spiralis temporarily lodged before they re-enter into circulation for their final distribution in the striated muscle?*

▶ They are lodged in various tissues and body cavities.

Q *For how many years do these encysted larvae remain alive?*

▶ The encysted larvae remain alive for many years.

Q *How is the cyst wall formed?*

▶ The cyst wall is formed due to host tissue reaction.

Q *How many principal maintenance cycles are there?*

▶ There are three principal maintenance cycles.

1. Pig to Pig
2. Rat to Rat
3. Sylvatic.

Q *How many pathogenic stages does it have?*

▶ There are three successive stages:

1. Invasion
2. Migration of the larvae
3. Encystations and tissue repair.

Q *What are the symptoms during the invasion stage?*

▶ The symptoms are nausea, vomiting, toxic dysentery or diarrhea, colic, sweating.

Q *What is the correct diagnosis of T. spiralis?*

▶ Demonstration of adult worm in feces, larvae in blood or mother's milk.

Q *Can xenodiagnosis be useful in the diagnosis?*

▶ It can be useful.

Trichuris trichiura

Q *What is the common name of T. trichiura?*

▶ It is called whipworm.

Q *Why is it called a whipworm?*
▶ It resembles a whip with a handle.

Q *Where was the egg of T. trichiura first observed?*
▶ It was first observed in the feces of a girl who had died 450 years ago and had been preserved.

Q *Which nematode has a retractile penial sheath?*
▶ *T. trichiura* has a retractile penial sheath.

Q *What is the shape of the egg of T. trichiura?*
▶ It is barrel-shaped with mucoid plugs at both ends.

Q *What is the egg laying capacity of T. trichiura?*
▶ Its egg laying capacity is 5000–7000 per day.

Q *What is its site of predilection?*
▶ Its site of predilection is the cecum.

Q *What are symptoms of T. trichiura?*
▶ The common symptoms are abdominal pain, vomiting, constipation, abdominal distension and systemic intoxication. The skin is dry and the patient is emaciated.

Capillaria philippinensis

Q *How does C. philippinensis remain burrowed in the mucosa of the jejunum?*
▶ They remain burrowed in the mucosa with both ends free.

Q *What is its mode of infection?*
▶ Its mode of infection is the fecal–oral route.

Q *What are its symptoms?*
▶ Its symptoms are diarrhea, emaciation, weakness and abdominal pain. Death may be due to cachexia.

Strongyloides stercoralis

Q *What is the common name of S. stercoralis?*
▶ Its common name is threadworm.

Q *What is its site of predilection?*
▶ Its site of predilection is the duodenum or the jejunum.

Q *What type of larvae is hatched from the egg of T. stercoralis?*
▶ Rhabditiform larvae are hatched out.

Q *Enumerate the different types of larvae of T. stercoralis.*
▶ There are two types of larvae.

1. Rhabditiform larvae
2. Filariform larvae.

Q *What are rhabditiform larvae?*
▶ If the esophagus is expanded posteriorly into a bulb which contains a valve mechanism it is referred to as rhabditiform larvae.

Q *What are filariform larvae?*
▶ If the muscular esophagus is of uniform caliber throughout, it is called filariform larvae, it is infective.

Q *Cite the main pathological changes produced by T. spiralis?*
▶ Skin lesion, pulmonary lesion and intestinal lesion are the main pathological changes.

Q *Why should T. spiralis filariform larvae enter the lungs before entering the intestine?*
▶ These filariform larvae should pass through the lungs, before further development takes place.

Superfamily: Strongyloidea

Q *What does the mouth cavity of this superfamily contain?*
▶ The mouth cavity contains teeth or cutting plates.

Q *How many families are included under this superfamily?*
▶ There are two families:

1. Family Ancylostomatidiae
2. Family Strongyloidae.

Q *How many subfamilies are there in the family Ancylostomatidiae?*
▶ There are two subfamilies:

1. Subfamily Ancylostominae.
2. Subfamily Uncinarinae.

Q *Give examples for each subfamily.*
▶ Subfamily Ancylostomatinae contains.
Ancylostoma duodenale (with two pairs of teeth);
A. braziliense (with one pair of teeth)
A. caninium (with two pairs of teeth)
Subfamiliy Uncinarinae – *Necator americanus* (with cutting plates)

Ancylostoma duodenale

Q *What is the common name of A. duodenale?*
▶ Its common name is 'Old World' hookworm.

Q *Where does the adult worm live?*
▶ The adult worm lives in the jejunum.

Q *Why is the living worm pinkish in colour?*
▶ It is pinkish due to ingested blood.

Q *Why is A. duodenale called hookworm?*

▶ It is called hookworm as its anterior end is bent dorsally like a hook.

Q *How is blood clotting prevented in ancylostomiasis?*

▶ Blood clotting is prevented by an enzyme secreted by its esophageal gland.

Q *During copulation why does the worm assume a Y-shaped figure?*

▶ It assumes a Y-shaped figure because of its genital opening.

Q *How are the rhabditiform larvae of A. duodenale distinguished from the strongyloides larvae and other free-living nematodes?*

▶ These larvae have a long, narrow buccal chamber, a flask-shaped muscular esophagus, a midgut and a short rectum.

Q *When does segmentation of the ovum to form blastomeres take place?*

▶ The segmentation takes place when the fertilized egg passes through the bowel.

Q *How many stages are there in their lifecycle?*

▶ There are five stages.

Q *During its lifecycle, why should its larvae migrate through the lungs.*

▶ They develop further during their migration through the lungs.

Q *What are the common sites of entry of the filariform larvae of A.duodenale?*

▶ The common sites of entry are:

1. the thin skin between the toes
2. the dorsum of the feet
3. the inner sides of the soles.

Q *What are the pathogenic effects of A. duodenale?*

▶ They are:

1. Cutaneous lesions
2. Pulmonary lesions.

Q *What is ground itch?*

▶ At the site where the filariform larvae of A. *duodenale* penetrate the skin, they produce ground itch.

Q *What are the characteristics of ground itch?*

▶ Ground itch is characterized by itching and burning, edema, erythema which develops into a papule, then a vesicle.

Q *What is cutaneous larva migrans?*

▶ Cutaneous larva migrans (creeping eruption) is a skin lesion produced by the entry of feline or canine ancylostoma.

Q *Why do the larvae of A. braziliense produce an itchy papule at the site of invasion?*

▶ An itchy papule is produced because they cannot enter below the stratum germinativum of the human skin.

Q *What is the serpiginous tunnel in stratum germinativum?*

▶ It is a tunnel formed with a corium as floor and stratum germinativum as the roof.

Q *Why are they called larva migrans?*

▶ Since these larvae move at the rate of several millimeters to a few centimeters per day within the tunnel, they are called larva migrans.

Q *Why can't these larvae penetrate below the stratum germinativum?*

▶ It may be due to the partial physiological inadaptability of the particular strain of human Ancylostoma.

Q *What type of anemia is observed in A. duodenale?*

▶ Microcytic hypochromic type of anemia is observed, which may be due to chronic loss of blood or nutritional defects.

Q *What are the different types of anemia and how are they caused?*

▶ In microcytic hypochromic anemia, there is iron deficiency; in the macrocytic type, there is deficiency of folic acid and vitamin B_{12}; in the dimorphic type, there is bulk iron, vitamin B_{12} or folic acid deficiency.

Q *Why is blood loss more in A. duodenale?*

▶ *A. duodenale* is a larger worm which is armed with teeth and is highly migratory therefore it leaves more bleeding points.

Q *How many types of symptoms are there?*

▶ There are three types of symptoms: mild, moderate and severe.

Q *Describe the severe type of symptoms?*

▶ Severe type presents a classical picture of hookworm disease. There is constipation or diarrhea and the food is undigested. The skin is dry. Even in hot climate, the patient is cold; the patient eats clay to relieve abdominal pain.

Q *What is pica or geophagy?*

▶ Pica or geophagy is eating clay or mud to relieve abdominal pain.

Necator americanus

Q *What is the common name of N. americanns?*

▶ Its common name is 'New World' hookworm.

Enterobius vermicularis

Q *What is the common name of E. vermicularis?*

▶ It is called pin worm or seat worm.

Q *What is its site of predilection?*

▶ Its site of predilection is the mucosa of the cecum, appendix, colon and ileum.

Q *Do E. vermicularis larvae enter and migrate through the lungs for their moulting?*

▶ Larvae of *E. vermicularis* do not migrate through the lungs for their moulting; but they moult twice en route to the intestine.

Q *How many eggs does a single female adult worm deposit?*
▶ It deposits 11,105 eggs.

Superfamily Ascaridoidea

Q *Describe the mouth of superfamily Ascaridoidea?*
▶ Its mouth has three lips without the buccal capsule.

Q *Describe the posterior end of the male adult worm of the superfamily.*
▶ Males do not have bursa copulatrix and caudal alae.

Ascaria lumbricoides

Q *What is the common name of A. lumbricoides?*
▶ Its common name is giant intestinal roundworm.

Q *What is ascarase?*
▶ Ascarase is proteose and is responsible for the allergy in the infected person. It is present in the body fluid of *A. lumbricoides*.

Q *What is the lifespan of the adult worm?*
▶ Its lifespan is less than two years.

Q *What is the indication of the presence of unfertilized eggs in the feces?*
▶ It shows that the host is harbouring the female.

Q *How long do Ascaris eggs remain infective?*
▶ They may remain infective for many months.

Q *Why should the larvae of A. lumbricoides migrate through the lungs?*
▶ They migrate through the lungs for further development.

Q *What is their migration period through the lungs?*
▶ Its migration is about 15 days.

Q *How many eggs are deposited by each female?*
▶ Each female deposits 2, 00,000 eggs per day.

Q *What are the pathological effects produced by migrating larvae, adult worm?*
▶ During migration through the lungs, the larvae cause trauma, hemorrhage, coughing, urticaria and fever. The adult worm obtains its food by sucking liquid nutrients, thus it deprives the host of its nutrition.

Q *What are Ascaris pneumonitis (Loeffler's syndrome), night blindness, spoliative action?*
▶ Ascaris pneumonitis is a condition in which there is consolidation of the lobule, spasms of coughing, urticaria, fever, difficulty in breathing.
Night blindness is caused by vitamin A deficiency caused by the adult worm.
Spoliative action occurs when the adult worms obtain their food by sucking liquid nutrient from the intestine, thereby depriving the host of its nutrition.

Q *How are adult worms protected from enzymatic digestion?*

▶ They are protected by the anti-enzymes liberated by them in the intestine.

Q *What is ectopic ascariasis?*

▶ Ectopic ascariasis occurs when the adult worms enter the Eustachian tube and cause otitis media due to fever which may cause the worms to be passed out.

Q *What are the symptoms of generalized toxemia?*

▶ Symptoms are insomnia, twisting, restlessness, meningitis, paraplegia, urticaria, cerebral symptoms in children.

Q *In whom can visceral larval migrans be seen?*

▶ Visceral larval migrans can be seen in children.

Superfamily Filarioidea

Q *What are the characteristics of this superfamily?*

▶ Its mouth is circular, simple and dorso-ventrally elongated and surrounded by papillae.

Wuchereria bancrofti

Q *What is nocturnal periodicity?*

▶ In the night (between 10 p.m. and 2 a.m.), the microfilariae of *W. bancrofti* appear in the circulation. This is called nocturnal periodicity.

Q *Why do microfilariae of W. bancrofti appear in the circulation at night?*

▶ The microfilarie may migrate to the periphery at night when the human body is relaxed; they respond to carbon dioxide and oxygen supply; they may adapt to the feeding habits of the mosquito; *Culex* is a night feeder and *Aedes* is a daytime feeder; they retire into the capillaries of the lungs during the day.

Q *How does the third stage larvae migrate in the wound?*

▶ They do so because they are attracted by the warmth of the skin.

Q *Why does W. bancrofti require the mosquito in its lifecycle?*

▶ It needs the mosquito for the complete development of the microfilaria.

Q *What are the pathological changes produced by the microfilaria lodged in the lymphatic vessels?*

▶ There will be infiltration of reticuloendothelial cells to attack these microfilariae, thickening and folding of the endothelial layer of lymph vessels, with fibrin deposition.

Q *What is pathogonomic of this disease?*

▶ Filarial granulation tissue is pathognomic.

Q *Enumerate the symptoms of W. bancrofti filariasis.*

▶ They are: 1. Lymphangitis 2. Lymphadenitis 3. Elephantiasis 4. Chyluria 5. Hydrocele

Q *Why is urine of chyluria milky in colour?*

▶ It is milky because it contains fat, albumin and fibrinogen.

Q *In complement fixation test, what antigen is used?*

▶ In CFT, alcoholic extract antigen of *Dirofilaria immitis* (*D. immitis* – dog heartworm) is used.

Q *Why is D. immitis used as antigen?*

▶ It is used because *D. immitis* and *W. bancrofti* are antigenically related.

Brugia malayi

Q *What is the common name of B. malayi?*

▶ It is called Malaysian filarial worm.

Q *Describe the main characteristics of Mf. malayi.*

▶ Its anterior end has two stylets; cephalic space is broader; its tail is constricted between two terminal nuclei, its appearance is stiff with secondary kinks. It is enveloped in a sheath.

Q *What are the main clinical features of B. malayi?*

▶ It causes lymphangitis and elephantiasis of the lower extremities.

Q *How is Malayan filariasis characterized?*

▶ It is characterized by the absence of chyuria and by the presence of scrotal swelling.

Q *Where does Mansonia sp. grow?*

▶ Mansonia sp.grows on water plants (*Pistia stratioides*).

Q *In which state of India does Mansonia grow?*

▶ Since water plants (*Pistia stratioides*) grow well in Kerala, Mansonia sp. breeds well and multiplies.

Q *How is Mansonia sp. controlled?*

▶ It can be controlled by destroying the water plant.

Onchocerca volvulus

Q *What is the common name of the filaria of O. volvulus*

▶ Its common name is bending filaria.

Q *What is the name of the disease caused by O. volvulus?*

▶ Its name is blinding filariases, river blindness.

Q *Where does the adult worm remain coiled?*

▶ It remains coiled in the subcutaneous connective tissue tumours (nodules)

Q *For how many years does the adult female of O. volvulus live?*

▶ It lives for more than 11 years.

Q *What is its intermediate host?*

▶ Its intermediate host is simulium (black fly).

Q *What are the ocular symptoms in O. volvulus infection?*

▶ They are conjunctivitis, corneal opacity, keratitis, iridocyclitis and glaucoma.

Dipetalonema perstans

Q *How is D. perstans called commonly?*
▶ It is called persistent filaria.

Q *Where does it live?*
▶ It lives in the body cavities (peritoneal, pleural, pericardium)

Q *What is its intermediate host?*
▶ Its intermediate host is *Culicoides austeni.*

Q *What are the symptoms of D. perstans?*
▶ They are fatal pericaditis, local irritation, toxic edema of the eyelid.

Mansonella ozzardi

Q *How is it known?*
▶ It is known as 'New World' filaria or Ozzard's filaria.

Q *What is its intermediate host?*
▶ Its intermediate host is *Culicoides furens.*

Loa loa

Q *What is the common name of Loa loa?*
▶ Its name is Loa worm or eye worm.

Q *What does it produce?*
▶ It produces fugitive swelling or Calabar swelling.

Q *What is its lifespan?*
▶ Its lifespan is 15 years.

Q *What is its intermediate host?*
▶ Its intermediate host is *Chrysops dimidiata* (deer fly) or mango fly.

Q *What are symptoms of Loa loa infection?*
▶ Creeping in and around the eye, calabar swelling of a hen's egg size, reddened giant urticarial swellings in the skin and mucous membrane, fever with eosinophilia.

Q *Enumerate human Dirofilaria?*
▶ They are *Dirofilaria immitis, D. conjunctivae, D. tenuis* and *D. crepens.*

Superfamily Dracunculoidea

Q *Describe this superfamily in short?*
▶ It is a long, cord-like worm, has a pore like mouth surrounded by papillae. The female is larger than the male. Its vulva is in the middle of the body.

Draculus medinensis

Q *What is its common name?*
▶ It is also called Medina worm, guinea worm, serpent worm.

Q *Why did the Arabian physician name this nematode vena medina?*
▶ It was so named because it was common in Medina.

Q *Which state of India has highest incidence of D.medinensis and why?*
▶ Gujarat has highest incidence of *D.medinensis* as step wells are very common in Gujarat.

Q *In which state of India was an adult worm, one metre long, removed from the eye of a patient.*
▶ It was in Orissa state.

Q *Where do the adult worms live?*
▶ They live in the subcutaneous tissue of the legs, arms and back.

Q *In which country was a single specimen of male D. medinensis recovered from a natural human infection?*
▶ From India.

Q *How are blisters caused in the subcutaneous tissue?*
▶ Toxic body fluid of *D.medinesis* causes blisters.

Q *Where are the blisters formed?*
▶ Blisters are formed only in those parts of the body which come in contact with water.

Q *When larvae of D. medinensis are discharged into water, for what do they swim in search of?*
▶ They swim in search of minute freshwater Cyclops for their further development.

Q *What will happen if they are not taken up by Cyclops?*
▶ They will die

Q *In which region of the body do their larvae grow and become sexually mature?*
▶ They grow and become sexually mature in the retroperitoneal connective tissue.

Q *What is the duration period of migration of the larvae from the intestine to retroperitoneal connective tissue?*
▶ The migration period of the larvae is one year.

Q *Where does copulation of D. medinensis takes place?*
▶ Their copulation takes place in the deeper connective tissue, not in the intestine.

Q *What is the fate of male D. medinensis after copulation?*
▶ The male *D. medinensis* dies after copulation.

Q *What is the duration for the complete development of the embryo?*
▶ It takes two weeks.

Q *How many larvae can kill the Cyclops?*
▶ More than 5-6 larvae can kill the Cyclops.

Q *What is the lifespan of the Cyclops?*
▶ Its lifespan is about three months.

Q *Within how many days can heavy infection of larvae kill the Cyclops?*
▶ Heavy infection may kill within 15 days.

Q *When will there be allergic reaction in D. medinensis infection?*
▶ When the gravid female worms begin to migrate to the skin, there will be allergic reaction.

Q *When will there be systemic reaction?*
▶ Before the formation of the blister, there will be systemic reaction.

Q *What are symptoms of systemic reaction?*
▶ They are erythema, urticaria, intensive pruritus, nausea, vomiting, diarrhea and giddiness.

Gnathostoma spinigerum

Q *Where do the adult worms live?*
▶ They live in tumours of the stomach wall of cats and dogs.

Q *What happens to the eggs of G. spinigerum when they are evacuated with feces?*
▶ In the water, the embryo is formed and hatches out. These larvae are ingested by Cyclops, in which the second stage larva is formed. When the infected cyclops is ingested by fish, third stage larva is formed in the flesh of fish. When the definite host (cat) eats the fish with infective larvae, it gets infected and a tumour is formed in the stomach of the cat.

Q *What is 1) gnathostomiasis externa and 2) interna?*
▶ 1) Gnathostomiasis externa is characterized by the development of pockets of abscesses; the formation of subcutaneous tunnels in which larva migrates (larva migrans causing creeping eruption).
2) Gnathostomiasis interna occurs when the adult worms are coiled in tumours of the digestive tract.

Gnathostoma hispidium

Q *In India, how many times has G. hispidium been found in human infection?*
▶ It has been found twice in human infection.

Angiostrongylodes cantonensis

Q *What is the common name of A. cantonensis and what does it cause in humans?*
▶ It is called rat lungworm. It causes eosinophilic meningo-encephalitis.

Q *How many eggs does a single female lay?*
▶ A single female may lay up to 15,000 eggs per day.

Q *Where are these eggs hatched out after ingestion by rats?*
▸ They hatch out in the lung of the rat.

Q *What is its intermediate host?*
▸ Its intermediate host is Cyclops.

Q *What happens in the rat when it ingests the Cyclops containing infective larvae?*
▸ The third (infective) stage larvae migrate to the rat brain, mature and migrate to the pulmonary arteries and begin to lay eggs. After swallowing, the larvae are passed out in the feces.

FIRST REPORT OF NEMATODES

Trichinella spiralis	Peacock (1828)
Trichuris trichiura	Linnaeus (1771)
Strongyloides stercoralis	Normand (1876)
Ancylostoma duodenale	Dubini (1843)
Ancylostoma caninum	Panjarathinam (1972)
Necator americanus	Stiles (1902)
Enterobius vermicularis	Panjarathinam (1978)
Ascaris lumbricoides	Known since ancient times
A. lumbricoides (in calf)	Panjarathinam (1972) Pondicherry
Wuchereria bancrofti	Demarguay (1863)
Brugia malayi	Brug (1927)
Onchocerca volvulus	Brumpt (1919)
Dipetalonema perstans	Daniels (1898)
Mansonella ozzardi	Ozzard
Loa loa	Mongin
Dracunculus medinensis	Bible (since antiquity)
Gnasthostoma spinigerum	Owen; Chandler (1827 in India)
Angiostrongyloides cantonensis	Chen (1935)

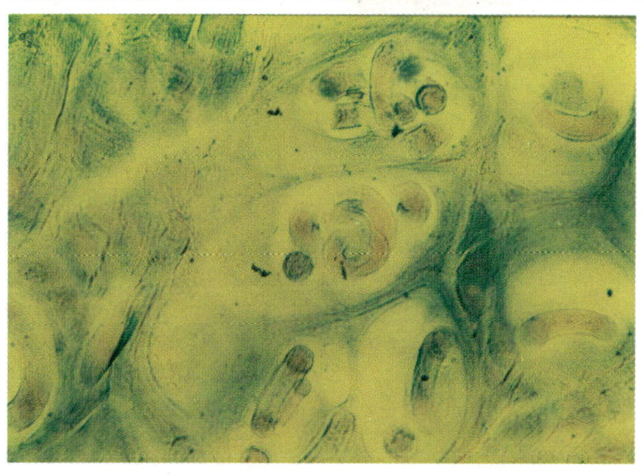

Cyst of *T. spiralis* in muscle fibre

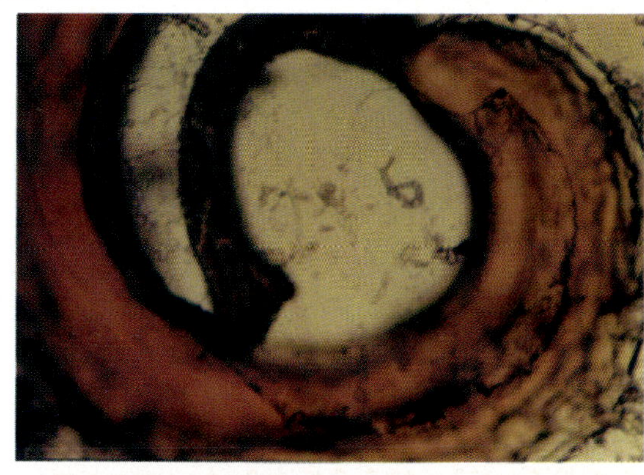

Posterior end of adult male of *T. trichiura*

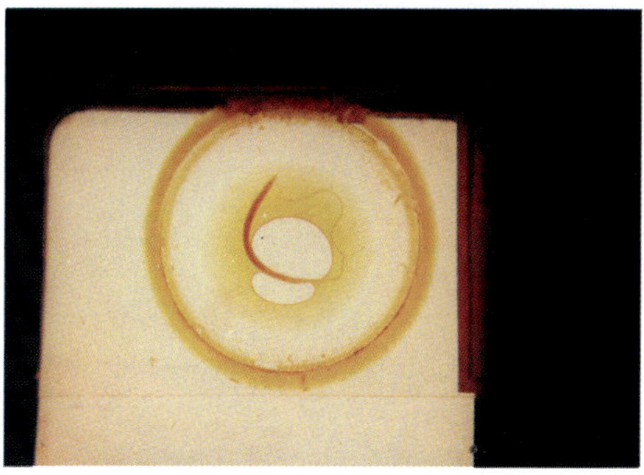

Adult female of *T. trichiura*

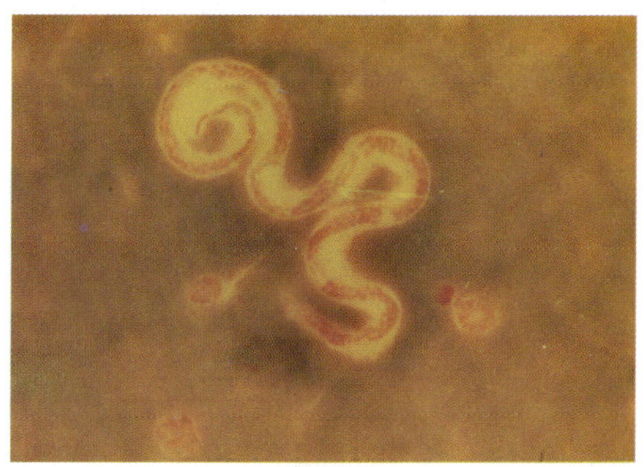

Sheathed microfilarea of *W. bancrofti*

Roundworm (natural size)

Female adult worm of *A. lumbricoides*

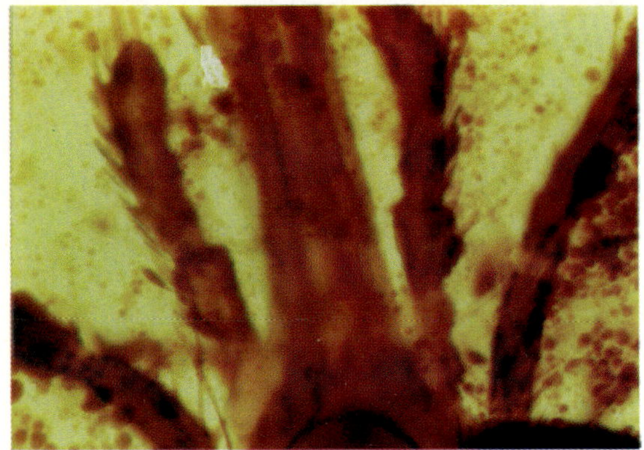
Mouth parts of female mosquito

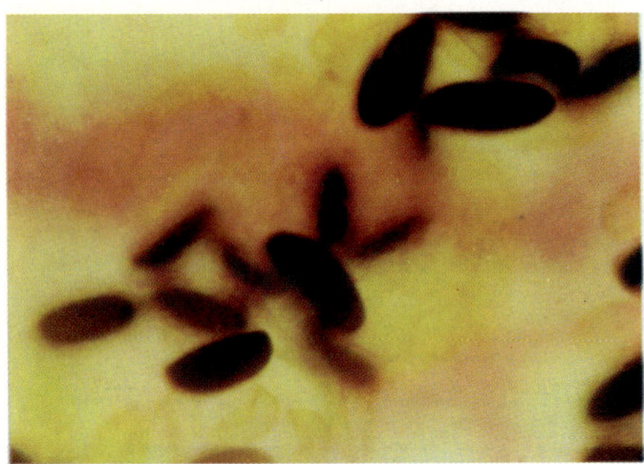
Egg of mosquito

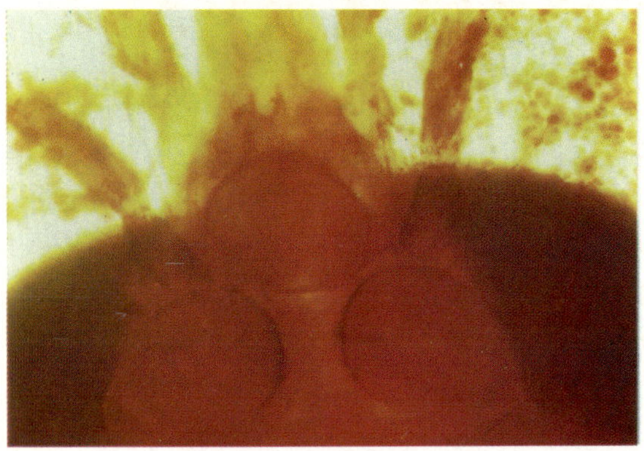
Head of mosquito

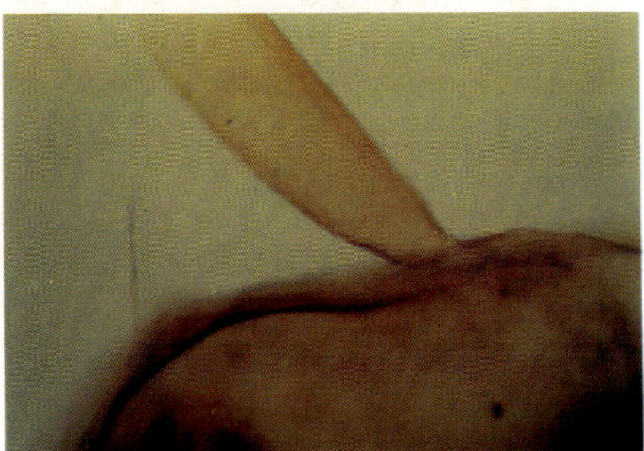
Pupa of mosquito

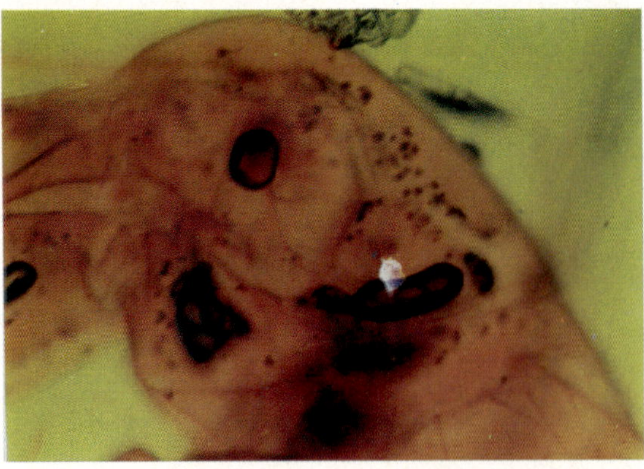
Head of *X. cheopsis*

9 IMMUNOPARASITOLOGY

Immunoparasitology is the study of host response to parasites and the parasites' evasion of the host's immune response. It has been demonstrated that numerous parasite species were capable of eliciting immune responses by stimulating B lymphoblasts in the lamina propria of the intestine to produce secretory IgA (sIgA). This immunoglobulin is believed to act nonspecifically by preventing parasites from attaching themselves to the mucosal cells. Further, intestinal parasites can cause the T-cells to migrate to the lamina propria via the mesenteric lymph nodes and thoracic duct.

Parasitic infections rarely confer lifelong or complete immunity after primary infection. The primary infection with cutaneous leishmaniasis is possibly an exception.

During most parasitic infections, the host is protected against hyperinfection by the same parasite species. However, subsequent infection can occur after the disappearance or expulsion of the parasite from the host. In malaria and toxoplasmosis, continuous low-level infection confers partial protection against the respective parasite species. This latter phenomenon is known as ***premunition***.

The immune responses may sometimes have detrimental effects on the host. For example, prolonged exposure to *A. lumbricoides* may cause delayed hypersensitivity reaction. Schistosome-soluble egg antigen produces extensive granuloma formation, an anaphylactic shock may ensue, due to hydatid cyst rupture and its fluid discharged into the visceral cavity of a sensitized patient. The crux of the problem is the antigenic complexity of the parasites themselves. When the host responds to multiple antigens, it is difficult to isolate pure antigens and to determine which antigens trigger either humoral or cell mediated immunity.

Antibodies produced in response to protozoan parasites ordinarily belong to the IgG and IgM classes. In most cases, it is nonspecific and therefore does not confer protection. Exceptions are antibodies produced against *Toxoplasma gondii,* possibly Plasmodia. It has been established that cell-mediated immunity determined by delayed hypersensitivity reaction is important in affording protection against many species of parasitic protozoa.

IMMUNITY TO PROTOZOA

Amebic dysentery Though the immunity to *E. histolytica* infection has not yet been clearly defined, the immunity to this infection may exist. The indigenous residents of highly endemic areas may possibly become immune to local strains. Symptomless carriers may develop considerable tolerance to the parasite. The complement fixation test may become positive when the blood serum of infected individuals is brought into contact with the antigen extracted from the cultures of ameba. When this antigen is injected into susceptible animals, it may protect these animals from *E. histolytica* infection; but it has been practically observed that a recovery from amebic dysentery does not confer immunity against reinfection.

E. histolytica regularly invades human tissues and does cause immune responses. Antibodies of IgG and IgM classes can be demonstrated by passive hemagglutination, precipitation, fluorescent antibody techniques. These antibodies can be used for the diagnosis of amebic dysentery. However, the presence of a specific antibody does not necessarily indicate active infection, but rather an exposure to the organism at some time. Skin tests give immediate responses in many patients indicating IgE production and Arthus phenomenon can also be demonstrated. Skin tests for immediate and delayed hypersensitivity indicate past or present infection. Delayed hypersensitivity is depressed with liver abscess. To date, there is little direct evidence that immunoglobulin is protective.

Cell mediated immunity to *E. histolytica* can be demonstrated by delayed hypersensitivity skin tests in human patients who do not have clinically evident disease, and patients with amebic abscess of the liver have depressed cell mediated immunity to amebic antigen while retaining their ability to respond to other skin test antigens.

Visceral leishmaniasis (*kala azar*) A long-lasting immunity appears after recovery from *kala azar*, as a second attack of the disease does not occur. In endemic areas, many exposed persons may develop a mild type of the disease and recover without appreciable symptoms. In visceral leishmaniasis, delayed hypersensitivity occurs only after spontaneous recovery or chemotheraphy, and there is increased nonspecific immunoglobulin level. Massive polyclonal hypergammaglobulinemia, with little or no evidence of cell mediated immunity, is the rule in visceral leishmaniasis.

Cutaneous leishmaniasis due to ***leishmania tropica*** results in immune response characterized by little or no specific antibody, but by strong cell-mediated immunity. In endemic areas, vaccination with virulent strains of the parasites derived from culture is a common practice to make certain that disfiguring lesions do not occur.

In American leishmaniasis (Espundia) due to *L. braziliensis*, both delayed hypersensitivity and elevated immunoglobulins are detected.

In malaria immunity, there is a combination of power and process. This combination

(a) Prevents plasmodial infection, reinfection or superinfection
(b) Destroys Plasmodium
(c) Limits its multiplication
(d) Modifies its effects on the body and
(e) Aids, specifically, in the repair of tissue.

The immunity may be natural or acquired. Natural immunity is genetic or innate, independent of previous infection e.g., humans are immune to avian malaria. Acquired immunity is due to antigenic stimulation by the parasite or its products. It protects against superinfection rather than against reinfection and it does not seem to persist much beyond the time when the Plasmodia are eliminated from the body. Acquired immunity may be active or passive. Actively acquired immunity is due to malarial infection. Active immunity may be concomitant, i.e. present while there is parasitemia, or it may be residual, persisting after eradication of parasites. Passive immunity is conferred by maternal transfer. Infants less than six months old are protected from antibodies received from their mother's milk (WHO, 1991).

Premunition is concomitant. Infection immunity tolerance is the term applied to an infection immunity which reduces the effects of a given number of parasites on the human host and also allows the infection without acute illness. There is variation in infection due to different strains of the same Plasmodium, as well as in different species. Malaria immunity is specific for homologous strains or species. In cellular immunity of malaria, the reticulo-endothelial system (lymphoid, macrophages) undergoes hyperplasia. Monocytes, especially the wandering cells found in the spleen, liver, bone marrow and general circulation originating as lymphocytes enlarge and become motile and phagocytic. They rapidly engulf merozoites, pigment, cellular debris and even whole parasitized red blood cells. As the disease continues, these macrophages also engulf apparently normal uninfected erythrocytes, thus further adding to the anemia caused by Plasmodium.

Humoral malaria immunity with the formation of protective antibodies is more important. Malaria antibodies are closely associated with the 7 S fraction of serum gammaglobulin and are developed during the infection. These antibodies have shown increased levels in the inhabitants of highly endemic areas. This immune gammaglobulin has been found to have a therapeutic and preventive effect in malaria of children. These malaria-protective antibodies have a powerful effect in stimulating the lymphoid–macrophage system. Besides, they seem to include lysins, aggulutinins, preceipitins, opsonins, complement fixing and cytoplasm modifying antibodies. Fluorescin-tagged antibodies can be used to differentiate strains of Plasmodia.

The exoerythrocytic forms induce little or no immune response, because *P. vivax* and other relapsing forms exist for extended periods in the exoerythrocytic phase. The parasites in the blood induce an array of humoral responses in the host as demonstrated by complement fixation, precipitation, agglutination and fluorescent antibody reaction. Specific protective IgG antibody was produced against merozoites.

The immune response that leads to protection is generally thought to be produced by complement independent antibodies, which inhibit the entry of the merozoites into the host erythrocytes. It has been shown that the people residing in endemic areas become increasingly less parasitemic with age and that children born in these areas appear to be protected during their first year of life by IgG, which crosses the placenta from the immune mother during gestation. Although all immune classes are elevated in the serum of malaria patients, it is the serum IgG levels which appear to correlate well with protection. The irradiated sporozoite antigens elicited an immune response in human volunteers, but did not cause disease in humans. Protection by this vaccine is fairly species specific.

In malarial infection, the reticuloendothelial system is hyperactive, resulting in the removal of affected red blood cells, parasitized cells and parasitic metabolic byproducts. An intact spleen may be needed, in addition to antibody production, because increased reticuloendothelial system clearance appears to be nonspecific, since enhanced clearance may augment the immune response.

In summary, it appears that noncomplement-dependent IgG antibodies to merozoite antigens are the main source of protection in malarial infection in the adult human, although the diverse antigens produced during the infection result in other types of immunity, not yet fully understood.

The earliest vaccine (synthetic peptide) against malaria was developed to prevent the invasion of red blood cells by raising antibodies against the micromerozoites. It is cheap and given in three doses against malaria caused by *P. vivax* and *P. falciparum*. In late 1991, this technology of vaccine preparation was transferred to India, free of cost.

Toxoplasmosis

Toxoplasma infection results in the production of IgG and IgM antibodies, which are readily demonstrated by hemagglutination, complement fixation, fluorescent antibody technique and Sabin–Feldman dye tests. The mere presence of antibody is not sufficient for protection, as shown by the ability of the parasite to persist in the presence of high antibody titres and by the fact that the passive transfer of antibody is not protective.

Cell mediated immunity is also involved in protection against Toxoplasma, because delayed hypersensitivity develops early in toxoplasmosis and protection results only from infection with living organisms. Interferon is also produced. Inhibition of the multiplication of organisms would effectively reduce the parasite burden. It now appears that the macrophages inhibit multiplication of Toxoplasma, either specifically or nonspecifically.

Vaccination of population with strains of low virulence would probably be effective in establishing protection against Toxoplasma, but most persons develop adequate protection after natural infection. In order to prevent the intrauterine transmission of Toxoplasma in uninfected women of child bearing age, this protection can be worthwhile.

African Trypanosomiasis

Greatly increased levels of immunoglobulins, especially of the IgM class, are regularly present in infected animals. Specific antibodies do arise in trypanosomal infection.

The specific antibody can either lyse the parasites or clump them. Clumping allows for more efficient removal of the parasites by the reticuloendothelial system.

Effective reduction of parasite numbers would protect the host. In fact, there are healthy carriers of Trypanosoma rhodesiense, which usually produces a fatal infection; it implies that some protective mechanism must exist. However, the precise immunologic nature of this protection is obscure.

The multiplicity of antigenic variants observed, makes vaccination an unlikely solution to African trypanosomiasis, unless a common antigen can be found. Antigenic variation produces specific antibody sequentially.

American Trypanosomiasis

An antibody that can be detected by a complement fixation test is produced during the course of the disease. This can be a guide for diagnosis, although the antibody cross-reacts with other flagellates i.e. leishmania. Antibody may persist after infection and therefore does not indicate active disease. High-titre antibody does not appear to limit the infection in humans. Acquired resistance to variant strains is probably the result of previous inapparent infection with strains of low virulence.

Activated macrophages can be demonstrated in *Trypanosoma cruzi* infection, although their role in protection is yet to be fully explained. Attempts to vaccinate against this disease might do more harm than good if such sensitized lymphocytes against shared antigens should develop.

IMMUNITY TO HELMINTHS

Helminths (trematodes, cestodes and nematodes) are metazoan (multicellular) organisms. The antigenic mosaics of these organisms are complex, making the isolation of medically important antigens difficult. Moreover, many helminths undergo lifecycles during which more than one level of IgE antibody are indicative of helminthic infection. Eosinophils readily attach to the cuticle of intestinal nematodes in the presence of specific antibody, because eosinophils are known to release substances such as enzymes and prostaglandins, it is hypothesized that they play a part in worm expulsion. Experimental studies using a rodent hookworm, *Nippastrongylus braziliensis*, showed that a soluble factor secreted by helper T cells stimulate B cells in the mesenteric lymph nodes to produce specific IgE antibody. IgE appears to be involved in the worm expulsion by interfering with the metabolism of the worm by rendering the worms susceptible to a population of T cells, capable of triggering worm expulsion.

Besides B and T cell involvement, immune responses to parasites may include inflammatory responses, macrophges activation, complement mediated cell lysis and interferon production. Thus, the parasites do indeed trigger immune response by their hosts.

The eggs of *Schistosoma mansoni* have been shown to secrete unique antigens that induce granuloma formation, the various stages of developing nematodes have stage-specific antigens to which the host responds in various ways and the special cells localized in the 'neck' of *Trichinella spiralis* elicit specific antibody.

Nematodes, cestodes and trematodes all share common antigens. The two most frequent responses to helminths – eosinophilia and reaginic antibody (IgE) – are both T cell dependent. In addition, certain helminths have been shown to potentiate the immune response to other antigens, perhaps by common metabolic byproducts, acting as a nonspecific adjuvant.

Nematodes

Trichinosis Specific immuno-diagnostic tests may be of great importance. The bentonite flocculation test for human trichinosis is of great value, because of its high degree of specificity. In addition, there are many other immuno-diagnostic tests, including complement fixation, hemagglutination, flocculation and skin tests. Skin tests produce both immediate and delayed hypersensitivity responses.

In humans, infection with *T. spiralis* initially elicits IgM antibody followed by IgG response. IgA antibody has not yet been reported, which is surprising, because the female worms are in the intestinal mucosa, a major site of IgA production. The immediate hypersensitivity response shows that IgE is also produced. Humans develop both immediate and delayed hypersensitivity to Trichinella antigens which suggests that IgE, alone or in combination with mononuclear cells, may mediate the protection. Although, Trichinella is extensively immunogenic in its hosts, it can also exert an immuno-suppressive action.

Ascariasis In *Ascaris lumbricoides* infection, specific antibody is detectable and IgE is elevated. During the infection with Ascaris, immune responses to other unrelated antigens are potentiated.

Toxocara infection *Toxocara canis*, the dog intestinal roundworm, is known to infect small children who ingest eggs in dirt. *T. canis* eggs produce a population of migrating larvae that are immobilized in the human tissue and consequently, never produce worms in the intestinal tract. The symptoms caused by the immobilized larvae are called visceral larva migrans. This visceral larva migrans is characterized by high eosinophilia and chronic granulomatous growth associated with the migrating larvae; such larvae in the eyes of the infected children have been confused with retinoblastoma, the diagnosis is only after enucleation of the affected eyeball. Specific immuno-diagnostic methods have been developed that should allow prompt diagnosis.

Filariasis The excretory, secretory antigen of *B. malayi* is effective in inducing resistance against filarial parasites and thus has potential in immuno-prophylaxis.

Trematodes

It is generally agreed that the protective immune response to schistosoma is mediated by antibody. However, in this disease and other helminth infections, there is evidence indicating that humoral and cellular protective mechanisms are interrelated. It is known that people residing in endemic areas become resistant to reinfection with schistosoma. It may be due to continuous exposure to a small number of cercariae of zoophilic species. Newly invading schistosomes are rapidly killed or immobilized by the action of the antibody. This concomitant immunity has been established as an important way in which host protection to reinfection may be achieved, while allowing the original parasite to persist.

IgG antibody that killed immobilized schistosoma has been demonstrated *in vitro*, but these antibodies do not protect against reinfection after passive transfer. At the other end, certain anti-sera have successfully produced protection. IgE production may be one of the mechanisms by which the protection is achieved.

Cell mediated immune response may produce many lesions. In *S. mansoni* and *S. japonicum*, fibrosis of the liver is the main cause of death. The fibrosis may result due to delayed hypersensitivity reaction to antigens produced by the secretions from the eggs.

In *S. haematobium* infection, a granulomatous reaction early in the diagnosis may spontaneously subside. This abatement results from desensitization by blocking antibody or antigen–antibody complex produced within the granuloma itself. It is generally agreed that antibodies formed to the developing worms produced the reaction.

Human IgE, IgG-4 are responsible for the resistance to the infection with *S. haematobium*. Immunity to reinfection is due to IgE, but IgG-4 acts as blocking antibody.

Cestodes

It is now established that the larval forms of the parasites which are tissue penetrators evoke humoral responses that protect the hyperimmunized host against new infection. Infection with cestodes is usually life-threatening to a human being, only when he acts as an unnatural intermediate host. *T. solium* from swine can develop extra-intestinally in humans and can be found in any organ of the body. When the encysted parasite dies in the brain, tissue reactions with resultant central nervous system disorders and even death can occur.

Echinococcosis Echinococcus granulosus normally forms fluid-filled cysts in the liver, but this can also occur in the lungs and in other parts of the body. These hydatid cysts are highly immunogenic and result in the production of high titres of reaginic antibody (IgE) and other immunoglobulins. Cystic fluid from a ruptured cyst can cause anaphylactic reaction and death. Little or no protection seems to be elicited by this highly immunogenic cestode, because the hydatid cysts remain alive for years.

Casoni's skin test indicates past or present echinococcosis, resulting in both immediate and delayed hypersensitivity. The specificity of this test is doubtful, because of cross-reaction with other helminths. Diagnosis can be made by hemagglutination, complement fixation and flocculation tests using the serum of the patient.

The lifecycle of protozoa and helminths are complicated and the immune response, to be effective, has to interrupt the cycle at a stage when the parasite is accessible to the immune process.

Malarial infection is initiated by sporozoites, which transform into exoerythrocytic schizonts in the liver and there is no recognizable immunity. The liver cells rupture and discharge their merozoites into the peripheral circulation, then they invade the erythrocytes. At this stage, it appears that there is alteration in the permeability of the red cell membrane, so that the immunoglobulin molecules can enter and attack the parasite, Plasmodium. Antibodies are readily detectable in the serum and increased until the crisis 7 to 10 days later, and then slowly decline. Because these antibodies are able to get across to the parasite only during a relatively short period of its lifecycle, the immunity is incomplete and the host usually fails to eliminate the parasite completely. Plasmodium-like trypanosome is subject to antigenic variation and antigenically distinct forms may appear after each relapse. Immunity probably depends on the gradual build up of antibodies to a group antigen, common to all variants. The state in which the organisms persist in small numbers in the tissue in the presence of an immune reaction is called 'preimmunition.'

The adaptive phenomenon of antigenic variation as seen in a trypanosome means that the immune response has great difficulty in coping with these parasitic variations, so that in African sleeping sickness, the parasite does not induce an effective immunity and the infected individuals develop a progressive infection with the invasion of the central nervous system, leading to death. Trypanosomiasis is associated with high levels of IgM immunoglobulin in both the blood and cerebrospinal fluid. It is not certain if this is due to repeated new antigenic stimuli resulting from the changes in the organisms or if the parasite in some way influences directly, the cells of the immune system. Increased immunoglobulin production is a common finding in protozoal infection and often affects all classes of immunoglobulins. Because usually less than 5% of the total immunoglobulin appears to react specially with the inducing parasite, it is probable that protozoa stimulate the lymphoid cells in a nonspecific way to over-produce immunoglobulins (called paraglobulins).

Helminth-like protozoa go through a complex lifecycle and protective immune mechanisms probably act only at an early stage in the cycle. The main stimulus seems to be due to the antigens derived from adult worms and the immune mechanisms act on new parasites entering the body. A noteworthy point regarding these infections is the appearance of IgE (reaginic) antibody with pulmonary eosinophilia and it seems likely that the immediate hypersensitivity reaction of anaphylactic type (type 1) is involved in the pathogenesis of helminth infection.

10

PARASITISM—OCCURRENCE, SYMPTOMS AND TREATMENT

PARASITES OF VARIOUS ORGANS

Intestinal Parasites

Intestinal parasites include protozoa, trematodes, cestodes and nematodes. Most of them gain entrance into the intestine by fecal contamination of food, water or fingers. Some of them may enter the body by skin penetration at the larval stage and, after migration through the tissue, mature in the gut. They are *Entameba histolytica, Fasciolopsis buski, Schistosoma mansoni, Schistosoma japonicum, Taenia saginata, Taenia solium, Hymenolepis nana, Diphyllobothrium latum, Ascaris lumbricoides, Ancylostoma duodenale, Necator americanus, Strongyloides stercoralis, Enterobius vermicularis, Trichuris trichiura* and *Balantidium coli.*

Genito-urinary Parasites

The genito-urinary system is not a frequent site of parasitism. However, there are two organisms which are exceptions: *Trichomonas vaginalis, Schistosoma haematobium.*

Tissue Parasites

Tissue parasites have the common feature of affecting some deeper organ (other than the gut) such as the liver, lungs and the central nervous systems. These are *Entameba histolytica, Toxoplasma gondii, Paragonimus westermani, Clonorchis sinensis, Taenia solium, Echinococcus granulosus, Trichinella spiralis* and *Pneumocystis carinii.*

Vascular Parasites

The vascular parasites constitute the major group of parasites. These are *Leishmania donovani, Trypanosoma gambiense, Trypanosoma cruzi, Plasmodium vivax, Plasmodium falciparum, Plasmodium malariae, Plasmodium ovale, Wuchereria bancrofti, Brugia malayi* and *Loa loa.*

Tumour Associated Parasites

Class Rhizopoda *Entameba histolytica*: Granulomatous tumor mass develops on the wall of the large intestine due to amebic ulcers.

Acanthameba castellani: Coprozoic or free living ameba cause perivascular granulomas and thrombi of pulmonary veins following inoculation through different routes in experimental animals. Granulomatous brain tumor is also caused by Acanthameba.

Class Mastigophora In Leishmania tropica infection, a nest of cells resembling epithelioma are observed.

In post *kala-azar* dermal leishmanoid, nodules may contain *L. donovani.*

L. braziliensis causes granulomatous lesions in patients suffering from espundia, i.e. bulbous granulomas affecting the lips, nares or cheeks.

Trypanosoma cruzi produces characteristic fibriotic encapsulation (Chagoma).

Class Sporozoa *Toxoplasma gondii* causes lesions consisting of microscopic granuloma in the brain and spinal chord.

Helminths

Class Cestoda *Hymenolepis nana* was found in a tumor removed from the chest wall of a 75-year-old Japanese woman.

Multiceps serialis: Cutaneous tumors were removed from a woman. They contained a coenurus (bladder worm) of *Multiceps serialis.* Similar tumor, excised from the intercostal muscle of a northern Nigerian, contained coenurus of *Multiceps glomeratus.*

Cysticercus fasciolaris, the larval stage of the cat tapeworm, *Taenia taeniaeformis*, stimulates the development of metastasing sarcoma in the liver of the rodent intermediate host.

OCCURRENCE

PROTOZOA

Rhizopoda	
1. *Entameba histolytica*	Various parts of India
2. *Entameba coli*	Various parts of India
3. *Acanthameba castellani*	Baroda, Mumbai
Mastigophora	
4. *Giardia intestinalis*	Various parts of India
5. *Trichomonas vaginalis*	Various parts of India
6. *Leishmania donovani*	Assam, Bengal (Dum Dum), Bihar, Orissa, Tamil Nadu, eastern Uttar Pradesh
7. *Leishmania tropica*	Kolkata, Western India
Sporozoa	
8. *Cryptosporidium*	Vellore, Kolkata, Bangalore, Chandigarh
9. *Isospora hominis*	Bengal (Arakan) (14 cases)
10. *Plasmodium*	Very common in India
11. *Sarcocystis lindemanni*	Mumbai (one case)
Ciliata	
12. *Balantidium coli*	Pondicherry (pig)

HELMINTHS

Cestoda	
13. *Taenia saginata*	Muslim community (India)
14. *Taenia solium*	Other than Muslim community (India)
15. *Echinococcus granulosus*	Many parts of India
16. *Hymenolepis nana*	Some parts of India
Trematoda	
17. *Schistosoma haematobium*	Maharashtra (Ratnagiri Dist.)
18. *Schistosoma nasalis* (Animal trematode)	Pondicherry
19. *Gastrodiscoides hominis*	Assam, Bengal
20. *Fasciola hepatica*	Some parts of India
21. *Fasciolopsis buski*	Assam, Bengal, eastern India
22. *Clonorchis sinensis*	Kolkata (one case)
23. *Opisthorchis felineus*	Kolkata (cat), human cases from some parts of India
24. *Paragonimus westermani*	Assam, Bengal, South India
Nematoda	
25. *Ancylostoma duodenale*	Punjab, Uttar Pradesh
26. *Necator americanus*	South India
27. *Enterobius vermicularis*	Common in India
28. *Ascaris lumbricoides*	Very common in India
29. *Wuchereria bancrofti*	Rajasthan, Gujarat, Punjab, Uttar Pradesh, Delhi
30. *Brugia malayi*	Kerala, Orissa, Madhya Pradesh, Assam, Hyderabad
31. *Dracunculus medinensis*	Rajasthan (Jodhpur), Tamil Nadu, Andhra Pradesh, Karnataka, Punjab, Madhya Pradesh, Maharashtra (Mumbai), Gujarat (Panchmahals, Valsad, Sabarkantha, Banaskantha)
32. *Gnathostoma spinigerum*	Few human cases and two cases of spurious parasitism

Class Nematoda *Stronglyoides stercoralis* causes rarely granulomatous intestinal lymphangitis due to migrating larvae and consequent dilatation of lymphatic vessels.

Toxocara canis: Larvae produce most commonly granulomatous lesions in the liver (millet seed size whitish nodules under the liver capsule), other organs involved are lungs, kidneys, heart, striated muscle, brain, eyeball, during their migration in the viscera in the unnatural host (human).

Onchocerca volvulus causes the tumours (onchocercoma) which are usually located on the scalp of American children; whereas in African patients they are situated on the chest or lower trunk; these tumour locations depend on the topographic distribution of biting by the simulium fly, above the ground level.

Dirofilaria immitis has been reported in a Japanese woman in a tumour-like growth removed from a subcutaneous lesion of the breast.

Dirofilaria conjunctivae have been removed from tumors in various anatomical locations on the human body; whereas *D. repens* was found in a subcutaneous nodule of the right lower eyelid of a female patient in Russia.

Gongyglonema neoplasticum and *G. orientle* provoke malignant gastric tumours in rats which have been inoculated with the larval stage of these worms.

Gnathostoma spinigerum was found in the gastric tumour of a tiger. Later, it was reported in two Indian human cases.

Class Trematoda Several species of Trematoda have been involved in the development of carcinoma. Among these species are *Fasciola hepatica*, *Clonorchis sinensis* and *Opistorchis felineus* which inhabit the biliary tract and species of Schistosoma or blood flukes which live in the mesenteric, pelvic or vesicle venous blood vessels.

The flukes of bile ducts cause, occasionally, adeno-carcinoma and solid primary carcinoma of the liver. Colonic, rectal, hepatic carcinoma was due to flukes of the large intestine and liver.

Around the eggs of *Schistosoma haematobium*, there is hyperplasia and inflammation of the mucous membrane of the urinary bladder resulting in pseudo-tubercles or papillomatous growth or visceral carcinoma.

In *S. japonicum* infection, there is formation of pseudo-tubercles around the eggs of *S. japonicum*, which transform into papillomatous growth in the extensive segments of the intestine. In case of *S. mansoni*, there is delayed production of granulomas around the eggs in the tissue (colon and rectum). In chronic *S. japonicum* infection, there is development of hepatocellular carcinoma with the association of hepatitis C virus infection.

S. nasalis (animal trematode) causes nasal granuloma in cattle. It is common in India and responds to Anthiomalin therapy.

The presence of the adult worm of *C. sinensis* in the distal bile passage provokes considerable proliferation of the biliary epithelium and later its desquamation resulting in Cholangio-carcinoma.

In *Opisthorchis felineus* infection, hypertrophy of the epithelium of the large bile passage or of the pancreas may develop with metastases into the epigastric lymph nodes which are responsible for the death of the patient. *Paragonimus westermani* typically provokes a granulomatous reaction leading to the development of fibrotic encapsulation.

Parasitic Opportunists Associated with HIV Infection

The spectrum of parasitic opportunists found in association with Human Immunodeficiency Virus (HIV) infection or Acquired Immunodeficiency Syndrome (AIDS) are protoza – *Pneumocystis carinii, Toxoplasma gondii, Isospora belli, Leishmania sp*. cryptosporidium and Microsporidia.

Parasites of Radiological Importance

E. histolytica (ultrasonography, X-ray of abdomen are done), *G. lamblia* (X-ray, sonography may reveal mucosal defects), *P. falciparum* (recent MRI can be used to diagnose cerebral malaria), *T. gondii* (X-ray, MRI of skull to show cerebral calcification - ventriculogram).

Pneumocystis carinii (radiological appearance of pneumocystis pneumonia), *E. granulosus* (X-ray, MRI, CT and ultrasonography are useful in the diagnosis), *T. solium* (cysticercus cellulosae – cerebral cysticercosis can be diagnosed by CT, MRI or sonography).

S. haematobium (bladder calcification, characteristic feature of urinary schistosomiasis and urinary tract pathology are detected by ultrasonography). *P. westermani* (ultrasonography, chest radiographs early in the disease show patchy cloudy infiltration. Pleural thickening and calcification may be seen late in the disease).

T. solium (in ocular cysticercosis – calcified larvae are detected by X-ray diagnosis). Calcified adult worm of *W. bancrofti* can be detected by X-ray. *D. medinensis* (X-ray can detect dead calcified worms of *D. medinensis*).

Parasites of Ophthalmic Importance

T. cruzi (edema of eyelids – Romana's sign).

T. gondii (pseudo-cysts in the eyes).

E. granulosus (hydatid cyst may develop in orbital capillary).

Multiceps brauni was found located in the eye.

T. solium causes ocular cysticercosis.

F. hepatica is seldom found in the eye.

The larvae of *A. lumbricoides* which migrate through the capillaries of the eyeball may cause retinitis.

Microfilariae of *O.volvulus* circulate into the eyeball and cause corneal opacity. Keratitis, iridocyclitis and secondary glaucoma are irreversible damages to the optic nerve leading to blindness.

The migrating adult worms of *Loa loa* are troublesome while passing in front of the eyeball and they have been removed from the eyelids, the anterior chamber of the eye and the bulba conjunctiva.

Thelazia callipaeda (oriental eye worm) and *T. californiensis* have a predilection for the conjunctiva.

D. medinensis (guinea worm) was removed from the subconjunctival space of the eye of an Indian patient.

Parasites of Cardiac Importance

T. cruzi (cardiac rhythm is disturbed; cardiomyopathy).

P. falciparum (coronary edema and thrombosis).

T. solium (cysticercus cellulosae may rarely produce myocarditis or congestive heart failure).

E. granulosus (hydatid cyst may develop on the heart valve).

C. sinensis produces the symptoms of palpitation of the heart, tachycardia.

In *T. spiralis* infection, blood pressure falls rapidly, myocarditis is a serious complication.

S. stercoralis larvae may be found in the heart.

Larvae of *T. canis* and *T. catis* may cause cardiac dysfunction. In *A. duodenale* infection, palpitation of the heart and signs and symptoms of high output, congestive heart failure are evident.

The wandering worm of *A. lumbricoides* may invade the heart.

Parasites of Gynecological Importance

Trichomonas vaginalis causes trichomonas vaginitis (a sexually transmitted disease).

Arthropod borne protozoal diseases: African sleeping sickness (glossina palpalis, tse tse fly); South American trypanosomiasis (Chagas' disease) – Triatoma infestans, reduvid bug; *kala azar* and Delhi boil (Phlebotomus argentipes, sand fly); Malaria (female Anopheles mosquito).

Arthropod borne taeniasis: *Dipylidium caninum* infestation (*Ctenocephalus canis*, dog flea).

Arthropod borne helminthic diseases: Filariasis (*Culex, Aedes, Anopheles* mosquito); Onchocerciasis; (Simulium, black fly); Dipetalonemiasis (*Culicoides austeni*, biting midges); Mansonelliasis ozzardi (*culicoides furens*); Loaiasis (*Chrysops dimidiata*, mango fly); Dracunculosis (*Diaptomus vulgaris*, Cyclops).

Zoonotic Parasites

Protozoa Cryptosporidium (Parasite of fowl, rodents and cattle) is unrecognized because of self limited mild gastroenteritis and diarrhea in humans.

Encephalitozoon cuniculi, a new, recent species that has a wide host range in mammals (rodents, rabbits, carnivores and primates) has been diagnosed once in Japan, in Sweden in children with neurological illness.

Leishmania identical to *L. tropica* causes Oriental sore in dogs in Iraq, Iran, Turkistan, Mumbai and northern Africa.

L. donovani is transmitted secondarily from dog to sand fly to humans in some endemic areas of China, Mediterranean countries and Brazil. Cat, horse and sheep have been reported infected with Leishmania morphologically similar to *L. donovani.*

T. gambiense There is no proof that any of the game animals of Africa acts as reservoirs of *T. gambiense* infection for humans, but domestic animals (cattle, pigs and goats) carry this infection for long periods of time without apparent symptoms.

T. rhodesiense The reservoirs of infection of *T. rhodesiense* for humans are believed to be game animals in Africa.

T. cruzi. In South America, various animals (dogs, cats, armadillos, bats, ferrets, foxes) have been found to be naturally infected with *T. cruzi.* Dogs and cats may be the common reservoirs of *T. cruzi* infection in South America.

Entameba histolytica Animal reservoirs of *E. histolytica* include monkeys, dogs and possibly dogs, but these animals at most constitute a minor source of human exposure compared with human beings.

E. coli. Although monkeys and occasionally dogs have been found to be naturally infected with Entameba morphologically similar to *E. coli*, human infection results from a human source.

Isospora hominis Dogs are suspected to be reservoir hosts of *I. hominis.*

Toxoplasma gondii infection may occur in humans or in any warm-blooded vertebrate animals (cats). Apparent toxoplasmosis is common in reservoir hosts and in humans.

Balantidium coli Humans are relatively refractory to infection with *B. coli* of porcine origin. In New Guinea, where the pigs are the principal domestic animals, human infection in pig farmers is common to some extent.

Helminths

Nematodes *Trichinellas spiralis* Pigs, rats, carnivorous, omnivorous wild hosts are primarily infected with trichinosis, whereas pigs, wild boar, bears, cats, dogs and other mammals which eat flesh became secondarily infected. Polar bears are probably the usual source of human infection in Alaska. Epidemic outbreaks due to consumption of sausage from infected hogs are common.

Strongyloides stercoralis The human being is an important host of *S. stercoralis*, dogs and chimpanzees have been found to be naturally infected with strains indistinguishable from those in humans.

Ancylostoma duodenale Humans are the only normal definite hosts of *A. duodenalde*, although a single female worm from a tiger (Kolkata) and hookworms identified as *A. duodenale* have been reported from the pig, dog and several species of wild animals in captivity.

A. ceylanicum, described from the intestine of a civet cat from Sri Lanka, parasitizes to a lesser extent, the dogs and humans.

A. braziliense Though first reported from cats and dogs in southern Brazil, it has been incorrectly reported from humans in many countries, including India and Sri Lanka.

A. caninum is a common parasite of dogs and cats and has been reported once as a parasite of humans in the Philippine islands.

Necator americanus is a parasite of the human small intestine (natural host). A hookworm, morphologically indistinguishable from *N. americanus* of humans, has been recovered from several species of simian hosts, rhinoceros, pangolin (Indonesia), rodent (Africa).

Trichostrongylus are the commonest parasites in the digestive tract of herbivorous animals throughout the world (Egypt, India - Assam, America). The majority of species occur only as an accidental human infection.

Haemonchus contortus is the most common parasite of domestic sheep throughout the world. Human infection is less common.

Metastrongylus elongates: Commonly parasitizes the respiratory tract of hogs, less commonly of sheep and cattle. Few human infections are on record.

Angiostrongylus cantonensis, originally described from the rats, is less commonly reported as human infection.

Syphacia muris and *S. obvelata:* These oxyurids are cosmopolitan in rats and mice, their eggs occur rarely in human feces.

Toxocara canis is a cosmopolitan parasite of dogs. Intestinal infection with the adult worm has been reported from the fox and twice from humans, although the authenticity of the human infection is questionable.

T. cati is the common ascarid of the domestic cat and some of its wild relatives. Some cases of this infection in humans have been recorded.

Gongylonema pulchrum This thread-like nematode is a cosmopolitan parasite of a ruminant and has been diagnosed from pigs, bears, monkeys and occasionally from humans. It was first recovered as a human parasite in Italy, since then additional infections in humans have been reported.

Gnathostoma spinigerum has been reported from domestic cats, wild cat, lion, leopard, mink and the dog in India and in other countries. Human cases are reported from India and other countries.

Dipetalonema perstans Humans are the important definite host for this species, although primates in Africa and New World monkeys act as reservoir hosts.

Thelazia Callipaeda (oriental eye worm) is a spiruroid nematode of the conjunctiva of dog, rabbit and humans.

T. Californiensis In addition to *T. callipaeda*, many species of this genus have a predilection for the conjunctiva of mammals, birds, and many human cases have been reported.

Dirofilaria immitis, D. conjunctivae, D. tenuis, D. repens are microfilariae of animals and they may become adults in humans without producing microfilaria.

Trematode *Schistosoma japonicum*. Dogs, cats, rats, mice, field mice, cattle, water buffaloes, pigs, horse, sheep and goats are naturally infected with *S. japonicum* in many endemic foci.

S. mansoni Human infection is mostly derived from human sources, although monkeys, baboons, gerbils, wild rodents, rats have occasionally been found infected with *S. mansoni* in endemic areas.

S. haematobium In addition to humans, the usual host, the monkey, baboon and chimpanzee, have been found naturally infected.

S. bovis, common parasite of cattle, sheep, goats and equines has been reported from baboons. Isolated cases of recovery of *S. bovis* eggs from human urine and stools in South Africa, Southern Rhodesia and Congo lack satisfactory proof. In Italy, this species causes cercarial dermatitis in humans. Eggs are longer and much narrower than those of *S. haematobium*.

S. mattheei is a natural parasite of sheep, goat, cattle, monkey and rarely in humans, in South Africa, Rhodesia. The eggs of this worm were found in human urine and adult forms were also found associated with those of *S. haemoatobium* in two human autopsies. In Rhodesia, over 1% of persons were infected with *S. mattheei;* eggs are found in stool and urine with equal frequency.

S. nasalis is a common parasite of cattle in India (Pondicherry, Panjarathinam, 1972), but there has been no record of human infection.

S. rhodhaini is the parasite of African wild rodents, dogs, cats. Human infection with *S. rhodhaini* has been reported in Congo.

S. incognitum is the natural parasite of Indian pigs and dogs. The eggs were twice recovered from human feces.

Trichobilharzia ocellate, Schistosoma spindale are animal schistosomes, which cause cercarial dermatitis in humans.

Gastrodiscoides hominis, common human parasites in India and other countries, has been found to infect pigs (common reservoir hosts) and monkeys in India.

Fasciola hepatica Reservoir hosts (primarily sheep) play the important role in the propagation of this infection in nature and hence, human infection occurs.

Fasciolopsis buski is a common parasite of humans and pigs in Central and South China and other countries. Dogs are occasionally infected. Other domestic animals, with the possible exception of rabbits, are probably refractory.

Echinostoma ilocanum (Garrison's fluke). Rats and dogs are reservoirs of *E. ilocanum* infection. Human infection is acquired from the consumption of raw snails containing encysted metacercariae.

Echinochasmus perfoliatus This echinostome has also been recovered from pig and fox and a human infection has been reported in Japan.

Plagiorchis muris is a natural parasite of several groups of birds at Douglas Lake, and has been reported once from a human patient in Japan.

Dicrocoelium dendriticum is a common parasite in the biliary passage of sheep, deer, herbivorous and omnivorous mammals. Many genuine human cases have been diagnosed from Europe, Asia and Africa.

Troglotrema salmincola Human infection is incidental to human and reservoir hosts (dogs, fox, raccoon and mink).

Paragonimus westermani The natural definite hosts are humans, tiger, cat, civet cat, leopard, panther, fox, wolf, dog, pig.

Opisthorchis felineus Humans, dog, cat, red, silver and polar foxes, domestic and wild swine, Norway rat, water rat are infected. The definite hosts acquire infection from consumption of infected raw fish.

Clonorchis sinensis In addition to humans, many reservoir hosts (principally the dog, cat) are naturally infected.

Heterophyes heterophyses In addition to humans, *H. heterophyses* has been found as a natural infection in the cat, dog, fox and other fish eating mammals in endemic areas.

Metagonimus yokogawai Fish-eating mammals and even the pelican are reservoir hosts of the infection.

Cestodes *Diphyllobotrium latum* Humans, domestic dog, cat, leopard, mangoose, foxes, seals, sea lions, bears, minks, domestic pigs have been found infected with *D. latum.*

Dipylidium caninum Dogs and cats are available sources of infection for humans, to whom it is uncommon.

Hymenolepis nana fraternal. The variety in murine hosts is infective for humans only under exceptional circumstances.

H. diminuta The tapeworm is a common parasite of the rat, mouse and dog (rarely), however, authentic human cases have been reported.

Taenia solium The human being is the usual definite host and gets infected by eating inadequately heated pork. Pigs, less frequently, sheep, dogs and cats harbour the cysticercus stage of *T. solium.*

T. saginata Human infection is acquired by consumption of inadequately cooked beef containing the viable cysticercus larvae.

T. taeniaeformis is a normal parasite of the intestine of the cat, which becomes infected from eating infected rats. A single human infection has been reported.

Multiceps multiceps Dog, wolf and fox are definite hosts of this worm. The larval stage is usually found in herbivorous animals (sheep, goats, cattle, horse). Human infection results from the ingestion of eggs passed in dog's feces.

Multiceps glomeratus is reported from the gerbil and humans.

Multiceps serialis is a parasite of dog, wolf and fox, rodents. Human infection is also on record.

Multiceps brauni This cestode was described from the intestine of dog. Infection with the coenurus (bladder worm) has been recorded in humans. In two patients, the parasite was located in the eye.

Echinococcus granulosus The dog is the optimum definite host, although humans, the wolf, jackal, fox, domestic cat have been found infected in nature. Cattle, sheep and pigs are the common reservoirs of the hydatid cyst.

E. multilocularis Humans get infected sporadically from eggs of *E. multilocularis* that have infected fox's excreta.

SYMPTOMATOLOGY OF PARASITIC DISEASES

The following are the important signs and symptoms of parasitic diseases:

Abscess, amebic: The liver is tender and enlarged. There is intense pain and fever, with night sweats when the abscess is formed.

Abscess, filarial: Along the lymphatics, filarial abscesses may appear and segments of adult worms may be seen in the abscess drainage which is free from bacteria.

Anemia: In malaria, ancylostomiasis, diphyllobothriasis, *kala azar*, trypanosomiasis, schistosomiasis and fasciolopsiasis, anemia is common. Microcytic hypochromic anemia is common in ancylostomiasis and malaria because of blood loss. In the case of hookworm infection, dietary intake of iron may prevent anemia. A microcytic anemia may develop in diphyllobothriasis, because of vitamin B_{12} deprivation by the worm attached to the jejunal wall. The proliferation of infected reticuloendothelial cells in the bone marrow is responsible for anemia in *kala azar* and Chagas' disease. In trypanosomiasis, schistosomiasis and fasciolopsiasis, systemic toxicity and nutritional defects may result in anemia.

Appendicitis: The blockage of the lumen of the appendix by Ascaris and Trichuris causes appendicitis. In amebiasis, acute appendicitis may occur.

Ascites: Tissue proliferation around the eggs leading to fibrosis of the liver may cause ascites in infection with *Schistosoma mansoni* and S. *japonicum*.

Asthma, bronchial: Migration of the larva of *Ascaris lumbricoides* through the lungs may cause bronchial asthma.

Calabar swellings: In loiasis, subcutaneous swellings are observed. They are painful and pruritic.

Chagoma: A hard, reddened, raised, primary lesion develops on the face, neck, abdomen or limbs in Chagas' disease.

Chorio-retinitis: Toxoplasma may infect the retina and choroid, and this affects eyesight.

Chyluria: The lymphatic fluid is passed in the urine which is milky white and contains microfilariae of *Wuchereria bancrofti*.

Coma: It is observed in falciparum malaria and in African trypanosomiasis.

Conjunctivitis: Onchocercal infection produces chronic conjunctivitis.

Convulsions: These may be seen in malarial paroxysms and in Ascaris infection in children.

Dermatitis: Strongyloides larvae, hookworm larvae and schistosoma cercariae penetrate through the skin and cause localized edema and pruritus leading to dermatitis. The cutaneous larva migrans reaction caused by the larvae of *Ancylostoma branziliense* is indicated by a red papule at the site of entry and there is severe itching. Adult *Loa loa* beneath the skin may cause dermatitis. The adult female *Dracunculus medinensis,* beneath the skin produces a blister.

Microfilariae of *Onchocerca volvulus* in the skin may cause pruritus. *Sarcoptes scabei* under the skin causes lesions similar to those of cutaneous larva migrans.

Diarrhea: Infiltration of the intestinal submucosa by macrophages containing *Leishmania donovani* may cause mucosal ulceration and diarrhea in *kala azar*. The mucosal capillaries of the intestine plugged with parasitized red blood cells cause profuse, watery diarrhea in falciparum malaria. Mucosal ulceration in amebiasis or balantidiasis may produce diarrhea. Mild mucoid diarrhea caused by giardiasis may lead to malabsorption of fat or 'steatorrhea' (diarrhea with fat). Mucous diarrhea may be caused by the development of the cysticercoids of *Hymenolepis nana* within the intestinal villi. Mild diarrhea followed by constipation or severe diarrhea may be observed in strongyloides infection. Diarrhea of toxic origin, characterized by nausea, vomiting, hepatic tenderness and fever, is caused by *Schistosoma mansoni* and S. *japonicum* infections. Egg deposition in the intestinal wall may be responsible for the profuse diarrhea or dysentery in schistosomiasis. Nausea, vomiting and diarrhea are indicated in heavy hookworm and whipworm infections. In fasciolopsiasis, diarrhea with undigested food is observed. Sometimes, there may be diarrhea in taeniasis and diphyllobothriasis.

Dysentery: The passage of 6–8 or more mucoid, blood-flecked stools per day is characteristic of acute amebic dysentery. There may be abdominal pain and tenderness.

Elephantiasis: Filarial elephantiasis is a chronic enlargement of the limb, scrotum, breast or vulva with hyperplasia of the connective tissue and skin. Rarely, there is blockage of the lymphatic drainage due to fibrosis caused by eggs deposited by *Schistosoma haematobium* in the vesicle plexus of the veins.

Eosinophilia: In many helminthic infections, eosinophilia is common. Tissue parasites provoke a higher eosinophilia than intestinal parasites. It is not characteristic in protozoan infections.

Epididymitis: It is seen in filarial infection.

Funiculitis: Inflammation of the spermatic cord occurs as an early symptom of filariasis.

Hematuria: There may be terminal hematuria in the last few drops of urine in *Schistosoma haematobium* infection.

Hydrocele: It is common in filariasis.

Hydrocephalus: In congenital toxoplasmosis, hydrocephalus or microcephaly is common.

Hyperpigmentation: Hyperpigmentation of the skin over the cheeks, temples and around the mouth is seen in *kala azar*. In onchocercosis, allergic dermatitis may result in hyper pigmentation of the area on the face, neck or ears.

Jaundice: In severe liver fluke infection, obstructive jaundice may be observed. In falciparum malaria, there is marked enlargement and tenderness of the liver, with jaundice appearing on the second day.

Leucocytosis: It is common only in amebic abscess. Leucocytosis, followed by leucopenia, is common in many protozoan and helminthic infections.

Leucopenia: It is generally seen in *kala azar.*

Lymphadenitis: It is common in filariasis. The axillary and inguinal lymph nodes are enlarged, painful and tender. In the acute stage of Chagas' disease, there is generalized adenopathy.

Lymphangitis: Acute lymphangitis is an early symptom of filariasis. It is followed by fever. When it occurs on a limb, it progresses distally.

Lymphocytosis: It is generally seen in Chagas' disease.

Lymph varices: Due to the lymphatic blockage in filariasis, the lymphatic vessels of the inguinal and femoral areas are dilated. The soft lobulated swellings may rupture and drain.

Meningo-encephalitis: In African sleeping sickness, the symptoms of meningo-encephalitis may result due to the invasion of the central nervous system by trypanosomes. There may be confusion, headache, drowsiness and finally, coma. In Chagas' disease, the symptoms are similar but milder. Meningo-encephalitis is also observed in falciparum malaria.

Microcephalus: See *Hydrocephalus.*

Monocytosis: In both protozoal and helminthic infections, monocytosis is a frequent finding.

Myocarditis: It is characteristic of Chagas' disease and trichinosis. In trichinosis, the migration of the larvae through the myocardium causes myocarditis. It is also seen in toxoplasmosis, as a result of the invasion of toxoplasma in the myocardium.

Myositis: Migration of *Trichinella spiralis* larva in the muscles causes myositis.

Neurological symptoms: See under *Meningoencephalitis.*

Nodules, subcutaneous: Onchocercomas, cysticercus larvae of *Taenia solium* and *Echinococcus* cysts may be found in the subcutaneous tissues forming nodules 0.5–3.0 cm in diameter.

Obstruction, intestinal: Ascaris may cause complete intestinal obstruction in children, causing abdominal pain, vomiting, distension and hyperperistalsis.

Ocular symptoms: See *Conjunctivitis.*

Edema: Migrating larvae of *Trichinella spiralis* may cause vasculitis leading to edema. The migration of adult *Loa loa* across the eyeball or lid may cause unilateral edema with local pruritus and intense pain. Calabar swellings are also seen in loiasis, while in onchocerciasis, there is edema of face, neck, ears followed by an intense pruritus and erythema. The most common type is unilateral edema of the eyelids (Romana's sign). Edema of the face and legs is seen in severe hookworm infection, fasciolopsis and diphyllobothriasis.

Onchocercoma: Adult worms of *Onchocerca volvulus* remain coiled underneath the skin, enclosed in a fibrous tissue capsule.

Orchitis: Recurrent attacks of hydrocele may cause orchitis in filariasis.

Pain: Abdominal pain is said to accompany many of the intestinal parasitic infections. Severe pain may indicate intestinal obstruction, perforation and peritonitis or bile duct blockage as in ascariasis.

Peritonitis: Penetration of Ascaris through the wall of the intestine leads to peritonitis, with pain, abdominal distension and tenderness. The ulcers in severe amebic dysentery may erode through the wall of the intestine to initiate peritonitis.

Pneumonitis: When the larvae of *Ascaris lumbricoides* break out of the capillaries into the alveoli, it can cause pneumonitis.

In the neonatal period, acute toxoplasmosis causes pneumonitis.

Proteinuria: Proteinuria with hyaline and granular casts in the urine is common in falciparum malaria.

Pruritus ani: It accompanies pinworm infection. Sometimes, it may also be associated with migration of the gravid proglottids of *Taenia saginata* out of the anus.

Pulmonary symptoms, chronic: Pseudo-tubercles are formed in the lungs around the ova of Schistosoma which are carried to the lungs. Chronic cough is characteristic of paragonimiasis. Cough is the primary symptom in pulmonary echinococcosis.

Rash: In the early stage of schistosome infection and in ascariasis, an allergic urticarial rash may appear. In the course of trichina infection, a macular or maculo-papular eruption may be seen.

Romana's sign: In the early stage of *Trypanosoma cruzi* infection (Chagas' disease), unilateral edema involving both the eyelids may appear.

Splenomegaly: In South African and American sleeping sickness, splenomegaly may be present. The spleen is said to enlarge downwards about an inch per month in *kala azar*. The spleen enlarges and becomes tender during an acute attack of malaria. Hepatic fibrosis caused by the eggs deposited by *Schistosoma mansoni* and S. *japonicum* in the liver may result in splenomegaly.

Tachycardia: It may be observed in African and American sleeping sickness, characterized by a fast pulse.

Ulcers, cutaneous: Oriental sore or Delhi boil, caused by *Leishmania tropica*, is characterized by a shallow ulcer. *L. braziliensis* also produces cutaneous ulcerations which involve the nasal mucosa, the soft and hard palates, nasal septum, the pharynx and larynx. *Dracunculus medinensis* initially produces a blister which transforms into an ulcer. Adult worms can be seen in the centre of the ulcer.

Urethritis: *Trichomonas vaginalis* causes nonspecific urethritis.

Vaginitis: In *Trichomonas vaginalis* infection, the vagina is congested and there is a yellowish discharge.

Winterbottom's sign: See *Lymphadenitis*.

TREATMENT

The following chemotherapeutic agents have proved useful in the treatment of protozoan and helmintic infections:

ALBENDAZOLE (single dose chewable vanilla flavoured most recent anthelmintic)

G. lamblia (protozoon)	
E. vermicularis	100%
A. lumbricoides	95.3

T. trichuria	95.3
A. duodenale	92.2
N. americanus	90
S. stercoralis	81
C. sinensis	80
G. lamblia (protozoon)	

Allopurinol (oral)

Use — Recent chemotherapeutic agent, effective as nitrofurans and benznidazole for Chagas' disease.

General toxicity — Well tolerated, no side-effect.

Dose regimen — 600–900 mg/day for 60 days.

Aminosidine, effective against *kala azar*.

Azardirachtine

Use — Substance from neem tree seed effective against Chagas' diseases by blocking the development of *T. cruzi*

Dose regimen — few mg; under experiment.

Bephenium Hydroxynaphtholate (Alcopar)

Use — Hookworm (ancylostomiasis), especially if patient also has ascariasis.

General toxicity — Well tolerated.

Dose regimen — Single 5 g oral dose empty stomach.

Bithionol Bitin

Use — Paragonimiasis.

General toxicity — Usually well tolerated.

Dose regimen — 2 g daily for 15 days.

Chloroquine Diphosphate (Aralen)

Use — Extra-intestinal amebiasis; malaria.

General toxicity — Well tolerated, but visual disturbances in some patients.

Dose regimen — Amebiasis-1g (500 mg b.i.d.) for 2 days, followed by 500 mg per day for 14 days. (malaria - therapeutic) 1.0 g initially 500 mg 6 hrs later, then 500 mg daily for 2 days. (malaria - suppressive) 500 mg once weekly.

Chlorsalicylamide (Yomesan)

Use — Intestinal taeniasis.

General toxicity — Usually well tolerated.

Dose regimen — 1.0 g chewed and taken with water; repeated 1 hr later, and followed by saline purge 2 hrs later.

Clotrimazole (Surfaz, 100 mg)

Use	Trichomonas vaginilis as a vaginal tablet.
General Toxicity	Well tolerated.
Dose regimen	To be inserted in the vagina at bedtime for 6 days. Also a single course of 4 tablets of Tinidazole to be taken at bedtime on the first day of treatment with clotrimozole vaginal tablets.

Diethylcarbamazine (Hetrazan)

Use	Filariasis.
General toxicity	Well tolerated.
Dose regimen	6.0 mg per kg (2 mg per kg t.i.d.) daily, after meals for 3–4 weeks (10–100 mg tablets).

Diodohydroxyquin (Diodoquin)

Use	Chronic intestinal amebiasis; balantidiasis.
General toxicity	Well tolerated, but not to be used in hyperthyroidic patients.
Dose regimen	(Whipworm) - 300 mg (100 t.i.d.) after meals on first day; followed by 600 mg (200 t.i.d.) after meals for 5 days; children receive half the above doses. (Strongyloidiasis) - same doses as for whipworm, but treatment is for 2–3 weeks.

Ethylstibamine (Neostibosan)

Use	Leishmaniasis, especially *kala azar.*
General toxicity	Gastro-intestinal upset; not to be used in patients with pulmonary or renal disorders.
Dose regimen	(300) mg ampoules 6.0 ml sterile distilled water added to make a fresh 5% solution. Initial 4.0 ml intravenous dose of 5% solution, followed by 6.0 ml of fresh 5% solution every 24 hr. for 15–20 days.

Emetine hydrochloride

Use	Amebic dysentery and liver amebiasis when chloroquine unsuccessful.
General toxicity	General toxin, especially to vascular system.
Dose regimen	(ampoules – 150 mg in 3.0 ml fluid) Not more than 65 mg per day intramuscularly or subcutaneously for 2-3 days

Hexyl resorcinol

Use	Hookworm, intestinal flukes and whipworm.
General toxicity	Well tolerated, but causes superficial burns if chewed.
Dose regimen	100 or 200 mg gelatin capsules, or in crystals. (orally) –100 mg per each year of age (up to 1.0 g - adult dose) on empty stomach following saline purge.

Ivermectin (Mectizan)

Use	Onchocerciasis, filaricais, a recent anthelminthic drug.
General toxicity	Some side effects.

Dose regimen — Onchocerciasis: single dose of 50 mg/kg body weight well tolerated, filariasis > 100 mg/kg body weight.

Ketoconazole

Use — *Kala azar*, Delhi boil-recent chemotherapeutic.

General toxicity — Well tolerated

Dose regimen — 600 mg daily in 3 divided doses for 4 weeks cure clinically and parasitologically.

Halofantrine

Use — Chloroquin-resistant Falciparum malaria

Contraindications — It is not advocated for pregnant women.

Dose regimen — 8 mg base 1 kg body weight every 6 hours for 3 days.

Lucanthone hydrochloride (Miracil D)

Use — Urinary and mansoni schistosomiasis.

General toxicity — Gastro-intestinal upset; turns skin yellow; not to be used in kidney or liver patients.

Dose regimen — (200 mg tablets) 15 mg per kg (5 mg per kg t.i.d.) for 7 days.

Mebendazole (Wormin)

Use — It is a new broadspectrum, anthelminthic with high activity against various helminths.

Contraindications — As a precautionary measure, it should not be given to a woman during pregnancy and to persons who are hypersensitive to the drug.

Dose — 1 tablet twice a day for 3 days.

Mefloquine

Use — Chloroquine-resistant Plasmodium falciparum malaria.

Contra — It should not be given to pregnant indications. Women in the first trimester.

Dose — 15 mg/kg body weight up to 1000 mg in two doses 12 hours apart.

Mefloquine-sufadoxine-pyrimethemaine (Fansimel)

Use — Chloroquine-resistant *P. falciparum* malaria.

General toxicity — Safe for 24 weeks, comparable with standard antimalarials.

Melarsen oxide

Use — Early and late African trypanosomiasis.

General toxicity — Gastro-intestinal upset and symptoms of arsenic toxicity.

Dose regimen — Intravenous injection of 5.0 ml of 5% solution once daily for four days; then after a week's interval, the same dose regimen repeated.

Mel B (Arsobal)

Use Early and late African trypanosomiasis.

General toxicity Symptoms of arsenic toxicity.

Dose regimen (15% solution in propylene glycol) Intravenous injection, 3.6 mg per kg for 4 days, followed by rest of 7 days, followed by 3.6 mg per kg for 4 days.

Methyl benzimidazole

Use New broadspectrum anthelmintic against *H. nana*, hookworm, trichostrongyloides, oxyrids, taenia, filaria.

Dose High cure rate when used in regimen in minute amount.

Metronidazole (Flagyl)

Use Trichomoniasis.

General toxicity Well tolerated, but some have diarrhea.

Dose regimen Females - 750 mg (250 mg t.i.d.) for 10 days, along with daily 500 mg vaginal insert.

Dose regimen Males - 500 mg (250 mg t.i.d.) for 10 days.

Oxytetracycline (Terramycin)

Use Acute intestinal amebiasis; balantidiasis, (given alone, or in combination with diodohydroxyquin).

General toxicity Possible increase of diarrhea; also possible fungal overgrowth of gut or vagina.

Dose regimen 1–2 g per day (250 to 500 mg q.i.d.) for 5–10 days.

Paromomycin (Humatin)

Use Amebic colitis (given alone, or in combination with diodohydroxyquin). Cryptosporidiosis in patients with AIDS

General toxicity Usually well tolerated.

Dose regimen 1.5 g (500 mg t.i.d.) for 7 days.

Pentamidine (Lomidine)

Use Early African trypanosomiasis, *kala azar*.

General toxicity Hypotensive reactions.

Dose regimen (2% solution) (early trypanosomiasis) – 4 mg per kg intramuscularly once daily or every other day: for 5 to 10 injections. (chemoprophylaxis) – 5 mg per kg intramuscularly once every few months.

Piperazine (Antepar)

Use Pinworm; ascariasis.

General toxicity Well tolerated.

Dose regimen (Pinworm) – 65 mg per kg (with maximum of 2 g) (syrup containing 100 mg per m\) once daily for 7 days. (ascariasis) – 150 mg per kg once daily for 2 days.

Potassium antimony tartarate (Tartar emetic)

Use	Schistosomiasis, especially japonicum schistosomiasis.
General toxicity	Highly toxic, affecting circulatory and respiratory systems in some patients; not to be used in patients with heart, renal, pulmonary, or hepatic disorders or in children; causes tissue necrosis if solution spills out of vein.
Dose regimen	(0.5% solution in sterile distilled water to be made fresh). Slow (3–4 ml per min) intravenous injection of 0.5% solution is given once daily, every other day, beginning with 8.0 ml and increasing the volume injected by 4.0 ml each day until 28 ml is administered; 28 ml is then administered every other day for 9–12 additional injections; a syringe of epinephrine solution should always be ready in case of medical emergency due to toxicity of the drug.

Praziquantel (derivative of prazinoisoquineline)

Use	It is a recent broadspectrum anthelmintic, effective against all species of trematodes.
General toxicity	Well tolerated, safe, easy to use and has high degree of efficacy with low toxicity.
Dose regimen	75 mg/kg of body weight divided into 3 doses daily for 3 days.

Primaquine diphosphate

Use	Radical cure of malaria.
General toxicity	May cause acute hemolytic anemia, especially in heavily pigmented races, not to be used following quinacrine, as the latter drug potentiates its toxicity.
Dose regimen	26.5 mg once daily for 14 days.

Pyrantel Pamoate

Use	Trichinelliasis, ancylostomiasis, ascariasis
General toxicity	Well tolerated, not advocated in pregnancy.
Dose regimen	Trichenelliasis, ancyclostomiasis –10 mg per kg body weight for 4 days. Ascariasis – single dose of 11 mg per 1 kg.

Pyronaridine

Use	Chloroquine-resistant falciparum malaria as promising candidate.
General toxicity	Clinical trials in China showed higher efficiency

Pyrimethamine (Daraprim)

Use	Active acquired toxoplasmosis; malaria suppression.
General toxicity	Some gastro-intestinal upset, but well tolerated at low doses.
Dose regimen	(toxoplasmosis) – 50 mg initially followed by 25 mg once daily for 14 days; (malaria suppression) 25 mg once weekly.

Pyrvinium pamoate (Povan)

Use	Usually well tolerated.
Dose regimen	(Oral-flavoured suspension) (pinworm) – 5 mg per kg as single oral dose (trichuriasis and strongyloidiasis) – 1.0 mg per kg daily for 7 days.

Quinacrine hydrochloride (Atabrine)

Use	Intestinal tapeworms; giardiasis.
General toxicity	Well tolerated over the short term, but may cause gastro-intestinal upset and mental disturbances in some patients; long term administration turns skin and eyeballs yellow.

Quinine sulfate

Use	Malaria (for cases resistant to chloroquine treatment).
General toxicity	Various side reactions as dizziness, cardiac irregularity and visual disturbances.
Dose regimen	(300 mg tablets) 1.8 g (600 mg t.i.d.) for 5–7 days.

Secnidazole

Use	Very effective recent antigiardial agent
General toxicity	Well tolerated.
Dose regimen	30 mg/kg body weight; parasitologically cured in 95.8% patients.

Sodium Antimony Gluconate

Use	Effective for visceral leishmaniasis in India
General toxicity	less toxic
Dose regimen	20 mg/kg body weight twice daily for 20 days.

Stibophen (Fuadin)

Use	Urinary and mansoni schistosomiasis.
General toxicity	Gastro-intestinal upset; not to be used in liver, heart, and kidney patients.
Dose regimen	(5.0 ml ampoules of 6% solution) Intramuscular injection of 1.5, 3.5 and 5.0 ml on days 1, 2 and 3, respectively, followed by 5.0 ml daily every other day for 18 injections. Children receive 20 to 30% less volume of the 6.3% solution.

Stilbamidine

Use	Visceral leishmaniasis.
General toxicity	Damage to trigeminal nerve, solution becomes highly toxic when exposed to light.
Dose regimen	(100 mg ampoules; 10 ml sterile distilled water added to make up fresh 1 % solution) Slow intravenous injections, 2.5 ml of 1 % solution initially, followed at 24 hr intervals for 10 to 15 days of increasing doses up to 13 ml per dose; average total dose of about 100 ml.

Sulfadoxine/Pyrimethamine (Fansidar)

Use	Chloroquine-resistant Falciparum malaria.
Dose	Single dose following shorter course of quinine.

Suramin (Bayer 205)

Use	Chemo-prophylactic and therapeutic for early African trypanosomiasis; onchocercosis, filariasis.
General toxicity	Kidney irritant and not to be used in patients with renal disorders; may also cause circulatory failure.
Dose regimen	(1.0 g ampoules, 10 ml sterile distilled water added to make up a fresh 1 % solution. Trial intravenous dose of 3 to 5 ml of 10% solution for possible toxicity; then at 4 day intervals, 10 ml of 10% solution are given at each injection.

Tinidazole (tridazole, 500 mg)

Use	Trichomonas vaginilis. General toxicity. Well tolerated.
Dose regimen	Single dose of 4 tables for sexual partner

Tetrachlorethylene

Use	Hookworm (when Ascaris is absent); intestinal flukes.
Dose regimen	(0.5 ml and 1.0 ml capsules) up to 5 ml maximum single dose, on an empty stomach.

Tryparsamide

Use	Late African trypanosomiasis.
General toxicity	May cause ocular disorders, not to be used in patients with ocular disease and in pregnancy.
Dose regimen	(2.0 mg; 10 ml sterile distilled water added to make 20% solution). Initial intravenous dose of 5.0 ml of 20% solution, followed by 5.0 ml a week later; then at 15 weekly intervals doses are gradually increased to 10–15 ml per dose for a total dose of 160 ml of the 20% solution.

Recent anthelmintic drugs and their clinical application

Some human helminthic infections which are susceptible to one or more of the benzimidazole compounds

Helminths		*Albendazole*	*Thiobendazole*	*Mebendazole*
Small intestine	Hook worm	±	+	+
	A. lumbricoldes	+	+	+
	S. stercoralis	+	–	+
Colorectal	*T. trichura*	±	+	+
	E. vermicularis	±	+	+
Systemic nematode	*Trichinella spiralis*	+	±	+
	Gnathostoma spinigerum	±	±	+

Angiostrongylus cantonensis		±	±	+
	Cutaneous larva migrans	+	–	+
	Visceral larva migrans	±	±	
Systemic cestode	*E. granulosus*	+	±	+
	E. multilocularis	+	±	+
	Neurocysticercosis (*T. solium*)	+	–	+

Section III

ENTOMOLOGY

Entomology is that branch of biological science which deals with the study of insects. Only insects (vectors) of medical importance are briefly described here, so as to enable medical students and physicians to identify them in a very short time.

11 VECTORS AND DISEASES

1. Order DIPTERA has one pair of membranous wings attached to the second thoracic segment and the second pair of wings replaced by minute club-shaped balancing organs, (halteres). The mouth parts are adapted for sucking. The metamorphosis is complete (egg → larva → pupa → adult).

Class INSECTA

Species *Anopheles culicifacies, Culex fatigans, Aedes polynesiensis* (mosquito), *Phlebotomus argentipes* (sand fly), *Culicoides austeni* (biting midges), *Simulium damnosum* (black fly), *Musca domestica* (house fly), *Glossina palpalis* (tse tse fly)

2. Order SIPHONAPTERA is wingless, its body strongly compressed laterally with an especially long pair of hind legs adapted for jumping. The mouth parts are adapted for sucking. The metamorphosis is complete (egg → larva → pupa → adult).

Species *Xenopsylla cheopis* (rat flea)

3. Order ANOPLURA (sucking louse) are, literally, insects which have an 'unarmed' tail. They are wingless, their body compressed dorsoventrally. The tarsi are one clawed, and the mouth parts are adapted for piercing and sucking. There is no metamorphosis (egg → nymph → adult).

Species *Pediculus humanus - var.capitis* (head louse) *Pediculus humanus - var.corporis* (body louse) *Phthirus pubis* (pubic louse)

4. Order ACARI (Ticks and mites). Their cephalo-thorax and abdomen are united. They are not externally segmented. The adults have four pairs of legs, and the larvae have three pairs of legs.

Superfamily IXODOIDEA (Ticks) have a large hypostome, ventral re-curved teeth, leathery skin and furrowed venter. The adults have tracheae and one pair of stigmal plates near the bases of legs III or IV. Representatives: *Ixodes, Dermacentor.*

Superfamily SARCOPTOIDEA have small three-jointed palpi; there is no eye. The tracheae, lacking tarsi, often end in suckers. The ventral suckers are at the genital opening or near the anal opening. The body is entire, its surface provided with fine parallel lines or folds. It is parasitic in all stages. Representative: *Sarcoptes scabiei.*

Subclass CRUSTACEA have two pairs of pre-oral antenniform appendages and three pairs of post-oral jaw-like appendages. They are chiefly aquatic, breathing through gills.

5. Order EUCOPEPODA (water flea): These lack compound eyes. The females carry egg sacs. Representatives: *Diaptomus, Cyclops.* These species are almost microscopically small, simple and aquatic with a pair of maxillae and five pairs of swimming legs. They lack compound eyes. They are elongated, convex on the dorsum, pyriform through the cephalic and thoracic regions, narrowed in the abdominal region and have two caudal furci. Medically, the genera *Diaptomus* and *Cyclops* are important.

	Diaptomus are important intermediate hosts of *Diphyllobothrium latum.* Many species of cyclops are intermediate hosts of *Dracunculus medinensis.*
6. Order	HETEROPTERA (true bugs): Typically these have two pairs of wings, with the basal part of the front wings thickened, more or less leathery, but are wingless in some families (i.e., bed bugs). The body is somewhat compressed dorso-ventrally. The tarsi are two-clawed, and the mouth parts adapted for piercing and sucking. The beak arises from the front part of the head. The metamorphosis is gradual (egg → larva → pupa → adult).
Species	*Triatoma infestans* (kissing bug, assassin bug).

The order DIPTERA is divided into three suborders: Nematocera, Brachycera and Cyclorrhapha.

MOSQUITO

Order	DIPTERA
Suborder	NEMATACERA
Class	INSECTA
Family	CULICIDAE (mosquito)

Adult mosquito (Fig. 11.1) The body of the adult mosquito consists of a head, a three-segmented thorax and a ten-segmented abdomen. The head bears a pair of compound eyes, a pair of fifteen jointed antennae (plumosed in the male and pilosed in the female), a pair of four-jointed palps and a biting and sucking type of proboscis. The thorax is three segmented, the mesothorax bearing a pair of wings and the metathorax, a pair of halteres. Each thoracic segment bears a pair of jointed legs. The wings bear scales and the second, fourth and fifth wing veins are forked. The abdomen is ten segmented, and the last two are transformed into the sexual structure.

Mouth parts of a female mosquito The head bears compound eyes, a pair of fifteen-jointed antennae, which are scarcely hairy or pilosed, and a pair of four-jointed palps, about one third of the length of the proboscis. The proboscis is elongated and consists of the following structures: an elongated labium ending in labellae, a pair of maxilla which are distally serrated, a pair of mandibles distally serrated, labrum epipharynx and hypopharynx.

The proboscis (mouth parts) of the female mosquito is strong like a needle, so that it can pierce through the skin. The female mosquitoes are therefore voracious blood suckers (Fig. 11.2).

Mouth parts of a male mosquito The head of the male mosquito bears a pair of compound eyes, a pair of fifteen-jointed antennae which are thickly hairy or plumosed, a pair of four-jointed palps equal to the proboscis and a sucking tube or proboscis. The proboscis consists of the same structures as in the female, but the maxillae and mandibles are greatly reduced. Hence, male mosquitoes are not voracious blood suckers.

Egg of mosquito The raft is boat shaped and contains a large number of eggs, about 200. Each egg is ovoid, dark in colour, floats with the narrow end upward and the broad end on the surface of the water. A knob-like process is attached to the broad end (Fig. 11.3)

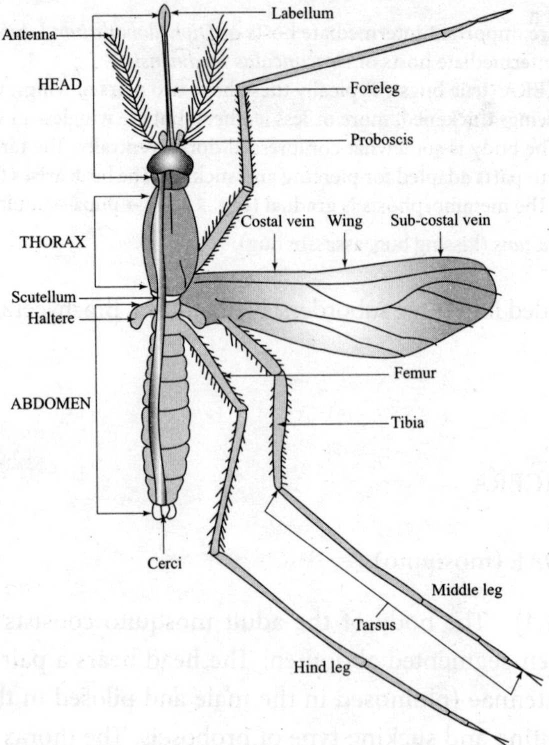

Fig. 11.1 Adult mosquito.

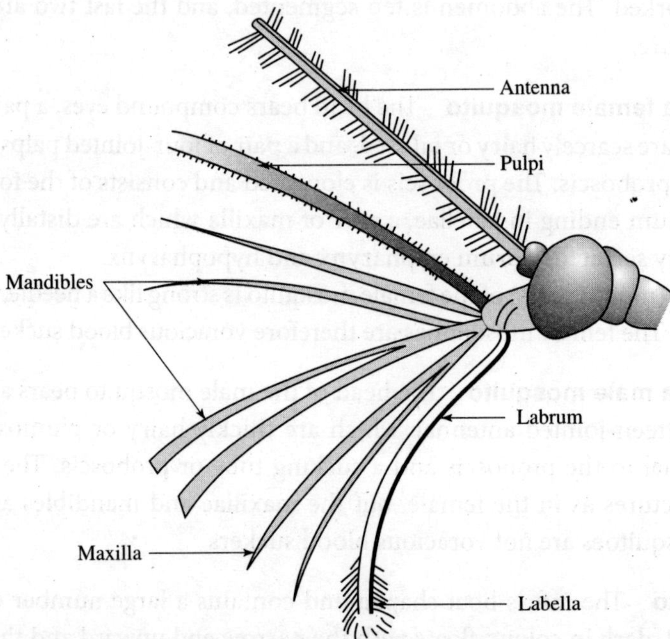

Fig. 11.2 Mouth parts of female mosquito.

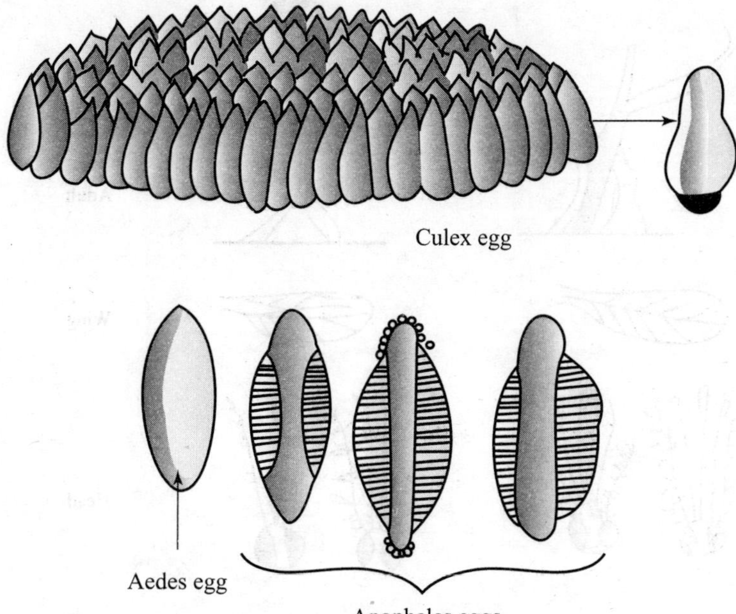

Fig. 11.3 Egg of mosquito.

Larva of mosquito (Fig 11.5) The round head of the larva has a pair of eyes and a pair of brushes near the mouth parts; there is a wide unsegmented thorax, and a nine-segmented abdomen ending in two pairs of gills. The eighth segment bears a cylindrical syphon tube. The larva rests, either hanging or parallel to the surface of water, with the syphon tube opening to the surface.

Pupa of mosquito (Fig. 11.6) The pupa has a characteristic comma shape. It has no mouth parts. Feeding is absent because the cephalothorax is unsheathed. It has a pair of trumpets and a pair of eyes. The segmented abdomen is provided with a pair of paddles at the distal end which act as a propeller while moving.

Fig. 11.4 Head of mosquito.

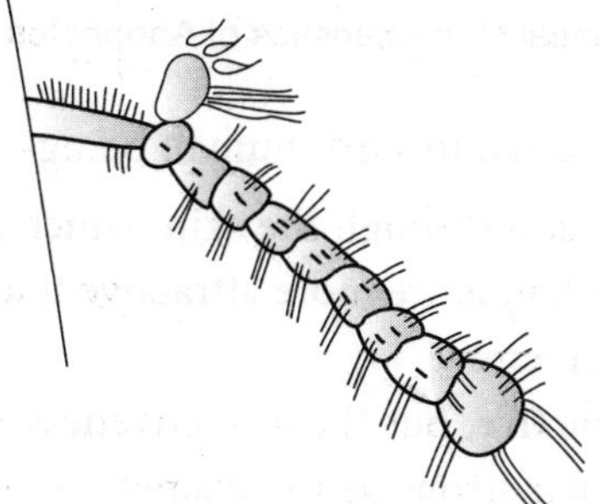

Fig. 11.5 Larva of mosquito.

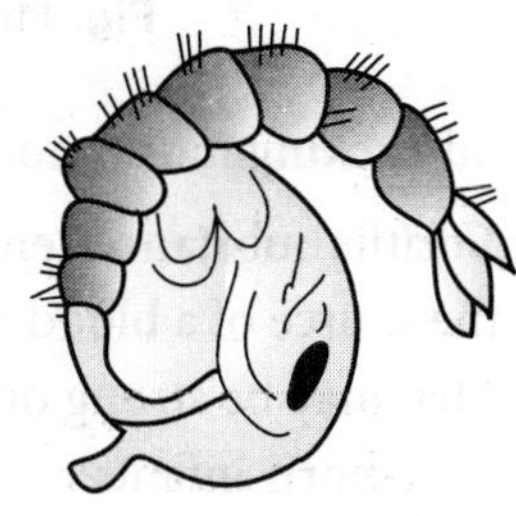

Fig. 11.6 Pupa of mosquito.

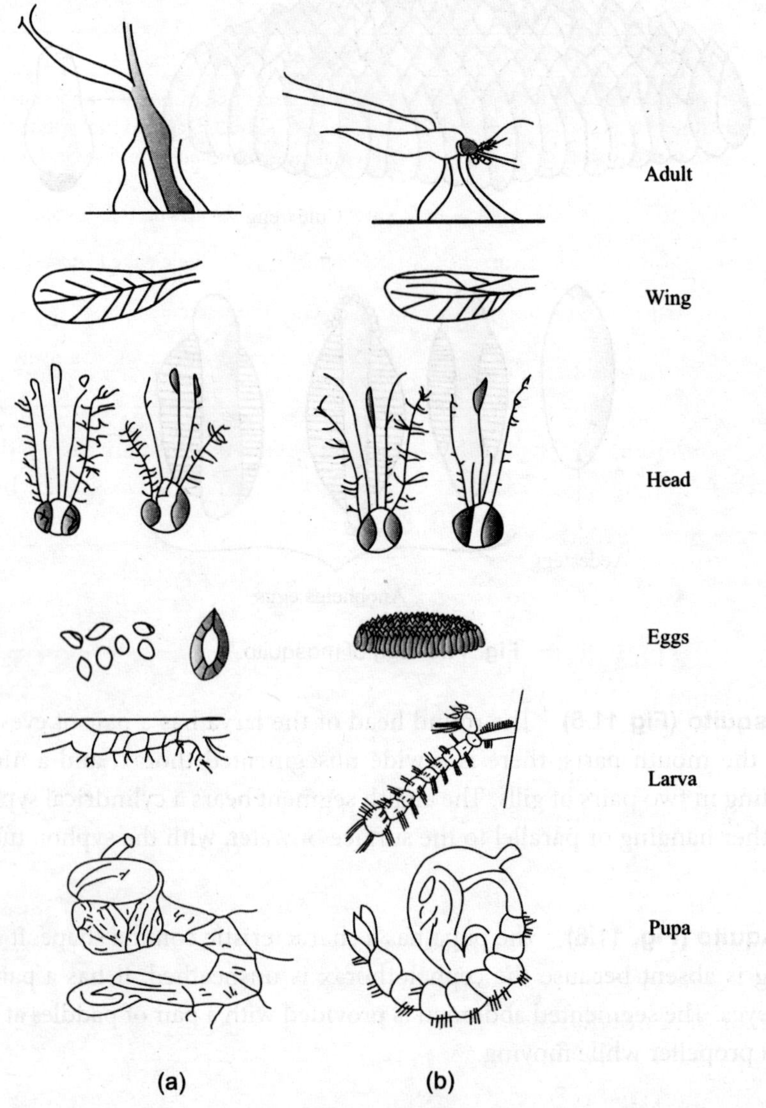

Fig. 11.7 Differential characteristics of Anopheles (a) Culex (b).

Blood-sucking mosquitoes are attracted towards human beings, because of

1. Volatile substances emitted by and through the skin, which enable the mosquitoes to find the source of a blood meal; the hands are more attractive than the arms,
2. Men may be strong or weak attractors;
3. New-born infants are less attractive, but the attractiveness increases during the first year of life and onwards. Besides, their strong sense of smell for human body odour, containing specific amino acids exuded through the sweat gland, they respond to sound vibrations

Identification of mosquitoes

Anopheles	*Culex, Aedes*
A. Adult. Rest at an oblique angle with proboscis and body in ***straight*** line; wings spotted or ***dotted***; palps of female as long as proboscis.	A. 1. Proboscis not in line with abdomen while resting; 2. Humped body; 3. Dappled (not spotted) wings; 4. Palps of female less than half of proboscis. I–*Culex* is brownish without banded legs; II–*Aedes* with white banded legs; silvery patches or scales on the thorax.
B. Eggs: Single naviculate with air sac (floats) in water.	B. In rafts (*Culex*), single naked (*Aedes*).
C. Larvae: Lie parallel to water surface while breathing.	C. Lie oblique to water surface.
D. Pupae: Breathing trumpets short and broad at margin.	D. Long, tubular breathing trumpets (*Culex*); short (*Aedes*)

through their antennal hairs, they make a sound near the human ear by their 600 wing movements per minute and travel 1–2 km per hour; they suck twice their body weight of blood during a single blood meal.

SAND FLY

Order DIPTERA
Suborder NEMATOCERA
Class INSECTA
Family PSYCHODIDAE
Species *Phlebotomus argentipes* (sand fly)

The sand fly is a delicately built, small insect. Its body consists of a head, a three-segmented thorax and a ten-segmented abdomen. The head bears a pair of sixteen-jointed antennae, equally hairy in both sexes, a pair of large compound eyes, a pair of five-jointed palps and a proboscis similar to that of the mosquito. The mesothorax bears a pair of wings, and the metathorax a pair of halteres. Each thoracic segment bears long jointed legs. The wings are lanceolate and the second wings is forked twice. The abdomen is ten segmented, and the last segment is rounded in the female, with claspers in the male. Both the body and the wings are covered with hair (Fig. 11.8).

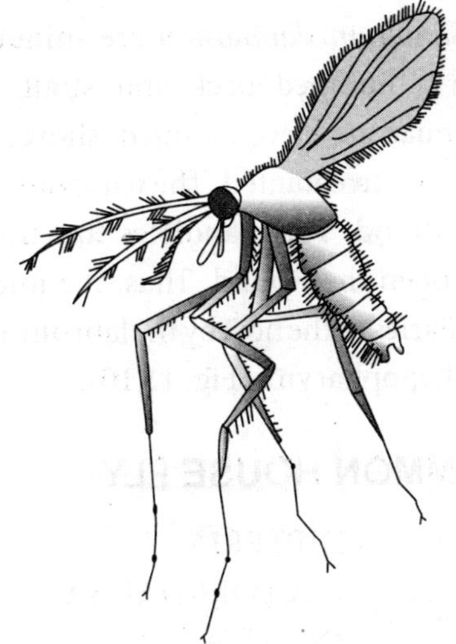

Fig. 11.8 Sand fly (*P. argentipes*).

BITING MIDGES

Suborder NEMATOCERA
Class INSECTA
Family CERATOPOGONIDAE
Species *Culicoides austeni* (biting midges)

Culicoides austeni is a minute insect. Its thorax is humped over the head. The long antennae are plumosed in the male and pylosed in the female. The proboscis is short and the wings are hairy and dappled (spotted). The wing venation is simple, the anterior veins being short (Fig. 11.9).

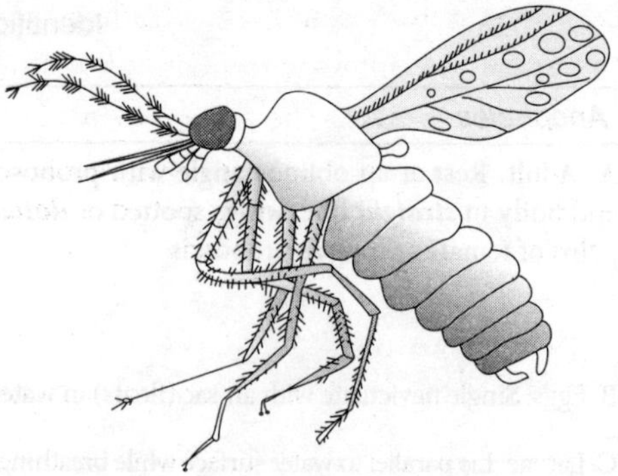

Fig. 11.9 Biting midges (*C. austeni*).

BLACK FLY

Order DIPTERIA
Suborder NEMATOCERA
Class INSECTA
Family SIMULIIDAE
Species *Simulium damnosum* (blackfly)

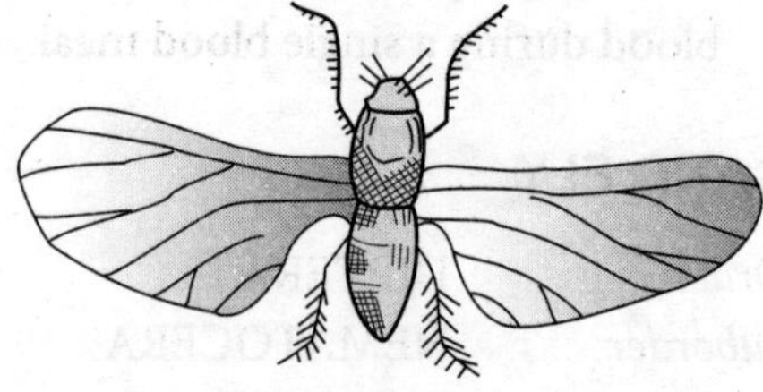

Fig. 11.10 Black fly (*S. damnosum*).

Simulium damnosum are minute, stout bodied, with a humped back and stout, short legs. The antennae are eleven jointed, short and naked. These have conspicuous eyes and the maxillary palps are five jointed. The wings are unspotted. Black flies breed in running water. Only females suck blood. The mandibles function as a pair of scissors in snipping the skin. The maxillae tear open the wound. Thus, the microfilariae of *Onchocerca* are removed from the peripheral capillaries of the host by the labrum-epipharynx and hypopharynx (Fig. 11.10).

COMMON HOUSE FLY

Order DIPTERIA
Suborder CYCLORRHAPHA
Class INSECTA
Family MUSCIDAE
Species *Musca domestica* (common house fly)

Musca domestica or the house fly is a medium-sized, slightly grey fly. Its body consists of a head, a three-segmented thorax

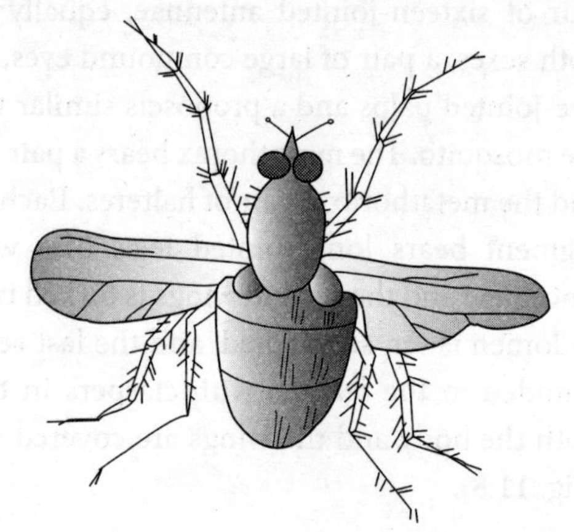

Fig. 11.11 Common house fly (*M. domestica*).

and a segmented abdomen. The head bears a pair of compound eyes, a pair of short three-segmented antennae, with bilaterally plumosed arista, a pair of two-jointed palps and a sucking type of mouth part. The thorax bears a few longitudinal stripes on the dorsum, three pairs of jointed legs and a pair of mesothoracic wings. The wings are bare and the fourth wing vein curves anteriorly, forming a closed apical cell. The abdomen is segmented, tapering posteriorly (Fig. 11.11).

Mouth Parts of Musca

The rostrum is retractile. The haustellum consists of the fulcrum, two-jointed palps, labrum-epipharynx and the labium. The fleshy labella are provided with pseudo-trachial tubes.

TSE TSE FLY

Order DIPTERIA
Suborder CYCLORRHAPHA
Class INSECTA
Family GLOSSINIDAE
Species *Glossina palpalis* (tse tse fly)

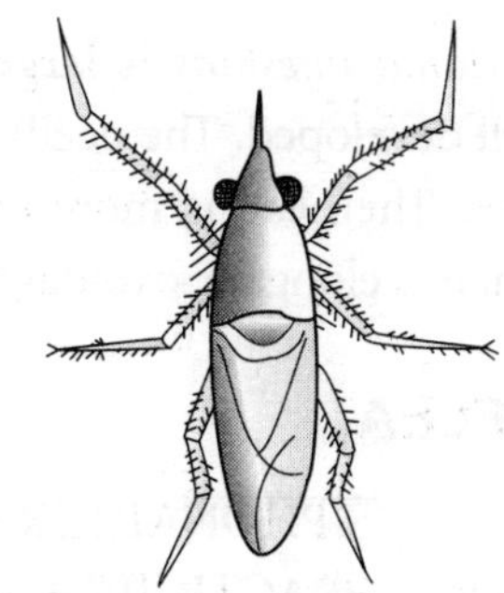

Fig. 11.12 Tse-tse fly (*G. palpalis*).

Glossina palpalis is honey brown in colour and is of the size of a house fly. The proboscis extends in front of the head. The wings have a characteristic venation and fold over one another, straight back across the abdomen. The antennae are larger and the bristles of the arista are branched. The maxillary palps are long, stout, extended organs with a flattened channel on their inner surface, in which the proboscis lies. The proboscis consists of a short, pyramidal rostrum and inconspicuous labella with rasps or teeth.

The labium enters the puncture wound made by the labellar teeth. Both males and females are voracious blood feeders. The piercing organs are flexible, like those of mosquitoes. They feed on capillary blood and the blood which escapes from the vessel (Fig. 11.12).

MANGO FLY

Order DIPTERA
Suborder BRACHYCERA
Class INSECTA
Family TABANIDAE
Species *Chrysops dimidiata* (mango fly)

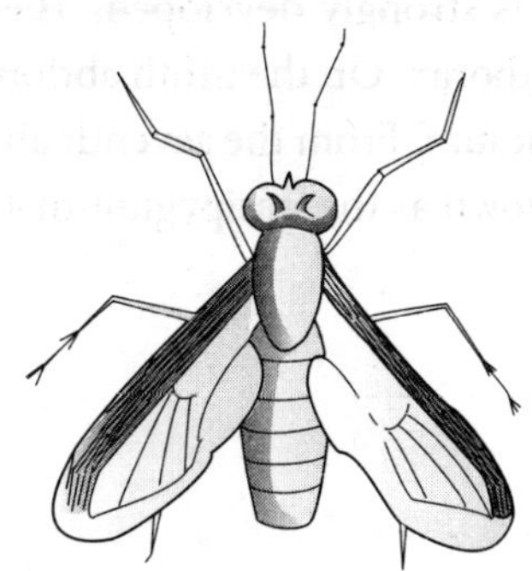

Fig. 11.13 Mango fly (*C. dimidiata*).

Chrysops dimidiata is about the size of a house fly or larger. The third segment of its long antennae is divided into five annulations, while the first and second antennal segments are both long. The hind tibiae are terminally spurred, and the wings are usually black banded. It has secondary eye-spots (Fig. 11.13).

ASSASSIN BUG

Order HETEROPTERA
Suborder GYMNOCERATA
Class INSECTA
Family TRIATOMIDAE
Species *Triatoma infestans* (assassin bug, kissing bug)

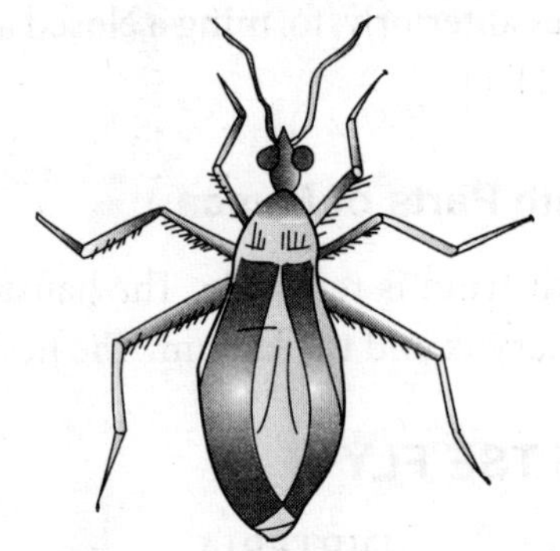

Fig. 11.14 Assassin bug (*T. infestans*).

Triatoma infestans is large in size, and its wings are well developed. The ocelli are present posterior to the eyes. The head is more or less cone shaped. The abdomen is elongate, ovoidal and is not conspicuously flattened (Fig. 11.14).

RAT FLEA

Order SIPHONAPTERA
Suborder FRACTICIPTA and INTEGRECIPTA
Class INSECTA
Family PULICIDAE
Species *Xenopsylla cheopis* (rat flea)

The body of *X. cheopis* is laterally flattened and consists of a head, a three-segmented thorax and a ten-segmented abdomen. The head is roughly triangular and anteriorly rounded and bears two pairs of three-jointed antennae in the antennal groove, and a pair of pigmented eyes. The mouth parts are of the biting and sucking types. There is the genal comb at the ventral border of the head. The thorax bears three pairs of jointed legs, of which the mesothorax pair is strongly developed. There are sixteen pro-natal combs at the posterior border of the pro-thorax. On the ninth abdominal segment, there is a saddle-shaped structure known as the 'pygidium'. From the seventh abdominal segment, a pair of bristles overhang the pygidium and is known as the 'antipygidium' (Fig. 11.15).

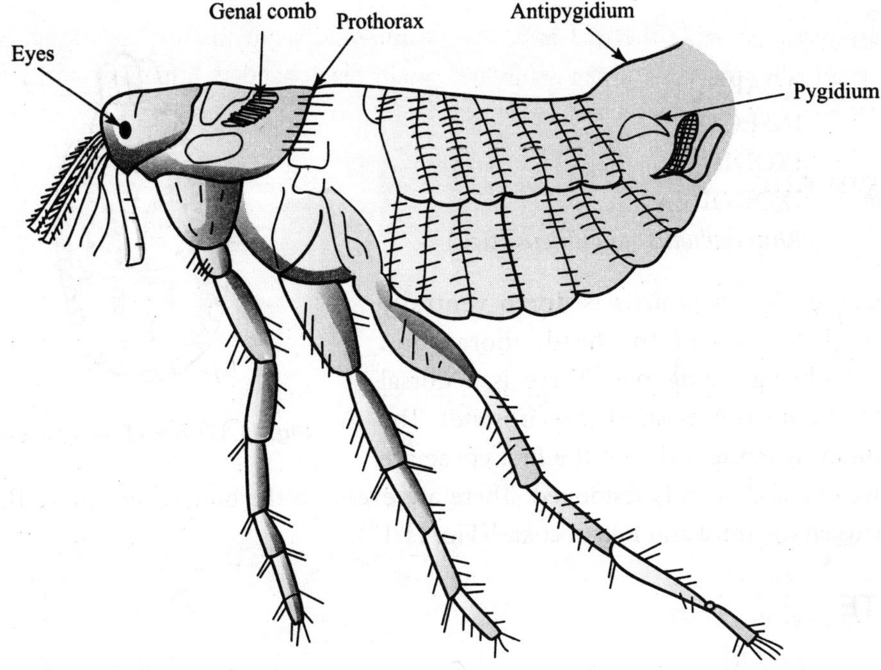

Fig. 11.15 Rat flea (*X. cheopsis*).

SUCKING LOUSE

Order ANOPLURA
Class INSECTA
Species *Pediculus humanus* (sucking louse)

Pediculus humanus is a small insect with a dorsoventrally flattened body which consists of a head, a three-segmented thorax and a ten-segmented abdomen. The head is roughly conical, bears a pair of five-jointed antennae, and biting and sucking types of mouth parts. The thorax bears three pairs of jointed legs ending in claws. There are mesothoracic spiracles, a large oval spiracle from the second to the seventh segment. The abdomen is broad with a festooned border, and the legs are provided with claws adapted for clinging to hairs or fibres (Fig. 11.16).

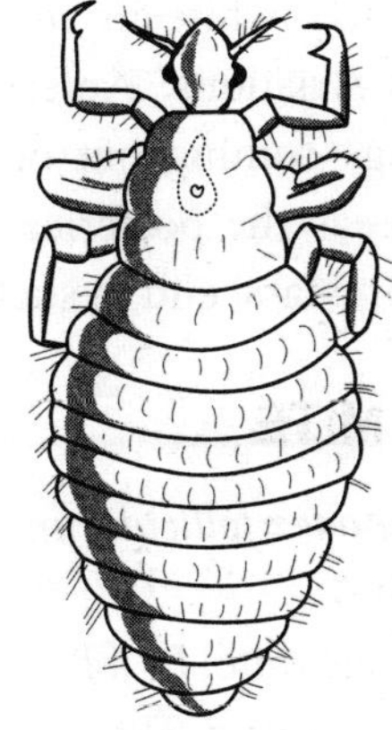

Fig. 11.16 Sucking louse (*P. humanus*).

TICK

Order	ACARI
Class	INSECTA
Family	IXODIDAE
Superfamily	IXODODEA
Species	*Rhipicephalus sanguineus* (tick)

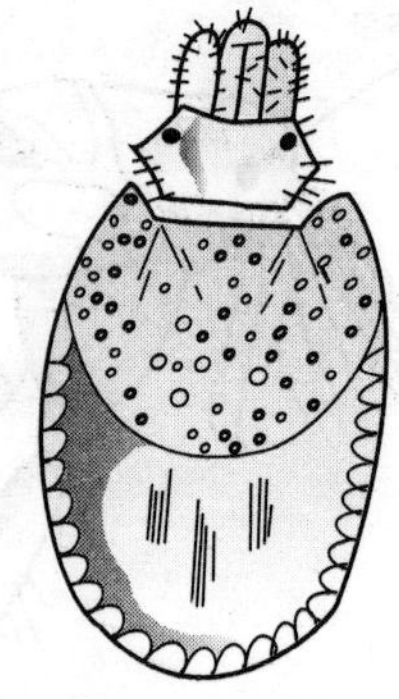

Fig. 11.17 Tick (*T. sanguineus*).

The body of *R. sanguineus* is dorso-ventrally flattened and consists of the head, thorax and abdomen, all being contiguous. There is a dorsal scutum and the rostrum is short (brevirostate). The basis capitulum is hexagonal, and the first coxae are deeply bifid. The abdomen is festooned. There are eyes and the body is inornate. There is a spiracle between the third and fourth coxae (Fig. 11.17).

ITCH MITE

Order	ACARI
Class	INSECTA
Superfamily	SARCOPTOIDEA
Family	SARCOPTIDAE
Species	*Sarcoptes scabiei* (itch mite)

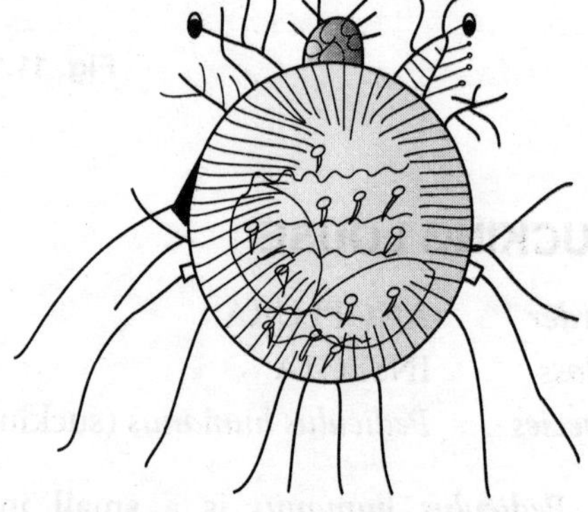

Fig. 11.18 Itch mite (*S. scabiei*).

Sarcoptes scabiei has a round or globular body, which is dirty white in colour with numerous scales and striations. Anteriorly, there are two pairs of legs coming out of the margin of the body, whereas the posterior legs remain within the body. The tarsi end in suckers (Fig. 11.18).

MANGE MITE

Species Demodex folliculorum
(Mange mite)

The mange mite, *D. folliculorum,* has a spindle-shaped body, which is anteriorly round and posteriorly tapering. The head, thorax and abdomen are clearly differentiated. The abdomen is elongated, posteriorly tapering, with numerous transverse striations (Fig. 11.19).

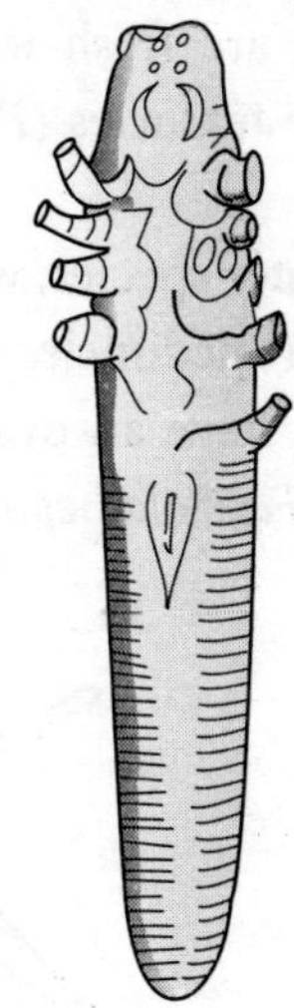

Fig. 11.19 Mange mite (*D. folliculorum*).

PHYLUM MOLLUSCA (SNAIL)

Mollusca are fleshy invertebrates lacking segmentation, with reduced body cavity, and usually an exoskeleton which frequently takes the form of a shell.

Gastropoda (Snails)

Gastropoda have asymmetrical organization, a well-developed head with contractile tentacles and a shell spirally coiled, at least in the larval stage.

Vectors And Diseases Transmitted

Genus	*Common name*	*Diseases*
Anopheles (female) Anopheles, Culex,	mosquito	Malaria
Aedes (female)	mosquito	Filariasis
Glossina	tse tse fly	African sleeping sickness
Phlebotomus	sand fly	Leishmaniasis (kala azar, oriental sore)
Culicoides	biting midges	Loiasis, non-periodic filariasis in Africa
Simulium (female)	black fly	Onchocerciasis
Chrysops (female)	mango or deer fly	Loiasis
Cyclops	water copepod	Diphyllobothriasis Dracunculosis
Musca	house fly	Amebiasis
Xenopsylla	rat flea	Hymenolepsiasis
Triatoma	kissing or assassin bug	American sleeping sickness
Pediculus	louse	Typhus fever
Ixodex	tick	Typhus fever
Sarcoptes	mite	Scabies

Many species are essential intermediate hosts of important human trematodes.

Family Melaniidae (Fig. 11.20): These are fresh-water species with a broad snout and pedunculated eyes at the outer base of the tentacles *(Paragonimus westermani, Metagonimus yokogawai).*

Family Cerithiidae: These are marine water species, with a broad, short contractile rostrum, and widely separated tentacles, eyes or short peduncles *(Heterophyes heterophyes).*

Family Lymnaeidae (Fig. 11.21): These have an oval or elongated shell. Many species of Lymnaea are intermediate hosts of flukes *(Fasciola hepatica).*

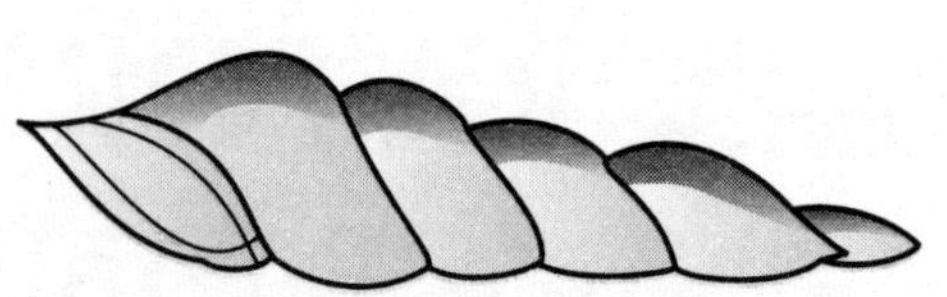

Fig. 11.20 *Melania libertina.*

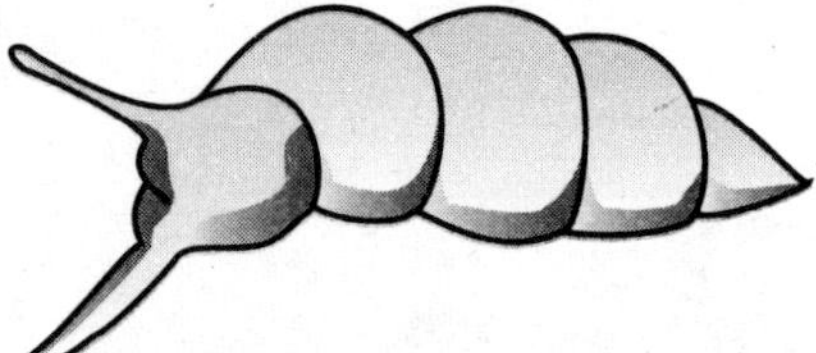

Fig. 11.21 *Lymnaea truncaluta.*

Subfamily Segmentininae (Fig. 11.22): These have small discoidal shiny shells, with or without internal partition *(Fasciolopsis huski).*

Family Ancylidae (Fig. 11.23): These have oval, large feet. The tentacles are short, blunt, and cylindrical. They have eyes at the inner base. The shell is usually cap-like *Ferrissia tenuis* (*Schistosoma haematobium*) in the endemic areas in India.

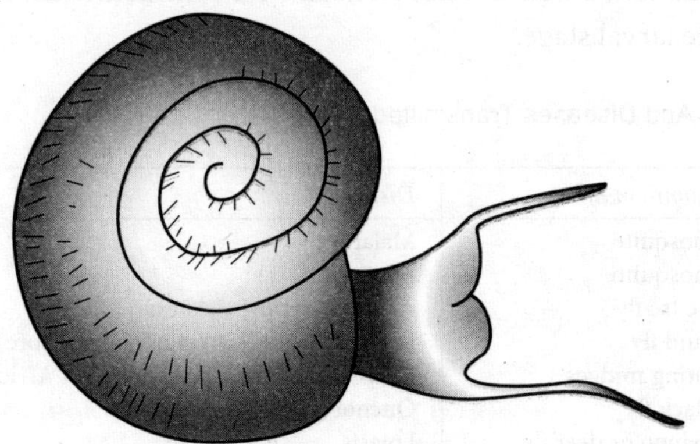

Fig. 11.22 *Segmentina.*

Fig. 11.23 *Ferrissia tenuis.*

12 LABORATORY EXAMINATIONS

BLOOD EXAMINATION FOR PARASITES

Next to the feces, the blood provides the most common medium for recovery of human parasites at various stages. From this source, routine diagnosis is made of malaria, African trypanosomiasis and most types of filariasis, less frequently Chagas' disease, and rarely, *kala azar* and toxoplasmosis.

Stains

1. LEISHMAN'S STAIN The materials required are:
1) A ground glass-stoppered bottle of 150 ml capacity,
2) A 100 ml graduated cylinder and
3) Glass pestle and mortar.

Method of preparation: All articles should be thoroughly cleaned and rinsed with methyl alcohol. First, 100 ml of methyl alcohol should be measured in the graduated cylinder. The weighed amount of Leishman powder (0.15 g) should be placed in a glass mortar and ground in a pestle, by adding methyl alcohol in small quantities. The dissolved stain should be carefully decanted off from time to time into a glass-stoppered bottle. The undissolved stain should be ground again with methyl alcohol till no residue is left and all the methyl alcohol is used up. The stoppered glass bottle with the stain should be kept in an incubator at 37°C for 24 hours before it is used.

Method of Leishman staining: Leishman's stain should be poured from the dropper bottle and diluted to twice its volume with neutral distilled water. Drying should be prevented by covering the stained slide with a petri-dish. The diluted stain should be allowed to remain over the slide for 10–15 minutes. And then the slide should be washed with running tap water, dried and examined under an oil immersion lens.

To bring out Schuffner's dots in Plasmodium: Alkaline buffer saline (sodium phosphate, 2.0 g, potassium hydrogen phosphate 1.0 mg, thymol 1.0 mg and distilled water 100 ml) is preferred for this. Leishman's stain is the best of all the Romanowsky stains for Plasmodium (Shute PG and Maryon, ME (1966) *Laboratory Techniques for the study of Malaria*, 2nd Ed. J & A Churchill Ltd, London, p: 112).

2. GIEMSA STAIN (prepared from Azure blue and eosin)

Composition

Concentrated Giemsa stain	10	ml
Methyl alcohol	10	ml
Acetone	10	ml
Phosphate buffer distilled water	100	ml

Method of Giemsa staining: The film is first fixed in pure methyl alcohol for 3–5 minutes and allowed to dry. Concentrated Giemsa stain is diluted by adding one drop of stain to each 1.0 ml of neutral distilled water. The diluted stain is poured over the film (about 5.0 ml per film is required) and kept for 30–45 minutes. The film is then washed with running tap water and dried. The stain is examined under an oil immersion lens.

3. FIELD'S STAIN This stain was developed by Field (1941) for thick blood films in the diagnosis of malaria. As in the Giemsa method for staining thick blood films, no preliminary fixation is required, but the films must be dried completely and freshly prepared.

Preparation of Field's stain: Two solutions are utilized, both isotonic and adjusted to a pH of 6.6.

Solution I

Methylene blue	0.8 g
Azure B	0.5 g
Disodium hydrogen phosphate (anhydrous)	5.0 g
Potassium dihydrogen phosphate	6.25 g
Distilled water	500 ml

Solution II

Eosin	1.0 g
Disodium hydrogen phosphate (anhydrous)	5.0 g
Potassium dihydrogen phosphate	6.25 g
Distilled water	500 ml

The phosphate salts are first made up in solution in the distilled water and the respective stains are added. (The azure B should be first ground in a mortar with a little of the phosphate solution). Each dye solution is stored for 24 hours, and then filtered. If any scum or precipitate forms later, refilteration is required. The stains may be kept for several weeks and used over and over, if they are kept in covered staining jars. When the eosin solution becomes greenish, it is no longer useful and should be replaced with fresh solution.

Technique of Field staining: The film is dipped just for a second in solution I. It is immediately cleaned with water until the stain ceases to flow from the film. The film is again dipped for a second in solution II and rinsed in clean water. It is then placed in a vertical position to dry.

4. JSB STAIN (Singh and Bhattacharji, 1944)

This is the rapid Romanowsky's method of staining malarial parasites.

Solution I	
Methylene blue	0.5 g
Potassium dichromate	0.5 g
Sulphuric acid (one per cent)	3.0 ml
Potassium hydroxide (one per cent)	10 ml
Distilled water	500 ml

Methylene blue is dissolved in 500 ml of distilled water in a narrow mouth flask. Sulphuric acid and potassium dichromate are added one after another. The solution is heated up in a water bath to boiling point for a period of 2–3 hours, till it turns blue. The solution is allowed to cool at room temperature till steel blue, needle-like crystals appear. At this stage, 10 ml of 1% potassium hydroxide is added, drop by drop, the flask being shaken continuously. A greater portion of the precipitate is dissolved and the liquid is filtered several times till the dye remaining on the filter paper is completely dissolved. The solution is left to mature at room temperature for 48 hours and then used.

Solution II	
Eosin	1.0 g
Distilled water	500 ml.

Method of JSB staining thick blood film: The slide is immersed in solution I for 10 seconds and washed for two seconds in a jar containing acidulated tap water adjusted to pH 6.2–6.6 by addition of 5% acetic or citric acid. The film is stained with solution II for one second and washed in the same jar for five seconds. It is immersed in solution I again for 10 seconds and washed as above for 10 seconds or till the smear gives a pink background. The film is then dried and examined.

Method of JSB staining for thick and thin films on the same slide: The thin smear is fixed in methyl alcohol for a second or two and dried. The whole slide is immersed in solution I for 30 seconds and washed in a jar containing acidulated tap water (ph 6.2–6.6). It is stained with solution II for a second and washed again in the same jar for four seconds. It is immersed in solution I again for 30 seconds and washed in acidulated water for 10 seconds or till the smear gives a pink background. It is then dried and examined.

Preparation of combined thick and thin films on the same slide: This method is of special value in survey work. Two drops of blood are taken on one slide with one about half an inch from the right end of the slide and the other, one inch from the same end of the slide. The former is made into a thick film and the latter into a thin film.

Preparation of films

Thin film on one slide: A drop of blood is taken at one end of the slide. A spreader is held at an angle of 45° and pushed in the opposite direction to make a smear.

Thick film on one slide: Four drops of blood are placed at the corners of a half inch square slide and joined to form a thick film. A glass slide with corners cut at one end or the coverslip of a hemocytometer can be used as spreaders.

Dehemoglobination of a thick film may be done as follows:

1. With glacial acetic acid and tartaric acid mixture:

Glacial acetic acid (2%)	4 parts
Crystal tartaric acid (2%)	1 part

   The film should be flooded with the mixture and as soon as the dehemoglobination is complete (as indicated by the greyish white colour of the film), the fluid is drained off by tilting. It is then fixed with methyl alcohol for 3–5 minutes. The slide is then washed thoroughly with neutral or slightly alkaline distilled water, so that every trace of the acid is removed.
2. In distilled water: The film is placed in a vertical position in a glass cylinder for 5–10 minutes. After dehemoglobination, the film is stained with Leishman's or Giemsa's stain in the same way as the thin film.

Examination of Blood for Malarial Parasites

Time for taking blood The blood specimen should be obtained several hours after the paroxysm has reached its peak, because the parasites are more easily detected in the film.

The schizogony of *Plasmodium vivax, P. malariae* and *P. ovale* can readily be demonstrated in the peripheral blood during both the febrile and afebrile periods. The best time for demonstrating *P. falciparum* is a few hours after the febrile paroxysm reaches its peak, because *P. falciparum* disappears from the peripheral blood during the afebrile period. Generally, the blood film should be taken when the patient is seen first and thereafter.

While drawing blood films for demonstrating malarial parasites, it will be useful to have both thin and thick films, either on one slide or on two different slides, and to examine them after staining. The thin film is examined first. If the parasites are identified, there is no need for examining the thick film. The thick film is examined if the parasites are not found in the thin film. If the parasites are found in the thick film but cannot be identified, then the thin smear is to be examined thoroughly to determine the species of Plasmodium.

Remarks on the examination of thin blood film Before a thin film slide is declared 'negative' for malarial parasites, it is necessary to observe certain rules:

1. The area of the film examined should be along the upper and lower margins of the 'tail' end of the film, because the parasites are more numerous there.
2. A minimum of 100 fields should be examined and the time taken for such examination should be about 8–10 minutes. The clinical attacks of malaria are associated with the presence of at least one parasite per 100 fields.

Remarks on the examination of thick blood film When the red blood cells are 'laked' by dehemoglobination, they remain unstained. The only elements seen in the film are the stained parasites and leucocytes. In the thick film, the morphology of the malarial parasites is distorted, and the relationship between the parasites and the red blood cells cannot be observed. Hence, it is difficult to identify the species of parasites in a thick film. Examination of the thick film is not the method of choice and can be considered as a concentration method for detecting the parasites, as it contains a larger amount of blood in a given area than does a thin film. The thick film saves a lot of time as one microscopic field is equivalent to 50 microscopic fields of a thin film. Thick films are often employed in mass surveys for quick diagnosis.

On severe falciparum malaria, it is important to know the degree of parasitemia so that the patient can be given appropriate treatment.

Malarial parasite density
1–10/100 high power fields .... +
11–20/100 high power fields .... + +
1–10 in every high power field .... + + +
More than 10 in every high power field... + + +

Parasitic Count

WBC count × Parasites count against 100 WBC/100

Examination of Blood for Microfilariae

Blood Culture

Blood for cultures should be collected between 10 p.m. and 2 a.m. in areas where the microfilaria shows nocturnal periodicity. In case of non-nocturnal periodicity, the blood may be taken at any time, preferably in the morning.

Examination of unstained preparation Two or three drops of blood are taken on a clean glass slide and a coverslip is put on. The rim of the coverslip is then smeared with vaseline to prevent drying up of the blood. The slide should be examined the next morning under the

SEROLOGICAL TESTS IN PARASITIC DISEASES

PARTICULATE AGGLUTINATION TESTS

	CFT	*Precipitin Flocculation*	*Bentonite Flocculation*	*Hemaggluti-nation*	*Latex Agglutination*	*Cholestrol Flocculation*	*Fluorescent Antibody*
Trichinosis	+	+	+	D	+	+	+
Echinococcus	+	D	+	+	+		E
Schistosomiasis	+	+	D	D	D	+	.
Ascariasis	E	D	+	+			.
Filariasis	D		+	+			.
Cysticercosis	+	+		+			D
Chagas' disease	+			+	E		E
Leishmaniasis	D			D			+
Toxoplasmosis	+			+			D
Amebiasis	+	+	+	+			+
Malaria	E			D	E		+

+ Generally accepted.

D Requires further development.

E Under experimental investigation.

low power objective of the microscope. The microfilaria, if present, may be seen wriggling about in the blood (the microfilaria may remain alive for a period of 24–48 hours in such a preparation).

Examination of stained preparation A thick film of blood is prepared and kept covered. The next morning, it is dehemoglobinised by the slide being put in water, dried and fixed in methyl alcohol and then stained with Leishman's stain or Giemsa stain. Microfilaria may be detected occasionally even in a thin film.

Vital staining Fresh blood or the sediment after dehemoglobination is mixed with methylene blue solution (1:5000 in physiological saline). The living microfilariae of *L. loa* and O. *volvulus* take up the stain in 10 minutes, whereas the microfilariae of *W. bancrofti* and *B. malayi* take up the stain much more slowly.

Recent Parasitic Serology

Serological tests are most helpful when the diagnostic forms cannot be readily demonstrated as in tissue infection like amebic liver abscess (ALA), trichinosis, visceral larval migrans and toxoplasmosis.

Immuno-diagnostic tests to detect parasitic antigens have been described for a number of infections and could eventually replace morphological diagnosis of many parasites. Monoclonal antibodies may be particularly helpful in developing sensitive and specific antigen detection tests.

Antigenic structure of parasites is complex and cross reactions in serological tests are common. Newer tests using different or more purified antigens have given better results. Various types of tests have been described. Agglutination tests use whole organisms or antigen-coated particles such as in bentonite flocculation (BF), indirect hemagglutination (IHA) and latex agglutination (LA). Complement fixation (CF) test has been widely used, but it is being superseded by newer tests. Precipitin tests include capillary precipitin, double gel diffusion, counter-immunoelectrophoresis (CIE) and circumlarval precipitation. Indirect immunofluorescence (IIF) has been widely used in parasitic serology and is readily adapted to detect IgM antibody. Recent test development has emphasized Enzyme linked immunosorbent assay (ELISA) and Soluble antigen fluorescent antibody (SAFA) such as Automated fluoroimmunoassay (FLAX) system, although some improved tests are based on the modification of older methods (e.g. IIF, CIE). Thus, improvements in serological methods and antigens are causing rapid changes in parasitic serology.

Cross reactions are common and the sensitivity and/or specificity of some tests may be poor. In addition, serology may not distinguish between previous and active infection, thus for some infections, serology may be useful in screening persons who have visited an endemic area, whereas they are of little value in diagnosing infection in residents of the endemic area. The presence of antibody does not necessarily indicate immunity.

Immuno-diagnostic procedures for detecting antigen or antibody in parasitic diseases are numerous and are changing rapidly.

ELISA technique In the micro-ELISA for detection of antibody, the antigen is coated on to the surface of wells in a micro-titration plate. The patient's serum is then added and time allowed for an antigen–antibody reaction to occur. An enzyme labeled specific antiglobulin is then added, which attaches to the antigen–antibody complexes. Any unattached, antiglobulin is washed away. An enzyme substrate is then added, which is acted upon by the attached enzyme producing a colour, which can be measured colorimetrically or interpreted visually. Commonly used enzymes are peroxidase or phosphatase. Penicillinase is found to be useful, cheaper and can be prepared in India.

In recent years, ELISA is used to assist in the diagnosis of malaria, amebiasis, schistosomiasis, onchocerciasis, leishmaniasis, echinococcosis, trypanosomiasis, trichinellosis and toxoplasmosis. ELISA is more sensitive and specific than other serological tests.

Amebiasis Serodiagnostic procedure depends on the type of infection present, a very low degree of sensitivity is found with sera from asymptomatic carriers, increased sensitivity from patients with amebic dysentery and the greatest sensitivity with sera from those patients with extra-intestinal disease. The CF has been generally replaced by IHA, CIF and indirect fluorescent antibody (IFA) procedures. These three tests have more or less the same degree of sensitivity.

A new fluorescence (FIAX) technique, in which the fluorescence is measured in a fluorometer, is a new test that has been adapted to routine diagnosis of amebiasis. The technique has been developed for the detection of antigen in feces. The sensitivity of this test is quite good, although the only parasite detected is *E. histolytica.*

Invasive amebiasis by *E. histolytica* can be detected by a very recent technique – cellulose acetate precipitin (CAP) test.

Dot immunobinding assay (DIB) and sandwich ELISA can be used in the diagnosis of invasive amebiasis. Both tests are equally specific and sensitive. DIB is easier to perform, is less expensive and recommended for detection of antibody in patients with invasive amebiasis (amebic liver abscess ALA) in India (1992).

Western blot of *E. histolytica* may become one of the very recent, more accurate methods for the successful immunodiagnosis and epidemiology of acute intestinal amebiasis.

Giardiasis ELISA is compared with microscopy for the detection of Giardia fecal antigens. ELISA was highly sensitive and specific, either visually (95 and 97% respectively) or by optical density determination (99 and 96% respectively). ELISA is extremely effective for epidemiology study.

Toxoplasmosis The methylene blue dye (MBD) test, Sabin–Feldman dye test, has been used for many years for the serological diagnosis of toxoplasmosis. This procedure has been replaced by the IHA and IFA procedures, both of them are technically simple to perform and utilize a killed antigen rather than live organisms (used in the MBD test). All these procedures are equally sensitive and specific between procedures and can be performed using specific conjugates of IgM, although the interpretations of the results are difficult. Congenital infections are generally indicated when sera from newborns are positive with IgM conjugates.

IgM antibody methods may give both false positive and false negative results, because of the rheumatoid factor, blocking antibody and the induction of factor IgM antibody against maternal globulin. The double sandwich ELISA test has eliminated many of these problems. The combination of IFA and IHA procedures allows more accurate interpretation, because a different type of antigen is used for each test.

Tests for IgM antibody (IgM fluorescent antibody or double sandwich ELISA technique) are particularly useful for establishing recent toxoplasma infection, because titres appear early (as early as five days after infection) and disappear within several months. IgM antibodies are elevated in acute disease. CFT using soluble, toxoplasma antigen becomes positive three to six weeks after infection, rises for two to eight months and falls to a very low level after one to two years.

Very recently, the direct agglutination test with 2-mercaptoethanol (AD-2ME) and immunofluorescent antibody test (IFAT) are used in the diagnosis of toxoplasmosis. The former is a little superior to the latter.

Pneumocystosis The tests of choice for pneumocystis are the CF and IFA tests and can detect in 85% of infected patients. A direct fluorescent antibody test has been developed for the detection of organisms in mucus and sputum smears and tissue biopsies.

During the last few years, CIE and ELISA were evaluated. They are still not easily available. They lack specificity and sensitivity, so they are not used successfully in routine clinical diagnosis. The development of culture technique for this organism may lead to more specific antigen production.

Leishmaniasis The serological procedures (IHA, IFA and CF) are available for visceral leishmaniasis and are quite helpful in making diagnosis and IFA is being used routinely with excellent results using amastigote antigen for cutaneous leishmaniasis. The IFA test is more specific than ELISA for diagnosis of cutaneous leishmaniasis, but neither is satisfactory as microscopic examination. Both methods were acceptable for the diagnosis of visceral leishmaniasis when promastigote forms of *L. donovani* were used as antigen. ELISA test, using promastigotes as antigen, is probably the most practical for testing the number of sera. The IFA technique employing either amastigotes or promastigotes as antigen has been used as direct agglutination test (DAT) of fixed promastigotes. There may be cross reaction with serum of patient infected with *T. cruzi*. The leishmanin skin (delayed hypersensitivity) test is negative in cases of active visceral leishmaniasis (AVL).

An immunodot assay has been very recently developed for serodiagnosis of AVL which utilizes protein A colloidal gold as the visualizing agent. The test is simple, requires few reagents and can be completed in two hours. It is sensitive and specific for AVL and generally correlates with ELISA. Either whole blood or sera in minute quantities may be used as test antibody.

Besides, recent indirect ELISA tests for *L. donovani* antibody was carried out with enzyme labelled protein A or protein G, instead of anti-immunogloubulin. It was found that this modification improved the positive/negative discrimination. In addition, antibody could be measured in human sera.

Most recently, monoclonal antibody L_{12} F_7 against the antigen of *L. donovani* promastigotes was labeled with peroxidase and used in the dot–ELISA test for detecting circulating antigen in sera of cases with visceral leishmaniasis. The results showed that monoclonal antibody can be used in dot–ELISA for diagnosis of visceral leishmaniasis. It is of special significance that this method can be used as a simple and reliable tool for field evaluation of therapeutic effectiveness for visceral leishmaniasis.

A recent technique that may permit direct and rapid diagnosis of cutaneous leishmaniasis, as well as differentiation of leishmania, is blotting with radiolabelled DNA probes.

A positive leishmanin skin test and serum antibody can be demonstrated in patients by the time a cutaneous lesion has ulcerated. These tests remain positive in mucocutaneous disease. Serological tests are not useful in the diagnosis, because antibody levels are low. Positive skin test and serological test can reflect a previous rather than a current leishmanial infection. A direct agglutination test (DAT) is useful and sensitive in the diagnosis of cutaneous leishmaniasis.

Chagas' disease Serological testing is generally not needed for diagnosis of acute disease. Parasite specific IgM antibody detected by immunofluorescence or direct agglutination does not become positive until 20 to 40 days after the onset of symptoms. The diagnosis of chronic Chagas' disease requires demonstration of antibody to *T. cruzi* in the presence of characteristic cardiac abnormalities. Very recently, in Brazil, American trypanosomiasis (*T. cruzi*) can be diagnosed by testing blood donors for infection by G-agglutination test (WHO). HIA and IIF tests are also used.

African sleeping sickness Several immuno-diagnostic tests have been developed for African trypanosomiasis – IFA, ELISA, Capillary hemagglutination (HA) tests that are useful for epidemiological surveys. However, at present, no serological test provides sufficient definite information for treatment of a patient without demonstration of the organism. A card agglutination test (CATT) has been recently produced. It is simple, specific, sensitive. It is yet to be fully evaluated.

Malaria A variety of serological tests have been developed for malaria, but are not usually used for the diagnosis of clinical infection. They are particularly useful for epidemiological survey and detection of infected blood donors. Those most commonly used are indirect immunofluorescent (IIF) and IHA tests. IIF titres, equal to or greater than 1:64, are suggestive of recent infection with Plasmodium. These serological tests showed a false positive rate of 1% or less and have a sensitivity of over 95%. Development of natural immunity in *P. falciparum* malaria can be detected by Western blot. The rather innovative test 'ABC–ELISA' is merely a novel abbreviation for avidin–biotin complex ELISA. It is a useful method for malaria serology in the field and is most recent. A conventional ELISA is carried out, but instead of enzyme-labeled antiglobulin, biotin-labelled antigloublin is followed by avidin-labeled enzyme (one additional step). The results of this new test correlated well with those obtained by immunofluorescence and was better than those of the conventional ELISA.

The IFA test and micro-ELISA test for detection of antimalarial antibodies have little value in endemic areas. Recently, monoclonal antibody has been introduced for the detection of plasmodial antigen in human blood for the diagnosis of malaria by IFA technique.

In India, the IIF test is used for the diagnosis of malaria by using *P. falciparum* antigen. The diagnostic titre is 1:80. Besides, 80% seropositivity was observed by mean ELISA – optical density values to both *P. falciparum* and *P. vivax*.

Plasmodial antigen can be detected by monoclonal antibody as a routine screening procedure for blood donors in transfusion medicine in endemic countries like India.

Cryptosporidiosis A serological test has been described (*J Clin Microbiol* 18:165, 1983).

Trichinellosis Diagnosis is often established indirectly by serological tests, some are commercially available. The most commonly used are bentonite flocculation (BF), fluorescent antibody (IIF) and complement fixation (CF). BF is very sensitive and usually becomes negative, two or three years after an infection; thus, a positive test usually indicates active infection. The test becomes positive after the third week of infection and is most helpful when a four-fold increase in titre in paired sera can be demonstrated. The CF test detects antibodies slightly earlier than the BF test. IIF is considered to be as good as the BF test and most sensitive.

Filariasis Serological tests using extracts of *Dirofilaria immitis* as antigen include IHA and BF, but they allow only a diagnosis of filarial group rather than the species. Moreover, there is cross reactivity with other parasites (false positive).

Western blot technique and ELISA can be used to detect antibody for *B. malayi* in filarial endemic area of different groups of patients.

Schistosomiasis Several serological tests (cholestrol–lecithin flocculation, BF, CF and IFA) are used for the diagnosis of schistosomiasis, all share problems of specificity and sensitivity. There has been increased use of IFA procedure which uses sections of an adult worm for the antigen and has proved to be a most sensitive technique (less cross reactivity with other sera).

The circumoval precipitin test is used extensively for diagnosis of *S. japonicum* infection. ELISA technique is sensitive as the IFA and CF titres with adult worm using an antigen, but indicates that ELISA was more specific.

Cysticercosis IHA was 85% reactive with sera from proved cases of human infection. The double diffusion was sensitive, using both animal and human sera. Cross reaction with sera from patients infected with Echinococcus species, *T. saginata* and Coenurus species have been reported.

Echinococcosis The IHA, IFA and immunoelectrophoresis (IE) procedures are considered to be the tests of choice for the diagnosis of echinococcosis. IHA and BF are routinely used at the Centre for Disease Control (CDC), USA. Of these, the IHA is most sensitive. Much of the IHA titres usually indicate the presence of hydatid disease. IE test has been evaluated in many countries, a double diffusion band 5 (DD^5) test has been reported to be more sensitive and more specific than the IE test. CIE test has also been reported to be specific and sensitive and ELISA has also been evaluated. IHA titre of 1:256 is considered significant and is positive in 88% of people with non-calcified hepatic cyst. Low titre with any of these tests do not necessarily mean infection, since sera from patients with other conditions, such as liver cirrhosis and collagen diseases, cross react. Cross reaction with cestode larvae, such as cysticercus, are also common. In addition, patients with calcified hepatic cysts or cysts of the lung, frequently have negative serology. Immunoblot test for human *E. granulosus* infection is under trial. Use of capture ELISA can be advocated to detect specific immune complex in serum and could be available in monitoring a certain endemic areas of active *E. granulosus* infection.

Visceral larva migrans Serological tests may aid in establishing the diagnosis. Different methods vary in sensitivity and specificity. The ELISA using embryonated egg extract as antigen offers much better sensitivity and specificity, and cross reacting with an Ascaris antibody can be removed by preadsorption. In visceral larva migrans, a significant titre is 1:32, whereas if ocular toxocariasis is suspected, a titre of 1:8 is significant.

Strongyloidiasis The results of the indirect agglutination test with newly developed gelatin particles were found quite comparable to those of IHA and ELISA. The test is simple and rapid to perform for mass screening for human strongyloidiasis. Very recently, the sensitivity, specificity, positive and negative predicted values of ELISA test using F_2, protein fraction from *S. stercoralis* were 95, 96.4, 95 and 96.4% respectively, as the latest observation. Immunoblot can be useful in the diagnosis of human strongyloidiasis.

Filariasis In India, very recently, Dot–ELISA in the detection of *W. bancrofti* filarial antibody was compared with standard ELISA, the dot–ELISA was found more sensitive. Besides, ELISA developed using soluble antigen of adult *B. malayi* gave positive responses in 95% of cases in India.

Onchocercosis can be diagnosed by recent immunoblot test.

Dracunculosis Most recently, the Falcon assay screening test–enzyme linked immunosorbent assay (FAST-ELISA) and enzyme linked immunoelectrotransfer blot (EITB) techniques are used to test human sera with *D. medinensis* adult worm antigen.

Serological tests performed at the Centre for Disease Control (CDC), USA (1990).

Diseases	*Tests*	*Diagnostic titres*
Amebiasis	IHA	1:256
Ascariasis	ELISA	1:128
Babesiosis	IIF	1:16
Chagas' disease	CF	1:8
Cysticercosis	IHA	1:128
Echinococcosis	IHA	1:256
Filariasis	IHA	1:128
Leishmaniasis	DAT	1:64
Malaria	IIF	1:64
Paragomoniasis	CF	1:8
Pneumocystosis	IIF	1:16
Schistosomiasis	IIF	Positive
Strongyloidiasis	IHA	1:64
Toxocariasis	ELISA	1:32
Toxoplasmosis	IIF, IIF – IgM+	1:256; 1:64
Trichinellosis	BFT	1:5

IHA – Indirect hemagglutination; CF – Complement fixation;

DAT – Direct agglutination test; IIF – Indirect immunofluorescence;

BFT – Bentonite flocculation test;

ELISA – Enzyme Linked Immunosorbent Assay;

+ Any IIF – IgM titre to toxoplasmosis in an infant less than two years old is strongly suggestive of infection.

The diagnostic titres given are highly suggestive of clinical disease, but a four-fold rise in titre is stronger evidence.

Infections due to Toxoplasma gondii and Trypanosoma cruzi

The advent of Polymerase Chain Reaction (PCR) has opened up the possibility of isolating DNA sequence from ancient samples from museum specimens and archeological findings. As a majority of these molecules in these ancient samples are degraded to such an extent as to preclude any other molecular technique, PCR with its remarkable sensitivity can be employed to amplify the existing few molecules to an appreciable extent, which can then be further studied.

For example, for the diagnosis of infections caused by RNA viruses by PCR, RNA has to be first converted into the complementary DNA (CDNA). CDNA is obtained by a reverse transcriptase assay, using RNA as the template. This step takes two hours. The CDNA thus obtained is next used as the template in the PCR assay.

Serological tests which have wider use are commonly carried out and most of these tests are well standardized. However, serological tests are essentially indirect tests, except when antigens are detected. The more direct tests involve demonstration of the pathogen or pathogen-specific nucleic acid (DNA or RNA) in the clinical diagnosis.

Therefore, the Polymerase Chain Reaction offers a rapid, sensitive and a very specific diagnostic approach for protozoal diseases caused by *Toxoplasma gondii* or *Trypanosoma cruzi*.

Microfilaria count About 20 mm^3 of blood should be placed on a clean glass slide with the help of the hemoglobinometer pipette, dried as a thick film, dehemoglobinised and stained as usual. The total number of microfilaria in the thick smear, multiplied by 50, will give the number per ml of blood.

Survey work Two new techniques for detecting and counting microfilaria are as follows:

1) Counting chamber technique in which a measured quantity (20 mm^3) of hemolysed blood is directly examined, and
2) Membrane filter concentration technique using a millipore membrane or nucleopore filter, where the microfilaria liberated from a measured quantity (10 ml) of the heparinised blood are examined, fresh or after staining.

STOOL EXAMINATION FOR PARASITES

Responsibility for laboratory diagnosis requires special training, skill and sound knowledge to be able to recognize true parasites and differentiate them from pseudo-parasites.

Specimens submitted for examination should be fresh and uncontaminated. They should be free of oil droplets, magnesia, powdered aluminum salts, barium or bismuth, and examined in a fresh condition or preserved properly. At least three separate specimens collected at intervals of 24 to 48 hours should be used for diagnosis. The reason for collecting more than one specimen is that gastrointestinal parasites often reproduce sporadically or at times, are not very abundant in stool specimens. The gastrointestinal parasites may not be discovered in a single stool specimen.

Before the fecal film is made, the entire specimen should be examined grossly to determine its consistency and component elements (feces, mucus, blood tissue elements and undigested food) and to look for macroscopic, parasitic segments of *Taenia saginata, T. solium,* whole adult worm of *Ascaris lumbricoides, Ancylostoma duodenale, Trichuris trichiura, Enterobius vermicularis* and various intestinal flukes.

During the identification of eggs, one should pay attention to shape, size, colour and marking on the surface of the egg shell, the presence of yolk granules, ovum or a differentiated embryo, the existence of an operculum and, in specific cases as in cestodes, the three pairs of embryonic hooklets. For detection of helminthic eggs, only an unstained preparation is necessary (Fig. 12.1).

A normal stool consists almost exclusively of feces, but in cases with a diseased intestine, a portion of the stool may contain a bloody mucous discharge.

Specimen Container A suitable type of container is a two ounce glass bottle with an aluminum or plastic screw cap. It can be used for stool, urine and sputum samples. For shipment, it should be placed securely in a mailing cylinder of heavy cardboard.

Preservation of stool sample

(MIF) fixative:

Reagents:

1. Lugol's iodine solution:

Iodine crystal (powdered)	5 g
Potassium iodide	10 g
Distilled water	100 ml

2. Merthiolate formaldehyde (MF) stock solution

Tincture of Merthiolate (1:1000)	200 ml
Formaldehyde	25 ml
Glycerol	5 ml
Distilled water	250 ml

To prepare the *Merthiolate Iodine Fixative* (MIF), 10–15 parts of freshly prepared Lugol's iodine solution is to be added into the merthiolate formaldehyde solution. This fixative may be used

1) In making direct fecal smears, or
2) For the collection and preservation of bulk stool specimens.

   1. Direct fecal smears: One drop of distilled water is added into the MIF solution taken on the slide. A small amount of feces is then added, mixed thoroughly and examined, after covering with a coverslip, under the low and high power objectives of the microscope.

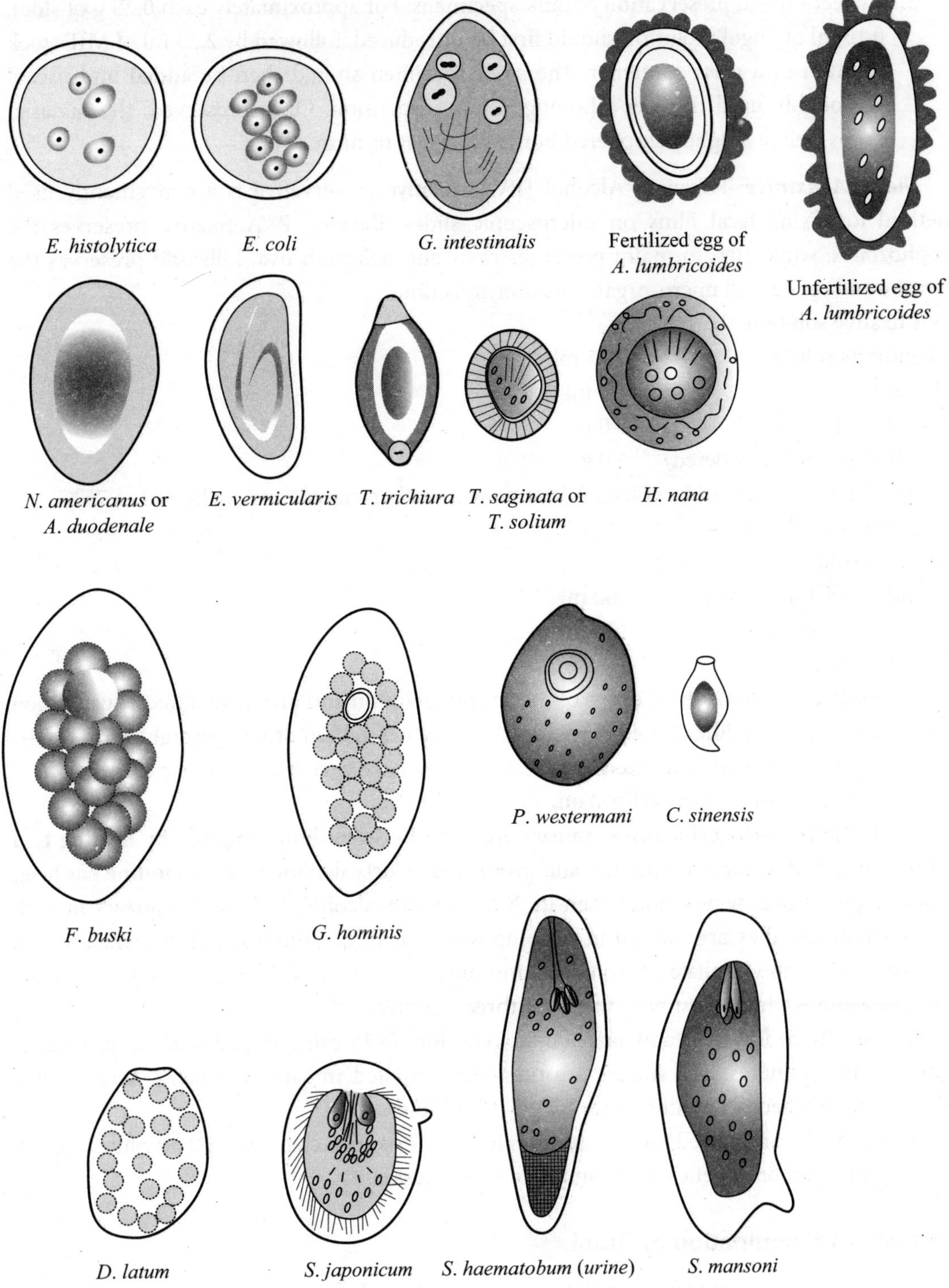

Fig. 12.1 Protozoan cyst and helminthic eggs.

2. Collection and preservation of bulk specimens: For approximately each 0.25 g of stool, 0.15 ml of Lugol's solution should first be introduced, followed by 2.35 ml of MIF stock solution in a glass container. The stool specimen should then be added and mixed thoroughly until there is a homogeneous suspension. Once preserved, the material keeps well in a tightly stoppered bottle for a year or more.

The PVA fixative: Polyvinyl Alcohol (PVA) fixative-preservative is a conveniently used method for fixing fecal films on microscopic slides. Besides, PVA fixative preserves the trophozoites, while 10% formalin preserves cysts and helminth ova, kills and preserves the parasite and renders all micro-organisms non-infectious.

PVA fixative solution:

Schaudinn's solution	93.5 ml
Glycerol	1.5 ml
Glacial acetic acid	5.0 ml
Polyvinyl alcohol (powdered)	5.0 g

Polyvinyl alcohol is added by constant stirring when other ingredients are heated to 75°C.

Schaudinn's fluid consists of:

Saturated solution of mercuric chloride in distilled water	200 ml
95% absolute alcohol	100 ml
Glacial acetic acid	15 ml

PVA fixative method: Three drops of the fixative solution and one drop of fecal suspension are spread over the middle of the microscopic slide, which is then dried overnight at 37°C. The dried film is then placed in iodized 70% alcohol to remove excessive mercuric chloride, then stained by Faust' iron-hematoxylin stain.

Faust's iron-hematoxylin stain: Smears are fixed in Schaudinn's solution by heating to a temperature of 60°C for two minutes, and immersed in 70% alcohol, to which iodine has been added to give a port wine colour, then in 70% and 50% alcohol, leaving the smears in each for two minutes. They are washed in running water for three minutes, and immersed in 2% aqueous iron alum (sulphate of iron and ammonium, 2.0 g; distilled water, 50 ml) solution. They are again washed in running water for three minutes.

They are stained in 0.5% aqueous hematoxylin for 10–15 minutes and washed in running water for two minutes. The smears are then differentiated in saturated picric acid for five minutes and washed in running water for 10–15 minutes.

The smears are immersed for two minutes in 70%, 95% (two changes) and absolute alcohol, cleared with xylol or toluene and mounted in xylol-balsam.

Methods of Examination of Stool

The object of the examination is to detect any parasitic infection by finding helminthic eggs and protozoan cysts and oocysts which may be passed along with the stool.

The methods of examination of stool used in detecting parasitic infection are as follows:

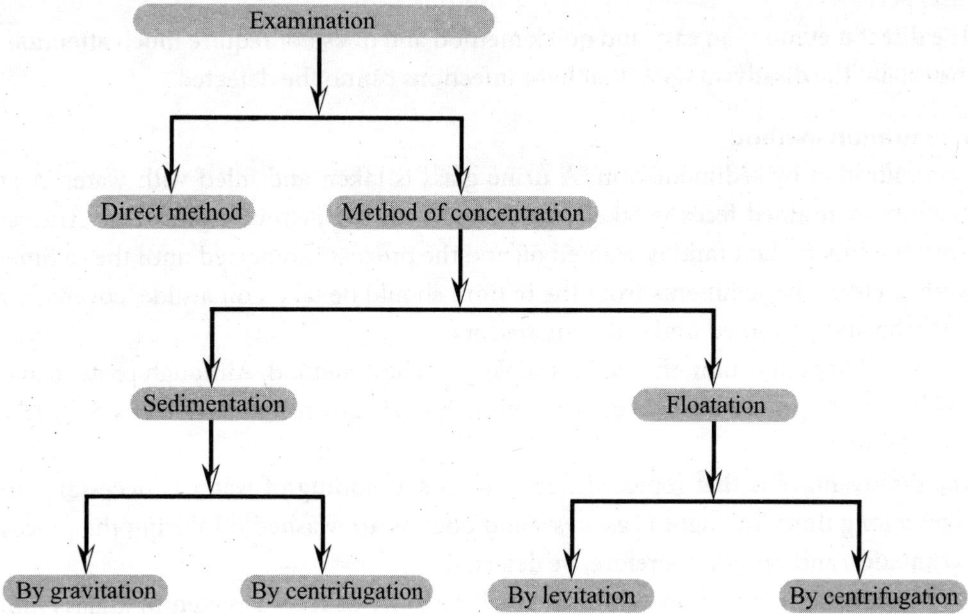

1. Direct method: Two cover glass preparations are prepared on one microscopic slide, far apart from each other:

1) Saline preparation: 1–2 mg of the fecal material should be mixed in a drop or two of physiological salt solution for the left hand preparation; and
2) Iodine preparation: 1–2 drops of iodine solution (filtered saturated solution of iodine in 1% potassium iodine, not in Lugol's iodine which is too strong for parasites) should be mixed with 1–2 mg of the fecal material for right hand preparation. Lugol's iodine can be used if it is diluted five times in distilled water. These films should be free from air bubbles, macroscopic debris and should be thin so that the newsprint can be read. Cyst forms can be detected in the saline preparation. While examining the unstained preparation, the light in the microscope should be carefully adjusted to get a clear view. For this purpose, the condenser should be racked down and the iris diaphragm is to be partially closed in order to cut down the illumination. It is convenient to use the mechanical stage of the microscope to adjust the light. After examination, the used slides should be discarded in a vessel containing five per cent lysol.

   The saline preparation is valuable for the study of living parasites (protozoan trophozoites, helminth eggs, nematode eggs and chromatoid bars of cyst). The iodine preparation is useful to study the characteristic features (nucleus, glycogen mass) of the protozoan cyst of *E. histolytica* and the flagella on the parasite.

   As the film dries, the feces clear more rapidly than do the eggs, but eggs also eventually become clear. Thus, the optimum time for drying under different conditions should be determined. In over-dried films, gas pockets form and the delicate eggs (e.g., hookworm) disappear.

The direct method is an easy and quick method and does not require much attention and materials. The disadvantage is that light infections cannot be detected.

2. Concentration method

a) Concentration by sedimentation: A urine glass is taken and filled with water. A small quantity of strained feces is taken and mixed with the help of a glass rod. After some time, the supernatant fluid is drained off and the process is repeated until the sediment is washed clear. The sediments from the bottom should be taken on a slide, covered with a coverslip and examined under the microscope.

In cases of light infection, this is the simplest and best method. Although protozoan cysts and helminth eggs are recovered, this method is especially recommended for Schistosoma and Clonorchis.

The disadvantage is that repeated decantation and adding of water is necessary, and it takes a long time. The light eggs, cysts and oocysts are washed off during the process of decantation and cannot, therefore, be detected.

i) Sedimentation by gravitation: A small quantity of feces is taken in a glass mortar, with the help of forceps, and some water is added. It is thoroughly mixed with a glass pestle and filtered through a strainer to remove the coarse debris. The filtrate is transferred into the urine glass for sedimentation. The heavier eggs settle down at the bottom of the jar within 10-15 minutes. The supernatant fluid is decanted off. It is again diluted and mixed thoroughly and allowed to settle down. The process is repeated several times for the removal of fecal debris or coarser matter. The heavier eggs settle down. A drop from the sediment is taken with the help of a pipette and put on a slide and a coverslip is placed over it. Then it is examined under the microscope, under low power first and then under high power.

This method is helpful in detecting heavy eggs, but it is generally not used for the detection of light eggs. It takes a lot of time, as much as 20–25 minutes, for each washing.

ii) Sedimentation by centrifugation: In a beaker, a small quantity of feces is dissolved and a little of it is transferred to one of the two tubes of the centrifuge machine. The machine should be started at 500–1000 rotations per minute. After 2–3 minutes, the fecal material settles at the bottom accompanied by the heavy eggs. Then the machine is stopped. The supernatant fluid is decanted off and the process is repeated several times, till the sediment is washed clear. A drop from the sediment is taken on a slide and examined under the microscope.

However light the infection may be, it can be detected by this method which is fairly useful for the concentration of protozoan cysts and helminth eggs in the stool.

If physiological salt solution is substituted for tap water, amebic trophozoites are concentrated in the living state.

However, this method is not simple and takes a long time to complete. The light eggs, cysts and oocysts are thrown off during the process of decantation and cannot therefore be detected.

b) Concentration by floatation: In this method, the floating medium originally used was brine, i.e., concentrated solution of sodium chloride with a specific gravity of 1.200. Eggs of common intestinal helminths such as hookworm, *Ascaris lumbricoides* and *Trichuris trichiura* are not damaged by this process, but the eggs of Schistosoma, strongyloides larvae and protozoan cysts become badly shrunken; moreover, the eggs of Clonorchis have a specific gravity higher than 1.200 and do not float in brine, as in the case of the unfertilized eggs of *Ascaris lumbricoides,* the eggs of *Taenia saginata, T. solium* and the eggs of all the intestinal flukes which do not float.

i) Floatation by levitation: A small quantity of feces is taken in a suitable cup, a little saturated solution of sodium chloride is added and an emulsion is made. More solution is added up to the brim of the cup. A glass slide is kept on the cup, so that the surface fluid touches the glass slide. After about 15 minutes, the slide is taken out upwards and turned upside down. A coverslip is placed over it and it is examined under the microscope.

Almost all the heavier particles settle at the bottom and the lighter helminth eggs, protozoan eggs, cysts and oocysts float on the surface, being completely separated from the mass of debris. It is the method of choice for detection of light infection of protozoan cysts, oocysts and light helminth eggs. No costly equipment is required. A large number of eggs, cysts and oocysts are concentrated on the surface and only a short time is required to search out the cysts.

The disadvantage is that heavy eggs cannot be detected by this process and it takes more time than floatation by centrifugation.

ii) Floatation by centrifugation: The fecal sample is dissolved in saturated sodium chloride solution. Then the two tubes of the centrifuge machine are filled up and fitted. The machine is rotated at 500–1000 rotations per minute for 2–3 minutes. In the tubes, the light eggs float on the liquid surface. Surface of the liquid is then touched with a small coverslip. Eggs, if present, will adhere to the coverslip. Then the coverslip is placed on a glass slide and examined under the microscope.

This method is effective for the diagnosis of light eggs, cysts and oocysts. It is also the most precise and delicate method to concentrate in the surface films, all but a negligible amount of the eggs of the hookworm, Ascaris and Trichuris.

This method is, however, complicated and requires costly equipment which may not be available everywhere.

Quantitative egg count technique Methods have been developed for the relatively accurate calculation of the hookworm, *Ascaris,* and, to a lesser degree, of *Trichuris* worm burden by counting the eggs, in the stool.

1. Beaver's direct egg count technique: A wooden block, 18 mm in thickness and of any convenient diameter, is fitted to the window of the photo-electric type of light meter and a 16 mm hole is drilled into the centre of the block. This serves as a platform for the microscope slide on which the smear is made and provides a mask which reduces the window to a convenient size for preparing and spreading the smear. An electric lamp is suspended directly over the reduced window and made adjustable, so that arbitrary whole number readings can be obtained. For routine smears, 1/500 ml (2.0 mg) of fecal suspension is most useful. For the number of eggs per ml of stool, the egg count is multiplied by the denominator, *viz.,* when the smear contains 1/200 ml, the factor is 200, and when 1/500 it is 500, etc.
2. Stoll's dilution egg count technique: Four grams of feces is placed in a large graded test tube with a mark indicating 56 and 60 ml levels. Decinormal sodium hydroxide is poured up to the 56 ml mark. Several small glass beads are added, the container is closed with a stopper and the content is shaken until the feces are thoroughly comminuted. A hard fecal specimen should be left in the liquid overnight to secure adequate disintegration. When proper comminution has been obtained, the mixture is shaken well, and 0.75 ml of the suspension is drawn up into a calibrated capillary pipette, discharged onto a clean microscope slide and covered with a 22 x 40 mm coverglass. The total number of eggs of the particular species of helminth under observation is then counted, and this number is multiplied by 200 to obtain the number of eggs per gram of feces. The estimated daily output of eggs can then be obtained by multiplying the number per gram by the total weight of a 24 hour fecal specimen. The estimate obtained depends on the consistency of the feces, so that correction factors are employed to convert the estimate to a formed stool basis, *viz.,* mushy-formed, 1.5; mushy, 2.0; mushy diarrheic, 3.0; frankly diarrheic, 4.0; and watery, 5.0.

Modified Ziehl-Neelsen Technique for Cryptosporidium Oocysts in Stool

1. Prepare a thin smear of a fresh fecal specimen.
2. Air-dry the smear. Fix the smear in an absolute methanol for 3 minutes.
3. Stain the smear with cold carbol fuchsin for 5–10 minutes. Wash off the stain with tap water.
4. Decolourize the smear using 3% hydrochloric acid in 95% ethanol, until no more colour floods from the smear.
5. Rinse off the decolouriser with clean tap water
6. Counterstain with 0.25% w/w malachite green for about 30 seconds
7. Wash off the stain with clean tap water. Wipe the back of the slide clean and place in a draining rack for smear to dry.
8. Examine the smear microscopically for oocysts, using the 40× objective to identify the oocysts.

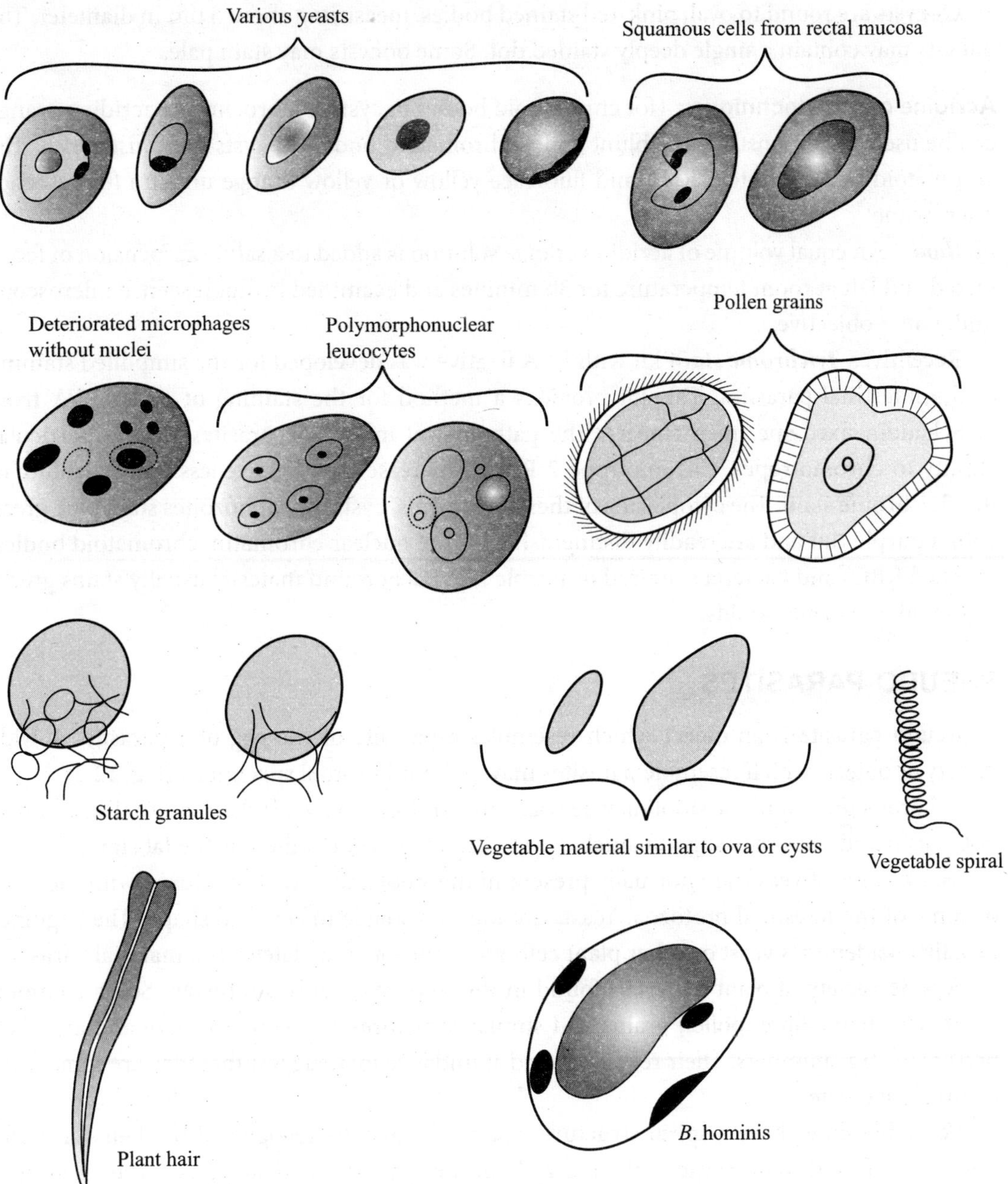

Fig. 12.2 Pseudo-parasites.

Oocysts are round to oval, pink-red stained bodies, measuring about 5 μm in diameter. The oocysts may contain a single deeply stained dot. Some oocysts may stain pale.

Acridine orange technique (for chromatoid bodies in cysts) Fluorochrome acridine orange can be used to demonstrate the blunt ended chromatoid bodies in cysts of *E. histolytica*. The chromatoid bodies contain RNA and fluoresce yellow or yellow orange under a fluorescence microscope.

Method An equal volume of acridine orange solution is added to a saline suspension of feces, mixed and left at room temperature for 30 minutes and examined by fluorescence microscopy under 40 × objective.

Recently, a ***Trichrome stain*** kit with PVA fixative was developed for the simplified staining of the intestinal parasites. This kit provides a method for the staining of either PVA fixed or Schaudin fixed specimen smears. The pathological intestinal parasites show a particular affinity to chromotropes. Chromotrope 2 R dyes increase the effectiveness and reliability of this Trichrome stain. The cytoplasms of these organisms, cysts or trophozoites stain blue green with a purple tint and are readily distinguishable. The nuclear chromatin, chromatoid bodies, ingested RBCs and bacteria stain red or purple red. Background material usually stains green, as should yeast and moulds.

PSEUDO-PARASITES

A pseudo-parasite is an object which resembles a parasite or the egg of a parasite. A wide variety of objects which resemble parasites may be found in stool specimens (Fig. 12.2).

Oil drops present in the stool may be small and uniform in size. If their internal structure is not considered, they may suggest amebic cysts. They can be identified by the fat stain.

Many kinds of yeasts are normally present in the stool and may be confused with the cysts of some of the intestinal protozoa. Yeasts are highly variable in size and shape. The beginner usually misidentifies yeast or other plant cells as an ameba, or a platelet as a malarial parasite.

A wide variety of plant materials found in the feces may cause confusion. Some common plant cells, hairs, fibre, pollen grains and similar structures are regular in size and are often present in large numbers. Their regularity and abundance may suggest that they are some form of animal parasite.

Vegetable fibres have a spiral structure. Plant cells may be recognized by their thick and frequently smooth wall. Some of them are about the same size and shape as certain helminth ova, but seldom possess the regularity of shape which characterizes the ova.

Vegetable hairs may be confused with larval nematodes. They have a homogeneous thick refractile wall and a minute central canal extending through the entire length of the structure.

Starch granules may be spherical and composed of concentric layers of white material. Potato starch frequently occurs in irregular sac-like aggregates of granules.

A frequent source of confusion is the presence of undigested citrus fruit vesicles in the feces. They resemble the gravid female pinworm in size and general outline. Close observation will show that they do not possess any internal structure.

More frequently, body parts or whole larvae and adult insects are seen in the stool as a result of having been ingested with food.

Various cellular elements in the stool may be mistaken for intestinal amebae. Most important in this regard are the polymorphonuclear leucocytes, macrophages, columnar epithelial cells from the intestinal mucosa or squamous cells from the anal mucosa. Identification of these cells depends upon the observation of their structure and the relative size of the nuclei in relation to the cytoplasm.

In the examination of thin blood smears for malarial parasites, the beginner is often misled by the superimposition of platelets on red cells. The malarial parasite has blue cytoplasm and red chromatin and is usually quite sharp in outline, whereas the platelets stain in varying shades of purple and are rather unclear in outline.

EXAMINATION OF SKIN SCRAPING FOR IDENTIFICATION OF MITES

Procedure A small quantity of skin scraping is taken in a test tube to which 10% potassium hydroxide is added. The material is boiled for 10 minutes and kept in a stand to settle the sediment. A drop of sediment should be taken on a slide with the help of a pipette, covered with a coverslip and examined under low and high power objectives.

13 CULTURE MEDIA

Cultural methods have been developed for a wide variety of protozoan parasites of humans and for the development of the larvae of *S. stercoralis* and hookworm. Some, used for cultivation of ameba, may be diagnostic aids, although they are not widely used. Procedures have been developed with difficulty for culturing Plasmodia, Leishmania and pneumocystis. Infection with experimental animals is not widely used for diagnosis. Relatively few helminths have been studied *in vitro* so far.

The purpose of culturing the parasite is manifold:

1. To diagnose accurately the organisms
2. To obtain more organisms to prepare antigen for immunological diagnosis
3. For teaching purposes when clinical material is scarce
4. For animal experimentation
5. For *in vitro* screening of drugs
6. To study the physiology of the parasite.

Types of media that have been widely used are:

A. For ameba (*E. histolytica*)
    1. Balamuth's monophasic medium containing egg yolk (dehydrated), Balamuth's buffer solution, rice powder (sterile), liver extract (*Medical Parasitology* (1981). 5th Ed. WB Saunders, Philadelphia.)
    2. Modified Boeck and Drobohlav's diphasic medium consists of whole egg; Ringer's solution, crude liver extract, rice powder (sterile).
    3. Shaffer, Ryden and Frege's transparent medium (composition – saline, horse serum, supernate of streptobacilli, penicillin).
    4. Philip's medium differs from all other *in vitro* culture media for *E. histolytica*, in which *T. cruzi* is substituted as metabolic associate.

B. For Giardia intestinalis. It can be cultivated in Diamond's medium or modified TYL-S-33 medium with bile salts and antibiotics (lyopholised TYL-S-33 medium obtainable from HVP Laboratories, Ralston, NE, USA).

C. For *Trichomonas vaginalis*.

1. Trussel and Johnson's medium contains peptone, sodium chloride, normal human serum, sodium thioglycollate.
2. Another trichomonas medium developed for isolation of human protozoa contains antibiotic (chloramphenicol) to inhibit the growth of contaminating bacteria; pH 6.0, favours the growth of trichomonas. Nutrients are provided by peptone, maltose and cystaine.
3. Lash's casein hydrolysate serum medium (*Clinical Laboratory Manual* (1979) 2nd Edition CV Mosby Co., St.Louis).
4. Feinberg medium for *T. vaginalis*. (*J Clin Parasitology* (1957) 10:327)
5. A modified Liquid medium (Fuji) was developed based on Diamond medium. In preparing the broth for *T. vaginalis* cultivation,

Trypticase peptone	10g
Yeast extract	10g
Maltose	20g
L–cysteine	1g
Ascorbic acid	1g
Neutral red	20mg

were dissolved and pH adjusted to 5.6 to 5.8, 1g agar was added. The medium was autoclaved and then 100 ml of horse serum and antibiotics (streptomycin, 2000 mg; gentamycin, 350 mg; penicillin, 2,000,000 units) were added. Finally, 6 ml volume of the mixture was pipetted into a screw-capped bottle.

D. For Leishmania

1. Leishmania can be cultivated in : Novy, Mac Neal and Nicolle's (NNN) medium which contains:

   Agar 14 g.
   Sodium chloride 6 g.
   Distilled water 900 ml. which is autoclaved

   Then the sterile defrinated rabbit blood is added and distributed in test tubes. The tube is rotated and slanted on ice to get more water of condensation only. In this supernatant water at the bottom of the tube, Leishmania can grow.

2. Scheider's enriched medium is also recommended for the *in vitro* culture of Leishmania.

   Composition:
   Schneider's Drosophila medium 80 ml.
   (Obtainable from Difco Ltd., USA)
   Fetal calf serum 20 ml.

Antibiotic – antimycotic solution 1–2 ml.
(Penicillin, Streptomycin, Fungizone)

Schneider's enriched medium is more sensitive than the NNN medium and has additional advantages, that is, it can be lyophilised and reconstituted with distilled water as required.

L. donovani (Indian strain) can be propagated in chemically defined media suitable for cultivation and cloning of promastigotes; defined medium – (S – α - MEM) based on α - minimum essential medium supplemented with glutamine, glucose, folic acid, biotin, hematin, HEPES and adenine; another defined medium – (S – RPMI - 1640), based on S-RPMI – 1640, suitably supplemented. Better growth in S-α -MEM and improved by addition of heat inactivated fetal bovine serum. Very recently, nutrient broth is commercially available in powder form, containing inactivated fetal calf serum and antibiotics; this is used for the cultivation of Leishmania. It is a cheap, easily prepared medium satisfactory for the growth, at 24°C of promastigotes of five strains of Leishmania sp. including *L. donovani.*

3. Basically, there are two different kinds of media (monophasic and diphasic)
   Senekjie's medium, a standard diphasic blood agar medium similar to NNN medium (1 litre)

Difco Bacto beef	50 g
Bacto agar	20 g
Bacto peptone	20 g
Sodium Chloride	5 g
Defrinated rabbit blood	150 ml

4. Amastigote *L. donovani* can be cultivated in a murine tumour cell, dog sarcoma cell, vero cell.
5. RBLM (liquid medium) for axenie cultivation of amastigote *L. donovani* as Alder medium. It is best for both amastigote and promastigote forms.

E. For trypanosoma
   1. Weinman's medium was developed to grow *T. gambiense*. It consists of: sodium chloride 8 g, distilled water 900 ml, citrated human plasma 100 ml and human globulin 20 ml. pH 7.4–7.5. It is dispensed in rubber stoppered test tubes and when inoculated, incubated at 26–28°C, the culture becomes positive in 7 to 10 days.
   2. Tobie, Von Brand and Mehlman's diphasic medium was developed for the culture of African trypanosomes and is also satisfactory for the culture of *T. cruzi* and Leishmania sp.
      This medium has two phases:
      a) Solid phase and
      b) Liquid overlay.

      This medium provides high yield of organisms.

3. *T. cruzi* grows in blood agar culture medium. The preparation and use of this medium are given below:

   Preparation of medium

Bacto blood agar base	1.4 g.
Bacto tryptose	0.5 g.
Agar	0.3 g.
Sodium chloride	0.6 g.
Distilled water	100 ml.

   All ingredients are mixed, dispensed in 4 ml. quantity in each test tube and autoclaved; when the medium is cooled, 0.3 ml. of sterile defrinated rabbit blood, previously heat inactivated is added. The medium is cooled to set in a sloped position; then benzyl penicillin (400 units) and streptomycin sulphate (400 units per ml.) are added to each tube; the medium is tested for sterility and then used.

F. For *Toxoplasma gondii.*

   In vitro culture and closing of *T. gondii* is done in a newly established line, derived from TG 180.

G. For *Balantidium coli.*

   1. Rees' medium for *B. coli.*

      To each sterile test tube containing sterile 18 ml. of Ringer's solution, two ml of sterile human serum and a small sprinkling of sterile rice powder are added. The medium is inoculated and incubated at 36°C, and transfers are made every 72 hours.

   2. For abundant *in vitro* growth of *B. coli*, rice flour is to be added to Balamuth's medium.

H. For Plasmodium.

   Very recently, *P. falciparum* was cultivated *in vitro* in the human umbilical cord erythrocytes in China.

   In vitro continuous cultivation of *P. falciparum* can also be carried out by using the candle jar method and type AB Rh+ plasma. The antigen from this *P. falciparum* can be used for the malaria fluorescent antibody test.

   Sorbitol synchronistion of *P. falciparum* culture has proved a reliable and simple method and has achieved worldwidc use.

In vitro cultivation of parasitic helminths

Attempts have been made to culture parasitic helminths in nutrient media, with partial success in some instances. The techniques for culture and isolation of some of the helminths are most difficult and often reserved for research purpose. *Necator americanus* can be cultivated successfully in undefined media based on chick embryo extract (CEE), serum, tissue extract.

For *W. bancrofti* microfilariae:

These microfilariae can be kept in an artificial medium (Franke's N I medium) with 10% human serum under 5% CO_2 atmosphere for 20 days. *Wuchereria bancrofti* can be cultured with 95% viability for 10 days in medium 199 with Hank's salts, supplemented with organic acids and sugars of Grace's insect medium. Adequate amount of ES (excretory and secretory) antigen was produced from supernatant fluid of the medium.

Using this antigen in ELISA, 90% microfilaria carriers, 90.35% chronic filarial patients were positive.

MICROSPORIDA (NEW HUMAN PROTOZOA)

Microsporida are an unnatural group of unicellular parasites (protozoa) with unusual biologic characteristics, especially with respect to their subcellular organisation and spore structure. They lack mitochondria and have ribosomes that resemble those of bacteria in subunit size and nucleotide sequences. It has been suggested that microsporidia arose as an early branch from the stock leading from the prokaryotes of the higher cells and have been accorded status as a separate phylum – Microsporidia.

Microsporidian lifecycles are composed of proliferative (merogonic) and spore producing (sporogony) phases. In the latter phase, a sporont divides into sporoblasts that mature into thick-walled Gram positive spores.

The spores have an extrusion apparatus consisting of a coiled polar filament and an anchoring disk and contain the infective agent known as sporoplasm. The obligate intracellular habitat is reached in a new host when the coiled polar filament is extruded, usually in the gut of the host, to form a hollow tube through which the sporoplasm passes to be inoculated in the host cell. Microsporidia have a great reproductive potential, multiplying within cells and spreading from cell to cell. Although they have long been known as parasites of widespread occurrence in populations of invertebrates and fish, the potential of Microsporidia for infecting warm-blooded vertebrates is only now being recognized. Infection with *Encephalitozoon cuniculi*, a species that has a wide host range in mammals (rodents, rabbits, carnivores and primates) has been diagnosed once in Japan, and even in Sweden in children with neurological illness.

Microsporidia are ubiquitous obligate intracellular protozoan parasites found commonly in laboratory animals. They are unicellular Gram positive organisms with mature spores 0.5–2 × 1–4 μm in diameter. Significant microsporidiosis in humans is increasing in association with the increase in patients with Acquired Immunodeficiency Syndrome (AIDS). There are four genera of microsporidia known to infect human beings:

1. *Enterocytozoon bieneusi*, the most common microsporidian observed in AIDS patients, infects the intestinal mucosa and causes diarrhea. Its estimated prevalence may be as high as 10% in AIDS patients.
2. *Pleistophora* species was reported in an immuno-compromised Human Immunodeficiency Virus (HIV) negative patient with myositis. Its spores are arranged in large groups enclosed by a membrane (Pansporoblastic membrane).
3. *Encephalitozoon cuniculi*, most common in laboratory animals, was reported in several immuno-compromised patients and also in AIDS patients with peritonitis; hepatitis.

Previously, *E. cuniculi* was the only available mammalian microsporidian for use in serological tests. Antibodies to *E. cuniculi* were found in patients. *E. cuniculi* was characterized by its development within a parasitophorous vacuole in macrophages, vascular endothelial and perithelial cells and kidney tubule cells and by its unpaired nuclei and disporous sporogony (i.e. sporont gives rise to two spores). Very recently, Didier *et al.* isolated and characterized a new human microsporidian, *E. hellum* (new species) from three AIDS patients.

4. *Nosema corneum* (new species), parasite causing ocular infection or nosematosis of the cornea, was first reported in HIV positive patients. *N. connori* was characterized by virtue of the paired (diplokaryotic) arrangement of its nuclei in the spores. It caused a generalized infection in a severely immuno-compromised infant, who died, in the U.S.A.

Besides, the infection with an *E. cuniculi*-like organism was reported in several AIDS patients with conjunctivitis and very recently, a new microsporidian, *E. hellum* (new species) was isolated and characterized from three AIDS patients with kerato-conjunctivitis as follows:

In vitro Growth of Microsporidia

E. cuniculi, N. corneum and *N. algerae* were grown in Madin–Darby canine kidney (MDCK) cells, using RPMI 1640 culture medium, supplemented with 5% heat inactivated fetal bovine serum and antibiotics.

Corneal tissue and conjunctival scrapings from HIV seropositive patients with microsporidal kerato-conjunctivitis were mixed and added to monolayer MDCK cells. The culture was incubated at 37°C with 5% CO_2 except for *N. algerae* culture which was incubated at room temperature.

Electron Microscopy of Microsporidia

The larger proliferative stages (meronts) were attached to a parasitophorous vacuole membrane. The spores displayed relatively thick electron-lucent endospores and irregular electron dense exospore structures.

Serology

The new ocular isolated *E. hellum* displayed immunological reactivities and morphological similarities to *E. cuniculi*. The serological diagnosis of microsporidiosis in AIDS patients is possible, because in all cases, positive antibody binding to *E. hellum* could be demonstrated. The availability of new human isolate provides antigen for testing sera and increases the likelihood of detecting positive sera.

Cyclospora (recent parasite) are coccidian-like or cyanobacterium-like bodies (CLB – the name Cyclospora sp. has been proposed). They were found to cause prolonged diarrheal disease among travelers and foreign residents at Kathmandu, Nepal in 1993. Duration of diarrhea in those infected with CLB was seven weeks. Mode of infection is via contaminated drinking water or unboiled milk.

OPPORTUNISTIC PARASITES AND AIDS

Sex is a part of life. The Human Immunodeficiency Virus (HIV) spreads primarily through sex and, once it enters the body, there is no way to throw it out. The infection progresses silently, affects the cells of the body's defense system and finally manifests itself into different types of opportunistic infections.

The most common complications of AIDS may be due to some opportunistic parasites (*Pneumocystis carinii, Toxoplasma gondii, Cryptosporidium, Isospora belli,* Leishmania, Microsporidia).

I. ***Pneumocystosis*** is widely distributed and is the infection of rodents, dogs, goats, sheep, horses and a reservoir for human infection. It also occurs commonly in mammals, infants and in AIDS patients. It is a pulmonary disease characterized by dyspnea, tachpnea and hypoxemia that occurs in immuno-deficient patients in malnourished and premature infants. *Pneumocystis carinii* probably cause asymptomatic infections in healthy mammalian hosts. The insidious form is typically seen in adult AIDS patients. In AIDS patients, the T_4 lymphocytes count is characteristically below 20% millimetre.

   Though *Pneumocystis carinii* are seen intracellularly in the pulmonary alveoli, their lifecycle is not yet well established. They are probably protozoa. Morphologically, they have a thick-walled cyst and thinner walled trophozoites. The cyst is 5–6 μm in diameter and usually contains a cluster of 6 to 8 round trophozoites (1–2 μm in diameter). The cyst is identified in clinical specimens by means of a Gram-Weigert stain. Sporozoites can be identified in the sputum by Giemsa stain.

   Pentamidine isethionate is used in the treatment of pneumocystosis in the United States. It is now replaced by cotrimoxazole which appears to be as effective as pentamidine and is less toxic.

II. ***Toxoplasmosis*** is a common disease in birds and animals caused by the protozoon, *Toxoplasma gondii.* The name *T. gondii* (arc-shaped protozoon) is derived from the Greek word, *toxon,* meaning arc and from the name of the African rodent, *gondi,* in which the organism can proliferate and cause clinically important diseases in human beings. Fulminating fatal infection may develop in patients with AIDS. There may be cerebral toxoplasmosis complications in AIDS patients, congenital toxoplasmosis in pregnant women and acute lymphadenopathic toxoplasmosis.

   Three forms exist in the lifecycle of *T. gondii*: the cyst, the trophozoite and the oocyst. The trophozoite has an arc or oval form and is about 3–4 μm in diameter and 6–7 μm in length. It is an obligate intracellular form that proliferates in acute infection. Trophozoites can enter vacuoles in any nucleated mammalian cell. They divide asexually and continue till the cell ruptures, releasing trophozoites to infect other cells.

   Cysts are 10–200 μm, found in brain, skeletal tissue and cardiac muscle. The oocysts are 10–12 μm in diameter, found in the intestinal mucosa of cats, where they release toxoplasma, proliferate by gametogony into microgametocyes and macrogametocytes. Then a zygote is formed, and ultimately oocysts are passed out in the feces.

Toxoplasmosis is a worldwide zoonosis. Natural infection occurs by ingestion of cysts or oocysts. In nature, the lifecycle is maintained by cats, birds and small mammals. Children are likely to get infected when playing in sand or by inhalation of dried feces.

The frequency of Toxoplasma infection in any population depends on economic and environmental factors. It can occur as a disseminated disease in patients with immunodeficiencies. The disease occurs with particular frequency in patients with AIDS. Clinical manifestations are variable. Fever, hepatosplenomegaly, pneumonitis, maculopapular rash, myositis, myocarditis, meningoencephalitis and central nervous system mass lesions may be seen. The most common manifestation particularly in patients with AIDS is the central nervous system involvement with fever, headache and confusion, progressing to coma, focal neurological signs and seizures. Computed tomography usually shows one or more lesions that are contrast enhancing in a ring or nodular pattern.

The diagnosis of toxoplasma infection can be based on serologic tests, lymph node histology and demonstration of trophozoites in body fluids or tissues or isolation of *T. gondii* from certain sites. The Sabin–Feldman test is highly sensitive and specific and gives comparable results with the indirect fluorescent antibody (IFA) test. Complement fixation test and indirect haemagglutination (IHA) tests are also performed.

A combination of pyremethamine and sulfadiazine is effective in inhibiting the replication of trophozoites. There are no drugs that will kill trophozoites or eradicate the cyst form. Pyremethamine can be given orally. Sulfadiazine and pyremethamine are effective in the treatment of AIDS patients infected with *T. gondii*.

III. ***Coccidiosis*** is caused by *Isospora belli* which is a sporozoon of the human intestine. Many species of the intestinal sporozoa or coccidia in animals cause some of the most economically important disease of domestic mammals and fowls. *I. belli* is one of the few coccidia that multiply sexually in the human intestine. Humans are the definite hosts.

The oocyst of *I. Belli* is 25–33 × 12–16 μm, elongate, ovoid and often has an asymmetric cyst wall.

I. belli inhabits the small intestine. Signs and symptoms of coccidiosis are apparently due to the invasion and multiplication of the parasite in the intestinal mucosa. Oocysts are shed into the intestinal lumen and passed in the stool. A week after ingestion of viable cysts, a low grade fever, lassitude and malaise may appear, followed soon by mild diarrhea and vague abdominal pain. The infection is usually self limited after 1–2 weeks, but sometimes diarrhea, weight loss and fever may last for 6 weeks to 6 months. Symptomatic coccidiosis is more common in children than in adults. Chronic infection occurs in poorly malnourished people living under unsanitary condition where continued reinfection is more likely or in immuno-suppressed persons or in AIDS patients. Human coccidiosis occurs from the ingestion of cysts.

Treatment of mild cases consists of bed rest and a bland diet for a few days. More severe and chronic cases are treated with trimethoprim–sulfamethoxazole. Patients sensitive to sulfanomide (e.g., some AIDS patients) may respond to pyrimethamine daily. Immuno-suppressed patients may have to be treated continuously.

IV. ***Cryptosporidiosis*** Cryptosporidium belongs to the class sporozoa and is toxonomically related to other coccidia that infect humans including *T. gondii*, *I. belli* and Plasmodium sp. It resembles very closely the unclassified protozoon, *P. carinii* morphologically, and in its ability to parasitize the immuno-compromised host (e.g. AIDS patient).

Cryptosporidium cyst is 2–5 μm in diameter and is identified in clinical specimens, by its characteristic acid fast positivity. When fully sporulated (mature), the oocyst contains four naked sporozoites that are elliptical (2–4 × 6–8 μm), flat, motile and are thought to be an infective form of the organism. They are resistant to laboratory disinfectants.

Sporozoites are released (excystation) and implant on intestinal epithelium, where they develop into trophozoites, followed by asexual and sexual endogenous stages, finally resulting in the production of oocysts that are released in the feces and are immediately infective. Its lifecycle is completed within a single host; which distinguishes it from other coccidia and it has the potential for infection within the same host. This may explain the persistent illness of AIDS patients infected with cryptosporidium.

It causes gastrointestinal tract infection, characterized by watery diarrhea, abdominal cramp, malabsorption and weight loss. The infection is usually a severe illness in immuno-compromised patients, particularly those with AIDS and is a self limited disease in the immunologically normal host. Though this coccidian protozoon has long been associated with disease in animals, later it has been identified in 47 AIDS patients with severe enteritis during 1981–82; thereafter, it has become of great importance to both the medical community and to public health worldwide.

The prevalence of human cryptosporidiosis is not yet determined. Survey in 1985 in India indicated that it is 11.1% in diarrhea patients. It is more common in children than in adults; breast feeding may be protective. More than 50% of AIDS patients have cryptosporidium and another 15% are infected with *I. belli*.

Microscopic examination of wet preparation of stool reveals cryptoporidium oocysts which may be confused with yeasts. With acid fast stain, acid fast positive (red) oocysts may be distinguished from acid fast negative (green) yeast. Many species of animals (mammals, birds, reptile and fish) are infected with cryptosporidium. There are seventeen species and lack host specificity: thus, only one species may parasitize many different species of animals. Treatment is unnecessary for patients with normal immunity.

Spiramycin may be effective temporarily. Successful use of Diclazuril (benzene–acetonitrite compound) in crysporidium infection in a 20-year-old man (an intravenous temporary drug user) with AIDS and chronic persistent hepatitis B has been reported. However, success in a single case should be viewed cautiously.

V. Leishmaniasis (visceral leishmaniasis or *kala azar*) caused by *Leishmania donovani*

VI. Mircrosporidiosis. Microsporidia are ubiquitous obligate intracellular protozoan parasites and are unicellular Gram positive organisms with mature spores. The spores have an extrusion apparatus consisting of a coiled polar filament and anchoring disk and contain the infective agent known as sporoplasm. The potential of Microsporidia for the infection of warm-blooded vertebrates is only now being recognized. Significiant mircrosporidiosis in humans is increasing in association with the increase in patients with AIDS. There are four genera of microsporidia known to infect human beings:

1. *Enterocytozoon bieneusi*, the most common microsporidian observed in AIDS patients, infects the intestinal mucosa and causes diarrhea.
2. *Pleistophora* species was reported in an immuno-compromised Human Immuno deficiency Virus (HIV) negative patient with myositis.
3. *Encephalitozoon cuniculi* was reported in several immuno-compromised patients and also in AIDS patients with peritonitis, hepatitis.
4. *Nosema corneum*, parasites causing ocular infection or nosematosis of the cornea, was first reported in HIV positive patients. Besides, the infection with *E. cuniculi*-like organism was reported in several AIDS patients with keratoconjunctivitis. Enzyme Linked Immunosorbent assay (ELISA) can be used to detect antibody to *E. cuniculi* infection in humans.

1. Leptomyxid Ameba (newly discovered protozoa) was also responsible for primary amebic meningo-encephalitis, granulomatous amebic encephalitis and keratitis in contact lens wearers. Clotrimazole and bifonazole were amebastatic rather than amebicidal on a clinical isolate of Acanthameba polyphage associated with Acanthameba keratitis.
2. Cyclospora (recent parasite) are coccidian-like or cynobacterium-like bodies (CLB – the name Cyclospora sp. has been proposed). They were found to cause prolonged diarrheal diseases among travelers and foreign residents at Kathmandu, Nepal in 1993. Duration of diarrhea in those infected with CLB was seven weeks. Mode of infection is via contaminated drinking water or unboiled milk.
3. Parasites associated with pulmonary diseases.
   1. Protozoa. *L. donovani*. Pulmonary involvement is usually characterized by signs and symptoms of bronchitis and broncho-pneumonia.
   2. Trematodes. *S. mansoni*. Pulmonary hypertension and Corpulmonale induced by pulmonary arteritis as a result of *S. mansoni* egg deposition.
      P. westermani. Pathologically this lung fluke has a stage of infiltration, encysted stage, non-suppurative chronic granulomatous reaction with numerous ova.
   3. Nematodes. *A. lumbricoides, Toxacara canis* and capillaria acrophila cause pulmonary granulomas. Patient may present with a visceral larva migrans syndrome, asthmatic symptoms and esinophilia.

APPENDIX

I. TECHNICAL TERMS

Abscess	(Latin: *abscedere* to go away, to separate). Circumscribed collection of pus in tissue.
Accolé	(French: *accoler* to embrace). Referring to the form of *Plasmodium falciparum* which adheres to the surface of red cells as a thin strip of cytoplasm.
Acetabulum	(Latin: *acetabulum* a little cup to hold vinegar). The sucking cup of flukes.
Aedes	(Greek: *aedes* odious. annoying). A genus of mosquitoes.
Alae	(Latin: *ala wing*). Referring to the hyaline wings at the anterior end of Enterobius.
Ameba	(Greek: *amoibe* change). A genus of protozoa which changes shape by extending pseudopodia.
Ancylostoma	(Greek: *agkylos* curved, bent; *stoma* mouth. Referring to the head which is bent backward). A genus of hookworms.
Anopheles	(Greek: *an* without; *opheles* help. The harmful one). A genus of mosquitoes.
Antenna	(Latin: *antenna* sail, yard). The feeder of insects; Arthropoda. (Greek: *arthron* joint; *poda*, plural of *pous* foot). The phylum of animals having jointed limbs.
Ascaris lumbricoides	(Greek: *askaris* intestinal worm; Latin: *lumbricus* earthworm; Greek. *eidos* form). The large intestinal roundworm.
Axonema	(Greek: *axon* axis; *nema* thread). The intracellular portion of the flagellum in flagellates.
Axostyle	(Greek: *axon* axis; *stylos* pillar). The axial supporting structure in flagellates.
Babesia	In honour of Victor Babes. Rumanian bacteriologist, 1854–1926. A genus of the Hemosporidia, which contains the species causing Texas cattle fever.
Balantidium	(Greek: *balantidion* little bag). A genus of ciliata.
Bilharziasis	After Theodor Bilharz, helminthologist, 1825–62. Infection with *Schistosoma hematobium*.
Binary	(Latin: *Bini* two at a time). Referring to the equal parts into which protozoa divide.

Bursa	(Latin: *bursa* purse, sac). A posterior expansion of the cuticle of some nematodes which serves as a clasper.
Calabar	A district, river and town in Southern Nigeria.
Casoni's test	After Tommaso Casoni, Italian physician. Skin test for hydatid disease.
Cercaria	(Greek: *kerkos* tail). The tailed larval stage of flukes.
Cestado	(Greek: *kestos* girdle; *eidos* form) resembling tapeworm.
Chagas' disease	After Carlos Chagas, Institute Oswaldo Cruz, Rio de Janeiro. 1879–1934. Infection with *Trypanosoma cruzi.*
Charcot–Leyden crystals	After Jean Martin Charcot, French neurologist, 1825–93 and Ernst Victor Von Leyden, German physician, 1832–1910. Colourless, pointed crystals found in the sputum in bronchial asthma and in the feces in amebic dysentery and other ulcerative diseases of the colon.
Chromatin	(Greek: *chroma* colour). The deeply staining protoplasmic material within the nucleus of the cell.
Chromatoidal	(Greek: *chroma* colour; *eidos* form), Resembling chromatin in affinity for stains.
Chrysops	(Greek: *chrysos* gold; *ops* face). A genus of biting flies.
Ciliata	(Latin: *cilium* eyelash). A class of protozoa.
Cirrus	(Latin: *cirrus* curl). Slender, flexible appendage, the male copulatory organ of flatworms.
Clonorchis sinensis	(Greck: *klon* branch; *orchis* testicle; pertaining to Sinae, i.e. Latin name for Oriental people or Chinese). The Chinese liver fluke.
Coccidiosis	(Greek: diminutive of *kokkos* berry) Infection with Coccidia. e.g. *Isospora hominis.*
Commensal	(Latin: *cum* together; *mensa* table. Companion at the table.) An organism living in or on another, partaking of its food, but not harming it.
Copepoda	(Greek: *kope* oar, *podus* foot. *poda* feet). Small Crustacea.
Coracidium	(Greek: diminutive of *korax* hooklet, originally crow)) Larval stage of *Diphyllobothrium latum.*
Cosmopolitan	(Greek: *kosmos* world; *polites* citizen). At home in any country.
Crithidia	(Greek: diminutive of *krithai* barley). A stage in the lifecycle of *Trypanosoma.*
Crustacea	(Latin: *crusta* crust, the hard surface or shell of a body). Class of Arthropoda including lobster, crab, shrimp.
Cryptozoite	(Greek: *kryptos* hidden; *zoion* animal). A stage in the lifecycle of Plasmodium.
Culex	(Latin: *Culex* gnat). A genus of mosquitoes.
C. fatigans	(Latin: *fatigare* to hunt down).
C. pipiens	(Latin: *pipire* to chirp).
C. quinquefasciatus	(Latin: *quinque* five; *fasciatus* past participle of *fasciare* to envelop with hands; *fascia* band).
Culicoides	(Latin: *culex* gnat; Greek: *eidos* form). Resembling Culex. The punkies or biting midges.

Cyclops	(Greek: *kylops* round-eyed). A genus of small crustacea, the intermediate host of *Diphyllobothrium latum* and *Dracunculus medinensis*.
Cyst	(Greek: *kystis* bladder). The immotile, resistant stage of protozoa. In pathology, a sac with a distinct wall containing fluid or other material.
Cysticercoid	(Greek: *kystis* bladder; *kerkos* tail; *eidos* form). Resembling a cysticercus, but with a small bladder without fluid. A stage in the lifecycle of *Hymenolepis nana*.
Cysticercosis	Infection with cysticercus, the larval stage of *Taenia*.
Cysticercus	(Greek: *kystis* bladder; *kerkos* tail). The larval stage of Taenia.
C. bovis	(Latin: *bos* cattle). The larval stage of *Taenia saginata*.
C. cellulosae	(Latin: diminutive of *cella* cell). The cysticercus of 'cell tissue'. The larval stage of *Taenia solium*.
Cytoplasm	(Greek: *kytos* hollow vessel, hence, cell; *plasma* a thing molded, hence the viscous matter of a cell). The cytoplasm of a cell other than that of the nucleus and inclusions.
Cytopyge	(Greek: *kytos* hollow vessel. Hence, cell; *pyge* bullock). The excretory orifice of certain protozoa.
Diaptomus	(Greek: *diaptoma* from *diapiptein* to slip away). A genus of small Crustacea, the intermediate host of *Diphyllobothrium latum*.
Diphyllobothrium latum	(Greek: *dis* double; *phyllon* leaf; *bothrion* groove; Latin: *latus* broad). The broad fish tapeworm.
Diptera	(Greek: *dis* double; *pteron* wing). The order of the Arthropoda which includes mosquitoes and flies.
Dirofilaria immitis	(Latin: *dirus* terrible; *filum* thread; *immitis* merciless). The filaria of the dog, the dog heartworm.
Diurnal	(Latin: *dies* day). Relating to daytime.
Donovania	In honour of C. Donovan, born 1863, pathologist in Madras (now Chennai), India. Bacteria causing granuloma inguinale.
Dracunculus medinensis	(Greek: diminutive of *drakon* dragon; probably from Medine, French Sudan, or Medina, Saudi Arabia). A tissue roundworm, the guinea worm.
Echinococcus granulosus	(Greek: *echinos* hedgehog; *kokkos* berry; Latin *granulum* a little grain, a small particle). The hydatid worm.
Ectoplasm	(Greek: *ektos* outside, external; *plasma* a thing molded, hence the viscous matter of a cell). The outer, more compact layer of the cytoplasm.
Endemic	(Greek: *en* in; *demos* the people). Constantly present in the people of a certain area.
Endoplasm	(Greek: *endon* within; *plasma* a thing molded, hence the viscous matter of a cell). The inner portion of the cytoplasm of a cell.
Entameba histolytica	(Greek: *entos* within; *amoibe* change; *histos* web, hence the tissue; *lyein* to dissolve). The causative organism of amebiasis.
Enterobius vermicularis	(Greek: *enteron* intestine; *bios* life; Latin: *vermicularis* diminutive of *vermis* worm). The seatworm or pinworm.
Entomology	(Greek: *entomon* insect, past participle of *entemnein* to cut in, because insects appear cut in or almost divided; *logos* word, science). The study of insects or of arthropods in general.

Espundia	(Spanish: tumour, ulcer). Muco-cutaneous leishmaniasis.
Estivo-autumnal malaria	(Latin: *aestivus* belonging to the summer, *autumnus* fall). Falciparum malaria.
Fasciola	(Latin: diminutive of *fascis* bundle, referring to the appearance of the reproductive organs). A genus of hermaphroditic flukes.
Fasciolopsis buski	(Latin: diminutive of *fascis* bundle, Greek: *opsis* appearance, after George Busk, surgeon in London, 1807–86). The giant intestinal fluke.
Feces	(Latin: plural of *faex* yeast, i.e., residue after fermentation). Feces are the excrement.
Filaria	(Latin: *filum* thread). The tissue roundworms.
Fuadin	Antimony compound named in honour of Ahmed Fuad, Pasha, King of Egypt from 1922–36. Used in the treatment of a number of parasitic infections.
Gamete	(Greek: *gamein* to marry). The mature sexual cell in the lifecycle of Plasmodium.
Gametocyte	(Greek: *gamein* to marry; *kytos* hollow vessel, hence cell). The sexually differentiated but immature cell in the lifecycle of Plasmodium.
Genal	(Latin: *gena* cheek). Pertaining to the cheek, the anterior part of the side of the head of an insect.
Giardia lamblia	In honour of Professor. Alfred Giard, biologist in Paris, France, 1846–1908 and Dr. Wilhelm Dusan Lambl, Bohemian physician, 1824–95. An intestinal flagellate.
Glossina	(Greek: *glossa* tongue). A genus of biting flies. G. *palpalis*. (Latin: from *palpare* to touch).
Guinea worm	Guinea, a coastal region of West Africa, *Dracunculus medinensis*.
Helminths	(Greek: Plural of helminth worms). The parasitic worms.
Hematuria	(Greek: *haina* blood; *ouron* urine). Discharge of bloody urine.
Hermaphrodite	(Greek: *Hermaphroditos*, the son of Hermes and Aphrodite). Organism with male and female reproductive organs.
Hexacanth	(Greek: *hex* six; *pous* foot, *poda* feet).
Hyaline	(Greek: *hydatis* a watery vesicle) The larva of *Echinococcus granulosus*.
Hydrocephalus	(Greek: *hydro* water; *kephale* head). A condition in which the amount of cerebro-spinal fluid is increased.
Hymenolepis nana	(Greek: *hymen* membrane; *lepsis* shell; Latin: *nanus* dwarf). The dwarf tapeworm, the eggs of which have a thin membrane.
Infect	(Latin: *in* and *facere* to put into). The establishment of a pathogenic organism (except arthropods) upon or within a host.
Infest	(Latin: *infestare* to attack, to molest). The establishment of arthropods upon or within the host.
Kala azar	(Hindi: *kala* black; *azar* febrile disease) Infection with *Leishmania donovani*.
Karyosome	(Greek: *karyon* kernel, hence nucleus; *soma* body). The nucleolus-like body within the nucleus of Protozoa.
Kinetoplast	(Greek: *Kinetos* movable; *plastos* formed). Kinetonucleus closely associated with the blepharoplast of hemoflagellates.

Leishmania donovani	After Sir William Boog Leishman, British Army Surgeon, 1865–1926, and C. Donovan – 1863, pathologist in Madras (now Chennai), India. Species of hemoflagellates causing *kala azar*.
Leptomonas	(Greek: *leptos*. delicate; *monas* unit). The flagellate stage of Leishmania.
Loa	Congo dialect: worm. A genus of filarial worm.
Macrogametocyte	(Greek: *makros* large; *gamein* to marry; *kytos* hollow vessel, hence cell). The female sexual stage in the lifecycle of Sporozoa.
Malaria	(Italian: *mala* bad; *aria* air). Infection with Plasmodium sp.
Mastigophora	(Greek: *mastix* whip, flagellum; *pherein* to bear). A class of Protozoa.
Maurer's dots	After Georg Maurer, 1860–1919, German physician in Sumatra (1888–1905). Irregular, red-staining dots or lines in erythrocytes infected with *Plasmodium falciparum*. Maurer's dots were discovered and described by Schiiffner in 1889. Maurer devised an important staining technique for them in 1902.
Merozoite	(Greek: *meros* part; *zoion* animal). A stage in the lifecycle of Plasmodium.
Metacercaria	(Greek: *meta* after; *kerkos* tail). The larval stage of flukes which follows the cercaria stage.
Metazoa	(*Singular* metazoon) (Greek: *meta* after beyond; *zoion* animal). Animals that came after the Protozoa, characterized by segmentation of the ovum.
Microgametocyte	(Greek: *mikros* small; *gamein* to marry; *kytos* hollow vessel, cell). The male sexual stage in the lifecycle of sporozoa.
Miracidium	(Greek: *meirakidion*. little boy). The ciliated larva which hatches from the egg of flukes.
Mosquito	(Spanish: diminutive of mucosa fly). A member of the Family Culicidae, order Diptera.
Necator	(Latin: *necator* killer, slayer). A genus of hookworm
Nemathelminths	(Greek: *nema* thread; *helmins* worm). The roundworms.
Nematoda	(Greek: *nema* thread; *eidos* form). Roundworms.
NNN Medium	Devised for the culture of hemoflagellates by Novy and McNeal in 1904 and modified by Nicolle in 1908.
Onchocerca volvulus	(Greek: *onchos* hook, tumour; *kerkos* tail; Latin *volvere* to twist). A filarial worm.
Onchosphere	(Greek: *onkos* hook, tumour; *sphaira* sphere). A stage in the lifecycle of tapeworm.
Oocyst	(Greek: *oion* egg; *kystis* bladder). A stage in the lifecycle of Sporozoa.
Ookinete	(Greek: *oion* egg; *kinesis* motion). A stage in the lifecycle of Plasmodium.
Operculum	(Latin: *operculum* cover, lid). Referring to the lid of eggs of certain flatworms.
Paragonimus	(Greek: *para* bedside; *gonimos* generative). A genus of flukes.
Parasite	(Greek: *parasitos* he who eats at someone else's table). An animal or plant which lives upon or within another organism.
Parasitology	(Greek: *para* bedside; *sitos* food; *logos* word, science). The study of parasites.
Paroxysm	(Greek: *paroxynein* to sharpen). A sudden severe attack in a disease.
Pathogenesis	(Greek: *pathos* disease; *genesis* origination). The origination and development of a disease.
Pathogenic	Of or pertaining to pathogenesis. Causing disease.

Pathognomonic	(Greek: *pathos* disease; *gnome* a sign). Characteristic of a disease, distinguishing it from other diseases.
Phlebotomus argentipes	(Greek: *phlebs* vein; *tommein* to cut; Latin: *argentum* silver; *pedes* feet). A genus of blood sucking flies, the sand flies.
Planorbis	(Latin: *planus* flat; *orbis* circle). A genus of snails, the intermediate host of *Schistosoma mansoni.*
Plasmodium	(Greek: *plasma* a thing molded, hence the viscous matter of a cell; *eidos* form, resemblance). A genus of sporozoa which contains the parasites causing malaria.
Plasmodium falciparum	(Latin: *falx* sickle; *pario* to bring forth).
Plasmodium vivax	(Latin: *vivax* vigorous). Platyhelminths. (Greek: *platys* wide, flat; *helmins* worm). Flatworms.
Proboscis	(Greek: *proboskis* trunk of an elephant). The tubular process of the head, especially of insects and arachnids, made up of various mouth parts.
Procercoid	(Greek: *pro* (occurring) before; *kerkos* tail; *eidos* form). A stage in the lifecycle of some tapeworms.
Proglottid	(Greek: *proglottis* the tip of the tongue). A segment of Taenia.
Protozoa	(*Singular* protozoon) (Greek: *protos* first; *zoion* animal). The phylum of uninuclear animals.
Pseudopodia	(Greek: *pseudes* false; *poda* plural of *pous* foot). Foot-like. A temporary protrusion of the cytoplasm of ameboid cells serving locomotion and feeding.
Pyrogenic	(Greek: *pyr* fire, hence fever; *gennan* to produce). Producing fever.
Redia	After Francesco Redi, Italian naturalist, 1626–97. Larval stage of flukes, found in snails.
Rhabditiform	(Greek: *rhabdos* rod; *eidos* form). A stage in the lifecycle of some roundworms.
Rhizopoda	(Greek: *rhiza* root; *poda* plural of *pous* foot). The class of Protozoa which move by means of pseudopodia: the ameba.
Rostellum	(Latin: *rostellum* the little beak). A prolongation of the scolex.
Schistosoma	(Greek: *schistoz* split; *soma* body). A genus of flukes, the blood flukes.
Schistosoma hematobium	(Greek: *haima* blood; *bios* life).
Schistosoma mansoni	After Sir Patrick Manson, 'the Father of Tropical Medicine', 1844–1922.
Schizogony	(Greek: *schizein* to split; *gonos*; generation). Asexual multiplication by multiple fission. The nucleus divides into several, after which the cell divides into as many nuclei as there are.
Schizont	(Greek: present participle of *schizein* to split). The stage in the lifecycle of Plasmodium, which precedes the merozoite stage.
Schiiffner's dots or granules	After Wilheim Schuffner, German pathologist, 1867–1949, who discovered and described acidophilic stippling of erythrocytes parasitized by *Plasmodium vivax* or *ovale.*
Scolex	(Greek: *skolex* worm (plural scolices). The anterior end of a tapeworm, by which it attaches itself to the wall of the intestine, commonly referred to as the head.
Simulium	(Latin: *simulare* to stimulate). This genus includes the black flies and buffalo gnats.

Sparganum	(Greek: *Spargana* diaper, referring to early childhood). The larval stage of the fish tapeworm, which is infective to humans.
Sporocyst	(Greek: *sporos* seed; *kytos* cell). The oocyst of Plasmodia, after sporozoites have developed within it, the larval stage of flukes in snails from which eventually cercariae develop.
Sporogony	(Greek: *sporos* seed; *gonos* generation). Sexual reproduction by the formation of spores. The lifecycle of Plasmodium in the mosquito.
Sporozoa	(Greek: *sporos* seed; *zoion* animal). The class of Plasmodium that form spores in their lifecycle.
Sporozoite	(Greek: *sporos* seed; *zoion* animal). The end product of sporogony. The stage of Plasmodium transmitted to humans by the mosquito.
Stoma	(Greek: *stoma* mouth). A minute opening.
Strobila	(Greek: *strobile* twisted). The complete tapeworm including scolex, neck and proglottids.
Stroma	(Greek: *stroma* bed). The supporting framework of an organ.
Strongyloides stercoralis	(Greek: *strongylos* round; *eidos* form; Latin; *stercus* dung). An intestinal round worm, the cause of strongyloidiasis.
Symbiosis	(Greek: *symbiosis* living together). The mutually advantageous association between organisms of different species.
Taenia	(Greek: *taina* ribbon). A genus of tapeworm.
Taenia solium	(Arabic: *sosi* chain). The pork tapeworm.
Tenesmus	(Greek: *teinein* to strain). Painful straining to empty the bowels or bladder, without the evacuation of feces or urine.
Toxoplasma gondii	(Greek: *toxon* bow; *plasma* a thing molded, hence the viscous matter of a cell); The gondii is a small North African rodent: a protozoon.
Trematoda	(Greek: *trema* hole; *eidos* form, i.e., having holes). Referring to acetabula. The flukes.
Triatoma	(Latin: *tria* three; Greek: *tomos* sectioned). A genus of Hemiptera (true bugs).
Trichinella	(Greek: diminutive of *thrix* hair). The Trichina worm.
Trichocephalus trichiurus	(Greek: *thrix* hair; *kephale* head; *thrix* hair, *oura* tail). Synonyms of *Trichuris trichiura*. The whipworm.
Trophozoite	(Greek: *trophe* nutrition; *zoion* animal). The motile stage of protozoa.
Trypanosoma	(Greek: *trypanon, auger*, borer, *soma*, body). A genus of hemoflagellates.
Tse tse	South African Dutch from Bantu. *Onomatopoeic* (imitative in origin) 'fly'. Species of genus Glossina.
Vacuole	(Latin: *vacuus* empty). Cavity in the cytoplasm.
Wuchereria bancrofti	After Otto Wucherer 1820–73, who described the microfilaria, in 1866, in Bahia, Brazil; after J. Bancroft, English physician, 1836–94, who discovered the adult worm of this species, in 1876, in Australia. A species of the filarial worm.
Xenodiagnosis	(Greek: *xenos* foreign, *diagnoskein* to learn thoroughly). Diagnosis by finding the causative organism in an arthropod infected from the patient.
Zoonosis	(Greek: *zoon* animal, *nosos* disease). Disease of animals transmitted to humans.
Zygote	(Greek: *zygon* yoke). A stage in the sexual lifecycle of sporozoa. The cell resulting from the union of microgamete and macrogamete.

II. FURTHER READING

1. Adams, ARD and Maegraith BG 1966. *Clinical Tropical Medicine.* Philadelphia: F.A. Davies Company.
2. Chatterjee, KD 1952. *Human parasites and parasitic diseases for students, laboratory workers, practioners of medicine and public health.* Kolkata: Saraswati Press Ltd.
3. Chatterjee, KD 1982. *Parasitology (Protozoology and Helminthology in relation to Clinical Medicine).* Kolkata: Chatterjee Medical Publishers.
4. Dawies, B, 1963. *Advances in Parasitology.* London and New York: Academic Press.
5. Dey, NC 1964. *Medical Parasitology.* Kolkata: Allied Agency.
6. Faust, EC, Beaver, PC and Jung, RC 1968. *Animal Agents and Vectors of Human Disease* (3rd Edn). Philadelphia: Lea and Febiger.
7. Faust, EC, Russel, PF and Jung, RC 1970. *Craig and Faust's Clinical Parasitology* (8th Edn). Philadelphia: Lea and Febiger.
8. Hunter, GW, Frye, WW and Swatzwedder, JC 1966. *A Manual of Tropical Medicine* (4th Edn). Philadelphia: W.B Saunders Company.
9. Larsh, J 1964. *Outline of Medical Parasitology.* New York: McGraw-Hill Book Company (Blakistan Division).
10. Shule, PG and Maryon, ME (1966) *Laboratory techniques for the study of Malaria.* 2nd Ed. ICA Churchill Ltd., London.
11. Mackie, TT, Hunter, GW and Brookworth, C 1954. *A Manual of Tropical Medicine.* Philadelphia and London: WB Saunders Company.
12. Markel, EK and Voge, M 1971. *Medical Parasitology.* Philadelphia and London: W.B Saunders Company.
13. Najarian, RH 1967. *Textbook of Medical Parasitology.* Baltimore, USA: The Williams and Wilkins Company.
14. Nnochiri, E 1975. *Medical Parasitology in the Tropics.* London, Nairobi, Ibadan: Oxford University Press.
15. Noble, ER and Noble, GA 1970. *Parasitology: The Biology of Animal Parasites.* Philadelphia: Lea and Febiger.
16. Piekarshi, G 1962. *Medical Parasitology.* England: University of Cambridge.
17. Sawitz, WG 1956. *Medical Parasitology* (2nd Edn). New York, Toronto, London: The Blakistan Division, McGraw-Hill Book Company.

III. REFERENCES

1. Garnhan, PCC, Donnelley, J, Hoogstraal, H, Kennedy, CC and Walton GA 1969. Human babesiosis in Ireland - Further observations and the medical significance of this infection, *Brit. Med. J.* 4: 768–770.
2. Panjarathinam, R 1970. Preliminary note on the incidence of coccidiosis in Pondicherry. *Gujvet* 4: 87–91.

3. Panjarathinam, R 1986. Hope for Malarial vaccine *Current Medical Practice.* 30: 247–249.
4. Panjarathinam, R 1972. Preliminary report on some animal diseases in Pondicherry region. *Gujvet.* 6: 32–33.
5. Panjarathinam, R 1983. Tropical disease: Filariasis. *Current Medical Practice.* 27: 63–66.
6. Panjarathinam, R 1991. Effect of Mebendazole on *Dipylidium caninum* (A short communication). *Current Medical Practice.* 38. 69–70.
7. Western, KA, Benson, GD, Gleason, NN, Healy, GR and. Schultz, MG 1970. Babesiosis in a Massachusettes resident, *New Eng. J. Med.* 283: 854–856.
8. WHO 1963. Terminology of malaria and malaria eradication, Geneva.
9. WHO 1968. Expert Committee on Malaria –14th report. Tech. Report Series No. 382, Geneva.

Index